THE FINANCIER, A NOVEL

THE FINANCIER, A NOVEL

Theodore Dreiser

www.General-Books.net

Publication Data:

Title: The Financier, a Novel
Author: Dreiser, Theodore, 1871-1945
Reprinted: 2010, General Books, Memphis, Tennessee, USA
Subjects: Fiction

How We Made This Book for You
We made this book exclusively for you using patented Print on Demand technology.
First we scanned the original rare book using a robot which automatically flipped and photographed each page.
We automated the typing, proof reading and design of this book using Optical Character Recognition (OCR) software on the scanned copy. That let us keep your cost as low as possible.
If a book is very old, worn and the type is faded, this can result in numerous typos or missing text. This is also why our books don't have illustrations; the OCR software can't distinguish between an illustration and a smudge.
We understand how annoying typos, missing text or illustrations, foot notes in the text or an index that doesn't work, can be. That's why we provide a free digital copy of most books exactly as they were originally published. You can also use this PDF edition to read the book on the go. Simply go to our website (www.general-books.net) to check availability. And we provide a free trial membership in our book club so you can get free copies of other editions or related books.
OCR is not a perfect solution but we feel it's more important to make books available for a low price than not at all. So we warn readers on our website and in the descriptions we provide to book sellers that our books don't have illustrations and may have numerous typos or missing text. We also provide excerpts from books to book sellers and on our website so you can preview the quality of the book before buying it.
If you would prefer that we manually type, proof read and design your book so that it's perfect, simply contact us for the cost. Since many of our books only sell one or two copies a year, unlike mass market books we have to split the production costs between those one or two buyers.

1

THE FINANCIER, A NOVEL

THE FINANCIER
Chapter I
The Philadelphia into which Frank Algernon Cowperwood was born was a city of two hundred and fifty thousand and more. It was set with handsome parks, notable buildings, and crowded with historic memories. Many of the things that we and he knew later were not then in existence–the telegraph, telephone, express company, ocean steamer, city delivery of mails. There were no postage-stamps or registered letters. The street car had not arrived. In its place were hosts of omnibuses, and for longer travel the slowly developing railroad system still largely connected by canals.

Cowperwood's father was a bank clerk at the time of Frank's birth, but ten years later, when the boy was already beginning to turn a very sensible, vigorous eye on the world, Mr. Henry Worthington Cowperwood, because of the death of the bank's president and the consequent moving ahead of the other officers, fell heir to the place vacated by the promoted teller, at the, to him, munificent salary of thirty-five hundred dollars a year. At once he decided, as he told his wife joyously, to remove his family from 21 Buttonwood Street to 124 New Market Street, a much better neighborhood, where there was a nice brick house of three stories in height as opposed to their present two-storied domicile. There was the probability that some day they would come into something even better, but for the present this was sufficient. He was exceedingly grateful.

Henry Worthington Cowperwood was a man who believed only what he saw and was content to be what he was–a banker, or a prospective one. He was at this time a significant figure–tall, lean, inquisitorial, clerkly–with nice, smooth, closely-cropped side whiskers coming to almost the lower lobes of his ears. His upper lip was smooth and curiously long, and he had a long, straight nose and a chin that tended to be pointed. His eyebrows were bushy, emphasizing vague, grayish-green eyes, and his hair was short and smooth and nicely parted. He wore a frock-coat always–it was quite the thing in financial circles in those days–and a high hat. And he kept his hands and nails immaculately clean. His manner might have been called severe, though really it was more cultivated than austere.

Being ambitious to get ahead socially and financially, he was very careful of whom or with whom he talked. He was as much afraid of expressing a rabid or unpopular political or social opinion as he was of being seen with an evil character, though he had really no opinion of great political significance to express. He was neither anti- nor pro-slavery, though the air was stormy with abolition sentiment and its opposition. He believed sincerely that vast fortunes were to be made out of railroads if one only had the capital and that curious thing, a magnetic personality–the ability to win the confidence of others. He was sure that Andrew Jackson was all wrong in his opposition to Nicholas Biddle and the United States Bank, one of the great issues of the day; and he was worried, as he might well be, by the perfect storm of wildcat money which was floating about and which was constantly coming to his bank–discounted, of course, and handed out again to anxious borrowers at a profit. His bank was the Third National of Philadelphia, located in that center of all Philadelphia and indeed, at that time, of practically all national finance–Third Street–and its owners conducted a brokerage business as a side line. There was a perfect plague of State banks, great and small, in those days, issuing notes practically without regulation upon insecure and unknown assets and failing and suspending with astonishing rapidity; and a knowledge of all these was an important requirement of Mr. Cowperwood's position. As a result, he had become the soul of caution. Unfortunately, for him, he lacked in a great measure the two things that are necessary for distinction in any field–magnetism and vision. He was not destined to be a great financier, though he was marked out to be a moderately successful one.

Mrs. Cowperwood was of a religious temperament–a small woman, with light-brown hair and clear, brown eyes, who had been very attractive in her day, but had become rather prim and matter-of-fact and inclined to take very seriously the maternal care of her three sons and one daughter. The former, captained by Frank, the eldest, were a source of considerable annoyance to her, for they were forever making expeditions to different parts of the city, getting in with bad boys, probably, and seeing and hearing things they should neither see nor hear.

Frank Cowperwood, even at ten, was a natural-born leader. At the day school he attended, and later at the Central High School, he was looked upon as one whose common sense could unquestionably be trusted in all cases. He was a sturdy youth, courageous and defiant. From the very start of his life, he wanted to know about economics and politics. He cared nothing for books. He was a clean, stalky, shapely boy, with a bright, clean-cut, incisive face; large, clear, gray eyes; a wide forehead; short, bristly, dark-brown hair. He had an incisive, quick-motioned, self-sufficient manner, and was forever asking questions with a keen desire for an intelligent reply. He never had an ache or pain, ate his food with gusto, and ruled his brothers with a rod of iron. "Come on, Joe!" "Hurry, Ed!" These commands were issued in no rough but always a sure way, and Joe and Ed came. They looked up to Frank from the first as a master, and what he had to say was listened to eagerly.

He was forever pondering, pondering–one fact astonishing him quite as much as another–for he could not figure out how this thing he had come into–this life–was organized. How did all these people get into the world? What were they doing here? Who started things, anyhow? His mother told him the story of Adam and Eve, but he didn't believe it. There was a fish-market not so very far from his home, and there, on his way to see his father at the bank, or conducting his brothers on after-school expeditions, he liked to look at a certain tank in front of one store where were kept odd specimens of sea-life brought in by the Delaware Bay fishermen. He saw once there a sea-horse–just a queer little sea-animal that looked somewhat like a horse– and another time he saw an electric eel which Benjamin Franklin's discovery had explained. One day he saw a squid and a lobster put in the tank, and in connection with them was witness to a tragedy which stayed with him all his life and cleared things up considerably intellectually. The lobster, it appeared from the talk of the idle bystanders, was offered no food, as the squid was considered his rightful prey. He lay at the bottom of the clear glass tank on the yellow sand, apparently seeing nothing– you could not tell in which way his beady, black buttons of eyes were looking–but apparently they were never off the body of the squid. The latter, pale and waxy in texture, looking very much like pork fat or jade, moved about in torpedo fashion; but his movements were apparently never out of the eyes of his enemy, for by degrees small portions of his body began to disappear, snapped off by the relentless claws of his pursuer. The lobster would leap like a catapult to where the squid was apparently idly dreaming, and the squid, very alert, would dart away, shooting out at the same time a cloud of ink, behind which it would disappear. It was not always completely successful, however. Small portions of its body or its tail were frequently left in the claws of the monster below. Fascinated by the drama, young Cowperwood came daily to watch.

One morning he stood in front of the tank, his nose almost pressed to the glass. Only a portion of the squid remained, and his ink-bag was emptier than ever. In the corner of the tank sat the lobster, poised apparently for action.

The boy stayed as long as he could, the bitter struggle fascinating him. Now, maybe, or in an hour or a day, the squid might die, slain by the lobster, and the lobster would eat him. He looked again at the greenish-copperish engine of destruction in the corner and wondered when this would be. To-night, maybe. He would come back to-night.

He returned that night, and lo! the expected had happened. There was a little crowd around the tank. The lobster was in the corner. Before him was the squid cut in two and partially devoured.

"He got him at last," observed one bystander. "I was standing right here an hour ago, and up he leaped and grabbed him. The squid was too tired. He wasn't quick enough. He did back up, but that lobster he calculated on his doing that. He's been figuring on his movements for a long time now. He got him to-day."

Frank only stared. Too bad he had missed this. The least touch of sorrow for the squid came to him as he stared at it slain. Then he gazed at the victor.

"That's the way it has to be, I guess," he commented to himself. "That squid wasn't quick enough." He figured it out.

"The squid couldn't kill the lobster–he had no weapon. The lobster could kill the squid–he was heavily armed. There was nothing for the squid to feed on; the lobster had the squid as prey. What was the result to be? What else could it be? He didn't have a chance," he concluded finally, as he trotted on homeward.

The incident made a great impression on him. It answered in a rough way that riddle which had been annoying him so much in the past: "How is life organized?" Things lived on each other–that was it. Lobsters lived on squids and other things. What lived on lobsters? Men, of course! Sure, that was it! And what lived on men? he asked himself. Was it other men? Wild animals lived on men. And there were Indians and cannibals. And some men were killed by storms and accidents. He wasn't so sure about men living on men; but men did kill each other. How about wars and street fights and mobs? He had seen a mob once. It attacked the Public Ledger building as he was coming home from school. His father had explained why. It was about the slaves. That was it! Sure, men lived on men. Look at the slaves. They were men. That's what all this excitement was about these days. Men killing other men–negroes.

He went on home quite pleased with himself at his solution.

"Mother!" he exclaimed, as he entered the house, "he finally got him!"

"Got who? What got what?" she inquired in amazement. "Go wash your hands."

"Why, that lobster got that squid I was telling you and pa about the other day."

"Well, that's too bad. What makes you take any interest in such things? Run, wash your hands."

"Well, you don't often see anything like that. I never did." He went out in the back yard, where there was a hydrant and a post with a little table on it, and on that a shining tin-pan and a bucket of water. Here he washed his face and hands.

"Say, papa," he said to his father, later, "you know that squid?"

"Yes."

"Well, he's dead. The lobster got him."

His father continued reading. "Well, that's too bad," he said, indifferently.

But for days and weeks Frank thought of this and of the life he was tossed into, for he was already pondering on what he should be in this world, and how he should get along. From seeing his father count money, he was sure that he would like banking; and Third Street, where his father's office was, seemed to him the cleanest, most fascinating street in the world.

Chapter II

The growth of young Frank Algernon Cowperwood was through years of what might be called a comfortable and happy family existence. Buttonwood Street, where he spent the first ten years of his life, was a lovely place for a boy to live. It contained mostly small two and three-story red brick houses, with small white marble steps leading up to the front door, and thin, white marble trimmings outlining the front door and windows. There were trees in the street–plenty of them. The road pavement was of big, round cobblestones, made bright and clean by the rains; and the sidewalks were of red brick, and always damp and cool. In the rear was a yard, with trees and grass and sometimes flowers, for the lots were almost always one hundred feet deep, and the house-fronts, crowding close to the pavement in front, left a comfortable space in the rear.

The Cowperwoods, father and mother, were not so lean and narrow that they could not enter into the natural tendency to be happy and joyous with their children; and so this family, which increased at the rate of a child every two or three years after Frank's birth until there were four children, was quite an interesting affair when he was ten and they were ready to move into the New Market Street home. Henry Worthington Cowperwood's connections were increased as his position grew more responsible, and gradually he was becoming quite a personage. He already knew a number of the more prosperous merchants who dealt with his bank, and because as a clerk his duties necessitated his calling at other banking-houses, he had come to be familiar with and favorably known in the Bank of the United States, the Drexels, the Edwards, and others. The brokers knew him as representing a very sound organization, and while he was not considered brilliant mentally, he was known as a most reliable and trustworthy individual.

In this progress of his father young Cowperwood definitely shared. He was quite often allowed to come to the bank on Saturdays, when he would watch with great interest the deft exchange of bills at the brokerage end of the business. He wanted to know where all the types of money came from, why discounts were demanded and received, what the men did with all the money they received. His father, pleased at his interest, was glad to explain so that even at this early age–from ten to fifteen–the boy gained a wide knowledge of the condition of the country financially–what a State bank was and what a national one; what brokers did; what stocks were, and why they fluctuated in value. He began to see clearly what was meant by money as a medium of exchange, and how all values were calculated according to one primary value, that of gold. He was a financier by instinct, and all the knowledge that pertained to that great art was as natural to him as the emotions and subtleties of life are to a poet. This medium of exchange, gold, interested him intensely. When his father explained to him how it was mined, he dreamed that he owned a gold mine and waked to wish that he did. He was likewise curious about stocks and bonds and he learned that some stocks and bonds were not worth the paper they were written on, and that others were worth much more than their face value indicated.

"There, my son," said his father to him one day, "you won't often see a bundle of those around this neighborhood." He referred to a series of shares in the British East India Company, deposited as collateral at two-thirds of their face value for a loan of one hundred thousand dollars. A Philadelphia magnate had hypothecated them for the use of the ready cash. Young Cowperwood looked at them curiously. "They don't look like much, do they?" he commented.

"They are worth just four times their face value," said his father, archly.

Frank reexamined them. "The British East India Company," he read. "Ten pounds–that's pretty near fifty dollars."

"Forty-eight, thirty-five," commented his father, dryly. "Well, if we had a bundle of those we wouldn't need to work very hard. You'll notice there are scarcely any pin-marks on them. They aren't sent around very much. I don't suppose these have ever been used as collateral before."

Young Cowperwood gave them back after a time, but not without a keen sense of the vast ramifications of finance. What was the East India Company? What did it do? His father told him.

At home also he listened to considerable talk of financial investment and adventure. He heard, for one thing, of a curious character by the name of Steemberger, a great beef speculator from Virginia, who was attracted to Philadelphia in those days by the hope of large and easy credits. Steemberger, so his father said, was close to Nicholas Biddle, Lardner, and others of the United States Bank, or at least friendly with them, and seemed to be able to obtain from that organization nearly all that he asked for. His operations in the purchase of cattle in Virginia, Ohio, and other States were vast, amounting, in fact, to an entire monopoly of the business of supplying beef to Eastern cities. He was a big man, enormous, with a face, his father said, something like that of a pig; and he wore a high beaver hat and a long frock-coat which hung loosely about his big chest and stomach. He had managed to force the price of beef up to thirty cents a pound, causing all the retailers and consumers to rebel, and this was what made him so conspicuous. He used to come to the brokerage end of the elder Cowperwood's bank, with as much as one hundred thousand or two hundred thousand dollars, in twelve months–post-notes of the United States Bank in denominations of one thousand, five thousand, and ten thousand dollars. These he would cash at from ten to twelve per cent. under their face value, having previously given the United States Bank his own note at four months for the entire amount. He would take his pay from the Third National brokerage counter in packages of Virginia, Ohio, and western Pennsylvania bank-notes at par, because he made his disbursements principally in those States. The Third National would in the first place realize a profit of from four to five per cent. on the original transaction; and as it took the Western bank-notes at a discount, it also made a profit on those.

There was another man his father talked about–one Francis J. Grund, a famous newspaper correspondent and lobbyist at Washington, who possessed the faculty of unearthing secrets of every kind, especially those relating to financial legislation. The secrets of the President and the Cabinet, as well as of the Senate and the House of Representatives, seemed to be open to him. Grund had been about, years before, purchasing through one or two brokers large amounts of the various kinds of Texas debt certificates and bonds. The Republic of Texas, in its struggle for independence from Mexico, had issued bonds and certificates in great variety, amounting in value to ten or fifteen million dollars. Later, in connection with the scheme to make Texas a State of the Union, a bill was passed providing a contribution on the part of the United States of five million dollars, to be applied to the extinguishment of this old debt. Grund knew of this, and also of the fact that some of this debt, owing to the peculiar conditions of issue, was to be paid in full, while other portions were to be scaled down, and there was to be a false or pre-arranged failure to pass the bill at one session in order to frighten off the outsiders who might have heard and begun to buy the old certificates for profit. He acquainted the Third National Bank with this fact, and of course the information came to Cowperwood as teller. He told his wife about it, and so his son, in this roundabout way, heard it, and his clear, big eyes glistened. He wondered why his father did not take advantage of the situation and buy some Texas certificates for himself. Grund, so his father said, and possibly three or four others, had made over a hundred thousand dollars apiece. It wasn't exactly legitimate, he seemed to think, and yet it was, too. Why shouldn't such inside information be rewarded? Somehow, Frank realized that his father was too honest, too cautious, but when he grew up, he told himself, he was going to be a broker, or a financier, or a banker, and do some of these things.

Just at this time there came to the Cowperwoods an uncle who had not previously appeared in the life of the family. He was a brother of Mrs. Cowperwood's–Seneca Davis by name–solid, unctuous, five feet ten in height, with a big, round body, a round, smooth head rather bald, a clear, ruddy complexion, blue eyes, and what little hair he had of a sandy hue. He was exceedingly well dressed according to standards prevailing in those days, indulging in flowered waistcoats, long, light-colored frock-coats, and the invariable (for a fairly prosperous man) high hat. Frank was fascinated by him at once. He had been a planter in Cuba and still owned a big ranch there and could tell him tales of Cuban life–rebellions, ambuscades, hand-to-hand fighting with machetes on his own plantation, and things of that sort. He brought with him a collection of Indian curies, to say nothing of an independent fortune and several slaves–one, named Manuel, a tall, raw-boned black, was his constant attendant, a bodyservant, as it were. He shipped raw sugar from his plantation in boat-loads to the Southwark wharves in Philadelphia. Frank liked him because he took life in a hearty, jovial way, rather rough and offhand for this somewhat quiet and reserved household.

"Why, Nancy Arabella," he said to Mrs Cowperwood on arriving one Sunday afternoon, and throwing the household into joyous astonishment at his unexpected and unheralded appearance, "you haven't grown an inch! I thought when you married old brother Hy here that you were going to fatten up like your brother. But look at you! I swear to Heaven you don't weigh five pounds." And he jounced her up and down by the waist, much to the perturbation of the children, who had never before seen their mother so familiarly handled.

Henry Cowperwood was exceedingly interested in and pleased at the arrival of this rather prosperous relative; for twelve years before, when he was married, Seneca Davis had not taken much notice of him.

"Look at these little putty-faced Philadelphians," he continued, "They ought to come down to my ranch in Cuba and get tanned up. That would take away this waxy look." And he pinched the cheek of Anna Adelaide, now five years old. "I tell you, Henry, you have a rather nice place here." And he looked at the main room of the rather conventional three-story house with a critical eye.

Measuring twenty by twenty-four and finished in imitation cherry, with a set of new Sheraton parlor furniture it presented a quaintly harmonious aspect. Since Henry had become teller the family had acquired a piano–a decided luxury in those days–

brought from Europe; and it was intended that Anna Adelaide, when she was old enough, should learn to play. There were a few uncommon ornaments in the room–a gas chandelier for one thing, a glass bowl with goldfish in it, some rare and highly polished shells, and a marble Cupid bearing a basket of flowers. It was summer time, the windows were open, and the trees outside, with their widely extended green branches, were pleasantly visible shading the brick sidewalk. Uncle Seneca strolled out into the back yard.

"Well, this is pleasant enough," he observed, noting a large elm and seeing that the yard was partially paved with brick and enclosed within brick walls, up the sides of which vines were climbing. "Where's your hammock? Don't you string a hammock here in summer? Down on my veranda at San Pedro I have six or seven."

"We hadn't thought of putting one up because of the neighbors, but it would be nice," agreed Mrs. Cowperwood. "Henry will have to get one."

"I have two or three in my trunks over at the hotel. My niggers make 'em down there. I'll send Manuel over with them in the morning."

He plucked at the vines, tweaked Edward's ear, told Joseph, the second boy, he would bring him an Indian tomahawk, and went back into the house.

"This is the lad that interests me," he said, after a time, laying a hand on the shoulder of Frank. "What did you name him in full, Henry?"

"Frank Algernon."

"Well, you might have named him after me. There's something to this boy. How would you like to come down to Cuba and be a planter, my boy?"

"I'm not so sure that I'd like to," replied the eldest.

"Well, that's straight-spoken. What have you against it?"

"Nothing, except that I don't know anything about it."

"What do you know?"

The boy smiled wisely. "Not very much, I guess."

"Well, what are you interested in?"

"Money!"

"Aha! What's bred in the bone, eh? Get something of that from your father, eh? Well, that's a good trait. And spoken like a man, too! We'll hear more about that later. Nancy, you're breeding a financier here, I think. He talks like one."

He looked at Frank carefully now. There was real force in that sturdy young body– no doubt of it. Those large, clear gray eyes were full of intelligence. They indicated much and revealed nothing.

"A smart boy!" he said to Henry, his brother-in-law. "I like his get-up. You have a bright family."

Henry Cowperwood smiled dryly. This man, if he liked Frank, might do much for the boy. He might eventually leave him some of his fortune. He was wealthy and single.

Uncle Seneca became a frequent visitor to the house–he and his negro body-guard, Manuel, who spoke both English and Spanish, much to the astonishment of the children; and he took an increasing interest in Frank.

"When that boy gets old enough to find out what he wants to do, I think I'll help him to do it," he observed to his sister one day; and she told him she was very grateful.

He talked to Frank about his studies, and found that he cared little for books or most of the study he was compelled to pursue. Grammar was an abomination. Literature silly. Latin was of no use. History–well, it was fairly interesting.

"I like bookkeeping and arithmetic," he observed. "I want to get out and get to work, though. That's what I want to do."

"You're pretty young, my son," observed his uncle. "You're only how old now? Fourteen?"

"Thirteen."

"Well, you can't leave school much before sixteen. You'll do better if you stay until seventeen or eighteen. It can't do you any harm. You won't be a boy again."

"I don't want to be a boy. I want to get to work."

"Don't go too fast, son. You'll be a man soon enough. You want to be a banker, do you?"

"Yes, sir!"

"Well, when the time comes, if everything is all right and you've behaved yourself and you still want to, I'll help you get a start in business. If I were you and were going to be a banker, I'd first spend a year or so in some good grain and commission house. There's good training to be had there. You'll learn a lot that you ought to know. And, meantime, keep your health and learn all you can. Wherever I am, you let me know, and I'll write and find out how you've been conducting yourself."

He gave the boy a ten-dollar gold piece with which to start a bank-account. And, not strange to say, he liked the whole Cowperwood household much better for this dynamic, self-sufficient, sterling youth who was an integral part of it.

Chapter III

It was in his thirteenth year that young Cowperwood entered into his first business venture. Walking along Front Street one day, a street of importing and wholesale establishments, he saw an auctioneer's flag hanging out before a wholesale grocery and from the interior came the auctioneer's voice: "What am I bid for this exceptional lot of Java coffee, twenty-two bags all told, which is now selling in the market for seven dollars and thirty-two cents a bag wholesale? What am I bid? What am I bid? The whole lot must go as one. What am I bid?"

"Eighteen dollars," suggested a trader standing near the door, more to start the bidding than anything else. Frank paused.

"Twenty-two!" called another.

"Thirty!" a third. "Thirty-five!" a fourth, and so up to seventy-five, less than half of what it was worth.

"I'm bid seventy-five! I'm bid seventy-five!" called the auctioneer, loudly. "Any other offers? Going once at seventy-five; am I offered eighty? Going twice at seventy-five, and"–he paused, one hand raised dramatically. Then he brought it down with a slap in the palm of the other–"sold to Mr. Silas Gregory for seventy-five. Make a note of that, Jerry," he called to his red-haired, freckle-faced clerk beside him. Then he turned to another lot of grocery staples–this time starch, eleven barrels of it.

Young Cowperwood was making a rapid calculation. If, as the auctioneer said, coffee was worth seven dollars and thirty-two cents a bag in the open market, and this buyer was getting this coffee for seventy-five dollars, he was making then and there eighty-six dollars and four cents, to say nothing of what his profit would be if he sold it at retail. As he recalled, his mother was paying twenty-eight cents a pound. He drew nearer, his books tucked under his arm, and watched these operations closely. The starch, as he soon heard, was valued at ten dollars a barrel, and it only brought six. Some kegs of vinegar were knocked down at one-third their value, and so on. He began to wish he could bid; but he had no money, just a little pocket change. The auctioneer noticed him standing almost directly under his nose, and was impressed with the stolidity–solidity–of the boy's expression.

"I am going to offer you now a fine lot of Castile soap–seven cases, no less–which, as you know, if you know anything about soap, is now selling at fourteen cents a bar. This soap is worth anywhere at this moment eleven dollars and seventy-five cents a case. What am I bid? What am I bid? What am I bid?" He was talking fast in the usual style of auctioneers, with much unnecessary emphasis; but Cowperwood was not unduly impressed. He was already rapidly calculating for himself. Seven cases at eleven dollars and seventy-five cents would be worth just eighty-two dollars and twenty-five cents; and if it went at half–if it went at half–

"Twelve dollars," commented one bidder.

"Fifteen," bid another.

"Twenty," called a third.

"Twenty-five," a fourth.

Then it came to dollar raises, for Castile soap was not such a vital commodity. "Twenty-six." "Twenty-seven." "Twenty-eight." "Twenty-nine." There was a pause. "Thirty," observed young Cowperwood, decisively.

The auctioneer, a short lean faced, spare man with bushy hair and an incisive eye, looked at him curiously and almost incredulously but without pausing. He had, somehow, in spite of himself, been impressed by the boy's peculiar eye; and now he felt, without knowing why, that the offer was probably legitimate enough, and that the boy had the money. He might be the son of a grocer.

"I'm bid thirty! I'm bid thirty! I'm bid thirty for this fine lot of Castile soap. It's a fine lot. It's worth fourteen cents a bar. Will any one bid thirty-one? Will any one bid thirty-one? Will any one bid thirty-one?"

"Thirty-one," said a voice.

"Thirty-two," replied Cowperwood. The same process was repeated.

"I'm bid thirty-two! I'm bid thirty-two! I'm bid thirty-two! Will anybody bid thirty-three? It's fine soap. Seven cases of fine Castile soap. Will anybody bid thirty-three?"

Young Cowperwood's mind was working. He had no money with him; but his father was teller of the Third National Bank, and he could quote him as reference. He could sell all of his soap to the family grocer, surely; or, if not, to other grocers. Other people were anxious to get this soap at this price. Why not he?

The auctioneer paused.

"Thirty-two once! Am I bid thirty-three? Thirty-two twice! Am I bid thirty-three? Thirty-two three times! Seven fine cases of soap. Am I bid anything more? Once, twice! Three times! Am I bid anything more?"–his hand was up again–"and sold to Mr.–?" He leaned over and looked curiously into the face of his young bidder.

"Frank Cowperwood, son of the teller of the Third National Bank," replied the boy, decisively.

"Oh, yes," said the man, fixed by his glance.

"Will you wait while I run up to the bank and get the money?"

"Yes. Don't be gone long. If you're not here in an hour I'll sell it again."

Young Cowperwood made no reply. He hurried out and ran fast; first, to his mother's grocer, whose store was within a block of his home.

Thirty feet from the door he slowed up, put on a nonchalant air, and strolling in, looked about for Castile soap. There it was, the same kind, displayed in a box and looking just as his soap looked.

"How much is this a bar, Mr. Dalrymple?" he inquired.

"Sixteen cents," replied that worthy.

"If I could sell you seven boxes for sixty-two dollars just like this, would you take them?"

"The same soap?"

"Yes, sir."

Mr. Dalrymple calculated a moment.

"Yes, I think I would," he replied, cautiously.

"Would you pay me to-day?"

"I'd give you my note for it. Where is the soap?"

He was perplexed and somewhat astonished by this unexpected proposition on the part of his neighbor's son. He knew Mr. Cowperwood well–and Frank also.

"Will you take it if I bring it to you to-day?"

"Yes, I will," he replied. "Are you going into the soap business?"

"No. But I know where I can get some of that soap cheap."

He hurried out again and ran to his father's bank. It was after banking hours; but he knew how to get in, and he knew that his father would be glad to see him make thirty dollars. He only wanted to borrow the money for a day.

"What's the trouble, Frank?" asked his father, looking up from his desk when he appeared, breathless and red faced.

"I want you to loan me thirty-two dollars! Will you?"

"Why, yes, I might. What do you want to do with it?"

"I want to buy some soap–seven boxes of Castile soap. I know where I can get it and sell it. Mr. Dalrymple will take it. He's already offered me sixty-two for it. I can get it for thirty-two. Will you let me have the money? I've got to run back and pay the auctioneer."

His father smiled. This was the most business-like attitude he had seen his son manifest. He was so keen, so alert for a boy of thirteen.

"Why, Frank," he said, going over to a drawer where some bills were, "are you going to become a financier already? You're sure you're not going to lose on this? You know what you're doing, do you?"

"You let me have the money, father, will you?" he pleaded. "I'll show you in a little bit. Just let me have it. You can trust me."

He was like a young hound on the scent of game. His father could not resist his appeal.

"Why, certainly, Frank," he replied. "I'll trust you." And he counted out six five-dollar certificates of the Third National's own issue and two ones. "There you are."

Frank ran out of the building with a briefly spoken thanks and returned to the auction room as fast as his legs would carry him. When he came in, sugar was being auctioned. He made his way to the auctioneer's clerk.

"I want to pay for that soap," he suggested.

"Now?"

"Yes. Will you give me a receipt?"

"Yep."

"Do you deliver this?"

"No. No delivery. You have to take it away in twenty-four hours."

That difficulty did not trouble him.

"All right," he said, and pocketed his paper testimony of purchase.

The auctioneer watched him as he went out. In half an hour he was back with a drayman—an idle levee-wharf hanger-on who was waiting for a job.

Frank had bargained with him to deliver the soap for sixty cents. In still another half-hour he was before the door of the astonished Mr. Dalrymple whom he had come out and look at the boxes before attempting to remove them. His plan was to have them carried on to his own home if the operation for any reason failed to go through. Though it was his first great venture, he was cool as glass.

"Yes," said Mr. Dalrymple, scratching his gray head reflectively. "Yes, that's the same soap. I'll take it. I'll be as good as my word. Where'd you get it, Frank?"

"At Bixom's auction up here," he replied, frankly and blandly.

Mr. Dalrymple had the drayman bring in the soap; and after some formality—because the agent in this case was a boy—made out his note at thirty days and gave it to him.

Frank thanked him and pocketed the note. He decided to go back to his father's bank and discount it, as he had seen others doing, thereby paying his father back and getting his own profit in ready money. It couldn't be done ordinarily on any day after business hours; but his father would make an exception in his case.

He hurried back, whistling; and his father glanced up smiling when he came in.

"Well, Frank, how'd you make out?" he asked.

"Here's a note at thirty days," he said, producing the paper Dalrymple had given him. "Do you want to discount that for me? You can take your thirty-two out of that."

His father examined it closely. "Sixty-two dollars!" he observed. "Mr. Dalrymple! That's good paper! Yes, I can. It will cost you ten per cent.," he added, jestingly. "Why don't you just hold it, though? I'll let you have the thirty-two dollars until the end of the month."

"Oh, no," said his son, "you discount it and take your money. I may want mine."

His father smiled at his business-like air. "All right," he said. "I'll fix it to-morrow. Tell me just how you did this." And his son told him.

At seven o'clock that evening Frank's mother heard about it, and in due time Uncle Seneca.

"What'd I tell you, Cowperwood?" he asked. "He has stuff in him, that youngster. Look out for him."

Mrs. Cowperwood looked at her boy curiously at dinner. Was this the son she had nursed at her bosom not so very long before? Surely he was developing rapidly.

"Well, Frank, I hope you can do that often," she said.

"I hope so, too, ma," was his rather noncommittal reply.

Auction sales were not to be discovered every day, however, and his home grocer was only open to one such transaction in a reasonable period of time, but from the very first young Cowperwood knew how to make money. He took subscriptions for a boys' paper; handled the agency for the sale of a new kind of ice-skate, and once organized a band of neighborhood youths into a union for the purpose of purchasing their summer straw hats at wholesale. It was not his idea that he could get rich by saving. From the first he had the notion that liberal spending was better, and that somehow he would get along.

It was in this year, or a little earlier, that he began to take an interest in girls. He had from the first a keen eye for the beautiful among them; and, being good-looking and magnetic himself, it was not difficult for him to attract the sympathetic interest of those in whom he was interested. A twelve-year old girl, Patience Barlow, who lived further up the street, was the first to attract his attention or be attracted by him. Black hair and snapping black eyes were her portion, with pretty pigtails down her back, and dainty feet and ankles to match a dainty figure. She was a Quakeress, the daughter of Quaker parents, wearing a demure little bonnet. Her disposition, however, was vivacious, and she liked this self-reliant, self-sufficient, straight-spoken boy. One day, after an exchange of glances from time to time, he said, with a smile and the courage that was innate in him: "You live up my way, don't you?"

"Yes," she replied, a little flustered–this last manifested in a nervous swinging of her school-bag–"I live at number one-forty-one."

"I know the house," he said. "I've seen you go in there. You go to the same school my sister does, don't you? Aren't you Patience Barlow?" He had heard some of the boys speak her name. "Yes. How do you know?"

"Oh, I've heard," he smiled. "I've seen you. Do you like licorice?"

He fished in his coat and pulled out some fresh sticks that were sold at the time.

"Thank you," she said, sweetly, taking one.

"It isn't very good. I've been carrying it a long time. I had some taffy the other day."

"Oh, it's all right," she replied, chewing the end of hers.

"Don't you know my sister, Anna Cowperwood?" he recurred, by way of self-introduction. "She's in a lower grade than you are, but I thought maybe you might have seen her."

"I think I know who she is. I've seen her coming home from school."

"I live right over there," he confided, pointing to his own home as he drew near to it, as if she didn't know. "I'll see you around here now, I guess."

"Do you know Ruth Merriam?" she asked, when he was about ready to turn off into the cobblestone road to reach his own door.

"No, why?"

"She's giving a party next Tuesday," she volunteered, seemingly pointlessly, but only seemingly.

"Where does she live?"

"There in twenty-eight."

"I'd like to go," he affirmed, warmly, as he swung away from her.

"Maybe she'll ask you," she called back, growing more courageous as the distance between them widened. "I'll ask her."

"Thanks," he smiled.

And she began to run gayly onward.

He looked after her with a smiling face. She was very pretty. He felt a keen desire to kiss her, and what might transpire at Ruth Merriam's party rose vividly before his eyes.

This was just one of the early love affairs, or puppy loves, that held his mind from time to time in the mixture of after events. Patience Barlow was kissed by him in secret ways many times before he found another girl. She and others of the street ran out to play in the snow of a winter's night, or lingered after dusk before her own door when the days grew dark early. It was so easy to catch and kiss her then, and to talk to her foolishly at parties. Then came Dora Fitler, when he was sixteen years old and she was fourteen; and Marjorie Stafford, when he was seventeen and she was fifteen. Dora Fitter was a brunette, and Marjorie Stafford was as fair as the morning, with bright-red cheeks, bluish-gray eyes, and flaxen hair, and as plump as a partridge.

It was at seventeen that he decided to leave school. He had not graduated. He had only finished the third year in high school; but he had had enough. Ever since his thirteenth year his mind had been on finance; that is, in the form in which he saw it manifested in Third Street. There had been odd things which he had been able to do to earn a little money now and then. His Uncle Seneca had allowed him to act as assistant weigher at the sugar-docks in Southwark, where three-hundred-pound bags were weighed into the government bonded warehouses under the eyes of United States inspectors. In certain emergencies he was called to assist his father, and was paid for it. He even made an arrangement with Mr. Dalrymple to assist him on Saturdays; but when his father became cashier of his bank, receiving an income of four thousand dollars a year, shortly after Frank had reached his fifteenth year, it was self-evident that Frank could no longer continue in such lowly employment.

Just at this time his Uncle Seneca, again back in Philadelphia and stouter and more domineering than ever, said to him one day:

"Now, Frank, if you're ready for it, I think I know where there's a good opening for you. There won't be any salary in it for the first year, but if you mind your p's and q's, they'll probably give you something as a gift at the end of that time. Do you know of Henry Waterman Company down in Second Street?"

"I've seen their place."

"Well, they tell me they might make a place for you as a bookkeeper. They're brokers in a way–grain and commission men. You say you want to get in that line. When school's out, you go down and see Mr. Waterman–tell him I sent you, and he'll make a place for you, I think. Let me know how you come out."

Uncle Seneca was married now, having, because of his wealth, attracted the attention of a poor but ambitious Philadelphia society matron; and because of this the general connections of the Cowperwoods were considered vastly improved. Henry Cowperwood was planning to move with his family rather far out on North Front Street, which commanded at that time a beautiful view of the river and was witnessing the construction of some charming dwellings. His four thousand dollars a year in these pre-Civil-War times was considerable. He was making what he considered judicious and conservative investments and because of his cautious, conservative, clock-like conduct it was thought he might reasonably expect some day to be vice-president and possibly president, of his bank.

This offer of Uncle Seneca to get him in with Waterman Company seemed to Frank just the thing to start him off right. So he reported to that organization at 74 South Second Street one day in June, and was cordially received by Mr. Henry Waterman, Sr. There was, he soon learned, a Henry Waterman, Jr., a young man of twenty-five, and a George Waterman, a brother, aged fifty, who was the confidential inside man. Henry Waterman, Sr., a man of fifty-five years of age, was the general head of the organization, inside and out–traveling about the nearby territory to see customers when that was necessary, coming into final counsel in cases where his brother could not adjust matters, suggesting and advising new ventures which his associates and hirelings carried out. He was, to look at, a phlegmatic type of man–short, stout, wrinkled about the eyes, rather protuberant as to stomach, red-necked, red-faced, the least bit popeyed, but shrewd, kindly, good-natured, and witty. He had, because of his naturally common-sense ideas and rather pleasing disposition built up a sound and successful business here. He was getting strong in years and would gladly have welcomed the hearty cooperation of his son, if the latter had been entirely suited to the business.

He was not, however. Not as democratic, as quick-witted, or as pleased with the work in hand as was his father, the business actually offended him. And if the trade had been left to his care, it would have rapidly disappeared. His father foresaw this, was grieved, and was hoping some young man would eventually appear who would be interested in the business, handle it in the same spirit in which it had been handled, and who would not crowd his son out.

Then came young Cowperwood, spoken of to him by Seneca Davis. He looked him over critically. Yes, this boy might do, he thought. There was something easy and sufficient about him. He did not appear to be in the least flustered or disturbed. He knew how to keep books, he said, though he knew nothing of the details of the grain and commission business. It was interesting to him. He would like to try it.

"I like that fellow," Henry Waterman confided to his brother the moment Frank had gone with instructions to report the following morning. "There's something to him. He's the cleanest, briskest, most alive thing that's walked in here in many a day."

"Yes," said George, a much leaner and slightly taller man, with dark, blurry, reflective eyes and a thin, largely vanished growth of brownish-black hair which contrasted strangely with the egg-shaped whiteness of his bald head. "Yes, he's a nice young man. It's a wonder his father don't take him in his bank."

"Well, he may not be able to," said his brother. "He's only the cashier there."

"That's right."

"Well, we'll give him a trial. I bet anything he makes good. He's a likely-looking youth."

Henry got up and walked out into the main entrance looking into Second Street. The cool cobble pavements, shaded from the eastern sun by the wall of buildings on the east–of which his was a part–the noisy trucks and drays, the busy crowds hurrying to and fro, pleased him. He looked at the buildings over the way–all three and four stories, and largely of gray stone and crowded with life–and thanked his stars that he had originally located in so prosperous a neighborhood. If he had only brought more property at the time he bought this!

"I wish that Cowperwood boy would turn out to be the kind of man I want," he observed to himself, meditatively. "He could save me a lot of running these days."

Curiously, after only three or four minutes of conversation with the boy, he sensed this marked quality of efficiency. Something told him he would do well.

Chapter IV

The appearance of Frank Cowperwood at this time was, to say the least, prepossessing and satisfactory. Nature had destined him to be about five feet ten inches tall. His head was large, shapely, notably commercial in aspect, thickly covered with crisp, dark-brown hair and fixed on a pair of square shoulders and a stocky body. Already his eyes had the look that subtle years of thought bring. They were inscrutable. You could tell nothing by his eyes. He walked with a light, confident, springy step. Life had given him no severe shocks nor rude awakenings. He had not been compelled to suffer illness or pain or deprivation of any kind. He saw people richer than himself, but he hoped to be rich. His family was respected, his father well placed. He owed no man anything. Once he had let a small note of his become overdue at the bank, but his father raised such a row that he never forgot it. "I would rather crawl on my hands and knees than let my paper go to protest," the old gentleman observed; and this fixed in his mind what scarcely needed to be so sharply emphasized–the significance of credit. No paper of his ever went to protest or became overdue after that through any negligence of his.

He turned out to be the most efficient clerk that the house of Waterman Co. had ever known. They put him on the books at first as assistant bookkeeper, vice Mr. Thomas Trixler, dismissed, and in two weeks George said: "Why don't we make Cowperwood head bookkeeper? He knows more in a minute than that fellow Sampson will ever know."

"All right, make the transfer, George, but don't fuss so. He won't be a bookkeeper long, though. I want to see if he can't handle some of these transfers for me after a bit."

The books of Messrs. Waterman Co., though fairly complicated, were child's play to Frank. He went through them with an ease and rapidity which surprised his erstwhile superior, Mr. Sampson.

"Why, that fellow," Sampson told another clerk on the first day he had seen Cowperwood work, "he's too brisk. He's going to make a bad break. I know that kind. Wait a little bit until we get one of those rush credit and transfer days." But the bad break Mr. Sampson anticipated did not materialize. In less than a week Cowperwood knew the financial condition of the Messrs. Waterman as well as they did–better–to a dollar. He knew how their accounts were distributed; from what section they drew the most business; who sent poor produce and good–the varying prices for a year told that. To satisfy himself he ran back over certain accounts in the ledger, verifying his suspicions. Bookkeeping did not interest him except as a record, a demonstration of a firm's life. He knew he would not do this long. Something else would happen; but he saw instantly what the grain and commission business was–every detail of it. He saw where, for want of greater activity in offering the goods consigned–quicker communication with shippers and buyers, a better working agreement with surrounding commission men–this house, or, rather, its customers, for it had nothing, endured severe losses. A man would ship a tow-boat or a car-load of fruit or vegetables against a supposedly rising or stable market; but if ten other men did the same thing at the same time, or other commission men were flooded with fruit or vegetables, and there was no way of disposing of them within a reasonable time, the price had to fall. Every day was bringing its special consignments. It instantly occurred to him that he would be of much more use to the house as an outside man disposing of heavy shipments, but he hesitated to say anything so soon. More than likely, things would adjust themselves shortly.

The Watermans, Henry and George, were greatly pleased with the way he handled their accounts. There was a sense of security in his very presence. He soon began to call Brother George's attention to the condition of certain accounts, making suggestions as to their possible liquidation or discontinuance, which pleased that individual greatly. He saw a way of lightening his own labors through the intelligence of this youth; while at the same time developing a sense of pleasant companionship with him.

Brother Henry was for trying him on the outside. It was not always possible to fill the orders with the stock on hand, and somebody had to go into the street or the Exchange to buy and usually he did this. One morning, when way-bills indicated a probable glut of flour and a shortage of grain–Frank saw it first–the elder Waterman called him into his office and said:

"Frank, I wish you would see what you can do with this condition that confronts us on the street. By to-morrow we're going to be overcrowded with flour. We can't be paying storage charges, and our orders won't eat it up. We're short on grain. Maybe you could trade out the flour to some of those brokers and get me enough grain to fill these orders."

"I'd like to try," said his employee.

He knew from his books where the various commission-houses were. He knew what the local merchants' exchange, and the various commission-merchants who dealt in these things, had to offer. This was the thing he liked to do–adjust a trade difficulty of this nature. It was pleasant to be out in the air again, to be going from door to door. He objected to desk work and pen work and poring over books. As he said in later years, his brain was his office. He hurried to the principal commission-merchants, learning what the state of the flour market was, and offering his surplus at the very rate he would have expected to get for it if there had been no prospective glut. Did they want to buy for immediate delivery (forty-eight hours being immediate) six hundred barrels of prime flour? He would offer it at nine dollars straight, in the barrel. They did not. He offered it in fractions, and some agreed to take one portion, and some another. In about an hour he was all secure on this save one lot of two hundred barrels, which he decided to offer in one lump to a famous operator named Genderman with whom his firm did no business. The latter, a big man with curly gray hair, a gnarled and yet pudgy face, and little eyes that peeked out shrewdly through fat eyelids, looked at Cowperwood curiously when he came in.

"What's your name, young man?" he asked, leaning back in his wooden chair.

"Cowperwood."

"So you work for Waterman Company? You want to make a record, no doubt. That's why you came to me?"

Cowperwood merely smiled.

"Well, I'll take your flour. I need it. Bill it to me."

Cowperwood hurried out. He went direct to a firm of brokers in Walnut Street, with whom his firm dealt, and had them bid in the grain he needed at prevailing rates. Then he returned to the office.

"Well," said Henry Waterman, when he reported, "you did that quick. Sold old Genderman two hundred barrels direct, did you? That's doing pretty well. He isn't on our books, is he?"

"No, sir."

"I thought not. Well, if you can do that sort of work on the street you won't be on the books long."

Thereafter, in the course of time, Frank became a familiar figure in the commission district and on 'change (the Produce Exchange), striking balances for his employer, picking up odd lots of things they needed, soliciting new customers, breaking gluts by disposing of odd lots in unexpected quarters. Indeed the Watermans were astonished at his facility in this respect. He had an uncanny faculty for getting appreciative hearings, making friends, being introduced into new realms. New life began to flow through the old channels of the Waterman company. Their customers were better satisfied. George was for sending him out into the rural districts to drum up trade, and this was eventually done.

Near Christmas-time Henry said to George: "We'll have to make Cowperwood a liberal present. He hasn't any salary. How would five hundred dollars do?"

"That's pretty much, seeing the way times are, but I guess he's worth it. He's certainly done everything we've expected, and more. He's cut out for this business."

"What does he say about it? Do you ever hear him say whether he's satisfied?"

"Oh, he likes it pretty much, I guess. You see him as much as I do."

"Well, we'll make it five hundred. That fellow wouldn't make a bad partner in this business some day. He has the real knack for it. You see that he gets the five hundred dollars with a word from both of us."

So the night before Christmas, as Cowperwood was looking over some way-bills and certificates of consignment preparatory to leaving all in order for the intervening holiday, George Waterman came to his desk.

"Hard at it," he said, standing under the flaring gaslight and looking at his brisk employee with great satisfaction.

It was early evening, and the snow was making a speckled pattern through the windows in front.

"Just a few points before I wind up," smiled Cowperwood.

"My brother and I have been especially pleased with the way you have handled the work here during the past six months. We wanted to make some acknowledgment, and we thought about five hundred dollars would be right. Beginning January first we'll give you a regular salary of thirty dollars a week."

"I'm certainly much obliged to you," said Frank. "I didn't expect that much. It's a good deal. I've learned considerable here that I'm glad to know."

"Oh, don't mention it. We know you've earned it. You can stay with us as long as you like. We're glad to have you with us."

Cowperwood smiled his hearty, genial smile. He was feeling very comfortable under this evidence of approval. He looked bright and cheery in his well-made clothes of English tweed.

On the way home that evening he speculated as to the nature of this business. He knew he wasn't going to stay there long, even in spite of this gift and promise of salary. They were grateful, of course; but why shouldn't they be? He was efficient, he knew that; under him things moved smoothly. It never occurred to him that he belonged in the realm of clerkdom. Those people were the kind of beings who ought to work for him, and who would. There was nothing savage in his attitude, no rage against fate, no dark fear of failure. These two men he worked for were already nothing more than characters in his eyes–their business significated itself. He could see their weaknesses and their shortcomings as a much older man might have viewed a boy's.

After dinner that evening, before leaving to call on his girl, Marjorie Stafford, he told his father of the gift of five hundred dollars and the promised salary.

"That's splendid," said the older man. "You're doing better than I thought. I suppose you'll stay there."

"No, I won't. I think I'll quit sometime next year."

"Why?"

"Well, it isn't exactly what I want to do. It's all right, but I'd rather try my hand at brokerage, I think. That appeals to me."

"Don't you think you are doing them an injustice not to tell them?"

"Not at all. They need me." All the while surveying himself in a mirror, straightening his tie and adjusting his coat.

"Have you told your mother?"

"No. I'm going to do it now."

He went out into the dining-room, where his mother was, and slipping his arms around her little body, said: "What do you think, Mammy?"

"Well, what?" she asked, looking affectionately into his eyes.

"I got five hundred dollars to-night, and I get thirty a week next year. What do you want for Christmas?"

"You don't say! Isn't that nice! Isn't that fine! They must like you. You're getting to be quite a man, aren't you?"

"What do you want for Christmas?"

"Nothing. I don't want anything. I have my children."

He smiled. "All right. Then nothing it is."

But she knew he would buy her something.

He went out, pausing at the door to grab playfully at his sister's waist, and saying that he'd be back about midnight, hurried to Marjorie's house, because he had promised to take her to a show.

"Anything you want for Christmas this year, Margy?" he asked, after kissing her in the dimly-lighted hall. "I got five hundred to-night."

She was an innocent little thing, only fifteen, no guile, no shrewdness.

"Oh, you needn't get me anything."

"Needn't I?" he asked, squeezing her waist and kissing her mouth again.

It was fine to be getting on this way in the world and having such a good time.

Chapter V

The following October, having passed his eighteenth year by nearly six months, and feeling sure that he would never want anything to do with the grain and commission business as conducted by the Waterman Company, Cowperwood decided to sever his relations with them and enter the employ of Tighe Company, bankers and brokers.

Cowperwood's meeting with Tighe Company had come about in the ordinary pursuance of his duties as outside man for Waterman Company. From the first Mr. Tighe took a keen interest in this subtle young emissary.

"How's business with you people?" he would ask, genially; or, "Find that you're getting many I.O.U.'s these days?"

Because of the unsettled condition of the country, the over-inflation of securities, the slavery agitation, and so forth, there were prospects of hard times. And Tighe–he could not have told you why–was convinced that this young man was worth talking to in regard to all this. He was not really old enough to know, and yet he did know.

"Oh, things are going pretty well with us, thank you, Mr. Tighe," Cowperwood would answer.

"I tell you," he said to Cowperwood one morning, "this slavery agitation, if it doesn't stop, is going to cause trouble."

A negro slave belonging to a visitor from Cuba had just been abducted and set free, because the laws of Pennsylvania made freedom the right of any negro brought into the state, even though in transit only to another portion of the country, and there was great excitement because of it. Several persons had been arrested, and the newspapers were discussing it roundly.

"I don't think the South is going to stand for this thing. It's making trouble in our business, and it must be doing the same thing for others. We'll have secession here, sure as fate, one of these days." He talked with the vaguest suggestion of a brogue.

"It's coming, I think," said Cowperwood, quietly. "It can't be healed, in my judgment. The negro isn't worth all this excitement, but they'll go on agitating for him–emotional people always do this. They haven't anything else to do. It's hurting our Southern trade."

"I thought so. That's what people tell me."

He turned to a new customer as young Cowperwood went out, but again the boy struck him as being inexpressibly sound and deep-thinking on financial matters. "If that young fellow wanted a place, I'd give it to him," he thought.

Finally, one day he said to him: "How would you like to try your hand at being a floor man for me in 'change? I need a young man here. One of my clerks is leaving."

"I'd like it," replied Cowperwood, smiling and looking intensely gratified. "I had thought of speaking to you myself some time."

"Well, if you're ready and can make the change, the place is open. Come any time you like."

"I'll have to give a reasonable notice at the other place," Cowperwood said, quietly. "Would you mind waiting a week or two?"

"Not at all. It isn't as important as that. Come as soon as you can straighten things out. I don't want to inconvenience your employers."

It was only two weeks later that Frank took his departure from Waterman Company, interested and yet in no way flustered by his new prospects. And great was the grief of Mr. George Waterman. As for Mr. Henry Waterman, he was actually irritated by this defection.

"Why, I thought," he exclaimed, vigorously, when informed by Cowperwood of his decision, "that you liked the business. Is it a matter of salary?"

"No, not at all, Mr. Waterman. It's just that I want to get into the straight-out brokerage business."

"Well, that certainly is too bad. I'm sorry. I don't want to urge you against your own best interests. You know what you are doing. But George and I had about agreed to offer you an interest in this thing after a bit. Now you're picking up and leaving. Why, damn it, man, there's good money in this business."

"I know it," smiled Cowperwood, "but I don't like it. I have other plans in view. I'll never be a grain and commission man." Mr. Henry Waterman could scarcely understand why obvious success in this field did not interest him. He feared the effect of his departure on the business.

And once the change was made Cowperwood was convinced that this new work was more suited to him in every way—as easy and more profitable, of course. In the first place, the firm of Tighe Co., unlike that of Waterman Co., was located in a handsome green-gray stone building at 66 South Third Street, in what was then, and for a number of years afterward, the heart of the financial district. Great institutions of national and international import and repute were near at hand—Drexel Co., Edward Clark Co., the Third National Bank, the First National Bank, the Stock Exchange, and similar institutions. Almost a score of smaller banks and brokerage firms were also in the vicinity. Edward Tighe, the head and brains of this concern, was a Boston Irishman, the son of an immigrant who had flourished and done well in that conservative city. He had come to Philadelphia to interest himself in the speculative life there. "Sure, it's a right good place for those of us who are awake," he told his friends, with a slight Irish accent, and he considered himself very much awake. He was a medium-tall man, not very stout, slightly and prematurely gray, and with a manner which was as lively and good-natured as it was combative and self-reliant. His upper lip was ornamented by a short, gray mustache.

"May heaven preserve me," he said, not long after he came there, "these Pennsylvanians never pay for anything they can issue bonds for." It was the period when Pennsylvania's credit, and for that matter Philadelphia's, was very bad in spite of its great wealth. "If there's ever a war there'll be battalions of Pennsylvanians marching around offering notes for their meals. If I could just live long enough I could get rich buyin' up Pennsylvania notes and bonds. I think they'll pay some time; but, my God, they're mortal slow! I'll be dead before the State government will ever catch up on the interest they owe me now."

It was true. The condition of the finances of the state and city was most reprehensible. Both State and city were rich enough; but there were so many schemes for looting the treasury in both instances that when any new work had to be undertaken bonds were necessarily issued to raise the money. These bonds, or warrants, as they were called, pledged interest at six per cent.; but when the interest fell due, instead of paying it, the city or State treasurer, as the case might be, stamped the same with the date of presentation, and the warrant then bore interest for not only its original face value, but the amount then due in interest. In other words, it was being slowly compounded. But this did not help the man who wanted to raise money, for as security they could not be hypothecated for more than seventy per cent. of their market value, and they were not selling at par, but at ninety. A man might buy or accept them in foreclosure, but he had a long wait. Also, in the final payment of most of them favoritism ruled, for it was only when the treasurer knew that certain warrants were in the hands of "a friend" that he would advertise that such and such warrants–those particular ones that he knew about–would be paid.

What was more, the money system of the United States was only then beginning slowly to emerge from something approximating chaos to something more nearly approaching order. The United States Bank, of which Nicholas Biddle was the progenitor, had gone completely in 1841, and the United States Treasury with its subtreasury system had come in 1846; but still there were many, many wildcat banks, sufficient in number to make the average exchange-counter broker a walking encyclopedia of solvent and insolvent institutions. Still, things were slowly improving, for the telegraph had facilitated stock-market quotations, not only between New York, Boston, and Philadelphia, but between a local broker's office in Philadelphia and his stock exchange. In other words, the short private wire had been introduced. Communication was quicker and freer, and daily grew better.

Railroads had been built to the South, East, North, and West. There was as yet no stock-ticker and no telephone, and the clearing-house had only recently been thought of in New York, and had not yet been introduced in Philadelphia. Instead of a clearing-house service, messengers ran daily between banks and brokerage firms, balancing accounts on pass-books, exchanging bills, and, once a week, transferring the gold coin, which was the only thing that could be accepted for balances due, since there was no stable national currency. "On 'change," when the gong struck announcing the close of the day's business, a company of young men, known as "settlement clerks," after a system borrowed from London, gathered in the center of the room and compared or gathered the various trades of the day in a ring, thus eliminating all those sales and resales between certain firms which naturally canceled each other. They carried long account books, and called out the transactions–"Delaware and Maryland sold to Beaumont and Company," "Delware and Maryland sold to Tighe and Company," and so on. This simplified the bookkeeping of the various firms, and made for quicker and more stirring commercial transactions.

Seats "on 'change" sold for two thousand dollars each. The members of the exchange had just passed rules limiting the trading to the hours between ten and three (before this they had been any time between morning and midnight), and had fixed the rates at which brokers could do business, in the face of cut-throat schemes which had previously held. Severe penalties were fixed for those who failed to obey. In other words, things were shaping up for a great 'change business, and Edward Tighe felt, with other brokers, that there was a great future ahead.

Chapter VI

The Cowperwood family was by this time established in its new and larger and more tastefully furnished house on North Front Street, facing the river. The house was four stories tall and stood twenty-five feet on the street front, without a yard.

Here the family began to entertain in a small way, and there came to see them, now and then, representatives of the various interests that Henry Cowperwood had encountered in his upward climb to the position of cashier. It was not a very distinguished company, but it included a number of people who were about as successful as himself–heads of small businesses who traded at his bank, dealers in dry-goods, leather, groceries (wholesale), and grain. The children had come to have intimacies of their own. Now and then, because of church connections, Mrs. Cowperwood ventured to have an afternoon tea or reception, at which even Cowperwood attempted the gallant in so far as to stand about in a genially foolish way and greet those whom his wife had invited. And so long as he could maintain his gravity very solemnly and greet people without being required to say much, it was not too painful for him. Singing was indulged in at times, a little dancing on occasion, and there was considerably more "company to dinner," informally, than there had been previously.

And here it was, during the first year of the new life in this house, that Frank met a certain Mrs. Semple, who interested him greatly. Her husband had a pretentious shoe store on Chestnut Street, near Third, and was planning to open a second one farther out on the same street.

The occasion of the meeting was an evening call on the part of the Semples, Mr. Semple being desirous of talking with Henry Cowperwood concerning a new transportation feature which was then entering the world–namely, street-cars. A tentative line, incorporated by the North Pennsylvania Railway Company, had been put into operation on a mile and a half of tracks extending from Willow Street along Front to Germantown Road, and thence by various streets to what was then known as the Cohocksink Depot; and it was thought that in time this mode of locomotion might drive out the hundreds of omnibuses which now crowded and made impassable the downtown streets. Young Cowperwood had been greatly interested from the start. Railway transportation, as a whole, interested him, anyway, but this particular phase was most fascinating. It was already creating widespread discussion, and he, with others, had gone to see it. A strange but interesting new type of car, fourteen feet long, seven feet wide, and nearly the same height, running on small iron car-wheels, was giving great satisfaction as being quieter and easier-riding than omnibuses; and

Alfred Semple was privately considering investing in another proposed line which, if it could secure a franchise from the legislature, was to run on Fifth and Sixth streets.

Cowperwood, Senior, saw a great future for this thing; but he did not see as yet how the capital was to be raised for it. Frank believed that Tighe Co. should attempt to become the selling agents of this new stock of the Fifth and Sixth Street Company in the event it succeeded in getting a franchise. He understood that a company was already formed, that a large amount of stock was to be issued against the prospective franchise, and that these shares were to be sold at five dollars, as against an ultimate par value of one hundred. He wished he had sufficient money to take a large block of them.

Meanwhile, Lillian Semple caught and held his interest. Just what it was about her that attracted him at this age it would be hard to say, for she was really not suited to him emotionally, intellectually, or otherwise. He was not without experience with women or girls, and still held a tentative relationship with Marjorie Stafford; but Lillian Semple, in spite of the fact that she was married and that he could have legitimate interest in her, seemed not wiser and saner, but more worth while. She was twenty-four as opposed to Frank's nineteen, but still young enough in her thoughts and looks to appear of his own age. She was slightly taller than he–though he was now his full height (five feet ten and one-half inches)–and, despite her height, shapely, artistic in form and feature, and with a certain unconscious placidity of soul, which came more from lack of understanding than from force of character. Her hair was the color of a dried English walnut, rich and plentiful, and her complexion waxen–cream wax—with lips of faint pink, and eyes that varied from gray to blue and from gray to brown, according to the light in which you saw them. Her hands were thin and shapely, her nose straight, her face artistically narrow. She was not brilliant, not active, but rather peaceful and statuesque without knowing it. Cowperwood was carried away by her appearance. Her beauty measured up to his present sense of the artistic. She was lovely, he thought–gracious, dignified. If he could have his choice of a wife, this was the kind of a girl he would like to have.

As yet, Cowperwood's judgment of women was temperamental rather than intellectual. Engrossed as he was by his desire for wealth, prestige, dominance, he was confused, if not chastened by considerations relating to position, presentability and the like. None the less, the homely woman meant nothing to him. And the passionate woman meant much. He heard family discussions of this and that sacrificial soul among women, as well as among men–women who toiled and slaved for their husbands or children, or both, who gave way to relatives or friends in crises or crucial moments, because it was right and kind to do so–but somehow these stories did not appeal to him. He preferred to think of people–even women–as honestly, frankly self-interested. He could not have told you why. People seemed foolish, or at the best very unfortunate not to know what to do in all circumstances and how to protect themselves. There was great talk concerning morality, much praise of virtue and decency, and much lifting of hands in righteous horror at people who broke or were even rumored to have broken the Seventh Commandment. He did not take this talk seriously. Already he had broken it secretly many times. Other young men did. Yet again, he was a little sick of the women of the streets and the bagnio. There were too many coarse, evil features in connection with such contacts. For a little while, the false tinsel-glitter of the house of ill repute appealed to him, for there was a certain force to its luxury–rich, as a rule, with red-plush furniture, showy red hangings, some coarse but showily-framed pictures, and, above all, the strong-bodied or sensuously lymphatic women who dwelt there, to (as his mother phrased it) prey on men. The strength of their bodies, the lust of their souls, the fact that they could, with a show of affection or good-nature, receive man after man, astonished and later disgusted him. After all, they were not smart. There was no vivacity of thought there. All that they could do, in the main, he fancied, was this one thing. He pictured to himself the dreariness of the mornings after, the stale dregs of things when only sleep and thought of gain could aid in the least; and more than once, even at his age, he shook his head. He wanted contact which was more intimate, subtle, individual, personal.

So came Lillian Semple, who was nothing more to him than the shadow of an ideal. Yet she cleared up certain of his ideas in regard to women. She was not physically as vigorous or brutal as those other women whom he had encountered in the lupanars, thus far–raw, unashamed contraveners of accepted theories and notions–and for that very reason he liked her. And his thoughts continued to dwell on her, notwithstanding the hectic days which now passed like flashes of light in his new business venture. For this stock exchange world in which he now found himself, primitive as it would seem to-day, was most fascinating to Cowperwood. The room that he went to in Third Street, at Dock, where the brokers or their agents and clerks gathered one hundred and fifty strong, was nothing to speak of artistically–a square chamber sixty by sixty, reaching from the second floor to the roof of a four-story building; but it was striking to him. The windows were high and narrow; a large-faced clock faced the west entrance of the room where you came in from the stairs; a collection of telegraph instruments, with their accompanying desks and chairs, occupied the northeast corner. On the floor, in the early days of the exchange, were rows of chairs where the brokers sat while various lots of stocks were offered to them. Later in the history of the exchange the chairs were removed and at different points posts or floor-signs indicating where certain stocks were traded in were introduced. Around these the men who were interested gathered to do their trading. From a hall on the third floor a door gave entrance to a visitor's gallery, small and poorly furnished; and on the west wall a large blackboard carried current quotations in stocks as telegraphed from New York and Boston. A wicket-like fence in the center of the room surrounded the desk and chair of the official recorder; and a very small gallery opening from the third floor on the west gave place for the secretary of the board, when he had any special announcement to make. There was a room off the southwest corner, where reports and annual compendiums of chairs were removed and at different signs indicating where certain stocks of various kinds were kept and were available for the use of members.

Young Cowperwood would not have been admitted at all, as either a broker or broker's agent or assistant, except that Tighe, feeling that he needed him and believing that he would be very useful, bought him a seat on 'change–charging the two thousand dollars it cost as a debt and then ostensibly taking him into partnership. It was against the rules of the exchange to sham a partnership in this way in order to put a man on the floor, but brokers did it. These men who were known to be minor partners and floor assistants were derisively called "eighth chasers" and "two-dollar brokers," because they were always seeking small orders and were willing to buy or sell for anybody on their commission, accounting, of course, to their firms for their work. Cowperwood, regardless of his intrinsic merits, was originally counted one of their number, and he was put under the direction of Mr. Arthur Rivers, the regular floor man of Tighe Company.

Rivers was an exceedingly forceful man of thirty-five, well-dressed, well-formed, with a hard, smooth, evenly chiseled face, which was ornamented by a short, black mustache and fine, black, clearly penciled eyebrows. His hair came to an odd point at the middle of his forehead, where he divided it, and his chin was faintly and attractively cleft. He had a soft voice, a quiet, conservative manner, and both in and out of this brokerage and trading world was controlled by good form. Cowperwood wondered at first why Rivers should work for Tighe–he appeared almost as able–but afterward learned that he was in the company. Tighe was the organizer and general hand-shaker, Rivers the floor and outside man.

It was useless, as Frank soon found, to try to figure out exactly why stocks rose and fell. Some general reasons there were, of course, as he was told by Tighe, but they could not always be depended on.

"Sure, anything can make or break a market"–Tighe explained in his delicate brogue–"from the failure of a bank to the rumor that your second cousin's grandmother has a cold. It's a most unusual world, Cowperwood. No man can explain it. I've seen breaks in stocks that you could never explain at all–no one could. It wouldn't be possible to find out why they broke. I've seen rises the same way. My God, the rumors of the stock exchange! They beat the devil. If they're going down in ordinary times some one is unloading, or they're rigging the market. If they're going up–God knows times must be good or somebody must be buying–that's sure. Beyond that–well, ask Rivers to show you the ropes. Don't you ever lose for me, though. That's the cardinal sin in this office." He grinned maliciously, even if kindly, at that.

Cowperwood understood–none better. This subtle world appealed to him. It answered to his temperament.

There were rumors, rumors, rumors–of great railway and street-car undertakings, land developments, government revision of the tariff, war between France and Turkey, famine in Russia or Ireland, and so on. The first Atlantic cable had not been laid as yet, and news of any kind from abroad was slow and meager. Still there were great financial figures in the held, men who, like Cyrus Field, or William H. Vanderbilt, or F. X. Drexel, were doing marvelous things, and their activities and the rumors concerning them counted for much.

Frank soon picked up all of the technicalities of the situation. A "bull," he learned, was one who bought in anticipation of a higher price to come; and if he was "loaded up" with a "line" of stocks he was said to be "long." He sold to "realize" his profit, or if his margins were exhausted he was "wiped out." A "bear" was one who sold stocks which most frequently he did not have, in anticipation of a lower price, at which he could buy and satisfy his previous sales. He was "short" when he had sold what he did not own, and he "covered" when he bought to satisfy his sales and to realize his profits or to protect himself against further loss in case prices advanced instead of declining.

He was in a "corner" when he found that he could not buy in order to make good the stock he had borrowed for delivery and the return of which had been demanded. He was then obliged to settle practically at a price fixed by those to whom he and other "shorts" had sold.

He smiled at first at the air of great secrecy and wisdom on the part of the younger men. They were so heartily and foolishly suspicious. The older men, as a rule, were inscrutable. They pretended indifference, uncertainty. They were like certain fish after a certain kind of bait, however. Snap! and the opportunity was gone. Somebody else had picked up what you wanted. All had their little note-books. All had their peculiar squint of eye or position or motion which meant "Done! I take you!" Sometimes they seemed scarcely to confirm their sales or purchases—they knew each other so well—but they did. If the market was for any reason active, the brokers and their agents were apt to be more numerous than if it were dull and the trading indifferent. A gong sounded the call to trading at ten o'clock, and if there was a noticeable rise or decline in a stock or a group of stocks, you were apt to witness quite a spirited scene. Fifty to a hundred men would shout, gesticulate, shove here and there in an apparently aimless manner; endeavoring to take advantage of the stock offered or called for.

"Five-eighths for five hundred P. and W.," some one would call—Rivers or Cowperwood, or any other broker.

"Five hundred at three-fourths," would come the reply from some one else, who either had an order to sell the stock at that price or who was willing to sell it short, hoping to pick up enough of the stock at a lower figure later to fill his order and make a little something besides. If the supply of stock at that figure was large Rivers would probably continue to bid five-eighths. If, on the other hand, he noticed an increasing demand, he would probably pay three-fourths for it. If the professional traders believed Rivers had a large buying order, they would probably try to buy the stock before he could at three-fourths, believing they could sell it out to him at a slightly higher price. The professional traders were, of course, keen students of psychology; and their success depended on their ability to guess whether or not a broker representing a big manipulator, like Tighe, had an order large enough to affect the market sufficiently to give them an opportunity to "get in and out," as they termed it, at a profit before he had completed the execution of his order. They were like hawks watching for an opportunity to snatch their prey from under the very claws of their opponents.

Four, five, ten, fifteen, twenty, thirty, forty, fifty, and sometimes the whole company would attempt to take advantage of the given rise of a given stock by either selling or offering to buy, in which case the activity and the noise would become deafening. Given groups might be trading in different things; but the large majority of them would abandon what they were doing in order to take advantage of a speciality. The eagerness of certain young brokers or clerks to discover all that was going on, and to take advantage of any given rise or fall, made for quick physical action, darting to and fro, the excited elevation of explanatory fingers. Distorted faces were shoved over shoulders or under arms. The most ridiculous grimaces were purposely or unconsciously indulged in. At times there were situations in which some individual was fairly smothered with arms, faces, shoulders, crowded toward him when he manifested any intention of either buying or selling at a profitable rate. At first it seemed quite a wonderful thing to young Cowperwood–the very physical face of it– for he liked human presence and activity; but a little later the sense of the thing as a picture or a dramatic situation, of which he was a part faded, and he came down to a clearer sense of the intricacies of the problem before him. Buying and selling stocks, as he soon learned, was an art, a subtlety, almost a psychic emotion. Suspicion, intuition, feeling–these were the things to be "long" on.

Yet in time he also asked himself, who was it who made the real money–the stock- brokers? Not at all. Some of them were making money, but they were, as he quickly saw, like a lot of gulls or stormy petrels, hanging on the lee of the wind, hungry and anxious to snap up any unwary fish. Back of them were other men, men with shrewd ideas, subtle resources. Men of immense means whose enterprise and holdings these stocks represented, the men who schemed out and built the railroads, opened the mines, organized trading enterprises, and built up immense manufactories. They might use brokers or other agents to buy and sell on 'change; but this buying and selling must be, and always was, incidental to the actual fact–the mine, the railroad, the wheat crop, the flour mill, and so on. Anything less than straight-out sales to realize quickly on assets, or buying to hold as an investment, was gambling pure and simple, and these men were gamblers. He was nothing more than a gambler's agent. It was not troubling him any just at this moment, but it was not at all a mystery now, what he was. As in the case of Waterman Company, he sized up these men shrewdly, judging some to be weak, some foolish, some clever, some slow, but in the main all small-minded or deficient because they were agents, tools, or gamblers. A man, a real man, must never be an agent, a tool, or a gambler–acting for himself or for others–he must employ such. A real man–a financier–was never a tool. He used tools. He created. He led.

Clearly, very clearly, at nineteen, twenty, and twenty-one years of age, he saw all this, but he was not quite ready yet to do anything about it. He was certain, however, that his day would come.

Chapter VII

In the meantime, his interest in Mrs. Semple had been secretly and strangely growing. When he received an invitation to call at the Semple home, he accepted with a great deal of pleasure. Their house was located not so very far from his own, on North Front Street, in the neighborhood of what is now known as No. 956. It had, in summer, quite a wealth of green leaves and vines. The little side porch which ornamented its south wall commanded a charming view of the river, and all the windows and doors were topped with lunettes of small-paned glass. The interior of the house was not as pleasing as he would have had it. Artistic impressiveness, as to the furniture at least, was wanting, although it was new and good. The pictures were–well, simply pictures. There were no books to speak of–the Bible, a few current novels, some of the more significant histories, and a collection of antiquated odds and ends in the shape of books inherited from relatives. The china was good–of a delicate pattern. The carpets and wall-paper were too high in key. So it went. Still, the personality of Lillian Semple was worth something, for she was really pleasing to look upon, making a picture wherever she stood or sat.

There were no children—a dispensation of sex conditions which had nothing to do with her, for she longed to have them. She was without any notable experience in social life, except such as had come to the Wiggin family, of which she was a member—relatives and a few neighborhood friends visiting. Lillian Wiggin, that was her maiden name—had two brothers and one sister, all living in Philadelphia and all married at this time. They thought she had done very well in her marriage.

It could not be said that she had wildly loved Mr. Semple at any time. Although she had cheerfully married him, he was not the kind of man who could arouse a notable passion in any woman. He was practical, methodic, orderly. His shoe store was a good one—well-stocked with styles reflecting the current tastes and a model of cleanliness and what one might term pleasing brightness. He loved to talk, when he talked at all, of shoe manufacturing, the development of lasts and styles. The ready-made shoe—machine-made to a certain extent—was just coming into its own slowly, and outside of these, supplies of which he kept, he employed bench-making shoemakers, satisfying his customers with personal measurements and making the shoes to order.

Mrs. Semple read a little—not much. She had a habit of sitting and apparently brooding reflectively at times, but it was not based on any deep thought. She had that curious beauty of body, though, that made her somewhat like a figure on an antique vase, or out of a Greek chorus. It was in this light, unquestionably, that Cowperwood saw her, for from the beginning he could not keep his eyes off her. In a way, she was aware of this but she did not attach any significance to it. Thoroughly conventional, satisfied now that her life was bound permanently with that of her husband, she had settled down to a staid and quiet existence.

At first, when Frank called, she did not have much to say. She was gracious, but the burden of conversation fell on her husband. Cowperwood watched the varying expression of her face from time to time, and if she had been at all psychic she must have felt something. Fortunately she was not. Semple talked to him pleasantly, because in the first place Frank was becoming financially significant, was suave and ingratiating, and in the next place he was anxious to get richer and somehow Frank represented progress to him in that line. One spring evening they sat on the porch and talked—nothing very important—slavery, street-cars, the panic—it was on then, that of 1857—the development of the West. Mr. Semple wanted to know all about the stock exchange. In return Frank asked about the shoe business, though he really did not care. All the while, inoffensively, he watched Mrs. Semple. Her manner, he thought, was soothing, attractive, delightful. She served tea and cake for them. They went inside after a time to avoid the mosquitoes. She played the piano. At ten o'clock he left.

Thereafter, for a year or so, Cowperwood bought his shoes of Mr. Semple. Occasionally also he stopped in the Chestnut Street store to exchange the time of the day. Semple asked his opinion as to the advisability of buying some shares in the Fifth and Sixth Street line, which, having secured a franchise, was creating great excitement. Cowperwood gave him his best judgment. It was sure to be profitable. He himself had purchased one hundred shares at five dollars a share, and urged Semple to do so. But he was not interested in him personally. He liked Mrs. Semple, though he did not see her very often.

About a year later, Mr. Semple died. It was an untimely death, one of those fortuitous and in a way insignificant episodes which are, nevertheless, dramatic in a dull way to those most concerned. He was seized with a cold in the chest late in the fall–one of those seizures ordinarily attributed to wet feet or to going out on a damp day without an overcoat–and had insisted on going to business when Mrs. Semple urged him to stay at home and recuperate. He was in his way a very determined person, not obstreperously so, but quietly and under the surface. Business was a great urge. He saw himself soon to be worth about fifty thousand dollars. Then this cold–nine more days of pneumonia–and he was dead. The shoe store was closed for a few days; the house was full of sympathetic friends and church people. There was a funeral, with burial service in the Callowhill Presbyterian Church, to which they belonged, and then he was buried. Mrs. Semple cried bitterly. The shock of death affected her greatly and left her for a time in a depressed state. A brother of hers, David Wiggin, undertook for the time being to run the shoe business for her. There was no will, but in the final adjustment, which included the sale of the shoe business, there being no desire on anybody's part to contest her right to all the property, she received over eighteen thousand dollars. She continued to reside in the Front Street house, and was considered a charming and interesting widow.

Throughout this procedure young Cowperwood, only twenty years of age, was quietly manifest. He called during the illness. He attended the funeral. He helped her brother, David Wiggin, dispose of the shoe business. He called once or twice after the funeral, then stayed away for a considerable time. In five months he reappeared, and thereafter he was a caller at stated intervals–periods of a week or ten days.

Again, it would be hard to say what he saw in Semple. Her prettiness, wax-like in its quality, fascinated him; her indifference aroused perhaps his combative soul. He could not have explained why, but he wanted her in an urgent, passionate way. He could not think of her reasonably, and he did not talk of her much to any one. His family knew that he went to see her, but there had grown up in the Cowperwood family a deep respect for the mental force of Frank. He was genial, cheerful, gay at most times, without being talkative, and he was decidedly successful. Everybody knew he was making money now. His salary was fifty dollars a week, and he was certain soon to get more. Some lots of his in West Philadelphia, bought three years before, had increased notably in value. His street-car holdings, augmented by still additional lots of fifty and one hundred and one hundred and fifty shares in new lines incorporated, were slowly rising, in spite of hard times, from the initiative five dollars in each case to ten, fifteen, and twenty-five dollars a share–all destined to go to par. He was liked in the financial district and he was sure that he had a successful future. Because of his analysis of the brokerage situation he had come to the conclusion that he did not want to be a stock gambler. Instead, he was considering the matter of engaging in bill-brokering, a business which he had observed to be very profitable and which involved no risk as long as one had capital. Through his work and his father's connections he had met many people–merchants, bankers, traders. He could get their business, or a part of it, he knew. People in Drexel Co. and Clark Co. were friendly to him. Jay Cooke, a rising banking personality, was a personal friend of his.

Meanwhile he called on Mrs. Semple, and the more he called the better he liked her. There was no exchange of brilliant ideas between them; but he had a way of being comforting and social when he wished. He advised her about her business affairs in so intelligent a way that even her relatives approved of it. She came to like him, because he was so considerate, quiet, reassuring, and so ready to explain over and over until everything was quite plain to her. She could see that he was looking on her affairs quite as if they were his own, trying to make them safe and secure.

"You're so very kind, Frank," she said to him, one night. "I'm awfully grateful. I don't know what I would have done if it hadn't been for you."

She looked at his handsome face, which was turned to hers, with child-like simplicity.

"Not at all. Not at all. I want to do it. I wouldn't have been happy if I couldn't."

His eyes had a peculiar, subtle ray in them–not a gleam. She felt warm toward him, sympathetic, quite satisfied that she could lean on him.

"Well, I am very grateful just the same. You've been so good. Come out Sunday again, if you want to, or any evening. I'll be home."

It was while he was calling on her in this way that his Uncle Seneca died in Cuba and left him fifteen thousand dollars. This money made him worth nearly twenty-five thousand dollars in his own right, and he knew exactly what to do with it. A panic had come since Mr. Semple had died, which had illustrated to him very clearly what an uncertain thing the brokerage business was. There was really a severe business depression. Money was so scarce that it could fairly be said not to exist at all. Capital, frightened by uncertain trade and money conditions, everywhere, retired to its hiding-places in banks, vaults, tea-kettles, and stockings. The country seemed to be going to the dogs. War with the South or secession was vaguely looming up in the distance. The temper of the whole nation was nervous. People dumped their holdings on the market in order to get money. Tighe discharged three of his clerks. He cut down his expenses in every possible way, and used up all his private savings to protect his private holdings. He mortgaged his house, his land holdings–everything; and in many instances young Cowperwood was his intermediary, carrying blocks of shares to different banks to get what he could on them.

"See if your father's bank won't loan me fifteen thousand on these," he said to Frank, one day, producing a bundle of Philadelphia Wilmington shares. Frank had heard his father speak of them in times past as excellent.

"They ought to be good," the elder Cowperwood said, dubiously, when shown the package of securities. "At any other time they would be. But money is so tight. We find it awfully hard these days to meet our own obligations. I'll talk to Mr. Kugel." Mr. Kugel was the president.

There was a long conversation–a long wait. His father came back to say it was doubtful whether they could make the loan. Eight per cent., then being secured for money, was a small rate of interest, considering its need. For ten per cent. Mr. Kugel might make a call-loan. Frank went back to his employer, whose commercial choler rose at the report.

"For Heaven's sake, is there no money at all in the town?" he demanded, contentiously. "Why, the interest they want is ruinous! I can't stand that. Well, take 'em back and bring me the money. Good God, this'll never do at all, at all!"

Frank went back. "He'll pay ten per cent.," he said, quietly.

Tighe was credited with a deposit of fifteen thousand dollars, with privilege to draw against it at once. He made out a check for the total fifteen thousand at once to the Girard National Bank to cover a shrinkage there. So it went.

During all these days young Cowperwood was following these financial complications with interest. He was not disturbed by the cause of slavery, or the talk of secession, or the general progress or decline of the country, except in so far as it affected his immediate interests. He longed to become a stable financier; but, now that he saw the inside of the brokerage business, he was not so sure that he wanted to stay in it. Gambling in stocks, according to conditions produced by this panic, seemed very hazardous. A number of brokers failed. He saw them rush in to Tighe with anguished faces and ask that certain trades be canceled. Their very homes were in danger, they said. They would be wiped out, their wives and children put out on the street.

This panic, incidentally, only made Frank more certain as to what he really wanted to do—now that he had this free money, he would go into business for himself. Even Tighe's offer of a minor partnership failed to tempt him.

"I think you have a nice business," he explained, in refusing, "but I want to get in the note-brokerage business for myself. I don't trust this stock game. I'd rather have a little business of my own than all the floor work in this world."

"But you're pretty young, Frank," argued his employer. "You have lots of time to work for yourself." In the end he parted friends with both Tighe and Rivers. "That's a smart young fellow," observed Tighe, ruefully.

"He'll make his mark," rejoined Rivers. "He's the shrewdest boy of his age I ever saw."

Chapter VIII

Cowperwood's world at this time was of roseate hue. He was in love and had money of his own to start his new business venture. He could take his street-car stocks, which were steadily increasing in value, and raise seventy per cent. of their market value. He could put a mortgage on his lots and get money there, if necessary. He had established financial relations with the Girard National Bank—President Davison there having taken a fancy to him—and he proposed to borrow from that institution some day. All he wanted was suitable investments—things in which he could realize surely, quickly. He saw fine prospective profits in the street-car lines, which were rapidly developing into local ramifications.

He purchased a horse and buggy about this time—the most attractive-looking animal and vehicle he could find—the combination cost him five hundred dollars—and invited Mrs. Semple to drive with him. She refused at first, but later consented. He had told her of his success, his prospects, his windfall of fifteen thousand dollars, his intention of going into the note-brokerage business. She knew his father was likely to succeed to the position of vice-president in the Third National Bank, and she liked the Cowperwoods. Now she began to realize that there was something more than mere friendship here. This erstwhile boy was a man, and he was calling on her. It was almost ridiculous in the face of things–her seniority, her widowhood, her placid, retiring disposition–but the sheer, quiet, determined force of this young man made it plain that he was not to be balked by her sense of convention.

Cowperwood did not delude himself with any noble theories of conduct in regard to her. She was beautiful, with a mental and physical lure for him that was irresistible, and that was all he desired to know. No other woman was holding him like that. It never occurred to him that he could not or should not like other women at the same time. There was a great deal of palaver about the sanctity of the home. It rolled off his mental sphere like water off the feathers of a duck. He was not eager for her money, though he was well aware of it. He felt that he could use it to her advantage. He wanted her physically. He felt a keen, primitive interest in the children they would have. He wanted to find out if he could make her love him vigorously and could rout out the memory of her former life. Strange ambition. Strange perversion, one might almost say.

In spite of her fears and her uncertainty, Lillian Semple accepted his attentions and interest because, equally in spite of herself, she was drawn to him. One night, when she was going to bed, she stopped in front of her dressing table and looked at her face and her bare neck and arms. They were very pretty. A subtle something came over her as she surveyed her long, peculiarly shaded hair. She thought of young Cowperwood, and then was chilled and shamed by the vision of the late Mr. Semple and the force and quality of public opinion.

"Why do you come to see me so often?" she asked him when he called the following evening.

"Oh, don't you know?" he replied, looking at her in an interpretive way.

"No."

"Sure you don't?"

"Well, I know you liked Mr. Semple, and I always thought you liked me as his wife. He's gone, though, now."

"And you're here," he replied.

"And I'm here?"

"Yes. I like you. I like to be with you. Don't you like me that way?"

"Why, I've never thought of it. You're so much younger. I'm five years older than you are."

"In years," he said, "certainly. That's nothing. I'm fifteen years older than you are in other ways. I know more about life in some ways than you can ever hope to learn–don't you think so?" he added, softly, persuasively.

"Well, that's true. But I know a lot of things you don't know." She laughed softly, showing her pretty teeth.

It was evening. They were on the side porch. The river was before them.

"Yes, but that's only because you're a woman. A man can't hope to get a woman's point of view exactly. But I'm talking about practical affairs of this world. You're not as old that way as I am."

"Well, what of it?"

"Nothing. You asked why I came to see you. That's why. Partly."

He relapsed into silence and stared at the water.

She looked at him. His handsome body, slowly broadening, was nearly full grown. His face, because of its full, clear, big, inscrutable eyes, had an expression which was almost babyish. She could not have guessed the depths it veiled. His cheeks were pink, his hands not large, but sinewy and strong. Her pale, uncertain, lymphatic body extracted a form of dynamic energy from him even at this range.

"I don't think you ought to come to see me so often. People won't think well of it." She ventured to take a distant, matronly air–the air she had originally held toward him.

"People," he said, "don't worry about people. People think what you want them to think. I wish you wouldn't take that distant air toward me."

"Why?"

"Because I like you."

"But you mustn't like me. It's wrong. I can't ever marry you. You're too young. I'm too old."

"Don't say that!" he said, imperiously. "There's nothing to it. I want you to marry me. You know I do. Now, when will it be?"

"Why, how silly! I never heard of such a thing!" she exclaimed. "It will never be, Frank. It can't be!"

"Why can't it?" he asked.

"Because–well, because I'm older. People would think it strange. I'm not long enough free."

"Oh, long enough nothing!" he exclaimed, irritably. "That's the one thing I have against you–you are so worried about what people think. They don't make your life. They certainly don't make mine. Think of yourself first. You have your own life to make. Are you going to let what other people think stand in the way of what you want to do?"

"But I don't want to," she smiled.

He arose and came over to her, looking into her eyes.

"Well?" she asked, nervously, quizzically.

He merely looked at her.

"Well?" she queried, more flustered.

He stooped down to take her arms, but she got up.

"Now you must not come near me," she pleaded, determinedly. "I'll go in the house, and I'll not let you come any more. It's terrible! You're silly! You mustn't interest yourself in me."

She did show a good deal of determination, and he desisted. But for the time being only. He called again and again. Then one night, when they had gone inside because of the mosquitoes, and when she had insisted that he must stop coming to see her, that his attentions were noticeable to others, and that she would be disgraced, he caught her, under desperate protest, in his arms.

"Now, see here!" she exclaimed. "I told you! It's silly! You mustn't kiss me! How dare you! Oh! oh! oh!–"

She broke away and ran up the near-by stairway to her room. Cowperwood followed her swiftly. As she pushed the door to he forced it open and recaptured her. He lifted her bodily from her feet and held her crosswise, lying in his arms.

"Oh, how could you!" she exclaimed. "I will never speak to you any more. I will never let you come here any more if you don't put me down this minute. Put me down!"

"I'll put you down, sweet," he said. "I'll take you down," at the same time pulling her face to him and kissing her. He was very much aroused, excited.

While she was twisting and protesting, he carried her down the stairs again into the living-room, and seated himself in the great armchair, still holding her tight in his arms.

"Oh!" she sighed, falling limp on his shoulder when he refused to let her go. Then, because of the set determination of his face, some intense pull in him, she smiled. "How would I ever explain if I did marry you?" she asked, weakly. "Your father! Your mother!"

"You don't need to explain. I'll do that. And you needn't worry about my family. They won't care."

"But mine," she recoiled.

"Don't worry about yours. I'm not marrying your family. I'm marrying you. We have independent means."

She relapsed into additional protests; but he kissed her the more. There was a deadly persuasion to his caresses. Mr. Semple had never displayed any such fire. He aroused a force of feeling in her which had not previously been there. She was afraid of it and ashamed.

"Will you marry me in a month?" he asked, cheerfully, when she paused.

"You know I won't!" she exclaimed, nervously. "The idea! Why do you ask?"

"What difference does it make? We're going to get married eventually." He was thinking how attractive he could make her look in other surroundings. Neither she nor his family knew how to live.

"Well, not in a month. Wait a little while. I will marry you after a while–after you see whether you want me."

He caught her tight. "I'll show you," he said.

"Please stop. You hurt me."

"How about it? Two months?"

"Certainly not."

"Three?"

"Well, maybe."

"No maybe in that case. We marry."

"But you're only a boy."

"Don't worry about me. You'll find out how much of a boy I am."

He seemed of a sudden to open up a new world to her, and she realized that she had never really lived before. This man represented something bigger and stronger than ever her husband had dreamed of. In his young way he was terrible, irresistible.

"Well, in three months then," she whispered, while he rocked her cozily in his arms.

Chapter IX

Cowperwood started in the note brokerage business with a small office at No. 64 South Third Street, where he very soon had the pleasure of discovering that his former excellent business connections remembered him. He would go to one house, where he suspected ready money might be desirable, and offer to negotiate their notes or any paper they might issue bearing six per cent. interest for a commission and then he would sell the paper for a small commission to some one who would welcome a secure investment. Sometimes his father, sometimes other people, helped him with suggestions as to when and how. Between the two ends he might make four and five per cent. on the total transaction. In the first year he cleared six thousand dollars over and above all expenses. That wasn't much, but he was augmenting it in another way which he believed would bring great profit in the future.

Before the first street-car line, which was a shambling affair, had been laid on Front Street, the streets of Philadelphia had been crowded with hundreds of springless omnibuses rattling over rough, hard, cobblestones. Now, thanks to the idea of John Stephenson, in New York, the double rail track idea had come, and besides the line on Fifth and Sixth Streets (the cars running out one street and back on another) which had paid splendidly from the start, there were many other lines proposed or under way. The city was as eager to see street-cars replace omnibuses as it was to see railroads replace canals. There was opposition, of course. There always is in such cases. The cry of probable monopoly was raised. Disgruntled and defeated omnibus owners and drivers groaned aloud.

Cowperwood had implicit faith in the future of the street railway. In support of this belief he risked all he could spare on new issues of stock shares in new companies. He wanted to be on the inside wherever possible, always, though this was a little difficult in the matter of the street-railways, he having been so young when they started and not having yet arranged his financial connections to make them count for much. The Fifth and Sixth Street line, which had been but recently started, was paying six hundred dollars a day. A project for a West Philadelphia line (Walnut and Chestnut) was on foot, as were lines to occupy Second and Third Streets, Race and Vine, Spruce and Pine, Green and Coates, Tenth and Eleventh, and so forth. They were engineered and backed by some powerful capitalists who had influence with the State legislature and could, in spite of great public protest, obtain franchises. Charges of corruption were in the air. It was argued that the streets were valuable, and that the companies should pay a road tax of a thousand dollars a mile. Somehow, however, these splendid grants were gotten through, and the public, hearing of the Fifth and Sixth Street line profits, was eager to invest. Cowperwood was one of these, and when the Second and Third Street line was engineered, he invested in that and in the Walnut and Chestnut Street line also. He began to have vague dreams of controlling a line himself some day, but as yet he did not see exactly how it was to be done, since his business was far from being a bonanza.

In the midst of this early work he married Mrs. Semple. There was no vast to-do about it, as he did not want any and his bride-to-be was nervous, fearsome of public opinion. His family did not entirely approve. She was too old, his mother and father thought, and then Frank, with his prospects, could have done much better. His sister

Anna fancied that Mrs. Semple was designing, which was, of course, not true. His brothers, Joseph and Edward, were interested, but not certain as to what they actually thought, since Mrs. Semple was good-looking and had some money.

It was a warm October day when he and Lillian went to the altar, in the First Presbyterian Church of Callowhill Street. His bride, Frank was satisfied, looked exquisite in a trailing gown of cream lace–a creation that had cost months of labor. His parents, Mrs. Seneca Davis, the Wiggin family, brothers and sisters, and some friends were present. He was a little opposed to this idea, but Lillian wanted it. He stood up straight and correct in black broadcloth for the wedding ceremony–because she wished it, but later changed to a smart business suit for traveling. He had arranged his affairs for a two weeks' trip to New York and Boston. They took an afternoon train for New York, which required five hours to reach. When they were finally alone in the Astor House, New York, after hours of make-believe and public pretense of indifference, he gathered her in his arms.

"Oh, it's delicious," he exclaimed, "to have you all to myself."

She met his eagerness with that smiling, tantalizing passivity which he had so much admired but which this time was tinged strongly with a communicated desire. He thought he should never have enough of her, her beautiful face, her lovely arms, her smooth, lymphatic body. They were like two children, billing and cooing, driving, dining, seeing the sights. He was curious to visit the financial sections of both cities. New York and Boston appealed to him as commercially solid. He wondered, as he observed the former, whether he should ever leave Philadelphia. He was going to be very happy there now, he thought, with Lillian and possibly a brood of young Cowperwoods. He was going to work hard and make money. With his means and hers now at his command, he might become, very readily, notably wealthy.

Chapter X

The home atmosphere which they established when they returned from their honeymoon was a great improvement in taste over that which had characterized the earlier life of Mrs. Cowperwood as Mrs. Semple. They had decided to occupy her house, on North Front Street, for a while at least. Cowperwood, aggressive in his current artistic mood, had objected at once after they were engaged to the spirit of the furniture and decorations, or lack of them, and had suggested that he be allowed to have it brought more in keeping with his idea of what was appropriate. During the years in which he had been growing into manhood he had come instinctively into sound notions of what was artistic and refined. He had seen so many homes that were more distinguished and harmonious than his own. One could not walk or drive about Philadelphia without seeing and being impressed with the general tendency toward a more cultivated and selective social life. Many excellent and expensive houses were being erected. The front lawn, with some attempt at floral gardening, was achieving local popularity. In the homes of the Tighes, the Leighs, Arthur Rivers, and others, he had noticed art objects of some distinction–bronzes, marbles, hangings, pictures, clocks, rugs.

It seemed to him now that his comparatively commonplace house could be made into something charming and for comparatively little money. The dining-room for instance which, through two plain windows set in a hat side wall back of the veranda, looked south over a stretch of grass and several trees and bushes to a dividing fence where the Semple property ended and a neighbor's began, could be made so much more attractive. That fence–sharp-pointed, gray palings–could be torn away and a hedge put in its place. The wall which divided the dining-room from the parlor could be knocked through and a hanging of some pleasing character put in its place. A bay-window could be built to replace the two present oblong windows–a bay which would come down to the floor and open out on the lawn via swiveled, diamond-shaped, lead-paned frames. All this shabby, nondescript furniture, collected from heaven knows where–partly inherited from the Semples and the Wiggins and partly bought–could be thrown out or sold and something better and more harmonious introduced. He knew a young man by the name of Ellsworth, an architect newly graduated from a local school, with whom he had struck up an interesting friendship–one of those inexplicable inclinations of temperament. Wilton Ellsworth was an artist in spirit, quiet, meditative, refined. From discussing the quality of a certain building on Chestnut Street which was then being erected, and which Ellsworth pronounced atrocious, they had fallen to discussing art in general, or the lack of it, in America. And it occurred to him that Ellsworth was the man to carry out his decorative views to a nicety. When he suggested the young man to Lillian, she placidly agreed with him and also with his own ideas of how the house could be revised.

So while they were gone on their honeymoon Ellsworth began the revision on an estimated cost of three thousand dollars, including the furniture. It was not completed for nearly three weeks after their return; but when finished made a comparatively new house. The dining-room bay hung low over the grass, as Frank wished, and the windows were diamond-paned and leaded, swiveled on brass rods. The parlor and dining-room were separated by sliding doors; but the intention was to hang in this opening a silk hanging depicting a wedding scene in Normandy. Old English oak was used in the dining-room, an American imitation of Chippendale and Sheraton for the sitting-room and the bedrooms. There were a few simple water-colors hung here and there, some bronzes of Hosmer and Powers, a marble venus by Potter, a now forgotten sculptor, and other objects of art–nothing of any distinction. Pleasing, appropriately colored rugs covered the floor. Mrs. Cowperwood was shocked by the nudity of the Venus which conveyed an atmosphere of European freedom not common to America; but she said nothing. It was all harmonious and soothing, and she did not feel herself capable to judge. Frank knew about these things so much better than she did. Then with a maid and a man of all work installed, a program of entertaining was begun on a small scale.

Those who recall the early years of their married life can best realize the subtle changes which this new condition brought to Frank, for, like all who accept the hymeneal yoke, he was influenced to a certain extent by the things with which he surrounded himself. Primarily, from certain traits of his character, one would have imagined him called to be a citizen of eminent respectability and worth. He appeared to be an ideal home man. He delighted to return to his wife in the evenings, leaving the crowded downtown section where traffic clamored and men hurried. Here he could feel that he was well-stationed and physically happy in life. The thought of the dinner-table with candles upon it (his idea); the thought of Lillian in a trailing gown of pale-blue or green silk–he liked her in those colors; the thought of a large fireplace flaming with solid lengths of cord-wood, and Lillian snuggling in his arms, gripped his immature imagination. As has been said before, he cared nothing for books, but life, pictures, trees, physical contact–these, in spite of his shrewd and already gripping financial calculations, held him. To live richly, joyously, fully–his whole nature craved that.

And Mrs. Cowperwood, in spite of the difference in their years, appeared to be a fit mate for him at this time. She was once awakened, and for the time being, clinging, responsive, dreamy. His mood and hers was for a baby, and in a little while that happy expectation was whispered to him by her. She had half fancied that her previous barrenness was due to herself, and was rather surprised and delighted at the proof that it was not so. It opened new possibilities–a seemingly glorious future of which she was not afraid. He liked it, the idea of self-duplication. It was almost acquisitive, this thought. For days and weeks and months and years, at least the first four or five, he took a keen satisfaction in coming home evenings, strolling about the yard, driving with his wife, having friends in to dinner, talking over with her in an explanatory way the things he intended to do. She did not understand his financial abstrusities, and he did not trouble to make them clear.

But love, her pretty body, her lips, her quiet manner–the lure of all these combined, and his two children, when they came–two in four years–held him. He would dandle Frank, Jr., who was the first to arrive, on his knee, looking at his chubby feet, his kindling eyes, his almost formless yet bud-like mouth, and wonder at the process by which children came into the world. There was so much to think of in this connection– the spermatozoic beginning, the strange period of gestation in women, the danger of disease and delivery. He had gone through a real period of strain when Frank, Jr., was born, for Mrs. Cowperwood was frightened. He feared for the beauty of her body–troubled over the danger of losing her; and he actually endured his first worry when he stood outside the door the day the child came. Not much–he was too self-sufficient, too resourceful; and yet he worried, conjuring up thoughts of death and the end of their present state. Then word came, after certain piercing, harrowing cries, that all was well, and he was permitted to look at the new arrival. The experience broadened his conception of things, made him more solid in his judgment of life. That old conviction of tragedy underlying the surface of things, like wood under its veneer, was emphasized. Little Frank, and later Lillian, blue-eyed and golden-haired, touched his imagination for a while. There was a good deal to this home idea, after all. That was the way life was organized, and properly so–its cornerstone was the home.

It would be impossible to indicate fully how subtle were the material changes which these years involved–changes so gradual that they were, like the lap of soft waters, unnoticeable. Considerable–a great deal, considering how little he had to begin with– wealth was added in the next five years. He came, in his financial world, to know fairly intimately, as commercial relationships go, some of the subtlest characters of the steadily enlarging financial world. In his days at Tighe's and on the exchange, many curious figures had been pointed out to him–State and city officials of one grade and another who were "making something out of politics," and some national figures who came from Washington to Philadelphia at times to see Drexel Co., Clark Co., and even Tighe Co. These men, as he learned, had tips or advance news of legislative or economic changes which were sure to affect certain stocks or trade opportunities. A young clerk had once pulled his sleeve at Tighe's.

"See that man going in to see Tighe?"

"Yes."

"That's Murtagh, the city treasurer. Say, he don't do anything but play a fine game. All that money to invest, and he don't have to account for anything except the principal. The interest goes to him."

Cowperwood understood. All these city and State officials speculated. They had a habit of depositing city and State funds with certain bankers and brokers as authorized agents or designated State depositories. The banks paid no interest–save to the officials personally. They loaned it to certain brokers on the officials' secret order, and the latter invested it in "sure winners." The bankers got the free use of the money a part of the time, the brokers another part: the officials made money, and the brokers received a fat commission. There was a political ring in Philadelphia in which the mayor, certain members of the council, the treasurer, the chief of police, the commissioner of public works, and others shared. It was a case generally of "You scratch my back and I'll scratch yours." Cowperwood thought it rather shabby work at first, but many men were rapidly getting rich and no one seemed to care. The newspapers were always talking about civic patriotism and pride but never a word about these things. And the men who did them were powerful and respected.

There were many houses, a constantly widening circle, that found him a very trustworthy agent in disposing of note issues or note payment. He seemed to know so quickly where to go to get the money. From the first he made it a principle to keep twenty thousand dollars in cash on hand in order to be able to take up a proposition instantly and without discussion. So, often he was able to say, "Why, certainly, I can do that," when otherwise, on the face of things, he would not have been able to do so. He was asked if he would not handle certain stock transactions on 'change. He had no seat, and he intended not to take any at first; but now he changed his mind, and bought one, not only in Philadelphia, but in New York also. A certain Joseph Zimmerman, a dry-goods man for whom he had handled various note issues, suggested that he undertake operating in street-railway shares for him, and this was the beginning of his return to the floor.

In the meanwhile his family life was changing–growing, one might have said, finer and more secure. Mrs. Cowperwood had, for instance, been compelled from time to time to make a subtle readjustment of her personal relationship with people, as he had with his. When Mr. Semple was alive she had been socially connected with tradesmen principally–retailers and small wholesalers–a very few. Some of the women of her own church, the First Presbyterian, were friendly with her. There had been church teas and sociables which she and Mr. Semple attended, and dull visits to his relatives and hers. The Cowperwoods, the Watermans, and a few families of that caliber, had been the notable exceptions. Now all this was changed. Young Cowperwood did not care very much for her relatives, and the Semples had been alienated by her second, and to them outrageous, marriage. His own family was closely interested by ties of affection and mutual prosperity, but, better than this, he was drawing to himself some really significant personalities. He brought home with him, socially–not to talk business, for he disliked that idea–bankers, investors, customers and prospective customers. Out on the Schuylkill, the Wissahickon, and elsewhere, were popular dining places where one could drive on Sunday. He and Mrs. Cowperwood frequently drove out to Mrs. Seneca Davis's, to Judge Kitchen's, to the home of Andrew Sharpless, a lawyer whom he knew, to the home of Harper Steger, his own lawyer, and others. Cowperwood had the gift of geniality. None of these men or women suspected the depth of his nature–he was thinking, thinking, thinking, but enjoyed life as he went.

One of his earliest and most genuine leanings was toward paintings. He admired nature, but somehow, without knowing why, he fancied one could best grasp it through the personality of some interpreter, just as we gain our ideas of law and politics through individuals. Mrs. Cowperwood cared not a whit one way or another, but she accompanied him to exhibitions, thinking all the while that Frank was a little peculiar. He tried, because he loved her, to interest her in these things intelligently, but while she pretended slightly, she could not really see or care, and it was very plain that she could not.

The children took up a great deal of her time. However, Cowperwood was not troubled about this. It struck him as delightful and exceedingly worth while that she should be so devoted. At the same time, her lethargic manner, vague smile and her sometimes seeming indifference, which sprang largely from a sense of absolute security, attracted him also. She was so different from him! She took her second marriage quite as she had taken her first–a solemn fact which contained no possibility of mental alteration. As for himself, however, he was bustling about in a world which, financially at least, seemed all alteration–there were so many sudden and almost unheard-of changes. He began to look at her at times, with a speculative eye–not very critically, for he liked her–but with an attempt to weigh her personality. He had known her five years and more now. What did he know about her? The vigor of youth–those first years–had made up for so many things, but now that he had her safely...

There came in this period the slow approach, and finally the declaration, of war between the North and the South, attended with so much excitement that almost all current minds were notably colored by it. It was terrific. Then came meetings, public and stirring, and riots; the incident of John Brown's body; the arrival of Lincoln, the great commoner, on his way from Springfield, Illinois, to Washington via Philadelphia, to take the oath of office; the battle of Bull Run; the battle of Vicksburg; the battle of Gettysburg, and so on. Cowperwood was only twenty-five at the time, a cool, determined youth, who thought the slave agitation might be well founded in human rights–no doubt was–but exceedingly dangerous to trade. He hoped the North would win; but it might go hard with him personally and other financiers. He did not care to fight. That seemed silly for the individual man to do. Others might–there were many poor, thin-minded, half-baked creatures who would put themselves up to be shot; but they were only fit to be commanded or shot down. As for him, his life was sacred to himself and his family and his personal interests. He recalled seeing, one day, in one of the quiet side streets, as the working-men were coming home from their work, a small enlisting squad of soldiers in blue marching enthusiastically along, the Union flag flying, the drummers drumming, the fifes blowing, the idea being, of course, to so impress the hitherto indifferent or wavering citizen, to exalt him to such a pitch, that he would lose his sense of proportion, of self-interest, and, forgetting all–wife, parents, home, and children–and seeing only the great need of the country, fall in behind and enlist. He saw one workingman swinging his pail, and evidently not contemplating any such denouement to his day's work, pause, listen as the squad approached, hesitate as it drew close, and as it passed, with a peculiar look of uncertainty or wonder in his eyes, fall in behind and march solemnly away to the enlisting quarters. What was it that had caught this man, Frank asked himself. How was he overcome so easily? He had not intended to go. His face was streaked with the grease and dirt of his work–he looked like a foundry man or machinist, say twenty-five years of age. Frank watched the little squad disappear at the end of the street round the corner under the trees.

This current war-spirit was strange. The people seemed to him to want to hear nothing but the sound of the drum and fife, to see nothing but troops, of which there were thousands now passing through on their way to the front, carrying cold steel in the shape of guns at their shoulders, to hear of war and the rumors of war. It was a thrilling sentiment, no doubt, great but unprofitable. It meant self-sacrifice, and he could not see that. If he went he might be shot, and what would his noble emotion amount to then? He would rather make money, regulate current political, social and financial affairs. The poor fool who fell in behind the enlisting squad–no, not fool, he would not call him that–the poor overwrought working-man–well, Heaven pity him! Heaven pity all of them! They really did not know what they were doing.

One day he saw Lincoln–a tall, shambling man, long, bony, gawky, but tremendously impressive. It was a raw, slushy morning of a late February day, and the great war President was just through with his solemn pronunciamento in regard to the bonds that might have been strained but must not be broken. As he issued from the doorway of Independence Hall, that famous birthplace of liberty, his face was set in a sad, meditative calm. Cowperwood looked at him fixedly as he issued from the doorway surrounded by chiefs of staff, local dignitaries, detectives, and the curious, sympathetic faces of the public. As he studied the strangely rough-hewn countenance a sense of the great worth and dignity of the man came over him.

"A real man, that," he thought; "a wonderful temperament." His every gesture came upon him with great force. He watched him enter his carriage, thinking "So that is the railsplitter, the country lawyer. Well, fate has picked a great man for this crisis."

For days the face of Lincoln haunted him, and very often during the war his mind reverted to that singular figure. It seemed to him unquestionable that fortuitously he had been permitted to look upon one of the world's really great men. War and statesmanship were not for him; but he knew how important those things were–at times.

Chapter XI

It was while the war was on, and after it was perfectly plain that it was not to be of a few days' duration, that Cowperwood's first great financial opportunity came to him. There was a strong demand for money at the time on the part of the nation, the State, and the city. In July, 1861, Congress had authorized a loan of fifty million dollars, to be secured by twenty-year bonds with interest not to exceed seven per cent., and the State authorized a loan of three millions on much the same security, the first being handled by financiers of Boston, New York, and Philadelphia, the second by Philadelphia financiers alone. Cowperwood had no hand in this. He was not big enough. He read in the papers of gatherings of men whom he knew personally or by reputation, "to consider the best way to aid the nation or the State"; but he was not included. And yet his soul yearned to be of them. He noticed how often a rich man's word sufficed–no money, no certificates, no collateral, no anything–just his word. If Drexel Co., or Jay Cooke Co., or Gould Fiske were rumored to be behind anything, how secure it was! Jay Cooke, a young man in Philadelphia, had made a great strike taking this State loan in company with Drexel Co., and selling it at par. The general opinion was that it ought to be and could only be sold at ninety. Cooke did not believe this. He believed that State pride and State patriotism would warrant offering the loan to small banks and private citizens, and that they would subscribe it fully and more. Events justified Cooke magnificently, and his public reputation was assured. Cowperwood wished he could make some such strike; but he was too practical to worry over anything save the facts and conditions that were before him.

His chance came about six months later, when it was found that the State would have to have much more money. Its quota of troops would have to be equipped and paid. There were measures of defense to be taken, the treasury to be replenished. A call for a loan of twenty-three million dollars was finally authorized by the legislature and issued. There was great talk in the street as to who was to handle it–Drexel Co. and Jay Cooke Co., of course.

Cowperwood pondered over this. If he could handle a fraction of this great loan now–he could not possibly handle the whole of it, for he had not the necessary connections–he could add considerably to his reputation as a broker while making a tidy sum. How much could he handle? That was the question. Who would take portions of it? His father's bank? Probably. Waterman Co.? A little. Judge Kitchen? A small fraction. The Mills-David Company? Yes. He thought of different individuals and concerns who, for one reason and another–personal friendship, good-nature, gratitude for past favors, and so on–would take a percentage of the seven-percent. bonds through him. He totaled up his possibilities, and discovered that in all likelihood, with a little preliminary missionary work, he could dispose of one million dollars if personal influence, through local political figures, could bring this much of the loan his way.

One man in particular had grown strong in his estimation as having some subtle political connection not visible on the surface, and this was Edward Malia Butler. Butler was a contractor, undertaking the construction of sewers, water-mains, foundations for buildings, street-paving, and the like. In the early days, long before Cowperwood had known him, he had been a garbage-contractor on his own account. The city at that time had no extended street-cleaning service, particularly in its outlying sections and some of the older, poorer regions. Edward Butler, then a poor young Irishman, had begun by collecting and hauling away the garbage free of charge, and feeding it to his pigs and cattle. Later he discovered that some people were willing to pay a small charge for this service. Then a local political character, a councilman friend of his–they were both Catholics–saw a new point in the whole thing. Butler could be made official garbage-collector. The council could vote an annual appropriation for this service. Butler could employ more wagons than he did now–dozens of them, scores. Not only that, but no other garbage-collector would be allowed. There were others, but the official contract awarded him would also, officially, be the end of the life of any and every disturbing rival. A certain amount of the profitable proceeds would have to be set aside to assuage the feelings of those who were not contractors. Funds would have to be loaned at election time to certain individuals and organizations–but no matter. The amount would be small. So Butler and Patrick Gavin Comiskey, the councilman (the latter silently) entered into business relations. Butler gave up driving a wagon himself. He hired a young man, a smart Irish boy of his neighborhood, Jimmy Sheehan, to be his assistant, superintendent, stableman, bookkeeper, and what not. Since he soon began to make between four and five thousand a year, where before he made two thousand, he moved into a brick house in an outlying section of the south side, and sent his children to school. Mrs. Butler gave up making soap and feeding pigs. And since then times had been exceedingly good with Edward Butler.

He could neither read nor write at first; but now he knew how, of course. He had learned from association with Mr. Comiskey that there were other forms of contracting–sewers, water-mains, gas-mains, street-paving, and the like. Who better than Edward Butler to do it? He knew the councilmen, many of them. Het met them in the back rooms of saloons, on Sundays and Saturdays at political picnics, at election councils and conferences, for as a beneficiary of the city's largess he was expected to contribute not only money, but advice. Curiously he had developed a strange political wisdom. He knew a successful man or a coming man when he saw one. So many of his bookkeepers, superintendents, time-keepers had graduated into councilmen and state legislators. His nominees–suggested to political conferences–were so often known to make good. First he came to have influence in his councilman's ward, then in his legislative district, then in the city councils of his party–Whig, of course–and then he was supposed to have an organization.

Mysterious forces worked for him in council. He was awarded significant contracts, and he always bid. The garbage business was now a thing of the past. His eldest boy, Owen, was a member of the State legislature and a partner in his business affairs. His second son, Callum, was a clerk in the city water department and an assistant to his father also. Aileen, his eldest daughter, fifteen years of age, was still in St. Agatha's, a convent school in Germantown. Norah, his second daughter and youngest child, thirteen years old, was in attendance at a local private school conducted by a Catholic sisterhood. The Butler family had moved away from South Philadelphia into Girard Avenue, near the twelve hundreds, where a new and rather interesting social life was beginning. They were not of it, but Edward Butler, contractor, now fifty-five years of age, worth, say, five hundred thousand dollars, had many political and financial friends. No longer a "rough neck," but a solid, reddish-faced man, slightly tanned, with broad shoulders and a solid chest, gray eyes, gray hair, a typically Irish face made wise and calm and undecipherable by much experience. His big hands and feet indicated a day when he had not worn the best English cloth suits and tanned leather, but his presence was not in any way offensive–rather the other way about. Though still possessed of a brogue, he was soft-spoken, winning, and persuasive.

He had been one of the first to become interested in the development of the street-car system and had come to the conclusion, as had Cowperwood and many others, that it was going to be a great thing. The money returns on the stocks or shares he had been induced to buy had been ample evidence of that, He had dealt through one broker and another, having failed to get in on the original corporate organizations. He wanted to pick up such stock as he could in one organization and another, for he believed they all had a future, and most of all he wanted to get control of a line or two. In connection with this idea he was looking for some reliable young man, honest and capable, who would work under his direction and do what he said. Then he learned of Cowperwood, and one day sent for him and asked him to call at his house.

Cowperwood responded quickly, for he knew of Butler, his rise, his connections, his force. He called at the house as directed, one cold, crisp February morning. He remembered the appearance of the street afterward–broad, brick-paved sidewalks, macadamized roadway, powdered over with a light snow and set with young, leafless, scrubby trees and lamp-posts. Butler's house was not new–he had bought and repaired it–but it was not an unsatisfactory specimen of the architecture of the time. It was fifty feet wide, four stories tall, of graystone and with four wide, white stone steps leading up to the door. The window arches, framed in white, had U-shaped keystones. There were curtains of lace and a glimpse of red plush through the windows, which gleamed warm against the cold and snow outside. A trim Irish maid came to the door and he gave her his card and was invited into the house.

"Is Mr. Butler home?"

"I'm not sure, sir. I'll find out. He may have gone out."

In a little while he was asked to come upstairs, where he found Butler in a somewhat commercial-looking room. It had a desk, an office chair, some leather furnishings, and a bookcase, but no completeness or symmetry as either an office or a living room. There were several pictures on the wall–an impossible oil painting, for one thing, dark and gloomy; a canal and barge scene in pink and nile green for another; some daguerreotypes of relatives and friends which were not half bad. Cowperwood noticed one of two girls, one with reddish-gold hair, another with what appeared to be silky brown. The beautiful silver effect of the daguerreotype had been tinted. They were pretty girls, healthy, smiling, Celtic, their heads close together, their eyes looking straight out at you. He admired them casually, and fancied they must be Butler's daughters.

"Mr. Cowperwood?" inquired Butler, uttering the name fully with a peculiar accent on the vowels. (He was a slow-moving man, solemn and deliberate.) Cowperwood noticed that his body was hale and strong like seasoned hickory, tanned by wind and rain. The flesh of his cheeks was pulled taut and there was nothing soft or flabby about him.

"I'm that man."

"I have a little matter of stocks to talk over with you" ("matter" almost sounded like "mather"), "and I thought you'd better come here rather than that I should come down to your office. We can be more private-like, and, besides, I'm not as young as I used to be."

He allowed a semi-twinkle to rest in his eye as he looked his visitor over.

Cowperwood smiled.

"Well, I hope I can be of service to you," he said, genially.

"I happen to be interested just at present in pickin' up certain street-railway stocks on 'change. I'll tell you about them later. Won't you have somethin' to drink? It's a cold morning."

"No, thanks; I never drink."

"Never? That's a hard word when it comes to whisky. Well, no matter. It's a good rule. My boys don't touch anything, and I'm glad of it. As I say, I'm interested in pickin' up a few stocks on 'change; but, to tell you the truth, I'm more interested in findin' some clever young felly like yourself through whom I can work. One thing leads to another, you know, in this world." And he looked at his visitor non-committally, and yet with a genial show of interest.

"Quite so," replied Cowperwood, with a friendly gleam in return.

"Well," Butler meditated, half to himself, half to Cowperwood, "there are a number of things that a bright young man could do for me in the street if he were so minded. I have two bright boys of my own, but I don't want them to become stock-gamblers, and I don't know that they would or could if I wanted them to. But this isn't a matter of stock-gambling. I'm pretty busy as it is, and, as I said awhile ago, I'm getting along. I'm not as light on my toes as I once was. But if I had the right sort of a young man–I've been looking into your record, by the way, never fear–he might handle a number of little things–investments and loans–which might bring us each a little somethin'. Sometimes the young men around town ask advice of me in one way and another–they have a little somethin' to invest, and so–"

He paused and looked tantalizingly out of the window, knowing full well Cowperwood was greatly interested, and that this talk of political influence and connections could only whet his appetite. Butler wanted him to see clearly that fidelity was the point in this case–fidelity, tact, subtlety, and concealment.

"Well, if you have been looking into my record," observed Cowperwood, with his own elusive smile, leaving the thought suspended.

Butler felt the force of the temperament and the argument. He liked the young man's poise and balance. A number of people had spoken of Cowperwood to him. (It was now Cowperwood Co. The company was fiction purely.) He asked him something about the street; how the market was running; what he knew about street-railways. Finally he outlined his plan of buying all he could of the stock of two given lines–the Ninth and Tenth and the Fifteenth and Sixteenth–without attracting any attention, if possible. It was to be done slowly, part on 'change, part from individual holders. He did not tell him that there was a certain amount of legislative pressure he hoped to bring to bear to get him franchises for extensions in the regions beyond where the lines now ended, in order that when the time came for them to extend their facilities they would have to see him or his sons, who might be large minority stockholders in these very concerns. It was a far-sighted plan, and meant that the lines would eventually drop into his or his sons' basket.

"I'll be delighted to work with you, Mr. Butler, in any way that you may suggest," observed Cowperwood. "I can't say that I have so much of a business as yet–merely prospects. But my connections are good. I am now a member of the New York and Philadelphia exchanges. Those who have dealt with me seem to like the results I get."

"I know a little something about your work already," reiterated Butler, wisely.

"Very well, then; whenever you have a commission you can call at my office, or write, or I will call here. I will give you my secret operating code, so that anything you say will be strictly confidential."

"Well, we'll not say anything more now. In a few days I'll have somethin' for you. When I do, you can draw on my bank for what you need, up to a certain amount." He got up and looked out into the street, and Cowperwood also arose.

"It's a fine day now, isn't it?"

"It surely is."

"Well, we'll get to know each other better, I'm sure."

He held out his hand.

"I hope so."

Cowperwood went out, Butler accompanying him to the door. As he did so a young girl bounded in from the street, red-cheeked, blue-eyed, wearing a scarlet cape with the peaked hood thrown over her red-gold hair.

"Oh, daddy, I almost knocked you down."

She gave her father, and incidentally Cowperwood, a gleaming, radiant, inclusive smile. Her teeth were bright and small, and her lips bud-red.

"You're home early. I thought you were going to stay all day?"

"I was, but I changed my mind."

She passed on in, swinging her arms.

"Yes, well–" Butler continued, when she had gone. "Then well leave it for a day or two. Good day."

"Good day."

Cowperwood, warm with this enhancing of his financial prospects, went down the steps; but incidentally he spared a passing thought for the gay spirit of youth that had manifested itself in this red-cheeked maiden. What a bright, healthy, bounding girl! Her voice had the subtle, vigorous ring of fifteen or sixteen. She was all vitality. What a fine catch for some young fellow some day, and her father would make him rich, no doubt, or help to.

Chapter XII

It was to Edward Malia Butler that Cowperwood turned now, some nineteen months later when he was thinking of the influence that might bring him an award of a portion of the State issue of bonds. Butler could probably be interested to take some of them himself, or could help him place some. He had come to like Cowperwood very much and was now being carried on the latter's books as a prospective purchaser of large blocks of stocks. And Cowperwood liked this great solid Irishman. He liked his history. He had met Mrs. Butler, a rather fat and phlegmatic Irish woman with a world of hard sense who cared nothing at all for show and who still liked to go into the kitchen and superintend the cooking. He had met Owen and Callum Butler, the boys, and Aileen and Norah, the girls. Aileen was the one who had bounded up the steps the first day he had called at the Butler house several seasons before.

There was a cozy grate-fire burning in Butler's improvised private office when Cowperwood called. Spring was coming on, but the evenings were cool. The older man invited Cowperwood to make himself comfortable in one of the large leather chairs before the fire and then proceeded to listen to his recital of what he hoped to accomplish.

"Well, now, that isn't so easy," he commented at the end. "You ought to know more about that than I do. I'm not a financier, as you well know." And he grinned apologetically.

"It's a matter of influence," went on Cowperwood. "And favoritism. That I know. Drexel Company and Cooke Company have connections at Harrisburg. They have men of their own looking after their interests. The attorney-general and the State treasurer are hand in glove with them. Even if I put in a bid, and can demonstrate that I can handle the loan, it won't help me to get it. Other people have done that. I have to have friends–influence. You know how it is."

"Them things," Butler said, "is easy enough if you know the right parties to approach. Now there's Jimmy Oliver–he ought to know something about that." Jimmy Oliver was the whilom district attorney serving at this time, and incidentally free adviser to Mr. Butler in many ways. He was also, accidentally, a warm personal friend of the State treasurer.

"How much of the loan do you want?"

"Five million."

"Five million!" Butler sat up. "Man, what are you talking about? That's a good deal of money. Where are you going to sell all that?"

"I want to bid for five million," assuaged Cowperwood, softly. "I only want one million but I want the prestige of putting in a bona fide bid for five million. It will do me good on the street."

Butler sank back somewhat relieved.

"Five million! Prestige! You want one million. Well, now, that's different. That's not such a bad idea. We ought to be able to get that."

He rubbed his chin some more and stared into the fire.

And Cowperwood felt confident when he left the house that evening that Butler would not fail him but would set the wheels working. Therefore, he was not surprised, and knew exactly what it meant, when a few days later he was introduced to City Treasurer Julian Bode, who promised to introduce him to State Treasurer Van Nostrand and to see that his claims to consideration were put before the people. "Of course, you know," he said to Cowperwood, in the presence of Butler, for it was at the latter's home that the conference took place, "this banking crowd is very powerful. You know who they are. They don't want any interference in this bond issue business. I was talking to Terrence Relihan, who represents them up there"–meaning Harrisburg, the State capital–"and he says they won't stand for it at all. You may have trouble right here in Philadelphia after you get it–they're pretty powerful, you know. Are you sure just where you can place it?"

"Yes, I'm sure," replied Cowperwood.

"Well, the best thing in my judgment is not to say anything at all. Just put in your bid. Van Nostrand, with the governor's approval, will make the award. We can fix the governor, I think. After you get it they may talk to you personally, but that's your business."

Cowperwood smiled his inscrutable smile. There were so many ins and outs to this financial life. It was an endless network of underground holes, along which all sorts of influences were moving. A little wit, a little nimbleness, a little luck-time and opportunity–these sometimes availed. Here he was, through his ambition to get on, and nothing else, coming into contact with the State treasurer and the governor. They were going to consider his case personally, because he demanded that it be considered–nothing more. Others more influential than himself had quite as much right to a share, but they didn't take it. Nerve, ideas, aggressiveness, how these counted when one had luck!

He went away thinking how surprised Drexel Co. and Cooke Co. would be to see him appearing in the field as a competitor. In his home, in a little room on the second floor next his bedroom, which he had fixed up as an office with a desk, a safe, and a leather chair, he consulted his resources. There were so many things to think of. He went over again the list of people whom he had seen and whom he could count on to subscribe, and in so far as that was concerned–the award of one million dollars–he was safe. He figured to make two per cent. on the total transaction, or twenty thousand dollars. If he did he was going to buy a house out on Girard Avenue beyond the Butlers', or, better yet, buy a piece of ground and erect one; mortgaging house and property so to do. His father was prospering nicely. He might want to build a house next to him, and they could live side by side. His own business, aside from this deal, would yield him ten thousand dollars this year. His street-car investments, aggregating fifty thousand, were paying six per cent. His wife's property, represented by this house, some government bonds, and some real estate in West Philadelphia amounted to forty thousand more. Between them they were rich; but he expected to be much richer. All he needed now was to keep cool. If he succeeded in this bond-issue matter, he could do it again and on a larger scale. There would be more issues. He turned out the light after a while and went into his wife's boudoir, where she was sleeping. The nurse and the children were in a room beyond.

"Well, Lillian," he observed, when she awoke and turned over toward him, "I think I have that bond matter that I was telling you about arranged at last. I think I'll get a million of it, anyhow. That'll mean twenty thousand. If I do we'll build out on Girard Avenue. That's going to be the street. The college is making that neighborhood."

"That'll be fine, won't it, Frank!" she observed, and rubbed his arm as he sat on the side of the bed.

Her remark was vaguely speculative.

"We'll have to show the Butlers some attention from now on. He's been very nice to me and he's going to be useful–I can see that. He asked me to bring you over some time. We must go. Be nice to his wife. He can do a lot for me if he wants to. He has two daughters, too. We'll have to have them over here."

"I'll have them to dinner sometime," she agreed cheerfully and helpfully, "and I'll stop and take Mrs. Butler driving if she'll go, or she can take me."

She had already learned that the Butlers were rather showy–the younger generation–that they were sensitive as to their lineage, and that money in their estimation was supposed to make up for any deficiency in any other respect. "Butler himself is a very presentable man," Cowperwood had once remarked to her, "but Mrs. Butler–well, she's all right, but she's a little commonplace. She's a fine woman, though, I think, good-natured and good-hearted." He cautioned her not to overlook Aileen and Norah, because the Butlers, mother and father, were very proud of them.

Mrs. Cowperwood at this time was thirty-two years old; Cowperwood twenty-seven. The birth and care of two children had made some difference in her looks. She was no longer as softly pleasing, more angular. Her face was hollow-cheeked, like so many of Rossetti's and Burne-Jones's women. Her health was really not as good as it had been—the care of two children and a late undiagnosed tendency toward gastritis having reduced her. In short she was a little run down nervously and suffered from fits of depression. Cowperwood had noticed this. He tried to be gentle and considerate, but he was too much of a utilitarian and practical-minded observer not to realize that he was likely to have a sickly wife on his hands later. Sympathy and affection were great things, but desire and charm must endure or one was compelled to be sadly conscious of their loss. So often now he saw young girls who were quite in his mood, and who were exceedingly robust and joyous. It was fine, advisable, practical, to adhere to the virtues as laid down in the current social lexicon, but if you had a sickly wife—And anyhow, was a man entitled to only one wife? Must he never look at another woman? Supposing he found some one? He pondered those things between hours of labor, and concluded that it did not make so much difference. If a man could, and not be exposed, it was all right. He had to be careful, though. Tonight, as he sat on the side of his wife's bed, he was thinking somewhat of this, for he had seen Aileen Butler again, playing and singing at her piano as he passed the parlor door. She was like a bright bird radiating health and enthusiasm—a reminder of youth in general.

"It's a strange world," he thought; but his thoughts were his own, and he didn't propose to tell any one about them.

The bond issue, when it came, was a curious compromise; for, although it netted him his twenty thousand dollars and more and served to introduce him to the financial notice of Philadelphia and the State of Pennsylvania, it did not permit him to manipulate the subscriptions as he had planned. The State treasurer was seen by him at the office of a local lawyer of great repute, where he worked when in the city. He was gracious to Cowperwood, because he had to be. He explained to him just how things were regulated at Harrisburg. The big financiers were looked to for campaign funds. They were represented by henchmen in the State assembly and senate. The governor and the treasurer were foot-free; but there were other influences—prestige, friendship, social power, political ambitions, etc. The big men might constitute a close corporation, which in itself was unfair; but, after all, they were the legitimate sponsors for big money loans of this kind. The State had to keep on good terms with them, especially in times like these. Seeing that Mr. Cowperwood was so well able to dispose of the million he expected to get, it would be perfectly all right to award it to him; but Van Nostrand had a counter-proposition to make. Would Cowperwood, if the financial crowd now handling the matter so desired, turn over his award to them for a consideration—a sum equal to what he expected to make—in the event the award was made to him? Certain financiers desired this. It was dangerous to oppose them. They were perfectly willing he should put in a bid for five million and get the prestige of that; to have him awarded one million and get the prestige of that was well enough also, but they desired to handle the twenty-three million dollars in an unbroken lot. It looked better. He need not be advertised as having withdrawn. They would be content to have him achieve the glory of having done what he started out to do. Just the same the example was bad. Others might wish to imitate him. If it were known in the street privately that he had been coerced, for a consideration, into giving up, others would be deterred from imitating him in the future. Besides, if he refused, they could cause him trouble. His loans might be called. Various banks might not be so friendly in the future. His constituents might be warned against him in one way or another.

Cowperwood saw the point. He acquiesced. It was something to have brought so many high and mighties to their knees. So they knew of him! They were quite well aware of him! Well and good. He would take the award and twenty thousand or thereabouts and withdraw. The State treasurer was delighted. It solved a ticklish proposition for him.

"I'm glad to have seen you," he said. "I'm glad we've met. I'll drop in and talk with you some time when I'm down this way. We'll have lunch together."

The State treasurer, for some odd reason, felt that Mr. Cowperwood was a man who could make him some money. His eye was so keen; his expression was so alert, and yet so subtle. He told the governor and some other of his associates about him.

So the award was finally made; Cowperwood, after some private negotiations in which he met the officers of Drexel Co., was paid his twenty thousand dollars and turned his share of the award over to them. New faces showed up in his office now from time to time—among them that of Van Nostrand and one Terrence Relihan, a representative of some other political forces at Harrisburg. He was introduced to the governor one day at lunch. His name was mentioned in the papers, and his prestige grew rapidly.

Immediately he began working on plans with young Ellsworth for his new house. He was going to build something exceptional this time, he told Lillian. They were going to have to do some entertaining—entertaining on a larger scale than ever. North Front Street was becoming too tame. He put the house up for sale, consulted with his father and found that he also was willing to move. The son's prosperity had redounded to the credit of the father. The directors of the bank were becoming much more friendly to the old man. Next year President Kugel was going to retire. Because of his son's noted coup, as well as his long service, he was going to be made president. Frank was a large borrower from his father's bank. By the same token he was a large depositor. His connection with Edward Butler was significant. He sent his father's bank certain accounts which it otherwise could not have secured. The city treasurer became interested in it, and the State treasurer. Cowperwood, Sr., stood to earn twenty thousand a year as president, and he owed much of it to his son. The two families were now on the best of terms. Anna, now twenty-one, and Edward and Joseph frequently spent the night at Frank's house. Lillian called almost daily at his mother's. There was much interchange of family gossip, and it was thought well to build side by side. So Cowperwood, Sr., bought fifty feet of ground next to his son's thirty-five, and together they commenced the erection of two charming, commodious homes, which were to be connected by a covered passageway, or pergola, which could be inclosed with glass in winter.

The most popular local stone, a green granite was chosen; but Mr. Ellsworth promised to present it in such a way that it would be especially pleasing. Cowperwood, Sr., decided that he could afford to spent seventy-five thousand dollars–he was now worth two hundred and fifty thousand; and Frank decided that he could risk fifty, seeing that he could raise money on a mortgage. He planned at the same time to remove his office farther south on Third Street and occupy a building of his own. He knew where an option was to be had on a twenty-five-foot building, which, though old, could be given a new brownstone front and made very significant. He saw in his mind's eye a handsome building, fitted with an immense plate-glass window; inside his hardwood fixtures visible; and over the door, or to one side of it, set in bronze letters, Cowperwood Co. Vaguely but surely he began to see looming before him, like a fleecy tinted cloud on the horizon, his future fortune. He was to be rich, very, very rich.

Chapter XIII

During all the time that Cowperwood had been building himself up thus steadily the great war of the rebellion had been fought almost to its close. It was now October, 1864. The capture of Mobile and the Battle of the Wilderness were fresh memories. Grant was now before Petersburg, and the great general of the South, Lee, was making that last brilliant and hopeless display of his ability as a strategist and a soldier. There had been times–as, for instance, during the long, dreary period in which the country was waiting for Vicksburg to fall, for the Army of the Potomac to prove victorious, when Pennsylvania was invaded by Lee–when stocks fell and commercial conditions were very bad generally. In times like these Cowperwood's own manipulative ability was taxed to the utmost, and he had to watch every hour to see that his fortune was not destroyed by some unexpected and destructive piece of news.

His personal attitude toward the war, however, and aside from his patriotic feeling that the Union ought to be maintained, was that it was destructive and wasteful. He was by no means so wanting in patriotic emotion and sentiment but that he could feel that the Union, as it had now come to be, spreading its great length from the Atlantic to the Pacific and from the snows of Canada to the Gulf, was worth while. Since his birth in 1837 he had seen the nation reach that physical growth–barring Alaska–which it now possesses. Not so much earlier than his youth Florida had been added to the Union by purchase from Spain; Mexico, after the unjust war of 1848, had ceded Texas and the territory to the West. The boundary disputes between England and the United States in the far Northwest had been finally adjusted. To a man with great social and financial imagination, these facts could not help but be significant; and if they did nothing more, they gave him a sense of the boundless commercial possibilities which existed potentially in so vast a realm. His was not the order of speculative financial enthusiasm which, in the type known as the "promoter," sees endless possibilities for gain in every unexplored rivulet and prairie reach; but the very vastness of the country suggested possibilities which he hoped might remain undisturbed. A territory covering the length of a whole zone and between two seas, seemed to him to possess potentialities which it could not retain if the States of the South were lost.

At the same time, the freedom of the negro was not a significant point with him. He had observed that race from his boyhood with considerable interest, and had been struck with virtues and defects which seemed inherent and which plainly, to him, conditioned their experiences.

He was not at all sure, for instance, that the negroes could be made into anything much more significant than they were. At any rate, it was a long uphill struggle for them, of which many future generations would not witness the conclusion. He had no particular quarrel with the theory that they should be free; he saw no particular reason why the South should not protest vigorously against the destruction of their property and their system. It was too bad that the negroes as slaves should be abused in some instances. He felt sure that that ought to be adjusted in some way; but beyond that he could not see that there was any great ethical basis for the contentions of their sponsors. The vast majority of men and women, as he could see, were not essentially above slavery, even when they had all the guarantees of a constitution formulated to prevent it. There was mental slavery, the slavery of the weak mind and the weak body. He followed the contentions of such men as Sumner, Garrison, Phillips, and Beecher, with considerable interest; but at no time could he see that the problem was a vital one for him. He did not care to be a soldier or an officer of soldiers; he had no gift for polemics; his mind was not of the disputatious order–not even in the realm of finance. He was concerned only to see what was of vast advantage to him, and to devote all his attention to that. This fratricidal war in the nation could not help him. It really delayed, he thought, the true commercial and financial adjustment of the country, and he hoped that it would soon end. He was not of those who complained bitterly of the excessive war taxes, though he knew them to be trying to many. Some of the stories of death and disaster moved him greatly; but, alas, they were among the unaccountable fortunes of life, and could not be remedied by him. So he had gone his way day by day, watching the coming in and the departing of troops, seeing the bands of dirty, disheveled, gaunt, sickly men returning from the fields and hospitals; and all he could do was to feel sorry. This war was not for him. He had taken no part in it, and he felt sure that he could only rejoice in its conclusion–not as a patriot, but as a financier. It was wasteful, pathetic, unfortunate.

The months proceeded apace. A local election intervened and there was a new city treasurer, a new assessor of taxes, and a new mayor; but Edward Malia Butler continued to have apparently the same influence as before. The Butlers and the Cowperwoods had become quite friendly. Mrs. Butler rather liked Lillian, though they were of different religious beliefs; and they went driving or shopping together, the younger woman a little critical and ashamed of the elder because of her poor grammar, her Irish accent, her plebeian tastes–as though the Wiggins had not been as plebeian as any. On the other hand the old lady, as she was compelled to admit, was good-natured and good-hearted. She loved to give, since she had plenty, and sent presents here and there to Lillian, the children, and others. "Now youse must come over and take dinner with us"–the Butlers had arrived at the evening-dinner period–or "Youse must come drive with me to-morrow."

"Aileen, God bless her, is such a foine girl," or "Norah, the darlin', is sick the day."

But Aileen, her airs, her aggressive disposition, her love of attention, her vanity, irritated and at times disgusted Mrs. Cowperwood. She was eighteen now, with a figure which was subtly provocative. Her manner was boyish, hoydenish at times, and although convent-trained, she was inclined to balk at restraint in any form. But there was a softness lurking in her blue eyes that was most sympathetic and human.

St. Timothy's and the convent school in Germantown had been the choice of her parents for her education—what they called a good Catholic education. She had learned a great deal about the theory and forms of the Catholic ritual, but she could not understand them. The church, with its tall, dimly radiant windows, its high, white altar, its figure of St. Joseph on one side and the Virgin Mary on the other, clothed in golden-starred robes of blue, wearing haloes and carrying scepters, had impressed her greatly. The church as a whole—any Catholic church—was beautiful to look at—soothing. The altar, during high mass, lit with a half-hundred or more candles, and dignified and made impressive by the rich, lacy vestments of the priests and the acolytes, the impressive needlework and gorgeous colorings of the amice, chasuble, cope, stole, and maniple, took her fancy and held her eye. Let us say there was always lurking in her a sense of grandeur coupled with a love of color and a love of love. From the first she was somewhat sex-conscious. She had no desire for accuracy, no desire for precise information. Innate sensuousness rarely has. It basks in sunshine, bathes in color, dwells in a sense of the impressive and the gorgeous, and rests there. Accuracy is not necessary except in the case of aggressive, acquisitive natures, when it manifests itself in a desire to seize. True controlling sensuousness cannot be manifested in the most active dispositions, nor again in the most accurate.

There is need of defining these statements in so far as they apply to Aileen. It would scarcely be fair to describe her nature as being definitely sensual at this time. It was too rudimentary. Any harvest is of long growth. The confessional, dim on Friday and Saturday evenings, when the church was lighted by but a few lamps, and the priest's warnings, penances, and ecclesiastical forgiveness whispered through the narrow lattice, moved her as something subtly pleasing. She was not afraid of her sins. Hell, so definitely set forth, did not frighten her. Really, it had not laid hold on her conscience. The old women and old men hobbling into church, bowed in prayer, murmuring over their beads, were objects of curious interest like the wood-carvings in the peculiar array of wood-reliefs emphasizing the Stations of the Cross. She herself had liked to confess, particularly when she was fourteen and fifteen, and to listen to the priest's voice as he admonished her with, "Now, my dear child." A particularly old priest, a French father, who came to hear their confessions at school, interested her as being kind and sweet. His forgiveness and blessing seemed sincere—better than her prayers, which she went through perfunctorily. And then there was a young priest at St. Timothy's, Father David, hale and rosy, with a curl of black hair over his forehead, and an almost jaunty way of wearing his priestly hat, who came down the aisle Sundays sprinkling holy water with a definite, distinguished sweep of the hand, who took her fancy. He heard confessions and now and then she liked to whisper her strange thoughts to him while she actually speculated on what he might privately be thinking. She could not, if she tried, associate him with any divine authority. He was too young, too human. There was something a little malicious, teasing, in the way she delighted to tell him about herself, and then walk demurely, repentantly out. At St. Agatha's she had been rather a difficult person to deal with. She was, as the good sisters of the school had readily perceived, too full of life, too active, to be easily controlled. "That Miss Butler," once observed Sister Constantia, the Mother Superior, to Sister Sempronia, Aileen's immediate mentor, "is a very spirited girl, you may have a great deal of trouble with her unless you use a good deal of tact. You may have to coax her with little gifts. You will get on better." So Sister Sempronia had sought to find what Aileen was most interested in, and bribe her therewith. Being intensely conscious of her father's competence, and vain of her personal superiority, it was not so easy to do. She had wanted to go home occasionally, though; she had wanted to be allowed to wear the sister's rosary of large beads with its pendent cross of ebony and its silver Christ, and this was held up as a great privilege. For keeping quiet in class, walking softly, and speaking softly—as much as it was in her to do—for not stealing into other girl's rooms after lights were out, and for abandoning crushes on this and that sympathetic sister, these awards and others, such as walking out in the grounds on Saturday afternoons, being allowed to have all the flowers she wanted, some extra dresses, jewels, etc., were offered. She liked music and the idea of painting, though she had no talent in that direction; and books, novels, interested her, but she could not get them. The rest—grammar, spelling, sewing, church and general history—she loathed. Deportment—well, there was something in that. She had liked the rather exaggerated curtsies they taught her, and she had often reflected on how she would use them when she reached home.

When she came out into life the little social distinctions which have been indicated began to impress themselves on her, and she wished sincerely that her father would build a better home—a mansion—such as those she saw elsewhere, and launch her properly in society. Failing in that, she could think of nothing save clothes, jewels, riding-horses, carriages, and the appropriate changes of costume which were allowed her for these. Her family could not entertain in any distinguished way where they were, and so already, at eighteen, she was beginning to feel the sting of a blighted ambition. She was eager for life. How was she to get it?

Her room was a study in the foibles of an eager and ambitious mind. It was full of clothes, beautiful things for all occasions—jewelry—which she had small opportunity to wear—shoes, stockings, lingerie, laces. In a crude way she had made a study of perfumes and cosmetics, though she needed the latter not at all, and these were present in abundance. She was not very orderly, and she loved lavishness of display; and her curtains, hangings, table ornaments, and pictures inclined to gorgeousness, which did not go well with the rest of the house.

Aileen always reminded Cowperwood of a high-stepping horse without a check-rein. He met her at various times, shopping with her mother, out driving with her father, and he was always interested and amused at the affected, bored tone she assumed before him—the "Oh, dear! Oh, dear! Life is so tiresome, don't you know," when, as a matter of fact, every moment of it was of thrilling interest to her. Cowperwood took her mental measurement exactly. A girl with a high sense of life in her, romantic, full of the thought of love and its possibilities. As he looked at her he had the sense of seeing the best that nature can do when she attempts to produce physical perfection. The thought came to him that some lucky young dog would marry her pretty soon and carry her away; but whoever secured her would have to hold her by affection and subtle flattery and attention if he held her at all.

"The little snip"–she was not at all–"she thinks the sun rises and sets in her father's pocket," Lillian observed one day to her husband. "To hear her talk, you'd think they were descended from Irish kings. Her pretended interest in art and music amuses me."

"Oh, don't be too hard on her," coaxed Cowperwood diplomatically. He already liked Aileen very much. "She plays very well, and she has a good voice."

"Yes, I know; but she has no real refinement. How could she have? Look at her father and mother."

"I don't see anything so very much the matter with her," insisted Cowperwood. "She's bright and good-looking. Of course, she's only a girl, and a little vain, but she'll come out of that. She isn't without sense and force, at that."

Aileen, as he knew, was most friendly to him. She liked him. She made a point of playing the piano and singing for him in his home, and she sang only when he was there. There was something about his steady, even gait, his stocky body and handsome head, which attracted her. In spite of her vanity and egotism, she felt a little overawed before him at times–keyed up. She seemed to grow gayer and more brilliant in his presence.

The most futile thing in this world is any attempt, perhaps, at exact definition of character. All individuals are a bundle of contradictions–none more so than the most capable.

In the case of Aileen Butler it would be quite impossible to give an exact definition. Intelligence, of a raw, crude order she had certainly–also a native force, tamed somewhat by the doctrines and conventions of current society, still showed clear at times in an elemental and not entirely unattractive way. At this time she was only eighteen years of age–decidedly attractive from the point of view of a man of Frank Cowperwood's temperament. She supplied something he had not previously known or consciously craved. Vitality and vivacity. No other woman or girl whom he had ever known had possessed so much innate force as she. Her red-gold hair–not so red as decidedly golden with a suggestion of red in it–looped itself in heavy folds about her forehead and sagged at the base of her neck. She had a beautiful nose, not sensitive, but straight-cut with small nostril openings, and eyes that were big and yet noticeably sensuous. They were, to him, a pleasing shade of blue-gray-blue, and her toilet, due to her temperament, of course, suggested almost undue luxury, the bangles, anklets, ear-rings, and breast-plates of the odalisque, and yet, of course, they were not there. She confessed to him years afterward that she would have loved to have stained her nails and painted the palms of her hands with madder-red. Healthy and vigorous, she was chronically interested in men–what they would think of her–and how she compared with other women.

The fact that she could ride in a carriage, live in a fine home on Girard Avenue, visit such homes as those of the Cowperwoods and others, was of great weight; and yet, even at this age, she realized that life was more than these things. Many did not have them and lived.

But these facts of wealth and advantage gripped her; and when she sat at the piano and played or rode in her carriage or walked or stood before her mirror, she was conscious of her figure, her charms, what they meant to men, how women envied her. Sometimes she looked at poor, hollow-chested or homely-faced girls and felt sorry for them; at other times she flared into inexplicable opposition to some handsome girl or woman who dared to brazen her socially or physically. There were such girls of the better families who, in Chestnut Street, in the expensive shops, or on the drive, on horseback or in carriages, tossed their heads and indicated as well as human motions can that they were better-bred and knew it. When this happened each stared defiantly at the other. She wanted ever so much to get up in the world, and yet namby-pamby men of better social station than herself did not attract her at all. She wanted a man. Now and then there was one "something like," but not entirely, who appealed to her, but most of them were politicians or legislators, acquaintances of her father, and socially nothing at all–and so they wearied and disappointed her. Her father did not know the truly elite. But Mr. Cowperwood–he seemed so refined, so forceful, and so reserved. She often looked at Mrs. Cowperwood and thought how fortunate she was.

Chapter XIV

The development of Cowperwood as Cowperwood Co. following his arresting bond venture, finally brought him into relationship with one man who was to play an important part in his life, morally, financially, and in other ways. This was George W. Stener, the new city treasurer-elect, who, to begin with, was a puppet in the hands of other men, but who, also in spite of this fact, became a personage of considerable importance, for the simple reason that he was weak. Stener had been engaged in the real estate and insurance business in a small way before he was made city treasurer. He was one of those men, of whom there are so many thousands in every large community, with no breadth of vision, no real subtlety, no craft, no great skill in anything. You would never hear a new idea emanating from Stener. He never had one in his life. On the other hand, he was not a bad fellow. He had a stodgy, dusty, commonplace look to him which was more a matter of mind than of body. His eye was of vague gray-blue; his hair a dusty light-brown and thin. His mouth–there was nothing impressive there. He was quite tall, nearly six feet, with moderately broad shoulders, but his figure was anything but shapely. He seemed to stoop a little, his stomach was the least bit protuberant, and he talked commonplaces–the small change of newspaper and street and business gossip. People liked him in his own neighborhood. He was thought to be honest and kindly; and he was, as far as he knew. His wife and four children were as average and insignificant as the wives and children of such men usually are.

Just the same, and in spite of, or perhaps, politically speaking, because of all this, George W. Stener was brought into temporary public notice by certain political methods which had existed in Philadelphia practically unmodified for the previous half hundred years. First, because he was of the same political faith as the dominant local political party, he had become known to the local councilman and ward-leader of his ward as a faithful soul–one useful in the matter of drumming up votes. And next–although absolutely without value as a speaker, for he had no ideas–you could send him from door to door, asking the grocer and the blacksmith and the butcher how he felt about things and he would make friends, and in the long run predict fairly accurately the probable vote. Furthermore, you could dole him out a few platitudes and he would repeat them. The Republican party, which was the new-born party then, but dominant in Philadelphia, needed your vote; it was necessary to keep the rascally Democrats out–he could scarcely have said why. They had been for slavery. They were for free trade. It never once occurred to him that these things had nothing to do with the local executive and financial administration of Philadelphia. Supposing they didn't? What of it?

In Philadelphia at this time a certain United States Senator, one Mark Simpson, together with Edward Malia Butler and Henry A. Mollenhauer, a rich coal dealer and investor, were supposed to, and did, control jointly the political destiny of the city. They had representatives, benchmen, spies, tools–a great company. Among them was this same Stener–a minute cog in the silent machinery of their affairs.

In scarcely any other city save this, where the inhabitants were of a deadly average in so far as being commonplace was concerned, could such a man as Stener have been elected city treasurer. The rank and file did not, except in rare instances, make up their political program. An inside ring had this matter in charge. Certain positions were allotted to such and such men or to such and such factions of the party for such and such services rendered–but who does not know politics?

In due course of time, therefore, George W. Stener had become persona grata to Edward Strobik, a quondam councilman who afterward became ward leader and still later president of council, and who, in private life was a stone-dealer and owner of a brickyard. Strobik was a benchman of Henry A. Mollenhauer, the hardest and coldest of all three of the political leaders. The latter had things to get from council, and Strobik was his tool. He had Stener elected; and because he was faithful in voting as he was told the latter was later made an assistant superintendent of the highways department.

Here he came under the eyes of Edward Malia Butler, and was slightly useful to him. Then the central political committee, with Butler in charge, decided that some nice, docile man who would at the same time be absolutely faithful was needed for city treasurer, and Stener was put on the ticket. He knew little of finance, but was an excellent bookkeeper; and, anyhow, was not corporation counsel Regan, another political tool of this great triumvirate, there to advise him at all times? He was. It was a very simple matter. Being put on the ticket was equivalent to being elected, and so, after a few weeks of exceedingly trying platform experiences, in which he had stammered through platitudinous declarations that the city needed to be honestly administered, he was inducted into office; and there you were.

Now it wouldn't have made so much difference what George W. Stener's executive and financial qualifications for the position were, but at this time the city of Philadelphia was still hobbling along under perhaps as evil a financial system, or lack of it, as any city ever endured–the assessor and the treasurer being allowed to collect and hold moneys belonging to the city, outside of the city's private vaults, and that without any demand on the part of anybody that the same be invested by them at interest for the city's benefit. Rather, all they were expected to do, apparently, was to restore the principal and that which was with them when they entered or left office. It was not understood or publicly demanded that the moneys so collected, or drawn from any source, be maintained intact in the vaults of the city treasury. They could be loaned out, deposited in banks or used to further private interests of any one, so long as the principal was returned, and no one was the wiser. Of course, this theory of finance was not publicly sanctioned, but it was known politically and journalistically, and in high finance. How were you to stop it?

Cowperwood, in approaching Edward Malia Butler, had been unconsciously let in on this atmosphere of erratic and unsatisfactory speculation without really knowing it. When he had left the office of Tighe Co., seven years before, it was with the idea that henceforth and forever he would have nothing to do with the stock-brokerage proposition; but now behold him back in it again, with more vim than he had ever displayed, for now he was working for himself, the firm of Cowperwood Co., and he was eager to satisfy the world of new and powerful individuals who by degrees were drifting to him. All had a little money. All had tips, and they wanted him to carry certain lines of stock on margin for them, because he was known to other political men, and because he was safe. And this was true. He was not, or at least up to this time had not been, a speculator or a gambler on his own account. In fact he often soothed himself with the thought that in all these years he had never gambled for himself, but had always acted strictly for others instead. But now here was George W. Stener with a proposition which was not quite the same thing as stock-gambling, and yet it was.

During a long period of years preceding the Civil War, and through it, let it here be explained and remembered, the city of Philadelphia had been in the habit, as a corporation, when there were no available funds in the treasury, of issuing what were known as city warrants, which were nothing more than notes or I.O.U.'s bearing six per cent. interest, and payable sometimes in thirty days, sometimes in three, sometimes in six months–all depending on the amount and how soon the city treasurer thought there would be sufficient money in the treasury to take them up and cancel them. Small tradesmen and large contractors were frequently paid in this way; the small tradesman who sold supplies to the city institutions, for instance, being compelled to discount his notes at the bank, if he needed ready money, usually for ninety cents on the dollar, while the large contractor could afford to hold his and wait. It can readily be seen that this might well work to the disadvantage of the small dealer and merchant, and yet prove quite a fine thing for a large contractor or note-broker, for the city was sure to pay the warrants at some time, and six per cent. interest was a fat rate, considering the absolute security. A banker or broker who gathered up these things from small tradesmen at ninety cents on the dollar made a fine thing of it all around if he could wait.

Originally, in all probability, there was no intention on the part of the city treasurer to do any one an injustice, and it is likely that there really were no funds to pay with at the time. However that may have been, there was later no excuse for issuing the warrants, seeing that the city might easily have been managed much more economically. But these warrants, as can readily be imagined, had come to be a fine source of profit for note-brokers, bankers, political financiers, and inside political manipulators generally and so they remained a part of the city's fiscal policy.

There was just one drawback to all this. In order to get the full advantage of this condition the large banker holding them must be an "inside banker," one close to the political forces of the city, for if he was not and needed money and he carried his warrants to the city treasurer, he would find that he could not get cash for them. But if he transferred them to some banker or note-broker who was close to the political force of the city, it was quite another matter. The treasury would find means to pay. Or, if so desired by the note-broker or banker–the right one–notes which were intended to be met in three months, and should have been settled at that time, were extended to run on years and years, drawing interest at six per cent. even when the city had ample funds to meet them. Yet this meant, of course, an illegal interest drain on the city, but that was all right also. "No funds" could cover that. The general public did not know. It could not find out. The newspapers were not at all vigilant, being pro-political. There were no persistent, enthusiastic reformers who obtained any political credence. During the war, warrants outstanding in this manner arose in amount to much over two million dollars, all drawing six per cent. interest, but then, of course, it began to get a little scandalous. Besides, at least some of the investors began to want their money back.

In order, therefore, to clear up this outstanding indebtedness and make everything shipshape again, it was decided that the city must issue a loan, say for two million dollars–no need to be exact about the amount. And this loan must take the shape of interest-bearing certificates of a par value of one hundred dollars, redeemable in six, twelve, or eighteen months, as the case may be. These certificates of loan were then ostensibly to be sold in the open market, a sinking-fund set aside for their redemption, and the money so obtained used to take up the long-outstanding warrants which were now such a subject of public comment.

It is obvious that this was merely a case of robbing Peter to pay Paul. There was no real clearing up of the outstanding debt. It was the intention of the schemers to make it possible for the financial politicians on the inside to reap the same old harvest by allowing the certificates to be sold to the right parties for ninety or less, setting up the claim that there was no market for them, the credit of the city being bad. To a certain extent this was true. The war was just over. Money was high. Investors could get more than six per cent. elsewhere unless the loan was sold at ninety. But there were a few watchful politicians not in the administration, and some newspapers and non-political financiers who, because of the high strain of patriotism existing at the time, insisted that the loan should be sold at par. Therefore a clause to that effect had to be inserted in the enabling ordinance.

This, as one might readily see, destroyed the politicians' little scheme to get this loan at ninety. Nevertheless since they desired that the money tied up in the old warrants and now not redeemable because of lack of funds should be paid them, the only way this could be done would be to have some broker who knew the subtleties of the stock market handle this new city loan on 'change in such a way that it would be made to seem worth one hundred and to be sold to outsiders at that figure. Afterward, if, as it was certain to do, it fell below that, the politicians could buy as much of it as they pleased, and eventually have the city redeem it at par.

George W. Stener, entering as city treasurer at this time, and bringing no special financial intelligence to the proposition, was really troubled. Henry A. Mollenhauer, one of the men who had gathered up a large amount of the old city warrants, and who now wanted his money, in order to invest it in bonanza offers in the West, called on Stener, and also on the mayor. He with Simpson and Butler made up the Big Three.

"I think something ought to be done about these warrants that are outstanding," he explained. "I am carrying a large amount of them, and there are others. We have helped the city a long time by saying nothing; but now I think that something ought to be done. Mr. Butler and Mr. Simpson feel the same way. Couldn't these new loan certificates be listed on the stock exchange and the money raised that way? Some clever broker could bring them to par."

Stener was greatly flattered by the visit from Mollenhauer. Rarely did he trouble to put in a personal appearance, and then only for the weight and effect his presence would have. He called on the mayor and the president of council, much as he called on Stener, with a lofty, distant, inscrutable air. They were as office-boys to him.

In order to understand exactly the motive for Mollenhauer's interest in Stener, and the significance of this visit and Stener's subsequent action in regard to it, it will be necessary to scan the political horizon for some little distance back. Although George W. Stener was in a way a political henchman and appointee of Mollenhauer's, the latter was only vaguely acquainted with him. He had seen him before; knew of him; had agreed that his name should be put on the local slate largely because he had been assured by those who were closest to him and who did his bidding that Stener was "all right," that he would do as he was told, that he would cause no one any trouble, etc. In fact, during several previous administrations, Mollenhauer had maintained a subsurface connection with the treasury, but never so close a one as could easily be traced. He was too conspicuous a man politically and financially for that. But he was not above a plan, in which Simpson if not Butler shared, of using political and commercial stool-pigeons to bleed the city treasury as much as possible without creating a scandal. In fact, for some years previous to this, various agents had already been employed–Edward Strobik, president of council, Asa Conklin, the then incumbent of the mayor's chair, Thomas Wycroft, alderman, Jacob Harmon, alderman, and others–to organize dummy companies under various names, whose business it was to deal in those things which the city needed–lumber, stone, steel, iron, cement–a long list–and of course, always at a fat profit to those ultimately behind the dummy companies, so organized. It saved the city the trouble of looking far and wide for honest and reasonable dealers.

Since the action of at least three of these dummies will have something to do with the development of Cowperwood's story, they may be briefly described. Edward Strobik, the chief of them, and the one most useful to Mollenhauer, in a minor way, was a very spry person of about thirty-five at this time–lean and somewhat forceful, with black hair, black eyes, and an inordinately large black mustache. He was dapper, inclined to noticeable clothing–a pair of striped trousers, a white vest, a black cutaway coat and a high silk hat. His markedly ornamental shoes were always polished to perfection, and his immaculate appearance gave him the nickname of "The Dude" among some. Nevertheless he was quite able on a small scale, and was well liked by many.

His two closest associates, Messrs. Thomas Wycroft and Jacob Harmon, were rather less attractive and less brilliant. Jacob Harmon was a thick wit socially, but no fool financially. He was big and rather doleful to look upon, with sandy brown hair and brown eyes, but fairly intelligent, and absolutely willing to approve anything which was not too broad in its crookedness and which would afford him sufficient protection to keep him out of the clutches of the law. He was really not so cunning as dull and anxious to get along.

Thomas Wycroft, the last of this useful but minor triumvirate, was a tall, lean man, candle-waxy, hollow-eyed, gaunt of face, pathetic to look at physically, but shrewd. He was an iron-molder by trade and had gotten into politics much as Stener had—because he was useful; and he had managed to make some money—via this triumvirate of which Strobik was the ringleader, and which was engaged in various peculiar businesses which will now be indicated.

The companies which these several henchmen had organized under previous administrations, and for Mollenhauer, dealt in meat, building material, lamp-posts, highway supplies, anything you will, which the city departments or its institutions needed. A city contract once awarded was irrevocable, but certain councilmen had to be fixed in advance and it took money to do that. The company so organized need not actually slaughter any cattle or mold lamp-posts. All it had to do was to organize to do that, obtain a charter, secure a contract for supplying such material to the city from the city council (which Strobik, Harmon, and Wycroft would attend to), and then sublet this to some actual beef-slaughterer or iron-founder, who would supply the material and allow them to pocket their profit which in turn was divided or paid for to Mollenhauer and Simpson in the form of political donations to clubs or organizations. It was so easy and in a way so legitimate. The particular beef-slaughterer or iron-founder thus favored could not hope of his own ability thus to obtain a contract. Stener, or whoever was in charge of the city treasury at the time, for his services in loaning money at a low rate of interest to be used as surety for the proper performance of contract, and to aid in some instances the beef-killer or iron-founder to carry out his end, was to be allowed not only the one or two per cent. which he might pocket (other treasurers had), but a fair proportion of the profits. A complacent, confidential chief clerk who was all right would be recommended to him. It did not concern Stener that Strobik, Harmon, and Wycroft, acting for Mollenhauer, were incidentally planning to use a little of the money loaned for purposes quite outside those indicated. It was his business to loan it.

However, to be going on. Some time before he was even nominated, Stener had learned from Strobik, who, by the way, was one of his sureties as treasurer (which suretyship was against the law, as were those of Councilmen Wycroft and Harmon, the law of Pennsylvania stipulating that one political servant might not become surety for another), that those who had brought about this nomination and election would by no means ask him to do anything which was not perfectly legal, but that he must be complacent and not stand in the way of big municipal perquisites nor bite the hands that fed him. It was also made perfectly plain to him, that once he was well in office a little money for himself was to be made. As has been indicated, he had always been a poor man. He had seen all those who had dabbled in politics to any extent about him heretofore do very well financially indeed, while he pegged along as an insurance and real-estate agent. He had worked hard as a small political henchman. Other politicians were building themselves nice homes in newer portions of the city. They were going off to New York or Harrisburg or Washington on jaunting parties. They were seen in happy converse at road-houses or country hotels in season with their wives or their women favorites, and he was not, as yet, of this happy throng. Naturally now that he was promised something, he was interested and compliant. What might he not get?

When it came to this visit from Mollenhauer, with its suggestion in regard to bringing city loan to par, although it bore no obvious relation to Mollenhauer's subsurface connection with Stener, through Strobik and the others, Stener did definitely recognize his own political subservience–his master's stentorian voice–and immediately thereafter hurried to Strobik for information.

"Just what would you do about this?" he asked of Strobik, who knew of Mollenhauer's visit before Stener told him, and was waiting for Stener to speak to him. "Mr. Mollenhauer talks about having this new loan listed on 'change and brought to par so that it will sell for one hundred."

Neither Strobik, Harmon, nor Wycroft knew how the certificates of city loan, which were worth only ninety on the open market, were to be made to sell for one hundred on 'change, but Mollenhauer's secretary, one Abner Sengstack, had suggested to Strobik that, since Butler was dealing with young Cowperwood and Mollenhauer did not care particularly for his private broker in this instance, it might be as well to try Cowperwood.

So it was that Cowperwood was called to Stener's office. And once there, and not as yet recognizing either the hand of Mollenhauer or Simpson in this, merely looked at the peculiarly shambling, heavy-cheeked, middle-class man before him without either interest or sympathy, realizing at once that he had a financial baby to deal with. If he could act as adviser to this man–be his sole counsel for four years!

"How do you do, Mr. Stener?" he said in his soft, ingratiating voice, as the latter held out his hand. "I am glad to meet you. I have heard of you before, of course."

Stener was long in explaining to Cowperwood just what his difficulty was. He went at it in a clumsy fashion, stumbling through the difficulties of the situation he was suffered to meet.

"The main thing, as I see it, is to make these certificates sell at par. I can issue them in any sized lots you like, and as often as you like. I want to get enough now to clear away two hundred thousand dollars' worth of the outstanding warrants, and as much more as I can get later."

Cowperwood felt like a physician feeling a patient's pulse–a patient who is really not sick at all but the reassurance of whom means a fat fee. The abstrusities of the stock exchange were as his A B C's to him. He knew if he could have this loan put in his hands–all of it, if he could have the fact kept dark that he was acting for the city, and that if Stener would allow him to buy as a "bull" for the sinking-fund while selling judiciously for a rise, he could do wonders even with a big issue. He had to have all of it, though, in order that he might have agents under him. Looming up in his mind was a scheme whereby he could make a lot of the unwary speculators about 'change go short of this stock or loan under the impression, of course, that it was scattered freely in various persons' hands, and that they could buy as much of it as they wanted. Then they would wake to find that they could not get it; that he had it all. Only he would not risk his secret that far. Not he, oh, no. But he would drive the city loan to par and then sell. And what a fat thing for himself among others in so doing. Wisely enough he sensed that there was politics in all this–shrewder and bigger men above and behind Stener. But what of that? And how slyly and shrewdly they were sending Stener to him. It might be that his name was becoming very potent in their political world here. And what might that not mean!

"I tell you what I'd like to do, Mr. Stener," he said, after he had listened to his explanation and asked how much of the city loan he would like to sell during the coming year. "I'll be glad to undertake it. But I'd like to have a day or two in which to think it over."

"Why, certainly, certainly, Mr. Cowperwood," replied Stener, genially. "That's all right. Take your time. If you know how it can be done, just show me when you're ready. By the way, what do you charge?"

"Well, the stock exchange has a regular scale of charges which we brokers are compelled to observe. It's one-fourth of one per cent. on the par value of bonds and loans. Of course, I may hav to add a lot of fictitious selling–I'll explain that to you later–but I won't charge you anything for that so long as it is a secret between us. I'll give you the best service I can, Mr. Stener. You can depend on that. Let me have a day or two to think it over, though."

He shook hands with Stener, and they parted. Cowperwood was satisfied that he was on the verge of a significant combination, and Stener that he had found someone on whom he could lean.

Chapter XV

The plan Cowperwood developed after a few days' meditation will be plain enough to any one who knows anything of commercial and financial manipulation, but a dark secret to those who do not. In the first place, the city treasurer was to use his (Cowperwood's) office as a bank of deposit. He was to turn over to him, actually, or set over to his credit on the city's books, subject to his order, certain amounts of city loans–two hundred thousand dollars at first, since that was the amount it was desired to raise quickly–and he would then go into the market and see what could be done to have it brought to par. The city treasurer was to ask leave of the stock exchange at once to have it listed as a security. Cowperwood would then use his influence to have this application acted upon quickly. Stener was then to dispose of all city loan certificates through him, and him only. He was to allow him to buy for the sinking-fund, supposedly, such amounts as he might have to buy in order to keep the price up to par. To do this, once a considerable number of the loan certificates had been unloaded on the public, it might be necessary to buy back a great deal. However, these would be sold again. The law concerning selling only at par would have to be abrogated to this extent–i.e., that the wash sales and preliminary sales would have to be considered no sales until par was reached.

There was a subtle advantage here, as Cowperwood pointed out to Stener. In the first place, since the certificates were going ultimately to reach par anyway, there was no objection to Stener or any one else buying low at the opening price and holding for a rise. Cowperwood would be glad to carry him on his books for any amount, and he would settle at the end of each month. He would not be asked to buy the certificates outright. He could be carried on the books for a certain reasonable margin, say ten points. The money was as good as made for Stener now. In the next place, in buying for the sinking-fund it would be possible to buy these certificates very cheap, for, having the new and reserve issue entirely in his hands, Cowperwood could throw such amounts as he wished into the market at such times as he wished to buy, and consequently depress the market. Then he could buy, and, later, up would go the price. Having the issues totally in his hands to boost or depress the market as he wished, there was no reason why the city should not ultimately get par for all its issues, and at the same time considerable money be made out of the manufactured fluctuations. He, Cowperwood, would be glad to make most of his profit that way. The city should allow him his normal percentage on all his actual sales of certificates for the city at par (he would have to have that in order to keep straight with the stock exchange); but beyond that, and for all the other necessary manipulative sales, of which there would be many, he would depend on his knowledge of the stock market to reimburse him. And if Stener wanted to speculate with him—well.

Dark as this transaction may seem to the uninitiated, it will appear quite clear to those who know. Manipulative tricks have always been worked in connection with stocks of which one man or one set of men has had complete control. It was no different from what subsequently was done with Erie, Standard Oil, Copper, Sugar, Wheat, and what not. Cowperwood was one of the first and one of the youngest to see how it could be done. When he first talked to Stener he was twenty-eight years of age. When he last did business with him he was thirty-four.

The houses and the bank-front of Cowperwood Co. had been proceeding apace. The latter was early Florentine in its decorations with windows which grew narrower as they approached the roof, and a door of wrought iron set between delicately carved posts, and a straight lintel of brownstone. It was low in height and distinguished in appearance. In the center panel had been hammered a hand, delicately wrought, thin and artistic, holding aloft a flaming brand. Ellsworth informed him that this had formerly been a money-changer's sign used in old Venice, the significance of which had long been forgotten.

The interior was finished in highly-polished hardwood, stained in imitation of the gray lichens which infest trees. Large sheets of clear, beveled glass were used, some oval, some oblong, some square, and some circular, following a given theory of eye movement. The fixtures for the gas-jets were modeled after the early Roman flame-brackets, and the office safe was made an ornament, raised on a marble platform at the back of the office and lacquered a silver-gray, with Cowperwood Co. lettered on it in gold. One had a sense of reserve and taste pervading the place, and yet it was also inestimably prosperous, solid and assuring. Cowperwood, when he viewed it at its completion, complimented Ellsworth cheerily. "I like this. It is really beautiful. It will be a pleasure to work here. If those houses are going to be anything like this, they will be perfect."

"Wait till you see them. I think you will be pleased, Mr. Cowperwood. I am taking especial pains with yours because it is smaller. It is really easier to treat your father's. But yours—" He went off into a description of the entrance-hall, reception-room and parlor, which he was arranging and decorating in such a way as to give an effect of size and dignity not really conformable to the actual space.

And when the houses were finished, they were effective and arresting–quite different from the conventional residences of the street. They were separated by a space of twenty feet, laid out as greensward. The architect had borrowed somewhat from the Tudor school, yet not so elaborated as later became the style in many of the residences in Philadelphia and elsewhere. The most striking features were rather deep-recessed doorways under wide, low, slightly floriated arches, and three projecting windows of rich form, one on the second floor of Frank's house, two on the facade of his father's. There were six gables showing on the front of the two houses, two on Frank's and four on his father's. In the front of each house on the ground floor was a recessed window unconnected with the recessed doorways, formed by setting the inner external wall back from the outer face of the building. This window looked out through an arched opening to the street, and was protected by a dwarf parapet or balustrade. It was possible to set potted vines and flowers there, which was later done, giving a pleasant sense of greenery from the street, and to place a few chairs there, which were reached via heavily barred French casements.

On the ground floor of each house was placed a conservatory of flowers, facing each other, and in the yard, which was jointly used, a pool of white marble eight feet in diameter, with a marble Cupid upon which jets of water played. The yard which was enclosed by a high but pierced wall of green-gray brick, especially burnt for the purpose the same color as the granite of the house, and surmounted by a white marble coping which was sown to grass and had a lovely, smooth, velvety appearance. The two houses, as originally planned, were connected by a low, green-columned pergola which could be enclosed in glass in winter.

The rooms, which were now slowly being decorated and furnished in period styles were very significant in that they enlarged and strengthened Frank Cowperwood's idea of the world of art in general. It was an enlightening and agreeable experience– one which made for artistic and intellectual growth–to hear Ellsworth explain at length the styles and types of architecture and furniture, the nature of woods and ornaments employed, the qualities and peculiarities of hangings, draperies, furniture panels, and door coverings. Ellsworth was a student of decoration as well as of architecture, and interested in the artistic taste of the American people, which he fancied would some day have a splendid outcome. He was wearied to death of the prevalent Romanesque composite combinations of country and suburban villa. The time was ripe for something new. He scarcely knew what it would be; but this that he had designed for Cowperwood and his father was at least different, as he said, while at the same time being reserved, simple, and pleasing. It was in marked contrast to the rest of the architecture of the street. Cowperwood's dining-room, reception-room, conservatory, and butler's pantry he had put on the first floor, together with the general entry-hall, staircase, and coat-room under the stairs. For the second floor he had reserved the library, general living-room, parlor, and a small office for Cowperwood, together with a boudoir for Lillian, connected with a dressing-room and bath.

On the third floor, neatly divided and accommodated with baths and dressing-rooms, were the nursery, the servants' quarters, and several guest-chambers.

Ellsworth showed Cowperwood books of designs containing furniture, hangings, etageres, cabinets, pedestals, and some exquisite piano forms. He discussed woods

with him–rosewood, mahogany, walnut, English oak, bird's-eye maple, and the manufactured effects such as ormolu, marquetry, and Boule, or buhl. He explained the
latter–how difficult it was to produce, how unsuitable it was in some respects for this
climate, the brass and tortoise-shell inlay coming to swell with the heat or damp, and
so bulging or breaking. He told of the difficulties and disadvantages of certain finishes,
but finally recommended ormolu furniture for the reception room, medallion tapestry
for the parlor, French renaissance for the dining-room and library, and bird's-eye maple
(dyed blue in one instance, and left its natural color in another) and a rather lightly
constructed and daintily carved walnut for the other rooms. The hangings, wall-paper,
and floor coverings were to harmonize–not match–and the piano and music-cabinet
for the parlor, as well as the etagere, cabinets, and pedestals for the reception-rooms,
were to be of buhl or marquetry, if Frank cared to stand the expense.

Ellsworth advised a triangular piano–the square shapes were so inexpressibly wearisome to the initiated. Cowperwood listened fascinated. He foresaw a home which
would be chaste, soothing, and delightful to look upon. If he hung pictures, gilt
frames were to be the setting, large and deep; and if he wished a picture-gallery, the
library could be converted into that, and the general living-room, which lay between
the library and the parlor on the second-floor, could be turned into a combination
library and living-room. This was eventually done; but not until his taste for pictures
had considerably advanced.

It was now that he began to take a keen interest in objects of art, pictures, bronzes,
little carvings and figurines, for his cabinets, pedestals, tables, and etageres. Philadelphia did not offer much that was distinguished in this realm–certainly not in the open
market. There were many private houses which were enriched by travel; but his connection with the best families was as yet small. There were then two famous American
sculptors, Powers and Hosmer, of whose work he had examples; but Ellsworth told
him that they were not the last word in sculpture and that he should look into the merits
of the ancients. He finally secured a head of David, by Thorwaldsen, which delighted
him, and some landscapes by Hunt, Sully, and Hart, which seemed somewhat in the
spirit of his new world.

The effect of a house of this character on its owner is unmistakable. We think we
are individual, separate, above houses and material objects generally; but there is a
subtle connection which makes them reflect us quite as much as we reflect them. They
lend dignity, subtlety, force, each to the other, and what beauty, or lack of it, there is,
is shot back and forth from one to the other as a shuttle in a loom, weaving, weaving.
Cut the thread, separate a man from that which is rightfully his own, characteristic
of him, and you have a peculiar figure, half success, half failure, much as a spider
without its web, which will never be its whole self again until all its dignities and
emoluments are restored.

The sight of his new house going up made Cowperwood feel of more weight in the
world, and the possession of his suddenly achieved connection with the city treasurer
was as though a wide door had been thrown open to the Elysian fields of opportunity.
He rode about the city those days behind a team of spirited bays, whose glossy hides
and metaled harness bespoke the watchful care of hostler and coachman. Ellsworth
was building an attractive stable in the little side street back of the houses, for the

joint use of both families. He told Mrs. Cowperwood that he intended to buy her a victoria–as the low, open, four-wheeled coach was then known–as soon as they were well settled in their new home, and that they were to go out more. There was some talk about the value of entertaining–that he would have to reach out socially for certain individuals who were not now known to him. Together with Anna, his sister, and his two brothers, Joseph and Edward, they could use the two houses jointly. There was no reason why Anna should not make a splendid match. Joe and Ed might marry well, since they were not destined to set the world on fire in commerce. At least it would not hurt them to try.

"Don't you think you will like that?" he asked his wife, referring to his plans for entertaining.

She smiled wanly. "I suppose so," she said.

Chapter XVI

It was not long after the arrangement between Treasurer Stener and Cowperwood had been made that the machinery for the carrying out of that political-financial relationship was put in motion. The sum of two hundred and ten thousand dollars in six per cent. interest-bearing certificates, payable in ten years, was set over to the credit of Cowperwood Co. on the books of the city, subject to his order. Then, with proper listing, he began to offer it in small amounts at more than ninety, at the same time creating the impression that it was going to be a prosperous investment. The certificates gradually rose and were unloaded in rising amounts until one hundred was reached, when all the two hundred thousand dollars' worth–two thousand certificates in all–was fed out in small lots. Stener was satisfied. Two hundred shares had been carried for him and sold at one hundred, which netted him two thousand dollars. It was illegitimate gain, unethical; but his conscience was not very much troubled by that. He had none, truly. He saw visions of a halcyon future.

It is difficult to make perfectly clear what a subtle and significant power this suddenly placed in the hands of Cowperwood. Consider that he was only twenty-eight–nearing twenty-nine. Imagine yourself by nature versed in the arts of finance, capable of playing with sums of money in the forms of stocks, certificates, bonds, and cash, as the ordinary man plays with checkers or chess. Or, better yet, imagine yourself one of those subtle masters of the mysteries of the higher forms of chess–the type of mind so well illustrated by the famous and historic chess-players, who could sit with their backs to a group of rivals playing fourteen men at once, calling out all the moves in turn, remembering all the positions of all the men on all the boards, and winning. This, of course, would be an overstatement of the subtlety of Cowperwood at this time, and yet it would not be wholly out of bounds. He knew instinctively what could be done with a given sum of money–how as cash it could be deposited in one place, and yet as credit and the basis of moving checks, used in not one but many other places at the same time. When properly watched and followed this manipulation gave him the constructive and purchasing power of ten and a dozen times as much as his original sum might have represented. He knew instinctively the principles of "pyramiding" and "kiting." He could see exactly not only how he could raise and lower the value of these certificates of loan, day after day and year after year–if he were so fortunate as to retain his hold on the city treasurer–but also how this would give him a credit with the banks hitherto beyond his wildest dreams. His father's bank was one of the first to profit by this and to extend him loans. The various local politicians and bosses–Mollenhauer, Butler, Simpson, and others–seeing the success of his efforts in this direction, speculated in city loan. He became known to Mollenhauer and Simpson, by reputation, if not personally, as the man who was carrying this city loan proposition to a successful issue. Stener was supposed to have done a clever thing in finding him. The stock exchange stipulated that all trades were to be compared the same day and settled before the close of the next; but this working arrangement with the new city treasurer gave Cowperwood much more latitude, and now he had always until the first of the month, or practically thirty days at times, in which to render an accounting for all deals connected with the loan issue.

And, moreover, this was really not an accounting in the sense of removing anything from his hands. Since the issue was to be so large, the sum at his disposal would always be large, and so-called transfers and balancing at the end of the month would be a mere matter of bookkeeping. He could use these city loan certificates deposited with him for manipulative purposes, deposit them at any bank as collateral for a loan, quite as if they were his own, thus raising seventy per cent. of their actual value in cash, and he did not hesitate to do so. He could take this cash, which need not be accounted for until the end of the month, and cover other stock transactions, on which he could borrow again. There was no limit to the resources of which he now found himself possessed, except the resources of his own energy, ingenuity, and the limits of time in which he had to work. The politicians did not realize what a bonanza he was making of it all for himself, because they were as yet unaware of the subtlety of his mind. When Stener told him, after talking the matter over with the mayor, Strobik, and others that he would formally, during the course of the year, set over on the city's books all of the two millions in city loan, Cowperwood was silent–but with delight. Two millions! His to play with! He had been called in as a financial adviser, and he had given his advice and it had been taken! Well. He was not a man who inherently was troubled with conscientious scruples. At the same time he still believed himself financially honest. He was no sharper or shrewder than any other financier–certainly no sharper than any other would be if he could.

It should be noted here that this proposition of Stener's in regard to city money had no connection with the attitude of the principal leaders in local politics in regard to street-railway control, which was a new and intriguing phase of the city's financial life. Many of the leading financiers and financier-politicians were interested in that. For instance, Messrs. Mollenhauer, Butler, and Simpson were interested in street-railways separately on their own account. There was no understanding between them on this score. If they had thought at all on the matter they would have decided that they did not want any outsider to interfere. As a matter of fact the street-railway business in Philadelphia was not sufficiently developed at this time to suggest to any one the grand scheme of union which came later. Yet in connection with this new arrangement between Stener and Cowperwood, it was Strobik who now came forward to Stener with an idea of his own. All were certain to make money through Cowperwood–he and Stener, especially. What was amiss, therefore, with himself and Stener and with Cowperwood as their–or rather Stener's secret representative, since Strobik did not dare to appear in the matter–buying now sufficient street-railway shares in some one line to control it, and then, if he, Strobik, could, by efforts of his own, get the city council to set aside certain streets for its extension, why, there you were–they would own it. Only, later, he proposed to shake Stener out if he could. But this preliminary work had to be done by some one, and it might as well be Stener. At the same time, as he saw, this work had to be done very carefully, because naturally his superiors were watchful, and if they found him dabbling in affairs of this kind to his own advantage, they might make it impossible for him to continue politically in a position where he could help himself just the same. Any outside organization such as a street-railway company already in existence had a right to appeal to the city council for privileges which would naturally further its and the city's growth, and, other things being equal, these could not be refused. It would not do for him to appear, however, both as a shareholder and president of the council. But with Cowperwood acting privately for Stener it would be another thing.

The interesting thing about this proposition as finally presented by Stener for Strobik to Cowperwood, was that it raised, without appearing to do so, the whole question of Cowperwood's attitude toward the city administration. Although he was dealing privately for Edward Butler as an agent, and with this same plan in mind, and although he had never met either Mollenhauer or Simpson, he nevertheless felt that in so far as the manipulation of the city loan was concerned he was acting for them. On the other hand, in this matter of the private street-railway purchase which Stener now brought to him, he realized from the very beginning, by Stener's attitude, that there was something untoward in it, that Stener felt he was doing something which he ought not to do.

"Cowperwood," he said to him the first morning he ever broached this matter–it was in Stener's office, at the old city hall at Sixth and Chestnut, and Stener, in view of his oncoming prosperity, was feeling very good indeed–"isn't there some street-railway property around town here that a man could buy in on and get control of if he had sufficient money?"

Cowperwood knew that there were such properties. His very alert mind had long since sensed the general opportunities here. The omnibuses were slowly disappearing. The best routes were already preempted. Still, there were other streets, and the city was growing. The incoming population would make great business in the future. One could afford to pay almost any price for the short lines already built if one could wait and extend the lines into larger and better areas later. And already he had conceived in his own mind the theory of the "endless chain," or "argeeable formula," as it was later termed, of buying a certain property on a long-time payment and issuing stocks or bonds sufficient not only to pay your seller, but to reimburse you for your trouble, to say nothing of giving you a margin wherewith to invest in other things–allied properties, for instance, against which more bonds could be issued, and so on, ad infinitum. It became an old story later, but it was new at that time, and he kept the thought closely to himself. None the less he was glad to have Stener speak of this, since street-railways were his hobby, and he was convinced that he would be a great master of them if he ever had an opportunity to control them.

"Why, yes, George," he said, noncommittally, "there are two or three that offer a good chance if a man had money enough. I notice blocks of stock being offered on 'change now and then by one person and another. It would be good policy to pick these things up as they're offered, and then to see later if some of the other stockholders won't want to sell out. Green and Coates, now, looks like a good proposition to me. If I had three or four hundred thousand dollars that I thought I could put into that by degrees I would follow it up. It only takes about thirty per cent. of the stock of any railroad to control it. Most of the shares are scattered around so far and wide that they never vote, and I think two or three hundred thousand dollars would control that road." He mentioned one other line that might be secured in the same way in the course of time.

Stener meditated. "That's a good deal of money," he said, thoughtfully. "I'll talk to you about that some more later." And he was off to see Strobik none the less.

Cowperwood knew that Stener did not have any two or three hundred thousand dollars to invest in anything. There was only one way that he could get it–and that was to borrow it out of the city treasury and forego the interest. But he would not do that on his own initiative. Some one else must be behind him and who else other than Mollenhauer, or Simpson, or possibly even Butler, though he doubted that, unless the triumvirate were secretly working together. But what of it? The larger politicians were always using the treasury, and he was thinking now, only, of his own attitude in regard to the use of this money. No harm could come to him, if Stener's ventures were successful; and there was no reason why they should not be. Even if they were not he would be merely acting as an agent. In addition, he saw how in the manipulation of this money for Stener he could probably eventually control certain lines for himself.

There was one line being laid out to within a few blocks of his new home–the Seventeenth and Nineteenth Street line it was called–which interested him greatly. He rode on it occasionally when he was delayed or did not wish to trouble about a vehicle. It ran through two thriving streets of red-brick houses, and was destined to have a great future once the city grew large enough. As yet it was really not long enough. If he could get that, for instance, and combine it with Butler's lines, once they were secured–or Mollenhauer's, or Simpson's, the legislature could be induced to give them additional franchises. He even dreamed of a combination between Butler, Mollenhauer, Simpson, and himself. Between them, politically, they could get anything. But Butler was not a philanthropist. He would have to be approached with a very sizable bird in hand. The combination must be obviously advisable. Besides, he was dealing for Butler in street-railway stocks, and if this particular line were such a good thing Butler might wonder why it had not been brought to him in the first place. It would be better, Frank thought, to wait until he actually had it as his own, in which case it would be a different matter. Then he could talk as a capitalist. He began to dream of a city-wide street-railway system controlled by a few men, or preferably himself alone.

Chapter XVII

The days that had been passing brought Frank Cowperwood and Aileen Butler somewhat closer together in spirit. Because of the pressure of his growing affairs he had not paid so much attention to her as he might have, but he had seen her often this past year. She was now nineteen and had grown into some subtle thoughts of her own. For one thing, she was beginning to see the difference between good taste and bad taste in houses and furnishings.

"Papa, why do we stay in this old barn?" she asked her father one evening at dinner, when the usual family group was seated at the table.

"What's the matter with this house, I'd like to know?" demanded Butler, who was drawn up close to the table, his napkin tucked comfortably under his chin, for he insisted on this when company was not present. "I don't see anything the matter with this house. Your mother and I manage to live in it well enough."

"Oh, it's terrible, papa. You know it," supplemented Norah, who was seventeen and quite as bright as her sister, though a little less experienced. "Everybody says so. Look at all the nice houses that are being built everywhere about here."

"Everybody! Everybody! Who is 'everybody,' I'd like to know?" demanded Butler, with the faintest touch of choler and much humor. "I'm somebody, and I like it. Those that don't like it don't have to live in it. Who are they? What's the matter with it, I'd like to know?"

The question in just this form had been up a number of times before, and had been handled in just this manner, or passed over entirely with a healthy Irish grin. To-night, however, it was destined for a little more extended thought.

"You know it's bad, papa," corrected Aileen, firmly. "Now what's the use getting mad about it? It's old and cheap and dingy. The furniture is all worn out. That old piano in there ought to be given away. I won't play on it any more. The Cowperwoods–"

"Old is it!" exclaimed Butler, his accent sharpening somewhat with his self-induced rage. He almost pronounced it "owled." "Dingy, hi! Where do you get that? At your convent, I suppose. And where is it worn? Show me where it's worn."

He was coming to her reference to Cowperwood, but he hadn't reached that when Mrs. Butler interfered. She was a stout, broad-faced woman, smiling-mouthed most of the time, with blurry, gray Irish eyes, and a touch of red in her hair, now modified by grayness. Her cheek, below the mouth, on the left side, was sharply accented by a large wen.

"Children! children!" (Mr. Butler, for all his commercial and political responsibility, was as much a child to her as any.) "Youse mustn't quarrel now. Come now. Give your father the tomatoes."

There was an Irish maid serving at table; but plates were passed from one to the other just the same. A heavily ornamented chandelier, holding sixteen imitation candles in white porcelain, hung low over the table and was brightly lighted, another offense to Aileen.

"Mama, how often have I told you not to say 'youse'?" pleaded Norah, very much disheartened by her mother's grammatical errors. "You know you said you wouldn't."

"And who's to tell your mother what she should say?" called Butler, more incensed than ever at this sudden and unwarranted rebellion and assault. "Your mother talked before ever you was born, I'd have you know. If it weren't for her workin' and slavin' you wouldn't have any fine manners to be paradin' before her. I'd have you know that. She's a better woman nor any you'll be runnin' with this day, you little baggage, you!"

"Mama, do you hear what he's calling me?" complained Norah, hugging close to her mother's arm and pretending fear and dissatisfaction.

"Eddie! Eddie!" cautioned Mrs. Butler, pleading with her husband. "You know he don't mean that, Norah, dear. Don't you know he don't?"

She was stroking her baby's head. The reference to her grammar had not touched her at all.

Butler was sorry that he had called his youngest a baggage; but these children–God bless his soul–were a great annoyance. Why, in the name of all the saints, wasn't this house good enough for them?

"Why don't you people quit fussing at the table?" observed Callum, a likely youth, with black hair laid smoothly over his forehead in a long, distinguished layer reaching from his left to close to his right ear, and his upper lip carrying a short, crisp mustache. His nose was short and retrousse, and his ears were rather prominent; but he was bright and attractive. He and Owen both realized that the house was old and poorly arranged; but their father and mother liked it, and business sense and family peace dictated silence on this score.

"Well, I think it's mean to have to live in this old place when people not one-fourth as good as we are are living in better ones. The Cowperwoods–why, even the Cowperwoods–"

"Yes, the Cowperwoods! What about the Cowperwoods?" demanded Butler, turning squarely to Aileen–she was sitting beside him—his big, red face glowing.

"Why, even they have a better house than we have, and he's merely an agent of yours."

"The Cowperwoods! The Cowperwoods! I'll not have any talk about the Cowperwoods. I'm not takin' my rules from the Cowperwoods. Suppose they have a fine house, what of it? My house is my house. I want to live here. I've lived here too long to be pickin' up and movin' away. If you don't like it you know what else you can do. Move if you want to. I'll not move."

It was Butler's habit when he became involved in these family quarrels, which were as shallow as puddles, to wave his hands rather antagonistically under his wife's or his children's noses.

"Oh, well, I will get out one of these days," Aileen replied. "Thank heaven I won't have to live here forever."

There flashed across her mind the beautiful reception-room, library, parlor, and boudoirs of the Cowperwoods, which were now being arranged and about which Anna Cowperwood talked to her so much–their dainty, lovely triangular grand piano in gold and painted pink and blue. Why couldn't they have things like that? Her father was unquestionably a dozen times as wealthy. But no, her father, whom she loved dearly, was of the old school. He was just what people charged him with being, a rough Irish contractor. He might be rich. She flared up at the injustice of things–why couldn't he have been rich and refined, too? Then they could have–but, oh, what was the use of complaining? They would never get anywhere with her father and mother in charge. She would just have to wait. Marriage was the answer–the right marriage. But whom was she to marry?

"You surely are not going to go on fighting about that now," pleaded Mrs. Butler, as strong and patient as fate itself. She knew where Aileen's trouble lay.

"But we might have a decent house," insisted Aileen. "Or this one done over," whispered Norah to her mother.

"Hush now! In good time," replied Mrs. Butler to Norah. "Wait. We'll fix it all up some day, sure. You run to your lessons now. You've had enough."

Norah arose and left. Aileen subsided. Her father was simply stubborn and impossible. And yet he was sweet, too. She pouted in order to compel him to apologize.

"Come now," he said, after they had left the table, and conscious of the fact that his daughter was dissatisfied with him. He must do something to placate her. "Play me somethin' on the piano, somethin' nice." He preferred showy, clattery things which exhibited her skill and muscular ability and left him wondering how she did it. That was what education was for—to enable her to play these very difficult things quickly and forcefully. "And you can have a new piano any time you like. Go and see about it. This looks pretty good to me, but if you don't want it, all right." Aileen squeezed his arm. What was the use of arguing with her father? What good would a lone piano do, when the whole house and the whole family atmosphere were at fault? But she played Schumann, Schubert, Offenbach, Chopin, and the old gentleman strolled to and fro and mused, smiling. There was real feeling and a thoughtful interpretation given to some of these things, for Aileen was not without sentiment, though she was so strong, vigorous, and withal so defiant; but it was all lost on him. He looked on her, his bright, healthy, enticingly beautiful daughter, and wondered what was going to become of her. Some rich man was going to many her—some fine, rich young man with good business instincts—and he, her father, would leave her a lot of money.

There was a reception and a dance to be given to celebrate the opening of the two Cowperwood homes—the reception to be held in Frank Cowperwood's residence, and the dance later at his father's. The Henry Cowperwood domicile was much more pretentious, the reception-room, parlor, music-room, and conservatory being in this case all on the ground floor and much larger. Ellsworth had arranged it so that those rooms, on occasion, could be thrown into one, leaving excellent space for promenade, auditorium, dancing—anything, in fact, that a large company might require. It had been the intention all along of the two men to use these houses jointly. There was, to begin with, a combination use of the various servants, the butler, gardener, laundress, and maids. Frank Cowperwood employed a governess for his children. The butler was really not a butler in the best sense. He was Henry Cowperwood's private servitor. But he could carve and preside, and he could be used in either house as occasion warranted. There was also a hostler and a coachman for the joint stable. When two carriages were required at once, both drove. It made a very agreeable and satisfactory working arrangement.

The preparation of this reception had been quite a matter of importance, for it was necessary for financial reasons to make it as extensive as possible, and for social reasons as exclusive. It was therefore decided that the afternoon reception at Frank's house, with its natural overflow into Henry W.'s, was to be for all—the Tighes, Steners, Butlers, Mollenhauers, as well as the more select groups to which, for instance, belonged Arthur Rivers, Mrs. Seneca Davis, Mr. and Mrs. Trenor Drake, and some of the younger Drexels and Clarks, whom Frank had met. It was not likely that the latter would condescend, but cards had to be sent. Later in the evening a less democratic group if possible was to be entertained, albeit it would have to be extended to include the friends of Anna, Mrs. Cowperwood, Edward, and Joseph, and any list which Frank might personally have in mind. This was to be the list. The best that could be persuaded, commanded, or influenced of the young and socially elect were to be invited here.

It was not possible, however, not to invite the Butlers, parents and children, particularly the children, for both afternoon and evening, since Cowperwood was personally attracted to Aileen and despite the fact that the presence of the parents would be most unsatisfactory. Even Aileen as he knew was a little unsatisfactory to Anna and Mrs. Frank Cowperwood; and these two, when they were together supervising the list of invitations, often talked about it.

"She's so hoidenish," observed Anna, to her sister-in-law, when they came to the name of Aileen. "She thinks she knows so much, and she isn't a bit refined. Her father! Well, if I had her father I wouldn't talk so smart."

Mrs. Cowperwood, who was before her secretaire in her new boudoir, lifted her eyebrows.

"You know, Anna, I sometimes wish that Frank's business did not compel me to have anything to do with them. Mrs. Butler is such a bore. She means well enough, but she doesn't know anything. And Aileen is too rough. She's too forward, I think. She comes over here and plays upon the piano, particularly when Frank's here. I wouldn't mind so much for myself, but I know it must annoy him. All her pieces are so noisy. She never plays anything really delicate and refined."

"I don't like the way she dresses," observed Anna, sympathetically. "She gets herself up too conspicuously. Now, the other day I saw her out driving, and oh, dear! you should have seen her! She had on a crimson Zouave jacket heavily braided with black about the edges, and a turban with a huge crimson feather, and crimson ribbons reaching nearly to her waist. Imagine that kind of a hat to drive in. And her hands! You should have seen the way she held her hands–oh–just so–self-consciously. They were curved just so"–and she showed how. "She had on yellow gauntlets, and she held the reins in one hand and the whip in the other. She drives just like mad when she drives, anyhow, and William, the footman, was up behind her. You should just have seen her. Oh, dear! oh, dear! she does think she is so much!" And Anna giggled, half in reproach, half in amusement.

"I suppose we'll have to invite her; I don't see how we can get out of it. I know just how she'll do, though. She'll walk about and pose and hold her nose up."

"Really, I don't see how she can," commented Anna. "Now, I like Norah. She's much nicer. She doesn't think she's so much."

"I like Norah, too," added Mrs. Cowperwood. "She's really very sweet, and to me she's prettier."

"Oh, indeed, I think so, too."

It was curious, though, that it was Aileen who commanded nearly all their attention and fixed their minds on her so-called idiosyncrasies. All they said was in its peculiar way true; but in addition the girl was really beautiful and much above the average intelligence and force. She was running deep with ambition, and she was all the more conspicuous, and in a way irritating to some, because she reflected in her own consciousness her social defects, against which she was inwardly fighting. She resented the fact that people could justly consider her parents ineligible, and for that reason her also. She was intrinsically as worth while as any one. Cowperwood, so able, and rapidly becoming so distinguished, seemed to realize it. The days that had been passing had brought them somewhat closer together in spirit. He was nice to her and liked to talk to her. Whenever he was at her home now, or she was at his and he was present, he managed somehow to say a word. He would come over quite near and look at her in a warm friendly fashion.

"Well, Aileen"–she could see his genial eyes–"how is it with you? How are your father and mother? Been out driving? That's fine. I saw you to-day. You looked beautiful."

"Oh, Mr. Cowperwood!"

"You did. You looked stunning. A black riding-habit becomes you. I can tell your gold hair a long way off."

"Oh, now, you mustn't say that to me. You'll make me vain. My mother and father tell me I'm too vain as it is."

"Never mind your mother and father. I say you looked stunning, and you did. You always do."

"Oh!"

She gave a little gasp of delight. The color mounted to her cheeks and temples. Mr. Cowperwood knew of course. He was so informed and intensely forceful. And already he was so much admired by so many, her own father and mother included, and by Mr. Mollenhauer and Mr. Simpson, so she heard. And his own home and office were so beautiful. Besides, his quiet intensity matched her restless force.

Aileen and her sister were accordingly invited to the reception but the Butlers mere and pere were given to understand, in as tactful a manner as possible, that the dance afterward was principally for young people.

The reception brought a throng of people. There were many, very many, introductions. There were tactful descriptions of little effects Mr. Ellsworth had achieved under rather trying circumstances; walks under the pergola; viewings of both homes in detail. Many of the guests were old friends. They gathered in the libraries and dining-rooms and talked. There was much jesting, some slappings of shoulders, some good story-telling, and so the afternoon waned into evening, and they went away.

Aileen had created an impression in a street costume of dark blue silk with velvet pelisse to match, and trimmed with elaborate pleatings and shirrings of the same materials. A toque of blue velvet, with high crown and one large dark-red imitation orchid, had given her a jaunty, dashing air. Beneath the toque her red-gold hair was arranged in an enormous chignon, with one long curl escaping over her collar. She was not exactly as daring as she seemed, but she loved to give that impression.

"You look wonderful," Cowperwood said as she passed him.

"I'll look different to-night," was her answer.

She had swung herself with a slight, swaggering stride into the dining-room and disappeared. Norah and her mother stayed to chat with Mrs. Cowperwood.

"Well, it's lovely now, isn't it?" breathed Mrs. Butler. "Sure you'll be happy here. Sure you will. When Eddie fixed the house we're in now, says I: 'Eddie, it's almost too fine for us altogether–surely it is,' and he says, says 'e, 'Norah, nothin' this side o' heavin or beyond is too good for ye'–and he kissed me. Now what d'ye think of that fer a big, hulkin' gossoon?"

"It's perfectly lovely, I think, Mrs. Butler," commented Mrs. Cowperwood, a little bit nervous because of others.

"Mama does love to talk so. Come on, mama. Let's look at the dining-room." It was Norah talking.

"Well, may ye always be happy in it. I wish ye that. I've always been happy in mine. May ye always be happy." And she waddled good-naturedly along.

The Cowperwood family dined hastily alone between seven and eight. At nine the evening guests began to arrive, and now the throng was of a different complexion– girls in mauve and cream-white and salmon-pink and silver-gray, laying aside lace shawls and loose dolmans, and the men in smooth black helping them. Outside in the cold, the carriage doors were slamming, and new guests were arriving constantly. Mrs. Cowperwood stood with her husband and Anna in the main entrance to the reception room, while Joseph and Edward Cowperwood and Mr. and Mrs. Henry W. Cowperwood lingered in the background. Lillian looked charming in a train gown of old rose, with a low, square neck showing a delicate chemisette of fine lace. Her face and figure were still notable, though her face was not as smoothly sweet as it had been years before when Cowperwood had first met her. Anna Cowperwood was not pretty, though she could not be said to be homely. She was small and dark, with a turned-up nose, snapping black eyes, a pert, inquisitive, intelligent, and alas, somewhat critical, air. She had considerable tact in the matter of dressing. Black, in spite of her darkness, with shining beads of sequins on it, helped her complexion greatly, as did a red rose in her hair. She had smooth, white well-rounded arms and shoulders. Bright eyes, a pert manner, clever remarks–these assisted to create an illusion of charm, though, as she often said, it was of little use. "Men want the dolly things."

In the evening inpour of young men and women came Aileen and Norah, the former throwing off a thin net veil of black lace and a dolman of black silk, which her brother Owen took from her. Norah was with Callum, a straight, erect, smiling young Irishman, who looked as though he might carve a notable career for himself. She wore a short, girlish dress that came to a little below her shoe-tops, a pale-figured lavender and white silk, with a fluffy hoop-skirt of dainty laced-edged ruffles, against which tiny bows of lavender stood out in odd places. There was a great sash of lavender about her waist, and in her hair a rosette of the same color. She looked exceedingly winsome–eager and bright-eyed.

But behind her was her sister in ravishing black satin, scaled as a fish with glistening crimsoned-silver sequins, her round, smooth arms bare to the shoulders, her corsage cut as low in the front and back as her daring, in relation to her sense of the proprieties, permitted. She was naturally of exquisite figure, erect, full-breasted, with somewhat more than gently swelling hips, which, nevertheless, melted into lovely, harmonious lines; and this low-cut corsage, receding back and front into a deep V, above a short, gracefully draped overskirt of black tulle and silver tissue, set her off to perfection. Her full, smooth, roundly modeled neck was enhanced in its cream-pink whiteness by an inch-wide necklet of black jet cut in many faceted black squares. Her complexion, naturally high in tone because of the pink of health, was enhanced by the tiniest speck of black court-plaster laid upon her cheekbone; and her hair, heightened in its reddish-gold by her dress, was fluffed loosely and adroitly about her eyes. The main mass of this treasure was done in two loose braids caught up in a black spangled net at the back of her neck; and her eyebrows had been emphasized by a pencil into something almost as significant as her hair. She was, for the occasion, a little too emphatic, perhaps, and yet more because of her burning vitality than of her costume. Art for her should have meant subduing her physical and spiritual significance. Life for her meant emphasizing them.

"Lillian!" Anna nudged her sister-in-law. She was grieved to think that Aileen was wearing black and looked so much better than either of them.

"I see," Lillian replied, in a subdued tone.

"So you're back again." She was addressing Aileen. "It's chilly out, isn't it?"

"I don't mind. Don't the rooms look lovely?"

She was gazing at the softly lighted chambers and the throng before her.

Norah began to babble to Anna. "You know, I just thought I never would get this old thing on." She was speaking of her dress. "Aileen wouldn't help me–the mean thing!"

Aileen had swept on to Cowperwood and his mother, who was near him. She had removed from her arm the black satin ribbon which held her train and kicked the skirts loose and free. Her eyes gleamed almost pleadingly for all her hauteur, like a spirited collie's, and her even teeth showed beautifully.

Cowperwood understood her precisely, as he did any fine, spirited animal.

"I can't tell you how nice you look," he whispered to her, familiarly, as though there was an old understanding between them. "You're like fire and song."

He did not know why he said this. He was not especially poetic. He had not formulated the phrase beforehand. Since his first glimpse of her in the hall, his feelings and ideas had been leaping and plunging like spirited horses. This girl made him set his teeth and narrow his eyes. Involuntarily he squared his jaw, looking more defiant, forceful, efficient, as she drew near.

But Aileen and her sister were almost instantly surrounded by young men seeking to be introduced and to write their names on dance-cards, and for the time being she was lost to view.

Chapter XVIII

The seeds of change–subtle, metaphysical–are rooted deeply. From the first mention of the dance by Mrs. Cowperwood and Anna, Aileen had been conscious of a desire toward a more effective presentation of herself than as yet, for all her father's money, she had been able to achieve. The company which she was to encounter, as she well knew, was to be so much more impressive, distinguished than anything she had heretofore known socially. Then, too, Cowperwood appeared as something more definite in her mind than he had been before, and to save herself she could not get him out of her consciousness.

A vision of him had come to her but an hour before as she was dressing. In a way she had dressed for him. She was never forgetful of the times he had looked at her in an interested way. He had commented on her hands once. To-day he had said that she looked "stunning," and she had thought how easy it would be to impress him to-night–to show him how truly beautiful she was.

She had stood before her mirror between eight and nine–it was nine-fifteen before she was really ready–and pondered over what she should wear. There were two tall pier-glasses in her wardrobe–an unduly large piece of furniture–and one in her closet door. She stood before the latter, looking at her bare arms and shoulders, her shapely figure, thinking of the fact that her left shoulder had a dimple, and that she had selected garnet garters decorated with heart-shaped silver buckles. The corset could not be made quite tight enough at first, and she chided her maid, Kathleen Kelly. She studied how to arrange her hair, and there was much ado about that before it was finally adjusted. She penciled her eyebrows and plucked at the hair about her forehead to make it loose and shadowy. She cut black court-plaster with her nail-shears and tried different-sized pieces in different places. Finally, she found one size and one place that suited her. She turned her head from side to side, looking at the combined effect of her hair, her penciled brows, her dimpled shoulder, and the black beauty-spot. If some one man could see her as she was now, some time! Which man? That thought scurried back like a frightened rat into its hole. She was, for all her strength, afraid of the thought of the one–the very deadly–the man.

And then she came to the matter of a train-gown. Kathleen laid out five, for Aileen had come into the joy and honor of these things recently, and she had, with the permission of her mother and father, indulged herself to the full. She studied a golden-yellow silk, with cream-lace shoulder-straps, and some gussets of garnet beads in the train that shimmered delightfully, but set it aside. She considered favorably a black-and-white striped silk of odd gray effect, and, though she was sorely tempted to wear it, finally let it go. There was a maroon dress, with basque and overskirt over white silk; a rich cream-colored satin; and then this black sequined gown, which she finally chose. She tried on the cream-colored satin first, however, being in much doubt about it; but her penciled eyes and beauty-spot did not seem to harmonize with it. Then she put on the black silk with its glistening crimsoned-silver sequins, and, lo, it touched her. She liked its coquettish drapery of tulle and silver about the hips. The "overskirt," which was at that time just coming into fashion, though avoided by the more conservative, had been adopted by Aileen with enthusiasm. She thrilled a little at the rustle of this black dress, and thrust her chin and nose forward to make it set right. Then after having Kathleen tighten her corsets a little more, she gathered the train over her arm by its train-band and looked again. Something was wanting. Oh, yes, her neck! What to wear–red coral? It did not look right. A string of pearls? That would not do either. There was a necklace made of small cameos set in silver which her mother had purchased, and another of diamonds which belonged to her mother, but they were not right. Finally, her jet necklet, which she did not value very highly, came into her mind, and, oh, how lovely it looked! How soft and smooth and glistening her chin looked above it. She caressed her neck affectionately, called for her black lace mantilla, her long, black silk dolman lined with red, and she was ready.

The ball-room, as she entered, was lovely enough. The young men and young women she saw there were interesting, and she was not wanting for admirers. The most aggressive of these youths–the most forceful–recognized in this maiden a fillip to life, a sting to existence. She was as a honey-jar surrounded by too hungry flies.

But it occurred to her, as her dance-list was filling up, that there was not much left for Mr. Cowperwood, if he should care to dance with her.

Cowperwood was meditating, as he received the last of the guests, on the subtlety of this matter of the sex arrangement of life. Two sexes. He was not at all sure that there was any law governing them. By comparison now with Aileen Butler, his wife looked rather dull, quite too old, and when he was ten years older she would look very much older.

"Oh, yes, Ellsworth had made quite an attractive arrangement out of these two houses–better than we ever thought he could do." He was talking to Henry Hale Sanderson, a young banker. "He had the advantage of combining two into one, and I think he's done more with my little one, considering the limitations of space, than he has with this big one. Father's has the advantage of size. I tell the old gentleman he's simply built a lean-to for me."

His father and a number of his cronies were over in the dining-room of his grand home, glad to get away from the crowd. He would have to stay, and, besides, he wanted to. Had he better dance with Aileen? His wife cared little for dancing, but he would have to dance with her at least once. There was Mrs. Seneca Davis smiling at him, and Aileen. By George, how wonderful! What a girl!

"I suppose your dance-list is full to overflowing. Let me see." He was standing before her and she was holding out the little blue-bordered, gold-monogrammed booklet. An orchestra was playing in the music room. The dance would begin shortly. There were delicately constructed, gold-tinted chairs about the walls and behind palms.

He looked down into her eyes–those excited, life-loving, eager eyes.

"You're quite full up. Let me see. Nine, ten, eleven. Well, that will be enough. I don't suppose I shall want to dance very much. It's nice to be popular."

"I'm not sure about number three. I think that's a mistake. You might have that if you wish."

She was falsifying.

"It doesn't matter so much about him, does it?"

His cheeks flushed a little as he said this.

"No."

Her own flamed.

"Well, I'll see where you are when it's called. You're darling. I'm afraid of you." He shot a level, interpretive glance into her eyes, then left. Aileen's bosom heaved. It was hard to breathe sometimes in this warm air.

While he was dancing first with Mrs. Cowperwood and later with Mrs. Seneca Davis, and still later with Mrs. Martyn Walker, Cowperwood had occasion to look at Aileen often, and each time that he did so there swept over him a sense of great vigor there, of beautiful if raw, dynamic energy that to him was irresistible and especially so to-night. She was so young. She was beautiful, this girl, and in spite of his wife's repeated derogatory comments he felt that she was nearer to his clear, aggressive, unblinking attitude than any one whom he had yet seen in the form of woman. She was unsophisticated, in a way, that was plain, and yet in another way it would take so little to make her understand so much. Largeness was the sense he had of her–not physically, though she was nearly as tall as himself–but emotionally. She seemed so intensely alive. She passed close to him a number of times, her eyes wide and smiling, her lips parted, her teeth agleam, and he felt a stirring of sympathy and companionship for her which he had not previously experienced. She was lovely, all of her–delightful.

"I'm wondering if that dance is open now," he said to her as he drew near toward the beginning of the third set. She was seated with her latest admirer in a far corner of the general living-room, a clear floor now waxed to perfection. A few palms here and there made embrasured parapets of green. "I hope you'll excuse me," he added, deferentially, to her companion.

"Surely," the latter replied, rising.

"Yes, indeed," she replied. "And you'd better stay here with me. It's going to begin soon. You won't mind?" she added, giving her companion a radiant smile.

"Not at all. I've had a lovely waltz." He strolled off.

Cowperwood sat down. "That's young Ledoux, isn't it? I thought so. I saw you dancing. You like it, don't you?"

"I'm crazy about it."

"Well, I can't say that myself. It's fascinating, though. Your partner makes such a difference. Mrs. Cowperwood doesn't like it as much as I do."

His mention of Lillian made Aileen think of her in a faintly derogative way for a moment.

"I think you dance very well. I watched you, too." She questioned afterwards whether she should have said this. It sounded most forward now–almost brazen.

"Oh, did you?"

"Yes."

He was a little keyed up because of her–slightly cloudy in his thoughts–because she was generating a problem in his life, or would if he let her, and so his talk was a little tame. He was thinking of something to say–some words which would bring them a little nearer together. But for the moment he could not. Truth to tell, he wanted to say a great deal.

"Well, that was nice of you," he added, after a moment. "What made you do it?"

He turned with a mock air of inquiry. The music was beginning again. The dancers were rising. He arose.

He had not intended to give this particular remark a serious turn; but, now that she was so near him, he looked into her eyes steadily but with a soft appeal and said, "Yes, why?"

They had come out from behind the palms. He had put his hand to her waist. His right arm held her left extended arm to arm, palm to palm. Her right hand was on his shoulder, and she was close to him, looking into his eyes. As they began the gay undulations of the waltz she looked away and then down without answering. Her movements were as light and airy as those of a butterfly. He felt a sudden lightness himself, communicated as by an invisible current. He wanted to match the suppleness of her body with his own, and did. Her arms, the flash and glint of the crimson sequins against the smooth, black silk of her closely fitting dress, her neck, her glowing, radiant hair, all combined to provoke a slight intellectual intoxication. She was so vigorously young, so, to him, truly beautiful.

"But you didn't answer," he continued.

"Isn't this lovely music?"

He pressed her fingers.

She lifted shy eyes to him now, for, in spite of her gay, aggressive force, she was afraid of him. His personality was obviously so dominating. Now that he was so close to her, dancing, she conceived of him as something quite wonderful, and yet she experienced a nervous reaction—a momentary desire to run away.

"Very well, if you won't tell me," he smiled, mockingly.

He thought she wanted him to talk to her so, to tease her with suggestions of this concealed feeling of his—this strong liking. He wondered what could come of any such understanding as this, anyhow?

"Oh, I just wanted to see how you danced," she said, tamely, the force of her original feeling having been weakened by a thought of what she was doing. He noted the change and smiled. It was lovely to be dancing with her. He had not thought mere dancing could hold such charm.

"You like me?" he said, suddenly, as the music drew to its close.

She thrilled from head to toe at the question. A piece of ice dropped down her back could not have startled her more. It was apparently tactless, and yet it was anything but tactless. She looked up quickly, directly, but his strong eyes were too much for her.

"Why, yes," she answered, as the music stopped, trying to keep an even tone to her voice. She was glad they were walking toward a chair.

"I like you so much," he said, "that I have been wondering if you really like me." There was an appeal in his voice, soft and gentle. His manner was almost sad.

"Why, yes," she replied, instantly, returning to her earlier mood toward him. "You know I do."

"I need some one like you to like me," he continued, in the same vein. "I need some one like you to talk to. I didn't think so before—but now I do. You are beautiful—wonderful."

"We mustn't," she said. "I mustn't. I don't know what I'm doing." She looked at a young man strolling toward her, and asked: "I have to explain to him. He's the one I had this dance with."

Cowperwood understood. He walked away. He was quite warm and tense now—almost nervous. It was quite clear to him that he had done or was contemplating perhaps a very treacherous thing. Under the current code of society he had no right to do it. It was against the rules, as they were understood by everybody. Her father, for instance—his father—every one in this particular walk of life. However, much breaking of the rules under the surface of things there might be, the rules were still there. As he had heard one young man remark once at school, when some story had been told of a boy leading a girl astray and to a disastrous end, "That isn't the way at all."

Still, now that he had said this, strong thoughts of her were in his mind. And despite his involved social and financial position, which he now recalled, it was interesting to him to see how deliberately and even calculatingly–and worse, enthusiastically–he was pumping the bellows that tended only to heighten the flames of his desire for this girl; to feed a fire that might ultimately consume him–and how deliberately and resourcefully!

Aileen toyed aimlessly with her fan as a black-haired, thin-faced young law student talked to her, and seeing Norah in the distance she asked to be allowed to run over to her.

"Oh, Aileen," called Norah, "I've been looking for you everywhere. Where have you been?"

"Dancing, of course. Where do you suppose I've been? Didn't you see me on the floor?"

"No, I didn't," complained Norah, as though it were most essential that she should. "How late are you going to stay?"

"Until it's over, I suppose. I don't know."

"Owen says he's going at twelve."

"Well, that doesn't matter. Some one will take me home. Are you having a good time?"

"Fine. Oh, let me tell you. I stepped on a lady's dress over there, last dance. She was terribly angry. She gave me such a look."

"Well, never mind, honey. She won't hurt you. Where are you going now?"

Aileen always maintained a most guardian-like attitude toward her sister.

"I want to find Callum. He has to dance with me next time. I know what he's trying to do. He's trying to get away from me. But he won't."

Aileen smiled. Norah looked very sweet. And she was so bright. What would she think of her if she knew? She turned back, and her fourth partner sought her. She began talking gayly, for she felt that she had to make a show of composure; but all the while there was ringing in her ears that definite question of his, "You like me, don't you?" and her later uncertain but not less truthful answer, "Yes, of course I do."

Chapter XIX

The growth of a passion is a very peculiar thing. In highly organized intellectual and artistic types it is so often apt to begin with keen appreciation of certain qualities, modified by many, many mental reservations. The egoist, the intellectual, gives but little of himself and asks much. Nevertheless, the lover of life, male or female, finding himself or herself in sympathetic accord with such a nature, is apt to gain much.

Cowperwood was innately and primarily an egoist and intellectual, though blended strongly therewith, was a humane and democratic spirit. We think of egoism and intellectualism as closely confined to the arts. Finance is an art. And it presents the operations of the subtlest of the intellectuals and of the egoists. Cowperwood was a financier. Instead of dwelling on the works of nature, its beauty and subtlety, to his material disadvantage, he found a happy mean, owing to the swiftness of his intellectual operations, whereby he could, intellectually and emotionally, rejoice in the beauty of life without interfering with his perpetual material and financial calculations. And when it came to women and morals, which involved so much relating to beauty, happiness, a sense of distinction and variety in living, he was but now beginning to suspect for himself at least that apart from maintaining organized society in its present form there was no basis for this one-life, one-love idea. How had it come about that so many people agreed on this single point, that it was good and necessary to marry one woman and cleave to her until death? He did not know. It was not for him to bother about the subtleties of evolution, which even then was being noised abroad, or to ferret out the curiosities of history in connection with this matter. He had no time. Suffice it that the vagaries of temperament and conditions with which he came into immediate contact proved to him that there was great dissatisfaction with that idea. People did not cleave to each other until death; and in thousands of cases where they did, they did not want to. Quickness of mind, subtlety of idea, fortuitousness of opportunity, made it possible for some people to right their matrimonial and social infelicities; whereas for others, because of dullness of wit, thickness of comprehension, poverty, and lack of charm, there was no escape from the slough of their despond. They were compelled by some devilish accident of birth or lack of force or resourcefulness to stew in their own juice of wretchedness, or to shuffle off this mortal coil–which under other circumstances had such glittering possibilities–via the rope, the knife, the bullet, or the cup of poison.

"I would die, too," he thought to himself, one day, reading of a man who, confined by disease and poverty, had lived for twelve years alone in a back bedroom attended by an old and probably decrepit housekeeper. A darning-needle forced into his heart had ended his earthly woes. "To the devil with such a life! Why twelve years? Why not at the end of the second or third?"

Again, it was so very evident, in so many ways, that force was the answer–great mental and physical force. Why, these giants of commerce and money could do as they pleased in this life, and did. He had already had ample local evidence of it in more than one direction. Worse–the little guardians of so-called law and morality, the newspapers, the preachers, the police, and the public moralists generally, so loud in their denunciation of evil in humble places, were cowards all when it came to corruption in high ones. They did not dare to utter a feeble squeak until some giant had accidentally fallen and they could do so without danger to themselves. Then, O Heavens, the palaver! What beatings of tom-toms! What mouthings of pharisaical moralities–platitudes! Run now, good people, for you may see clearly how evil is dealt with in high places! It made him smile. Such hypocrisy! Such cant! Still, so the world was organized, and it was not for him to set it right. Let it wag as it would. The thing for him to do was to get rich and hold his own–to build up a seeming of virtue and dignity which would pass muster for the genuine thing. Force would do that. Quickness of wit. And he had these. "I satisfy myself," was his motto; and it might well have been emblazoned upon any coat of arms which he could have contrived to set forth his claim to intellectual and social nobility.

But this matter of Aileen was up for consideration and solution at this present moment, and because of his forceful, determined character he was presently not at all disturbed by the problem it presented. It was a problem, like some of those knotty financial complications which presented themselves daily; but it was not insoluble. What did he want to do? He couldn't leave his wife and fly with Aileen, that was certain. He had too many connections. He had too many social, and thinking of his children and parents, emotional as well as financial ties to bind him. Besides, he was not at all sure that he wanted to. He did not intend to leave his growing interests, and at the same time he did not intend to give up Aileen immediately. The unheralded manifestation of interest on her part was too attractive. Mrs. Cowperwood was no longer what she should be physically and mentally, and that in itself to him was sufficient to justify his present interest in this girl. Why fear anything, if only he could figure out a way to achieve it without harm to himself? At the same time he thought it might never be possible for him to figure out any practical or protective program for either himself or Aileen, and that made him silent and reflective. For by now he was intensely drawn to her, as he could feel–something chemic and hence dynamic was uppermost in him now and clamoring for expression.

At the same time, in contemplating his wife in connection with all this, he had many qualms, some emotional, some financial. While she had yielded to his youthful enthusiasm for her after her husband's death, he had only since learned that she was a natural conservator of public morals–the cold purity of the snowdrift in so far as the world might see, combined at times with the murky mood of the wanton. And yet, as he had also learned, she was ashamed of the passion that at times swept and dominated her. This irritated Cowperwood, as it would always irritate any strong, acquisitive, direct-seeing temperament. While he had no desire to acquaint the whole world with his feelings, why should there be concealment between them, or at least mental evasion of a fact which physically she subscribed to? Why do one thing and think another? To be sure, she was devoted to him in her quiet way, not passionately (as he looked back he could not say that she had ever been that), but intellectually. Duty, as she understood it, played a great part in this. She was dutiful. And then what people thought, what the time-spirit demanded–these were the great things. Aileen, on the contrary, was probably not dutiful, and it was obvious that she had no temperamental connection with current convention. No doubt she had been as well instructed as many another girl, but look at her. She was not obeying her instructions.

In the next three months this relationship took on a more flagrant form. Aileen, knowing full well what her parents would think, how unspeakable in the mind of the current world were the thoughts she was thinking, persisted, nevertheless, in so thinking and longing. Cowperwood, now that she had gone thus far and compromised herself in intention, if not in deed, took on a peculiar charm for her. It was not his body–great passion is never that, exactly. The flavor of his spirit was what attracted and compelled, like the glow of a flame to a moth. There was a light of romance in his eyes, which, however governed and controlled–was directive and almost all-powerful to her.

When he touched her hand at parting, it was as though she had received an electric shock, and she recalled that it was very difficult for her to look directly into his eyes. Something akin to a destructive force seemed to issue from them at times. Other people, men particularly, found it difficult to face Cowperwood's glazed stare. It was as though there were another pair of eyes behind those they saw, watching through thin, obscuring curtains. You could not tell what he was thinking.

And during the next few months she found herself coming closer and closer to Cowperwood. At his home one evening, seated at the piano, no one else being present at the moment, he leaned over and kissed her. There was a cold, snowy street visible through the interstices of the hangings of the windows, and gas-lamps flickering outside. He had come in early, and hearing Aileen, he came to where she was seated at the piano. She was wearing a rough, gray wool cloth dress, ornately banded with fringed Oriental embroidery in blue and burnt-orange, and her beauty was further enhanced by a gray hat planned to match her dress, with a plume of shaded orange and blue. On her fingers were four or five rings, far too many–an opal, an emerald, a ruby, and a diamond–flashing visibly as she played.

She knew it was he, without turning. He came beside her, and she looked up smiling, the reverie evoked by Schubert partly vanishing–or melting into another mood. Suddenly he bent over and pressed his lips firmly to hers. His mustache thrilled her with its silky touch. She stopped playing and tried to catch her breath, for, strong as she was, it affected her breathing. Her heart was beating like a triphammer. She did not say, "Oh," or, "You mustn't," but rose and walked over to a window, where she lifted a curtain, pretending to look out. She felt as though she might faint, so intensely happy was she.

Cowperwood followed her quickly. Slipping his arms about her waist, he looked at her flushed cheeks, her clear, moist eyes and red mouth.

"You love me?" he whispered, stern and compelling because of his desire.

"Yes! Yes! You know I do."

He crushed her face to his, and she put up her hands and stroked his hair.

A thrilling sense of possession, mastery, happiness and understanding, love of her and of her body, suddenly overwhelmed him.

"I love you," he said, as though he were surprised to hear himself say it. "I didn't think I did, but I do. You're beautiful. I'm wild about you."

"And I love you" she answered. "I can't help it. I know I shouldn't, but–oh–" Her hands closed tight over his ears and temples. She put her lips to his and dreamed into his eyes. Then she stepped away quickly, looking out into the street, and he walked back into the living-room. They were quite alone. He was debating whether he should risk anything further when Norah, having been in to see Anna next door, appeared and not long afterward Mrs. Cowperwood. Then Aileen and Norah left.

Chapter XX

This definite and final understanding having been reached, it was but natural that this liaison should proceed to a closer and closer relationship. Despite her religious upbringing, Aileen was decidedly a victim of her temperament. Current religious feeling and belief could not control her. For the past nine or ten years there had been slowly forming in her mind a notion of what her lover should be like. He should be strong, handsome, direct, successful, with clear eyes, a ruddy glow of health, and a certain native understanding and sympathy–a love of life which matched her own. Many young men had approached her. Perhaps the nearest realization of her ideal was Father David, of St. Timothy's, and he was, of course, a priest and sworn to celibacy. No word had ever passed between them but he had been as conscious of her as she of him. Then came Frank Cowperwood, and by degrees, because of his presence and contact, he had been slowly built up in her mind as the ideal person. She was drawn as planets are drawn to their sun.

It is a question as to what would have happened if antagonistic forces could have been introduced just at this time. Emotions and liaisons of this character can, of course, occasionally be broken up and destroyed. The characters of the individuals can be modified or changed to a certain extent, but the force must be quite sufficient. Fear is a great deterrent–fear of material loss where there is no spiritual dread–but wealth and position so often tend to destroy this dread. It is so easy to scheme with means. Aileen had no spiritual dread whatever. Cowperwood was without spiritual or religious feeling. He looked at this girl, and his one thought was how could he so deceive the world that he could enjoy her love and leave his present state undisturbed. Love her he did surely.

Business necessitated his calling at the Butlers' quite frequently, and on each occasion he saw Aileen. She managed to slip forward and squeeze his hand the first time he came–to steal a quick, vivid kiss; and another time, as he was going out, she suddenly appeared from behind the curtains hanging at the parlor door.

"Honey!"

The voice was soft and coaxing. He turned, giving her a warning nod in the direction of her father's room upstairs.

She stood there, holding out one hand, and he stepped forward for a second. Instantly her arms were about his neck, as he slipped his about her waist.

"I long to see you so."

"I, too. I'll fix some way. I'm thinking."

He released her arms, and went out, and she ran to the window and looked out after him. He was walking west on the street, for his house was only a few blocks away, and she looked at the breadth of his shoulders, the balance of his form. He stepped so briskly, so incisively. Ah, this was a man! He was her Frank. She thought of him in that light already. Then she sat down at the piano and played pensively until dinner.

And it was so easy for the resourceful mind of Frank Cowperwood, wealthy as he was, to suggest ways and means. In his younger gallivantings about places of ill repute, and his subsequent occasional variations from the straight and narrow path, he had learned much of the curious resources of immorality. Being a city of five hundred thousand and more at this time, Philadelphia had its nondescript hotels, where one might go, cautiously and fairly protected from observation; and there were houses of a conservative, residential character, where appointments might be made, for a consideration. And as for safeguards against the production of new life–they were not mysteries to him any longer. He knew all about them. Care was the point of caution. He had to be cautious, for he was so rapidly coming to be an influential and a distinguished man. Aileen, of course, was not conscious, except in a vague way, of the drift of her passion; the ultimate destiny to which this affection might lead was not clear to her. Her craving was for love–to be fondled and caressed–and she really did not think so much further. Further thoughts along this line were like rats that showed their heads out of dark holes in shadowy corners and scuttled back at the least sound. And, anyhow, all that was to be connected with Cowperwood would be beautiful. She really did not think that he loved her yet as he should; but he would. She did not know that she wanted to interfere with the claims of his wife. She did not think she did. But it would not hurt Mrs. Cowperwood if Frank loved her–Aileen–also.

How shall we explain these subtleties of temperament and desire? Life has to deal with them at every turn. They will not down, and the large, placid movements of nature outside of man's little organisms would indicate that she is not greatly concerned. We see much punishment in the form of jails, diseases, failures, and wrecks; but we also see that the old tendency is not visibly lessened. Is there no law outside of the subtle will and power of the individual to achieve? If not, it is surely high time that we knew it–one and all. We might then agree to do as we do; but there would be no silly illusion as to divine regulation. Vox populi, vox Dei.

So there were other meetings, lovely hours which they soon began to spend the moment her passion waxed warm enough to assure compliance, without great fear and without thought of the deadly risk involved. From odd moments in his own home, stolen when there was no one about to see, they advanced to clandestine meetings beyond the confines of the city. Cowperwood was not one who was temperamentally inclined to lose his head and neglect his business. As a matter of fact, the more he thought of this rather unexpected affectional development, the more certain he was that he must not let it interfere with his business time and judgment. His office required his full attention from nine until three, anyhow. He could give it until five-thirty with profit; but he could take several afternoons off, from three-thirty until five-thirty or six, and no one would be the wiser. It was customary for Aileen to drive alone almost every afternoon a spirited pair of bays, or to ride a mount, bought by her father for her from a noted horse-dealer in Baltimore. Since Cowperwood also drove and rode, it was not difficult to arrange meeting-places far out on the Wissahickon or the Schuylkill road. There were many spots in the newly laid-out park, which were as free from interruption as the depths of a forest. It was always possible that they might encounter some one; but it was also always possible to make a rather plausible explanation, or none at all, since even in case of such an encounter nothing, ordinarily, would be suspected.

So, for the time being there was love-making, the usual billing and cooing of lovers in a simple and much less than final fashion; and the lovely horseback rides together under the green trees of the approaching spring were idyllic. Cowperwood awakened to a sense of joy in life such as he fancied, in the blush of this new desire, he had never experienced before. Lillian had been lovely in those early days in which he had first called on her in North Front Street, and he had fancied himself unspeakably happy at that time; but that was nearly ten years since, and he had forgotten. Since then he had had no great passion, no notable liaison; and then, all at once, in the midst of his new, great business prosperity, Aileen. Her young body and soul, her passionate illusions. He could see always, for all her daring, that she knew so little of the calculating, brutal world with which he was connected. Her father had given her all the toys she wanted without stint; her mother and brothers had coddled her, particularly her mother. Her young sister thought she was adorable. No one imagined for one moment that Aileen would ever do anything wrong. She was too sensible, after all, too eager to get up in the world. Why should she, when her life lay open and happy before her–a delightful love-match, some day soon, with some very eligible and satisfactory lover?

"When you marry, Aileen," her mother used to say to her, "we'll have a grand time here. Sure we'll do the house over then, if we don't do it before. Eddie will have to fix it up, or I'll do it meself. Never fear."

"Yes–well, I'd rather you'd fix it now," was her reply.

Butler himself used to strike her jovially on the shoulder in a rough, loving way, and ask, "Well, have you found him yet?" or "Is he hanging around the outside watchin' for ye?"

If she said, "No," he would reply: "Well, he will be, never fear–worse luck. I'll hate to see ye go, girlie! You can stay here as long as ye want to, and ye want to remember that you can always come back."

Aileen paid very little attention to this bantering. She loved her father, but it was all such a matter of course. It was the commonplace of her existence, and not so very significant, though delightful enough.

But how eagerly she yielded herself to Cowperwood under the spring trees these days! She had no sense of that ultimate yielding that was coming, for now he merely caressed and talked to her. He was a little doubtful about himself. His growing liberties for himself seemed natural enough, but in a sense of fairness to her he began to talk to her about what their love might involve. Would she? Did she understand? This phase of it puzzled and frightened Aileen a little at first. She stood before him one afternoon in her black riding-habit and high silk riding-hat perched jauntily on her red-gold hair; and striking her riding-skirt with her short whip, pondering doubtfully as she listened. He had asked her whether she knew what she was doing? Whither they were drifting? If she loved him truly enough? The two horses were tethered in a thicket a score of yards away from the main road and from the bank of a tumbling stream, which they had approached. She was trying to discover if she could see them. It was pretense. There was no interest in her glance. She was thinking of him and the smartness of his habit, and the exquisiteness of this moment. He had such a charming calico pony. The leaves were just enough developed to make a diaphanous lacework of green. It was like looking through a green-spangled arras to peer into the woods beyond or behind. The gray stones were already faintly messy where the water rippled and sparkled, and early birds were calling–robins and blackbirds and wrens.

"Baby mine," he said, "do you understand all about this? Do you know exactly what you're doing when you come with me this way?"

"I think I do."

She struck her boot and looked at the ground, and then up through the trees at the blue sky.

"Look at me, honey."

"I don't want to."

"But look at me, sweet. I want to ask you something."

"Don't make me, Frank, please. I can't."

"Oh yes, you can look at me."

"No."

She backed away as he took her hands, but came forward again, easily enough.

"Now look in my eyes."

"I can't."

"See here."

"I can't. Don't ask me. I'll answer you, but don't make me look at you."

His hand stole to her cheek and fondled it. He petted her shoulder, and she leaned her head against him.

"Sweet, you're so beautiful," he said finally, "I can't give you up. I know what I ought to do. You know, too, I suppose; but I can't. I must have you. If this should end in exposure, it would be quite bad for you and me. Do you understand?"

"Yes."

"I don't know your brothers very well; but from looking at them I judge they're pretty determined people. They think a great deal of you."

"Indeed, they do." Her vanity prinked slightly at this.

"They would probably want to kill me, and very promptly, for just this much. What do you think they would want to do if—well, if anything should happen, some time?"

He waited, watching her pretty face.

"But nothing need happen. We needn't go any further."

"Aileen!"

"I won't look at you. You needn't ask. I can't."

"Aileen! Do you mean that?"

"I don't know. Don't ask me, Frank."

"You know it can't stop this way, don't you? You know it. This isn't the end. Now, if—" He explained the whole theory of illicit meetings, calmly, dispassionately. "You are perfectly safe, except for one thing, chance exposure. It might just so happen; and then, of course, there would be a great deal to settle for. Mrs. Cowperwood would never give me a divorce; she has no reason to. If I should clean up in the way I hope to—if I should make a million—I wouldn't mind knocking off now. I don't expect to work all my days. I have always planned to knock off at thirty-five. I'll have enough by that time. Then I want to travel. It will only be a few more years now. If you were free—if your father and mother were dead"—curiously she did not wince at this practical reference—"it would be a different matter."

He paused. She still gazed thoughtfully at the water below, her mind running out to a yacht on the sea with him, a palace somewhere—just they two. Her eyes, half closed, saw this happy world; and, listening to him, she was fascinated.

"Hanged if I see the way out of this, exactly. But I love you!" He caught her to him. "I love you—love you!"

"Oh, yes," she replied intensely, "I want you to. I'm not afraid."

"I've taken a house in North Tenth Street," he said finally, as they walked over to the horses and mounted them. "It isn't furnished yet; but it will be soon. I know a woman who will take charge."

"Who is she?"

"An interesting widow of nearly fifty. Very intelligent—she is attractive, and knows a good deal of life. I found her through an advertisement. You might call on her some afternoon when things are arranged, and look the place over. You needn't meet her except in a casual way. Will you?"

She rode on, thinking, making no reply. He was so direct and practical in his calculations.

"Will you? It will be all right. You might know her. She isn't objectionable in any way. Will you?"

"Let me know when it is ready," was all she said finally.

Chapter XXI

The vagaries of passion! Subtleties! Risks! What sacrifices are not laid willfully upon its altar! In a little while this more than average residence to which Cowperwood had referred was prepared solely to effect a satisfactory method of concealment. The house was governed by a seemingly recently-bereaved widow, and it was possible for Aileen to call without seeming strangely out of place. In such surroundings, and under such circumstances, it was not difficult to persuade her to give herself wholly to her lover, governed as she was by her wild and unreasoning affection and passion. In a way, there was a saving element of love, for truly, above all others, she wanted this man. She had no thought or feeling toward any other. All her mind ran toward visions of the future, when, somehow, she and he might be together for all time. Mrs. Cowperwood might die, or he might run away with her at thirty-five when he had a million. Some adjustment would be made, somehow. Nature had given her this man. She relied on him implicitly. When he told her that he would take care of her so that nothing evil should befall, she believed him fully. Such sins are the commonplaces of the confessional.

It is a curious fact that by some subtlety of logic in the Christian world, it has come to be believed that there can be no love outside the conventional process of courtship and marriage. One life, one love, is the Christian idea, and into this sluice or mold it has been endeavoring to compress the whole world. Pagan thought held no such belief. A writing of divorce for trivial causes was the theory of the elders; and in the primeval world nature apparently holds no scheme for the unity of two beyond the temporary care of the young. That the modern home is the most beautiful of schemes, when based upon mutual sympathy and understanding between two, need not be questioned. And yet this fact should not necessarily carry with it a condemnation of all love not so fortunate as to find so happy a denouement. Life cannot be put into any mold, and the attempt might as well be abandoned at once. Those so fortunate as to find harmonious companionship for life should congratulate themselves and strive to be worthy of it. Those not so blessed, though they be written down as pariahs, have yet some justification. And, besides, whether we will or not, theory or no theory, the basic facts of chemistry and physics remain. Like is drawn to like. Changes in temperament bring changes in relationship. Dogma may bind some minds; fear, others. But there are always those in whom the chemistry and physics of life are large, and in whom neither dogma nor fear is operative. Society lifts its hands in horror; but from age to age the Helens, the Messalinas, the Du Barrys, the Pompadours, the Maintenons, and the Nell Gwyns flourish and point a freer basis of relationship than we have yet been able to square with our lives.

These two felt unutterably bound to each other. Cowperwood, once he came to understand her, fancied that he had found the one person with whom he could live happily the rest of his life. She was so young, so confident, so hopeful, so undismayed. All these months since they had first begun to reach out to each other he had been hourly contrasting her with his wife. As a matter of fact, his dissatisfaction, though it may be said to have been faint up to this time, was now surely tending to become real enough. Still, his children were pleasing to him; his home beautiful. Lillian, phlegmatic and now thin, was still not homely. All these years he had found her satisfactory enough; but now his dissatisfaction with her began to increase. She was not like Aileen–not young, not vivid, not as unschooled in the commonplaces of life. And while ordinarily, he was not one who was inclined to be querulous, still now on occasion, he could be. He began by asking questions concerning his wife's appearance–irritating little whys which are so trivial and yet so exasperating and discouraging to a woman. Why didn't she get a mauve hat nearer the shade of her dress? Why didn't she go out more? Exercise would do her good. Why didn't she do this, and why didn't she do that? He scarcely noticed that he was doing this; but she did, and she felt the undertone–the real significance–and took umbrage.

"Oh, why–why?" she retorted, one day, curtly. "Why do you ask so many questions? You don't care so much for me any more; that's why. I can tell."

He leaned back startled by the thrust. It had not been based on any evidence of anything save his recent remarks; but he was not absolutely sure. He was just the least bit sorry that he had irritated her, and he said so.

"Oh, it's all right," she replied. "I don't care. But I notice that you don't pay as much attention to me as you used to. It's your business now, first, last, and all the time. You can't get your mind off of that."

He breathed a sigh of relief. She didn't suspect, then.

But after a little time, as he grew more and more in sympathy with Aileen, he was not so disturbed as to whether his wife might suspect or not. He began to think on occasion, as his mind followed the various ramifications of the situation, that it would be better if she did. She was really not of the contentious fighting sort. He now decided because of various calculations in regard to her character that she might not offer as much resistance to some ultimate rearrangement, as he had originally imagined. She might even divorce him. Desire, dreams, even in him were evoking calculations not as sound as those which ordinarily generated in his brain.

No, as he now said to himself, the rub was not nearly so much in his own home, as it was in the Butler family. His relations with Edward Malia Butler had become very intimate. He was now advising with him constantly in regard to the handling of his securities, which were numerous. Butler held stocks in such things as the Pennsylvania Coal Company, the Delaware and Hudson Canal, the Morris and Essex Canal, the Reading Railroad. As the old gentleman's mind had broadened to the significance of the local street-railway problem in Philadelphia, he had decided to close out his other securities at such advantageous terms as he could, and reinvest the money in local lines. He knew that Mollenhauer and Simpson were doing this, and they were excellent judges of the significance of local affairs. Like Cowperwood, he had the idea that if he controlled sufficient of the local situation in this field, he could at last effect a joint relationship with Mollenhauer and Simpson. Political legislation, advantageous to the combined lines, could then be so easily secured. Franchises and necessary extensions to existing franchises could be added. This conversion of his outstanding stock in other fields, and the picking up of odd lots in the local street-railway, was the business of Cowperwood. Butler, through his sons, Owen and

Callum, was also busy planning a new line and obtaining a franchise, sacrificing, of course, great blocks of stock and actual cash to others, in order to obtain sufficient influence to have the necessary legislation passed. Yet it was no easy matter, seeing that others knew what the general advantages of the situation were, and because of this Cowperwood, who saw the great source of profit here, was able, betimes, to serve himself–buying blocks, a part of which only went to Butler, Mollenhauer or others. In short he was not as eager to serve Butler, or any one else, as he was to serve himself if he could.

In this connection, the scheme which George W. Stener had brought forward, representing actually in the background Strobik, Wycroft, and Harmon, was an opening wedge for himself. Stener's plan was to loan him money out of the city treasury at two per cent., or, if he would waive all commissions, for nothing (an agent for self-protective purposes was absolutely necessary), and with it take over the North Pennsylvania Company's line on Front Street, which, because of the shortness of its length, one mile and a half, and the brevity of the duration of its franchise, was neither doing very well nor being rated very high. Cowperwood in return for his manipulative skill was to have a fair proportion of the stock–twenty per cent. Strobik and Wycroft knew the parties from whom the bulk of the stock could be secured if engineered properly. Their plan was then, with this borrowed treasury money, to extend its franchise and then the line itself, and then later again, by issuing a great block of stock and hypothecating it with a favored bank, be able to return the principal to the city treasury and pocket their profits from the line as earned. There was no trouble in this, in so far as Cowperwood was concerned, except that it divided the stock very badly among these various individuals, and left him but a comparatively small share–for his thought and pains.

But Cowperwood was an opportunist. And by this time his financial morality had become special and local in its character. He did not think it was wise for any one to steal anything from anybody where the act of taking or profiting was directly and plainly considered stealing. That was unwise–dangerous–hence wrong. There were so many situations wherein what one might do in the way of taking or profiting was open to discussion and doubt. Morality varied, in his mind at least, with conditions, if not climates. Here, in Philadelphia, the tradition (politically, mind you–not generally) was that the city treasurer might use the money of the city without interest so long as he returned the principal intact. The city treasury and the city treasurer were like a honey-laden hive and a queen bee around which the drones–the politicians–swarmed in the hope of profit. The one disagreeable thing in connection with this transaction with Stener was that neither Butler, Mollenhauer nor Simpson, who were the actual superiors of Stener and Strobik, knew anything about it. Stener and those behind him were, through him, acting for themselves. If the larger powers heard of this, it might alienate them. He had to think of this. Still, if he refused to make advantageous deals with Stener or any other man influential in local affairs, he was cutting off his nose to spite his face, for other bankers and brokers would, and gladly. And besides it was not at all certain that Butler, Mollenhauer, and Simpson would ever hear.

In this connection, there was another line, which he rode on occasionally, the Seventeenth and Nineteenth Street line, which he felt was a much more interesting thing for him to think about, if he could raise the money. It had been originally capitalized for five hundred thousand dollars; but there had been a series of bonds to the value of two hundred and fifty thousand dollars added for improvements, and the company was finding great difficulty in meeting the interest. The bulk of the stock was scattered about among small investors, and it would require all of two hundred and fifty thousand dollars to collect it and have himself elected president or chairman of the board of directors. Once in, however, he could vote this stock as he pleased, hypothecating it meanwhile at his father's bank for as much as he could get, and issuing more stocks with which to bribe legislators in the matter of extending the line, and in taking up other opportunities to either add to it by purchase or supplement it by working agreements. The word "bribe" is used here in this matter-of-fact American way, because bribery was what was in every one's mind in connection with the State legislature. Terrence Relihan–the small, dark-faced Irishman, a dandy in dress and manners–who represented the financial interests at Harrisburg, and who had come to Cowperwood after the five million bond deal had been printed, had told him that nothing could be done at the capital without money, or its equivalent, negotiable securities. Each significant legislator, if he yielded his vote or his influence, must be looked after. If he, Cowperwood, had any scheme which he wanted handled at any time, Relihan had intimated to him that he would be glad to talk with him. Cowperwood had figured on this Seventeenth and Nineteenth Street line scheme more than once, but he had never felt quite sure that he was willing to undertake it. His obligations in other directions were so large. But the lure was there, and he pondered and pondered.

Stener's scheme of loaning him money wherewith to manipulate the North Pennsylvania line deal put this Seventeenth and Nineteenth Street dream in a more favorable light. As it was he was constantly watching the certificates of loan issue, for the city treasury,–buying large quantities when the market was falling to protect it and selling heavily, though cautiously, when he saw it rising and to do this he had to have a great deal of free money to permit him to do it. He was constantly fearful of some break in the market which would affect the value of all his securities and result in the calling of his loans. There was no storm in sight. He did not see that anything could happen in reason; but he did not want to spread himself out too thin. As he saw it now, therefore if he took one hundred and fifty thousand dollars of this city money and went after this Seventeenth and Nineteenth Street matter it would not mean that he was spreading himself out too thin, for because of this new proposition could he not call on Stener for more as a loan in connection with these other ventures? But if anything should happen–well–

"Frank," said Stener, strolling into his office one afternoon after four o'clock when the main rush of the day's work was over–the relationship between Cowperwood and Stener had long since reached the "Frank" and "George" period–"Strobik thinks he has that North Pennsylvania deal arranged so that we can take it up if we want to. The principal stockholder, we find, is a man by the name of Coltan–not Ike Colton, but Ferdinand. How's that for a name?" Stener beamed fatly and genially.

Things had changed considerably for him since the days when he had been fortu-itously and almost indifferently made city treasurer. His method of dressing had so much improved since he had been inducted into office, and his manner expressed so much more good feeling, confidence, aplomb, that he would not have recognized himself if he had been permitted to see himself as had those who had known him before. An old, nervous shifting of the eyes had almost ceased, and a feeling of restfulness, which had previously been restlessness, and had sprung from a sense of necessity, had taken its place. His large feet were incased in good, square-toed, soft-leather shoes; his stocky chest and fat legs were made somewhat agreeable to the eye by a well-cut suit of brownish-gray cloth; and his neck was now surrounded by a low, wing-point white collar and brown-silk tie. His ample chest, which spread out a little lower in around and constantly enlarging stomach, was ornamented by a heavy-link gold chain, and his white cuffs had large gold cuff-buttons set with rubies of a very notable size. He was rosy and decidedly well fed. In fact, he was doing very well indeed.

He had moved his family from a shabby two-story frame house in South Ninth Street to a very comfortable brick one three stories in height, and three times as large, on Spring Garden Street. His wife had a few acquaintances–the wives of other politicians. His children were attending the high school, a thing he had hardly hoped for in earlier days. He was now the owner of fourteen or fifteen pieces of cheap real estate in different portions of the city, which might eventually become very valuable, and he was a silent partner in the South Philadelphia Foundry Company and the American Beef and Pork Company, two corporations on paper whose principal business was subletting contracts secured from the city to the humble butchers and foundrymen who would carry out orders as given and not talk too much or ask questions.

"Well, that is an odd name," said Cowperwood, blandly. "So he has it? I never thought that road would pay, as it was laid out. It's too short. It ought to run about three miles farther out into the Kensington section."

"You're right," said Stener, dully.

"Did Strobik say what Colton wants for his shares?"

"Sixty-eight, I think."

"The current market rate. He doesn't want much, does he? Well, George, at that rate it will take about"–he calculated quickly on the basis of the number of shares Cotton was holding–"one hundred and twenty thousand to get him out alone. That isn't all. There's Judge Kitchen and Joseph Zimmerman and Senator Donovan"–he was referring to the State senator of that name. "You'll be paying a pretty fair price for that stud when you get it. It will cost considerable more to extend the line. It's too much, I think."

Cowperwood was thinking how easy it would be to combine this line with his dreamed-of Seventeenth and Nineteenth Street line, and after a time and with this in view he added:

"Say, George, why do you work all your schemes through Strobik and Harmon and Wycroft? Couldn't you and I manage some of these things for ourselves alone instead of for three or four? It seems to me that plan would be much more profitable to you."

"It would, it would!" exclaimed Stener, his round eyes fixed on Cowperwood in a rather helpless, appealing way. He liked Cowperwood and had always been hoping that mentally as well as financially he could get close to him. "I've thought of that. But these fellows have had more experience in these matters than I have had, Frank.

They've been longer at the game. I don't know as much about these things as they do."

Cowperwood smiled in his soul, though his face remained passive.

"Don't worry about them, George," he continued genially and confidentially. "You and I together can know and do as much as they ever could and more. I'm telling you. Take this railroad deal you're in on now, George; you and I could manipulate that just as well and better than it can be done with Wycroft, Strobik, and Harmon in on it. They're not adding anything to the wisdom of the situation. They're not putting up any money. You're doing that. All they're doing is agreeing to see it through the legislature and the council, and as far as the legislature is concerned, they can't do any more with that than any one else could—than I could, for instance. It's all a question of arranging things with Relihan, anyhow, putting up a certain amount of money for him to work with. Here in town there are other people who can reach the council just as well as Strobik." He was thinking (once he controlled a road of his own) of conferring with Butler and getting him to use his influence. It would serve to quiet Strobik and his friends. "I'm not asking you to change your plans on this North Pennsylvania deal. You couldn't do that very well. But there are other things. In the future why not let's see if you and I can't work some one thing together? You'll be much better off, and so will I. We've done pretty well on the city-loan proposition so far, haven't we?"

The truth was, they had done exceedingly well. Aside from what the higher powers had made, Stener's new house, his lots, his bank-account, his good clothes, and his changed and comfortable sense of life were largely due to Cowperwood's successful manipulation of these city-loan certificates. Already there had been four issues of two hundred thousand dollars each. Cowperwood had bought and sold nearly three million dollars' worth of these certificates, acting one time as a "bull" and another as a "bear." Stener was now worth all of one hundred and fifty thousand dollars.

"There's a line that I know of here in the city which could be made into a splendidly paying property," continued Cowperwood, meditatively, "if the right things could be done with it. Just like this North Pennsylvania line, it isn't long enough. The territory it serves isn't big enough. It ought to be extended; but if you and I could get it, it might eventually be worked with this North Pennsylvania Company or some other as one company. That would save officers and offices and a lot of things. There is always money to be made out of a larger purchasing power."

He paused and looked out the window of his handsome little hardwood office, speculating upon the future. The window gave nowhere save into a back yard behind another office building which had formerly been a residence. Some grass grew feebly there. The red wall and old-fashioned brick fence which divided it from the next lot reminded him somehow of his old home in New Market Street, to which his Uncle Seneca used to come as a Cuban trader followed by his black Portuguese servitor. He could see him now as he sat here looking at the yard.

"Well," asked Stener, ambitiously, taking the bait, "why don't we get hold of that— you and me? I suppose I could fix it so far as the money is concerned. How much would it take?"

Cowperwood smiled inwardly again.

"I don't know exactly," he said, after a time. "I want to look into it more carefully. The one trouble is that I'm carrying a good deal of the city's money as it is. You see, I have that two hundred thousand dollars against your city-loan deals. And this new scheme will take two or three hundred thousand more. If that were out of the way–"

He was thinking of one of the inexplicable stock panics–those strange American depressions which had so much to do with the temperament of the people, and so little to do with the basic conditions of the country. "If this North Pennsylvania deal were through and done with–"

He rubbed his chin and pulled at his handsome silky mustache.

"Don't ask me any more about it, George," he said, finally, as he saw that the latter was beginning to think as to which line it might be. "Don't say anything at all about it. I want to get my facts exactly right, and then I'll talk to you. I think you and I can do this thing a little later, when we get the North Pennsylvania scheme under way. I'm so rushed just now I'm not sure that I want to undertake it at once; but you keep quiet and we'll see." He turned toward his desk, and Stener got up.

"I'll make any sized deposit with you that you wish, the moment you think you're ready to act, Frank," exclaimed Stener, and with the thought that Cowperwood was not nearly as anxious to do this as he should be, since he could always rely on him (Stener) when there was anything really profitable in the offing. Why should not the able and wonderful Cowperwood be allowed to make the two of them rich? "Just notify Stires, and he'll send you a check. Strobik thought we ought to act pretty soon."

"I'll tend to it, George," replied Cowperwood, confidently. "It will come out all right. Leave it to me."

Stener kicked his stout legs to straighten his trousers, and extended his hand. He strolled out in the street thinking of this new scheme. Certainly, if he could get in with Cowperwood right he would be a rich man, for Cowperwood was so successful and so cautious. His new house, this beautiful banking office, his growing fame, and his subtle connections with Butler and others put Stener in considerable awe of him. Another line! They would control it and the North Pennsylvania! Why, if this went on, he might become a magnate–he really might–he, George W. Stener, once a cheap real-estate and insurance agent. He strolled up the street thinking, but with no more idea of the importance of his civic duties and the nature of the social ethics against which he was offending than if they had never existed.

Chapter XXII

The services which Cowperwood performed during the ensuing year and a half for Stener, Strobik, Butler, State Treasurer Van Nostrand, State Senator Relihan, representative of "the interests," so-called, at Harrisburg, and various banks which were friendly to these gentlemen, were numerous and confidential. For Stener, Strobik, Wycroft, Harmon and himself he executed the North Pennsylvania deal, by which he became a holder of a fifth of the controlling stock. Together he and Stener joined to purchase the Seventeenth and Nineteenth Street line and in the concurrent gambling in stocks.

By the summer of 1871, when Cowperwood was nearly thirty-four years of age, he had a banking business estimated at nearly two million dollars, personal holdings aggregating nearly half a million, and prospects which other things being equal looked to wealth which might rival that of any American. The city, through its treasurer–still Mr. Stener–was a depositor with him to the extent of nearly five hundred thousand dollars. The State, through its State treasurer, Van Nostrand, carried two hundred thousand dollars on his books. Bode was speculating in street-railway stocks to the extent of fifty thousand dollars. Relihan to the same amount. A small army of politicians and political hangers-on were on his books for various sums. And for Edward Malia Butler he occasionally carried as high as one hundred thousand dollars in margins. His own loans at the banks, varying from day to day on variously hypothecated securities, were as high as seven and eight hundred thousand dollars. Like a spider in a spangled net, every thread of which he knew, had laid, had tested, he had surrounded and entangled himself in a splendid, glittering network of connections, and he was watching all the details.

His one pet idea, the thing he put more faith in than anything else, was his street-railway manipulations, and particularly his actual control of the Seventeenth and Nineteenth Street line. Through an advance to him, on deposit, made in his bank by Stener at a time when the stock of the Seventeenth and Nineteenth Street line was at a low ebb, he had managed to pick up fifty-one per cent. of the stock for himself and Stener, by virtue of which he was able to do as he pleased with the road. To accomplish this, however, he had resorted to some very "peculiar" methods, as they afterward came to be termed in financial circles, to get this stock at his own valuation. Through agents he caused suits for damages to be brought against the company for non-payment of interest due. A little stock in the hands of a hireling, a request made to a court of record to examine the books of the company in order to determine whether a receivership were not advisable, a simultaneous attack in the stock market, selling at three, five, seven, and ten points off, brought the frightened stockholders into the market with their holdings. The banks considered the line a poor risk, and called their loans in connection with it. His father's bank had made one loan to one of the principal stockholders, and that was promptly called, of course. Then, through an agent, the several heaviest shareholders were approached and an offer was made to help them out. The stocks would be taken off their hands at forty. They had not really been able to discover the source of all their woes; and they imagined that the road was in bad condition, which it was not. Better let it go. The money was immediately forthcoming, and Cowperwood and Stener jointly controlled fifty-one per cent. But, as in the case of the North Pennsylvania line, Cowperwood had been quietly buying all of the small minority holdings, so that he had in reality fifty-one per cent. of the stock, and Stener twenty-five per cent. more.

This intoxicated him, for immediately he saw the opportunity of fulfilling his long-contemplated dream–that of reorganizing the company in conjunction with the North Pennsylvania line, issuing three shares where one had been before and after unloading all but a control on the general public, using the money secured to buy into other lines which were to be boomed and sold in the same way. In short, he was one of those early, daring manipulators who later were to seize upon other and ever larger phases of American natural development for their own aggrandizement.

In connection with this first consolidation, his plan was to spread rumors of the coming consolidation of the two lines, to appeal to the legislature for privileges of extension, to get up an arresting prospectus and later annual reports, and to boom the stock on the stock exchange as much as his swelling resources would permit. The trouble is that when you are trying to make a market for a stock–to unload a large issue such as his was (over five hundred thousand dollars' worth)–while retaining five hundred thousand for yourself, it requires large capital to handle it. The owner in these cases is compelled not only to go on the market and do much fictitious buying, thus creating a fictitious demand, but once this fictitious demand has deceived the public and he has been able to unload a considerable quantity of his wares, he is, unless he rids himself of all his stock, compelled to stand behind it. If, for instance, he sold five thousand shares, as was done in this instance, and retained five thousand, he must see that the public price of the outstanding five thousand shares did not fall below a certain point, because the value of his private shares would fall with it. And if, as is almost always the case, the private shares had been hypothecated with banks and trust companies for money wherewith to conduct other enterprises, the falling of their value in the open market merely meant that the banks would call for large margins to protect their loans or call their loans entirely. This meant that his work was a failure, and he might readily fail. He was already conducting one such difficult campaign in connection with this city-loan deal, the price of which varied from day to day, and which he was only too anxious to have vary, for in the main he profited by these changes.

But this second burden, interesting enough as it was, meant that he had to be doubly watchful. Once the stock was sold at a high price, the money borrowed from the city treasurer could be returned; his own holdings created out of foresight, by capitalizing the future, by writing the shrewd prospectuses and reports, would be worth their face value, or little less. He would have money to invest in other lines. He might obtain the financial direction of the whole, in which case he would be worth millions. One shrewd thing he did, which indicated the foresight and subtlety of the man, was to make a separate organization or company of any extension or addition which he made to his line. Thus, if he had two or three miles of track on a street, and he wanted to extend it two or three miles farther on the same street, instead of including this extension in the existing corporation, he would make a second corporation to control the additional two or three miles of right of way. This corporation he would capitalize at so much, and issue stocks and bonds for its construction, equipment, and manipulation. Having done this he would then take the sub-corporation over into the parent concern, issuing more stocks and bonds of the parent company wherewith to do it, and, of course, selling these bonds to the public. Even his brothers who worked for him did not know the various ramifications of his numerous deals, and executed his orders blindly. Sometimes Joseph said to Edward, in a puzzled way, "Well, Frank knows what he is about, I guess."

On the other hand, he was most careful to see that every current obligation was instantly met, and even anticipated, for he wanted to make a great show of regularity. Nothing was so precious as reputation and standing. His forethought, caution, and promptness pleased the bankers. They thought he was one of the sanest, shrewdest men they had ever met.

However, by the spring and summer of 1871, Cowperwood had actually, without being in any conceivable danger from any source, spread himself out very thin. Because of his great success he had grown more liberal–easier–in his financial ventures. By degrees, and largely because of his own confidence in himself, he had induced his father to enter upon his street-car speculations, to use the resources of the Third National to carry a part of his loans and to furnish capital at such times as quick resources were necessary. In the beginning the old gentleman had been a little nervous and skeptical, but as time had worn on and nothing but profit eventuated, he grew bolder and more confident.

"Frank," he would say, looking up over his spectacles, "aren't you afraid you're going a little too fast in these matters? You're carrying a lot of loans these days."

"No more than I ever did, father, considering my resources. You can't turn large deals without large loans. You know that as well as I do."

"Yes, I know, but–now that Green and Coates–aren't you going pretty strong there?"

"Not at all. I know the inside conditions there. The stock is bound to go up eventually. I'll bull it up. I'll combine it with my other lines, if necessary."

Cowperwood stared at his boy. Never was there such a defiant, daring manipulator.

"You needn't worry about me, father. If you are going to do that, call my loans. Other banks will loan on my stocks. I'd like to see your bank have the interest."

So Cowperwood, Sr., was convinced. There was no gainsaying this argument. His bank was loaning Frank heavily, but not more so than any other. And as for the great blocks of stocks he was carrying in his son's companies, he was to be told when to get out should that prove necessary. Frank's brothers were being aided in the same way to make money on the side, and their interests were also now bound up indissolubly with his own.

With his growing financial opportunities, however, Cowperwood had also grown very liberal in what might be termed his standard of living. Certain young art dealers in Philadelphia, learning of his artistic inclinations and his growing wealth, had followed him up with suggestions as to furniture, tapestries, rugs, objects of art, and paintings–at first the American and later the foreign masters exclusively. His own and his father's house had not been furnished fully in these matters, and there was that other house in North Tenth Street, which he desired to make beautiful. Aileen had always objected to the condition of her own home. Love of distinguished surroundings was a basic longing with her, though she had not the gift of interpreting her longings. But this place where they were secretly meeting must be beautiful. She was as keen for that as he was. So it became a veritable treasure-trove, more distinguished in furnishings than some of the rooms of his own home. He began to gather here some rare examples of altar cloths, rugs, and tapestries of the Middle Ages. He bought furniture after the Georgian theory–a combination of Chippendale, Sheraton, and Heppelwhite modified by the Italian Renaissance and the French Louis. He learned of handsome examples of porcelain, statuary, Greek vase forms, lovely collections of Japanese ivories and netsukes. Fletcher Gray, a partner in Cable Gray, a local firm of importers of art objects, called on him in connection with a tapestry of the fourteenth century weaving. Gray was an enthusiast and almost instantly he conveyed some of his suppressed and yet fiery love of the beautiful to Cowperwood.

"There are fifty periods of one shade of blue porcelain alone, Mr. Cowperwood," Gray informed him. "There are at least seven distinct schools or periods of rugs–Persian, Armenian, Arabian, Flemish, Modern Polish, Hungarian, and so on. If you ever went into that, it would be a distinguished thing to get a complete–I mean a representative–collection of some one period, or of all these periods. They are beautiful. I have seen some of them, others I've read about."

"You'll make a convert of me yet, Fletcher," replied Cowperwood. "You or art will be the ruin of me. I'm inclined that way temperamentally as it is, I think, and between you and Ellsworth and Gordon Strake"–another young man intensely interested in painting–"you'll complete my downfall. Strake has a splendid idea. He wants me to begin right now–I'm using that word 'right' in the sense of 'properly,'" he commented–"and get what examples I can of just the few rare things in each school or period of art which would properly illustrate each. He tells me the great pictures are going to increase in value, and what I could get for a few hundred thousand now will be worth millions later. He doesn't want me to bother with American art."

"He's right," exclaimed Gray, "although it isn't good business for me to praise another art man. It would take a great deal of money, though."

"Not so very much. At least, not all at once. It would be a matter of years, of course. Strake thinks that some excellent examples of different periods could be picked up now and later replaced if anything better in the same held showed up."

His mind, in spite of his outward placidity, was tinged with a great seeking. Wealth, in the beginning, had seemed the only goal, to which had been added the beauty of women. And now art, for art's sake–the first faint radiance of a rosy dawn–had begun to shine in upon him, and to the beauty of womanhood he was beginning to see how necessary it was to add the beauty of life–the beauty of material background–how, in fact, the only background for great beauty was great art. This girl, this Aileen Butler, her raw youth and radiance, was nevertheless creating in him a sense of the distinguished and a need for it which had never existed in him before to the same degree. It is impossible to define these subtleties of reaction, temperament on temperament, for no one knows to what degree we are marked by the things which attract us. A love affair such as this had proved to be was little less or more than a drop of coloring added to a glass of clear water, or a foreign chemical agent introduced into a delicate chemical formula.

In short, for all her crudeness, Aileen Butler was a definite force personally. Her nature, in a way, a protest against the clumsy conditions by which she found herself surrounded, was almost irrationally ambitious. To think that for so long, having been born into the Butler family, she had been the subject, as well as the victim of such commonplace and inartistic illusions and conditions, whereas now, owing to her contact with, and mental subordination to Cowperwood, she was learning so many wonderful phases of social, as well as financial, refinement of which previously she had guessed nothing. The wonder, for instance, of a future social career as the wife of such a man as Frank Cowperwood. The beauty and resourcefulness of his mind, which, after hours of intimate contact with her, he was pleased to reveal, and which, so definite were his comments and instructions, she could not fail to sense. The wonder of his financial and artistic and future social dreams. And, oh, oh, she was his, and he was hers. She was actually beside herself at times with the glory, as well as the delight of all this.

At the same time, her father's local reputation as a quondam garbage contractor ("slop-collector" was the unfeeling comment of the vulgarian cognoscenti); her own unavailing efforts to right a condition of material vulgarity or artistic anarchy in her own home; the hopelessness of ever being admitted to those distinguished portals which she recognized afar off as the last sanctum sanctorum of established respectability and social distinction, had bred in her, even at this early age, a feeling of deadly opposition to her home conditions as they stood. Such a house compared to Cowperwood's! Her dear, but ignorant, father! And this great man, her lover, had now condescended to love her–see in her his future wife. Oh, God, that it might not fail! Through the Cowperwoods at first she had hoped to meet a few people, young men and women–and particularly men–who were above the station in which she found herself, and to whom her beauty and prospective fortune would commend her; but this had not been the case. The Cowperwoods themselves, in spite of Frank Cowperwood's artistic proclivities and growing wealth, had not penetrated the inner circle as yet. In fact, aside from the subtle, preliminary consideration which they were receiving, they were a long way off.

None the less, and instinctively in Cowperwood Aileen recognized a way out–a door–and by the same token a subtle, impending artistic future of great magnificence. This man would rise beyond anything he now dreamed of–she felt it. There was in him, in some nebulous, unrecognizable form, a great artistic reality which was finer than anything she could plan for herself. She wanted luxury, magnificence, social station. Well, if she could get this man they would come to her. There were, apparently, insuperable barriers in the way; but hers was no weakling nature, and neither was his. They ran together temperamentally from the first like two leopards. Her own thoughts–crude, half formulated, half spoken–nevertheless matched his to a degree in the equality of their force and their raw directness.

"I don't think papa knows how to do," she said to him, one day. "It isn't his fault. He can't help it. He knows that he can't. And he knows that I know it. For years I wanted him to move out of that old house there. He knows that he ought to. But even that wouldn't do much good."

She paused, looking at him with a straight, clear, vigorous glance. He liked the medallion sharpness of her features–their smooth, Greek modeling.

"Never mind, pet," he replied. "We will arrange all these things later. I don't see my way out of this just now; but I think the best thing to do is to confess to Lillian some day, and see if some other plan can't be arranged. I want to fix it so the children won't suffer. I can provide for them amply, and I wouldn't be at all surprised if Lillian would be willing to let me go. She certainly wouldn't want any publicity."

He was counting practically, and man-fashion, on her love for her children.

Aileen looked at him with clear, questioning, uncertain eyes. She was not wholly without sympathy, but in a way this situation did not appeal to her as needing much. Mrs. Cowperwood was not friendly in her mood toward her. It was not based on anything save a difference in their point of view. Mrs. Cowperwood could never understand how a girl could carry her head so high and "put on such airs," and Aileen could not understand how any one could be so lymphatic and lackadaisical as Lillian Cowperwood. Life was made for riding, driving, dancing, going. It was made for airs and banter and persiflage and coquetry. To see this woman, the wife of a young, forceful man like Cowperwood, acting, even though she were five years older and the mother of two children, as though life on its romantic and enthusiastic pleasurable side were all over was too much for her. Of course Lillian was unsuited to Frank; of course he needed a young woman like herself, and fate would surely give him to her. Then what a delicious life they would lead!

"Oh, Frank," she exclaimed to him, over and over, "if we could only manage it. Do you think we can?"

"Do I think we can? Certainly I do. It's only a matter of time. I think if I were to put the matter to her clearly, she wouldn't expect me to stay. You look out how you conduct your affairs. If your father or your brother should ever suspect me, there'd be an explosion in this town, if nothing worse. They'd fight me in all my money deals, if they didn't kill me. Are you thinking carefully of what you are doing?"

"All the time. If anything happens I'll deny everything. They can't prove it, if I deny it. I'll come to you in the long run, just the same."

They were in the Tenth Street house at the time. She stroked his cheeks with the loving fingers of the wildly enamored woman.

"I'll do anything for you, sweetheart," she declared. "I'd die for you if I had to. I love you so."

"Well, pet, no danger. You won't have to do anything like that. But be careful."

Chapter XXIII

Then, after several years of this secret relationship, in which the ties of sympathy and understanding grew stronger instead of weaker, came the storm. It burst unexpectedly and out of a clear sky, and bore no relation to the intention or volition of any individual. It was nothing more than a fire, a distant one–the great Chicago fire, October 7th, 1871, which burned that city–its vast commercial section–to the ground, and instantly and incidentally produced a financial panic, vicious though of short duration in various other cities in America. The fire began on Saturday and continued apparently unabated until the following Wednesday. It destroyed the banks, the commercial houses, the shipping conveniences, and vast stretches of property. The heaviest loss fell naturally upon the insurance companies, which instantly, in many cases–the majority–closed their doors. This threw the loss back on the manufacturers and wholesalers in other cities who had had dealings with Chicago as well as the merchants of that city. Again, very grievous losses were borne by the host of eastern capitalists which had for years past partly owned, or held heavy mortgages on, the magnificent buildings for business purposes and residences in which Chicago was already rivaling every city on the continent. Transportation was disturbed, and the keen scent of Wall Street, and Third Street in Philadelphia, and State Street in Boston, instantly perceived in the early reports the gravity of the situation. Nothing could be done on Saturday or Sunday after the exchange closed, for the opening reports came too late. On Monday, however, the facts were pouring in thick and fast; and the owners of railroad securities, government securities, street-car securities, and, indeed, all other forms of stocks and bonds, began to throw them on the market in order to raise cash. The banks naturally were calling their loans, and the result was a stock stampede which equaled the Black Friday of Wall Street of two years before.

Cowperwood and his father were out of town at the time the fire began. They had gone with several friends–bankers–to look at a proposed route of extension of a local steam-railroad, on which a loan was desired. In buggies they had driven over a good portion of the route, and were returning to Philadelphia late Sunday evening when the cries of newsboys hawking an "extra" reached their ears.

"Ho! Extra! Extra! All about the big Chicago fire!"

"Ho! Extra! Extra! Chicago burning down! Extra! Extra!"

The cries were long-drawn-out, ominous, pathetic. In the dusk of the dreary Sunday afternoon, when the city had apparently retired to Sabbath meditation and prayer, with that tinge of the dying year in the foliage and in the air, one caught a sense of something grim and gloomy.

"Hey, boy," called Cowperwood, listening, seeing a shabbily clothed misfit of a boy with a bundle of papers under his arm turning a corner. "What's that? Chicago burning!"

He looked at his father and the other men in a significant way as he reached for the paper, and then, glancing at the headlines, realized the worst.

ALL CHICAGO BURNING

FIRE RAGES UNCHECKED IN COMMERCIAL SECTION SINCE YESTERDAY EVENING. BANKS, COMMERCIAL HOUSES, PUBLIC BUILDINGS IN RUINS. DIRECT TELEGRAPHIC COMMUNICATION SUSPENDED SINCE THREE O'CLOCK TO-DAY. NO END TO PROGRESS OF DISASTER IN SIGHT.

"That looks rather serious," he said, calmly, to his companions, a cold, commanding force coming into his eyes and voice. To his father he said a little later, "It's panic, unless the majority of the banks and brokerage firms stand together."

He was thinking quickly, brilliantly, resourcefully of his own outstanding obligations. His father's bank was carrying one hundred thousand dollars' worth of his street-railway securities at sixty, and fifty thousand dollars' worth of city loan at seventy. His father had "up with him" over forty thousand dollars in cash covering market manipulations in these stocks. The banking house of Drexel Co. was on his books as a creditor for one hundred thousand, and that loan would be called unless they were especially merciful, which was not likely. Jay Cooke Co. were his creditors for another one hundred and fifty thousand. They would want their money. At four smaller banks and three brokerage companies he was debtor for sums ranging from fifty thousand dollars down. The city treasurer was involved with him to the extent of nearly five hundred thousand dollars, and exposure of that would create a scandal; the State treasurer for two hundred thousand. There were small accounts, hundreds of them, ranging from one hundred dollars up to five and ten thousand. A panic would mean not only a withdrawal of deposits and a calling of loans, but a heavy depression of securities. How could he realize on his securities?–that was the question–how without selling so many points off that his fortune would be swept away and he would be ruined?

He figured briskly the while he waved adieu to his friends, who hurried away, struck with their own predicament.

"You had better go on out to the house, father, and I'll send some telegrams." (The telephone had not yet been invented.) "I'll be right out and we'll go into this thing together. It looks like black weather to me. Don't say anything to any one until after we have had our talk; then we can decide what to do."

Cowperwood, Sr., was already plucking at his side-whiskers in a confused and troubled way. He was cogitating as to what might happen to him in case his son failed, for he was deeply involved with him. He was a little gray in his complexion now, frightened, for he had already strained many points in his affairs to accommodate his son. If Frank should not be able promptly on the morrow to meet the call which the bank might have to make for one hundred and fifty thousand dollars, the onus and scandal of the situation would be on him.

On the other hand, his son was meditating on the tangled relation in which he now found himself in connection with the city treasurer and the fact that it was not possible for him to support the market alone. Those who should have been in a position to help him were now as bad off as himself. There were many unfavorable points in the whole situation. Drexel Co. had been booming railway stocks–loaning heavily on them. Jay Cooke Co. had been backing Northern Pacific–were practically doing their best to build that immense transcontinental system alone. Naturally, they were long on that and hence in a ticklish position. At the first word they would throw over their surest securities–government bonds, and the like–in order to protect their more speculative holdings. The bears would see the point. They would hammer and hammer, selling short all along the line. But he did not dare to do that. He would be breaking his own back quickly, and what he needed was time. If he could only get time–three days, a week, ten days–this storm would surely blow over.

The thing that was troubling him most was the matter of the half-million invested with him by Stener. A fall election was drawing near. Stener, although he had served two terms, was slated for reelection. A scandal in connection with the city treasury would be a very bad thing. It would end Stener's career as an official–would very likely send him to the penitentiary. It might wreck the Republican party's chances to win. It would certainly involve himself as having much to do with it. If that happened, he would have the politicians to reckon with. For, if he were hard pressed, as he would be, and failed, the fact that he had been trying to invade the city street-railway preserves which they held sacred to themselves, with borrowed city money, and that this borrowing was liable to cost them the city election, would all come out. They would not view all that with a kindly eye. It would be useless to say, as he could, that he had borrowed the money at two per cent. (most of it, to save himself, had been covered by a protective clause of that kind), or that he had merely acted as an agent for Stener. That might go down with the unsophisticated of the outer world, but it would never be swallowed by the politicians. They knew better than that.

There was another phase to this situation, however, that encouraged him, and that was his knowledge of how city politics were going in general. It was useless for any politician, however loftily, to take a high and mighty tone in a crisis like this. All of them, great and small, were profiting in one way and another through city privileges. Butler, Mollenhauer, and Simpson, he knew, made money out of contracts–legal enough, though they might be looked upon as rank favoritism–and also out of vast sums of money collected in the shape of taxes–land taxes, water taxes, etc.–which were deposited in the various banks designated by these men and others as legal depositories for city money. The banks supposedly carried the city's money in their vaults as a favor, without paying interest of any kind, and then reinvested it–for whom? Cowperwood had no complaint to make, for he was being well treated, but these men could scarcely expect to monopolize all the city's benefits. He did not know either Mollenhauer or Simpson personally–but he knew they as well as Butler had made money out of his own manipulation of city loan. Also, Butler was most friendly to him. It was not unreasonable for him to think, in a crisis like this, that if worst came to worst, he could make a clean breast of it to Butler and receive aid. In case he could not get through secretly with Stener's help, Cowperwood made up his mind that he would do this.

His first move, he decided, would be to go at once to Stener's house and demand the loan of an additional three or four hundred thousand dollars. Stener had always been very tractable, and in this instance would see how important it was that his shortage of half a million should not be made public. Then he must get as much more as possible. But where to get it? Presidents of banks and trust companies, large stock jobbers, and the like, would have to be seen. Then there was a loan of one hundred thousand dollars he was carrying for Butler. The old contractor might be induced to leave that. He hurried to his home, secured his runabout, and drove rapidly to Stener's.

As it turned out, however, much to his distress and confusion, Stener was out of town–down on the Chesapeake with several friends shooting ducks and fishing, and was not expected back for several days. He was in the marshes back of some small town. Cowperwood sent an urgent wire to the nearest point and then, to make assurance doubly sure, to several other points in the same neighborhood, asking him to return immediately. He was not at all sure, however, that Stener would return in time and was greatly nonplussed and uncertain for the moment as to what his next step would be. Aid must be forthcoming from somewhere and at once.

Suddenly a helpful thought occurred to him. Butler and Mollenhauer and Simpson were long on local street-railways. They must combine to support the situation and protect their interests. They could see the big bankers, Drexel Co. and Cooke Co., and others and urge them to sustain the market. They could strengthen things generally by organizing a buying ring, and under cover of their support, if they would, he might sell enough to let him out, and even permit him to go short and make something–a whole lot. It was a brilliant thought, worthy of a greater situation, and its only weakness was that it was not absolutely certain of fulfillment.

He decided to go to Butler at once, the only disturbing thought being that he would now be compelled to reveal his own and Stener's affairs. So reentering his runabout he drove swiftly to the Butler home.

When he arrived there the famous contractor was at dinner. He had not heard the calling of the extras, and of course, did not understand as yet the significance of the fire. The servant's announcement of Cowperwood brought him smiling to the door.

"Won't you come in and join us? We're just havin' a light supper. Have a cup of coffee or tea, now–do."

"I can't," replied Cowperwood. "Not to-night, I'm in too much of a hurry. I want to see you for just a few moments, and then I'll be off again. I won't keep you very long."

"Why, if that's the case, I'll come right out." And Butler returned to the dining-room to put down his napkin. Aileen, who was also dining, had heard Cowperwood's voice, and was on the qui vive to see him. She wondered what it was that brought him at this time of night to see her father. She could not leave the table at once, but hoped to before he went. Cowperwood was thinking of her, even in the face of this impending storm, as he was of his wife, and many other things. If his affairs came down in a heap it would go hard with those attached to him. In this first clouding of disaster, he could not tell how things would eventuate. He meditated on this desperately, but he was not panic-stricken. His naturally even-molded face was set in fine, classic lines; his eyes were as hard as chilled steel.

"Well, now," exclaimed Butler, returning, his countenance manifesting a decidedly comfortable relationship with the world as at present constituted. "What's up with you to-night? Nawthin' wrong, I hope. It's been too fine a day."

"Nothing very serious, I hope myself," replied Cowperwood, "But I want to talk with you a few minutes, anyhow. Don't you think we had better go up to your room?"

"I was just going to say that," replied Butler–"the cigars are up there."

They started from the reception-room to the stairs, Butler preceding and as the contractor mounted, Aileen came out from the dining-room in a frou-frou of silk. Her splendid hair was drawn up from the base of the neck and the line of the forehead into some quaint convolutions which constituted a reddish-gold crown. Her complexion was glowing, and her bare arms and shoulders shone white against the dark red of her evening gown. She realized there was something wrong.

"Oh, Mr. Cowperwood, how do you do?" she exclaimed, coming forward and holding out her hand as her father went on upstairs. She was delaying him deliberately in order to have a word with him and this bold acting was for the benefit of the others.

"What's the trouble, honey?" she whispered, as soon as her father was out of hearing. "You look worried."

"Nothing much, I hope, sweet," he said. "Chicago is burning up and there's going to be trouble to-morrow. I have to talk to your father."

She had time only for a sympathetic, distressed "Oh," before he withdrew his hand and followed Butler upstairs. She squeezed his arm, and went through the reception-room to the parlor. She sat down, thinking, for never before had she seen Cowperwood's face wearing such an expression of stern, disturbed calculation. It was placid, like fine, white wax, and quite as cold; and those deep, vague, inscrutable eyes! So Chicago was burning. What would happen to him? Was he very much involved? He had never told her in detail of his affairs. She would not have understood fully any more than would have Mrs. Cowperwood. But she was worried, nevertheless, because it was her Frank, and because she was bound to him by what to her seemed indissoluble ties.

Literature, outside of the masters, has given us but one idea of the mistress, the subtle, calculating siren who delights to prey on the souls of men. The journalism and the moral pamphleteering of the time seem to foster it with almost partisan zeal.

It would seem that a censorship of life had been established by divinity, and the care of its execution given into the hands of the utterly conservative. Yet there is that other form of liaison which has nothing to do with conscious calculation. In the vast majority of cases it is without design or guile. The average woman, controlled by her affections and deeply in love, is no more capable than a child of anything save sacrificial thought–the desire to give; and so long as this state endures, she can only do this. She may change–Hell hath no fury, etc.–but the sacrificial, yielding, solicitous attitude is more often the outstanding characteristic of the mistress; and it is this very attitude in contradistinction to the grasping legality of established matrimony that has caused so many wounds in the defenses of the latter. The temperament of man, either male or female, cannot help falling down before and worshiping this nonseeking, sacrificial note. It approaches vast distinction in life. It appears to be related to that last word in art, that largeness of spirit which is the first characteristic of the great picture, the great building, the great sculpture, the great decoration–namely, a giving, freely and without stint, of itself, of beauty. Hence the significance of this particular mood in Aileen.

All the subtleties of the present combination were troubling Cowperwood as he followed Butler into the room upstairs.

"Sit down, sit down. You won't take a little somethin'? You never do. I remember now. Well, have a cigar, anyhow. Now, what's this that's troublin' you to-night?"

Voices could be heard faintly in the distance, far off toward the thicker residential sections.

"Extra! Extra! All about the big Chicago fire! Chicago burning down!"

"Just that," replied Cowperwood, hearkening to them. "Have you heard the news?"

"No. What's that they're calling?"

"It's a big fire out in Chicago."

"Oh," replied Butler, still not gathering the significance of it.

"It's burning down the business section there, Mr. Butler," went on Cowperwood ominously, "and I fancy it's going to disturb financial conditions here to-morrow. That is what I have come to see you about. How are your investments? Pretty well drawn in?"

Butler suddenly gathered from Cowperwood's expression that there was something very wrong. He put up his large hand as he leaned back in his big leather chair, and covered his mouth and chin with it. Over those big knuckles, and bigger nose, thick and cartilaginous, his large, shaggy-eyebrowed eyes gleamed. His gray, bristly hair stood up stiffly in a short, even growth all over his head.

"So that's it," he said. "You're expectin' trouble to-morrow. How are your own affairs?"

"I'm in pretty good shape, I think, all told, if the money element of this town doesn't lose its head and go wild. There has to be a lot of common sense exercised to-morrow, or to-night, even. You know we are facing a real panic. Mr. Butler, you may as well know that. It may not last long, but while it does it will be bad. Stocks are going to drop to-morrow ten or fifteen points on the opening. The banks are going to call their loans unless some arrangement can be made to prevent them. No one man can do that. It will have to be a combination of men. You and Mr. Simpson and Mr. Mollenhauer might do it–that is, you could if you could persuade the big banking people to combine to back the market. There is going to be a raid on local street-railways–all of them. Unless they are sustained the bottom is going to drop out. I have always known that you were long on those. I thought you and Mr. Mollenhauer and some of the others might want to act. If you don't I might as well confess that it is going to go rather hard with me. I am not strong enough to face this thing alone."

He was meditating on how he should tell the whole truth in regard to Stener.

"Well, now, that's pretty bad," said Butler, calmly and meditatively. He was thinking of his own affairs. A panic was not good for him either, but he was not in a desperate state. He could not fail. He might lose some money, but not a vast amount–before he could adjust things. Still he did not care to lose any money.

"How is it you're so bad off?" he asked, curiously. He was wondering how the fact that the bottom was going to drop out of local street-railways would affect Cowperwood so seriously. "You're not carryin' any of them things, are you?" he added.

It was now a question of lying or telling the truth, and Cowperwood was literally afraid to risk lying in this dilemma. If he did not gain Butler's comprehending support he might fail, and if he failed the truth would come out, anyhow.

"I might as well make a clean breast of this, Mr. Butler," he said, throwing himself on the old man's sympathies and looking at him with that brisk assurance which Butler so greatly admired. He felt as proud of Cowperwood at times as he did of his own sons. He felt that he had helped to put him where he was.

"The fact is that I have been buying street-railway stocks, but not for myself exactly. I am going to do something now which I think I ought not to do, but I cannot help myself. If I don't do it, it will injure you and a lot of people whom I do not wish to injure. I know you are naturally interested in the outcome of the fall election. The truth is I have been carrying a lot of stocks for Mr. Stener and some of his friends. I do not know that all the money has come from the city treasury, but I think that most of it has. I know what that means to Mr. Stener and the Republican party and your interests in case I fail. I don't think Mr. Stener started this of his own accord in the first place–I think I am as much to blame as anybody–but it grew out of other things. As you know, I handled that matter of city loan for him and then some of his friends wanted me to invest in street-railways for them. I have been doing that ever since. Personally I have borrowed considerable money from Mr. Stener at two per cent. In fact, originally the transactions were covered in that way. Now I don't want to shift the blame on any one. It comes back to me and I am willing to let it stay there, except that if I fail Mr. Stener will be blamed and that will reflect on the administration. Naturally, I don't want to fail. There is no excuse for my doing so. Aside from this panic I have never been in a better position in my life. But I cannot weather this storm without assistance, and I want to know if you won't help me. If I pull through I will give you my word that I will see that the money which has been taken from the treasury is put back there. Mr. Stener is out of town or I would have brought him here with me."

Cowperwood was lying out of the whole cloth in regard to bringing Stener with him, and he had no intention of putting the money back in the city treasury except by degrees and in such manner as suited his convenience; but what he had said sounded well and created a great seeming of fairness.

"How much money is it Stener has invested with you?" asked Butler. He was a little confused by this curious development. It put Cowperwood and Stener in an odd light.

"About five hundred thousand dollars," replied Cowperwood.

The old man straightened up. "Is it as much as that?" he said.

"Just about–a little more or a little less; I'm not sure which."

The old contractor listened solemnly to all Cowperwood had to say on this score, thinking of the effect on the Republican party and his own contracting interests. He liked Cowperwood, but this was a rough thing the latter was telling him–rough, and a great deal to ask. He was a slow-thinking and a slow-moving man, but he did well enough when he did think. He had considerable money invested in Philadelphia street-railway stocks–perhaps as much as eight hundred thousand dollars. Mollenhauer had perhaps as much more. Whether Senator Simpson had much or little he could not tell. Cowperwood had told him in the past that he thought the Senator had a good deal. Most of their holdings, as in the case of Cowperwood's, were hypothecated at the various banks for loans and these loans invested in other ways. It was not advisable or comfortable to have these loans called, though the condition of no one of the triumvirate was anything like as bad as that of Cowperwood. They could see themselves through without much trouble, though not without probable loss unless they took hurried action to protect themselves.

He would not have thought so much of it if Cowperwood had told him that Stener was involved, say, to the extent of seventy-five or a hundred thousand dollars. That might be adjusted. But five hundred thousand dollars!

"That's a lot of money," said Butler, thinking of the amazing audacity of Stener, but failing at the moment to identify it with the astute machinations of Cowperwood. "That's something to think about. There's no time to lose if there's going to be a panic in the morning. How much good will it do ye if we do support the market?"

"A great deal," returned Cowperwood, "although of course I have to raise money in other ways. I have that one hundred thousand dollars of yours on deposit. Is it likely that you'll want that right away?"

"It may be," said Butler.

"It's just as likely that I'll need it so badly that I can't give it up without seriously injuring myself," added Cowperwood. "That's just one of a lot of things. If you and Senator Simpson and Mr. Mollenhauer were to get together–you're the largest holders of street-railway stocks–and were to see Mr. Drexel and Mr. Cooke, you could fix things so that matters would be considerably easier. I will be all right if my loans are not called, and my loans will not be called if the market does not slump too heavily. If it does, all my securities are depreciated, and I can't hold out."

Old Butler got up. "This is serious business," he said. "I wish you'd never gone in with Stener in that way. It don't look quite right and it can't be made to. It's bad, bad business," he added dourly. "Still, I'll do what I can. I can't promise much, but I've always liked ye and I'll not be turning on ye now unless I have to. But I'm sorry–very. And I'm not the only one that has a hand in things in this town." At the same time he was thinking it was right decent of Cowperwood to forewarn him this way in regard to his own affairs and the city election, even though he was saving his own neck by so doing. He meant to do what he could.

"I don't suppose you could keep this matter of Stener and the city treasury quiet for a day or two until I see how I come out?" suggested Cowperwood warily.

"I can't promise that," replied Butler. "I'll have to do the best I can. I won't lave it go any further than I can help–you can depend on that." He was thinking how the effect of Stener's crime could be overcome if Cowperwood failed.

"Owen!"

He stepped to the door, and, opening it, called down over the banister.

"Yes, father."

"Have Dan hitch up the light buggy and bring it around to the door. And you get your hat and coat. I want you to go along with me."

"Yes, father."

He came back.

"Sure that's a nice little storm in a teapot, now, isn't it? Chicago begins to burn, and I have to worry here in Philadelphia. Well, well–" Cowperwood was up now and moving to the door. "And where are you going?"

"Back to the house. I have several people coming there to see me. But I'll come back here later, if I may."

"Yes, yes," replied Butler. "To be sure I'll be here by midnight, anyhow. Well, good night. I'll see you later, then, I suppose. I'll tell you what I find out."

He went back in his room for something, and Cowperwood descended the stair alone. From the hangings of the reception-room entryway Aileen signaled him to draw near.

"I hope it's nothing serious, honey?" she sympathized, looking into his solemn eyes.

It was not time for love, and he felt it.

"No," he said, almost coldly, "I think not."

"Frank, don't let this thing make you forget me for long, please. You won't, will you? I love you so."

"No, no, I won't!" he replied earnestly, quickly and yet absently.

"I can't! Don't you know I won't?" He had started to kiss her, but a noise disturbed him. "Sh!"

He walked to the door, and she followed him with eager, sympathetic eyes.

What if anything should happen to her Frank? What if anything could? What would she do? That was what was troubling her. What would, what could she do to help him? He looked so pale–strained.

Chapter XXIV

The condition of the Republican party at this time in Philadelphia, its relationship to George W. Stener, Edward Malia Butler, Henry A. Mollenhauer, Senator Mark Simpson, and others, will have to be briefly indicated here, in order to foreshadow Cowperwood's actual situation. Butler, as we have seen, was normally interested in and friendly to Cowperwood. Stener was Cowperwood's tool. Mollenhauer and Senator Simpson were strong rivals of Butler for the control of city affairs. Simpson represented the Republican control of the State legislature, which could dictate to the city if necessary, making new election laws, revising the city charter, starting political investigations, and the like. He had many influential newspapers, corporations, banks, at his beck and call. Mollenhauer represented the Germans, some Americans, and some large stable corporations–a very solid and respectable man. All three were strong, able, and dangerous politically. The two latter counted on Butler's influence, particularly with the Irish, and a certain number of ward leaders and Catholic politicians and laymen, who were as loyal to him as though he were a part of the church itself. Butler's return to these followers was protection, influence, aid, and good-will generally. The city's return to him, via Mollenhauer and Simpson, was in the shape of contracts–fat ones–street-paving, bridges, viaducts, sewers. And in order for him to get these contracts the affairs of the Republican party, of which he was a beneficiary as well as a leader, must be kept reasonably straight. At the same time it was no more a part of his need to keep the affairs of the party straight than it was of either Mollenhauer's or Simpson's, and Stener was not his appointee. The latter was more directly responsible to Mollenhauer than to any one else.

As Butler stepped into the buggy with his son he was thinking about this, and it was puzzling him greatly.

"Cowperwood's just been here," he said to Owen, who had been rapidly coming into a sound financial understanding of late, and was already a shrewder man politically and socially than his father, though he had not the latter's magnetism. "He's been tellin' me that he's in a rather tight place. You hear that?" he continued, as some voice in the distance was calling "Extra! Extra!" "That's Chicago burnin', and there's goin' to be trouble on the stock exchange to-morrow. We have a lot of our street-railway stocks around at the different banks. If we don't look sharp they'll be callin' our loans. We have to 'tend to that the first thing in the mornin'. Cowperwood has a hundred thousand of mine with him that he wants me to let stay there, and he has some money that belongs to Stener, he tells me."

"Stener?" asked Owen, curiously. "Has he been dabbling in stocks?" Owen had heard some rumors concerning Stener and others only very recently, which he had not credited nor yet communicated to his father. "How much money of his has Cowperwood?" he asked.

Butler meditated. "Quite a bit, I'm afraid," he finally said. "As a matter of fact, it's a great deal–about five hundred thousand dollars. If that should become known, it would be makin' a good deal of noise, I'm thinkin'."

"Whew!" exclaimed Owen in astonishment. "Five hundred thousand dollars! Good Lord, father! Do you mean to say Stener has got away with five hundred thousand dollars? Why, I wouldn't think he was clever enough to do that. Five hundred thousand dollars! It will make a nice row if that comes out."

"Aisy, now! Aisy, now!" replied Butler, doing his best to keep all phases of the situation in mind. "We can't tell exactly what the circumstances were yet. He mayn't have meant to take so much. It may all come out all right yet. The money's invested. Cowperwood hasn't failed yet. It may be put back. The thing to be settled on now is whether anything can be done to save him. If he's tellin' me the truth–and I never knew him to lie–he can get out of this if street-railway stocks don't break too heavy in the mornin'. I'm going over to see Henry Mollenhauer and Mark Simpson. They're in on this. Cowperwood wanted me to see if I couldn't get them to get the bankers together and have them stand by the market. He thought we might protect our loans by comin' on and buyin' and holdin' up the price."

Owen was running swiftly in his mind over Cowperwood's affairs–as much as he knew of them. He felt keenly that the banker ought to be shaken out. This dilemma was his fault, not Stener's–he felt. It was strange to him that his father did not see it and resent it.

"You see what it is, father," he said, dramatically, after a time. "Cowperwood's been using this money of Stener's to pick up stocks, and he's in a hole. If it hadn't been for this fire he'd have got away with it; but now he wants you and Simpson and Mollenhauer and the others to pull him out. He's a nice fellow, and I like him fairly well; but you're a fool if you do as he wants you to. He has more than belongs to him already. I heard the other day that he has the Front Street line, and almost all of Green and Coates; and that he and Stener own the Seventeenth and Nineteenth; but I didn't believe it. I've been intending to ask you about it. I think Cowperwood has a majority for himself stowed away somewhere in every instance. Stener is just a pawn. He moves him around where he pleases."

Owen's eyes gleamed avariciously, opposingly. Cowperwood ought to be punished, sold out, driven out of the street-railway business in which Owen was anxious to rise.

"Now you know," observed Butler, thickly and solemnly, "I always thought that young felly was clever, but I hardly thought he was as clever as all that. So that's his game. You're pretty shrewd yourself, aren't you? Well, we can fix that, if we think well of it. But there's more than that to all this. You don't want to forget the Republican party. Our success goes with the success of that, you know"–and he paused and looked at his son. "If Cowperwood should fail and that money couldn't be put back–" He broke off abstractedly. "The thing that's troublin' me is this matter of Stener and the city treasury. If somethin' ain't done about that, it may go hard with the party this fall, and with some of our contracts. You don't want to forget that an election is comin' along in November. I'm wonderin' if I ought to call in that one hundred thousand dollars. It's goin' to take considerable money to meet my loans in the mornin'."

It is a curious matter of psychology, but it was only now that the real difficulties of the situation were beginning to dawn on Butler. In the presence of Cowperwood he was so influenced by that young man's personality and his magnetic presentation of his need and his own liking for him that he had not stopped to consider all the phases of his own relationship to the situation. Out here in the cool night air, talking to Owen, who was ambitious on his own account and anything but sentimentally considerate of Cowperwood, he was beginning to sober down and see things in their true light. He had to admit that Cowperwood had seriously compromised the city treasury and the Republican party, and incidentally Butler's own private interests. Nevertheless, he liked Cowperwood. He was in no way prepared to desert him. He was now going to see Mollenhauer and Simpson as much to save Cowperwood really as the party and his own affairs. And yet a scandal. He did not like that–resented it. This young scalawag! To think he should be so sly. None the less he still liked him, even here and now, and was feeling that he ought to do something to help the young man, if anything could help him. He might even leave his hundred-thousand-dollar loan with him until the last hour, as Cowperwood had requested, if the others were friendly.

"Well, father," said Owen, after a time, "I don't see why you need to worry any more than Mollenhauer or Simpson. If you three want to help him out, you can; but for the life of me I don't see why you should. I know this thing will have a bad effect on the election, if it comes out before then; but it could be hushed up until then, couldn't it? Anyhow, your street-railway holdings are more important than this election, and if you can see your way clear to getting the street-railway lines in your hands you won't need to worry about any elections. My advice to you is to call that one-hundred-thousand-dollar loan of yours in the morning, and meet the drop in your stocks that way. It may make Cowperwood fail, but that won't hurt you any. You can go into the market and buy his stocks. I wouldn't be surprised if he would run to you and ask you to take them. You ought to get Mollenhauer and Simpson to scare Stener so that he won't loan Cowperwood any more money. If you don't, Cowperwood will run there and get more. Stener's in too far now. If Cowperwood won't sell out, well and good; the chances are he will bust, anyhow, and then you can pick up as much on the market as any one else. I think he'll sell. You can't afford to worry about Stener's five hundred thousand dollars. No one told him to loan it. Let him look out for himself. It may hurt the party, but you can look after that later. You and Mollenhauer can fix the newspapers so they won't talk about it till after election."

"Aisy! Aisy!" was all the old contractor would say. He was thinking hard.

Chapter XXV

The residence of Henry A. Mollenhauer was, at that time, in a section of the city which was almost as new as that in which Butler was living. It was on South Broad Street, near a handsome library building which had been recently erected. It was a spacious house of the type usually affected by men of new wealth in those days–a structure four stories in height of yellow brick and white stone built after no school which one could readily identify, but not unattractive in its architectural composition. A broad flight of steps leading to a wide veranda gave into a decidedly ornate door, which was set on either side by narrow windows and ornamented to the right and left with pale-blue jardinieres of considerable charm of outline. The interior, divided into twenty rooms, was paneled and parqueted in the most expensive manner for homes of that day. There was a great reception-hall, a large parlor or drawing-room, a dining-room at least thirty feet square paneled in oak; and on the second floor were a music-room devoted to the talents of Mollenhauer's three ambitious daughters, a library and private office for himself, a boudoir and bath for his wife, and a conservatory.

Mollenhauer was, and felt himself to be, a very important man. His financial and political judgment was exceedingly keen. Although he was a German, or rather an American of German parentage, he was a man of a rather impressive American presence. He was tall and heavy and shrewd and cold. His large chest and wide shoulders supported a head of distinguished proportions, both round and long when seen from different angles. The frontal bone descended in a protruding curve over the nose, and projected solemnly over the eyes, which burned with a shrewd, inquiring gaze. And the nose and mouth and chin below, as well as his smooth, hard cheeks,

confirmed the impression that he knew very well what he wished in this world, and was very able without regard to let or hindrance to get it. It was a big face, impressive, well modeled. He was an excellent friend of Edward Malia Butler's, as such friendships go, and his regard for Mark Simpson was as sincere as that of one tiger for another. He respected ability; he was willing to play fair when fair was the game. When it was not, the reach of his cunning was not easily measured.

When Edward Butler and his son arrived on this Sunday evening, this distinguished representative of one-third of the city's interests was not expecting them. He was in his library reading and listening to one of his daughters playing the piano. His wife and his other two daughters had gone to church. He was of a domestic turn of mind. Still, Sunday evening being an excellent one for conference purposes generally in the world of politics, he was not without the thought that some one or other of his distinguished confreres might call, and when the combination footman and butler announced the presence of Butler and his son, he was well pleased.

"So there you are," he remarked to Butler, genially, extending his hand. "I'm certainly glad to see you. And Owen! How are you, Owen? What will you gentlemen have to drink, and what will you smoke? I know you'll have something. John"–to the servitor—"see if you can find something for these gentlemen. I have just been listening to Caroline play; but I think you've frightened her off for the time being."

He moved a chair into position for Butler, and indicated to Owen another on the other side of the table. In a moment his servant had returned with a silver tray of elaborate design, carrying whiskies and wines of various dates and cigars in profusion. Owen was the new type of young financier who neither smoked nor drank. His father temperately did both.

"It's a comfortable place you have here," said Butler, without any indication of the important mission that had brought him. "I don't wonder you stay at home Sunday evenings. What's new in the city?"

"Nothing much, so far as I can see," replied Mollenhauer, pacifically. "Things seem to be running smooth enough. You don't know anything that we ought to worry about, do you?"

"Well, yes," said Butler, draining off the remainder of a brandy and soda that had been prepared for him. "One thing. You haven't seen an avenin' paper, have you?"

"No, I haven't," said Mollenhauer, straightening up. "Is there one out? What's the trouble anyhow?"

"Nothing–except Chicago's burning, and it looks as though we'd have a little money-storm here in the morning."

"You don't say! I didn't hear that. There's a paper out, is there? Well, well–is it much of a fire?"

"The city is burning down, so they say," put in Owen, who was watching the face of the distinguished politician with considerable interest.

"Well, that is news. I must send out and get a paper. John!" he called. His man-servant appeared. "See if you can get me a paper somewhere." The servant disappeared. "What makes you think that would have anything to do with us?" observed Mollenhauer, returning to Butler.

"Well, there's one thing that goes with that that I didn't know till a little while ago and that is that our man Stener is apt to be short in his accounts, unless things come out better than some people seem to think," suggested Butler, calmly. "That might not look so well before election, would it?" His shrewd gray Irish eyes looked into Mollenhauer's, who returned his gaze.

"Where did you get that?" queried Mr. Mollenhauer icily. "He hasn't deliberately taken much money, has he? How much has he taken–do you know?"

"Quite a bit," replied Butler, quietly. "Nearly five hundred thousand, so I understand. Only I wouldn't say that it has been taken as yet. It's in danger of being lost."

"Five hundred thousand!" exclaimed Mollenhauer in amazement, and yet preserving his usual calm. "You don't tell me! How long has this been going on? What has he been doing with the money?"

"He's loaned a good deal–about five hundred thousand dollars to this young Cowperwood in Third Street, that's been handlin' city loan. They've been investin' it for themselves in one thing and another–mostly in buyin' up street-railways." (At the mention of street-railways Mollenhauer's impassive countenance underwent a barely perceptible change.) "This fire, accordin' to Cowperwood, is certain to produce a panic in the mornin', and unless he gets considerable help he doesn't see how he's to hold out. If he doesn't hold out, there'll be five hundred thousand dollars missin' from the city treasury which can't be put back. Stener's out of town and Cowperwood's come to me to see what can be done about it. As a matter of fact, he's done a little business for me in times past, and he thought maybe I could help him now–that is, that I might get you and the Senator to see the big bankers with me and help support the market in the mornin'. If we don't he's goin' to fail, and he thought the scandal would hurt us in the election. He doesn't appear to me to be workin' any game–just anxious to save himself and do the square thing by me–by us, if he can." Butler paused.

Mollenhauer, sly and secretive himself, was apparently not at all moved by this unexpected development. At the same time, never having thought of Stener as having any particular executive or financial ability, he was a little stirred and curious. So his treasurer was using money without his knowing it, and now stood in danger of being prosecuted! Cowperwood he knew of only indirectly, as one who had been engaged to handle city loan. He had profited by his manipulation of city loan. Evidently the banker had made a fool of Stener, and had used the money for street-railway shares! He and Stener must have quite some private holdings then. That did interest Mollenhauer greatly.

"Five hundred thousand dollars!" he repeated, when Butler had finished. "That is quite a little money. If merely supporting the market would save Cowperwood we might do that, although if it's a severe panic I do not see how anything we can do will be of very much assistance to him. If he's in a very tight place and a severe slump is coming, it will take a great deal more than our merely supporting the market to save him. I've been through that before. You don't know what his liabilities are?"

"I do not," said Butler.

"He didn't ask for money, you say?"

"He wants me to l'ave a hundred thousand he has of mine until he sees whether he can get through or not."

"Stener is really out of town, I suppose?" Mollenhauer was innately suspicious.

"So Cowperwood says. We can send and find out."

Mollenhauer was thinking of the various aspects of the case. Supporting the market would be all very well if that would save Cowperwood, and the Republican party and his treasurer. At the same time Stener could then be compelled to restore the five hundred thousand dollars to the city treasury, and release his holdings to some one—preferably to him—Mollenhauer. But here was Butler also to be considered in this matter. What might he not want? He consulted with Butler and learned that Cowperwood had agreed to return the five hundred thousand in case he could get it together. The various street-car holdings were not asked after. But what assurance had any one that Cowperwood could be so saved? And could, or would get the money together? And if he were saved would he give the money back to Stener? If he required actual money, who would loan it to him in a time like this—in case a sharp panic was imminent? What security could he give? On the other hand, under pressure from the right parties he might be made to surrender all his street-railway holdings for a song—his and Stener's. If he (Mollenhauer) could get them he would not particularly care whether the election was lost this fall or not, although he felt satisfied, as had Owen, that it would not be lost. It could be bought, as usual. The defalcation—if Cowperwood's failure made Stener's loan into one—could be concealed long enough, Mollenhauer thought, to win. Personally as it came to him now he would prefer to frighten Stener into refusing Cowperwood additional aid, and then raid the latter's street-railway stock in combination with everybody else's, for that matter—Simpson's and Butler's included. One of the big sources of future wealth in Philadelphia lay in these lines. For the present, however, he had to pretend an interest in saving the party at the polls.

"I can't speak for the Senator, that's sure," pursued Mollenhauer, reflectively. "I don't know what he may think. As for myself, I am perfectly willing to do what I can to keep up the price of stocks, if that will do any good. I would do so naturally in order to protect my loans. The thing that we ought to be thinking about, in my judgment, is how to prevent exposure, in case Mr. Cowperwood does fail, until after election. We have no assurance, of course, that however much we support the market we will be able to sustain it."

"We have not," replied Butler, solemnly.

Owen thought he could see Cowperwood's approaching doom quite plainly. At that moment the door-bell rang. A maid, in the absence of the footman, brought in the name of Senator Simpson.

"Just the man," said Mollenhauer. "Show him up. You can see what he thinks."

"Perhaps I had better leave you alone now," suggested Owen to his father. "Perhaps I can find Miss Caroline, and she will sing for me. I'll wait for you, father," he added.

Mollenhauer cast him an ingratiating smile, and as he stepped out Senator Simpson walked in.

A more interesting type of his kind than Senator Mark Simpson never flourished in the State of Pennsylvania, which has been productive of interesting types. Contrasted with either of the two men who now greeted him warmly and shook his hand, he was physically unimpressive. He was small–five feet nine inches, to Mollenhauer's six feet and Butler's five feet eleven inches and a half, and then his face was smooth, with a receding jaw. In the other two this feature was prominent. Nor were his eyes as frank as those of Butler, nor as defiant as those of Mollenhauer; but for subtlety they were unmatched by either–deep, strange, receding, cavernous eyes which contemplated you as might those of a cat looking out of a dark hole, and suggesting all the artfulness that has ever distinguished the feline family. He had a strange mop of black hair sweeping down over a fine, low, white forehead, and a skin as pale and bluish as poor health might make it; but there was, nevertheless, resident here a strange, resistant, capable force that ruled men–the subtlety with which he knew how to feed cupidity with hope and gain and the ruthlessness with which he repaid those who said him nay. He was a still man, as such a man might well have been–feeble and fish-like in his handshake, wan and slightly lackadaisical in his smile, but speaking always with eyes that answered for every defect.

"Av'nin', Mark, I'm glad to see you," was Butler's greeting.

"How are you, Edward?" came the quiet reply.

"Well, Senator, you're not looking any the worse for wear. Can I pour you something?"

"Nothing to-night, Henry," replied Simpson. "I haven't long to stay. I just stopped by on my way home. My wife's over here at the Cavanaghs', and I have to stop by to fetch her."

"Well, it's a good thing you dropped in, Senator, just when you did," began Mollenhauer, seating himself after his guest. "Butler here has been telling me of a little political problem that has arisen since I last saw you. I suppose you've heard that Chicago is burning?"

"Yes; Cavanagh was just telling me. It looks to be quite serious. I think the market will drop heavily in the morning."

"I wouldn't be surprised myself," put in Mollenhauer, laconically.

"Here's the paper now," said Butler, as John, the servant, came in from the street bearing the paper in his hand. Mollenhauer took it and spread it out before them. It was among the earliest of the "extras" that were issued in this country, and contained a rather impressive spread of type announcing that the conflagration in the lake city was growing hourly worse since its inception the day before.

"Well, that is certainly dreadful," said Simpson. "I'm very sorry for Chicago. I have many friends there. I shall hope to hear that it is not so bad as it seems."

The man had a rather grandiloquent manner which he never abandoned under any circumstances.

"The matter that Butler was telling me about," continued Mollenhauer, "has something to do with this in a way. You know the habit our city treasurers have of loaning out their money at two per cent.?"

"Yes?" said Simpson, inquiringly.

"Well, Mr. Stener, it seems, has been loaning out a good deal of the city's money to this young Cowperwood, in Third Street, who has been handling city loans."

"You don't say!" said Simpson, putting on an air of surprise. "Not much, I hope?" The Senator, like Butler and Mollenhauer, was profiting greatly by cheap loans from the same source to various designated city depositories.

"Well, it seems that Stener has loaned him as much as five hundred thousand dollars, and if by any chance Cowperwood shouldn't be able to weather this storm, Stener is apt to be short that amount, and that wouldn't look so good as a voting proposition to the people in November, do you think? Cowperwood owes Mr. Butler here one hundred thousand dollars, and because of that he came to see him to-night. He wanted Butler to see if something couldn't be done through us to tide him over. If not"–he waved one hand suggestively–"well, he might fail."

Simpson fingered his strange, wide mouth with his delicate hand. "What have they been doing with the five hundred thousand dollars?" he asked.

"Oh, the boys must make a little somethin' on the side," said Butler, cheerfully. "I think they've been buyin' up street-railways, for one thing." He stuck his thumbs in the armholes of his vest. Both Mollenhauer and Simpson smiled wan smiles.

"Quite so," said Mollenhauer. Senator Simpson merely looked the deep things that he thought.

He, too, was thinking how useless it was for any one to approach a group of politicians with a proposition like this, particularly in a crisis such as bid fair to occur. He reflected that if he and Butler and Mollenhauer could get together and promise Cowperwood protection in return for the surrender of his street-railway holdings it would be a very different matter. It would be very easy in this case to carry the city treasury loan along in silence and even issue more money to support it; but it was not sure, in the first place, that Cowperwood could be made to surrender his stocks, and in the second place that either Butler or Mollenhauer would enter into any such deal with him, Simpson. Butler had evidently come here to say a good word for Cowperwood. Mollenhauer and himself were silent rivals. Although they worked together politically it was toward essentially different financial ends. They were allied in no one particular financial proposition, any more than Mollenhauer and Butler were. And besides, in all probability Cowperwood was no fool. He was not equally guilty with Stener; the latter had loaned him money. The Senator reflected on whether he should broach some such subtle solution of the situation as had occurred to him to his colleagues, but he decided not. Really Mollenhauer was too treacherous a man to work with on a thing of this kind. It was a splendid chance but dangerous. He had better go it alone. For the present they should demand of Stener that he get Cowperwood to return the five hundred thousand dollars if he could. If not, Stener could be sacrificed for the benefit of the party, if need be. Cowperwood's stocks, with this tip as to his condition, would, Simpson reflected, offer a good opportunity for a little stock-exchange work on the part of his own brokers. They could spread rumors as to Cowperwood's condition and then offer to take his shares off his hands–for a song, of course. It was an evil moment that led Cowperwood to Butler.

"Well, now," said the Senator, after a prolonged silence, "I might sympathize with Mr. Cowperwood in his situation, and I certainly don't blame him for buying up street-railways if he can; but I really don't see what can be done for him very well in this crisis. I don't know about you, gentlemen, but I am rather certain that I am not in a position to pick other people's chestnuts out of the fire if I wanted to, just now. It all depends on whether we feel that the danger to the party is sufficient to warrant our going down into our pockets and assisting him."

At the mention of real money to be loaned Mollenhauer pulled a long face. "I can't see that I will be able to do very much for Mr. Cowperwood," he sighed.

"Begad," said Buler, with a keen sense of humor, "it looks to me as if I'd better be gettin' in my one hundred thousand dollars. That's the first business of the early mornin'." Neither Simpson nor Mollenhauer condescended on this occasion to smile even the wan smile they had smiled before. They merely looked wise and solemn.

"But this matter of the city treasury, now," said Senator Simpson, after the atmosphere had been allowed to settle a little, "is something to which we shall have to devote a little thought. If Mr. Cowperwood should fail, and the treasury lose that much money, it would embarrass us no little. What lines are they," he added, as an afterthought, "that this man has been particularly interested in?"

"I really don't know," replied Butler, who did not care to say what Owen had told him on the drive over.

"I don't see," said Mollenhauer, "unless we can make Stener get the money back before this man Cowperwood fails, how we can save ourselves from considerable annoyance later; but if we did anything which would look as though we were going to compel restitution, he would probably shut up shop anyhow. So there's no remedy in that direction. And it wouldn't be very kind to our friend Edward here to do it until we hear how he comes out on his affair." He was referring to Butler's loan.

"Certainly not," said Senator Simpson, with true political sagacity and feeling.

"I'll have that one hundred thousand dollars in the mornin'," said Butler, "and never fear."

"I think," said Simpson, "if anything comes of this matter that we will have to do our best to hush it up until after the election. The newspapers can just as well keep silent on that score as not. There's one thing I would suggest"–and he was now thinking of the street-railway properties which Cowperwood had so judiciously collected–"and that is that the city treasurer be cautioned against advancing any more money in a situation of this kind. He might readily be compromised into advancing much more. I suppose a word from you, Henry, would prevent that."

"Yes; I can do that," said Mollenhauer, solemnly.

"My judgement would be," said Butler, in a rather obscure manner, thinking of Cowperwood's mistake in appealing to these noble protectors of the public, "that it's best to let sleepin' dogs run be themselves."

Thus ended Frank Cowperwood's dreams of what Butler and his political associates might do for him in his hour of distress.

The energies of Cowperwood after leaving Butler were devoted to the task of seeing others who might be of some assistance to him. He had left word with Mrs. Stener that if any message came from her husband he was to be notified at once. He hunted up Walter Leigh, of Drexel Co., Avery Stone of Jay Cooke Co., and President Davison of the Girard National Bank. He wanted to see what they thought of the situation and to negotiate a loan with President Davison covering all his real and personal property.

"I can't tell you, Frank," Walter Leigh insisted, "I don't know how things will be running by to-morrow noon. I'm glad to know how you stand. I'm glad you're doing what you're doing–getting all your affairs in shape. It will help a lot. I'll favor you all I possibly can. But if the chief decides on a certain group of loans to be called, they'll have to be called, that's all. I'll do my best to make things look better. If the whole of Chicago is wiped out, the insurance companies–some of them, anyhow–are sure to go, and then look out. I suppose you'll call in all your loans?"

"Not any more than I have to."

"Well, that's just the way it is here–or will be."

The two men shook hands. They liked each other. Leigh was of the city's fashionable coterie, a society man to the manner born, but with a wealth of common sense and a great deal of worldly experience.

"I'll tell you, Frank," he observed at parting, "I've always thought you were carrying too much street-railway. It's great stuff if you can get away with it, but it's just in a pinch like this that you're apt to get hurt. You've been making money pretty fast out of that and city loans."

He looked directly into his long-time friend's eyes, and they smiled.

It was the same with Avery Stone, President Davison, and others. They had all already heard rumors of disaster when he arrived. They were not sure what the morrow would bring forth. It looked very unpromising.

Cowperwood decided to stop and see Butler again for he felt certain his interview with Mollenhauer and Simpson was now over. Butler, who had been meditating what he should say to Cowperwood, was not unfriendly in his manner. "So you're back," he said, when Cowperwood appeared.

"Yes, Mr. Butler."

"Well, I'm not sure that I've been able to do anything for you. I'm afraid not," Butler said, cautiously. "It's a hard job you set me. Mollenhauer seems to think that he'll support the market, on his own account. I think he will. Simpson has interests which he has to protect. I'm going to buy for myself, of course."

He paused to reflect.

"I couldn't get them to call a conference with any of the big moneyed men as yet," he added, warily. "They'd rather wait and see what happens in the mornin'. Still, I wouldn't be down-hearted if I were you. If things turn out very bad they may change their minds. I had to tell them about Stener. It's pretty bad, but they're hopin' you'll come through and straighten that out. I hope so. About my own loan–well, I'll see how things are in the mornin'. If I raisonably can I'll lave it with you. You'd better see me again about it. I wouldn't try to get any more money out of Stener if I were you. It's pretty bad as it is."

Cowperwood saw at once that he was to get no aid from the politicians. The one thing that disturbed him was this reference to Stener. Had they already communicated with him–warned him? If so, his own coming to Butler had been a bad move; and yet from the point of view of his possible failure on the morrow it had been advisable. At least now the politicians knew where he stood. If he got in a very tight corner he would come to Butler again–the politicians could assist him or not, as they chose. If they did not help him and he failed, and the election were lost, it was their own fault.

Anyhow, if he could see Stener first the latter would not be such a fool as to stand in his own light in a crisis like this.

"Things look rather dark to-night, Mr. Butler," he said, smartly, "but I still think I'll come through. I hope so, anyhow. I'm sorry to have put you to so much trouble. I wish, of course, that you gentlemen could see your way clear to assist me, but if you can't, you can't. I have a number of things that I can do. I hope that you will leave your loan as long as you can."

He went briskly out, and Butler meditated. "A clever young chap that," he said. "It's too bad. But he may come out all right at that."

Cowperwood hurried to his own home only to find his father awake and brooding. To him he talked with that strong vein of sympathy and understanding which is usually characteristic of those drawn by ties of flesh and blood. He liked his father. He sympathized with his painstaking effort to get up in the world. He could not forget that as a boy he had had the loving sympathy and interest of his father. The loan which he had from the Third National, on somewhat weak Union Street Railway shares he could probably replace if stocks did not drop too tremendously. He must replace this at all costs. But his father's investments in street-railways, which had risen with his own ventures, and which now involved an additional two hundred thousand–how could he protect those? The shares were hypothecated and the money was used for other things. Additional collateral would have to be furnished the several banks carrying them. It was nothing except loans, loans, loans, and the need of protecting them. If he could only get an additional deposit of two or three hundred thousand dollars from Stener. But that, in the face of possible financial difficulties, was rank criminality. All depended on the morrow.

Monday, the ninth, dawned gray and cheerless. He was up with the first ray of light, shaved and dressed, and went over, under the gray-green pergola, to his father's house. He was up, also, and stirring about, for he had not been able to sleep. His gray eyebrows and gray hair looked rather shaggy and disheveled, and his side-whiskers anything but decorative. The old gentleman's eyes were tired, and his face was gray. Cowperwood could see that he was worrying. He looked up from a small, ornate escritoire of buhl, which Ellsworth had found somewhere, and where he was quietly tabulating a list of his resources and liabilities. Cowperwood winced. He hated to see his father worried, but he could not help it. He had hoped sincerely, when they built their houses together, that the days of worry for his father had gone forever.

"Counting up?" he asked, familiarly, with a smile. He wanted to hearten the old gentleman as much as possible.

"I was just running over my affairs again to see where I stood in case–" He looked quizzically at his son, and Frank smiled again.

"I wouldn't worry, father. I told you how I fixed it so that Butler and that crowd will support the market. I have Rivers and Targool and Harry Eltinge on 'change helping me sell out, and they are the best men there. They'll handle the situation carefully. I couldn't trust Ed or Joe in this case, for the moment they began to sell everybody would know what was going on with me. This way my men will seem like bears hammering the market, but not hammering too hard. I ought to be able to unload enough at ten points off to raise five hundred thousand. The market may not go lower than that. You can't tell. It isn't going to sink indefinitely. If I just knew what the big insurance companies were going to do! The morning paper hasn't come yet, has it?"

He was going to pull a bell, but remembered that the servants would scarcely be up as yet. He went to the front door himself. There were the Press and the Public Ledger lying damp from the presses. He picked them up and glanced at the front pages. His countenance fell. On one, the Press, was spread a great black map of Chicago, a most funereal-looking thing, the black portion indicating the burned section. He had never seen a map of Chicago before in just this clear, definite way. That white portion was Lake Michigan, and there was the Chicago River dividing the city into three almost equal portions–the north side, the west side, the south side. He saw at once that the city was curiously arranged, somewhat like Philadelphia, and that the business section was probably an area of two or three miles square, set at the juncture of the three sides, and lying south of the main stem of the river, where it flowed into the lake after the southwest and northwest branches had united to form it. This was a significant central area; but, according to this map, it was all burned out. "Chicago in Ashes" ran a great side-heading set in heavily leaded black type. It went on to detail the sufferings of the homeless, the number of the dead, the number of those whose fortunes had been destroyed. Then it descanted upon the probable effect in the East. Insurance companies and manufacturers might not be able to meet the great strain of all this.

"Damn!" said Cowperwood gloomily. "I wish I were out of this stock-jobbing business. I wish I had never gotten into it." He returned to his drawing-room and scanned both accounts most carefully.

Then, though it was still early, he and his father drove to his office. There were already messages awaiting him, a dozen or more, to cancel or sell. While he was standing there a messenger-boy brought him three more. One was from Stener and said that he would be back by twelve o'clock, the very earliest he could make it. Cowperwood was relieved and yet distressed. He would need large sums of money to meet various loans before three. Every hour was precious. He must arrange to meet Stener at the station and talk to him before any one else should see him. Clearly this was going to be a hard, dreary, strenuous day.

Third Street, by the time he reached there, was stirring with other bankers and brokers called forth by the exigencies of the occasion. There was a suspicious hurrying of feet–that intensity which makes all the difference in the world between a hundred people placid and a hundred people disturbed. At the exchange, the atmosphere was feverish. At the sound of the gong, the staccato uproar began. Its metallic vibrations were still in the air when the two hundred men who composed this local organization at its utmost stress of calculation, threw themselves upon each other in a gibbering struggle to dispose of or seize bargains of the hour. The interests were so varied that it was impossible to say at which pole it was best to sell or buy.

Targool and Rivers had been delegated to stay at the center of things, Joseph and Edward to hover around on the outside and to pick up such opportunities of selling as might offer a reasonable return on the stock. The "bears" were determined to jam things down, and it all depended on how well the agents of Mollenhauer, Simpson, Butler, and others supported things in the street-railway world whether those stocks retained any strength or not. The last thing Butler had said the night before was that they would do the best they could. They would buy up to a certain point. Whether they would support the market indefinitely he would not say. He could not vouch for Mollenhauer and Simpson. Nor did he know the condition of their affairs.

While the excitement was at its highest Cowperwood came in. As he stood in the door looking to catch the eye of Rivers, the 'change gong sounded, and trading stopped. All the brokers and traders faced about to the little balcony, where the secretary of the 'change made his announcements; and there he stood, the door open behind him, a small, dark, clerkly man of thirty-eight or forty, whose spare figure and pale face bespoke the methodic mind that knows no venturous thought. In his right hand he held a slip of white paper.

"The American Fire Insurance Company of Boston announces its inability to meet its obligations." The gong sounded again.

Immediately the storm broke anew, more voluble than before, because, if after one hour of investigation on this Monday morning one insurance company had gone down, what would four or five hours or a day or two bring forth? It meant that men who had been burned out in Chicago would not be able to resume business. It meant that all loans connected with this concern had been, or would be called now. And the cries of frightened "bulls" offering thousand and five thousand lot holdings in Northern Pacific, Illinois Central, Reading, Lake Shore, Wabash; in all the local streetcar lines; and in Cowperwood's city loans at constantly falling prices was sufficient to take the heart out of all concerned. He hurried to Arthur Rivers's side in the lull; but there was little he could say.

"It looks as though the Mollenhauer and Simpson crowds aren't doing much for the market," he observed, gravely.

"They've had advices from New York," explained Rivers solemnly. "It can't be supported very well. There are three insurance companies over there on the verge of quitting, I understand. I expect to see them posted any minute."

They stepped apart from the pandemonium, to discuss ways and means. Under his agreement with Stener, Cowperwood could buy up to one hundred thousand dollars of city loan, above the customary wash sales, or market manipulation, by which they were making money. This was in case the market had to be genuinely supported. He decided to buy sixty thousand dollars worth now, and use this to sustain his loans elsewhere. Stener would pay him for this instantly, giving him more ready cash. It might help him in one way and another; and, anyhow, it might tend to strengthen the other securities long enough at least to allow him to realize a little something now at better than ruinous rates. If only he had the means "to go short" on this market! If only doing so did not really mean ruin to his present position. It was characteristic of the man that even in this crisis he should be seeing how the very thing that of necessity, because of his present obligations, might ruin him, might also, under slightly different conditions, yield him a great harvest. He could not take advantage of it, however. He could not be on both sides of this market. It was either "bear" or "bull," and of necessity he was "bull." It was strange but true. His subtlety could not avail him here. He was about to turn and hurry to see a certain banker who might loan him something on his house, when the gong struck again. Once more trading ceased. Arthur Rivers, from his position at the State securities post, where city loan was sold, and where he had started to buy for Cowperwood, looked significantly at him. Newton Targool hurried to Cowperwood's side.

"You're up against it," he exclaimed. "I wouldn't try to sell against this market. It's no use. They're cutting the ground from under you. The bottom's out. Things are bound to turn in a few days. Can't you hold out? Here's more trouble."

He raised his eyes to the announcer's balcony.

"The Eastern and Western Fire Insurance Company of New York announces that it cannot meet its obligations."

A low sound something like "Haw!" broke forth. The announcer's gavel struck for order.

"The Erie Fire Insurance Company of Rochester announces that it cannot meet its obligations."

Again that "H-a-a-a-w!"

Once more the gavel.

"The American Trust Company of New York has suspended payment."

"H-a-a-a-w!"

The storm was on.

"What do you think?" asked Targool. "You can't brave this storm. Can't you quit selling and hold out for a few days? Why not sell short?"

"They ought to close this thing up," Cowperwood said, shortly. "It would be a splendid way out. Then nothing could be done."

He hurried to consult with those who, finding themselves in a similar predicament with himself, might use their influence to bring it about. It was a sharp trick to play on those who, now finding the market favorable to their designs in its falling condition, were harvesting a fortune. But what was that to him? Business was business. There was no use selling at ruinous figures, and he gave his lieutenants orders to stop. Unless the bankers favored him heavily, or the stock exchange was closed, or Stener could be induced to deposit an additional three hundred thousand with him at once, he was ruined. He hurried down the street to various bankers and brokers suggesting that they do this—close the exchange. At a few minutes before twelve o'clock he drove rapidly to the station to meet Stener; but to his great disappointment the latter did not arrive. It looked as though he had missed his train. Cowperwood sensed something, some trick; and decided to go to the city hall and also to Stener's house. Perhaps he had returned and was trying to avoid him.

Not finding him at his office, he drove direct to his house. Here he was not surprised to meet Stener just coming out, looking very pale and distraught. At the sight of Cowperwood he actually blanched.

"Why, hello, Frank," he exclaimed, sheepishly, "where do you come from?"

"What's up, George?" asked Cowperwood. "I thought you were coming into Broad Street."

"So I was," returned Stener, foolishly, "but I thought I would get off at West Philadelphia and change my clothes. I've a lot of things to 'tend to yet this afternoon. I was coming in to see you." After Cowperwood's urgent telegram this was silly, but the young banker let it pass.

"Jump in, George," he said. "I have something very important to talk to you about. I told you in my telegram about the likelihood of a panic. It's on. There isn't a moment to lose. Stocks are 'way down, and most of my loans are being called. I want to know if you won't let me have three hundred and fifty thousand dollars for a few days at four or five per cent. I'll pay it all back to you. I need it very badly. If I don't get it I'm likely to fail. You know what that means, George. It will tie up every dollar I have. Those street-car holdings of yours will be tied up with me. I won't be able to let you realize on them, and that will put those loans of mine from the treasury in bad shape. You won't be able to put the money back, and you know what that means. We're in this thing together. I want to see you through safely, but I can't do it without your help. I had to go to Butler last night to see about a loan of his, and I'm doing my best to get money from other sources. But I can't see my way through on this, I'm afraid, unless you're willing to help me." Cowperwood paused. He wanted to put the whole case clearly and succinctly to him before he had a chance to refuse–to make him realize it as his own predicament.

As a matter of fact, what Cowperwood had keenly suspected was literally true. Stener had been reached. The moment Butler and Simpson had left him the night before, Mollenhauer had sent for his very able secretary, Abner Sengstack, and despatched him to learn the truth about Stener's whereabouts. Sengstack had then sent a long wire to Strobik, who was with Stener, urging him to caution the latter against Cowperwood. The state of the treasury was known. Stener and Strobik were to be met by Sengstack at Wilmington (this to forefend against the possibility of Cowperwood's reaching Stener first)–and the whole state of affairs made perfectly plain. No more money was to be used under penalty of prosecution. If Stener wanted to see any one he must see Mollenhauer. Sengstack, having received a telegram from Strobik informing him of their proposed arrival at noon the next day, had proceeded to Wilmington to meet them. The result was that Stener did not come direct into the business heart of the city, but instead got off at West Philadelphia, proposing to go first to his house to change his clothes and then to see Mollenhauer before meeting Cowperwood. He was very badly frightened and wanted time to think.

"I can't do it, Frank," he pleaded, piteously. "I'm in pretty bad in this matter. Mollenhauer's secretary met the train out at Wilmington just now to warn me against this situation, and Strobik is against it. They know how much money I've got outstanding. You or somebody has told them. I can't go against Mollenhauer. I owe everything I've got to him, in a way. He got me this place."

"Listen, George. Whatever you do at this time, don't let this political loyalty stuff cloud your judgment. You're in a very serious position and so am I. If you don't act for yourself with me now no one is going to act for you–now or later–no one. And later will be too late. I proved that last night when I went to Butler to get help for the two of us. They all know about this business of our street-railway holdings and they want to shake us out and that's the big and little of it–nothing more and nothing less. It's a case of dog eat dog in this game and this particular situation and it's up to us to save ourselves against everybody or go down together, and that's just what I'm here to tell you. Mollenhauer doesn't care any more for you to-day than he does for that lamp-post. It isn't that money you've paid out to me that's worrying him, but who's getting something for it and what. Well they know that you and I are getting street-railways, don't you see, and they don't want us to have them. Once they get those out of our hands they won't waste another day on you or me. Can't you see that? Once we've lost all we've invested, you're down and so am I–and no one is going to turn a hand for you or me politically or in any other way. I want you to understand that, George, because it's true. And before you say you won't or you will do anything because Mollenhauer says so, you want to think over what I have to tell you."

He was in front of Stener now, looking him directly in the eye and by the kinetic force of his mental way attempting to make Stener take the one step that might save him–Cowperwood–however little in the long run it might do for Stener. And, more interesting still, he did not care. Stener, as he saw him now, was a pawn in whosoever's hands he happened to be at the time, and despite Mr. Mollenhauer and Mr. Simpson and Mr. Butler he proposed to attempt to keep him in his own hands if possible. And so he stood there looking at him as might a snake at a bird determined to galvanize him into selfish self-interest if possible. But Stener was so frightened that at the moment it looked as though there was little to be done with him. His face was a grayish-blue: his eyelids and eye rings puffy and his hands and lips moist. God, what a hole he was in now!

"Say that's all right, Frank," he exclaimed desperately. "I know what you say is true. But look at me and my position, if I do give you this money. What can't they do to me, and won't. If you only look at it from my point of view. If only you hadn't gone to Butler before you saw me."

"As though I could see you, George, when you were off duck shooting and when I was wiring everywhere I knew to try to get in touch with you. How could I? The situation had to be met. Besides, I thought Butler was more friendly to me than he proved. But there's no use being angry with me now, George, for going to Butler as I did, and anyhow you can't afford to be now. We're in this thing together. It's a case of sink or swim for just us two–not any one else–just us–don't you get that? Butler couldn't or wouldn't do what I wanted him to do–get Mollenhauer and Simpson to support the market. Instead of that they are hammering it. They have a game of their own. It's to shake us out–can't you see that? Take everything that you and I have gathered. It is up to you and me, George, to save ourselves, and that's what I'm here for now. If you don't let me have three hundred and fifty thousand dollars–three hundred thousand, anyhow–you and I are ruined. It will be worse for you, George, than for me, for I'm not involved in this thing in any way–not legally, anyhow. But that's not what I'm thinking of. What I want to do is to save us both–put us on easy street for the rest of our lives, whatever they say or do, and it's in your power, with my help, to do that for both of us. Can't you see that? I want to save my business so then I can help you to save your name and money." He paused, hoping this had convinced Stener, but the latter was still shaking.

"But what can I do, Frank?" he pleaded, weakly. "I can't go against Mollenhauer. They can prosecute me if I do that. They can do it, anyhow. I can't do that. I'm not strong enough. If they didn't know, if you hadn't told them, it might be different, but this way–" He shook his head sadly, his gray eyes filled with a pale distress.

"George," replied Cowperwood, who realized now that only the sternest arguments would have any effect here, "don't talk about what I did. What I did I had to do. You're in danger of losing your head and your nerve and making a serious mistake here, and I don't want to see you make it. I have five hundred thousand of the city's money invested for you–partly for me, and partly for you, but more for you than for me"–which, by the way, was not true–"and here you are hesitating in an hour like this as to whether you will protect your interest or not. I can't understand it. This is a crisis, George. Stocks are tumbling on every side–everybody's stocks. You're not alone in this–neither am I. This is a panic, brought on by a fire, and you can't expect to come out of a panic alive unless you do something to protect yourself. You say you owe your place to Mollenhauer and that you're afraid of what he'll do. If you look at your own situation and mine, you'll see that it doesn't make much difference what he does, so long as I don't fail. If I fail, where are you? Who's going to save you from prosecution? Will Mollenhauer or any one else come forward and put five hundred thousand dollars in the treasury for you? He will not. If Mollenhauer and the others have your interests at heart, why aren't they helping me on 'change today? I'll tell you why. They want your street-railway holdings and mine, and they don't care whether you go to jail afterward or not. Now if you're wise you will listen to me. I've been loyal to you, haven't I? You've made money through me–lots of it. If you're wise, George, you'll go to your office and write me your check for three hundred thousand dollars, anyhow, before you do a single other thing. Don't see anybody and don't do anything till you've done that. You can't be hung any more for a sheep than you can for a lamb. No one can prevent you from giving me that check. You're the city treasurer. Once I have that I can see my way out of this, and I'll pay it all back to you next week or the week after–this panic is sure to end in that time. With that put back in the treasury we can see them about the five hundred thousand a little later. In three months, or less, I can fix it so that you can put that back. As a matter of fact, I can do it in fifteen days once I am on my feet again. Time is all I want. You won't have lost your holdings and nobody will cause you any trouble if you put the money back. They don't care to risk a scandal any more than you do. Now what'll you do, George? Mollenhauer can't stop you from doing this any more than I can make you. Your life is in your own hands. What will you do?"

Stener stood there ridiculously meditating when, as a matter of fact, his very financial blood was oozing away. Yet he was afraid to act. He was afraid of Mollenhauer, afraid of Cowperwood, afraid of life and of himself. The thought of panic, loss, was not so much a definite thing connected with his own property, his money, as it was with his social and political standing in the community. Few people have the sense of financial individuality strongly developed. They do not know what it means to be a controller of wealth, to have that which releases the sources of social action–its medium of exchange. They want money, but not for money's sake. They want it for what it will buy in the way of simple comforts, whereas the financier wants it for what it will control–for what it will represent in the way of dignity, force, power. Cowperwood wanted money in that way; Stener not. That was why he had been so ready to let Cowperwood act for him; and now, when he should have seen more clearly than ever the significance of what Cowperwood was proposing, he was frightened and his reason obscured by such things as Mollenhauer's probable opposition and rage, Cowperwood's possible failure, his own inability to face a real crisis. Cowperwood's innate financial ability did not reassure Stener in this hour. The banker was too young, too new. Mollenhauer was older, richer. So was Simpson; so was Butler. These men, with their wealth, represented the big forces, the big standards in his world. And besides, did not Cowperwood himself confess that he was in great danger–that he was in a corner. That was the worst possible confession to make to Stener–although under the circumstances it was the only one that could be made–for he had no courage to face danger.

So it was that now, Stener stood by Cowperwood meditating–pale, flaccid; unable to see the main line of his interests quickly, unable to follow it definitely, surely, vigorously–while they drove to his office. Cowperwood entered it with him for the sake of continuing his plea.

"Well, George," he said earnestly, "I wish you'd tell me. Time's short. We haven't a moment to lose. Give me the money, won't you, and I'll get out of this quick. We haven't a moment, I tell you. Don't let those people frighten you off. They're playing their own little game; you play yours."

"I can't, Frank," said Stener, finally, very weakly, his sense of his own financial future, overcome for the time being by the thought of Mollenhauer's hard, controlling face. "I'll have to think. I can't do it right now. Strobik just left me before I saw you, and–"

"Good God, George," exclaimed Cowperwood, scornfully, "don't talk about Strobik! What's he got to do with it? Think of yourself. Think of where you will be. It's your future–not Strobik's–that you have to think of."

"I know, Frank," persisted Stener, weakly; "but, really, I don't see how I can. Honestly I don't. You say yourself you're not sure whether you can come out of things all right, and three hundred thousand more is three hundred thousand more. I can't, Frank. I really can't. It wouldn't be right. Besides, I want to talk to Mollenhauer first, anyhow."

"Good God, how you talk!" exploded Cowperwood, angrily, looking at him with ill-concealed contempt. "Go ahead! See Mollenhauer! Let him tell you how to cut your own throat for his benefit. It won't be right to loan me three hundred thousand dollars more, but it will be right to let the five hundred thousand dollars you have loaned stand unprotected and lose it. That's right, isn't it? That's just what you propose to do–lose it, and everything else besides. I want to tell you what it is, George–you've lost your mind. You've let a single message from Mollenhauer frighten you to death, and because of that you're going to risk your fortune, your reputation, your standing–everything. Do you really realize what this means if I fail? You will be a convict, I tell you, George. You will go to prison. This fellow Mollenhauer, who is so quick to tell you what not to do now, will be the last man to turn a hand for you once you're down. Why, look at me–I've helped you, haven't I? Haven't I handled your affairs satisfactorily for you up to now? What in Heaven's name has got into you? What have you to be afraid of?"

Stener was just about to make another weak rejoinder when the door from the outer office opened, and Albert Stires, Stener's chief clerk, entered. Stener was too flustered to really pay any attention to Stires for the moment; but Cowperwood took matters in his own hands.

"What is it, Albert?" he asked, familiarly.

"Mr. Sengstack from Mr. Mollenhauer to see Mr. Stener."

At the sound of this dreadful name Stener wilted like a leaf. Cowperwood saw it. He realized that his last hope of getting the three hundred thousand dollars was now probably gone. Still he did not propose to give up as yet.

"Well, George," he said, after Albert had gone out with instructions that Stener would see Sengstack in a moment. "I see how it is. This man has got you mesmerized. You can't act for yourself now—you're too frightened. I'll let it rest for the present; I'll come back. But for Heaven's sake pull yourself together. Think what it means. I'm telling you exactly what's going to happen if you don't. You'll be independently rich if you do. You'll be a convict if you don't."

And deciding he would make one more effort in the street before seeing Butler again, he walked out briskly, jumped into his light spring runabout waiting outside—a handsome little yellow-glazed vehicle, with a yellow leather cushion seat, drawn by a young, high-stepping bay mare—and sent her scudding from door to door, throwing down the lines indifferently and bounding up the steps of banks and into office doors.

But all without avail. All were interested, considerate; but things were very uncertain. The Girard National Bank refused an hour's grace, and he had to send a large bundle of his most valuable securities to cover his stock shrinkage there. Word came from his father at two that as president of the Third National he would have to call for his one hundred and fifty thousand dollars due there. The directors were suspicious of his stocks. He at once wrote a check against fifty thousand dollars of his deposits in that bank, took twenty-five thousand of his available office funds, called a loan of fifty thousand against Tighe Co., and sold sixty thousand Green Coates, a line he had been tentatively dabbling in, for one-third their value—and, combining the general results, sent them all to the Third National. His father was immensely relieved from one point of view, but sadly depressed from another. He hurried out at the noon-hour to see what his own holdings would bring. He was compromising himself in a way by doing it, but his parental heart, as well as is own financial interests, were involved. By mortgaging his house and securing loans on his furniture, carriages, lots, and stocks, he managed to raise one hundred thousand in cash, and deposited it in his own bank to Frank's credit; but it was a very light anchor to windward in this swirling storm, at that. Frank had been counting on getting all of his loans extended three or four days at least. Reviewing his situation at two o'clock of this Monday afternoon, he said to himself thoughtfully but grimly: "Well, Stener has to loan me three hundred thousand—that's all there is to it. And I'll have to see Butler now, or he'll be calling his loan before three."

He hurried out, and was off to Butler's house, driving like mad.

Chapter XXVI

Things had changed greatly since last Cowperwood had talked with Butler. Although most friendly at the time the proposition was made that he should combine with Mollenhauer and Simpson to sustain the market, alas, now on this Monday morning at nine o'clock, an additional complication had been added to the already tangled situation which had changed Butler's attitude completely. As he was leaving his home to enter his runabout, at nine o'clock in the morning of this same day in which Cowperwood was seeking Stener's aid, the postman, coming up, had handed Butler four letters, all of which he paused for a moment to glance at. One was from a sub-contractor by the name of O'Higgins, the second was from Father Michel, his confessor, of St. Timothy's, thanking him for a contribution to the parish poor fund; a third was from Drexel Co. relating to a deposit, and the fourth was an anonymous communication, on cheap stationery from some one who was apparently not very literate–a woman most likely–written in a scrawling hand, which read:

DEAR SIR–This is to warn you that your daughter
Aileen is running around with a man that she shouldn't,
Frank A. Cowperwood, the banker. If you don't believe
it, watch the house at 931 North Tenth Street. Then you
can see for yourself.

There was neither signature nor mark of any kind to indicate from whence it might have come. Butler got the impression strongly that it might have been written by some one living in the vicinity of the number indicated. His intuitions were keen at times. As a matter of fact, it was written by a girl, a member of St. Timothy's Church, who did live in the vicinity of the house indicated, and who knew Aileen by sight and was jealous of her airs and her position. She was a thin, anemic, dissatisfied creature who had the type of brain which can reconcile the gratification of personal spite with a comforting sense of having fulfilled a moral duty. Her home was some five doors north of the unregistered Cowperwood domicile on the opposite side of the street, and by degrees, in the course of time, she made out, or imagined that she had, the significance of this institution, piecing fact to fancy and fusing all with that keen intuition which is so closely related to fact. The result was eventually this letter which now spread clear and grim before Butler's eyes.

The Irish are a philosophic as well as a practical race. Their first and strongest impulse is to make the best of a bad situation–to put a better face on evil than it normally wears. On first reading these lines the intelligence they conveyed sent a peculiar chill over Butler's sturdy frame. His jaw instinctively closed, and his gray eyes narrowed. Could this be true? If it were not, would the author of the letter say so practically, "If you don't believe it, watch the house at 931 North Tenth Street"? Wasn't that in itself proof positive–the hard, matter-of-fact realism of it? And this was the man who had come to him the night before seeking aid–whom he had done so much to assist. There forced itself into his naturally slow-moving but rather accurate mind a sense of the distinction and charm of his daughter–a considerably sharper picture than he had ever had before, and at the same time a keener understanding of the personality of Frank Algernon Cowperwood. How was it he had failed to detect the real subtlety of this man? How was it he had never seen any sign of it, if there had been anything between Cowperwood and Aileen?

Parents are frequently inclined, because of a time-flattered sense of security, to take their children for granted. Nothing ever has happened, so nothing ever will happen. They see their children every day, and through the eyes of affection; and despite their natural charm and their own strong parental love, the children are apt to become not only commonplaces, but ineffably secure against evil. Mary is naturally a good girl–a little wild, but what harm can befall her? John is a straight-forward, steady-going boy–how could he get into trouble? The astonishment of most parents at the sudden accidental revelation of evil in connection with any of their children is almost invariably pathetic. "My John! My Mary! Impossible!" But it is possible. Very possible. Decidedly likely. Some, through lack of experience or understanding, or both, grow hard and bitter on the instant. They feel themselves astonishingly abased in the face of notable tenderness and sacrifice. Others collapse before the grave manifestation of the insecurity and uncertainty of life–the mystic chemistry of our being. Still others, taught roughly by life, or endowed with understanding or intuition, or both, see in this the latest manifestation of that incomprehensible chemistry which we call life and personality, and, knowing that it is quite vain to hope to gainsay it, save by greater subtlety, put the best face they can upon the matter and call a truce until they can think. We all know that life is unsolvable–we who think. The remainder imagine a vain thing, and are full of sound and fury signifying nothing.

So Edward Butler, being a man of much wit and hard, grim experience, stood there on his doorstep holding in his big, rough hand his thin slip of cheap paper which contained such a terrific indictment of his daughter. There came to him now a picture of her as she was when she was a very little girl–she was his first baby girl–and how keenly he had felt about her all these years. She had been a beautiful child–her red-gold hair had been pillowed on his breast many a time, and his hard, rough fingers had stroked her soft cheeks, lo, these thousands of times. Aileen, his lovely, dashing daughter of twenty-three! He was lost in dark, strange, unhappy speculations, without any present ability to think or say or do the right thing. He did not know what the right thing was, he finally confessed to himself. Aileen! Aileen! His Aileen! If her mother knew this it would break her heart. She mustn't! She mustn't! And yet mustn't she?

The heart of a father! The world wanders into many strange by-paths of affection. The love of a mother for her children is dominant, leonine, selfish, and unselfish. It is concentric. The love of a husband for his wife, or of a lover for his sweetheart, is a sweet bond of agreement and exchange trade in a lovely contest. The love of a father for his son or daughter, where it is love at all, is a broad, generous, sad, contemplative giving without thought of return, a hail and farewell to a troubled traveler whom he would do much to guard, a balanced judgment of weakness and strength, with pity for failure and pride in achievement. It is a lovely, generous, philosophic blossom which rarely asks too much, and seeks only to give wisely and plentifully. "That my boy may succeed! That my daughter may be happy!" Who has not heard and dwelt upon these twin fervors of fatherly wisdom and tenderness?

As Butler drove downtown his huge, slow-moving, in some respects chaotic mind turned over as rapidly as he could all of the possibilities in connection with this unexpected, sad, and disturbing revelation. Why had Cowperwood not been satisfied with his wife? Why should he enter into his (Butler's) home, of all places, to establish a clandestine relationship of this character? Was Aileen in any way to blame? She was not without mental resources of her own. She must have known what she was doing. She was a good Catholic, or, at least, had been raised so. All these years she had been going regularly to confession and communion. True, of late Butler had noticed that she did not care so much about going to church, would sometimes make excuses and stay at home on Sundays; but she had gone, as a rule. And now, now–his thoughts would come to the end of a blind alley, and then he would start back, as it were, mentally, to the center of things, and begin all over again.

He went up the stairs to his own office slowly. He went in and sat down, and thought and thought. Ten o'clock came, and eleven. His son bothered him with an occasional matter of interest, but, finding him moody, finally abandoned him to his own speculations. It was twelve, and then one, and he was still sitting there thinking, when the presence of Cowperwood was announced.

Cowperwood, on finding Butler not at home, and not encountering Aileen, had hurried up to the office of the Edward Butler Contracting Company, which was also the center of some of Butler's street-railway interests. The floor space controlled by the company was divided into the usual official compartments, with sections for the bookkeepers, the road-managers, the treasurer, and so on. Owen Butler, and his father had small but attractively furnished offices in the rear, where they transacted all the important business of the company.

During this drive, curiously, by reason of one of those strange psychologic intuitions which so often precede a human difficulty of one sort or another, he had been thinking of Aileen. He was thinking of the peculiarity of his relationship with her, and of the fact that now he was running to her father for assistance. As he mounted the stairs he had a peculiar sense of the untoward; but he could not, in his view of life, give it countenance. One glance at Butler showed him that something had gone amiss. He was not so friendly; his glance was dark, and there was a certain sternness to his countenance which had never previously been manifested there in Cowperwood's memory. He perceived at once that here was something different from a mere intention to refuse him aid and call his loan. What was it? Aileen? It must be that. Somebody had suggested something. They had been seen together. Well, even so, nothing could be proved. Butler would obtain no sign from him. But his loan–that was to be called, surely. And as for an additional loan, he could see now, before a word had been said, that that thought was useless.

"I came to see you about that loan of yours, Mr. Butler," he observed, briskly, with an old-time, jaunty air. You could not have told from his manner or his face that he had observed anything out of the ordinary.

Butler, who was alone in the room–Owen having gone into an adjoining room–merely stared at him from under his shaggy brows.

"I'll have to have that money," he said, brusquely, darkly.

An old-time Irish rage suddenly welled up in his bosom as he contemplated this jaunty, sophisticated undoer of his daughter's virtue. He fairly glared at him as he thought of him and her.

"I judged from the way things were going this morning that you might want it," Cowperwood replied, quietly, without sign of tremor. "The bottom's out, I see."

"The bottom's out, and it'll not be put back soon, I'm thinkin'. I'll have to have what's belongin' to me to-day. I haven't any time to spare."

"Very well," replied Cowperwood, who saw clearly how treacherous the situation was. The old man was in a dour mood. His presence was an irritation to him, for some reason–a deadly provocation. Cowperwood felt clearly that it must be Aileen, that he must know or suspect something.

He must pretend business hurry and end this. "I'm sorry. I thought I might get an extension; but that's all right. I can get the money, though. I'll send it right over."

He turned and walked quickly to the door.

Butler got up. He had thought to manage this differently.

He had thought to denounce or even assault this man. He was about to make some insinuating remark which would compel an answer, some direct charge; but Cowperwood was out and away as jaunty as ever.

The old man was flustered, enraged, disappointed. He opened the small office door which led into the adjoining room, and called, "Owen!"

"Yes, father."

"Send over to Cowperwood's office and get that money."

"You decided to call it, eh?"

"I have."

Owen was puzzled by the old man's angry mood. He wondered what it all meant, but thought he and Cowperwood might have had a few words. He went out to his desk to write a note and call a clerk. Butler went to the window and stared out. He was angry, bitter, brutal in his vein.

"The dirty dog!" he suddenly exclaimed to himself, in a low voice. "I'll take every dollar he's got before I'm through with him. I'll send him to jail, I will. I'll break him, I will. Wait!"

He clinched his big fists and his teeth.

"I'll fix him. I'll show him. The dog! The damned scoundrel!"

Never in his life before had he been so bitter, so cruel, so relentless in his mood.

He walked his office floor thinking what he could do. Question Aileen–that was what he would do. If her face, or her lips, told him that his suspicion was true, he would deal with Cowperwood later. This city treasurer business, now. It was not a crime in so far as Cowperwood was concerned; but it might be made to be.

So now, telling the clerk to say to Owen that he had gone down the street for a few moments, he boarded a street-car and rode out to his home, where he found his elder daughter just getting ready to go out. She wore a purple-velvet street dress edged with narrow, flat gilt braid, and a striking gold-and-purple turban. She had on dainty new boots of bronze kid and long gloves of lavender suede. In her ears was one of her latest affectations, a pair of long jet earrings. The old Irishman realized on this occasion, when he saw her, perhaps more clearly than he ever had in his life, that he had grown a bird of rare plumage.

"Where are you going, daughter?" he asked, with a rather unsuccessful attempt to conceal his fear, distress, and smoldering anger.

"To the library," she said easily, and yet with a sudden realization that all was not right with her father. His face was too heavy and gray. He looked tired and gloomy.

"Come up to my office a minute," he said. "I want to see you before you go."

Aileen heard this with a strange feeling of curiosity and wonder. It was not customary for her father to want to see her in his office just when she was going out; and his manner indicated, in this instance, that the exceptional procedure portended a strange revelation of some kind. Aileen, like every other person who offends against a rigid convention of the time, was conscious of and sensitive to the possible disastrous results which would follow exposure. She had often thought about what her family would think if they knew what she was doing; she had never been able to satisfy herself in her mind as to what they would do. Her father was a very vigorous man. But she had never known him to be cruel or cold in his attitude toward her or any other member of the family, and especially not toward her. Always he seemed too fond of her to be completely alienated by anything that might happen; yet she could not be sure.

Butler led the way, planting his big feet solemnly on the steps as he went up. Aileen followed with a single glance at herself in the tall pier-mirror which stood in the hall, realizing at once how charming she looked and how uncertain she was feeling about what was to follow. What could her father want? It made the color leave her cheeks for the moment, as she thought what he might want.

Butler strolled into his stuffy room and sat down in the big leather chair, disproportioned to everything else in the chamber, but which, nevertheless, accompanied his desk. Before him, against the light, was the visitor's chair, in which he liked to have those sit whose faces he was anxious to study. When Aileen entered he motioned her to it, which was also ominous to her, and said, "Sit down there."

She took the seat, not knowing what to make of his procedure. On the instant her promise to Cowperwood to deny everything, whatever happened, came back to her. If her father was about to attack her on that score, he would get no satisfaction, she thought. She owed it to Frank. Her pretty face strengthened and hardened on the instant. Her small, white teeth set themselves in two even rows; and her father saw quite plainly that she was consciously bracing herself for an attack of some kind. He feared by this that she was guilty, and he was all the more distressed, ashamed, outraged, made wholly unhappy. He fumbled in the left-hand pocket of his coat and drew forth from among the various papers the fatal communication so cheap in its physical texture. His big fingers fumbled almost tremulously as he fished the letter-sheet out of the small envelope and unfolded it without saying a word. Aileen watched his face and his hands, wondering what it could be that he had here. He handed the paper over, small in his big fist, and said, "Read that."

Aileen took it, and for a second was relieved to be able to lower her eyes to the paper. Her relief vanished in a second, when she realized how in a moment she would have to raise them again and look him in the face.

DEAR SIR–This is to warn you that your daughter
Aileen is running around with a man that she shouldn't,
Frank A. Cowperwood, the banker. If you don't believe
it, watch the house at 931 North Tenth Street. Then you
can see for yourself.

In spite of herself the color fled from her cheeks instantly, only to come back in a hot, defiant wave.

"Why, what a lie!" she said, lifting her eyes to her father's. "To think that any one should write such a thing of me! How dare they! I think it's a shame!"

Old Butler looked at her narrowly, solemnly. He was not deceived to any extent by her bravado. If she were really innocent, he knew she would have jumped to her feet in her defiant way. Protest would have been written all over her. As it was, she only stared haughtily. He read through her eager defiance to the guilty truth.

"How do ye know, daughter, that I haven't had the house watched?" he said, quizzically. "How do ye know that ye haven't been seen goin' in there?"

Only Aileen's solemn promise to her lover could have saved her from this subtle thrust. As it was, she paled nervously; but she saw Frank Cowperwood, solemn and distinguished, asking her what she would say if she were caught.

"It's a lie!" she said, catching her breath. "I wasn't at any house at that number, and no one saw me going in there. How can you ask me that, father?"

In spite of his mixed feelings of uncertainty and yet unshakable belief that his daughter was guilty, he could not help admiring her courage–she was so defiant, as she sat there, so set in her determination to lie and thus defend herself. Her beauty helped her in his mood, raised her in his esteem. After all, what could you do with a woman of this kind? She was not a ten-year-old girl any more, as in a way he sometimes continued to fancy her.

"Ye oughtn't to say that if it isn't true, Aileen," he said. "Ye oughtn't to lie. It's against your faith. Why would anybody write a letter like that if it wasn't so?"

"But it's not so," insisted Aileen, pretending anger and outraged feeling, "and I don't think you have any right to sit there and say that to me. I haven't been there, and I'm not running around with Mr. Cowperwood. Why, I hardly know the man except in a social way."

Butler shook his head solemnly.

"It's a great blow to me, daughter. It's a great blow to me," he said. "I'm willing to take your word if ye say so; but I can't help thinkin' what a sad thing it would be if ye were lyin' to me. I haven't had the house watched. I only got this this mornin'. And what's written here may not be so. I hope it isn't. But we'll not say any more about that now. If there is anythin' in it, and ye haven't gone too far yet to save yourself, I want ye to think of your mother and your sister and your brothers, and be a good girl. Think of the church ye was raised in, and the name we've got to stand up for in the world. Why, if ye were doin' anything wrong, and the people of Philadelphy got a hold of it, the city, big as it is, wouldn't be big enough to hold us. Your brothers have got a reputation to make, their work to do here. You and your sister want to get married sometime. How could ye expect to look the world in the face and do anythin' at all if ye are doin' what this letter says ye are, and it was told about ye?"

The old man's voice was thick with a strange, sad, alien emotion. He did not want to believe that his daughter was guilty, even though he knew she was. He did not want to face what he considered in his vigorous, religious way to be his duty, that of reproaching her sternly. There were some fathers who would have turned her out, he fancied. There were others who might possibly kill Cowperwood after a subtle investigation. That course was not for him. If vengeance he was to have, it must be through politics and finance–he must drive him out. But as for doing anything desperate in connection with Aileen, he could not think of it.

"Oh, father," returned Aileen, with considerable histrionic ability in her assumption of pettishness, "how can you talk like this when you know I'm not guilty? When I tell you so?"

The old Irishman saw through her make-believe with profound sadness—the feeling that one of his dearest hopes had been shattered. He had expected so much of her socially and matrimonially. Why, any one of a dozen remarkable young men might have married her, and she would have had lovely children to comfort him in his old age.

"Well, we'll not talk any more about it now, daughter," he said, wearily. "Ye've been so much to me during all these years that I can scarcely belave anythin' wrong of ye. I don't want to, God knows. Ye're a grown woman, though, now; and if ye are doin' anythin' wrong I don't suppose I could do so much to stop ye. I might turn ye out, of course, as many a father would; but I wouldn't like to do anythin' like that. But if ye are doin' anythin' wrong"—and he put up his hand to stop a proposed protest on the part of Aileen—"remember, I'm certain to find it out in the long run, and Philadelphy won't be big enough to hold me and the man that's done this thing to me. I'll get him," he said, getting up dramatically. "I'll get him, and when I do—" He turned a livid face to the wall, and Aileen saw clearly that Cowperwood, in addition to any other troubles which might beset him, had her father to deal with. Was this why Frank had looked so sternly at her the night before?

"Why, your mother would die of a broken heart if she thought there was anybody could say the least word against ye," pursued Butler, in a shaken voice. "This man has a family—a wife and children, Ye oughtn't to want to do anythin' to hurt them. They'll have trouble enough, if I'm not mistaken—facin' what's comin' to them in the future," and Butler's jaw hardened just a little. "Ye're a beautiful girl. Ye're young. Ye have money. There's dozens of young men'd be proud to make ye their wife. Whatever ye may be thinkin' or doin', don't throw away your life. Don't destroy your immortal soul. Don't break my heart entirely."

Aileen, not ungenerous—fool of mingled affection and passion—could now have cried. She pitied her father from her heart; but her allegiance was to Cowperwood, her loyalty unshaken. She wanted to say something, to protest much more; but she knew that it was useless. Her father knew that she was lying.

"Well, there's no use of my saying anything more, father," she said, getting up. The light of day was fading in the windows. The downstairs door closed with a light slam, indicating that one of the boys had come in. Her proposed trip to the library was now without interest to her. "You won't believe me, anyhow. I tell you, though, that I'm innocent just the same."

Butler lifted his big, brown hand to command silence. She saw that this shameful relationship, as far as her father was concerned, had been made quite clear, and that this trying conference was now at an end. She turned and walked shamefacedly out. He waited until he heard her steps fading into faint nothings down the hall toward her room. Then he arose. Once more he clinched his big fists.

"The scoundrel!" he said. "The scoundrel! I'll drive him out of Philadelphy, if it takes the last dollar I have in the world."

Chapter XXVII

For the first time in his life Cowperwood felt conscious of having been in the presence of that interesting social phenomenon–the outraged sentiment of a parent. While he had no absolute knowledge as to why Butler had been so enraged, he felt that Aileen was the contributing cause. He himself was a father. His boy, Frank, Jr., was to him not so remarkable. But little Lillian, with her dainty little slip of a body and bright-aureoled head, had always appealed to him. She was going to be a charming woman one day, he thought, and he was going to do much to establish her safely. He used to tell her that she had "eyes like buttons," "feet like a pussy-cat," and hands that were "just five cents' worth," they were so little. The child admired her father and would often stand by his chair in the library or the sitting-room, or his desk in his private office, or by his seat at the table, asking him questions.

This attitude toward his own daughter made him see clearly how Butler might feel toward Aileen. He wondered how he would feel if it were his own little Lillian, and still he did not believe he would make much fuss over the matter, either with himself or with her, if she were as old as Aileen. Children and their lives were more or less above the willing of parents, anyhow, and it would be a difficult thing for any parent to control any child, unless the child were naturally docile-minded and willing to be controlled.

It also made him smile, in a grim way, to see how fate was raining difficulties on him. The Chicago fire, Stener's early absence, Butler, Mollenhauer, and Simpson's indifference to Stener's fate and his. And now this probable revelation in connection with Aileen. He could not be sure as yet, but his intuitive instincts told him that it must be something like this.

Now he was distressed as to what Aileen would do, say if suddenly she were confronted by her father. If he could only get to her! But if he was to meet Butler's call for his loan, and the others which would come yet to-day or on the morrow, there was not a moment to lose. If he did not pay he must assign at once. Butler's rage, Aileen, his own danger, were brushed aside for the moment. His mind concentrated wholly on how to save himself financially.

He hurried to visit George Waterman; David Wiggin, his wife's brother, who was now fairly well to do; Joseph Zimmerman, the wealthy dry-goods dealer who had dealt with him in the past; Judge Kitchen, a private manipulator of considerable wealth; Frederick Van Nostrand, the State treasurer, who was interested in local street-railway stocks, and others. Of all those to whom he appealed one was actually not in a position to do anything for him; another was afraid; a third was calculating eagerly to drive a hard bargain; a fourth was too deliberate, anxious to have much time. All scented the true value of his situation, all wanted time to consider, and he had no time to consider. Judge Kitchen did agree to lend him thirty thousand dollars–a paltry sum. Joseph Zimmerman would only risk twenty-five thousand dollars. He could see where, all told, he might raise seventy-five thousand dollars by hypothecating double the amount in shares; but this was ridiculously insufficient. He had figured again, to a dollar, and he must have at least two hundred and fifty thousand dollars above all his present holdings, or he must close his doors. To-morrow at two o'clock he would know. If he didn't he would be written down as "failed" on a score of ledgers in Philadelphia.

What a pretty pass for one to come to whose hopes had so recently run so high! There was a loan of one hundred thousand dollars from the Girard National Bank which he was particularly anxious to clear off. This bank was the most important in the city, and if he retained its good will by meeting this loan promptly he might hope for favors in the future whatever happened. Yet, at the moment, he did not see how he could do it. He decided, however, after some reflection, that he would deliver the stocks which Judge Kitchen, Zimmerman, and others had agreed to take and get their checks or cash yet this night. Then he would persuade Stener to let him have a check for the sixty thousand dollars' worth of city loan he had purchased this morning on 'change. Out of it he could take twenty-five thousand dollars to make up the balance due the bank, and still have thirty-five thousand for himself.

The one unfortunate thing about such an arrangement was that by doing it he was building up a rather complicated situation in regard to these same certificates. Since their purchase in the morning, he had not deposited them in the sinking-fund, where they belonged (they had been delivered to his office by half past one in the afternoon), but, on the contrary, had immediately hypothecated them to cover another loan. It was a risky thing to have done, considering that he was in danger of failing and that he was not absolutely sure of being able to take them up in time.

But, he reasoned, he had a working agreement with the city treasurer (illegal of course), which would make such a transaction rather plausible, and almost all right, even if he failed, and that was that none of his accounts were supposed necessarily to be put straight until the end of the month. If he failed, and the certificates were not in the sinking-fund, he could say, as was the truth, that he was in the habit of taking his time, and had forgotten. This collecting of a check, therefore, for these as yet undeposited certificates would be technically, if not legally and morally, plausible. The city would be out only an additional sixty thousand dollars–making five hundred and sixty thousand dollars all told, which in view of its probable loss of five hundred thousand did not make so much difference. But his caution clashed with his need on this occasion, and he decided that he would not call for the check unless Stener finally refused to aid him with three hundred thousand more, in which case he would claim it as his right. In all likelihood Stener would not think to ask whether the certificates were in the sinking-fund or not. If he did, he would have to lie–that was all.

He drove rapidly back to his office, and, finding Butler's note, as he expected, wrote a check on his father's bank for the one hundred thousand dollars which had been placed to his credit by his loving parent, and sent it around to Butler's office. There was another note, from Albert Stires, Stener's secretary, advising him not to buy or sell any more city loan–that until further notice such transactions would not be honored. Cowperwood immediately sensed the source of this warning. Stener had been in conference with Butler or Mollenhauer, and had been warned and frightened. Nevertheless, he got in his buggy again and drove directly to the city treasurer's office.

Since Cowperwood's visit Stener had talked still more with Sengstack, Strobik, and others, all sent to see that a proper fear of things financial had been put in his heart. The result was decidedly one which spelled opposition to Cowperwood.

Strobik was considerably disturbed himself. He and Wycroft and Harmon had also been using money out of the treasury–much smaller sums, of course, for they had not

Cowperwood's financial imagination–and were disturbed as to how they would return what they owed before the storm broke. If Cowperwood failed, and Stener was short in his accounts, the whole budget might be investigated, and then their loans would be brought to light. The thing to do was to return what they owed, and then, at least, no charge of malfeasance would lie against them.

"Go to Mollenhauer," Strobik had advised Stener, shortly after Cowperwood had left the latter's office, "and tell him the whole story. He put you here. He was strong for your nomination. Tell him just where you stand and ask him what to do. He'll probably be able to tell you. Offer him your holdings to help you out. You have to. You can't help yourself. Don't loan Cowperwood another damned dollar, whatever you do. He's got you in so deep now you can hardly hope to get out. Ask Mollenhauer if he won't help you to get Cowperwood to put that money back. He may be able to influence him."

There was more in this conversation to the same effect, and then Stener hurried as fast as his legs could carry him to Mollenhauer's office. He was so frightened that he could scarcely breathe, and he was quite ready to throw himself on his knees before the big German-American financier and leader. Oh, if Mr. Mollenhauer would only help him! If he could just get out of this without going to jail!

"Oh, Lord! Oh, Lord! Oh, Lord!" he repeated, over and over to himself, as he walked. "What shall I do?"

The attitude of Henry A. Mollenhauer, grim, political boss that he was–trained in a hard school–was precisely the attitude of every such man in all such trying circumstances.

He was wondering, in view of what Butler had told him, just how much he could advantage himself in this situation. If he could, he wanted to get control of whatever street-railway stock Stener now had, without in any way compromising himself. Stener's shares could easily be transferred on 'change through Mollenhauer's brokers to a dummy, who would eventually transfer them to himself (Mollenhauer). Stener must be squeezed thoroughly, though, this afternoon, and as for his five hundred thousand dollars' indebtedness to the treasury, Mollenhauer did not see what could be done about that. If Cowperwood could not pay it, the city would have to lose it; but the scandal must be hushed up until after election. Stener, unless the various party leaders had more generosity than Mollenhauer imagined, would have to suffer exposure, arrest, trial, confiscation of his property, and possibly sentence to the penitentiary, though this might easily be commuted by the governor, once public excitement died down. He did not trouble to think whether Cowperwood was criminally involved or not. A hundred to one he was not. Trust a shrewd man like that to take care of himself. But if there was any way to shoulder the blame on to Cowperwood, and so clear the treasurer and the skirts of the party, he would not object to that. He wanted to hear the full story of Stener's relations with the broker first. Meanwhile, the thing to do was to seize what Stener had to yield.

The troubled city treasurer, on being shown in Mr. Mollenhauer's presence, at once sank feebly in a chair and collapsed. He was entirely done for mentally. His nerve was gone, his courage exhausted like a breath.

"Well, Mr. Stener?" queried Mr. Mollenhauer, impressively, pretending not to know what brought him.

"I came about this matter of my loans to Mr. Cowperwood."

"Well, what about them?"

"Well, he owes me, or the city treasury rather, five hundred thousand dollars, and I understand that he is going to fail and that he can't pay it back."

"Who told you that?"

"Mr. Sengstack, and since then Mr. Cowperwood has been to see me. He tells me he must have more money or he will fail and he wants to borrow three hundred thousand dollars more. He says he must have it."

"So!" said Mr. Mollenhauer, impressively, and with an air of astonishment which he did not feel. "You would not think of doing that, of course. You're too badly involved as it is. If he wants to know why, refer him to me. Don't advance him another dollar. If you do, and this case comes to trial, no court would have any mercy on you. It's going to be difficult enough to do anything for you as it is. However, if you don't advance him any more—we will see. It may be possible, I can't say, but at any rate, no more money must leave the treasury to bolster up this bad business. It's much too difficult as it now is." He stared at Stener warningly. And he, shaken and sick, yet because of the faint suggestion of mercy involved somewhere in Mollenhauer's remarks, now slipped from his chair to his knees and folded his hands in the uplifted attitude of a devotee before a sacred image.

"Oh, Mr. Mollenhauer," he choked, beginning to cry, "I didn't mean to do anything wrong. Strobik and Wycroft told me it was all right. You sent me to Cowperwood in the first place. I only did what I thought the others had been doing. Mr. Bode did it, just like I have been doing. He dealt with Tighe and Company. I have a wife and four children, Mr. Mollenhauer. My youngest boy is only seven years old. Think of them, Mr. Mollenhauer! Think of what my arrest will mean to them! I don't want to go to jail. I didn't think I was doing anything very wrong—honestly I didn't. I'll give up all I've got. You can have all my stocks and houses and lots—anything—if you'll only get me out of this. You won't let 'em send me to jail, will you?"

His fat, white lips were trembling—wabbling nervously—and big hot tears were coursing down his previously pale but now flushed cheeks. He presented one of those almost unbelievable pictures which are yet so intensely human and so true. If only the great financial and political giants would for once accurately reveal the details of their lives!

Mollenhauer looked at him calmly, meditatively. How often had he seen weaklings no more dishonest than himself, but without his courage and subtlety, pleading to him in this fashion, not on their knees exactly, but intellectually so! Life to him, as to every other man of large practical knowledge and insight, was an inexplicable tangle. What were you going to do about the so-called morals and precepts of the world? This man Stener fancied that he was dishonest, and that he, Mollenhauer, was honest. He was here, self-convicted of sin, pleading to him, Mollenhauer, as he would to a righteous, unstained saint. As a matter of fact, Mollenhauer knew that he was simply shrewder, more far-seeing, more calculating, not less dishonest. Stener was lacking in force and brains—not morals. This lack was his principal crime. There were people who believed in some esoteric standard of right–some ideal of conduct absolutely and very far removed from practical life; but he had never seen them practice it save to their own financial (not moral–he would not say that) destruction. They were never significant, practical men who clung to these fatuous ideals. They were always poor, nondescript, negligible dreamers. He could not have made Stener understand all this if he had wanted to, and he certainly did not want to. It was too bad about Mrs. Stener and the little Steners. No doubt she had worked hard, as had Stener, to get up in the world and be something–just a little more than miserably poor; and now this unfortunate complication had to arise to undo them–this Chicago fire. What a curious thing that was! If any one thing more than another made him doubt the existence of a kindly, overruling Providence, it was the unheralded storms out of clear skies– financial, social, anything you choose–that so often brought ruin and disaster to so many.

"Get Up, Stener," he said, calmly, after a few moments. "You mustn't give way to your feelings like this. You must not cry. These troubles are never unraveled by tears. You must do a little thinking for yourself. Perhaps your situation isn't so bad."

As he was saying this Stener was putting himself back in his chair, getting out his handkerchief, and sobbing hopelessly in it.

"I'll do what I can, Stener. I won't promise anything. I can't tell you what the result will be. There are many peculiar political forces in this city. I may not be able to save you, but I am perfectly willing to try. You must put yourself absolutely under my direction. You must not say or do anything without first consulting with me. I will send my secretary to you from time to time. He will tell you what to do. You must not come to me unless I send for you. Do you understand that thoroughly?"

"Yes, Mr. Mollenhauer."

"Well, now, dry your eyes. I don't want you to go out of this office crying. Go back to your office, and I will send Sengstack to see you. He will tell you what to do. Follow him exactly. And whenever I send for you come at once."

He got up, large, self-confident, reserved. Stener, buoyed up by the subtle reassurance of his remarks, recovered to a degree his equanimity. Mr. Mollenhauer, the great, powerful Mr. Mollenhauer was going to help him out of his scrape. He might not have to go to jail after all. He left after a few moments, his face a little red from weeping, but otherwise free of telltale marks, and returned to his office.

Three-quarters of an hour later, Sengstack called on him for the second time that day–Abner Sengstack, small, dark-faced, club-footed, a great sole of leather three inches thick under his short, withered right leg, his slightly Slavic, highly intelligent countenance burning with a pair of keen, piercing, inscrutable black eyes. Sengstack was a fit secretary for Mollenhauer. You could see at one glance that he would make Stener do exactly what Mollenhauer suggested. His business was to induce Stener to part with his street-railway holdings at once through Tighe Co., Butler's brokers, to the political sub-agent who would eventually transfer them to Mollenhauer. What little Stener received for them might well go into the treasury. Tighe Co. would manage the "'change" subtleties of this without giving any one else a chance to bid, while at the same time making it appear an open-market transaction. At the same time Sengstack went carefully into the state of the treasurer's office for his master's benefit–finding out what it was that Strobik, Wycroft, and Harmon had been doing with their loans. Via another source they were ordered to disgorge at once or face prosecution. They were a part of Mollenhauer's political machine. Then, having cautioned Stener not to set over the remainder of his property to any one, and not to listen to any one, most of all to the Machiavellian counsel of Cowperwood, Sengstack left.

Needless to say, Mollenhauer was greatly gratified by this turn of affairs. Cowperwood was now most likely in a position where he would have to come and see him, or if not, a good share of the properties he controlled were already in Mollenhauer's possession. If by some hook or crook he could secure the remainder, Simpson and Butler might well talk to him about this street-railway business. His holdings were now as large as any, if not quite the largest.

Chapter XXVIII

It was in the face of this very altered situation that Cowperwood arrived at Stener's office late this Monday afternoon.

Stener was quite alone, worried and distraught. He was anxious to see Cowperwood, and at the same time afraid.

"George," began Cowperwood, briskly, on seeing him, "I haven't much time to spare now, but I've come, finally, to tell you that you'll have to let me have three hundred thousand more if you don't want me to fail. Things are looking very bad today. They've caught me in a corner on my loans; but this storm isn't going to last. You can see by the very character of it that it can't."

He was looking at Stener's face, and seeing fear and a pained and yet very definite necessity for opposition written there. "Chicago is burning, but it will be built up again. Business will be all the better for it later on. Now, I want you to be reasonable and help me. Don't get frightened."

Stener stirred uneasily. "Don't let these politicians scare you to death. It will all blow over in a few days, and then we'll be better off than ever. Did you see Mollenhauer?"

"Yes."

"Well, what did he have to say?"

"He said just what I thought he'd say. He won't let me do this. I can't, Frank, I tell you!" exclaimed Stener, jumping up. He was so nervous that he had had a hard time keeping his seat during this short, direct conversation. "I can't! They've got me in a corner! They're after me! They all know what we've been doing. Oh, say, Frank"–he threw up his arms wildly–"you've got to get me out of this. You've got to let me have that five hundred thousand back and get me out of this. If you don't, and you should fail, they'll send me to the penitentiary. I've got a wife and four children, Frank. I can't go on in this. It's too big for me. I never should have gone in on it in the first place. I never would have if you hadn't persuaded me, in a way. I never thought when I began that I would ever get in as bad as all this. I can't go on, Frank. I can't! I'm willing you should have all my stock. Only give me back that five hundred thousand, and we'll call it even." His voice rose nervously as he talked, and he wiped his wet forehead with his hand and stared at Cowperwood pleadingly, foolishly.

Cowperwood stared at him in return for a few moments with a cold, fishy eye. He knew a great deal about human nature, and he was ready for and expectant of any queer shift in an individual's attitude, particularly in time of panic; but this shift of Stener's was quite too much. "Whom else have you been talking to, George, since I saw you? Whom have you seen? What did Sengstack have to say?"

"He says just what Mollenhauer does, that I mustn't loan any more money under any circumstances, and he says I ought to get that five hundred thousand back as quickly as possible."

"And you think Mollenhauer wants to help you, do you?" inquired Cowperwood, finding it hard to efface the contempt which kept forcing itself into his voice.

"I think he does, yes. I don't know who else will, Frank, if he don't. He's one of the big political forces in this town."

"Listen to me," began Cowperwood, eyeing him fixedly. Then he paused. "What did he say you should do about your holdings?"

"Sell them through Tighe Company and put the money back in the treasury, if you won't take them."

"Sell them to whom?" asked Cowperwood, thinking of Stener's last words.

"To any one on 'change who'll take them, I suppose. I don't know."

"I thought so," said Cowperwood, comprehendingly. "I might have known as much. They're working you, George. They're simply trying to get your stocks away from you. Mollenhauer is leading you on. He knows I can't do what you want–give you back the five hundred thousand dollars. He wants you to throw your stocks on the market so that he can pick them up. Depend on it, that's all arranged for already. When you do, he's got me in his clutches, or he thinks he has–he and Butler and Simpson. They want to get together on this local street-railway situation, and I know it, I feel it. I've felt it coming all along. Mollenhauer hasn't any more intention of helping you than he has of flying. Once you've sold your stocks he's through with you–mark my word. Do you think he'll turn a hand to keep you out of the penitentiary once you're out of this street-railway situation? He will not. And if you think so, you're a bigger fool than I take you to be, George. Don't go crazy. Don't lose your head. Be sensible. Look the situation in the face. Let me explain it to you. If you don't help me now–if you don't let me have three hundred thousand dollars by to-morrow noon, at the very latest, I'm through, and so are you. There is not a thing the matter with our situation. Those stocks of ours are as good to-day as they ever were. Why, great heavens, man, the railways are there behind them. They're paying. The Seventeenth and Nineteenth Street line is earning one thousand dollars a day right now. What better evidence do you want than that? Green Coates is earning five hundred dollars. You're frightened, George. These damned political schemers have scared you. Why, you've as good a right to loan that money as Bode and Murtagh had before you. They did it. You've been doing it for Mollenhauer and the others, only so long as you do it for them it's all right. What's a designated city depository but a loan?"

Cowperwood was referring to the system under which certain portions of city money, like the sinking-fund, were permitted to be kept in certain banks at a low rate of interest or no rate–banks in which Mollenhauer and Butler and Simpson were interested. This was their safe graft.

"Don't throw your chances away, George. Don't quit now. You'll be worth millions in a few years, and you won't have to turn a hand. All you will have to do will be to keep what you have. If you don't help me, mark my word, they'll throw you over the moment I'm out of this, and they'll let you go to the penitentiary. Who's going to put up five hundred thousand dollars for you, George? Where is Mollenhauer going to get it, or Butler, or anybody, in these times? They can't. They don't intend to. When I'm through, you're through, and you'll be exposed quicker than any one else. They can't hurt me, George. I'm an agent. I didn't ask you to come to me. You came to me in the first place of your own accord. If you don't help me, you're through, I tell you, and you're going to be sent to the penitentiary as sure as there are jails. Why don't you take a stand, George? Why don't you stand your ground? You have your wife and children to look after. You can't be any worse off loaning me three hundred thousand more than you are right now. What difference does it make–five hundred thousand or eight hundred thousand? It's all one and the same thing, if you're going to be tried for it. Besides, if you loan me this, there isn't going to be any trial. I'm not going to fail. This storm will blow over in a week or ten days, and we'll be rich again. For Heaven's sake, George, don't go to pieces this way! Be sensible! Be reasonable!"

He paused, for Stener's face had become a jelly-like mass of woe.

"I can't, Frank," he wailed. "I tell you I can't. They'll punish me worse than ever if I do that. They'll never let up on me. You don't know these people."

In Stener's crumpling weakness Cowperwood read his own fate. What could you do with a man like that? How brace him up? You couldn't! And with a gesture of infinite understanding, disgust, noble indifference, he threw up his hands and started to walk out. At the door he turned.

"George," he said, "I'm sorry. I'm sorry for you, not for myself. I'll come out of things all right, eventually. I'll be rich. But, George, you're making the one great mistake of your life. You'll be poor; you'll be a convict, and you'll have only yourself to blame. There isn't a thing the matter with this money situation except the fire. There isn't a thing wrong with my affairs except this slump in stocks–this panic. You sit there, a fortune in your hands, and you allow a lot of schemers, highbinders, who don't know any more of your affairs or mine than a rabbit, and who haven't any interest in you except to plan what they can get out of you, to frighten you and prevent you from doing the one thing that will save your life. Three hundred thousand paltry dollars that in three or four weeks from now I can pay back to you four and five times over, and for that you will see me go broke and yourself to the penitentiary. I can't understand it, George. You're out of your mind. You're going to rue this the longest day that you live."

He waited a few moments to see if this, by any twist of chance, would have any effect; then, noting that Stener still remained a wilted, helpless mass of nothing, he shook his head gloomily and walked out.

It was the first time in his life that Cowperwood had ever shown the least sign of weakening or despair. He had felt all along as though there were nothing to the Greek theory of being pursued by the furies. Now, however, there seemed an untoward fate which was pursuing him. It looked that way. Still, fate or no fate, he did not propose to be daunted. Even in this very beginning of a tendency to feel despondent he threw back his head, expanded his chest, and walked as briskly as ever.

In the large room outside Stener's private office he encountered Albert Stires, Stener's chief clerk and secretary. He and Albert had exchanged many friendly greetings in times past, and all the little minor transactions in regard to city loan had been discussed between them, for Albert knew more of the intricacies of finance and financial bookkeeping than Stener would ever know.

At the sight of Stires the thought in regard to the sixty thousand dollars' worth of city loan certificates, previously referred to, flashed suddenly through his mind. He had not deposited them in the sinking-fund, and did not intend to for the present—could not, unless considerable free money were to reach him shortly—for he had used them to satisfy other pressing demands, and had no free money to buy them back—or, in other words, release them. And he did not want to just at this moment. Under the law governing transactions of this kind with the city treasurer, he was supposed to deposit them at once to the credit of the city, and not to draw his pay therefor from the city treasurer until he had. To be very exact, the city treasurer, under the law, was not supposed to pay him for any transaction of this kind until he or his agents presented a voucher from the bank or other organization carrying the sinking-fund for the city showing that the certificates so purchased had actually been deposited there. As a matter of fact, under the custom which had grown up between him and Stener, the law had long been ignored in this respect. He could buy certificates of city loan for the sinking-fund up to any reasonable amount, hypothecate them where he pleased, and draw his pay from the city without presenting a voucher. At the end of the month sufficient certificates of city loan could usually be gathered from one source and another to make up the deficiency, or the deficiency could actually be ignored, as had been done on more than one occasion, for long periods of time, while he used money secured by hypothecating the shares for speculative purposes. This was actually illegal; but neither Cowperwood nor Stener saw it in that light or cared.

The trouble with this particular transaction was the note that he had received from Stener ordering him to stop both buying and selling, which put his relations with the city treasury on a very formal basis. He had bought these certificates before receiving this note, but had not deposited them. He was going now to collect his check; but perhaps the old, easy system of balancing matters at the end of the month might not be said to obtain any longer. Stires might ask him to present a voucher of deposit. If so, he could not now get this check for sixty thousand dollars, for he did not have the certificates to deposit. If not, he might get the money; but, also, it might constitute the basis of some subsequent legal action. If he did not eventually deposit the certificates before failure, some charge such as that of larceny might be brought against him. Still, he said to himself, he might not really fail even yet. If any of his banking associates should, for any reason, modify their decision in regard to calling his loans, he would not. Would Stener make a row about this if he so secured this check? Would the city officials pay any attention to him if he did? Could you get any district attorney to take cognizance of such a transaction, if Stener did complain? No, not in all likelihood; and, anyhow, nothing would come of it. No jury would punish him in the face of the understanding existing between him and Stener as agent or broker and principal. And, once he had the money, it was a hundred to one Stener would think no more about it. It would go in among the various unsatisfied liabilities, and nothing more would be thought about it. Like lightning the entire situation hashed through his mind. He would risk it. He stopped before the chief clerk's desk.

"Albert," he said, in a low voice, "I bought sixty thousand dollars' worth of city loan for the sinking-fund this morning. Will you give my boy a check for it in the morning, or, better yet, will you give it to me now? I got your note about no more purchases. I'm going back to the office. You can just credit the sinking-fund with eight hundred certificates at from seventy-five to eighty. I'll send you the itemized list later."

"Certainly, Mr. Cowperwood, certainly," replied Albert, with alacrity. "Stocks are getting an awful knock, aren't they? I hope you're not very much troubled by it?"

"Not very, Albert," replied Cowperwood, smiling, the while the chief clerk was making out his check. He was wondering if by any chance Stener would appear and attempt to interfere with this. It was a legal transaction. He had a right to the check provided he deposited the certificates, as was his custom, with the trustee of the fund. He waited tensely while Albert wrote, and finally, with the check actually in his hand, breathed a sigh of relief. Here, at least, was sixty thousand dollars, and to-night's work would enable him to cash the seventy-five thousand that had been promised him. To-morrow, once more he must see Leigh, Kitchen, Jay Cooke Co., Edward Clark Co.–all the long list of people to whom he owed loans and find out what could be done. If he could only get time! If he could get just a week!

Chapter XXIX

But time was not a thing to be had in this emergency. With the seventy-five thousand dollars his friends had extended to him, and sixty thousand dollars secured from Stires, Cowperwood met the Girard call and placed the balance, thirty-five thousand dollars, in a private safe in his own home. He then made a final appeal to the bankers and financiers, but they refused to help him. He did not, however, commiserate himself in this hour. He looked out of his office window into the little court, and sighed. What more could he do? He sent a note to his father, asking him to call for lunch. He sent a note to his lawyer, Harper Steger, a man of his own age whom he liked very much, and asked him to call also. He evolved in his own mind various plans of delay, addresses to creditors and the like, but alas! he was going to fail. And the worst of it was that this matter of the city treasurer's loans was bound to become a public, and more than a public, a political, scandal. And the charge of conniving, if not illegally, at least morally, at the misuse of the city's money was the one thing that would hurt him most.

How industriously his rivals would advertise this fact! He might get on his feet again if he failed; but it would be uphill work. And his father! His father would be pulled down with him. It was probable that he would be forced out of the presidency of his bank. With these thoughts Cowperwood sat there waiting. As he did so Aileen Butler was announced by his office-boy, and at the same time Albert Stires.

"Show in Miss Butler," he said, getting up. "Tell Mr. Stires to wait." Aileen came briskly, vigorously in, her beautiful body clothed as decoratively as ever. The street suit that she wore was of a light golden-brown broadcloth, faceted with small, dark-red buttons. Her head was decorated with a brownish-red shake of a type she had learned was becoming to her, brimless and with a trailing plume, and her throat was graced by a three-strand necklace of gold beads. Her hands were smoothly gloved as usual, and her little feet daintily shod. There was a look of girlish distress in her eyes, which, however, she was trying hard to conceal.

"Honey," she exclaimed, on seeing him, her arms extended–"what is the trouble? I wanted so much to ask you the other night. You're not going to fail, are you? I heard father and Owen talking about you last night."

"What did they say?" he inquired, putting his arm around her and looking quietly into her nervous eyes.

"Oh, you know, I think papa is very angry with you. He suspects. Some one sent him an anonymous letter. He tried to get it out of me last night, but he didn't succeed. I denied everything. I was in here twice this morning to see you, but you were out. I was so afraid that he might see you first, and that you might say something."

"Me, Aileen?"

"Well, no, not exactly. I didn't think that. I don't know what I thought. Oh, honey, I've been so worried. You know, I didn't sleep at all. I thought I was stronger than that; but I was so worried about you. You know, he put me in a strong light by his desk, where he could see my face, and then he showed me the letter. I was so astonished for a moment I hardly know what I said or how I looked."

"What did you say?"

"Why, I said: 'What a shame! It isn't so!' But I didn't say it right away. My heart was going like a trip-hammer. I'm afraid he must have been able to tell something from my face. I could hardly get my breath."

"He's a shrewd man, your father," he commented. "He knows something about life. Now you see how difficult these situations are. It's a blessing he decided to show you the letter instead of watching the house. I suppose he felt too bad to do that. He can't prove anything now. But he knows. You can't deceive him."

"How do you know he knows?"

"I saw him yesterday."

"Did he talk to you about it?"

"No; I saw his face. He simply looked at me."

"Honey! I'm so sorry for him!"

"I know you are. So am I. But it can't be helped now. We should have thought of that in the first place."

"But I love you so. Oh, honey, he will never forgive me. He loves me so. He mustn't know. I won't admit anything. But, oh, dear!"

She put her hands tightly together on his bosom, and he looked consolingly into her eyes. Her eyelids, were trembling, and her lips. She was sorry for her father, herself, Cowperwood. Through her he could sense the force of Butler's parental affection; the volume and danger of his rage. There were so many, many things as he saw it now converging to make a dramatic denouement.

"Never mind," he replied; "it can't be helped now. Where is my strong, determined Aileen? I thought you were going to be so brave? Aren't you going to be? I need to have you that way now."

"Do you?"

"Yes."

"Are you in trouble?"

"I think I am going to fail, dear."

"Oh, no!"

"Yes, honey. I'm at the end of my rope. I don't see any way out just at present. I've sent for my father and my lawyer. You mustn't stay here, sweet. Your father may come in here at any time. We must meet somewhere–to-morrow, say–to-morrow afternoon. You remember Indian Rock, out on the Wissahickon?"

"Yes."

"Could you be there at four?"

"Yes."

"Look out for who's following. If I'm not there by four-thirty, don't wait. You know why. It will be because I think some one is watching. There won't be, though, if we work it right. And now you must run, sweet. We can't use Nine-thirty-one any more. I'll have to rent another place somewhere else."

"Oh, honey, I'm so sorry."

"Aren't you going to be strong and brave? You see, I need you to be."

He was almost, for the first time, a little sad in his mood.

"Yes, dear, yes," she declared, slipping her arms under his and pulling him tight. "Oh, yes! You can depend on me. Oh, Frank, I love you so! I'm so sorry. Oh, I do hope you don't fail! But it doesn't make any difference, dear, between you and me, whatever happens, does it? We will love each other just the same. I'll do anything for you, honey! I'll do anything you say. You can trust me. They sha'n't know anything from me."

She looked at his still, pale face, and a sudden strong determination to fight for him welled up in her heart. Her love was unjust, illegal, outlawed; but it was love, just the same, and had much of the fiery daring of the outcast from justice.

"I love you! I love you! I love you, Frank!" she declared. He unloosed her hands.

"Run, sweet. To-morrow at four. Don't fail. And don't talk. And don't admit anything, whatever you do."

"I won't."

"And don't worry about me. I'll be all right."

He barely had time to straighten his tie, to assume a nonchalant attitude by the window, when in hurried Stener's chief clerk–pale, disturbed, obviously out of key with himself.

"Mr. Cowperwood! You know that check I gave you last night? Mr. Stener says it's illegal, that I shouldn't have given it to you, that he will hold me responsible. He says I can be arrested for compounding a felony, and that he will discharge me and have me sent to prison if I don't get it back. Oh, Mr. Cowperwood, I am only a young man! I'm just really starting out in life. I've got my wife and little boy to look after. You won't let him do that to me? You'll give me that check back, won't you? I can't go back to the office without it. He says you're going to fail, and that you knew it, and that you haven't any right to it."

Cowperwood looked at him curiously. He was surprised at the variety and character of these emissaries of disaster. Surely, when troubles chose to multiply they had great skill in presenting themselves in rapid order. Stener had no right to make any such statement. The transaction was not illegal. The man had gone wild. True, he,

Cowperwood, had received an order after these securities were bought not to buy or sell any more city loan, but that did not invalidate previous purchases. Stener was browbeating and frightening his poor underling, a better man than himself, in order to get back this sixty-thousand-dollar check. What a petty creature he was! How true it was, as somebody had remarked, that you could not possibly measure the petty meannesses to which a fool could stoop!

"You go back to Mr. Stener, Albert, and tell him that it can't be done. The certificates of loan were purchased before his order arrived, and the records of the exchange will prove it. There is no illegality here. I am entitled to that check and could have collected it in any qualified court of law. The man has gone out of his head. I haven't failed yet. You are not in any danger of any legal proceedings; and if you are, I'll help defend you. I can't give you the check back because I haven't it to give; and if I had, I wouldn't. That would be allowing a fool to make a fool of me. I'm sorry, very, but I can't do anything for you."

"Oh, Mr. Cowperwood!" Tears were in Stires's eyes. "He'll discharge me! He'll forfeit my sureties. I'll be turned out into the street. I have only a little property of my own—outside of my salary!"

He wrung his hands, and Cowperwood shook his head sadly.

"This isn't as bad as you think, Albert. He won't do what he says. He can't. It's unfair and illegal. You can bring suit and recover your salary. I'll help you in that as much as I'm able. But I can't give you back this sixty-thousand-dollar check, because I haven't it to give. I couldn't if I wanted to. It isn't here any more. I've paid for the securities I bought with it. The securities are not here. They're in the sinking-fund, or will be."

He paused, wishing he had not mentioned that fact. It was a slip of the tongue, one of the few he ever made, due to the peculiar pressure of the situation. Stires pleaded longer. It was no use, Cowperwood told him. Finally he went away, crestfallen, fearsome, broken. There were tears of suffering in his eyes. Cowperwood was very sorry. And then his father was announced.

The elder Cowperwood brought a haggard face. He and Frank had had a long conversation the evening before, lasting until early morning, but it had not been productive of much save uncertainty.

"Hello, father!" exclaimed Cowperwood, cheerfully, noting his father's gloom. He was satisfied that there was scarcely a coal of hope to be raked out of these ashes of despair, but there was no use admitting it.

"Well?" said his father, lifting his sad eyes in a peculiar way.

"Well, it looks like stormy weather, doesn't it? I've decided to call a meeting of my creditors, father, and ask for time. There isn't anything else to do. I can't realize enough on anything to make it worth while talking about. I thought Stener might change his mind, but he's worse rather than better. His head bookkeeper just went out of here."

"What did he want?" asked Henry Cowperwood.

"He wanted me to give him back a check for sixty thousand that he paid me for some city loan I bought yesterday morning." Frank did not explain to his father, however, that he had hypothecated the certificates this check had paid for, and used the check itself to raise money enough to pay the Girard National Bank and to give himself thirty-five thousand in cash besides.

"Well, I declare!" replied the old man. "You'd think he'd have better sense than that. That's a perfectly legitimate transaction. When did you say he notified you not to buy city loan?"

"Yesterday noon."

"He's out of his mind," Cowperwood, Sr., commented, laconically.

"It's Mollenhauer and Simpson and Butler, I know. They want my street-railway lines. Well, they won't get them. They'll get them through a receivership, and after the panic's all over. Our creditors will have first chance at these. If they buy, they'll buy from them. If it weren't for that five-hundred-thousand-dollar loan I wouldn't think a thing of this. My creditors would sustain me nicely. But the moment that gets noised around!... And this election! I hypothecated those city loan certificates because I didn't want to get on the wrong side of Davison. I expected to take in enough by now to take them up. They ought to be in the sinking-fund, really."

The old gentleman saw the point at once, and winced.

"They might cause you trouble, there, Frank."

"It's a technical question," replied his son. "I might have been intending to take them up. As a matter of fact, I will if I can before three. I've been taking eight and ten days to deposit them in the past. In a storm like this I'm entitled to move my pawns as best I can."

Cowperwood, the father, put his hand over his mouth again. He felt very disturbed about this. He saw no way out, however. He was at the end of his own resources. He felt the side-whiskers on his left cheek. He looked out of the window into the little green court. Possibly it was a technical question, who should say. The financial relations of the city treasury with other brokers before Frank had been very lax. Every banker knew that. Perhaps precedent would or should govern in this case. He could not say. Still, it was dangerous—not straight. If Frank could get them out and deposit them it would be so much better.

"I'd take them up if I were you and I could," he added.

"I will if I can."

"How much money have you?"

"Oh, twenty thousand, all told. If I suspend, though, I'll have to have a little ready cash."

"I have eight or ten thousand, or will have by night, I hope."

He was thinking of some one who would give him a second mortgage on his house.

Cowperwood looked quietly at him. There was nothing more to be said to his father. "I'm going to make one more appeal to Stener after you leave here," he said. "I'm going over there with Harper Steger when he comes. If he won't change I'll send out notice to my creditors, and notify the secretary of the exchange. I want you to keep a stiff upper lip, whatever happens. I know you will, though. I'm going into the thing head down. If Stener had any sense—" He paused. "But what's the use talking about a damn fool?"

He turned to the window, thinking of how easy it would have been, if Aileen and he had not been exposed by this anonymous note, to have arranged all with Butler. Rather than injure the party, Butler, in extremis, would have assisted him. Now...!

His father got up to go. He was as stiff with despair as though he were suffering from cold.

"Well," he said, wearily.

Cowperwood suffered intensely for him. What a shame! His father! He felt a great surge of sorrow sweep over him but a moment later mastered it, and settled to his quick, defiant thinking. As the old man went out, Harper Steger was brought in. They shook hands, and at once started for Stener's office. But Stener had sunk in on himself like an empty gas-bag, and no efforts were sufficient to inflate him. They went out, finally, defeated.

"I tell you, Frank," said Steger, "I wouldn't worry. We can tie this thing up legally until election and after, and that will give all this row a chance to die down. Then you can get your people together and talk sense to them. They're not going to give up good properties like this, even if Stener does go to jail."

Steger did not know of the sixty thousand dollars' worth of hypothecated securities as yet. Neither did he know of Aileen Butler and her father's boundless rage.

Chapter XXX

There was one development in connection with all of this of which Cowperwood was as yet unaware. The same day that brought Edward Butler the anonymous communication in regard to his daughter, brought almost a duplicate of it to Mrs. Frank Algernon Cowperwood, only in this case the name of Aileen Butler had curiously been omitted.

Perhaps you don't know that your husband is running with another woman. If you don't believe it, watch the house at 931 North Tenth Street.

Mrs. Cowperwood was in the conservatory watering some plants when this letter was brought by her maid Monday morning. She was most placid in her thoughts, for she did not know what all the conferring of the night before meant. Frank was occasionally troubled by financial storms, but they did not see to harm him.

"Lay it on the table in the library, Annie. I'll get it."

She thought it was some social note.

In a little while (such was her deliberate way), she put down her sprinkling-pot and went into the library. There it was lying on the green leather sheepskin which constituted a part of the ornamentation of the large library table. She picked it up, glanced at it curiously because it was on cheap paper, and then opened it. Her face paled slightly as she read it; and then her hand trembled–not much. Hers was not a soul that ever loved passionately, hence she could not suffer passionately. She was hurt, disgusted, enraged for the moment, and frightened; but she was not broken in spirit entirely. Thirteen years of life with Frank Cowperwood had taught her a number of things. He was selfish, she knew now, self-centered, and not as much charmed by her as he had been. The fear she had originally felt as to the effect of her preponderance of years had been to some extent justified by the lapse of time. Frank did not love her as he had–he had not for some time; she had felt it. What was it?–she had asked herself at times–almost, who was it? Business was engrossing him so.

Finance was his master. Did this mean the end of her regime, she queried. Would he cast her off? Where would she go? What would she do? She was not helpless, of course, for she had money of her own which he was manipulating for her. Who was this other woman? Was she young, beautiful, of any social position? Was it–? Suddenly she stopped. Was it? Could it be, by any chance–her mouth opened–Aileen Butler?

She stood still, staring at this letter, for she could scarcely countenance her own thought. She had observed often, in spite of all their caution, how friendly Aileen had been to him and he to her. He liked her; he never lost a chance to defend her. Lillian had thought of them at times as being curiously suited to each other temperamentally. He liked young people. But, of course, he was married, and Aileen was infinitely beneath him socially, and he had two children and herself. And his social and financial position was so fixed and stable that he did not dare trifle with it. Still she paused; for forty years and two children, and some slight wrinkles, and the suspicion that we may be no longer loved as we once were, is apt to make any woman pause, even in the face of the most significant financial position. Where would she go if she left him? What would people think? What about the children? Could she prove this liaison? Could she entrap him in a compromising situation? Did she want to?

She saw now that she did not love him as some women love their husbands. She was not wild about him. In a way she had been taking him for granted all these years, had thought that he loved her enough not to be unfaithful to her; at least fancied that he was so engrossed with the more serious things of life that no petty liaison such as this letter indicated would trouble him or interrupt his great career. Apparently this was not true. What should she do? What say? How act? Her none too brilliant mind was not of much service in this crisis. She did not know very well how either to plan or to fight.

The conventional mind is at best a petty piece of machinery. It is oyster-like in its functioning, or, perhaps better, clam-like. It has its little siphon of thought-processes forced up or down into the mighty ocean of fact and circumstance; but it uses so little, pumps so faintly, that the immediate contiguity of the vast mass is not disturbed. Nothing of the subtlety of life is perceived. No least inkling of its storms or terrors is ever discovered except through accident. When some crude, suggestive fact, such as this letter proved to be, suddenly manifests itself in the placid flow of events, there is great agony or disturbance and clogging of the so-called normal processes. The siphon does not work right. It sucks in fear and distress. There is great grinding of maladjusted parts–not unlike sand in a machine–and life, as is so often the case, ceases or goes lamely ever after.

Mrs. Cowperwood was possessed of a conventional mind. She really knew nothing about life. And life could not teach her. Reaction in her from salty thought-processes was not possible. She was not alive in the sense that Aileen Butler was, and yet she thought that she was very much alive. All illusion. She wasn't. She was charming if you loved placidity. If you did not, she was not. She was not engaging, brilliant, or forceful. Frank Cowperwood might well have asked himself in the beginning why he married her. He did not do so now because he did not believe it was wise to question the past as to one's failures and errors. It was, according to him, most unwise to regret. He kept his face and thoughts to the future.

But Mrs. Cowperwood was truly distressed in her way, and she went about the house thinking, feeling wretchedly. She decided, since the letter asked her to see for herself, to wait. She must think how she would watch this house, if at all. Frank must not know. If it were Aileen Butler by any chance–but surely not–she thought she would expose her to her parents. Still, that meant exposing herself. She determined to conceal her mood as best she could at dinner-time–but Cowperwood was not able to be there. He was so rushed, so closeted with individuals, so closely in conference with his father and others, that she scarcely saw him this Monday night, nor the next day, nor for many days.

For on Tuesday afternoon at two-thirty he issued a call for a meeting of his creditors, and at five-thirty he decided to go into the hands of a receiver. And yet, as he stood before his principal creditors–a group of thirty men–in his office, he did not feel that his life was ruined. He was temporarily embarrassed. Certainly things looked very black. The city-treasurership deal would make a great fuss. Those hypothecated city loan certificates, to the extent of sixty thousand, would make another, if Stener chose. Still, he did not feel that he was utterly destroyed.

"Gentlemen," he said, in closing his address of explanation at the meeting, quite as erect, secure, defiant, convincing as he had ever been, "you see how things are. These securities are worth just as much as they ever were. There is nothing the matter with the properties behind them. If you will give me fifteen days or twenty, I am satisfied that I can straighten the whole matter out. I am almost the only one who can, for I know all about it. The market is bound to recover. Business is going to be better than ever. It's time I want. Time is the only significant factor in this situation. I want to know if you won't give me fifteen or twenty days–a month, if you can. That is all I want."

He stepped aside and out of the general room, where the blinds were drawn, into his private office, in order to give his creditors an opportunity to confer privately in regard to his situation. He had friends in the meeting who were for him. He waited one, two, nearly three hours while they talked. Finally Walter Leigh, Judge Kitchen, Avery Stone, of Jay Cooke Co., and several others came in. They were a committee appointed to gather further information.

"Nothing more can be done to-day, Frank," Walter Leigh informed him, quietly. "The majority want the privilege of examining the books. There is some uncertainty about this entanglement with the city treasurer which you say exists. They feel that you'd better announce a temporary suspension, anyhow; and if they want to let you resume later they can do so."

"I'm sorry for that, gentlemen," replied Cowperwood, the least bit depressed. "I would rather do anything than suspend for one hour, if I could help it, for I know just what it means. You will find assets here far exceeding the liabilities if you will take the stocks at their normal market value; but that won't help any if I close my doors. The public won't believe in me. I ought to keep open."

"Sorry, Frank, old boy," observed Leigh, pressing his hand affectionately. "If it were left to me personally, you could have all the time you want. There's a crowd of old fogies out there that won't listen to reason. They're panic-struck. I guess they're pretty hard hit themselves. You can scarcely blame them. You'll come out all right, though I wish you didn't have to shut up shop. We can't do anything with them, however. Why, damn it, man, I don't see how you can fail, really. In ten days these stocks will be all right."

Judge Kitchen commiserated with him also; but what good did that do? He was being compelled to suspend. An expert accountant would have to come in and go over his books. Butler might spread the news of this city-treasury connection. Stener might complain of this last city-loan transaction. A half-dozen of his helpful friends stayed with him until four o'clock in the morning; but he had to suspend just the same. And when he did that, he knew he was seriously crippled if not ultimately defeated in his race for wealth and fame.

When he was really and finally quite alone in his private bedroom he stared at himself in the mirror. His face was pale and tired, he thought, but strong and effective. "Pshaw!" he said to himself, "I'm not whipped. I'm still young. I'll get out of this in some way yet. Certainly I will. I'll find some way out."

And so, cogitating heavily, wearily, he began to undress. Finally he sank upon his bed, and in a little while, strange as it may seem, with all the tangle of trouble around him, slept. He could do that–sleep and gurgle most peacefully, the while his father paced the floor in his room, refusing to be comforted. All was dark before the older man–the future hopeless. Before the younger man was still hope.

And in her room Lillian Cowperwood turned and tossed in the face of this new calamity. For it had suddenly appeared from news from her father and Frank and Anna and her mother-in-law that Frank was about to fail, or would, or had–it was almost impossible to say just how it was. Frank was too busy to explain. The Chicago fire was to blame. There was no mention as yet of the city treasurership. Frank was caught in a trap, and was fighting for his life.

In this crisis, for the moment, she forgot about the note as to his infidelity, or rather ignored it. She was astonished, frightened, dumbfounded, confused. Her little, placid, beautiful world was going around in a dizzy ring. The charming, ornate ship of their fortune was being blown most ruthlessly here and there. She felt it a sort of duty to stay in bed and try to sleep; but her eyes were quite wide, and her brain hurt her. Hours before Frank had insisted that she should not bother about him, that she could do nothing; and she had left him, wondering more than ever what and where was the line of her duty. To stick by her husband, convention told her; and so she decided. Yes, religion dictated that, also custom. There were the children. They must not be injured. Frank must be reclaimed, if possible. He would get over this. But what a blow!

Chapter XXXI

The suspension of the banking house of Frank A. Cowperwood Co. created a great stir on 'change and in Philadelphia generally. It was so unexpected, and the amount involved was comparatively so large. Actually he failed for one million two hundred and fifty thousand dollars; and his assets, under the depressed condition of stock values, barely totaled seven hundred and fifty thousand dollars. There had been considerable work done on the matter of his balance-sheet before it was finally given to the public; but when it was, stocks dropped an additional three points generally, and the papers the next day devoted notable headlines to it. Cowperwood had no idea of failing permanently; he merely wished to suspend temporarily, and later, if possible, to persuade his creditors to allow him to resume. There were only two things which stood in the way of this: the matter of the five hundred thousand dollars borrowed from the city treasury at a ridiculously low rate of interest, which showed plainer than words what had been going on, and the other, the matter of the sixty-thousand-dollar check. His financial wit had told him there were ways to assign his holdings in favor of his largest creditors, which would tend to help him later to resume; and he had been swift to act. Indeed, Harper Steger had drawn up documents which named Jay Cooke Co., Edward Clark Co., Drexel Co., and others as preferred. He knew that even though dissatisfied holders of smaller shares in his company brought suit and compelled readjustment or bankruptcy later, the intention shown to prefer some of his most influential aids was important. They would like it, and might help him later when all this was over. Besides, suits in plenty are an excellent way of tiding over a crisis of this kind until stocks and common sense are restored, and he was for many suits. Harper Steger smiled once rather grimly, even in the whirl of the financial chaos where smiles were few, as they were figuring it out.

"Frank," he said, "you're a wonder. You'll have a network of suits spread here shortly, which no one can break through. They'll all be suing each other."

Cowperwood smiled.

"I only want a little time, that's all," he replied. Nevertheless, for the first time in his life he was a little depressed; for now this business, to which he had devoted years of active work and thought, was ended.

The thing that was troubling him most in all of this was not the five hundred thousand dollars which was owing the city treasury, and which he knew would stir political and social life to the center once it was generally known–that was a legal or semi-legal transaction, at least–but rather the matter of the sixty thousand dollars' worth of unrestored city loan certificates which he had not been able to replace in the sinking-fund and could not now even though the necessary money should fall from heaven. The fact of their absence was a matter of source. He pondered over the situation a good deal. The thing to do, he thought, if he went to Mollenhauer or Simpson, or both (he had never met either of them, but in view of Butler's desertion they were his only recourse), was to say that, although he could not at present return the five hundred thousand dollars, if no action were taken against him now, which would prevent his resuming his business on a normal scale a little later, he would pledge his word that every dollar of the involved five hundred thousand dollars would eventually be returned to the treasury. If they refused, and injury was done him, he proposed to let them wait until he was "good and ready," which in all probability would be never. But, really, it was not quite clear how action against him was to be prevented–even by them. The money was down on his books as owing the city treasury, and it was down on the city treasury's books as owing from him. Besides, there was a local organization known as the Citizens' Municipal Reform Association which occasionally conducted investigations in connection with public affairs. His defalcation would be sure to come to the ears of this body and a public investigation might well follow. Various private individuals knew of it already. His creditors, for instance, who were now examining his books.

This matter of seeing Mollenhauer or Simpson, or both, was important, anyhow, he thought; but before doing so he decided to talk it all over with Harper Steger. So several days after he had closed his doors, he sent for Steger and told him all about the transaction, except that he did not make it clear that he had not intended to put the certificates in the sinking-fund unless he survived quite comfortably.

Harper Steger was a tall, thin, graceful, rather elegant man, of gentle voice and perfect manners, who walked always as though he were a cat, and a dog were prowling somewhere in the offing. He had a longish, thin face of a type that is rather attractive to women. His eyes were blue, his hair brown, with a suggestion of sandy red in it. He had a steady, inscrutable gaze which sometimes came to you over a thin, delicate hand, which he laid meditatively over his mouth. He was cruel to the limit of the word, not aggressively but indifferently; for he had no faith in anything. He was not poor. He had not even been born poor. He was just innately subtle, with the rather constructive thought, which was about the only thing that compelled him to work, that he ought to be richer than he was–more conspicuous. Cowperwood was an excellent avenue toward legal prosperity. Besides, he was a fascinating customer. Of all his clients, Steger admired Cowperwood most.

"Let them proceed against you," he said on this occasion, his brilliant legal mind taking in all the phases of the situation at once. "I don't see that there is anything more here than a technical charge. If it ever came to anything like that, which I don't think it will, the charge would be embezzlement or perhaps larceny as bailee. In this instance, you were the bailee. And the only way out of that would be to swear that you had received the check with Stener's knowledge and consent. Then it would only be a technical charge of irresponsibility on your part, as I see it, and I don't believe any jury would convict you on the evidence of how this relationship was conducted. Still, it might; you never can tell what a jury is going to do. All this would have to come out at a trial, however. The whole thing, it seems to me, would depend on which of you two–yourself or Stener–the jury would be inclined to believe, and on how anxious this city crowd is to find a scapegoat for Stener. This coming election is the rub. If this panic had come at any other time–"

Cowperwood waved for silence. He knew all about that. "It all depends on what the politicians decide to do. I'm doubtful. The situation is too complicated. It can't be hushed up." They were in his private office at his house. "What will be will be," he added.

"What would that mean, Harper, legally, if I were tried on a charge of larceny as bailee, as you put it, and convicted? How many years in the penitentiary at the outside?"

Steger thought a minute, rubbing his chin with his hand. "Let me see," he said, "that is a serious question, isn't it? The law says one to five years at the outside; but the sentences usually average from one to three years in embezzlement cases. Of course, in this case–"

"I know all about that," interrupted Cowperwood, irritably. "My case isn't any different from the others, and you know it. Embezzlement is embezzlement if the politicians want to have it so." He fell to thinking, and Steger got up and strolled about leisurely. He was thinking also.

"And would I have to go to jail at any time during the proceedings–before a final adjustment of the case by the higher courts?" Cowperwood added, directly, grimly, after a time.

"Yes, there is one point in all legal procedure of the kind," replied Steger, cautiously, now rubbing his ear and trying to put the matter as delicately as possible. "You can avoid jail sentences all through the earlier parts of a case like this; but if you are once tried and convicted it's pretty hard to do anything–as a matter of fact, it becomes absolutely necessary then to go to jail for a few days, five or so, pending the motion for a new trial and the obtaining of a certificate of reasonable doubt. It usually takes that long."

The young banker sat there staring out of the window, and Steger observed, "It is a bit complicated, isn't it?"

"Well, I should say so," returned Frank, and he added to himself: "Jail! Five days in prison!" That would be a terrific slap, all things considered. Five days in jail pending the obtaining of a certificate of reasonable doubt, if one could be obtained! He must avoid this! Jail! The penitentiary! His commercial reputation would never survive that.

Chapter XXXII

The necessity of a final conference between Butler, Mollenhauer, and Simpson was speedily reached, for this situation was hourly growing more serious. Rumors were floating about in Third Street that in addition to having failed for so large an amount as to have further unsettled the already panicky financial situation induced by the Chicago fire, Cowperwood and Stener, or Stener working with Cowperwood, or the other way round, had involved the city treasury to the extent of five hundred thousand dollars. And the question was how was the matter to be kept quiet until after election, which was still three weeks away. Bankers and brokers were communicating odd rumors to each other about a check that had been taken from the city treasury after Cowperwood knew he was to fail, and without Stener's consent. Also that there was danger that it would come to the ears of that very uncomfortable political organization known as the Citizens' Municipal Reform Association, of which a well-known iron-manufacturer of great probity and moral rectitude, one Skelton C. Wheat, was president. Wheat had for years been following on the trail of the dominant Republican administration in a vain attempt to bring it to a sense of some of its political iniquities. He was a serious and austere man—one of those solemn, self-righteous souls who see life through a peculiar veil of duty, and who, undisturbed by notable animal passions of any kind, go their way of upholding the theory of the Ten Commandments over the order of things as they are.

The committee in question had originally been organized to protest against some abuses in the tax department; but since then, from election to election, it had been drift-ing from one subject to another, finding an occasional evidence of its worthwhileness in some newspaper comment and the frightened reformation of some minor political official who ended, usually, by taking refuge behind the skirts of some higher political power–in the last reaches, Messrs. Butler, Mollenhauer, and Simpson. Just now it was without important fuel or ammunition; and this assignment of Cowperwood, with its attendant crime, so far as the city treasury was concerned, threatened, as some politicians and bankers saw it, to give it just the club it was looking for.

However, the decisive conference took place between Cowperwood and the reigning political powers some five days after Cowperwood's failure, at the home of Senator Simpson, which was located in Rittenhouse Square–a region central for the older order of wealth in Philadelphia. Simpson was a man of no little refinement artistically, of Quaker extraction, and of great wealth-breeding judgment which he used largely to satisfy his craving for political predominance. He was most liberal where money would bring him a powerful or necessary political adherent. He fairly showered offices– commissionerships, trusteeships, judgeships, political nominations, and executive positions generally–on those who did his bidding faithfully and without question. Compared with Butler and Mollenhauer he was more powerful than either, for he represented the State and the nation. When the political authorities who were trying to swing a national election were anxious to discover what the State of Pennsylvania would do, so far as the Republican party was concerned, it was to Senator Simpson that they appealed. In the literal sense of the word, he knew. The Senator had long since graduated from State to national politics, and was an interesting figure in the United States Senate at Washington, where his voice in all the conservative and moneyed councils of the nation was of great weight.

The house that he occupied, of Venetian design, and four stories in height, bore many architectural marks of distinction, such as the floriated window, the door with the semipointed arch, and medallions of colored marble set in the walls. The Senator was a great admirer of Venice. He had been there often, as he had to Athens and Rome, and had brought back many artistic objects representative of the civilizations and refinements of older days. He was fond, for one thing, of the stern, sculptured heads of the Roman emperors, and the fragments of gods and goddesses which are the best testimony of the artistic aspirations of Greece. In the entresol of this house was one of his finest treasures–a carved and floriated base bearing a tapering monolith some four feet high, crowned by the head of a peculiarly goatish Pan, by the side of which were the problematic remains of a lovely nude nymph–just the little feet broken off at the ankles. The base on which the feet of the nymph and the monolith stood was ornamented with carved ox-skulls intertwined with roses. In his reception hall were replicas of Caligula, Nero, and other Roman emperors; and on his stair-walls reliefs of dancing nymphs in procession, and priests bearing offerings of sheep and swine to the sacrificial altars. There was a clock in some corner of the house which chimed the quarter, the half, the three-quarters, and the hour in strange, euphonious, and pathetic notes. On the walls of the rooms were tapestries of Flemish origin, and in the reception-hall, the library, the living-room, and the drawing-room, richly carved furniture after the standards of the Italian Renaissance. The Senator's taste in the matter of paintings was inadequate, and he mistrusted it; but such as he had were of distinguished origin and authentic. He cared more for his curio-cases filled with smaller imported bronzes, Venetian glass, and Chinese jade. He was not a collector of these in any notable sense–merely a lover of a few choice examples. Handsome tiger and leopard skin rugs, the fur of a musk-ox for his divan, and tanned and brown-stained goat and kid skins for his tables, gave a sense of elegance and reserved profusion. In addition the Senator had a dining-room done after the Jacobean idea of artistic excellence, and a wine-cellar which the best of the local vintners looked after with extreme care. He was a man who loved to entertain lavishly; and when his residence was thrown open for a dinner, a reception, or a ball, the best of local society was to be found there.

The conference was in the Senator's library, and he received his colleagues with the genial air of one who has much to gain and little to lose. There were whiskies, wines, cigars on the table, and while Mollenhauer and Simpson exchanged the commonplaces of the day awaiting the arrival of Butler, they lighted cigars and kept their inmost thoughts to themselves.

It so happened that upon the previous afternoon Butler had learned from Mr. David Pettie, the district attorney, of the sixty-thousand-dollar-check transaction. At the same time the matter had been brought to Mollenhauer's attention by Stener himself. It was Mollenhauer, not Butler who saw that by taking advantage of Cowperwood's situation, he might save the local party from blame, and at the same time most likely fleece Cowperwood out of his street-railway shares without letting Butler or Simpson know anything about it. The thing to do was to terrorize him with a private threat of prosecution.

Butler was not long in arriving, and apologized for the delay. Concealing his recent grief behind as jaunty an air as possible, he began with:

"It's a lively life I'm leadin', what with every bank in the city wantin' to know how their loans are goin' to be taken care of." He took a cigar and struck a match.

"It does look a little threatening," said Senator Simpson, smiling. "Sit down. I have just been talking with Avery Stone, of Jay Cooke Company, and he tells me that the talk in Third Street about Stener's connection with this Cowperwood failure is growing very strong, and that the newspapers are bound to take up the matter shortly, unless something is done about it. I am sure that the news will also reach Mr. Wheat, of the Citizens' Reform Association, very shortly. We ought to decide now, gentlemen, what we propose to do. One thing, I am sure, is to eliminate Stener from the ticket as quietly as possible. This really looks to me as if it might become a very serious issue, and we ought to be doing what we can now to offset its effect later."

Mollenhauer pulled a long breath through his cigar, and blew it out in a rolling steel-blue cloud. He studied the tapestry on the opposite wall but said nothing.

"There is one thing sure," continued Senator Simpson, after a time, seeing that no one else spoke, "and that is, if we do not begin a prosecution on our own account within a reasonable time, some one else is apt to; and that would put rather a bad face on the matter. My own opinion would be that we wait until it is very plain that prosecution is going to be undertaken by some one else–possibly the Municipal Reform Association–but that we stand ready to step in and act in such a way as to make it look as though we had been planning to do it all the time. The thing to do is to gain time; and so I would suggest that it be made as difficult as possible to get at the treasurer's books. An investigation there, if it begins at all–as I think is very likely–should be very slow in producing the facts."

The Senator was not at all for mincing words with his important confreres, when it came to vital issues. He preferred, in his grandiloquent way, to call a spade a spade.

"Now that sounds like very good sense to me," said Butler, sinking a little lower in his chair for comfort's sake, and concealing his true mood in regard to all this. "The boys could easily make that investigation last three weeks, I should think. They're slow enough with everything else, if me memory doesn't fail me." At the same time he was cogitating as to how to inject the personality of Cowperwood and his speedy prosecution without appearing to be neglecting the general welfare of the local party too much.

"Yes, that isn't a bad idea," said Mollenhauer, solemnly, blowing a ring of smoke, and thinking how to keep Cowperwood's especial offense from coming up at this conference and until after he had seen him.

"We ought to map out our program very carefully," continued Senator Simpson, "so that if we are compelled to act we can do so very quickly. I believe myself that this thing is certain to come to an issue within a week, if not sooner, and we have no time to lose. If my advice were followed now, I should have the mayor write the treasurer a letter asking for information, and the treasurer write the mayor his answer, and also have the mayor, with the authority of the common council, suspend the treasurer for the time being—I think we have the authority to do that—or, at least, take over his principal duties but without for the time being, anyhow, making any of these transactions public—until we have to, of course. We ought to be ready with these letters to show to the newspapers at once, in case this action is forced upon us."

"I could have those letters prepared, if you gentlemen have no objection," put in Mollenhauer, quietly, but quickly.

"Well, that strikes me as sinsible," said Butler, easily. "It's about the only thing we can do under the circumstances, unless we could find some one else to blame it on, and I have a suggestion to make in that direction. Maybe we're not as helpless as we might be, all things considered."

There was a slight gleam of triumph in his eye as he said this, at the same time that there was a slight shadow of disappointment in Mollenhauer's. So Butler knew, and probably Simpson, too.

"Just what do you mean?" asked the Senator, looking at Butler interestedly. He knew nothing of the sixty-thousand-dollar check transaction. He had not followed the local treasury dealings very closely, nor had he talked to either of his confreres since the original conference between them. "There haven't been any outside parties mixed up with this, have there?" His own shrewd, political mind was working.

"No-o. I wouldn't call him an outside party, exactly, Senator," went on Butler suavely. "It's Cowperwood himself I'm thinkin' of. There's somethin' that has come up since I saw you gentlemen last that makes me think that perhaps that young man isn't as innocent as he might be. It looks to me as though he was the ringleader in this business, as though he had been leadin' Stener on against his will. I've been lookin' into the matter on me own account, and as far as I can make out this man Stener isn't as much to blame as I thought. From all I can learn, Cowperwood's been threatenin' Stener with one thing and another if he didn't give him more money, and only the other day he got a big sum on false pretenses, which might make him equally guilty with Stener. There's sixty-thousand dollars of city loan certificates that has been paid for that aren't in the sinking-fund. And since the reputation of the party's in danger this fall, I don't see that we need to have any particular consideration for him." He paused, strong in the conviction that he had sent a most dangerous arrow flying in the direction of Cowperwood, as indeed he had. Yet at this moment, both the Senator and Mollenhauer were not a little surprised, seeing at their last meeting he had appeared rather friendly to the young banker, and this recent discovery seemed scarcely any occasion for a vicious attitude on his part. Mollenhauer in particular was surprised, for he had been looking on Butler's friendship for Cowperwood as a possible stumbling block.

"Um-m, you don't tell me," observed Senator Simpson, thoughtfully, stroking his mouth with his pale hand.

"Yes, I can confirm that," said Mollenhauer, quietly, seeing his own little private plan of browbeating Cowperwood out of his street-railway shares going glimmering. "I had a talk with Stener the other day about this very matter, and he told me that Cowperwood had been trying to force him to give him three hundred thousand dollars more, and that when he refused Cowperwood managed to get sixty thousand dollars further without his knowledge or consent."

"How could he do that?" asked Senator Simpson, incredulously. Mollenhauer explained the transaction.

"Oh," said the Senator, when Mollenhauer had finished, "that indicates a rather sharp person, doesn't it? And the certificates are not in the sinking-fund, eh?"

"They're not," chimed in Butler, with considerable enthusiasm.

"Well, I must say," said Simpson, rather relieved in his manner, "this looks like a rather good thing than not to me. A scapegoat possibly. We need something like this. I see no reason under the circumstances for trying to protect Mr. Cowperwood. We might as well try to make a point of that, if we have to. The newspapers might just as well talk loud about that as anything else. They are bound to talk; and if we give them the right angle, I think that the election might well come and go before the matter could be reasonably cleared up, even though Mr. Wheat does interfere. I will be glad to undertake to see what can be done with the papers."

"Well, that bein' the case," said Butler, "I don't see that there's so much more we can do now; but I do think it will be a mistake if Cowperwood isn't punished with the other one. He's equally guilty with Stener, if not more so, and I for one want to see him get what he deserves. He belongs in the penitentiary, and that's where he'll go if I have my say." Both Mollenhauer and Simpson turned a reserved and inquiring eye on their usually genial associate. What could be the reason for his sudden determination to have Cowperwood punished? Cowperwood, as Mollenhauer and Simpson saw it, and as Butler would ordinarily have seen it, was well within his human, if not his strictly legal rights. They did not blame him half as much for trying to do what he had done as they blamed Stener for letting him do it. But, since Butler felt as he did, and there was an actual technical crime here, they were perfectly willing that the party should have the advantage of it, even if Cowperwood went to the penitentiary.

"You may be right," said Senator Simpson, cautiously. "You might have those letters prepared, Henry; and if we have to bring any action at all against anybody before election, it would, perhaps, be advisable to bring it against Cowperwood. Include Stener if you have to but not unless you have to. I leave it to you two, as I am compelled to start for Pittsburg next Friday; but I know you will not overlook any point."

The Senator arose. His time was always valuable. Butler was highly gratified by what he had accomplished. He had succeeded in putting the triumvirate on record against Cowperwood as the first victim, in case of any public disturbance or demonstration against the party. All that was now necessary was for that disturbance to manifest itself; and, from what he could see of local conditions, it was not far off. There was now the matter of Cowperwood's disgruntled creditors to look into; and if by buying in these he should succeed in preventing the financier from resuming business, he would have him in a very precarious condition indeed. It was a sad day for Cowperwood, Butler thought–the day he had first tried to lead Aileen astray–and the time was not far off when he could prove it to him.

Chapter XXXIII

In the meantime Cowperwood, from what he could see and hear, was becoming more and more certain that the politicians would try to make a scapegoat of him, and that shortly. For one thing, Stires had called only a few days after he closed his doors and imparted a significant bit of information. Albert was still connected with the city treasury, as was Stener, and engaged with Sengstack and another personal appointee of Mollenhauer's in going over the treasurer's books and explaining their financial significance. Stires had come to Cowperwood primarily to get additional advice in regard to the sixty-thousand-dollar check and his personal connection with it. Stener, it seemed, was now threatening to have his chief clerk prosecuted, saying that he was responsible for the loss of the money and that his bondsmen could be held responsible. Cowperwood had merely laughed and assured Stires that there was nothing to this.

"Albert," he had said, smilingly, "I tell you positively, there's nothing in it. You're not responsible for delivering that check to me. I'll tell you what you do, now. Go and consult my lawyer–Steger. It won't cost you a cent, and he'll tell you exactly what to do. Now go on back and don't worry any more about it. I am sorry this move of mine has caused you so much trouble, but it's a hundred to one you couldn't have kept your place with a new city treasurer, anyhow, and if I see any place where you can possibly fit in later, I'll let you know."

Another thing that made Cowperwood pause and consider at this time was a letter from Aileen, detailing a conversation which had taken place at the Butler dinner table one evening when Butler, the elder, was not at home. She related how her brother Owen in effect had stated that they–the politicians–her father, Mollenhauer, and Simpson, were going to "get him yet" (meaning Cowperwood), for some criminal financial manipulation of something–she could not explain what–a check or something. Aileen was frantic with worry. Could they mean the penitentiary, she asked in her letter? Her dear lover! Her beloved Frank! Could anything like this really happen to him?

His brow clouded, and he set his teeth with rage when he read her letter. He would have to do something about this–see Mollenhauer or Simpson, or both, and make some offer to the city. He could not promise them money for the present–only notes–but they might take them. Surely they could not be intending to make a scapegoat of him over such a trivial and uncertain matter as this check transaction! When there was the five hundred thousand advanced by Stener, to say nothing of all the past shady transactions of former city treasurers! How rotten! How political, but how real and dangerous.

But Simpson was out of the city for a period of ten days, and Mollenhauer, having in mind the suggestion made by Butler in regard to utilizing Cowperwood's misdeed for the benefit of the party, had already moved as they had planned. The letters were ready and waiting. Indeed, since the conference, the smaller politicians, taking their cue from the overlords, had been industriously spreading the story of the sixty-thousand-dollar check, and insisting that the burden of guilt for the treasury defalcation, if any, lay on the banker. The moment Mollenhauer laid eyes on Cowperwood he realized, however, that he had a powerful personality to deal with. Cowperwood gave no evidence of fright. He merely stated, in his bland way, that he had been in the habit of borrowing money from the city treasury at a low rate of interest, and that this panic had involved him so that he could not possibly return it at present.

"I have heard rumors, Mr. Mollenhauer," he said, "to the effect that some charge is to be brought against me as a partner with Mr. Stener in this matter; but I am hoping that the city will not do that, and I thought I might enlist your influence to prevent it. My affairs are not in a bad way at all, if I had a little time to arrange matters. I am making all of my creditors an offer of fifty cents on the dollar now, and giving notes at one, two, and three years; but in this matter of the city treasury loans, if I could come to terms, I would be glad to make it a hundred cents—only I would want a little more time. Stocks are bound to recover, as you know, and, barring my losses at this time, I will be all right. I realize that the matter has gone pretty far already. The newspapers are likely to start talking at any time, unless they are stopped by those who can control them." (He looked at Mollenhauer in a complimentary way.) "But if I could be kept out of the general proceedings as much as possible, my standing would not be injured, and I would have a better chance of getting on my feet. It would be better for the city, for then I could certainly pay it what I owe it." He smiled his most winsome and engaging smile. And Mollenhauer seeing him for the first time, was not unimpressed. Indeed he looked at this young financial David with an interested eye. If he could have seen a way to accept this proposition of Cowperwood's, so that the money offered would have been eventually payable to him, and if Cowperwood had had any reasonable prospect of getting on his feet soon, he would have considered carefully what he had to say. For then Cowperwood could have assigned his recovered property to him. As it was, there was small likelihood of this situation ever being straightened out. The Citizens' Municipal Reform Association, from all he could hear, was already on the move—investigating, or about to, and once they had set their hands to this, would unquestionably follow it closely to the end.

"The trouble with this situation, Mr. Cowperwood," he said, affably, "is that it has gone so far that it is practically out of my hands. I really have very little to do with it. I don't suppose, though, really, it is this matter of the five-hundred-thousand-dollar loan that is worrying you so much, as it is this other matter of the sixty-thousand-dollar check you received the other day. Mr. Stener insists that you secured that illegally, and he is very much wrought up about it. The mayor and the other city officials know of it now, and they may force some action. I don't know."

Mollenhauer was obviously not frank in his attitude–a little bit evasive in his sly reference to his official tool, the mayor; and Cowperwood saw it. It irritated him greatly, but he was tactful enough to be quite suave and respectful.

"I did get a check for sixty thousand dollars, that's true," he replied, with apparent frankness, "the day before I assigned. It was for certificates I had purchased, however, on Mr. Stener's order, and was due me. I needed the money, and asked for it. I don't see that there is anything illegal in that."

"Not if the transaction was completed in all its details," replied Mollenhauer, blandly. "As I understand it, the certificates were bought for the sinking-fund, and they are not there. How do you explain that?"

"An oversight, merely," replied Cowperwood, innocently, and quite as blandly as Mollenhauer. "They would have been there if I had not been compelled to assign so unexpectedly. It was not possible for me to attend to everything in person. It has not been our custom to deposit them at once. Mr. Stener will tell you that, if you ask him."

"You don't say," replied Mollenhauer. "He did not give me that impression. However, they are not there, and I believe that that makes some difference legally. I have no interest in the matter one way or the other, more than that of any other good Republican. I don't see exactly what I can do for you. What did you think I could do?"

"I don't believe you can do anything for me, Mr. Mollenhauer," replied Cowperwood, a little tartly, "unless you are willing to deal quite frankly with me. I am not a beginner in politics in Philadelphia. I know something about the powers in command. I thought that you could stop any plan to prosecute me in this matter, and give me time to get on my feet again. I am not any more criminally responsible for that sixty thousand dollars than I am for the five hundred thousand dollars that I had as loan before it–not as much so. I did not create this panic. I did not set Chicago on fire. Mr. Stener and his friends have been reaping some profit out of dealing with me. I certainly was entitled to make some effort to save myself after all these years of service, and I can't understand why I should not receive some courtesy at the hands of the present city administration, after I have been so useful to it. I certainly have kept city loan at par; and as for Mr. Stener's money, he has never wanted for his interest on that, and more than his interest."

"Quite so," replied Mollenhauer, looking Cowperwood in the eye steadily and estimating the force and accuracy of the man at their real value. "I understand exactly how it has all come about, Mr. Cowperwood. No doubt Mr. Stener owes you a debt of gratitude, as does the remainder of the city administration. I'm not saying what the city administration ought or ought not do. All I know is that you find yourself wittingly or unwittingly in a dangerous situation, and that public sentiment in some quarters is already very strong against you. I personally have no feeling one way or the other, and if it were not for the situation itself, which looks to be out of hand, would not be opposed to assisting you in any reasonable way. But how? The Republican party is in a very bad position, so far as this election is concerned. In a way, however innocently, you have helped to put it there, Mr. Cowperwood. Mr. Butler, for some reason to which I am not a party, seems deeply and personally incensed. And Mr. Butler is a great power here–" (Cowperwood began to wonder whether by any chance Butler had indicated the nature of his social offense against himself, but he could not bring himself to believe that. It was not probable.) "I sympathize with you greatly, Mr. Cowperwood, but what I suggest is that you first See Mr. Butler and Mr. Simpson. If they agree to any program of aid, I will not be opposed to joining. But apart from that I do not know exactly what I can do. I am only one of those who have a slight say in the affairs of Philadelphia."

At this point, Mollenhauer rather expected Cowperwood to make an offer of his own holdings, but he did not. Instead he said, "I'm very much obliged to you, Mr. Mollenhauer, for the courtesy of this interview. I believe you would help me if you could. I shall just have to fight it out the best way I can. Good day."

And he bowed himself out. He saw clearly how hopeless was his quest.

In the meanwhile, finding that the rumors were growing in volume and that no one appeared to be willing to take steps to straighten the matter out, Mr. Skelton C. Wheat, President of the Citizens' Municipal Reform Association, was, at last and that by no means against his will, compelled to call together the committee of ten estimable Philadelphians of which he was chairman, in a local committee-hall on Market Street, and lay the matter of the Cowperwood failure before it.

"It strikes me, gentlemen," he announced, "that this is an occasion when this organization can render a signal service to the city and the people of Philadelphia, and prove the significance and the merit of the title originally selected for it, by making such a thoroughgoing investigation as will bring to light all the facts in this case, and then by standing vigorously behind them insist that such nefarious practices as we are informed were indulged in in this case shall cease. I know it may prove to be a difficult task. The Republican party and its local and State interests are certain to be against us. Its leaders are unquestionably most anxious to avoid comment and to have their ticket go through undisturbed, and they will not contemplate with any equanimity our opening activity in this matter; but if we persevere, great good will surely come of it. There is too much dishonesty in public life as it is. There is a standard of right in these matters which cannot permanently be ignored, and which must eventually be fulfilled. I leave this matter to your courteous consideration."

Mr. Wheat sat down, and the body before him immediately took the matter which he proposed under advisement. It was decided to appoint a subcommittee "to investigate" (to quote the statement eventually given to the public) "the peculiar rumors now affecting one of the most important and distinguished offices of our municipal government," and to report at the next meeting, which was set for the following evening at nine o'clock. The meeting adjourned, and the following night at nine reassembled, four individuals of very shrewd financial judgment having meantime been about the task assigned them. They drew up a very elaborate statement, not wholly in accordance with the facts, but as nearly so as could be ascertained in so short a space of time.

"It appears [read the report, after a preamble which explained why the committee had been appointed] that it has been the custom of city treasurers for years, when loans have been authorized by councils, to place them in the hands of some favorite broker for sale, the broker accounting to the treasurer for the moneys received by such sales at short periods, generally the first of each month. In the present case Frank A. Cowperwood has been acting as such broker for the city treasurer. But even this vicious and unbusiness-like system appears not to have been adhered to in the case of Mr. Cowperwood. The accident of the Chicago fire, the consequent depression of stock values, and the subsequent failure of Mr. Frank A. Cowperwood have so involved matters temporarily that the committee has not been able to ascertain with accuracy that regular accounts have been rendered; but from the manner in which Mr. Cowperwood has had possession of bonds (city loan) for hypothecation, etc., it would appear that he has been held to no responsibility in these matters, and that there have always been under his control several hundred thousand dollars of cash or securities belonging to the city, which he has manipulated for various purposes; but the details of the results of these transactions are not easily available.

"Some of the operations consisted of hypothecation of large amounts of these loans before the certificates were issued, the lender seeing that the order for the hypothecated securities was duly made to him on the books of the treasurer. Such methods appear to have been occurring for a long time, and it being incredible that the city treasurer could be unaware of the nature of the business, there is indication of a complicity between him and Mr. Cowperwood to benefit by the use of the city credit, in violation of the law.

"Furthermore, at the very time these hypothecations were being made, and the city paying interest upon such loans, the money representing them was in the hands of the treasurer's broker and bearing no interest to the city. The payment of municipal warrants was postponed, and they were being purchased at a discount in large amounts by Mr. Cowperwood with the very money that should have been in the city treasury. The bona fide holders of the orders for certificates of loans are now unable to obtain them, and thus the city's credit is injured to a greater extent than the present defalcation, which amounts to over five hundred thousand dollars. An accountant is now at work on the treasurer's books, and a few days should make clear the whole modus operandi. It is hoped that the publicity thus obtained will break up such vicious practices."

There was appended to this report a quotation from the law governing the abuse of a public trust; and the committee went on to say that, unless some taxpayer chose to initiate proceedings for the prosecution of those concerned, the committee itself would be called upon to do so, although such action hardly came within the object for which it was formed.

This report was immediately given to the papers. Though some sort of a public announcement had been anticipated by Cowperwood and the politicians, this was, nevertheless, a severe blow. Stener was beside himself with fear. He broke into a cold sweat when he saw the announcement which was conservatively headed, "Meeting of the Municipal Reform Association." All of the papers were so closely identified with the political and financial powers of the city that they did not dare to come out openly and say what they thought. The chief facts had already been in the hands of the various editors and publishers for a week and more, but word had gone around from Mollenhauer, Simpson, and Butler to use the soft pedal for the present. It was not good for Philadelphia, for local commerce, etc., to make a row. The fair name of the city would be smirched. It was the old story.

At once the question was raised as to who was really guilty, the city treasurer or the broker, or both. How much money had actually been lost? Where had it gone? Who was Frank Algernon Cowperwood, anyway? Why was he not arrested? How did he come to be identified so closely with the financial administration of the city? And though the day of what later was termed "yellow journalism" had not arrived, and the local papers were not given to such vital personal comment as followed later, it was not possible, even bound as they were, hand and foot, by the local political and social magnates, to avoid comment of some sort. Editorials had to be written. Some solemn, conservative references to the shame and disgrace which one single individual could bring to a great city and a noble political party had to be ventured upon.

That desperate scheme to cast the blame on Cowperwood temporarily, which had been concocted by Mollenhauer, Butler, and Simpson, to get the odium of the crime outside the party lines for the time being, was now lugged forth and put in operation. It was interesting and strange to note how quickly the newspapers, and even the Citizens' Municipal Reform Association, adopted the argument that Cowperwood was largely, if not solely, to blame. Stener had loaned him the money, it is true–had put bond issues in his hands for sale, it is true, but somehow every one seemed to gain the impression that Cowperwood had desperately misused the treasurer. The fact that he had taken a sixty-thousand-dollar check for certificates which were not in the sinking-fund was hinted at, though until they could actually confirm this for themselves both the newspapers and the committee were too fearful of the State libel laws to say so.

In due time there were brought forth several noble municipal letters, purporting to be a stern call on the part of the mayor, Mr. Jacob Borchardt, on Mr. George W. Stener for an immediate explanation of his conduct, and the latter's reply, which were at once given to the newspapers and the Citizens' Municipal Reform Association. These letters were enough to show, so the politicians figured, that the Republican party was anxious to purge itself of any miscreant within its ranks, and they also helped to pass the time until after election.

OFFICE OF THE MAYOR OF THE CITY OF PHILADELPHIA
GEORGE W. STENER, ESQ., October 18,
1871. City Treasurer.
DEAR SIR,–Information has been given
me that certificates of city loan to a large amount, issued
by you for sale on account of the city, and, I presume,
after the usual requisition from the mayor of the city, have
passed out of your custody, and that the proceeds of the
sale of said certificates have not been paid into the city
treasury.
I have also been informed that a large amount of the city's
money has been permitted to pass into the hands of some one
or more brokers or bankers doing business on Third Street,
and that said brokers or bankers have since met with
financial difficulties, whereby, and by reason of the above

generally, the interests of the city are likely to be very seriously affected.

I have therefore to request that you will promptly advise me of the truth or falsity of these statements, so that such duties as devolve upon me as the chief magistrate of the city, in view of such facts, if they exist, may be intelligently discharged. Yours respectfully, JACOB BORCHARDT, Mayor of Philadelphia.

OFFICE OF THE TREASURER OF THE CITY OF PHILADELPHIA HON. JACOB BORCHARDT. October 19, 1871.

DEAR SIR,–I have to acknowledge the receipt of your communication of the 21st instant, and to express my regret that I cannot at this time give you the information you ask. There is undoubtedly an embarrassment in the city treasury, owing to the delinquency of the broker who for several years past has negotiated the city loans, and I have been, since the discovery of this fact, and still am occupied in endeavoring to avert or lessen the loss with which the city is threatened. I am, very respectfully, GEORGE W. STENER.

OFFICE OF THE MAYOR OF THE CITY OF PHILADELPHIA GEORGE W. STENER, ESQ., October 21, 1871.

City Treasurer.

DEAR SIR–Under the existing circumstances you will consider this as a notice of withdrawal and revocation of any requisition or authority by me for the sale of loan, so far as the same has not been fulfilled. Applications for loans may for the present be made at this office. Very respectfully, JACOB BORCHARDT, Mayor of Philadelphia.

And did Mr. Jacob Borchardt write the letters to which his name was attached? He did not. Mr. Abner Sengstack wrote them in Mr. Mollenhauer's office, and Mr. Mollenhauer's comment when he saw them was that he thought they would do–that they were very good, in fact. And did Mr. George W. Stener, city treasurer of Philadelphia, write that very politic reply? He did not. Mr. Stener was in a state of complete collapse, even crying at one time at home in his bathtub. Mr. Abner Sengstack wrote that also, and had Mr. Stener sign it. And Mr. Mollenhauer's comment on that, before it was sent, was that he thought it was "all right." It was a time when all the little rats and mice were scurrying to cover because of the presence of a great, fiery-eyed public cat somewhere in the dark, and only the older and wiser rats were able to act.

Indeed, at this very time and for some days past now, Messrs. Mollenhauer, Butler, and Simpson were, and had been, considering with Mr. Pettie, the district attorney, just what could be done about Cowperwood, if anything, and in order to further emphasize the blame in that direction, and just what defense, if any, could be made for Stener. Butler, of course, was strong for Cowperwood's prosecution. Pettie did not see that any defense could be made for Stener, since various records of street-car stocks purchased for him were spread upon Cowperwood's books; but for Cowperwood—"Let me see," he said. They were speculating, first of all, as to whether it might not be good policy to arrest Cowperwood, and if necessary try him, since his mere arrest would seem to the general public, at least, positive proof of his greater guilt, to say nothing of the virtuous indignation of the administration, and in consequence might tend to divert attention from the evil nature of the party until after election.

So finally, on the afternoon of October 26, 1871, Edward Strobik, president of the common council of Philadelphia, appeared before the mayor, as finally ordered by Mollenhauer, and charged by affidavit that Frank A. Cowperwood, as broker, employed by the treasurer to sell the bonds of the city, had committed embezzlement and larceny as bailee. It did not matter that he charged George W. Stener with embezzlement at the same time. Cowperwood was the scapegoat they were after.

Chapter XXXIV

The contrasting pictures presented by Cowperwood and Stener at this time are well worth a moment's consideration. Stener's face was grayish-white, his lips blue. Cowperwood, despite various solemn thoughts concerning a possible period of incarceration which this hue and cry now suggested, and what that meant to his parents, his wife and children, his business associates, and his friends, was as calm and collected as one might assume his great mental resources would permit him to be. During all this whirl of disaster he had never once lost his head or his courage. That thing conscience, which obsesses and rides some people to destruction, did not trouble him at all. He had no consciousness of what is currently known as sin. There were just two faces to the shield of life from the point of view of his peculiar mind-strength and weakness. Right and wrong? He did not know about those. They were bound up in metaphysical abstrusities about which he did not care to bother. Good and evil? Those were toys of clerics, by which they made money. And as for social favor or social ostracism which, on occasion, so quickly followed upon the heels of disaster of any kind, well, what was social ostracism? Had either he or his parents been of the best society as yet? And since not, and despite this present mix-up, might not the future hold social restoration and position for him? It might. Morality and immorality? He never considered them. But strength and weakness—oh, yes! If you had strength you could protect yourself always and be something. If you were weak—pass quickly to the rear and get out of the range of the guns. He was strong, and he knew it, and somehow he always believed in his star. Something—he could not say what—it was the only metaphysics he bothered about—was doing something for him. It had always helped him. It made things come out right at times. It put excellent opportunities in his way. Why had he been given so fine a mind? Why always favored financially, personally? He had not deserved it—earned it. Accident, perhaps, but somehow the thought that he would always be protected—these intuitions, the "hunches" to act which he frequently had—could not be so easily explained. Life was a dark, insoluble mystery, but whatever it was, strength and weakness were its two constituents. Strength would win—weakness lose. He must rely on swiftness of thought, accuracy, his judgment, and on nothing else. He was really a brilliant picture of courage and energy—moving about briskly in a jaunty, dapper way, his mustaches curled, his clothes pressed, his nails manicured, his face clean-shaven and tinted with health.

In the meantime, Cowperwood had gone personally to Skelton C. Wheat and tried to explain his side of the situation, alleging that he had done no differently from many others before him, but Wheat was dubious. He did not see how it was that the sixty thousand dollars' worth of certificates were not in the sinking-fund. Cowperwood's explanation of custom did not avail. Nevertheless, Mr. Wheat saw that others in politics had been profiting quite as much as Cowperwood in other ways and he advised Cowperwood to turn state's evidence. This, however, he promptly refused to do–he was no "squealer," and indicated as much to Mr. Wheat, who only smiled wryly.

Butler, Sr., was delighted (concerned though he was about party success at the polls), for now he had this villain in the toils and he would have a fine time getting out of this. The incoming district attorney to succeed David Pettie if the Republican party won would be, as was now planned, an appointee of Butler's–a young Irishman who had done considerable legal work for him–one Dennis Shannon. The other two party leaders had already promised Butler that. Shannon was a smart, athletic, good-looking fellow, all of five feet ten inches in height, sandy-haired, pink-cheeked, blue-eyed, considerable of an orator and a fine legal fighter. He was very proud to be in the old man's favor–to be promised a place on the ticket by him–and would, he said, if elected, do his bidding to the best of his knowledge and ability.

There was only one fly in the ointment, so far as some of the politicians were concerned, and that was that if Cowperwood were convicted, Stener must needs be also. There was no escape in so far as any one could see for the city treasurer. If Cowperwood was guilty of securing by trickery sixty thousand dollars' worth of the city money, Stener guilty of securing five hundred thousand dollars. The prison term for this was five years. He might plead not guilty, and by submitting as evidence that what he did was due to custom save himself from the odious necessity of pleading guilty; but he would be convicted nevertheless. No jury could get by the fact in regard to him. In spite of public opinion, when it came to a trial there might be considerable doubt in Cowperwood's case. There was none in Stener's.

The practical manner in which the situation was furthered, after Cowperwood and Stener were formally charged may be quickly noted. Steger, Cowperwood's lawyer, learned privately beforehand that Cowperwood was to be prosecuted. He arranged at once to have his client appear before any warrant could be served, and to forestall the newspaper palaver which would follow it if he had to be searched for.

The mayor issued a warrant for Cowperwood's arrest, and, in accordance with Steger's plan, Cowperwood immediately appeared before Borchardt in company with his lawyer and gave bail in twenty thousand dollars (W. C. Davison, president of the Girard National Bank, being his surety), for his appearance at the central police station on the following Saturday for a hearing. Marcus Oldslaw, a lawyer, had been employed by Strobik as president of the common council, to represent him in prosecuting the case for the city. The mayor looked at Cowperwood curiously, for he, being comparatively new to the political world of Philadelphia, was not so familiar with him as others were; and Cowperwood returned the look pleasantly enough.

"This is a great dumb show, Mr. Mayor," he observed once to Borchardt, quietly, and the latter replied, with a smile and a kindly eye, that as far as he was concerned, it was a form of procedure which was absolutely unavoidable at this time.

"You know how it is, Mr. Cowperwood," he observed. The latter smiled. "I do, indeed," he said.

Later there followed several more or less perfunctory appearances in a local police court, known as the Central Court, where when arraigned he pleaded not guilty, and finally his appearance before the November grand jury, where, owing to the complicated nature of the charge drawn up against him by Pettie, he thought it wise to appear. He was properly indicted by the latter body (Shannon, the newly elected district attorney, making a demonstration in force), and his trial ordered for December 5th before a certain Judge Payderson in Part I of Quarter Sessions, which was the local branch of the State courts dealing with crimes of this character. His indictment did not occur, however, before the coming and going of the much-mooted fall election, which resulted, thanks to the clever political manipulations of Mollenhauer and Simpson (ballot-box stuffing and personal violence at the polls not barred), in another victory, by, however, a greatly reduced majority. The Citizens' Municipal Reform Association, in spite of a resounding defeat at the polls, which could not have happened except by fraud, continued to fire courageously away at those whom it considered to be the chief malefactors.

Aileen Butler, during all this time, was following the trend of Cowperwood's outward vicissitudes as heralded by the newspapers and the local gossip with as much interest and bias and enthusiasm for him as her powerful physical and affectional nature would permit. She was no great reasoner where affection entered in, but shrewd enough without it; and, although she saw him often and he told her much—as much as his natural caution would permit—she yet gathered from the newspapers and private conversation, at her own family's table and elsewhere, that, as bad as they said he was, he was not as bad as he might be. One item only, clipped from the Philadelphia Public Ledger soon after Cowperwood had been publicly accused of embezzlement, comforted and consoled her. She cut it out and carried it in her bosom; for, somehow, it seemed to show that her adored Frank was far more sinned against than sinning. It was a part of one of those very numerous pronunciamientos or reports issued by the Citizens' Municipal Reform Association, and it ran:

"The aspects of the case are graver than have yet been allowed to reach the public. Five hundred thousand dollars of the deficiency arises not from city bonds sold and not accounted for, but from loans made by the treasurer to his broker. The committee is also informed, on what it believes to be good authority, that the loans sold by the broker were accounted for in the monthly settlements at the lowest prices current during the month, and that the difference between this rate and that actually realized was divided between the treasurer and the broker, thus making it to the interest of both parties to 'bear' the market at some time during the month, so as to obtain a low quotation for settlement. Nevertheless, the committee can only regard the prosecution instituted against the broker, Mr. Cowperwood, as an effort to divert public attention from more guilty parties while those concerned may be able to 'fix' matters to suit themselves."

"There," thought Aileen, when she read it, "there you have it." These politicians– her father among them as she gathered after his conversation with her–were trying to put the blame of their own evil deeds on her Frank. He was not nearly as bad as he was painted. The report said so. She gloated over the words "an effort to divert public attention from more guilty parties." That was just what her Frank had been telling her in those happy, private hours when they had been together recently in one place and another, particularly the new rendezvous in South Sixth Street which he had established, since the old one had to be abandoned. He had stroked her rich hair, caressed her body, and told her it was all a prearranged political scheme to cast the blame as much as possible on him and make it as light as possible for Stener and the party generally. He would come out of it all right, he said, but he cautioned her not to talk. He did not deny his long and profitable relations with Stener. He told her exactly how it was. She understood, or thought she did. Anyhow, her Frank was telling her, and that was enough.

As for the two Cowperwood households, so recently and pretentiously joined in success, now so gloomily tied in failure, the life was going out of them. Frank Algernon was that life. He was the courage and force of his father: the spirit and opportunity of his brothers, the hope of his children, the estate of his wife, the dignity and significance of the Cowperwood name. All that meant opportunity, force, emolument, dignity, and happiness to those connected with him, he was. And his marvelous sun was waning apparently to a black eclipse.

Since the fatal morning, for instance, when Lillian Cowperwood had received that utterly destructive note, like a cannonball ripping through her domestic affairs, she had been walking like one in a trance. Each day now for weeks she had been going about her duties placidly enough to all outward seeming, but inwardly she was running with a troubled tide of thought. She was so utterly unhappy. Her fortieth year had come for her at a time when life ought naturally to stand fixed and firm on a solid base, and here she was about to be torn bodily from the domestic soil in which she was growing and blooming, and thrown out indifferently to wither in the blistering noonday sun of circumstance.

As for Cowperwood, Senior, his situation at his bank and elsewhere was rapidly nearing a climax. As has been said, he had had tremendous faith in his son; but he could not help seeing that an error had been committed, as he thought, and that Frank was suffering greatly for it now. He considered, of course, that Frank had been entitled to try to save himself as he had; but he so regretted that his son should have put his foot into the trap of any situation which could stir up discussion of the sort that was now being aroused. Frank was wonderfully brilliant. He need never have taken up with the city treasurer or the politicians to have succeeded marvelously. Local street-railways and speculative politicians were his undoing. The old man walked the floor all of the days, realizing that his sun was setting, that with Frank's failure he failed, and that this disgrace–these public charges–meant his own undoing. His hair had grown very gray in but a few weeks, his step slow, his face pallid, his eyes sunken. His rather showy side-whiskers seemed now like flags or ornaments of a better day that was gone. His only consolation through it all was that Frank had actually got out of his relationship with the Third National Bank without owing it a single dollar. Still as he knew the directors of that institution could not possibly tolerate the presence of a man whose son had helped loot the city treasury, and whose name was now in the public prints in this connection. Besides, Cowperwood, Sr., was too old. He ought to retire.

The crisis for him therefore came on the day when Frank was arrested on the embezzlement charge. The old man, through Frank, who had it from Steger, knew it was coming, still had the courage to go to the bank but it was like struggling under the weight of a heavy stone to do it. But before going, and after a sleepless night, he wrote his resignation to Frewen Kasson, the chairman of the board of directors, in order that he should be prepared to hand it to him, at once. Kasson, a stocky, well-built, magnetic man of fifty, breathed an inward sigh of relief at the sight of it.

"I know it's hard, Mr. Cowperwood," he said, sympathetically. "We–and I can speak for the other members of the board–we feel keenly the unfortunate nature of your position. We know exactly how it is that your son has become involved in this matter. He is not the only banker who has been involved in the city's affairs. By no means. It is an old system. We appreciate, all of us, keenly, the services you have rendered this institution during the past thirty-five years. If there were any possible way in which we could help to tide you over the difficulties at this time, we would be glad to do so, but as a banker yourself you must realize just how impossible that would be. Everything is in a turmoil. If things were settled–if we knew how soon this would blow over–" He paused, for he felt that he could not go on and say that he or the bank was sorry to be forced to lose Mr. Cowperwood in this way at present. Mr. Cowperwood himself would have to speak.

During all this Cowperwood, Sr., had been doing his best to pull himself together in order to be able to speak at all. He had gotten out a large white linen handkerchief and blown his nose, and had straightened himself in his chair, and laid his hands rather peacefully on his desk. Still he was intensely wrought up.

"I can't stand this!" he suddenly exclaimed. "I wish you would leave me alone now."

Kasson, very carefully dressed and manicured, arose and walked out of the room for a few moments. He appreciated keenly the intensity of the strain he had just witnessed. The moment the door was closed Cowperwood put his head in his hands and shook convulsively. "I never thought I'd come to this," he muttered. "I never thought it." Then he wiped away his salty hot tears, and went to the window to look out and to think of what else to do from now on.

Chapter XXXV

As time went on Butler grew more and more puzzled and restive as to his duty in regard to his daughter. He was sure by her furtive manner and her apparent desire to avoid him, that she was still in touch with Cowperwood in some way, and that this would bring about a social disaster of some kind. He thought once of going to Mrs. Cowperwood and having her bring pressure to bear on her husband, but afterwards he decided that that would not do. He was not really positive as yet that Aileen was secretly meeting Cowperwood, and, besides, Mrs. Cowperwood might not know of her husband's duplicity. He thought also of going to Cowperwood personally and threatening him, but that would be a severe measure, and again, as in the other case, he lacked proof. He hesitated to appeal to a detective agency, and he did not care to take the other members of the family into his confidence. He did go out and scan the neighborhood of 931 North Tenth Street once, looking at the house; but that helped him little. The place was for rent, Cowperwood having already abandoned his connection with it.

Finally he hit upon the plan of having Aileen invited to go somewhere some distance off–Boston or New Orleans, where a sister of his wife lived. It was a delicate matter to engineer, and in such matters he was not exactly the soul of tact; but he undertook it. He wrote personally to his wife's sister at New Orleans, and asked her if she would, without indicating in any way that she had heard from him, write his wife and ask if she would not permit Aileen to come and visit her, writing Aileen an invitation at the same time; but he tore the letter up. A little later he learned accidentally that Mrs. Mollenhauer and her three daughters, Caroline, Felicia, and Alta, were going to Europe early in December to visit Paris, the Riviera, and Rome; and he decided to ask Mollenhauer to persuade his wife to invite Norah and Aileen, or Aileen only, to go along, giving as an excuse that his own wife would not leave him, and that the girls ought to go. It would be a fine way of disposing of Aileen for the present. The party was to be gone six months. Mollenhauer was glad to do so, of course. The two families were fairly intimate. Mrs. Mollenhauer was willing–delighted from a politic point of view–and the invitation was extended. Norah was overjoyed. She wanted to see something of Europe, and had always been hoping for some such opportunity. Aileen was pleased from the point of view that Mrs. Mollenhauer should invite her. Years before she would have accepted in a flash. But now she felt that it only came as a puzzling interruption, one more of the minor difficulties that were tending to interrupt her relations with Cowperwood. She immediately threw cold water on the proposition, which was made one evening at dinner by Mrs. Butler, who did not know of her husband's share in the matter, but had received a call that afternoon from Mrs. Mollenhauer, when the invitation had been extended.

"She's very anxious to have you two come along, if your father don't mind," volunteered the mother, "and I should think ye'd have a fine time. They're going to Paris and the Riveera."

"Oh, fine!" exclaimed Norah. "I've always wanted to go to Paris. Haven't you, Ai? Oh, wouldn't that be fine?"

"I don't know that I want to go," replied Aileen. She did not care to compromise herself by showing any interest at the start. "It's coming on winter, and I haven't any clothes. I'd rather wait and go some other time."

"Oh, Aileen Butler!" exclaimed Norah. "How you talk! I've heard you say a dozen times you'd like to go abroad some winter. Now when the chance comes–besides you can get your clothes made over there."

"Couldn't you get somethin' over there?" inquired Mrs. Butler. "Besides, you've got two or three weeks here yet."

"They wouldn't want a man around as a sort of guide and adviser, would they, mother?" put in Callum.

"I might offer my services in that capacity myself," observed Owen, reservedly.

"I'm sure I don't know," returned Mrs. Butler, smiling, and at the same time chewing a lusty mouthful. "You'll have to ast 'em, my sons."

Aileen still persisted. She did not want to go. It was too sudden. It was this. It was that. Just then old Butler came in and took his seat at the head of the table. Knowing all about it, he was most anxious to appear not to.

"You wouldn't object, Edward, would you?" queried his wife, explaining the proposition in general.

"Object!" he echoed, with a well simulated but rough attempt at gayety. "A fine thing I'd be doing for meself–objectin'. I'd be glad if I could get shut of the whole pack of ye for a time."

"What talk ye have!" said his wife. "A fine mess you'd make of it livin' alone."

"I'd not be alone, belave me," replied Butler. "There's many a place I'd be welcome in this town–no thanks to ye."

"And there's many a place ye wouldn't have been if it hadn't been for me. I'm tellin' ye that," retorted Mrs. Butler, genially.

"And that's not stretchin' the troot much, aither," he answered, fondly.

Aileen was adamant. No amount of argument both on the part of Norah and her mother had any effect whatever. Butler witnessed the failure of his plan with considerable dissatisfaction, but he was not through. When he was finally convinced that there was no hope of persuading her to accept the Mollenhauer proposition, he decided, after a while, to employ a detective.

At that time, the reputation of William A. Pinkerton, of detective fame, and of his agency was great. The man had come up from poverty through a series of vicissitudes to a high standing in his peculiar and, to many, distasteful profession; but to any one in need of such in themselves calamitous services, his very famous and decidedly patriotic connection with the Civil War and Abraham Lincoln was a recommendation. He, or rather his service, had guarded the latter all his stormy incumbency at the executive mansion. There were offices for the management of the company's business in Philadelphia, Washington, and New York, to say nothing of other places. Butler was familiar with the Philadelphia sign, but did not care to go to the office there. He decided, once his mind was made up on this score, that he would go over to New York, where he was told the principal offices were.

He made the simple excuse one day of business, which was common enough in his case, and journeyed to New York–nearly five hours away as the trains ran then–arriving at two o'clock. At the offices on lower Broadway, he asked to see the manager, whom he found to be a large, gross-featured, heavy-bodied man of fifty, gray-eyed, gray-haired, puffily outlined as to countenance, but keen and shrewd, and with short, fat-fingered hands, which drummed idly on his desk as he talked. He was dressed in a suit of dark-brown wool cloth, which struck Butler as peculiarly showy, and wore a large horseshoe diamond pin. The old man himself invariably wore conservative gray.

"How do you do?" said Butler, when a boy ushered him into the presence of this worthy, whose name was Martinson–Gilbert Martinson, of American and Irish extraction. The latter nodded and looked at Butler shrewdly, recognizing him at once as a man of force and probably of position. He therefore rose and offered him a chair.

"Sit down," he said, studying the old Irishman from under thick, bushy eyebrows. "What can I do for you?"

"You're the manager, are you?" asked Butler, solemnly, eyeing the man with a shrewd, inquiring eye.

"Yes, sir," replied Martinson, simply. "That's my position here."

"This Mr. Pinkerton that runs this agency–he wouldn't be about this place, now, would he?" asked Butler, carefully. "I'd like to talk to him personally, if I might, meaning no offense to you."

"Mr. Pinkerton is in Chicago at present," replied Mr. Martinson. "I don't expect him back for a week or ten days. You can talk to me, though, with the same confidence that you could to him. I'm the responsible head here. However, you're the best judge of that."

Butler debated with himself in silence for a few moments, estimating the man before him. "Are you a family man yourself?" he asked, oddly.

"Yes, sir, I'm married," replied Martinson, solemnly. "I have a wife and two children."

Martinson, from long experience conceived that this must be a matter of family misconduct–a son, daughter, wife. Such cases were not infrequent.

"I thought I would like to talk to Mr. Pinkerton himself, but if you're the responsible head–" Butler paused.

"I am," replied Martinson. "You can talk to me with the same freedom that you could to Mr. Pinkerton. Won't you come into my private office? We can talk more at ease in there."

He led the way into an adjoining room which had two windows looking down into Broadway; an oblong table, heavy, brown, smoothly polished; four leather-backed chairs; and some pictures of the Civil War battles in which the North had been victorious. Butler followed doubtfully. He hated very much to take any one into his confidence in regard to Aileen. He was not sure that he would, even now. He wanted to "look these fellys over," as he said in his mind. He would decide then what he wanted to do. He went to one of the windows and looked down into the street, where there was a perfect swirl of omnibuses and vehicles of all sorts. Mr. Martinson quietly closed the door.

"Now then, if there's anything I can do for you," Mr. Martinson paused. He thought by this little trick to elicit Buder's real name–it often "worked"–but in this instance the name was not forthcoming. Butler was too shrewd.

"I'm not so sure that I want to go into this," said the old man solemnly. "Certainly not if there's any risk of the thing not being handled in the right way. There's somethin' I want to find out about–somethin' that I ought to know; but it's a very private matter with me, and–" He paused to think and conjecture, looking at Mr. Martinson the while. The latter understood his peculiar state of mind. He had seen many such cases.

"Let me say right here, to begin with, Mr.–"

"Scanlon," interpolated Butler, easily; "that's as good a name as any if you want to use one. I'm keepin' me own to meself for the present."

"Scanlon," continued Martinson, easily. "I really don't care whether it's your right name or not. I was just going to say that it might not be necessary to have your right name under any circumstances–it all depends upon what you want to know. But, so far as your private affairs are concerned, they are as safe with us, as if you had never told them to any one. Our business is built upon confidence, and we never betray it. We wouldn't dare. We have men and women who have been in our employ for over thirty years, and we never retire any one except for cause, and we don't pick people who are likely to need to be retired for cause. Mr. Pinkerton is a good judge of men. There are others here who consider that they are. We handle over ten thousand separate cases in all parts of the United States every year. We work on a case only so long as we are wanted. We try to find out only such things as our customers want. We do not pry unnecessarily into anybody's affairs. If we decide that we cannot find out what you want to know, we are the first to say so. Many cases are rejected right here in this office before we ever begin. Yours might be such a one. We don't want cases merely for the sake of having them, and we are frank to say so. Some matters that involve public policy, or some form of small persecution, we don't touch at all–we won't be a party to them. You can see how that is. You look to me to be a man of the world. I hope I am one. Does it strike you that an organization like ours would be likely to betray any one's confidence?" He paused and looked at Butler for confirmation of what he had just said.

"It wouldn't seem likely," said the latter; "that's the truth. It's not aisy to bring your private affairs into the light of day, though," added the old man, sadly.

They both rested.

"Well," said Butler, finally, "you look to me to be all right, and I'd like some advice. Mind ye, I'm willing to pay for it well enough; and it isn't anything that'll be very hard to find out. I want to know whether a certain man where I live is goin' with a certain woman, and where. You could find that out aisy enough, I belave–couldn't you?"

"Nothing easier," replied Martinson. "We are doing it all the time. Let me see if I can help you just a moment, Mr. Scanlon, in order to make it easier for you. It is very plain to me that you don't care to tell any more than you can help, and we don't care to have you tell any more than we absolutely need. We will have to have the name of the city, of course, and the name of either the man or the woman; but not necessarily both of them, unless you want to help us in that way. Sometimes if you give us the name of one party–say the man, for illustration–and the description of the woman–an accurate one–or a photograph, we can tell you after a little while exactly what you want to know. Of course, it's always better if we have full information. You suit yourself about that. Tell me as much or as little as you please, and I'll guarantee that we will do our best to serve you, and that you will be satisfied afterward."

He smiled genially.

"Well, that bein' the case," said Butler, finally taking the leap, with many mental reservations, however, "I'll be plain with you. My name's not Scanlon. It's Butler. I live in Philadelphy. There's a man there, a banker by the name of Cowperwood–Frank A. Cowperwood–"

"Wait a moment," said Martinson, drawing an ample pad out of his pocket and producing a lead-pencil; "I want to get that. How do you spell it?"

Butler told him.

"Yes; now go on."

"He has a place in Third Street–Frank A. Cowperwood–any one can show you where it is. He's just failed there recently."

"Oh, that's the man," interpolated Martinson. "I've heard of him. He's mixed up in some city embezzlement case over there. I suppose the reason you didn't go to our Philadelphia office is because you didn't want our local men over there to know anything about it. Isn't that it?"

"That's the man, and that's the reason," said Butler. "I don't care to have anything of this known in Philadelphy. That's why I'm here. This man has a house on Girard Avenue–Nineteen-thirty-seven. You can find that out, too, when you get over there."

"Yes," agreed Mr. Martinson.

"Well, it's him that I want to know about–him–and a certain woman, or girl, rather." The old man paused and winced at this necessity of introducing Aileen into the case. He could scarcely think of it–he was so fond of her. He had been so proud of Aileen. A dark, smoldering rage burned in his heart against Cowperwood.

"A relative of yours–possibly, I suppose," remarked Martinson, tactfully. "You needn't tell me any more–just give me a description if you wish. We may be able to work from that." He saw quite clearly what a fine old citizen in his way he was dealing with here, and also that the man was greatly troubled. Butler's heavy, meditative face showed it. "You can be quite frank with me, Mr. Butler," he added; "I think I understand. We only want such information as we must have to help you, nothing more."

"Yes," said the old man, dourly. "She is a relative. She's me daughter, in fact. You look to me like a sensible, honest man. I'm her father, and I wouldn't do anything for the world to harm her. It's tryin' to save her I am. It's him I want." He suddenly closed one big fist forcefully.

Martinson, who had two daughters of his own, observed the suggestive movement.

"I understand how you feel, Mr. Butler," he observed. "I am a father myself. We'll do all we can for you. If you can give me an accurate description of her, or let one of my men see her at your house or office, accidentally, of course, I think we can tell you in no time at all if they are meeting with any regularity. That's all you want to know, is it–just that?"

"That's all," said Butler, solemnly.

"Well, that oughtn't to take any time at all, Mr. Butler–three or four days possibly, if we have any luck–a week, ten days, two weeks. It depends on how long you want us to shadow him in case there is no evidence the first few days."

"I want to know, however long it takes," replied Butler, bitterly. "I want to know, if it takes a month or two months or three to find out. I want to know." The old man got up as he said this, very positive, very rugged. "And don't send me men that haven't sinse–lots of it, plase. I want men that are fathers, if you've got 'em–and that have sinse enough to hold their tongues–not b'ys."

"I understand, Mr. Butler," Martinson replied. "Depend on it, you'll have the best we have, and you can trust them. They'll be discreet. You can depend on that. The way I'll do will be to assign just one man to the case at first, some one you can see for yourself whether you like or not. I'll not tell him anything. You can talk to him. If you like him, tell him, and he'll do the rest. Then, if he needs any more help, he can get it. What is your address?"

Butler gave it to him.

"And there'll be no talk about this?"

"None whatever–I assure you."

"And when'll he be comin' along?"

"To-morrow, if you wish. I have a man I could send to-night. He isn't here now or I'd have him talk with you. I'll talk to him, though, and make everything clear. You needn't worry about anything. Your daughter's reputation will be safe in his hands."

"Thank you kindly," commented Butler, softening the least bit in a gingerly way. "I'm much obliged to you. I'll take it as a great favor, and pay you well."

"Never mind about that, Mr. Butler," replied Martinson. "You're welcome to anything this concern can do for you at its ordinary rates."

He showed Butler to the door, and the old man went out. He was feeling very depressed over this–very shabby. To think he should have to put detectives on the track of his Aileen, his daughter!

Chapter XXXVI

The very next day there called at Butler's office a long, preternaturally solemn man of noticeable height and angularity, dark-haired, dark-eyed, sallow, with a face that was long and leathery, and particularly hawk-like, who talked with Butler for over an hour and then departed. That evening he came to the Butler house around dinner-time, and, being shown into Butler's room, was given a look at Aileen by a ruse. Butler sent for her, standing in the doorway just far enough to one side to yield a good view of her. The detective stood behind one of the heavy curtains which had already been put up for the winter, pretending to look out into the street.

"Did any one drive Sissy this mornin'?" asked Butler of Aileen, inquiring after a favorite family horse. Butler's plan, in case the detective was seen, was to give the impression that he was a horseman who had come either to buy or to sell. His name was Jonas Alderson, and be looked sufficiently like a horsetrader to be one.

"I don't think so, father," replied Aileen. "I didn't. I'll find out."

"Never mind. What I want to know is did you intend using her to-morrow?"

"No, not if you want her. Jerry suits me just as well."

"Very well, then. Leave her in the stable." Butler quietly closed the door. Aileen concluded at once that it was a horse conference. She knew he would not dispose of any horse in which she was interested without first consulting her, and so she thought no more about it.

After she was gone Alderson stepped out and declared that he was satisfied. "That's all I need to know," he said. "I'll let you know in a few days if I find out anything."

He departed, and within thirty-six hours the house and office of Cowperwood, the house of Butler, the office of Harper Steger, Cowperwood's lawyer, and Cowperwood and Aileen separately and personally were under complete surveillance. It took six men to do it at first, and eventually a seventh, when the second meeting-place, which was located in South Sixth Street, was discovered. All the detectives were from New York. In a week all was known to Alderson. It bad been agreed between him and Butler that if Aileen and Cowperwood were discovered to have any particular rendezvous Butler was to be notified some time when she was there, so that he might go immediately and confront her in person, if he wished. He did not intend to kill Cowperwood–and Alderson would have seen to it that he did not in his presence at least, but he would give him a good tongue-lashing, fell him to the floor, in all likelihood, and march Aileen away. There would be no more lying on her part as to whether she was or was not going with Cowperwood. She would not be able to say after that what she would or would not do. Butler would lay down the law to her. She would reform, or he would send her to a reformatory. Think of her influence on her sister, or on any good girl–knowing what she knew, or doing what she was doing! She would go to Europe after this, or any place he chose to send her.

In working out his plan of action it was necessary for Butler to take Alderson into his confidence and the detective made plain his determination to safeguard Cowperwood's person.

"We couldn't allow you to strike any blows or do any violence," Alderson told Butler, when they first talked about it. "It's against the rules. You can go in there on a search-warrant, if we have to have one. I can get that for you without anybody's knowing anything about your connection with the case. We can say it's for a girl from New York. But you'll have to go in in the presence of my men. They won't permit any trouble. You can get your daughter all right–we'll bring her away, and him, too, if you say so; but you'll have to make some charge against him, if we do. Then there's the danger of the neighbors seeing. You can't always guarantee you won't collect a crowd that way." Butler had many misgivings about the matter. It was fraught with great danger of publicity. Still he wanted to know. He wanted to terrify Aileen if he could–to reform her drastically.

Within a week Alderson learned that Aileen and Cowperwood were visiting an apparently private residence, which was anything but that. The house on South Sixth Street was one of assignation purely; but in its way it was superior to the average establishment of its kind–of red brick, white-stone trimmings, four stories high, and all the rooms, some eighteen in number, furnished in a showy but cleanly way. It's patronage was highly exclusive, only those being admitted who were known to the mistress, having been introduced by others. This guaranteed that privacy which the illicit affairs of this world so greatly required. The mere phrase, "I have an appointment," was sufficient, where either of the parties was known, to cause them to be shown to a private suite. Cowperwood had known of the place from previous experiences, and when it became necessary to abandon the North Tenth Street house, he had directed Aileen to meet him here.

The matter of entering a place of this kind and trying to find any one was, as Alderson informed Butler on hearing of its character, exceedingly difficult. It involved the right of search, which was difficult to get. To enter by sheer force was easy enough in most instances where the business conducted was in contradistinction to the moral sentiment of the community; but sometimes one encountered violent opposition from the tenants themselves. It might be so in this case. The only sure way of avoiding such opposition would be to take the woman who ran the place into one's confidence, and by paying her sufficiently insure silence. "But I do not advise that in this instance," Alderson had told Butler, "for I believe this woman is particularly friendly to your man. It might be better, in spite of the risk, to take it by surprise." To do that, he explained, it would be necessary to have at least three men in addition to the leader–perhaps four, who, once one man had been able to make his entrance into the hallway, on the door being opened in response to a ring, would appear quickly and enter with and sustain him. Quickness of search was the next thing–the prompt opening of all doors. The servants, if any, would have to be overpowered and silenced in some way. Money sometimes did this; force accomplished it at other times. Then one of the detectives simulating a servant could tap gently at the different doors–Butler and the others standing by–and in case a face appeared identify it or not, as the case might be. If the door was not opened and the room was not empty, it could eventually be forced. The house was one of a solid block, so that there was no chance of escape save by the front and rear doors, which were to be safe-guarded. It was a daringly conceived scheme. In spite of all this, secrecy in the matter of removing Aileen was to be preserved.

When Butler heard of this he was nervous about the whole terrible procedure. He thought once that without going to the house he would merely talk to his daughter declaring that he knew and that she could not possibly deny it. He would then give her her choice between going to Europe or going to a reformatory. But a sense of the raw brutality of Aileen's disposition, and something essentially coarse in himself, made him eventually adopt the other method. He ordered Alderson to perfect his plan, and once he found Aileen or Cowperwood entering the house to inform him quickly. He would then drive there, and with the assistance of these men confront her.

It was a foolish scheme, a brutalizing thing to do, both from the point of view of affection and any corrective theory he might have had. No good ever springs from violence. But Butler did not see that. He wanted to frighten Aileen, to bring her by shock to a realization of the enormity of the offense she was committing. He waited fully a week after his word had been given; and then, one afternoon, when his nerves were worn almost thin from fretting, the climax came. Cowperwood had already been indicted, and was now awaiting trial. Aileen had been bringing him news, from time to time, of just how she thought her father was feeling toward him. She did not get this evidence direct from Butler, of course–he was too secretive, in so far as she was concerned, to let her know how relentlessly he was engineering Cowperwood's final downfall–but from odd bits confided to Owen, who confided them to Callum, who in turn, innocently enough, confided them to Aileen. For one thing, she had learned in this way of the new district attorney elect–his probable attitude–for he was a constant caller at the Butler house or office. Owen had told Callum that he thought Shannon was going to do his best to send Cowperwood "up"–that the old man thought he deserved it.

In the next place she had learned that her father did not want Cowperwood to resume business–did not feel he deserved to be allowed to. "It would be a God's blessing if the community were shut of him," he had said to Owen one morning, apropos of a notice in the papers of Cowperwood's legal struggles; and Owen had asked Callum why he thought the old man was so bitter. The two sons could not understand it. Cowperwood heard all this from her, and more–bits about Judge Payderson, the judge who was to try him, who was a friend of Butler's–also about the fact that Stener might be sent up for the full term of his crime, but that he would be pardoned soon afterward.

Apparently Cowperwood was not very much frightened. He told her that he had powerful financial friends who would appeal to the governor to pardon him in case he was convicted; and, anyhow, that he did not think that the evidence was strong enough to convict him. He was merely a political scapegoat through public clamor and her father's influence; since the latter's receipt of the letter about them he had been the victim of Butler's enmity, and nothing more. "If it weren't for your father, honey," he declared, "I could have this indictment quashed in no time. Neither Mollenhauer nor Simpson has anything against me personally, I am sure. They want me to get out of the street-railway business here in Philadelphia, and, of course, they wanted to make things look better for Stener at first; but depend upon it, if your father hadn't been against me they wouldn't have gone to any such length in making me the victim. Your father has this fellow Shannon and these minor politicians just where he wants them, too. That's where the trouble lies. They have to go on."

"Oh, I know," replied Aileen. "It's me, just me, that's all. If it weren't for me and what he suspects he'd help you in a minute. Sometimes, you know, I think I've been very bad for you. I don't know what I ought to do. If I thought it would help you any I'd not see you any more for a while, though I don't see what good that would do now. Oh, I love you, love you, Frank! I would do anything for you. I don't care what people think or say. I love you."

"Oh, you just think you do," he replied, jestingly. "You'll get over it. There are others."

"Others!" echoed Aileen, resentfully and contemptuously. "After you there aren't any others. I just want one man, my Frank. If you ever desert me, I'll go to hell. You'll see."

"Don't talk like that, Aileen," he replied, almost irritated. "I don't like to hear you. You wouldn't do anything of the sort. I love you. You know I'm not going to desert you. It would pay you to desert me just now."

"Oh, how you talk!" she exclaimed. "Desert you! It's likely, isn't it? But if ever you desert me, I'll do just what I say. I swear it."

"Don't talk like that. Don't talk nonsense."

"I swear it. I swear by my love. I swear by your success—my own happiness. I'll do just what I say. I'll go to hell."

Cowperwood got up. He was a little afraid now of this deep-seated passion he had aroused. It was dangerous. He could not tell where it would lead.

It was a cheerless afternoon in November, when Alderson, duly informed of the presence of Aileen and Cowperwood in the South Sixth Street house by the detective on guard drove rapidly up to Butler's office and invited him to come with him. Yet even now Butler could scarcely believe that he was to find his daughter there. The shame of it. The horror. What would he say to her? How reproach her? What would he do to Cowperwood? His large hands shook as he thought. They drove rapidly to within a few doors of the place, where a second detective on guard across the street approached. Butler and Alderson descended from the vehicle, and together they approached the door. It was now almost four-thirty in the afternoon. In a room within the house, Cowperwood, his coat and vest off, was listening to Aileen's account of her troubles.

The room in which they were sitting at the time was typical of the rather common-place idea of luxury which then prevailed. Most of the "sets" of furniture put on the market for general sale by the furniture companies were, when they approached in any way the correct idea of luxury, imitations of one of the Louis periods. The curtains were always heavy, frequently brocaded, and not infrequently red. The carpets were richly flowered in high colors with a thick, velvet nap. The furniture, of whatever wood it might be made, was almost invariably heavy, floriated, and cumbersome. This room contained a heavily constructed bed of walnut, with washstand, bureau, and wardrobe to match. A large, square mirror in a gold frame was hung over the washstand. Some poor engravings of landscapes and several nude figures were hung in gold frames on the wall. The gilt-framed chairs were upholstered in pink-and-white-flowered brocade, with polished brass tacks. The carpet was of thick Brussels, pale cream and pink in hue, with large blue jardinieres containing flowers woven in as ornaments. The general effect was light, rich, and a little stuffy.

"You know I get desperately frightened, sometimes," said Aileen. "Father might be watching us, you know. I've often wondered what I'd do if he caught us. I couldn't lie out of this, could I?"

"You certainly couldn't," said Cowperwood, who never failed to respond to the incitement of her charms. She had such lovely smooth arms, a full, luxuriously tapering throat and neck; her golden-red hair floated like an aureole about her head, and her large eyes sparkled. The wondrous vigor of a full womanhood was hers—errant, ill-balanced, romantic, but exquisite, "but you might as well not cross that bridge until you come to it," he continued. "I myself have been thinking that we had better not go on with this for the present. That letter ought to have been enough to stop us for the time."

He came over to where she stood by the dressing-table, adjusting her hair.

"You're such a pretty minx," he said. He slipped his arm about her and kissed her pretty mouth. "Nothing sweeter than you this side of Paradise," he whispered in her ear.

While this was enacting, Butler and the extra detective had stepped out of sight, to one side of the front door of the house, while Alderson, taking the lead, rang the bell. A negro servant appeared.

"Is Mrs. Davis in?" he asked, genially, using the name of the woman in control. "I'd like to see her."

"Just come in," said the maid, unsuspectingly, and indicated a reception-room on the right. Alderson took off his soft, wide-brimmed hat and entered. When the maid went up-stairs he immediately returned to the door and let in Butler and two detectives. The four stepped into the reception-room unseen. In a few moments the "madam" as the current word characterized this type of woman, appeared. She was tall, fair, rugged, and not at all unpleasant to look upon. She had light-blue eyes and a genial smile. Long contact with the police and the brutalities of sex in her early life had made her wary, a little afraid of how the world would use her. This particular method of making a living being illicit, and she having no other practical knowledge at her command, she was as anxious to get along peacefully with the police and the public generally as any struggling tradesman in any walk of life might have been.

She had on a loose, blue-flowered peignoir, or dressing-gown, open at the front, tied with blue ribbons and showing a little of her expensive underwear beneath. A large opal ring graced her left middle finger, and turquoises of vivid blue were pendent from her ears. She wore yellow silk slippers with bronze buckles; and altogether her appearance was not out of keeping with the character of the reception-room itself, which was a composite of gold-flowered wall-paper, blue and cream-colored Brussels carpet, heavily gold-framed engravings of reclining nudes, and a gilt-framed pier-glass, which rose from the floor to the ceiling. Needless to say, Butler was shocked to the soul of him by this suggestive atmosphere which was supposed to include his daughter in its destructive reaches.

Alderson motioned one of his detectives to get behind the woman–between her and the door–which he did.

"Sorry to trouble you, Mrs. Davis," he said, "but we are looking for a couple who are in your house here. We're after a runaway girl. We don't want to make any disturbance–merely to get her and take her away." Mrs. Davis paled and opened her mouth. "Now don't make any noise or try to scream, or we'll have to stop you. My men are all around the house. Nobody can get out. Do you know anybody by the name of Cowperwood?"

Mrs. Davis, fortunately from one point of view, was not of a particularly nervous nor yet contentious type. She was more or less philosophic. She was not in touch with the police here in Philadelphia, hence subject to exposure. What good would it do to cry out? she thought. The place was surrounded. There was no one in the house at the time to save Cowperwood and Aileen. She did not know Cowperwood by his name, nor Aileen by hers. They were a Mr. and Mrs. Montague to her.

"I don't know anybody by that name," she replied nervously.

"Isn't there a girl here with red hair?" asked one of Alderson's assistants. "And a man with a gray suit and a light-brown mustache? They came in here half an hour ago. You remember them, don't you?"

"There's just one couple in the house, but I'm not sure whether they're the ones you want. I'll ask them to come down if you wish. Oh, I wish you wouldn't make any disturbance. This is terrible."

"We'll not make any disturbance," replied Alderson, "if you don't. Just you be quiet. We merely want to see the girl and take her away. Now, you stay where you are. What room are they in?"

"In the second one in the rear up-stairs. Won't you let me go, though? It will be so much better. I'll just tap and ask them to come out."

"No. We'll tend to that. You stay where you are. You're not going to get into any trouble. You just stay where you are," insisted Alderson.

He motioned to Butler, who, however, now that he had embarked on his grim task, was thinking that he had made a mistake. What good would it do him to force his way in and make her come out, unless he intended to kill Cowperwood? If she were made to come down here, that would be enough. She would then know that he knew all. He did not care to quarrel with Cowperwood, in any public way, he now decided. He was afraid to. He was afraid of himself.

"Let her go," he said grimly, doggedly referring to Mrs. Davis, "But watch her. Tell the girl to come down-stairs to me."

Mrs. Davis, realizing on the moment that this was some family tragedy, and hoping in an agonized way that she could slip out of it peacefully, started upstairs at once with Alderson and his assistants who were close at his heels. Reaching the door of the room occupied by Cowperwood and Aileen, she tapped lightly. At the time Aileen and Cowperwood were sitting in a big arm-chair. At the first knock Aileen blanched and leaped to her feet. Usually not nervous, to-day, for some reason, she anticipated trouble. Cowperwood's eyes instantly hardened.

"Don't be nervous," he said, "no doubt it's only the servant. I'll go."

He started, but Aileen interfered. "Wait," she said. Somewhat reassured, she went to the closet, and taking down a dressing-gown, slipped it on. Meanwhile the tap came again. Then she went to the door and opened it the least bit.

"Mrs. Montague," exclaimed Mrs. Davis, in an obviously nervous, forced voice, "there's a gentleman downstairs who wishes to see you."

"A gentleman to see me!" exclaimed Aileen, astonished and paling. "Are you sure?"

"Yes; he says he wants to see you. There are several other men with him. I think it's some one who belongs to you, maybe."

Aileen realized on the instant, as did Cowperwood, what had in all likelihood happened. Butler or Mrs. Cowperwood had trailed them—in all probability her father. He wondered now what he should do to protect her, not himself. He was in no way deeply concerned for himself, even here. Where any woman was concerned he was too chivalrous to permit fear. It was not at all improbable that Butler might want to kill him; but that did not disturb him. He really did not pay any attention to that thought, and he was not armed.

"I'll dress and go down," he said, when he saw Aileen's pale face. "You stay here. And don't you worry in any way for I'll get you out of this—now, don't worry. This is my affair. I got you in it and I'll get you out of it." He went for his hat and coat and added, as he did so, "You go ahead and dress; but let me go first."

Aileen, the moment the door closed, had begun to put on her clothes swiftly and nervously. Her mind was working like a rapidly moving machine. She was wondering whether this really could be her father. Perhaps it was not. Might there be some other Mrs. Montague—a real one? Supposing it was her father—he had been so nice to her in not telling the family, in keeping her secret thus far. He loved her—she knew that. It makes all the difference in the world in a child's attitude on an occasion like this whether she has been loved and petted and spoiled, or the reverse. Aileen had been loved and petted and spoiled. She could not think of her father doing anything terrible physically to her or to any one else. But it was so hard to confront him—to look into his eyes. When she had attained a proper memory of him, her fluttering wits told her what to do.

"No, Frank," she whispered, excitedly; "if it's father, you'd better let me go. I know how to talk to him. He won't say anything to me. You stay here. I'm not afraid—really, I'm not. If I want you, I'll call you."

He had come over and taken her pretty chin in his hands, and was looking solemnly into her eyes.

"You mustn't be afraid," he said. "I'll go down. If it's your father, you can go away with him. I don't think he'll do anything either to you or to me. If it is he, write me something at the office. I'll be there. If I can help you in any way, I will. We can fix up something. There's no use trying to explain this. Say nothing at all."

He had on his coat and overcoat, and was standing with his hat in his hand. Aileen was nearly dressed, struggling with the row of red current-colored buttons which fastened her dress in the back. Cowperwood helped her. When she was ready–hat, gloves, and all–he said:

"Now let me go first. I want to see."

"No; please, Frank," she begged, courageously. "Let me, I know it's father. Who else could it be?" She wondered at the moment whether her father had brought her two brothers but would not now believe it. He would not do that, she knew. "You can come if I call." She went on. "Nothing's going to happen, though. I understand him. He won't do anything to me. If you go it will only make him angry. Let me go. You stand in the door here. If I don't call, it's all right. Will you?"

She put her two pretty hands on his shoulders, and he weighed the matter very carefully. "Very well," he said, "only I'll go to the foot of the stairs with you."

They went to the door and he opened it. Outside were Alderson with two other detectives and Mrs. Davis, standing perhaps five feet away.

"Well," said Cowperwood, commandingly, looking at Alderson.

"There's a gentleman down-stairs wishes to see the lady," said Alderson. "It's her father, I think," he added quietly.

Cowperwood made way for Aileen, who swept by, furious at the presence of men and this exposure. Her courage had entirely returned. She was angry now to think her father would make a public spectacle of her. Cowperwood started to follow.

"I'd advise you not to go down there right away," cautioned Alderson, sagely. "That's her father. Butler's her name, isn't it? He don't want you so much as he wants her."

Cowperwood nevertheless walked slowly toward the head of the stairs, listening.

"What made you come here, father?" he heard Aileen ask.

Butler's reply he could not hear, but he was now at ease for he knew how much Butler loved his daughter.

Confronted by her father, Aileen was now attempting to stare defiantly, to look reproachful, but Butler's deep gray eyes beneath their shaggy brows revealed such a weight of weariness and despair as even she, in her anger and defiance, could not openly flaunt. It was all too sad.

"I never expected to find you in a place like this, daughter," he said. "I should have thought you would have thought better of yourself." His voice choked and he stopped.

"I know who you're here with," he continued, shaking his head sadly. "The dog! I'll get him yet. I've had men watchin' you all the time. Oh, the shame of this day! The shame of this day! You'll be comin' home with me now."

"That's just it, father," began Aileen. "You've had men watching me. I should have thought—" She stopped, because he put up his hand in a strange, agonized, and yet dominating way.

"None of that! none of that!" he said, glowering under his strange, sad, gray brows. "I can't stand it! Don't tempt me! We're not out of this place yet. He's not! You'll come home with me now."

Aileen understood. It was Cowperwood he was referring to. That frightened her.

"I'm ready," she replied, nervously.

The old man led the way broken-heartedly. He felt he would never live to forget the agony of this hour.

Chapter XXXVII

In spite of Butler's rage and his determination to do many things to the financier, if he could, he was so wrought up and shocked by the attitude of Aileen that he could scarcely believe he was the same man he had been twenty-four hours before. She was so nonchalant, so defiant. He had expected to see her wilt completely when confronted with her guilt. Instead, he found, to his despair, after they were once safely out of the house, that he had aroused a fighting quality in the girl which was not incomparable to his own. She had some of his own and Owen's grit. She sat beside him in the little runabout—not his own—in which he was driving her home, her face coloring and blanching by turns, as different waves of thought swept over her, determined to stand her ground now that her father had so plainly trapped her, to declare for Cowperwood and her love and her position in general. What did she care, she asked herself, what her father thought now? She was in this thing. She loved Cowperwood; she was permanently disgraced in her father's eyes. What difference could it all make now? He had fallen so low in his parental feeling as to spy on her and expose her before other men—strangers, detectives, Cowperwood. What real affection could she have for him after this? He had made a mistake, according to her. He had done a foolish and a contemptible thing, which was not warranted however bad her actions might have been. What could he hope to accomplish by rushing in on her in this way and ripping the veil from her very soul before these other men—these crude detectives? Oh, the agony of that walk from the bedroom to the reception-room! She would never forgive her father for this—never, never, never! He had now killed her love for him—that was what she felt. It was to be a battle royal between them from now on. As they rode—in complete silence for a while—her hands clasped and unclasped defiantly, her nails cutting her palms, and her mouth hardened.

It is an open question whether raw opposition ever accomplishes anything of value in this world. It seems so inherent in this mortal scheme of things that it appears to have a vast validity. It is more than likely that we owe this spectacle called life to it, and that this can be demonstrated scientifically; but when that is said and done, what is the value? What is the value of the spectacle? And what the value of a scene such as this enacted between Aileen and her father?

The old man saw nothing for it, as they rode on, save a grim contest between them which could end in what? What could he do with her? They were riding away fresh from this awful catastrophe, and she was not saying a word! She had even asked him why he had come there! How was he to subdue her, when the very act of trapping her had failed to do so? His ruse, while so successful materially, had failed so utterly spiritually. They reached the house, and Aileen got out. The old man, too nonplussed to wish to go further at this time, drove back to his office. He then went out and walked–a peculiar thing for him to do; he had done nothing like that in years and years–walking to think. Coming to an open Catholic church, he went in and prayed for enlightenment, the growing dusk of the interior, the single everlasting lamp before the repository of the chalice, and the high, white altar set with candles soothing his troubled feelings.

He came out of the church after a time and returned home. Aileen did not appear at dinner, and he could not eat. He went into his private room and shut the door–thinking, thinking, thinking. The dreadful spectacle of Aileen in a house of ill repute burned in his brain. To think that Cowperwood should have taken her to such a place–his Aileen, his and his wife's pet. In spite of his prayers, his uncertainty, her opposition, the puzzling nature of the situation, she must be got out of this. She must go away for a while, give the man up, and then the law should run its course with him. In all likelihood Cowperwood would go to the penitentiary–if ever a man richly deserved to go, it was he. Butler would see that no stone was left unturned. He would make it a personal issue, if necessary. All he had to do was to let it be known in judicial circles that he wanted it so. He could not suborn a jury, that would be criminal; but he could see that the case was properly and forcefully presented; and if Cowperwood were convicted, Heaven help him. The appeal of his financial friends would not save him. The judges of the lower and superior courts knew on which side their bread was buttered. They would strain a point in favor of the highest political opinion of the day, and he certainly could influence that. Aileen meanwhile was contemplating the peculiar nature of her situation. In spite of their silence on the way home, she knew that a conversation was coming with her father. It had to be. He would want her to go somewhere. Most likely he would revive the European trip in some form–she now suspected the invitation of Mrs. Mollenhauer as a trick; and she had to decide whether she would go. Would she leave Cowperwood just when he was about to be tried? She was determined she would not. She wanted to see what was going to happen to him. She would leave home first–run to some relative, some friend, some stranger, if necessary, and ask to be taken in. She had some money–a little. Her father had always been very liberal with her. She could take a few clothes and disappear. They would be glad enough to send for her after she had been gone awhile. Her mother would be frantic; Norah and Callum and Owen would be beside themselves with wonder and worry; her father–she could see him. Maybe that would bring him to his senses. In spite of all her emotional vagaries, she was the pride and interest of this home, and she knew it.

It was in this direction that her mind was running when her father, a few days after the dreadful exposure in the Sixth Street house, sent for her to come to him in his room. He had come home from his office very early in the afternoon, hoping to find Aileen there, in order that he might have a private interview with her, and by good luck found her in. She had had no desire to go out into the world these last few days–she was too expectant of trouble to come. She had just written Cowperwood asking for a rendezvous out on the Wissahickon the following afternoon, in spite of the detectives.

She must see him. Her father, she said, had done nothing; but she was sure he would attempt to do something. She wanted to talk to Cowperwood about that.

"I've been thinkin' about ye, Aileen, and what ought to be done in this case," began her father without preliminaries of any kind once they were in his "office room" in the house together. "You're on the road to ruin if any one ever was. I tremble when I think of your immortal soul. I want to do somethin' for ye, my child, before it's too late. I've been reproachin' myself for the last month and more, thinkin', perhaps, it was somethin' I had done, or maybe had failed to do, aither me or your mother, that has brought ye to the place where ye are to-day. Needless to say, it's on me conscience, me child. It's a heartbroken man you're lookin' at this day. I'll never be able to hold me head up again. Oh, the shame–the shame! That I should have lived to see it!"

"But father," protested Aileen, who was a little distraught at the thought of having to listen to a long preachment which would relate to her duty to God and the Church and her family and her mother and him. She realized that all these were important in their way; but Cowperwood and his point of view had given her another outlook on life. They had discussed this matter of families–parents, children, husbands, wives, brothers, sisters–from almost every point of view. Cowperwood's laissez-faire attitude had permeated and colored her mind completely. She saw things through his cold, direct "I satisfy myself" attitude. He was sorry for all the little differences of personality that sprang up between people, causing quarrels, bickerings, oppositions, and separation; but they could not be helped. People outgrew each other. Their points of view altered at varying ratios–hence changes. Morals–those who had them had them; those who hadn't, hadn't. There was no explaining. As for him, he saw nothing wrong in the sex relationship. Between those who were mutually compatible it was innocent and delicious. Aileen in his arms, unmarried, but loved by him, and he by her, was as good and pure as any living woman–a great deal purer than most. One found oneself in a given social order, theory, or scheme of things. For purposes of social success, in order not to offend, to smooth one's path, make things easy, avoid useless criticism, and the like, it was necessary to create an outward seeming– ostensibly conform. Beyond that it was not necessary to do anything. Never fail, never get caught. If you did, fight your way out silently and say nothing. That was what he was doing in connection with his present financial troubles; that was what he had been ready to do the other day when they were caught. It was something of all this that was coloring Aileen's mood as she listened at present.

"But father," she protested, "I love Mr. Cowperwood. It's almost the same as if I were married to him. He will marry me some day when he gets a divorce from Mrs. Cowperwood. You don't understand how it is. He's very fond of me, and I love him. He needs me."

Butler looked at her with strange, non-understanding eyes. "Divorce, did you say," he began, thinking of the Catholic Church and its dogma in regard to that. "He'll divorce his own wife and children–and for you, will he? He needs you, does he?" he added, sarcastically. "What about his wife and children? I don't suppose they need him, do they? What talk have ye?"

Aileen flung her head back defiantly. "It's true, nevertheless," she reiterated. "You just don't understand."

Butler could scarcely believe his ears. He had never heard such talk before in his life from any one. It amazed and shocked him. He was quite aware of all the subtleties of politics and business, but these of romance were too much for him. He knew nothing about them. To think a daughter of his should be talking like this, and she a Catholic! He could not understand where she got such notions unless it was from the Machiavellian, corrupting brain of Cowperwood himself.

"How long have ye had these notions, my child?" he suddenly asked, calmly and soberly. "Where did ye get them? Ye certainly never heard anything like that in this house, I warrant. Ye talk as though ye had gone out of yer mind."

"Oh, don't talk nonsense, father," flared Aileen, angrily, thinking how hopeless it was to talk to her father about such things anyhow. "I'm not a child any more. I'm twenty-four years of age. You just don't understand. Mr. Cowperwood doesn't like his wife. He's going to get a divorce when he can, and will marry me. I love him, and he loves me, and that's all there is to it."

"Is it, though?" asked Butler, grimly determined by hook or by crook, to bring this girl to her senses. "Ye'll be takin' no thought of his wife and children then? The fact that he's goin' to jail, besides, is nawthin' to ye, I suppose. Ye'd love him just as much in convict stripes, I suppose–more, maybe." (The old man was at his best, humanly speaking, when he was a little sarcastic.) "Ye'll have him that way, likely, if at all."

Aileen blazed at once to a furious heat. "Yes, I know," she sneered. "That's what you would like. I know what you've been doing. Frank does, too. You're trying to railroad him to prison for something he didn't do–and all on account of me. Oh, I know. But you won't hurt him. You can't! He's bigger and finer than you think he is and you won't hurt him in the long run. He'll get out again. You want to punish him on my account; but he doesn't care. I'll marry him anyhow. I love him, and I'll wait for him and marry him, and you can do what you please. So there!"

"Ye'll marry him, will you?" asked Butler, nonplussed and further astounded. "So ye'll wait for him and marry him? Ye'll take him away from his wife and children, where, if he were half a man, he'd be stayin' this minute instead of gallivantin' around with you. And marry him? Ye'd disgrace your father and yer mother and yer family? Ye'll stand here and say this to me, I that have raised ye, cared for ye, and made somethin' of ye? Where would you be if it weren't for me and your poor, hard-workin' mother, schemin' and plannin' for you year in and year out? Ye're smarter than I am, I suppose. Ye know more about the world than I do, or any one else that might want to say anythin' to ye. I've raised ye to be a fine lady, and this is what I get. Talk about me not bein' able to understand, and ye lovin' a convict-to-be, a robber, an embezzler, a bankrupt, a lyin', thavin'–"

"Father!" exclaimed Aileen, determinedly. "I'll not listen to you talking that way. He's not any of the things that you say. I'll not stay here." She moved toward the door; but Butler jumped up now and stopped her. His face for the moment was flushed and swollen with anger.

"But I'm not through with him yet," he went on, ignoring her desire to leave, and addressing her direct–confident now that she was as capable as another of understanding him. "I'll get him as sure as I have a name. There's law in this land, and I'll have it on him. I'll show him whether he'll come sneakin' into dacent homes and robbin' parents of their children."

He paused after a time for want of breath and Aileen stared, her face tense and white. Her father could be so ridiculous. He was, contrasted with Cowperwood and his views, so old-fashioned. To think he could be talking of some one coming into their home and stealing her away from him, when she had been so willing to go. What silliness! And yet, why argue? What good could be accomplished, arguing with him here in this way? And so for the moment, she said nothing more–merely looked. But Butler was by no means done. His mood was too stormy even though he was doing his best now to subdue himself.

"It's too bad, daughter," he resumed quietly, once he was satisfied that she was going to have little, if anything, to say. "I'm lettin' my anger get the best of me. It wasn't that I intended talkin' to ye about when I ast ye to come in. It's somethin' else I have on me mind. I was thinkin', perhaps, ye'd like to go to Europe for the time bein' to study music. Ye're not quite yourself just at present. Ye're needin' a rest. It would be good for ye to go away for a while. Ye could have a nice time over there. Norah could go along with ye, if you would, and Sister Constantia that taught you. Ye wouldn't object to havin' her, I suppose?"

At the mention of this idea of a trip of Europe again, with Sister Constantia and music thrown in to give it a slightly new form, Aileen bridled, and yet half-smiled to herself now. It was so ridiculous–so tactless, really, for her father to bring up this now, and especially after denouncing Cowperwood and her, and threatening all the things he had. Had he no diplomacy at all where she was concerned? It was really too funny! But she restrained herself here again, because she felt as well as saw, that argument of this kind was all futile now.

"I wish you wouldn't talk about that, father," she began, having softened under his explanation. "I don't want to go to Europe now. I don't want to leave Philadelphia. I know you want me to go; but I don't want to think of going now. I can't."

Butler's brow darkened again. What was the use of all this opposition on her part? Did she really imagine that she was going to master him–her father, and in connection with such an issue as this? How impossible! But tempering his voice as much as possible, he went on, quite softly, in fact. "But it would be so fine for ye, Aileen. Ye surely can't expect to stay here after–" He paused, for he was going to say "what has happened." He knew she was very sensitive on that point. His own conduct in hunting her down had been such a breach of fatherly courtesy that he knew she felt resentful, and in a way properly so. Still, what could be greater than her own crime? "After," he concluded, "ye have made such a mistake ye surely wouldn't want to stay here. Ye won't be wantin' to keep up that–committin' a mortal sin. It's against the laws of God and man."

He did so hope the thought of sin would come to Aileen–the enormity of her crime from a spiritual point of view–but Aileen did not see it at all.

"You don't understand me, father," she exclaimed, hopelessly toward the end. "You can't. I have one idea, and you have another. But I don't seem to be able to make you understand now. The fact is, if you want to know it, I don't believe in the Catholic Church any more, so there."

The moment Aileen had said this she wished she had not. It was a slip of the tongue. Butler's face took on an inexpressibly sad, despairing look.

"Ye don't believe in the Church?" he asked.

"No, not exactly–not like you do."

He shook his head.

"The harm that has come to yer soul!" he replied. "It's plain to me, daughter, that somethin' terrible has happened to ye. This man has ruined ye, body and soul. Somethin' must be done. I don't want to be hard on ye, but ye must leave Philadelphy. Ye can't stay here. I can't permit ye. Ye can go to Europe, or ye can go to yer aunt's in New Orleans; but ye must go somewhere. I can't have ye stayin' here–it's too dangerous. It's sure to be comin' out. The papers'll be havin' it next. Ye're young yet. Yer life is before you. I tremble for yer soul; but so long as ye're young and alive ye may come to yer senses. It's me duty to be hard. It's my obligation to you and the Church. Ye must quit this life. Ye must lave this man. Ye must never see him any more. I can't permit ye. He's no good. He has no intintion of marrying ye, and it would be a crime against God and man if he did. No, no! Never that! The man's a bankrupt, a scoundrel, a thafe. If ye had him, ye'd soon be the unhappiest woman in the world. He wouldn't be faithful to ye. No, he couldn't. He's not that kind." He paused, sick to the depths of his soul. "Ye must go away. I say it once and for all. I mane it kindly, but I want it. I have yer best interests at heart. I love ye; but ye must. I'm sorry to see ye go–I'd rather have ye here. No one will be sorrier; but ye must. Ye must make it all seem natcheral and ordinary to yer mother; but ye must go–d'ye hear? Ye must."

He paused, looking sadly but firmly at Aileen under his shaggy eyebrows. She knew he meant this. It was his most solemn, his most religious expression. But she did not answer. She could not. What was the use? Only she was not going. She knew that–and so she stood there white and tense.

"Now get all the clothes ye want," went on Butler, by no means grasping her true mood. "Fix yourself up in any way you plase. Say where ye want to go, but get ready."

"But I won't, father," finally replied Aileen, equally solemnly, equally determinedly. "I won't go! I won't leave Philadelphia."

"Ye don't mane to say ye will deliberately disobey me when I'm asking ye to do somethin' that's intended for yer own good, will ye daughter?"

"Yes, I will," replied Aileen, determinedly. "I won't go! I'm sorry, but I won't!"

"Ye really mane that, do ye?" asked Butler, sadly but grimly.

"Yes, I do," replied Aileen, grimly, in return.

"Then I'll have to see what I can do, daughter," replied the old man. "Ye're still my daughter, whatever ye are, and I'll not see ye come to wreck and ruin for want of doin' what I know to be my solemn duty. I'll give ye a few more days to think this over, but go ye must. There's an end of that. There are laws in this land still. There are things that can be done to those who won't obey the law. I found ye this time–much as it hurt me to do it. I'll find ye again if ye try to disobey me. Ye must change yer ways. I can't have ye goin' on as ye are. Ye understand now. It's the last word. Give this man up, and ye can have anything ye choose. Ye're my girl–I'll do everything I can in this world to make ye happy. Why, why shouldn't I? What else have I to live for but me children? It's ye and the rest of them that I've been workin' and plannin' for all these years. Come now, be a good girl. Ye love your old father, don't ye? Why, I rocked ye in my arms as a baby, Aileen. I've watched over ye when ye were not bigger than what would rest in me two fists here. I've been a good father to ye–ye can't deny that. Look at the other girls you've seen. Have any of them had more nor what ye have had? Ye won't go against me in this. I'm sure ye won't. Ye can't. Ye love me too much–surely ye do–don't ye?" His voice weakened. His eyes almost filled.

He paused and put a big, brown, horny hand on Aileen's arm. She had listened to his plea not unmoved–really more or less softened–because of the hopelessness of it. She could not give up Cowperwood. Her father just did not understand. He did not know what love was. Unquestionably he had never loved as she had.

She stood quite silent while Butler appealed to her.

"I'd like to, father," she said at last and softly, tenderly. "Really I would. I do love you. Yes, I do. I want to please you; but I can't in this–I can't! I love Frank Cowperwood. You don't understand–really you don't!"

At the repetition of Cowperwood's name Butler's mouth hardened. He could see that she was infatuated–that his carefully calculated plea had failed. So he must think of some other way.

"Very well, then," he said at last and sadly, oh, so sadly, as Aileen turned away. "Have it yer own way, if ye will. Ye must go, though, willy-nilly. It can't be any other way. I wish to God it could."

Aileen went out, very solemn, and Butler went over to his desk and sat down. "Such a situation!" he said to himself. "Such a complication!"

Chapter XXXVIII

The situation which confronted Aileen was really a trying one. A girl of less innate courage and determination would have weakened and yielded. For in spite of her various social connections and acquaintances, the people to whom Aileen could run in an emergency of the present kind were not numerous. She could scarcely think of any one who would be likely to take her in for any lengthy period, without question. There were a number of young women of her own age, married and unmarried, who were very friendly to her, but there were few with whom she was really intimate. The only person who stood out in her mind, as having any real possibility of refuge for a period, was a certain Mary Calligan, better known as "Mamie" among her friends, who had attended school with Aileen in former years and was now a teacher in one of the local schools.

The Calligan family consisted of Mrs. Katharine Calligan, the mother, a dressmaker by profession and a widow–her husband, a house-mover by trade, having been killed by a falling wall some ten years before–and Mamie, her twenty-three-year-old daughter. They lived in a small two-story brick house in Cherry Street, near Fifteenth. Mrs. Calligan was not a very good dressmaker, not good enough, at least, for the Butler family to patronize in their present exalted state. Aileen went there occasionally for gingham house-dresses, underwear, pretty dressing-gowns, and alterations on some of her more important clothing which was made by a very superior modiste in Chestnut Street. She visited the house largely because she had gone to school with Mamie at St. Agatha's, when the outlook of the Calligan family was much more promising. Mamie was earning forty dollars a month as the teacher of a sixth-grade room in one of the nearby public schools, and Mrs. Calligan averaged on the whole about two dollars a day–sometimes not so much. The house they occupied was their own, free and clear, and the furniture which it contained suggested the size of their joint income, which was somewhere near eighty dollars a month.

Mamie Calligan was not good-looking, not nearly as good-looking as her mother had been before her. Mrs. Calligan was still plump, bright, and cheerful at fifty, with a fund of good humor. Mamie was somewhat duller mentally and emotionally. She was serious-minded–made so, perhaps, as much by circumstances as by anything else, for she was not at all vivid, and had little sex magnetism. Yet she was kindly, honest, earnest, a good Catholic, and possessed of that strangely excessive ingrowing virtue which shuts so many people off from the world–a sense of duty. To Mamie Calligan duty (a routine conformity to such theories and precepts as she had heard and worked by since her childhood) was the all-important thing, her principal source of comfort and relief; her props in a queer and uncertain world being her duty to her Church; her duty to her school; her duty to her mother; her duty to her friends, etc. Her mother often wished for Mamie's sake that she was less dutiful and more charming physically, so that the men would like her.

In spite of the fact that her mother was a dressmaker, Mamie's clothes never looked smart or attractive–she would have felt out of keeping with herself if they had. Her shoes were rather large, and ill-fitting; her skirt hung in lifeless lines from her hips to her feet, of good material but seemingly bad design. At that time the colored "jersey," so-called, was just coming into popular wear, and, being close-fitting, looked well on those of good form. Alas for Mamie Calligan! The mode of the time compelled her to wear one; but she had neither the arms nor the chest development which made this garment admirable. Her hat, by choice, was usually a pancake affair with a long, single feather, which somehow never seemed to be in exactly the right position, either to her hair or her face. At most times she looked a little weary; but she was not physically weary so much as she was bored. Her life held so little of real charm; and Aileen Butler was unquestionably the most significant element of romance in it.

Mamie's mother's very pleasant social disposition, the fact that they had a very cleanly, if poor little home, that she could entertain them by playing on their piano, and that Mrs. Calligan took an adoring interest in the work she did for her, made up the sum and substance of the attraction of the Calligan home for Aileen. She went there occasionally as a relief from other things, and because Mamie Calligan had a compatible and very understanding interest in literature. Curiously, the books Aileen liked she liked–Jane Eyre, Kenelm Chillingly, Tricotrin, and A Bow of Orange Ribbon. Mamie occasionally recommended to Aileen some latest effusion of this character; and Aileen, finding her judgment good, was constrained to admire her.

In this crisis it was to the home of the Calligans that Aileen turned in thought. If her father really was not nice to her, and she had to leave home for a time, she could go to the Calligans. They would receive her and say nothing. They were not sufficiently well known to the other members of the Butler family to have the latter suspect that she had gone there. She might readily disappear into the privacy of Cherry Street and not be seen or heard of for weeks. It is an interesting fact to contemplate that the

Calligans, like the various members of the Butler family, never suspected Aileen of the least tendency toward a wayward existence. Hence her flight from her own family, if it ever came, would be laid more to the door of a temperamental pettishness than anything else.

On the other hand, in so far as the Butler family as a unit was concerned, it needed Aileen more than she needed it. It needed the light of her countenance to keep it appropriately cheerful, and if she went away there would be a distinct gulf that would not soon be overcome.

Butler, senior, for instance, had seen his little daughter grow into radiantly beautiful womanhood. He had seen her go to school and convent and learn to play the piano–to him a great accomplishment. Also he had seen her manner change and become very showy and her knowledge of life broaden, apparently, and become to him, at least, impressive. Her smart, dogmatic views about most things were, to him, at least, well worth listening to. She knew more about books and art than Owen or Callum, and her sense of social manners was perfect. When she came to the table–breakfast, luncheon, or dinner–she was to him always a charming object to see. He had produced Aileen–he congratulated himself. He had furnished her the money to be so fine. He would continue to do so. No second-rate upstart of a man should be allowed to ruin her life. He proposed to take care of her always–to leave her so much money in a legally involved way that a failure of a husband could not possibly affect her. "You're the charming lady this evenin', I'm thinkin'," was one of his pet remarks; and also, "My, but we're that fine!" At table almost invariably she sat beside him and looked out for him. That was what he wanted. He had put her there beside him at his meals years before when she was a child.

Her mother, too, was inordinately fond of her, and Callum and Owen appropriately brotherly. So Aileen had thus far at least paid back with beauty and interest quite as much as she received, and all the family felt it to be so. When she was away for a day or two the house seemed glum–the meals less appetizing. When she returned, all were happy and gay again.

Aileen understood this clearly enough in a way. Now, when it came to thinking of leaving and shifting for herself, in order to avoid a trip which she did not care to be forced into, her courage was based largely on this keen sense of her own significance to the family. She thought over what her father had said, and decided she must act at once. She dressed for the street the next morning, after her father had gone, and decided to step in at the Calligans' about noon, when Mamie would be at home for luncheon. Then she would take up the matter casually. If they had no objection, she would go there. She sometimes wondered why Cowperwood did not suggest, in his great stress, that they leave for some parts unknown; but she also felt that he must know best what he could do. His increasing troubles depressed her.

Mrs. Calligan was alone when she arrived and was delighted to see her. After exchanging the gossip of the day, and not knowing quite how to proceed in connection with the errand which had brought her, she went to the piano and played a melancholy air.

"Sure, it's lovely the way you play, Aileen," observed Mrs. Calligan who was unduly sentimental herself. "I love to hear you. I wish you'd come oftener to see us. You're so rarely here nowadays."

"Oh, I've been so busy, Mrs. Calligan," replied Aileen. "I've had so much to do this fall, I just couldn't. They wanted me to go to Europe; but I didn't care to. Oh, dear!" she sighed, and in her playing swept off with a movement of sad, romantic significance. The door opened and Mamie came in. Her commonplace face brightened at the sight of Aileen.

"Well, Aileen Butler!" she exclaimed. "Where did you come from? Where have you been keeping yourself so long?"

Aileen rose to exchange kisses. "Oh, I've been very busy, Mamie. I've just been telling your mother. How are you, anyway? How are you getting along in your work?"

Mamie recounted at once some school difficulties which were puzzling her–the growing size of classes and the amount of work expected. While Mrs. Calligan was setting the table Mamie went to her room and Aileen followed her.

As she stood before her mirror arranging her hair Aileen looked at her meditatively.

"What's the matter with you, Aileen, to-day?" Mamie asked. "You look so–" She stopped to give her a second glance.

"How do I look?" asked Aileen.

"Well, as if you were uncertain or troubled about something. I never saw you look that way before. What's the matter?"

"Oh, nothing," replied Aileen. "I was just thinking." She went to one of the windows which looked into the little yard, meditating on whether she could endure living here for any length of time. The house was so small, the furnishings so very simple.

"There is something the matter with you to-day, Aileen," observed Mamie, coming over to her and looking in her face. "You're not like yourself at all."

"I've got something on my mind," replied Aileen–"something that's worrying me. I don't know just what to do–that's what's the matter."

"Well, whatever can it be?" commented Mamie. "I never saw you act this way before. Can't you tell me? What is it?"

"No, I don't think I can–not now, anyhow." Aileen paused. "Do you suppose your mother would object," she asked, suddenly, "if I came here and stayed a little while? I want to get away from home for a time for a certain reason."

"Why, Aileen Butler, how you talk!" exclaimed her friend. "Object! You know she'd be delighted, and so would I. Oh, dear–can you come? But what makes you want to leave home?"

"That's just what I can't tell you–not now, anyhow. Not you, so much, but your mother. You know, I'm afraid of what she'd think," replied Aileen. "But, you mustn't ask me yet, anyhow. I want to think. Oh, dear! But I want to come, if you'll let me. Will you speak to your mother, or shall I?"

"Why, I will," said Mamie, struck with wonder at this remarkable development; "but it's silly to do it. I know what she'll say before I tell her, and so do you. You can just bring your things and come. That's all. She'd never say anything or ask anything, either, and you know that–if you didn't want her to." Mamie was all agog and aglow at the idea. She wanted the companionship of Aileen so much.

Aileen looked at her solemnly, and understood well enough why she was so enthusiastic–both she and her mother. Both wanted her presence to brighten their world. "But neither of you must tell anybody that I'm here, do you hear? I don't want any one to know–particularly no one of my family. I've a reason, and a good one, but I can't tell you what it is–not now, anyhow. You'll promise not to tell any one."

"Oh, of course," replied Mamie eagerly. "But you're not going to run away for good, are you, Aileen?" she concluded curiously and gravely.

"Oh, I don't know; I don't know what I'll do yet. I only know that I want to get away for a while, just now–that's all." She paused, while Mamie stood before her, agape.

"Well, of all things," replied her friend. "Wonders never cease, do they, Aileen? But it will be so lovely to have you here. Mama will be so pleased. Of course, we won't tell anybody if you don't want us to. Hardly any one ever comes here; and if they do, you needn't see them. You could have this big room next to me. Oh, wouldn't that be nice? I'm perfectly delighted." The young school-teacher's spirits rose to a decided height. "Come on, why not tell mama right now?"

Aileen hesitated because even now she was not positive whether she should do this, but finally they went down the stairs together, Aileen lingering behind a little as they neared the bottom. Mamie burst in upon her mother with: "Oh, mama, isn't it lovely? Aileen's coming to stay with us for a while. She doesn't want any one to know, and she's coming right away." Mrs. Calligan, who was holding a sugarbowl in her hand, turned to survey her with a surprised but smiling face. She was immediately curious as to why Aileen should want to come–why leave home. On the other hand, her feeling for Aileen was so deep that she was greatly and joyously intrigued by the idea. And why not? Was not the celebrated Edward Butler's daughter a woman grown, capable of regulating her own affairs, and welcome, of course, as the honored member of so important a family. It was very flattering to the Calligans to think that she would want to come under any circumstances.

"I don't see how your parents can let you go, Aileen; but you're certainly welcome here as long as you want to stay, and that's forever, if you want to." And Mrs. Calligan beamed on her welcomingly. The idea of Aileen Butler asking to be permitted to come here! And the hearty, comprehending manner in which she said this, and Mamie's enthusiasm, caused Aileen to breathe a sigh of relief. The matter of the expense of her presence to the Calligans came into her mind.

"I want to pay you, of course," she said to Mrs. Calligan, "if I come."

"The very idea, Aileen Butler!" exclaimed Mamie. "You'll do nothing of the sort. You'll come here and live with me as my guest."

"No, I won't! If I can't pay I won't come," replied Aileen. "You'll have to let me do that." She knew that the Calligans could not afford to keep her.

"Well, we'll not talk about that now, anyhow," replied Mrs. Calligan. "You can come when you like and stay as long as you like. Reach me some clean napkins, Mamie." Aileen remained for luncheon, and left soon afterward to keep her suggested appointment with Cowperwood, feeling satisfied that her main problem had been solved. Now her way was clear. She could come here if she wanted to. It was simply a matter of collecting a few necessary things or coming without bringing anything. Perhaps Frank would have something to suggest.

In the meantime Cowperwood made no effort to communicate with Aileen since the unfortunate discovery of their meeting place, but had awaited a letter from her, which was not long in coming. And, as usual, it was a long, optimistic, affectionate, and defiant screed in which she related all that had occurred to her and her present plan of leaving home. This last puzzled and troubled him not a little.

Aileen in the bosom of her family, smart and well-cared for, was one thing. Aileen out in the world dependent on him was another. He had never imagined that she would be compelled to leave before he was prepared to take her; and if she did now, it might stir up complications which would be anything but pleasant to contemplate. Still he was fond of her, very, and would do anything to make her happy. He could support her in a very respectable way even now, if he did not eventually go to prison, and even there he might manage to make some shift for her. It would be so much better, though, if he could persuade her to remain at home until he knew exactly what his fate was to be. He never doubted but that some day, whatever happened, within a reasonable length of time, he would be rid of all these complications and well-to-do again, in which case, if he could get a divorce, he wanted to marry Aileen. If not, he would take her with him anyhow, and from this point of view it might be just as well as if she broke away from her family now. But from the point of view of present complications–the search Butler would make–it might be dangerous. He might even publicly charge him with abduction. He therefore decided to persuade Aileen to stay at home, drop meetings and communications for the time being, and even go abroad. He would be all right until she came back and so would she–common sense ought to rule in this case.

With all this in mind he set out to keep the appointment she suggested in her letter, nevertheless feeling it a little dangerous to do so.

"Are you sure," he asked, after he had listened to her description of the Calligan homestead, "that you would like it there? It sounds rather poor to me."

"Yes, but I like them so much," replied Aileen.

"And you're sure they won't tell on you?"

"Oh, no; never, never!"

"Very well," he concluded. "You know what you're doing. I don't want to advise you against your will. If I were you, though, I'd take your father's advice and go away for a while. He'll get over this then, and I'll still be here. I can write you occasionally, and you can write me."

The moment Cowperwood said this Aileen's brow clouded. Her love for him was so great that there was something like a knife thrust in the merest hint at an extended separation. Her Frank here and in trouble–on trial maybe and she away! Never! What could he mean by suggesting such a thing? Could it be that he didn't care for her as much as she did for him? Did he really love her? she asked herself. Was he going to desert her just when she was going to do the thing which would bring them nearer together? Her eyes clouded, for she was terribly hurt.

"Why, how you talk!" she exclaimed. "You know I won't leave Philadelphia now. You certainly don't expect me to leave you."

Cowperwood saw it all very clearly. He was too shrewd not to. He was immensely fond of her. Good heaven, he thought, he would not hurt her feelings for the world!

"Honey," he said, quickly, when he saw her eyes, "you don't understand. I want you to do what you want to do. You've planned this out in order to be with me; so now you do it. Don't think any more about me or anything I've said. I was merely thinking that it might make matters worse for both of us; but I don't believe it will. You think your father loves you so much that after you're gone he'll change his mind. Very good; go. But we must be very careful, sweet–you and I–really we must. This thing is getting serious. If you should go and your father should charge me with abduction–take the public into his confidence and tell all about this, it would be serious for both of us–as much for you as for me, for I'd be convicted sure then, just on that account, if nothing else. And then what? You'd better not try to see me often for the present–not any oftener than we can possibly help. If we had used common sense and stopped when your father got that letter, this wouldn't have happened. But now that it has happened, we must be as wise as we can, don't you see? So, think it over, and do what you think best and then write me and whatever you do will be all right with me–do you hear?" He drew her to him and kissed her. "You haven't any money, have you?" he concluded wisely.

Aileen, deeply moved by all he had just said, was none the less convinced once she had meditated on it a moment, that her course was best. Her father loved her too much. He would not do anything to hurt her publicly and so he would not attack Cowperwood through her openly. More than likely, as she now explained to Frank, he would plead with her to come back. And he, listening, was compelled to yield. Why argue? She would not leave him anyhow.

He went down in his pocket for the first time since he had known Aileen and produced a layer of bills. "Here's two hundred dollars, sweet," he said, "until I see or hear from you. I'll see that you have whatever you need; and now don't think that I don't love you. You know I do. I'm crazy about you."

Aileen protested that she did not need so much–that she did not really need any–she had some at home; but he put that aside. He knew that she must have money.

"Don't talk, honey," he said. "I know what you need." She had been so used to receiving money from her father and mother in comfortable amounts from time to time that she thought nothing of it. Frank loved her so much that it made everything right between them. She softened in her mood and they discussed the matter of letters, reaching the conclusion that a private messenger would be safest. When finally they parted, Aileen, from being sunk in the depths by his uncertain attitude, was now once more on the heights. She decided that he did love her, and went away smiling. She had her Frank to fall back on–she would teach her father. Cowperwood shook his head, following her with his eyes. She represented an additional burden, but give her up, he certainly could not. Tear the veil from this illusion of affection and make her feel so wretched when he cared for her so much? No. There was really nothing for him to do but what he had done. After all, he reflected, it might not work out so badly. Any detective work that Butler might choose to do would prove that she had not run to him. If at any moment it became necessary to bring common sense into play to save the situation from a deadly climax, he could have the Butlers secretly informed as to Aileen's whereabouts. That would show he had little to do with it, and they could try to persuade Aileen to come home again. Good might result–one could not tell. He would deal with the evils as they arose. He drove quickly back to his office, and Aileen returned to her home determined to put her plan into action. Her father had given her some little time in which to decide–possibly he would give her longer–but she would not wait. Having always had her wish granted in everything, she could not understand why she was not to have her way this time. It was about five o'clock now. She would wait until all the members of the family were comfortably seated at the dinner-table, which would be about seven o'clock, and then slip out.

On arriving home, however, she was greeted by an unexpected reason for suspending action. This was the presence of a certain Mr. and Mrs. Steinmetz–the former a well-known engineer who drew the plans for many of the works which Butler undertook. It was the day before Thanksgiving, and they were eager to have Aileen and Norah accompany them for a fortnight's stay at their new home in West Chester–a structure concerning the charm of which Aileen had heard much. They were exceedingly agreeable people–comparatively young and surrounded by a coterie of interesting friends. Aileen decided to delay her flight and go. Her father was most cordial. The presence and invitation of the Steinmetzes was as much a relief to him as it was to Aileen. West Chester being forty miles from Philadelphia, it was unlikely that Aileen would attempt to meet Cowperwood while there.

She wrote Cowperwood of the changed condition and departed, and he breathed a sigh of relief, fancying at the time that this storm had permanently blown over.

Chapter XXXIX

In the meanwhile the day of Cowperwood's trial was drawing near. He was under the impression that an attempt was going to be made to convict him whether the facts warranted it or not. He did not see any way out of his dilemma, however, unless it was to abandon everything and leave Philadelphia for good, which was impossible. The only way to guard his future and retain his financial friends was to stand trial as quickly as possible, and trust them to assist him to his feet in the future in case he failed. He discussed the possibilities of an unfair trial with Steger, who did not seem to think that there was so much to that. In the first place, a jury could not easily be suborned by any one. In the next place, most judges were honest, in spite of their political cleavage, and would go no further than party bias would lead them in their rulings and opinions, which was, in the main, not so far. The particular judge who was to sit in this case, one Wilbur Payderson, of the Court of Quarter Sessions, was a strict party nominee, and as such beholden to Mollenhauer, Simpson, and Butler; but, in so far as Steger had ever heard, he was an honest man.

"What I can't understand," said Steger, "is why these fellows should be so anxious to punish you, unless it is for the effect on the State at large. The election's over. I understand there's a movement on now to get Stener out in case he is convicted, which he will be. They have to try him. He won't go up for more than a year, or two or three, and if he does he'll be pardoned out in half the time or less. It would be the same in your case, if you were convicted. They couldn't keep you in and let him out.

But it will never get that far–take my word for it. We'll win before a jury, or we'll reverse the judgment of conviction before the State Supreme Court, certain. Those five judges up there are not going to sustain any such poppycock idea as this."

Steger actually believed what he said, and Cowperwood was pleased. Thus far the young lawyer had done excellently well in all of his cases. Still, he did not like the idea of being hunted down by Butler. It was a serious matter, and one of which Steger was totally unaware. Cowperwood could never quite forget that in listening to his lawyer's optimistic assurances.

The actual beginning of the trial found almost all of the inhabitants of this city of six hundred thousand "keyed up." None of the women of Cowperwood's family were coming into court. He had insisted that there should be no family demonstration for the newspapers to comment upon. His father was coming, for he might be needed as a witness. Aileen had written him the afternoon before saying she had returned from West Chester and wishing him luck. She was so anxious to know what was to become of him that she could not stay away any longer and had returned–not to go to the courtroom, for he did not want her to do that, but to be as near as possible when his fate was decided, adversely or otherwise. She wanted to run and congratulate him if he won, or to console with him if he lost. She felt that her return would be likely to precipitate a collision with her father, but she could not help that.

The position of Mrs. Cowperwood was most anomalous. She had to go through the formality of seeming affectionate and tender, even when she knew that Frank did not want her to be. He felt instinctively now that she knew of Aileen. He was merely awaiting the proper hour in which to spread the whole matter before her. She put her arms around him at the door on the fateful morning, in the somewhat formal manner into which they had dropped these later years, and for a moment, even though she was keenly aware of his difficulties, she could not kiss him. He did not want to kiss her, but he did not show it. She did kiss him, though, and added: "Oh, I do hope things come out all right."

"You needn't worry about that, I think, Lillian," he replied, buoyantly. "I'll be all right."

He ran down the steps and walked out on Girard Avenue to his former car line, where he bearded a car. He was thinking of Aileen and how keenly she was feeling for him, and what a mockery his married life now was, and whether he would face a sensible jury, and so on and so forth. If he didn't–if he didn't–this day was crucial!

He stepped off the car at Third and Market and hurried to his office. Steger was already there. "Well, Harper," observed Cowperwood, courageously, "today's the day."

The Court of Quarter Sessions, Part I, where this trial was to take place, was held in famous Independence Hall, at Sixth and Chestnut Streets, which was at this time, as it had been for all of a century before, the center of local executive and judicial life. It was a low two-story building of red brick, with a white wooden central tower of old Dutch and English derivation, compounded of the square, the circle, and the octagon. The total structure consisted of a central portion and two T-shaped wings lying to the right and left, whose small, oval-topped old-fashioned windows and doors were set with those many-paned sashes so much admired by those who love what

THE FINANCIER, A NOVEL

is known as Colonial architecture. Here, and in an addition known as State House Row (since torn down), which extended from the rear of the building toward Walnut Street, were located the offices of the mayor, the chief of police, the city treasurer, the chambers of council, and all the other important and executive offices of the city, together with the four branches of Quarter Sessions, which sat to hear the growing docket of criminal cases. The mammoth city hall which was subsequently completed at Broad and Market Streets was then building.

An attempt had been made to improve the reasonably large courtrooms by putting in them raised platforms of dark walnut surmounted by large, dark walnut desks, behind which the judges sat; but the attempt was not very successful. The desks, jury-boxes, and railings generally were made too large, and so the general effect was one of disproportion. A cream-colored wall had been thought the appropriate thing to go with black walnut furniture, but time and dust had made the combination dreary. There were no pictures or ornaments of any kind, save the stalky, over-elaborated gas-brackets which stood on his honor's desk, and the single swinging chandelier suspended from the center of the ceiling. Fat bailiffs and court officers, concerned only in holding their workless jobs, did not add anything to the spirit of the scene. Two of them in the particular court in which this trial was held contended hourly as to which should hand the judge a glass of water. One preceded his honor like a fat, stuffy, dusty majordomo to and from his dressing-room. His business was to call loudly, when the latter entered, "His honor the Court, hats off. Everybody please rise," while a second bailiff, standing at the left of his honor when he was seated, and between the jury-box and the witness-chair, recited in an absolutely unintelligible way that beautiful and dignified statement of collective society's obligation to the constituent units, which begins, "Hear ye! hear ye! hear ye!" and ends, "All those of you having just cause for complaint draw near and ye shall be heard." However, you would have thought it was of no import here. Custom and indifference had allowed it to sink to a mumble. A third bailiff guarded the door of the jury-room; and in addition to these there were present a court clerk–small, pale, candle-waxy, with colorless milk-and-water eyes, and thin, pork-fat-colored hair and beard, who looked for all the world like an Americanized and decidedly decrepit Chinese mandarin–and a court stenographer.

Judge Wilbur Payderson, a lean herring of a man, who had sat in this case originally as the examining judge when Cowperwood had been indicted by the grand jury, and who had bound him over for trial at this term, was a peculiarly interesting type of judge, as judges go. He was so meager and thin-blooded that he was arresting for those qualities alone. Technically, he was learned in the law; actually, so far as life was concerned, absolutely unconscious of that subtle chemistry of things that transcends all written law and makes for the spirit and, beyond that, the inutility of all law, as all wise judges know. You could have looked at his lean, pedantic body, his frizzled gray hair, his fishy, blue-gray eyes, without any depth of speculation in them, and his nicely modeled but unimportant face, and told him that he was without imagination; but he would not have believed you–would have fined you for contempt of court. By the careful garnering of all his little opportunities, the furbishing up of every meager advantage; by listening slavishly to the voice of party, and following as nearly as he could the behests of intrenched property, he had reached his present state. It was not very far along, at that. His salary was only six thousand dollars a year. His little fame did not extend beyond the meager realm of local lawyers and judges. But the sight of his name quoted daily as being about his duties, or rendering such and such a decision, was a great satisfaction to him. He thought it made him a significant figure in the world. "Behold I am not as other men," he often thought, and this comforted him. He was very much flattered when a prominent case came to his calendar; and as he sat enthroned before the various litigants and lawyers he felt, as a rule, very significant indeed. Now and then some subtlety of life would confuse his really limited intellect; but in all such cases there was the letter of the law. He could hunt in the reports to find out what really thinking men had decided. Besides, lawyers everywhere are so subtle. They put the rules of law, favorable or unfavorable, under the judge's thumb and nose. "Your honor, in the thirty-second volume of the Revised Reports of Massachusetts, page so and so, line so and so, in Arundel versus Bannerman, you will find, etc." How often have you heard that in a court of law? The reasoning that is left to do in most cases is not much. And the sanctity of the law is raised like a great banner by which the pride of the incumbent is strengthened.

Payderson, as Steger had indicated, could scarcely be pointed to as an unjust judge. He was a party judge–Republican in principle, or rather belief, beholden to the dominant party councils for his personal continuance in office, and as such willing and anxious to do whatever he considered that he reasonably could do to further the party welfare and the private interests of his masters. Most people never trouble to look into the mechanics of the thing they call their conscience too closely. Where they do, too often they lack the skill to disentangle the tangled threads of ethics and morals. Whatever the opinion of the time is, whatever the weight of great interests dictates, that they conscientiously believe. Some one has since invented the phrase "a corporation-minded judge." There are many such.

Payderson was one. He fairly revered property and power. To him Butler and Mollenhauer and Simpson were great men–reasonably sure to be right always because they were so powerful. This matter of Cowperwood's and Stener's defalcation he had long heard of. He knew by associating with one political light and another just what the situation was. The party, as the leaders saw it, had been put in a very bad position by Cowperwood's subtlety. He had led Stener astray–more than an ordinary city treasurer should have been led astray–and, although Stener was primarily guilty as the original mover in the scheme, Cowperwood was more so for having led him imaginatively to such disastrous lengths. Besides, the party needed a scapegoat–that was enough for Payderson, in the first place. Of course, after the election had been won, and it appeared that the party had not suffered so much, he did not understand quite why it was that Cowperwood was still so carefully included in the Proceedings; but he had faith to believe that the leaders had some just grounds for not letting him off. From one source and another he learned that Butler had some private grudge against Cowperwood. What it was no one seemed to know exactly. The general impression was that Cowperwood had led Butler into some unwholesome financial transactions. Anyhow, it was generally understood that for the good of the party, and in order to teach a wholesome lesson to dangerous subordinates–it had been decided to allow these several indictments to take their course. Cowperwood was to be punished quite as severely as Stener for the moral effect on the community. Stener was to be sentenced the maximum sentence for his crime in order that the party and the courts should appear properly righteous. Beyond that he was to be left to the mercy of the governor, who could ease things up for him if he chose, and if the leaders wished. In the silly mind of the general public the various judges of Quarter Sessions, like girls incarcerated in boarding-schools, were supposed in their serene aloofness from life not to know what was going on in the subterranean realm of politics; but they knew well enough, and, knowing particularly well from whence came their continued position and authority, they were duly grateful.

Chapter XL

When Cowperwood came into the crowded courtroom with his father and Steger, quite fresh and jaunty (looking the part of the shrewd financier, the man of affairs), every one stared. It was really too much to expect, most of them thought, that a man like this would be convicted. He was, no doubt, guilty; but, also, no doubt, he had ways and means of evading the law. His lawyer, Harper Steger, looked very shrewd and canny to them. It was very cold, and both men wore long, dark, bluish-gray overcoats, cut in the latest mode. Cowperwood was given to small boutonnieres in fair weather, but to-day he wore none. His tie, however, was of heavy, impressive silk, of lavender hue, set with a large, clear, green emerald. He wore only the thinnest of watch-chains, and no other ornament of any kind. He always looked jaunty and yet reserved, good-natured, and yet capable and self-sufficient. Never had he looked more so than he did to-day.

He at once took in the nature of the scene, which had a peculiar interest for him. Before him was the as yet empty judge's rostrum, and at its right the empty jury-box, between which, and to the judge's left, as he sat facing the audience, stood the witness-chair where he must presently sit and testify. Behind it, already awaiting the arrival of the court, stood a fat bailiff, one John Sparkheaver whose business it was to present the aged, greasy Bible to be touched by the witnesses in making oath, and to say, "Step this way," when the testimony was over. There were other bailiffs–one at the gate giving into the railed space before the judge's desk, where prisoners were arraigned, lawyers sat or pleaded, the defendant had a chair, and so on; another in the aisle leading to the jury-room, and still another guarding the door by which the public entered. Cowperwood surveyed Stener, who was one of the witnesses, and who now, in his helpless fright over his own fate, was without malice toward any one. He had really never borne any. He wished if anything now that he had followed Cowperwood's advice, seeing where he now was, though he still had faith that Mollenhauer and the political powers represented by him would do something for him with the governor, once he was sentenced. He was very pale and comparatively thin. Already he had lost that ruddy bulk which had been added during the days of his prosperity. He wore a new gray suit and a brown tie, and was clean-shaven. When his eye caught Cowperwood's steady beam, it faltered and drooped. He rubbed his ear foolishly. Cowperwood nodded.

"You know," he said to Steger, "I feel sorry for George. He's such a fool. Still I did all I could."

Cowperwood also watched Mrs. Stener out of the tail of his eye–an undersized, peaked, and sallow little woman, whose clothes fitted her abominably. It was just like

Stener to marry a woman like that, he thought. The scrubby matches of the socially unelect or unfit always interested, though they did not always amuse, him. Mrs. Stener had no affection for Cowperwood, of course, looking on him, as she did, as the unscrupulous cause of her husband's downfall. They were now quite poor again, about to move from their big house into cheaper quarters; and this was not pleasing for her to contemplate.

Judge Payderson came in after a time, accompanied by his undersized but stout court attendant, who looked more like a pouter-pigeon than a human being; and as they came, Bailiff Sparkheaver rapped on the judge's desk, beside which he had been slumbering, and mumbled, "Please rise!" The audience arose, as is the rule of all courts. Judge Payderson stirred among a number of briefs that were lying on his desk, and asked, briskly, "What's the first case, Mr. Protus?" He was speaking to his clerk.

During the long and tedious arrangement of the day's docket and while the various minor motions of lawyers were being considered, this courtroom scene still retained interest for Cowperwood. He was so eager to win, so incensed at the outcome of untoward events which had brought him here. He was always intensely irritated, though he did not show it, by the whole process of footing delays and queries and quibbles, by which legally the affairs of men were too often hampered. Law, if you had asked him, and he had accurately expressed himself, was a mist formed out of the moods and the mistakes of men, which befogged the sea of life and prevented plain sailing for the little commercial and social barques of men; it was a miasma of misinterpretation where the ills of life festered, and also a place where the accidentally wounded were ground between the upper and the nether millstones of force or chance; it was a strange, weird, interesting, and yet futile battle of wits where the ignorant and the incompetent and the shrewd and the angry and the weak were made pawns and shuttlecocks for men–lawyers, who were playing upon their moods, their vanities, their desires, and their necessities. It was an unholy and unsatisfactory disrupting and delaying spectacle, a painful commentary on the frailties of life, and men, a trick, a snare, a pit and gin. In the hands of the strong, like himself when he was at his best, the law was a sword and a shield, a trap to place before the feet of the unwary; a pit to dig in the path of those who might pursue. It was anything you might choose to make of it–a door to illegal opportunity; a cloud of dust to be cast in the eyes of those who might choose, and rightfully, to see; a veil to be dropped arbitrarily between truth and its execution, justice and its judgment, crime and punishment. Lawyers in the main were intellectual mercenaries to be bought and sold in any cause. It amused him to hear the ethical and emotional platitudes of lawyers, to see how readily they would lie, steal, prevaricate, misrepresent in almost any cause and for any purpose. Great lawyers were merely great unscrupulous subtleties, like himself, sitting back in dark, close-woven lairs like spiders and awaiting the approach of unwary human flies. Life was at best a dark, inhuman, unkind, unsympathetic struggle built of cruelties and the law, and its lawyers were the most despicable representatives of the whole unsatisfactory mess. Still he used law as he would use any other trap or weapon to rid him of a human ill; and as for lawyers, he picked them up as he would any club or knife wherewith to defend himself. He had no particular respect for any of them–not even Harper Steger, though he liked him. They were tools to be used–knives, keys, clubs, anything you will; but nothing more. When they were through they were paid and dropped–put aside and forgotten. As for judges, they were merely incompetent lawyers, at a rule, who were shelved by some fortunate turn of chance, and who would not, in all likelihood, be as efficient as the lawyers who pleaded before them if they were put in the same position. He had no respect for judges–he knew too much about them. He knew how often they were sycophants, political climbers, political hacks, tools, time-servers, judicial door-mats lying before the financially and politically great and powerful who used them as such. Judges were fools, as were most other people in this dusty, shifty world. Pah! His inscrutable eyes took them all in and gave no sign. His only safety lay, he thought, in the magnificent subtley of his own brain, and nowhere else. You could not convince Cowperwood of any great or inherent virtue in this mortal scheme of things. He knew too much; he knew himself.

When the judge finally cleared away the various minor motions pending, he ordered his clerk to call the case of the City of Philadelphia versus Frank A. Cowperwood, which was done in a clear voice. Both Dennis Shannon, the new district attorney, and Steger, were on their feet at once. Steger and Cowperwood, together with Shannon and Strobik, who had now come in and was standing as the representative of the State of Pennsylvania–the complainant–had seated themselves at the long table inside the railing which inclosed the space before the judge's desk. Steger proposed to Judge Payderson, for effect's sake more than anything else, that this indictment be quashed, but was overruled.

A jury to try the case was now quickly impaneled–twelve men out of the usual list called to serve for the month–and was then ready to be challenged by the opposing counsel. The business of impaneling a jury was a rather simple thing so far as this court was concerned. It consisted in the mandarin-like clerk taking the names of all the jurors called to serve in this court for the month–some fifty in all–and putting them, each written on a separate slip of paper, in a whirling drum, spinning it around a few times, and then lifting out the first slip which his hand encountered, thus glorifying chance and settling on who should be juror No. 1. His hand reaching in twelve times drew out the names of the twelve jurymen, who as their names were called, were ordered to take their places in the jury-box.

Cowperwood observed this proceeding with a great deal of interest. What could be more important than the men who were going to try him? The process was too swift for accurate judgment, but he received a faint impression of middle-class men. One man in particular, however, an old man of sixty-five, with iron-gray hair and beard, shaggy eyebrows, sallow complexion, and stooped shoulders, struck him as having that kindness of temperament and breadth of experience which might under certain circumstances be argumentatively swayed in his favor. Another, a small, sharp-nosed, sharp-chinned commercial man of some kind, he immediately disliked.

"I hope I don't have to have that man on my jury," he said to Steger, quietly.

"You don't," replied Steger. "I'll challenge him. We have the right to fifteen peremptory challenges on a case like this, and so has the prosecution."

When the jury-box was finally full, the two lawyers waited for the clerk to bring them the small board upon which slips of paper bearing the names of the twelve jurors were fastened in rows in order of their selection–jurors one, two, and three being in the first row; four, five, and six in the second, and so on. It being the prerogative of the attorney for the prosecution to examine and challenge the jurors first, Shannon arose, and, taking the board, began to question them as to their trades or professions, their knowledge of the case before the court, and their possible prejudice for or against the prisoner.

It was the business of both Steger and Shannon to find men who knew a little something of finance and could understand a peculiar situation of this kind without any of them (looking at it from Steger's point of view) having any prejudice against a man's trying to assist himself by reasonable means to weather a financial storm or (looking at it from Shannon's point of view) having any sympathy with such means, if they bore about them the least suspicion of chicanery, jugglery, or dishonest manipulation of any kind. As both Shannon and Steger in due course observed for themselves in connection with this jury, it was composed of that assorted social fry which the dragnets of the courts, cast into the ocean of the city, bring to the surface for purposes of this sort. It was made up in the main of managers, agents, tradesmen, editors, engineers, architects, furriers, grocers, traveling salesmen, authors, and every other kind of working citizen whose experience had fitted him for service in proceedings of this character. Rarely would you have found a man of great distinction; but very frequently a group of men who were possessed of no small modicum of that interesting quality known as hard common sense.

Throughout all this Cowperwood sat quietly examining the men. A young florist, with a pale face, a wide speculative forehead, and anemic hands, struck him as being sufficiently impressionable to his personal charm to be worth while. He whispered as much to Steger. There was a shrewd Jew, a furrier, who was challenged because he had read all of the news of the panic and had lost two thousand dollars in street-railway stocks. There was a stout wholesale grocer, with red cheeks, blue eyes, and flaxen hair, who Cowperwood said he thought was stubborn. He was eliminated. There was a thin, dapper manager of a small retail clothing store, very anxious to be excused, who declared, falsely, that he did not believe in swearing by the Bible. Judge Payderson, eyeing him severely, let him go. There were some ten more in all—men who knew of Cowperwood, men who admitted they were prejudiced, men who were hidebound Republicans and resentful of this crime, men who knew Stener—who were pleasantly eliminated.

By twelve o'clock, however, a jury reasonably satisfactory to both sides had been chosen.

Chapter XLI

At two o'clock sharp Dennis Shannon, as district attorney, began his opening address. He stated in a very simple, kindly way—for he had a most engaging manner—that the indictment as here presented charged Mr. Frank A. Cowperwood, who was sitting at the table inside the jury-rail, first with larceny, second with embezzlement, third with larceny as bailee, and fourth with embezzlement of a certain sum of money—a specific sum, to wit, sixty thousand dollars—on a check given him (drawn to his order) October 9, 1871, which was intended to reimburse him for a certain number of certificates of city loan, which he as agent or bailee of the check was supposed to have purchased for the city sinking-fund on the order of the city treasurer (under some form of agreement which had been in existence between them, and which had been in force for some time)–said fund being intended to take up such certificates as they might mature in the hands of holders and be presented for payment–for which purpose, however, the check in question had never been used.

"Now, gentlemen," said Mr. Shannon, very quietly, "before we go into this very simple question of whether Mr. Cowperwood did or did not on the date in question get from the city treasurer sixty thousand dollars, for which he made no honest return, let me explain to you just what the people mean when they charge him first with larceny, second with embezzlement, third with larceny as bailee, and fourth with embezzlement on a check. Now, as you see, there are four counts here, as we lawyers term them, and the reason there are four counts is as follows: A man may be guilty of larceny and embezzlement at the same time, or of larceny or embezzlement separately, and without being guilty of the other, and the district attorney representing the people might be uncertain, not that he was not guilty of both, but that it might not be possible to present the evidence under one count, so as to insure his adequate punishment for a crime which in a way involved both. In such cases, gentlemen, it is customary to indict a man under separate counts, as has been done in this case. Now, the four counts in this case, in a way, overlap and confirm each other, and it will be your duty, after we have explained their nature and character and presented the evidence, to say whether the defendant is guilty on one count or the other, or on two or three of the counts, or on all four, just as you see fit and proper–or, to put it in a better way, as the evidence warrants. Larceny, as you may or may not know, is the act of taking away the goods or chattels of another without his knowledge or consent, and embezzlement is the fraudulent appropriation to one's own use of what is intrusted to one's care and management, especially money. Larceny as bailee, on the other hand, is simply a more definite form of larceny wherein one fixes the act of carrying away the goods of another without his knowledge or consent on the person to whom the goods were delivered in trust that is, the agent or bailee. Embezzlement on a check, which constitutes the fourth charge, is simply a more definite form of fixing charge number two in an exact way and signifies appropriating the money on a check given for a certain definite purpose. All of these charges, as you can see, gentlemen, are in a way synonymous. They overlap and overlay each other. The people, through their representative, the district attorney, contend that Mr. Cowperwood, the defendant here, is guilty of all four charges. So now, gentlemen, we will proceed to the history of this crime, which proves to me as an individual that this defendant has one of the most subtle and dangerous minds of the criminal financier type, and we hope by witnesses to prove that to you, also."

Shannon, because the rules of evidence and court procedure here admitted of no interruption of the prosecution in presenting a case, then went on to describe from his own point of view how Cowperwood had first met Stener; how he had wormed himself into his confidence; how little financial knowledge Stener had, and so forth; coming down finally to the day the check for sixty thousand dollars was given Cowperwood; how Stener, as treasurer, claimed that he knew nothing of its delivery, which constituted the base of the charge of larceny; how Cowperwood, having it, misappropriated the certificates supposed to have been purchased for the sinking-fund, if they were purchased at all–all of which Shannon said constituted the crimes with which the defendant was charged, and of which he was unquestionably guilty.

"We have direct and positive evidence of all that we have thus far contended, gentlemen," Mr. Shannon concluded violently. "This is not a matter of hearsay or theory, but of fact. You will be shown by direct testimony which cannot be shaken just how it was done. If, after you have heard all this, you still think this man is innocent– that he did not commit the crimes with which he is charged–it is your business to acquit him. On the other hand, if you think the witnesses whom we shall put on the stand are telling the truth, then it is your business to convict him, to find a verdict for the people as against the defendant. I thank you for your attention."

The jurors stirred comfortably and took positions of ease, in which they thought they were to rest for the time; but their idle comfort was of short duration for Shannon now called out the name of George W. Stener, who came hurrying forward very pale, very flaccid, very tired-looking. His eyes, as he took his seat in the witness-chair, laying his hand on the Bible and swearing to tell the truth, roved in a restless, nervous manner.

His voice was a little weak as he started to give his testimony. He told first how he had met Cowperwood in the early months of 1866–he could not remember the exact day; it was during his first term as city treasurer–he had been elected to the office in the fall of 1864. He had been troubled about the condition of city loan, which was below par, and which could not be sold by the city legally at anything but par. Cowperwood had been recommended to him by some one–Mr. Strobik, he believed, though he couldn't be sure. It was the custom of city treasurers to employ brokers, or a broker, in a crisis of this kind, and he was merely following what had been the custom. He went on to describe, under steady promptings and questions from the incisive mind of Shannon, just what the nature of this first conversation was–he remembered it fairly well; how Mr. Cowperwood had said he thought he could do what was wanted; how he had gone away and drawn up a plan or thought one out; and how he had returned and laid it before Stener. Under Shannon's skillful guidance Stener elucidated just what this scheme was–which wasn't exactly so flattering to the honesty of men in general as it was a testimonial to their subtlety and skill.

After much discussion of Stener's and Cowperwood's relations the story finally got down to the preceding October, when by reason of companionship, long business understanding, mutually prosperous relationship, etc., the place bad been reached where, it was explained, Cowperwood was not only handling several millions of city loan annually, buying and selling for the city and trading in it generally, but in the bargain had secured one five hundred thousand dollars' worth of city money at an exceedingly low rate of interest, which was being invested for himself and Stener in profitable street-car ventures of one kind and another. Stener was not anxious to be altogether clear on this point; but Shannon, seeing that he was later to prosecute Stener himself for this very crime of embezzlement, and that Steger would soon follow in cross-examination, was not willing to let him be hazy. Shannon wanted to fix Cowperwood in the minds of the jury as a clever, tricky person, and by degrees he certainly managed to indicate a very subtle-minded man. Occasionally, as one sharp point after another of Cowperwood's skill was brought out and made moderately clear, one juror or another turned to look at Cowperwood. And he noting this and in order to impress them all as favorably as possible merely gazed Stenerward with a steady air of intelligence and comprehension.

The examination now came down to the matter of the particular check for sixty thousand dollars which Albert Stires had handed Cowperwood on the afternoon–late–of October 9, 1871. Shannon showed Stener the check itself. Had he ever seen it? Yes. Where? In the office of District Attorney Pettie on October 20th, or thereabouts last. Was that the first time he had seen it? Yes. Had he ever heard about it before then? Yes. When? On October 10th last. Would he kindly tell the jury in his own way just how and under what circumstances he first heard of it then? Stener twisted uncomfortably in his chair. It was a hard thing to do. It was not a pleasant commentary on his own character and degree of moral stamina, to say the least. However, he cleared his throat again and began a description of that small but bitter section of his life's drama in which Cowperwood, finding himself in a tight place and about to fail, had come to him at his office and demanded that he loan him three hundred thousand dollars more in one lump sum.

There was considerable bickering just at this point between Steger and Shannon, for the former was very anxious to make it appear that Stener was lying out of the whole cloth about this. Steger got in his objection at this point, and created a considerable diversion from the main theme, because Stener kept saying he "thought" or he "believed."

"Object!" shouted Steger, repeatedly. "I move that that be stricken from the record as incompetent, irrelevant, and immaterial. The witness is not allowed to say what he thinks, and the prosecution knows it very well."

"Your honor," insisted Shannon, "I am doing the best I can to have the witness tell a plain, straightforward story, and I think that it is obvious that he is doing so."

"Object!" reiterated Steger, vociferously. "Your honor, I insist that the district attorney has no right to prejudice the minds of the jury by flattering estimates of the sincerity of the witness. What he thinks of the witness and his sincerity is of no importance in this case. I must ask that your honor caution him plainly in this matter."

"Objection sustained," declared Judge Payderson, "the prosecution will please be more explicit"; and Shannon went on with his case.

Stener's testimony, in one respect, was most important, for it made plain what Cowperwood did not want brought out–namely, that he and Stener had had a dispute before this; that Stener had distinctly told Cowperwood that he would not loan him any more money; that Cowperwood had told Stener, on the day before he secured this check, and again on that very day, that he was in a very desperate situation financially, and that if he were not assisted to the extent of three hundred thousand dollars he would fail, and that then both he and Stener would be ruined. On the morning of this day, according to Stener, he had sent Cowperwood a letter ordering him to cease purchasing city loan certificates for the sinking-fund. It was after their conversation on the same afternoon that Cowperwood surreptitiously secured the check for sixty thousand dollars from Albert Stires without his (Stener's) knowledge; and it was subsequent to this latter again that Stener, sending Albert to demand the return of the check, was refused, though the next day at five o'clock in the afternoon Cowperwood made an assignment. And the certificates for which the check had been purloined were not in the sinking-fund as they should have been. This was dark testimony for Cowperwood.

If any one imagines that all this was done without many vehement objections and exceptions made and taken by Steger, and subsequently when he was cross-examining Stener, by Shannon, he errs greatly. At times the chamber was coruscating with these two gentlemen's bitter wrangles, and his honor was compelled to hammer his desk with his gavel, and to threaten both with contempt of court, in order to bring them to a sense of order. Indeed while Payderson was highly incensed, the jury was amused and interested.

"You gentlemen will have to stop this, or I tell you now that you will both be heavily fined. This is a court of law, not a bar-room. Mr. Steger, I expect you to apologize to me and your colleague at once. Mr. Shannon, I must ask that you use less aggressive methods. Your manner is offensive to me. It is not becoming to a court of law. I will not caution either of you again."

Both lawyers apologized as lawyers do on such occasions, but it really made but little difference. Their individual attitudes and moods continued about as before.

"What did he say to you," asked Shannon of Stener, after one of these troublesome interruptions, "on that occasion, October 9th last, when he came to you and demanded the loan of an additional three hundred thousand dollars? Give his words as near as you can remember–exactly, if possible."

"Object!" interposed Steger, vigorously. "His exact words are not recorded any-where except in Mr. Stener's memory, and his memory of them cannot be admitted in this case. The witness has testified to the general facts."

Judge Payderson smiled grimly. "Objection overruled," he returned.

"Exception!" shouted Steger.

"He said, as near as I can remember," replied Stener, drumming on the arms of the witness-chair in a nervous way, "that if I didn't give him three hundred thousand dollars he was going to fail, and I would be poor and go to the penitentiary."

"Object!" shouted Stager, leaping to his feet. "Your honor, I object to the whole manner in which this examination is being conducted by the prosecution. The evidence which the district attorney is here trying to extract from the uncertain memory of the witness is in defiance of all law and precedent, and has no definite bearing on the facts of the case, and could not disprove or substantiate whether Mr. Cowperwood thought or did not think that he was going to fail. Mr. Stener might give one version of this conversation or any conversation that took place at this time, and Mr. Cowperwood another. As a matter of fact, their versions are different. I see no point in Mr. Shannon's line of inquiry, unless it is to prejudice the jury's minds towards accepting certain allegations which the prosecution is pleased to make and which it cannot possibly substantiate. I think you ought to caution the witness to testify only in regard to things that he recalls exactly, not to what he thinks he remembers; and for my part I think that all that has been testified to in the last five minutes might be well stricken out."

"Objection overruled," replied Judge Payderson, rather indifferently; and Steger who had been talking merely to overcome the weight of Stener's testimony in the minds of the jury, sat down.

Shannon once more approached Stener.

"Now, as near as you can remember, Mr. Stener, I wish you would tell the jury what else it was that Mr. Cowperwood said on that occasion. He certainly didn't stop with the remark that you would be ruined and go to the penitentiary. Wasn't there other language that was employed on that occasion?"

"He said, as far as I can remember," replied Stener, "that there were a lot of political schemers who were trying to frighten me, that if I didn't give him three hundred thousand dollars we would both be ruined, and that I might as well be tried for stealing a sheep as a lamb."

"Ha!" yelled Shannon. "He said that, did he?"

"Yes, sir; he did," said Stener.

"How did he say it, exactly? What were his exact words?" Shannon demanded, emphatically, pointing a forceful forefinger at Stener in order to key him up to a clear memory of what had transpired.

"Well, as near as I can remember, he said just that," replied Stener, vaguely. "You might as well be tried for stealing a sheep as a lamb."

"Exactly!" exclaimed Shannon, whirling around past the jury to look at Cowperwood. "I thought so."

"Pure pyrotechnics, your honor," said Steger, rising to his feet on the instant. "All intended to prejudice the minds of the jury. Acting. I wish you would caution the counsel for the prosecution to confine himself to the evidence in hand, and not act for the benefit of his case."

The spectators smiled; and Judge Payderson, noting it, frowned severely. "Do you make that as an objection, Mr. Steger?" he asked.

"I certainly do, your honor," insisted Steger, resourcefully.

"Objection overruled. Neither counsel for the prosecution nor for the defense is limited to a peculiar routine of expression."

Steger himself was ready to smile, but he did not dare to.

Cowperwood fearing the force of such testimony and regretting it, still looked at Stener, pityingly. The feebleness of the man; the weakness of the man; the pass to which his cowardice had brought them both!

When Shannon was through bringing out this unsatisfactory data, Steger took Stener in hand; but he could not make as much out of him as he hoped. In so far as this particular situation was concerned, Stener was telling the exact truth; and it is hard to weaken the effect of the exact truth by any subtlety of interpretation, though it can, sometimes, be done. With painstaking care Steger went over all the ground of Stener's long relationship with Cowperwood, and tried to make it appear that Cowperwood was invariably the disinterested agent–not the ringleader in a subtle, really criminal adventure. It was hard to do, but he made a fine impression. Still the jury listened with skeptical minds. It might not be fair to punish Cowperwood for seizing with avidity upon a splendid chance to get rich quick, they thought; but it certainly was not worth while to throw a veil of innocence over such palpable human cupidity. Finally, both lawyers were through with Stener for the time being, anyhow, and then Albert Stires was called to the stand.

He was the same thin, pleasant, alert, rather agreeable soul that he had been in the heyday of his clerkly prosperity–a little paler now, but not otherwise changed. His small property had been saved for him by Cowperwood, who had advised Steger to inform the Municipal Reform Association that Stires' bondsmen were attempting to sequestrate it for their own benefit, when actually it should go to the city if there were any real claim against him–which there was not. That watchful organization had issued one of its numerous reports covering this point, and Albert had had the pleasure of seeing Strobik and the others withdraw in haste. Naturally he was grateful to Cowperwood, even though once he had been compelled to cry in vain in his presence. He was anxious now to do anything he could to help the banker, but his naturally truthful disposition prevented him from telling anything except the plain facts, which were partly beneficial and partly not.

Stires testified that he recalled Cowperwood's saying that he had purchased the certificates, that he was entitled to the money, that Stener was unduly frightened, and that no harm would come to him, Albert. He identified certain memoranda in the city treasurer's books, which were produced, as being accurate, and others in Cowperwood's books, which were also produced, as being corroborative. His testimony as to Stener's astonishment on discovering that his chief clerk had given Cowperwood a check was against the latter; but Cowperwood hoped to overcome the effect of this by his own testimony later.

Up to now both Steger and Cowperwood felt that they were doing fairly well, and that they need not be surprised if they won their case.

Chapter XLII

The trial moved on. One witness for the prosecution after another followed until the State had built up an arraignment that satisfied Shannon that he had established Cowperwood's guilt, whereupon he announced that he rested. Steger at once arose and began a long argument for the dismissal of the case on the ground that there was no evidence to show this, that and the other, but Judge Payderson would have none of it. He knew how important the matter was in the local political world.

"I don't think you had better go into all that now, Mr. Steger," he said, wearily, after allowing him to proceed a reasonable distance. "I am familiar with the custom of the city, and the indictment as here made does not concern the custom of the city. Your argument is with the jury, not with me. I couldn't enter into that now. You may renew your motion at the close of the defendants' case. Motion denied."

District-Attorney Shannon, who had been listening attentively, sat down. Steger, seeing there was no chance to soften the judge's mind by any subtlety of argument, returned to Cowperwood, who smiled at the result.

"We'll just have to take our chances with the jury," he announced.

"I was sure of it," replied Cowperwood.

Steger then approached the jury, and, having outlined the case briefly from his angle of observation, continued by telling them what he was sure the evidence would show from his point of view.

"As a matter of fact, gentlemen, there is no essential difference in the evidence which the prosecution can present and that which we, the defense, can present. We are not going to dispute that Mr. Cowperwood received a check from Mr. Stener for sixty thousand dollars, or that he failed to put the certificate of city loan which that sum of money represented, and to which he was entitled in payment as agent, in the sinking-fund, as the prosecution now claims he should have done; but we are going to claim and prove also beyond the shadow of a reasonable doubt that he had a right, as the agent of the city, doing business with the city through its treasury department for four years, to withhold, under an agreement which he had with the city treasurer, all payments of money and all deposits of certificates in the sinking-fund until the first day of each succeeding month—the first month following any given transaction. As a matter of fact we can and will bring many traders and bankers who have had dealings with the city treasury in the past in just this way to prove this. The prosecution is going to ask you to believe that Mr. Cowperwood knew at the time he received this check that he was going to fail; that he did not buy the certificates, as he claimed, with the view of placing them in the sinking-fund; and that, knowing he was going to fail, and that he could not subsequently deposit them, he deliberately went to Mr. Albert Stires, Mr. Stener's secretary, told him that he had purchased such certificates, and on the strength of a falsehood, implied if not actually spoken, secured the check, and walked away.

"Now, gentlemen, I am not going to enter into a long-winded discussion of these points at this time, since the testimony is going to show very rapidly what the facts are. We have a number of witnesses here, and we are all anxious to have them heard. What I am going to ask you to remember is that there is not one scintilla of testimony outside of that which may possibly be given by Mr. George W. Stener, which will show either that Mr. Cowperwood knew, at the time he called on the city treasurer, that he was going to fail, or that he had not purchased the certificates in question, or that he had not the right to withhold them from the sinking-fund as long as he pleased up to the first of the month, the time he invariably struck a balance with the city. Mr. Stener, the ex-city treasurer, may possibly testify one way. Mr. Cowperwood, on his own behalf, will testify another. It will then be for you gentlemen to decide between them, to decide which one you prefer to believe—Mr. George W. Stener, the ex-city treasurer, the former commercial associate of Mr. Cowperwood, who, after years and years of profit, solely because of conditions of financial stress, fire, and panic, preferred to turn on his one-time associate from whose labors he had reaped so much profit, or Mr. Frank A. Cowperwood, the well-known banker and financier, who did his best to weather the storm alone, who fulfilled to the letter every agreement he ever had with the city, who has even until this hour been busy trying to remedy the unfair financial difficulties forced upon him by fire and panic, and who only yesterday made an offer to the city that, if he were allowed to continue in uninterrupted control of his affairs he would gladly repay as quickly as possible every dollar of his indebtedness (which is really not all his), including the five hundred thousand dollars under discussion between him and Mr. Stener and the city, and so prove by his works, not talk, that there was no basis for this unfair suspicion of his motives. As you perhaps surmise, the city has not chosen to accept his offer, and I shall try and tell you why later, gentlemen. For the present we will proceed with the testimony, and for the defense all I ask is that you give very close attention to all that is testified to here to-day. Listen very carefully to Mr. W. C. Davison when he is put on the stand. Listen equally carefully to Mr. Cowperwood when we call him to testify. Follow the other testimony closely, and then you will be able to judge for yourselves. See if you can distinguish a just motive for this prosecution. I can't. I am very much obliged to you for listening to me, gentlemen, so attentively."

He then put on Arthur Rivers, who had acted for Cowperwood on 'change as special agent during the panic, to testify to the large quantities of city loan he had purchased to stay the market; and then after him, Cowperwood's brothers, Edward and Joseph, who testified to instructions received from Rivers as to buying and selling city loan on that occasion–principally buying.

The next witness was President W. C. Davison of the Girard National Bank. He was a large man physically, not so round of body as full and broad. His shoulders and chest were ample. He had a big blond head, with an ample breadth of forehead, which was high and sane-looking. He had a thick, squat nose, which, however, was forceful, and thin, firm, even lips. There was the faintest touch of cynical humor in his hard blue eyes at times; but mostly he was friendly, alert, placid-looking, without seeming in the least sentimental or even kindly. His business, as one could see plainly, was to insist on hard financial facts, and one could see also how he would naturally be drawn to Frank Algernon Cowperwood without being mentally dominated or upset by him. As he took the chair very quietly, and yet one might say significantly, it was obvious that he felt that this sort of legal-financial palaver was above the average man and beneath the dignity of a true financier–in other words, a bother. The drowsy Sparkheaver holding up a Bible beside him for him to swear by might as well have been a block of wood. His oath was a personal matter with him. It was good business to tell the truth at times. His testimony was very direct and very simple.

He had known Mr. Frank Algernon Cowperwood for nearly ten years. He had done business with or through him nearly all of that time. He knew nothing of his personal relations with Mr. Stener, and did not know Mr. Stener personally. As for the particular check of sixty thousand dollars–yes, he had seen it before. It had come into the bank on October 10th along with other collateral to offset an overdraft on the part of Cowperwood Co. It was placed to the credit of Cowperwood Co. on the books of the bank, and the bank secured the cash through the clearing-house. No money was drawn out of the bank by Cowperwood Co. after that to create an overdraft. The bank's account with Cowperwood was squared.

Nevertheless, Mr. Cowperwood might have drawn heavily, and nothing would have been thought of it. Mr. Davison did not know that Mr. Cowperwood was going to fail–did not suppose that he could, so quickly. He had frequently overdrawn his account with the bank; as a matter of fact, it was the regular course of his business to overdraw it. It kept his assets actively in use, which was the height of good business. His overdrafts were protected by collateral, however, and it was his custom to send bundles of collateral or checks, or both, which were variously distributed to keep things straight. Mr. Cowperwood's account was the largest and most active in the bank, Mr. Davison kindly volunteered. When Mr. Cowperwood had failed there had been over ninety thousand dollars' worth of certificates of city loan in the bank's possession which Mr Cowperwood had sent there as collateral. Shannon, on cross-examination, tried to find out for the sake of the effect on the jury, whether Mr. Davison was not for some ulterior motive especially favorable to Cowperwood. It was not possible for him to do that. Steger followed, and did his best to render the favorable points made by Mr. Davison in Cowperwood's behalf perfectly clear to the jury by having him repeat them. Shannon objected, of course, but it was of no use. Steger managed to make his point.

He now decided to have Cowperwood take the stand, and at the mention of his name in this connection the whole courtroom bristled.

Cowperwood came forward briskly and quickly. He was so calm, so jaunty, so defiant of life, and yet so courteous to it. These lawyers, this jury, this straw-and-water judge, these machinations of fate, did not basically disturb or humble or weaken him. He saw through the mental equipment of the jury at once. He wanted to assist his counsel in disturbing and confusing Shannon, but his reason told him that only an indestructible fabric of fact or seeming would do it. He believed in the financial rightness of the thing he had done. He was entitled to do it. Life was war–particularly financial life; and strategy was its keynote, its duty, its necessity. Why should he bother about petty, picayune minds which could not understand this? He went over his history for Steger and the jury, and put the sanest, most comfortable light on it that he could. He had not gone to Mr. Stener in the first place, he said–he had been called. He had not urged Mr. Stener to anything. He had merely shown him and his friends financial possibilities which they were only too eager to seize upon. And they had seized upon them. (It was not possible for Shannon to discover at this period how subtly he had organized his street-car companies so that he could have "shaken out" Stener and his friends without their being able to voice a single protest, so he talked of these things as opportunities which he had made for Stener and others. Shannon was not a financier, neither was Steger. They had to believe in a way, though they doubted it, partly–particularly Shannon.) He was not responsible for the custom prevailing in the office of the city treasurer, he said. He was a banker and broker.

The jury looked at him, and believed all except this matter of the sixty-thousand-dollar check. When it came to that he explained it all plausibly enough. When he had gone to see Stener those several last days, he had not fancied that he was really going to fail. He had asked Stener for some money, it is true–not so very much, all things considered–one hundred and fifty thousand dollars; but, as Stener should have testified, he (Cowperwood) was not disturbed in his manner. Stener had merely been one resource of his. He was satisfied at that time that he had many others. He had not used the forceful language or made the urgent appeal which Stener said he had, although he had pointed out to Stener that it was a mistake to become panic-stricken, also to withhold further credit. It was true that Stener was his easiest, his quickest resource, but not his only one. He thought, as a matter of fact, that his credit would be greatly extended by his principal money friends if necessary, and that he would have ample time to patch up his affairs and keep things going until the storm should blow over. He had told Stener of his extended purchase of city loan to stay the market on the first day of the panic, and of the fact that sixty thousand dollars was due him. Stener had made no objection. It was just possible that he was too mentally disturbed at the time to pay close attention. After that, to his, Cowperwood's, surprise, unexpected pressure on great financial houses from unexpected directions had caused them to be not willingly but unfortunately severe with him. This pressure, coming collectively the next day, had compelled him to close his doors, though he had not really expected to up to the last moment. His call for the sixty-thousand-dollar check at the time had been purely fortuitous. He needed the money, of course, but it was due him, and his clerks were all very busy. He merely asked for and took it personally to save time. Stener knew if it had been refused him he would have brought suit. The matter of depositing city loan certificates in the sinking-fund, when purchased for the city, was something to which he never gave any personal attention whatsoever. His bookkeeper, Mr. Stapley, attended to all that. He did not know, as a matter of fact, that they had not been deposited. (This was a barefaced lie. He did know.) As for the check being turned over to the Girard National Bank, that was fortuitous. It might just as well have been turned over to some other bank if the conditions had been different.

Thus on and on he went, answering all of Steger's and Shannon's searching questions with the most engaging frankness, and you could have sworn from the solemnity with which he took it all–the serious business attention–that he was the soul of so-called commercial honor. And to say truly, he did believe in the justice as well as the necessity and the importance of all that he had done and now described. He wanted the jury to see it as he saw it–put itself in his place and sympathize with him.

He was through finally, and the effect on the jury of his testimony and his personality was peculiar. Philip Moultrie, juror No. 1, decided that Cowperwood was lying. He could not see how it was possible that he could not know the day before that he was going to fail. He must have known, he thought. Anyhow, the whole series of transactions between him and Stener seemed deserving of some punishment, and all during this testimony he was thinking how, when he got in the jury-room, he would vote guilty. He even thought of some of the arguments he would use to convince the others that Cowperwood was guilty. Juror No. 2, on the contrary, Simon Glassberg, a clothier, thought he understood how it all came about, and decided to vote for acquittal. He did not think Cowperwood was innocent, but he did not think he deserved to be punished. Juror No. 3, Fletcher Norton, an architect, thought Cowperwood was guilty, but at the same time that he was too talented to be sent to prison. Juror No. 4, Charles Hillegan, an Irishman, a contractor, and a somewhat religious-minded person, thought Cowperwood was guilty and ought to be punished. Juror No. 5, Philip Lukash, a coal merchant, thought he was guilty. Juror No. 6, Benjamin Fraser, a mining expert, thought he was probably guilty, but he could not be sure. Uncertain what he would do, juror No. 7, J. J. Bridges, a broker in Third Street, small, practical, narrow, thought Cowperwood was shrewd and guilty and deserved to be punished. He would vote for his punishment. Juror No. 8, Guy E. Tripp, general manager of a small steamboat company, was uncertain. Juror No. 9, Joseph Tisdale, a retired glue manufacturer, thought Cowperwood was probably guilty as charged, but to Tisdale it was no crime. Cowperwood was entitled to do as he had done under the circumstances. Tisdale would vote for his acquittal. Juror No. 10, Richard Marsh, a young florist, was for Cowperwood in a sentimental way. He had, as a matter of fact, no real convictions.

Juror No. 11, Richard Webber, a grocer, small financially, but heavy physically, was for Cowperwood's conviction. He thought him guilty. Juror No. 12, Washington B. Thomas, a wholesale flour merchant, thought Cowperwood was guilty, but believed in a recommendation to mercy after pronouncing him so. Men ought to be reformed, was his slogan.

So they stood, and so Cowperwood left them, wondering whether any of his testimony had had a favorable effect.

Chapter XLIII

Since it is the privilege of the lawyer for the defense to address the jury first, Steger bowed politely to his colleague and came forward. Putting his hands on the jury-box rail, he began in a very quiet, modest, but impressive way:

"Gentlemen of the jury, my client, Mr. Frank Algernon Cowperwood, a well-known banker and financier of this city, doing business in Third Street, is charged by the State of Pennsylvania, represented by the district attorney of this district, with fraudulently transferring from the treasury of the city of Philadelphia to his own purse the sum of sixty thousand dollars, in the form of a check made out to his order, dated October 9, 1871, and by him received from one Albert Stires, the private secretary and head bookkeeper of the treasurer of this city, at the time in question. Now, gentlemen, what are the facts in this connection? You have heard the various witnesses and know the general outlines of the story. Take the testimony of George W. Stener, to begin with. He tells you that sometime back in the year 1866 he was greatly in need of some one, some banker or broker, who would tell him how to bring city loan, which was selling very low at the time, to par–who would not only tell him this, but proceed to demonstrate that his knowledge was accurate by doing it. Mr. Stener was an inexperienced man at the time in the matter of finance. Mr. Cowperwood was an active young man with an enviable record as a broker and a trader on 'change. He proceeded to demonstrate to Mr. Stener not only in theory, but in fact, how this thing of bringing city loan to par could be done. He made an arrangement at that time with Mr. Stener, the details of which you have heard from Mr. Stener himself, the result of which was that a large amount of city loan was turned over to Mr. Cowperwood by Mr. Stener for sale, and by adroit manipulation–methods of buying and selling which need not be gone into here, but which are perfectly sane and legitimate in the world in which Mr. Cowperwood operated, did bring that loan to par, and kept it there year after year as you have all heard here testified to.

"Now what is the bone of contention here, gentlemen, the significant fact which brings Mr. Stener into this court at this time charging his old-time agent and broker with larceny and embezzlement, and alleging that he has transferred to his own use without a shadow of return sixty thousand dollars of the money which belongs to the city treasury? What is it? Is it that Mr. Cowperwood secretly, with great stealth, as it were, at some time or other, unknown to Mr. Stener or to his assistants, entered the office of the treasurer and forcibly, and with criminal intent, carried away sixty thousand dollars' worth of the city's money? Not at all. The charge is, as you have heard the district attorney explain, that Mr. Cowperwood came in broad daylight at between four and five o'clock of the afternoon preceeding the day of his assignment; was closeted with Mr. Stener for a half or three-quarters of an hour; came out;

explained to Mr. Albert Stires that he had recently bought sixty thousand dollars' worth of city loan for the city sinking-fund, for which he had not been paid; asked that the amount be credited on the city's books to him, and that he be given a check, which was his due, and walked out. Anything very remarkable about that, gentlemen? Anything very strange? Has it been testified here to-day that Mr. Cowperwood was not the agent of the city for the transaction of just such business as he said on that occasion that he had transacted? Did any one say here on the witness-stand that he had not bought city loan as he said he had?

"Why is it then that Mr. Stener charges Mr. Cowperwood with larcenously securing and feloniously disposing of a check for sixty thousand dollars for certificates which he had a right to buy, and which it has not been contested here that he did buy? The reason lies just here–listen–just here. At the time my client asked for the check and took it away with him and deposited it in his own bank to his own account, he failed, so the prosecution insists, to put the sixty thousand dollars' worth of certificates for which he had received the check, in the sinking-fund; and having failed to do that, and being compelled by the pressure of financial events the same day to suspend payment generally, he thereby, according to the prosecution and the anxious leaders of the Republican party in the city, became an embezzler, a thief, a this or that–anything you please so long as you find a substitute for George W. Stener and the indifferent leaders of the Republican party in the eyes of the people."

And here Mr. Steger proceeded boldly and defiantly to outline the entire political situation as it had manifested itself in connection with the Chicago fire, the subsequent panic and its political consequences, and to picture Cowperwood as the unjustly ma-ligned agent, who before the fire was valuable and honorable enough to suit any of the political leaders of Philadelphia, but afterward, and when political defeat threatened, was picked upon as the most available scapegoat anywhere within reach.

And it took him a half hour to do that. And afterward but only after he had pointed to Stener as the true henchman and stalking horse, who had, in turn, been used by political forces above him to accomplish certain financial results, which they were not willing to have ascribed to themselves, he continued with:

"But now, in the light of all this, only see how ridiculous all this is! How silly! Frank A. Cowperwood had always been the agent of the city in these matters for years and years. He worked under certain rules which he and Mr. Stener had agreed upon in the first place, and which obviously came from others, who were above Mr. Stener, since they were hold-over customs and rules from administrations, which had been long before Mr. Stener ever appeared on the scene as city treasurer. One of them was that he could carry all transactions over until the first of the month following before he struck a balance. That is, he need not pay any money over for anything to the city treasurer, need not send him any checks or deposit any money or certificates in the sinking-fund until the first of the month because–now listen to this carefully, gentlemen; it is important–because his transactions in connection with city loan and everything else that he dealt in for the city treasurer were so numerous, so swift, so uncalculated beforehand, that he had to have a loose, easy system of this kind in order to do his work properly–to do business at all. Otherwise he could not very well have worked to the best advantage for Mr. Stener, or for any one else. It would have meant too much bookkeeping for him–too much for the city treasurer. Mr. Stener has testified to that in the early part of his story. Albert Stires has indicated that that was his understanding of it. Well, then what? Why, just this. Would any jury suppose, would any sane business man believe that if such were the case Mr. Cowperwood would be running personally with all these items of deposit, to the different banks or the sinking-fund or the city treasurer's office, or would be saying to his head bookkeeper, 'Here, Stapley, here is a check for sixty thousand dollars. See that the certificates of loan which this represents are put in the sinking-fund to-day'? And why not? What a ridiculous supposition any other supposition is! As a matter of course and as had always been the case, Mr. Cowperwood had a system. When the time came, this check and these certificates would be automatically taken care of. He handed his bookkeeper the check and forgot all about it. Would you imagine a banker with a vast business of this kind doing anything else?"

Mr. Steger paused for breath and inquiry, and then, having satisfied himself that his point had been sufficiently made, he continued:

"Of course the answer is that he knew he was going to fail. Well, Mr. Cowperwood's reply is that he didn't know anything of the sort. He has personally testified here that it was only at the last moment before it actually happened that he either thought or knew of such an occurrence. Why, then, this alleged refusal to let him have the check to which he was legally entitled? I think I know. I think I can give a reason if you will hear me out."

Steger shifted his position and came at the jury from another intellectual angle:

"It was simply because Mr. George W. Stener at that time, owing to a recent notable fire and a panic, imagined for some reason–perhaps because Mr. Cowperwood cautioned him not to become frightened over local developments generally–that Mr. Cowperwood was going to close his doors; and having considerable money on deposit with him at a low rate of interest, Mr. Stener decided that Mr. Cowperwood must not have any more money–not even the money that was actually due him for services rendered, and that had nothing whatsoever to do with the money loaned him by Mr. Stener at two and one-half per cent. Now isn't that a ridiculous situation? But it was because Mr. George W. Stener was filled with his own fears, based on a fire and a panic which had absolutely nothing to do with Mr. Cowperwood's solvency in the beginning that he decided not to let Frank A. Cowperwood have the money that was actually due him, because he, Stener, was criminally using the city's money to further his own private interests (through Mr. Cowperwood as a broker), and in danger of being exposed and possibly punished. Now where, I ask you, does the good sense of that decision come in? Is it apparent to you, gentlemen? Was Mr. Cowperwood still an agent for the city at the time he bought the loan certificates as here testified? He certainly was. If so, was he entitled to that money? Who is going to stand up here and deny it? Where is the question then, as to his right or his honesty in this matter? How does it come in here at all? I can tell you. It sprang solely from one source and from nowhere else, and that is the desire of the politicians of this city to find a scapegoat for the Republican party.

"Now you may think I am going rather far afield for an explanation of this very peculiar decision to prosecute Mr. Cowperwood, an agent of the city, for demanding and receiving what actually belonged to him. But I'm not. Consider the position of the Republican party at that time. Consider the fact that an exposure of the truth in regard to the details of a large defalcation in the city treasury would have a very unsatisfactory effect on the election about to be held. The Republican party had a new city treasurer to elect, a new district attorney. It had been in the habit of allowing its city treasurers the privilege of investing the funds in their possession at a low rate of interest for the benefit of themselves and their friends. Their salaries were small. They had to have some way of eking out a reasonable existence. Was Mr. George Stener responsible for this custom of loaning out the city money? Not at all. Was Mr. Cowperwood? Not at all. The custom had been in vogue long before either Mr. Cowperwood or Mr. Stener came on the scene. Why, then, this great hue and cry about it now? The entire uproar sprang solely from the fear of Mr. Stener at this juncture, the fear of the politicians at this juncture, of public exposure. No city treasurer had ever been exposed before. It was a new thing to face exposure, to face the risk of having the public's attention called to a rather nefarious practice of which Mr. Stener was taking advantage, that was all. A great fire and a panic were endangering the security and well-being of many a financial organization in the city–Mr. Cowperwood's among others. It meant many possible failures, and many possible failures meant one possible failure. If Frank A. Cowperwood failed, he would fail owing the city of Philadelphia five hundred thousand dollars, borrowed from the city treasurer at the very low rate of interest of two and one-half per cent. Anything very detrimental to Mr. Cowperwood in that? Had he gone to the city treasurer and asked to be loaned money at two and one-half per cent.? If he had, was there anything criminal in it from a business point of view? Isn't a man entitled to borrow money from any source he can at the lowest possible rate of interest? Did Mr. Stener have to loan it to Mr. Cowperwood if he did not want to? As a matter of fact didn't he testify here to-day that he personally had sent for Mr. Cowperwood in the first place? Why, then, in Heaven's name, this excited charge of larceny, larceny as bailee, embezzlement, embezzlement on a check, etc., etc.?

"Once more, gentlemen, listen. I'll tell you why. The men who stood behind Stener, and whose bidding he was doing, wanted to make a political scapegoat of some one–of Frank Algernon Cowperwood, if they couldn't get any one else. That's why. No other reason under God's blue sky, not one. Why, if Mr. Cowperwood needed more money just at that time to tide him over, it would have been good policy for them to have given it to him and hushed this matter up. It would have been illegal–though not any more illegal than anything else that has ever been done in this connection–but it would have been safer. Fear, gentlemen, fear, lack of courage, inability to meet a great crisis when a great crisis appears, was all that really prevented them from doing this. They were afraid to place confidence in a man who had never heretofore betrayed their trust and from whose loyalty and great financial ability they and the city had been reaping large profits. The reigning city treasurer of the time didn't have the courage to go on in the face of fire and panic and the rumors of possible failure, and stick by his illegal guns; and so he decided to draw in his horns as testified here to-day–to ask Mr. Cowperwood to return all or at least a big part of the five hundred thousand dollars he had loaned him, and which Cowperwood had been actually using for his, Stener's benefit, and to refuse him in addition the money that was actually due him for an authorized purchase of city loan. Was Cowperwood guilty as an agent in any of these transactions? Not in the least. Was there any suit pending to make him return the five hundred thousand dollars of city money involved in his present failure? Not at all. It was simply a case of wild, silly panic on the part of George W. Stener, and a strong desire on the part of the Republican party leaders, once they discovered what the situation was, to find some one outside of Stener, the party treasurer, upon whom they could blame the shortage in the treasury. You heard what Mr. Cowperwood testified to here in this case to-day–that he went to Mr. Stener to forfend against any possible action of this kind in the first place. And it was because of this very warning that Mr. Stener became wildly excited, lost his head, and wanted Mr. Cowperwood to return him all his money, all the five hundred thousand dollars he had loaned him at two and one-half per cent. Isn't that silly financial business at the best? Wasn't that a fine time to try to call a perfectly legal loan?

"But now to return to this particular check of sixty thousand dollars. When Mr. Cowperwood called that last afternoon before he failed, Mr. Stener testified that he told him that he couldn't have any more money, that it was impossible, and that then Mr. Cowperwood went out into his general office and without his knowledge or consent persuaded his chief clerk and secretary, Mr. Albert Stires, to give him a check for sixty thousand dollars, to which he was not entitled and on which he, Stener, would have stopped payment if he had known.

"What nonsense! Why didn't he know? The books were there, open to him. Mr. Stires told him the first thing the next morning. Mr. Cowperwood thought nothing of it, for he was entitled to it, and could collect it in any court of law having jurisdiction in such cases, failure or no failure. It is silly for Mr. Stener to say he would have stopped payment. Such a claim was probably an after-thought of the next morning after he had talked with his friends, the politicians, and was all a part, a trick, a trap, to provide the Republican party with a scapegoat at this time. Nothing more and nothing less; and you may be sure no one knew it better than the people who were most anxious to see Mr. Cowperwood convicted."

Steger paused and looked significantly at Shannon.

"Gentlemen of the jury [he finally concluded, quietly and earnestly], you are going to find, when you think it over in the jury-room this evening, that this charge of larceny and larceny as bailee, and embezzlement of a check for sixty thousand dollars, which are contained in this indictment, and which represent nothing more than the eager effort of the district attorney to word this one act in such a way that it will look like a crime, represents nothing more than the excited imagination of a lot of political refugees who are anxious to protect their own skirts at the expense of Mr. Cowperwood, and who care for nothing–honor, fair play, or anything else, so long as they are let off scot-free. They don't want the Republicans of Pennsylvania to think too ill of the Republican party management and control in this city. They want to protect George W. Stener as much as possible and to make a political scapegoat of my client. It can't be done, and it won't be done. As honorable, intelligent men you won't permit it to be done. And I think with that thought I can safely leave you."

Steger suddenly turned from the jury-box and walked to his seat beside Cowperwood, while Shannon arose, calm, forceful, vigorous, much younger.

As between man and man, Shannon was not particularly opposed to the case Steger had made out for Cowperwood, nor was he opposed to Cowperwood's having made money as he did. As a matter of fact, Shannon actually thought that if he had been in Cowperwood's position he would have done exactly the same thing. However, he was the newly elected district attorney. He had a record to make; and, besides, the political powers who were above him were satisfied that Cowperwood ought to be convicted for the looks of the thing. Therefore he laid his hands firmly on the rail at first, looked the jurors steadily in the eyes for a time, and, having framed a few thoughts in his mind began:

"Now, gentlemen of the jury, it seems to me that if we all pay strict attention to what has transpired here to-day, we will have no difficulty in reaching a conclusion; and it will be a very satisfactory one, if we all try to interpret the facts correctly. This defendant, Mr. Cowperwood, comes into this court to-day charged, as I have stated to you before, with larceny, with larceny as bailee, with embezzlement, and with embezzlement of a specific check–namely, one dated October 9, 1871, drawn to the order of Frank A. Cowperwood Company for the sum of sixty thousand dollars by the secretary of the city treasurer for the city treasurer, and by him signed, as he had a perfect right to sign it, and delivered to the said Frank A. Cowperwood, who claims that he was not only properly solvent at the time, but had previously purchased certificates of city loan to the value of sixty thousand dollars, and had at that time or would shortly thereafter, as was his custom, deposit them to the credit of the city in the city sinking-fund, and thus close what would ordinarily be an ordinary transaction–namely, that of Frank A. Cowperwood Company as bankers and brokers for the city buying city loan for the city, depositing it in the sinking-fund, and being promptly and properly reimbursed. Now, gentlemen, what are the actual facts in this case? Was the said Frank A. Cowperwood Company–there is no company, as you well know, as you have heard testified here to-day, only Frank A. Cowperwood–was the said Frank A. Cowperwood a fit person to receive the check at this time in the manner he received it–that is, was he authorized agent of the city at the time, or was he not? Was he solvent? Did he actually himself think he was going to fail, and was this sixty-thousand-dollar check a last thin straw which he was grabbing at to save his financial life regardless of what it involved legally, morally, or otherwise; or had he actually purchased certificates of city loan to the amount he said he had in the way he said he had, at the time he said he had, and was he merely collecting his honest due? Did he intend to deposit these certificates of loans in the city sinking-fund, as he said he would–as it was understood naturally and normally that he would–or did he not? Were his relations with the city treasurer as broker and agent the same as they had always been on the day that he secured this particular check for sixty thousand dollars, or were they not? Had they been terminated by a conversation fifteen minutes before or two days before or two weeks before–it makes no difference when, so long as they had been properly terminated–or had they not? A business man has a right to abrogate an agreement at any time where there is no specific form of contract and no fixed period of operation entered into–as you all must know. You must not forget that in considering the evidence in this case. Did George W. Stener, knowing or suspecting that Frank A. Cowperwood was in a tight place financially, unable to fulfill any longer properly and honestly the duties supposedly devolving on him by this agreement, terminate it then and there on October 9, 1871, before this check for sixty thousand dollars was given, or did he not? Did Mr. Frank A. Cowperwood then and there, knowing that he was no longer an agent of the city treasurer and the city, and knowing also that he was insolvent (having, as Mr. Stener contends, admitted to him that he was so), and having no intention of placing the certificates which he subsequently declared he had purchased in the sinking-fund, go out into Mr. Stener's general office, meet his secretary, tell him he had purchased sixty thousand dollars' worth of city loan, ask for the check, get it, put it in his pocket, walk off, and never make any return of any kind in any manner, shape, or form to the city, and then, subsequently, twenty-four hours later, fail, owing this and five hundred thousand dollars more to the city treasury, or did he not? What are the facts in this case? What have the witnesses testified to? What has George W. Stener testified to, Albert Stires, President Davison, Mr. Cowperwood himself? What are the interesting, subtle facts in this case, anyhow? Gentlemen, you have a very curious problem to decide."

He paused and gazed at the jury, adjusting his sleeves as he did so, and looking as though he knew for certain that he was on the trail of a slippery, elusive criminal who was in a fair way to foist himself upon an honorable and decent community and an honorable and innocent jury as an honest man.

Then he continued:

"Now, gentlemen, what are the facts? You can see for yourselves exactly how this whole situation has come about. You are sensible men. I don't need to tell you. Here are two men, one elected treasurer of the city of Philadelphia, sworn to guard the interests of the city and to manipulate its finances to the best advantage, and the other called in at a time of uncertain financial cogitation to assist in unraveling a possibly difficult financial problem; and then you have a case of a quiet, private financial understanding being reached, and of subsequent illegal dealings in which one man who is shrewder, wiser, more versed in the subtle ways of Third Street leads the other along over seemingly charming paths of fortunate investment into an accidental but none the less criminal mire of failure and exposure and public calumny and what not. And then they get to the place where the more vulnerable individual of the two–the man in the most dangerous position, the city treasurer of Philadelphia, no less–can no longer reasonably or, let us say, courageously, follow the other fellow; and then you have such a spectacle as was described here this afternoon in the witness-chair by Mr. Stener–that is, you have a vicious, greedy, unmerciful financial wolf standing over a cowering, unsophisticated commercial lamb, and saying to him, his white, shiny teeth glittering all the while, 'If you don't advance me the money I ask for–the three hundred thousand dollars I now demand–you will be a convict, your children will be thrown in the street, you and your wife and your family will be in poverty again, and there will be no one to turn a hand for you.' That is what Mr. Stener says Mr. Cowperwood said to him. I, for my part, haven't a doubt in the world that he did. Mr. Steger, in his very guarded references to his client, describes him as a nice, kind, gentlemanly agent, a broker merely on whom was practically forced the use of five hundred thousand dollars at two and a half per cent. when money was bringing from ten to fifteen per cent. in Third Street on call loans, and even more. But I for one don't choose to believe it. The thing that strikes me as strange in all of this is that if he was so nice and kind and gentle and remote–a mere hired and therefore subservient agent–how is it that he could have gone to Mr. Stener's office two or three days before the matter of this sixty-thousand-dollar check came up and say to him, as Mr. Stener testifies under oath that he did say to him, 'If you don't give me three hundred thousand dollars' worth more of the city's money at once, to-day, I will fail, and you will be a convict. You will go to the penitentiary.'? That's what he said to him. 'I will fail and you will be a convict. They can't touch me, but they will arrest you. I am an agent merely.' Does that sound like a nice, mild, innocent, well-mannered agent, a hired broker, or doesn't it sound like a hard, defiant, contemptuous master–a man in control and ready to rule and win by fair means or foul?

"Gentlemen, I hold no brief for George W. Stener. In my judgment he is as guilty as his smug co-partner in crime–if not more so–this oily financier who came smiling and in sheep's clothing, pointing out subtle ways by which the city's money could be made profitable for both; but when I hear Mr. Cowperwood described as I have just heard him described, as a nice, mild, innocent agent, my gorge rises. Why, gentlemen, if you want to get a right point of view on this whole proposition you will have to go back about ten or twelve years and see Mr. George W. Stener as he was then, a rather poverty-stricken beginner in politics, and before this very subtle and capable broker and agent came along and pointed out ways and means by which the city's money could be made profitable; George W. Stener wasn't very much of a personage then, and neither was Frank A. Cowperwood when he found Stener newly elected to the office of city treasurer. Can't you see him arriving at that time nice and fresh and young and well dressed, as shrewd as a fox, and saying: 'Come to me. Let me handle city loan. Loan me the city's money at two per cent. or less.' Can't you hear him suggesting this? Can't you see him?

"George W. Stener was a poor man, comparatively a very poor man, when he first became city treasurer. All he had was a small real-estate and insurance business which brought him in, say, twenty-five hundred dollars a year. He had a wife and four children to support, and he had never had the slightest taste of what for him might be called luxury or comfort. Then comes Mr. Cowperwood–at his request, to be sure, but on an errand which held no theory of evil gains in Mr. Stener's mind at the time–and proposes his grand scheme of manipulating all the city loan to their mutual advantage. Do you yourselves think, gentlemen, from what you have seen of George W. Stener here on the witness-stand, that it was he who proposed this plan of ill-gotten wealth to that gentleman over there?"

He pointed to Cowperwood.

"Does he look to you like a man who would be able to tell that gentleman anything about finance or this wonderful manipulation that followed? I ask you, does he look clever enough to suggest all the subtleties by which these two subsequently made so much money? Why, the statement of this man Cowperwood made to his creditors at the time of his failure here a few weeks ago showed that he considered himself to be worth over one million two hundred and fifty thousand dollars, and he is only a little over thirty-four years old to-day. How much was he worth at the time he first entered business relations with the ex-city treasurer? Have you any idea? I can tell. I had the matter looked up almost a month ago on my accession to office. Just a little over two hundred thousand dollars, gentlemen–just a little over two hundred thousand dollars. Here is an abstract from the files of Dun Company for that year. Now you can see how rapidly our Caesar has grown in wealth since then. You can see how profitable these few short years have been to him. Was George W. Stener worth any such sum up to the time he was removed from his office and indicted for embezzlement? Was he? I have here a schedule of his liabilities and assets made out at the time. You can see it for yourselves, gentlemen. Just two hundred and twenty thousand dollars measured the sum of all his property three weeks ago; and it is an accurate estimate, as I have reason to know. Why was it, do you suppose, that Mr. Cowperwood grew so fast in wealth and Mr. Stener so slowly? They were partners in crime. Mr. Stener was loaning Mr. Cowperwood vast sums of the city's money at two per cent. when call-rates for money in Third Street were sometimes as high as sixteen and seventeen per cent. Don't you suppose that Mr. Cowperwood sitting there knew how to use this very cheaply come-by money to the very best advantage? Does he look to you as though he didn't? You have seen him on the witness-stand. You have heard him testify. Very suave, very straightforward-seeming, very innocent, doing everything as a favor to Mr. Stener and his friends, of course, and yet making a million in a little over six years and allowing Mr. Stener to make one hundred and sixty thousand dollars or less, for Mr. Stener had some little money at the time this partnership was entered into–a few thousand dollars."

Shannon now came to the vital transaction of October 9th, when Cowperwood called on Stener and secured the check for sixty thousand dollars from Albert Stires. His scorn for this (as he appeared to think) subtle and criminal transaction was unbounded. It was plain larceny, stealing, and Cowperwood knew it when he asked Stires for the check.

"Think of it! [Shannon exclaimed, turning and looking squarely at Cowperwood, who faced him quite calmly, undisturbed and unashamed.] Think of it! Think of the colossal nerve of the man–the Machiavellian subtlety of his brain. He knew he was going to fail. He knew after two days of financial work–after two days of struggle to offset the providential disaster which upset his nefarious schemes–that he had exhausted every possible resource save one, the city treasury, and that unless he could compel aid there he was going to fail. He already owed the city treasury five hundred thousand dollars. He had already used the city treasurer as a cat's-paw so much, had involved him so deeply, that the latter, because of the staggering size of the debt, was becoming frightened. Did that deter Mr. Cowperwood? Not at all."

He shook his finger ominously in Cowperwood's face, and the latter turned irritably away. "He is showing off for the benefit of his future," he whispered to Steger. "I wish you could tell the jury that."

"I wish I could," replied Steger, smiling scornfully, "but my hour is over."

"Why [continued Mr. Shannon, turning once more to the jury], think of the colossal, wolfish nerve that would permit a man to say to Albert Stires that he had just purchased sixty thousand dollars' worth additional of city loan, and that he would then and there take the check for it! Had he actually purchased this city loan as he said he had? Who can tell? Could any human being wind through all the mazes of the complicated bookkeeping system which he ran, and actually tell? The best answer to that is that if he did purchase the certificates he intended that it should make no difference to the city, for he made no effort to put the certificates in the sinking-fund, where they belonged. His counsel says, and he says, that he didn't have to until the first of the month, although the law says that he must do it at once, and he knew well enough that legally he was bound to do it. His counsel says, and he says, that he didn't know he was going to fail. Hence there was no need of worrying about it. I wonder if any of you gentlemen really believed that? Had he ever asked for a check like that so quick before in his life? In all the history of these nefarious transactions was there another incident like that? You know there wasn't. He had never before, on any occasion, asked personally for a check for anything in this office, and yet on this occasion he did it. Why? Why should he ask for it this time? A few hours more, according to his own statement, wouldn't have made any difference one way or the other, would it? He could have sent a boy for it, as usual. That was the way it had always been done before. Why anything different now? I'll tell you why! [Shannon suddenly shouted, varying his voice tremendously.] I'll tell you why! He knew that he was a ruined man! He knew that his last semi-legitimate avenue of escape–the favor of George W. Stener–had been closed to him! He knew that honestly, by open agreement, he could not extract another single dollar from the treasury of the city of Philadelphia. He knew that if he left the office without this check and sent a boy for it, the aroused city treasurer would have time to inform his clerks, and that then no further money could be obtained. That's why! That's why, gentlemen, if you really want to know.

"Now, gentlemen of the jury, I am about done with my arraignment of this fine, honorable, virtuous citizen whom the counsel for the defense, Mr. Steger, tells you you cannot possibly convict without doing a great injustice. All I have to say is that you look to me like sane, intelligent men–just the sort of men that I meet everywhere in the ordinary walks of life, doing an honorable American business in an honorable American way. Now, gentlemen of the jury [he was very soft-spoken now], all I have to say is that if, after all you have heard and seen here to-day, you still think that Mr. Frank A. Cowperwood is an honest, honorable man–that he didn't steal, willfully and knowingly, sixty thousand dollars from the Philadelphia city treasury; that he had actually bought the certificates he said he had, and had intended to put them in the sinking-fund, as he said he did, then don't you dare to do anything except turn him loose, and that speedily, so that he can go on back to-day into Third Street, and start to straighten out his much-entangled financial affairs. It is the only thing for honest, conscientious men to do–to turn him instantly loose into the heart of this community, so that some of the rank injustice that my opponent, Mr. Steger, alleges has been done him will be a little made up to him. You owe him, if that is the way you feel, a prompt acknowledgment of his innocence. Don't worry about George W. Stener. His guilt is established by his own confession. He admits he is guilty. He will be sentenced without trial later on. But this man–he says he is an honest, honorable man. He says he didn't think he was going to fail. He says he used all that threatening, compelling, terrifying language, not because he was in danger of failing, but because he didn't want the bother of looking further for aid. What do you think? Do you really think that he had purchased sixty thousand dollars more of certificates for the sinking-fund, and that he was entitled to the money? If so, why didn't he put them in the sinking-fund? They're not there now, and the sixty thousand dollars is gone. Who got it? The Girard National Bank, where he was overdrawn to the extent of one hundred thousand dollars! Did it get it and forty thousand dollars more in other checks and certificates? Certainly. Why? Do you suppose the Girard National Bank might be in any way grateful for this last little favor before he closed his doors? Do you think that President Davison, whom you saw here testifying so kindly in this case feels at all friendly, and that that may possibly–I don't say that it does–explain his very kindly interpretation of Mr. Cowperwood's condition? It might be. You can think as well along that line as I can. Anyhow, gentlemen, President Davison says Mr. Cowperwood is an honorable, honest man, and so does his counsel, Mr. Steger. You have heard the testimony. Now you think it over. If you want to turn him loose–turn him loose. [He waved his hand wearily.] You're the judges. I wouldn't; but then I am merely a hard-working lawyer–one person, one opinion. You may think differently–that's your business. [He waved his hand suggestively, almost contemptuously.] However, I'm through, and I thank you for your courtesy. Gentlemen, the decision rests with you."

He turned away grandly, and the jury stirred–so did the idle spectators in the court. Judge Payderson sighed a sigh of relief. It was now quite dark, and the flaring gas forms in the court were all brightly lighted. Outside one could see that it was snowing. The judge stirred among his papers wearily, and turning to the jurors solemnly, began his customary explanation of the law, after which they filed out to the jury-room.

Cowperwood turned to his father who now came over across the fast-emptying court, and said:

"Well, we'll know now in a little while."

"Yes," replied Cowperwood, Sr., a little wearily. "I hope it comes out right. I saw Butler back there a little while ago."

"Did you?" queried Cowperwood, to whom this had a peculiar interest.

"Yes," replied his father. "He's just gone."

So, Cowperwood thought, Butler was curious enough as to his fate to want to come here and watch him tried. Shannon was his tool. Judge Payderson was his emissary, in a way. He, Cowperwood, might defeat him in the matter of his daughter, but it was not so easy to defeat him here unless the jury should happen to take a sympathetic attitude. They might convict him, and then Butler's Judge Payderson would have the privilege of sentencing him–giving him the maximum sentence. That would not be so nice–five years! He cooled a little as he thought of it, but there was no use worrying about what had not yet happened. Steger came forward and told him that his bail was now ended–had been the moment the jury left the room–and that he was at this moment actually in the care of the sheriff, of whom he knew–Sheriff Adlai Jaspers. Unless he were acquitted by the jury, Steger added, he would have to remain in the sheriff's care until an application for a certificate of reasonable doubt could be made and acted upon.

"It would take all of five days, Frank," Steger said, "but Jaspers isn't a bad sort. He'd be reasonable. Of course if we're lucky you won't have to visit him. You will have to go with this bailiff now, though. Then if things come out right we'll go home. Say, I'd like to win this case," he said. "I'd like to give them the laugh and see you do it. I consider you've been pretty badly treated, and I think I made that perfectly clear. I can reverse this verdict on a dozen grounds if they happen to decide against you."

He and Cowperwood and the latter's father now stalked off with the sheriff's subordinate—a small man by the name of "Eddie" Zanders, who had approached to take charge. They entered a small room called the pen at the back of the court, where all those on trial whose liberty had been forfeited by the jury's leaving the room had to wait pending its return. It was a dreary, high-ceiled, four-square place, with a window looking out into Chestnut Street, and a second door leading off into somewhere—one had no idea where. It was dingy, with a worn wooden floor, some heavy, plain, wooden benches lining the four sides, no pictures or ornaments of any kind. A single two-arm gas-pipe descended from the center of the ceiling. It was permeated by a peculiarly stale and pungent odor, obviously redolent of all the flotsam and jetsam of life—criminal and innocent—that had stood or sat in here from time to time, waiting patiently to learn what a deliberating fate held in store.

Cowperwood was, of course, disgusted; but he was too self-reliant and capable to show it. All his life he had been immaculate, almost fastidious in his care of himself. Here he was coming, perforce, in contact with a form of life which jarred upon him greatly. Steger, who was beside him, made some comforting, explanatory, apologetic remarks.

"Not as nice as it might be," he said, "but you won't mind waiting a little while. The jury won't be long, I fancy."

"That may not help me," he replied, walking to the window. Afterward he added: "What must be, must be."

His father winced. Suppose Frank was on the verge of a long prison term, which meant an atmosphere like this? Heavens! For a moment, he trembled, then for the first time in years he made a silent prayer.

Chapter XLIV

Meanwhile the great argument had been begun in the jury-room, and all the points that had been meditatively speculated upon in the jury-box were now being openly discussed.

It is amazingly interesting to see how a jury will waver and speculate in a case like this—how curious and uncertain is the process by which it makes up its so-called mind. So-called truth is a nebulous thing at best; facts are capable of such curious inversion and interpretation, honest and otherwise. The jury had a strongly complicated problem before it, and it went over it and over it.

Juries reach not so much definite conclusions as verdicts, in a curious fashion and for curious reasons. Very often a jury will have concluded little so far as its individual members are concerned and yet it will have reached a verdict. The matter of time, as all lawyers know, plays a part in this. Juries, speaking of the members collectively and frequently individually, object to the amount of time it takes to decide a case. They do not enjoy sitting and deliberating over a problem unless it is tremendously fascinating. The ramifications or the mystery of a syllogism can become a weariness and a bore. The jury-room itself may and frequently does become a dull agony.

On the other hand, no jury contemplates a disagreement with any degree of satisfaction. There is something so inherently constructive in the human mind that to leave a problem unsolved is plain misery. It haunts the average individual like any other important task left unfinished. Men in a jury-room, like those scientifically demonstrated atoms of a crystal which scientists and philosophers love to speculate upon, like finally to arrange themselves into an orderly and artistic whole, to present a compact, intellectual front, to be whatever they have set out to be, properly and rightly—a compact, sensible jury. One sees this same instinct magnificently displayed in every other phase of nature—in the drifting of sea-wood to the Sargasso Sea, in the geometric interrelation of air-bubbles on the surface of still water, in the marvelous unreasoned architecture of so many insects and atomic forms which make up the substance and the texture of this world. It would seem as though the physical substance of life—this apparition of form which the eye detects and calls real were shot through with some vast subtlety that loves order, that is order. The atoms of our so-called being, in spite of our so-called reason—the dreams of a mood—know where to go and what to do. They represent an order, a wisdom, a willing that is not of us. They build orderly in spite of us. So the subconscious spirit of a jury. At the same time, one does not forget the strange hypnotic effect of one personality on another, the varying effects of varying types on each other, until a solution—to use the word in its purely chemical sense—is reached. In a jury-room the thought or determination of one or two or three men, if it be definite enough, is likely to pervade the whole room and conquer the reason or the opposition of the majority. One man "standing out" for the definite thought that is in him is apt to become either the triumphant leader of a pliant mass or the brutally battered target of a flaming, concentrated intellectual fire. Men despise dull opposition that is without reason. In a jury-room, of all places, a man is expected to give a reason for the faith that is in him—if one is demanded. It will not do to say, "I cannot agree." Jurors have been known to fight. Bitter antagonisms lasting for years have been generated in these close quarters. Recalcitrant jurors have been hounded commercially in their local spheres for their unreasoned oppositions or conclusions.

After reaching the conclusion that Cowperwood unquestionably deserved some punishment, there was wrangling as to whether the verdict should be guilty on all four counts, as charged in the indictment. Since they did not understand how to differentiate between the various charges very well, they decided it should be on all four, and a recommendation to mercy added. Afterward this last was eliminated, however; either he was guilty or he was not. The judge could see as well as they could all the extenuating circumstances—perhaps better. Why tie his hands? As a rule no attention was paid to such recommendations, anyhow, and it only made the jury look wabbly.

So, finally, at ten minutes after twelve that night, they were ready to return a verdict; and Judge Payderson, who, because of his interest in the case and the fact that he lived not so far away, had decided to wait up this long, was recalled. Steger and Cowperwood were sent for. The court-room was fully lighted. The bailiff, the clerk, and the stenographer were there. The jury filed in, and Cowperwood, with Steger at his right, took his position at the gate which gave into the railed space where prisoners always stand to hear the verdict and listen to any commentary of the judge. He was accompanied by his father, who was very nervous.

For the first time in his life he felt as though he were walking in his sleep. Was this the real Frank Cowperwood of two months before–so wealthy, so progressive, so sure? Was this only December 5th or 6th now (it was after midnight)? Why was it the jury had deliberated so long? What did it mean? Here they were now, standing and gazing solemnly before them; and here now was Judge Payderson, mounting the steps of his rostrum, his frizzled hair standing out in a strange, attractive way, his familiar bailiff rapping for order. He did not look at Cowperwood–it would not be courteous–but at the jury, who gazed at him in return. At the words of the clerk, "Gentlemen of the jury, have you agreed upon a verdict?" the foreman spoke up, "We have."

"Do you find the defendant guilty or not guilty?"

"We find the defendant guilty as charged in the indictment."

How had they come to do this? Because he had taken a check for sixty thousand dollars which did not belong to him? But in reality it did. Good Lord, what was sixty thousand dollars in the sum total of all the money that had passed back and forth between him and George W. Stener? Nothing, nothing! A mere bagatelle in its way; and yet here it had risen up, this miserable, insignificant check, and become a mountain of opposition, a stone wall, a prison-wall barring his further progress. It was astonishing. He looked around him at the court-room. How large and bare and cold it was! Still he was Frank A. Cowperwood. Why should he let such queer thoughts disturb him? His fight for freedom and privilege and restitution was not over yet. Good heavens! It had only begun. In five days he would be out again on bail. Steger would take an appeal. He would be out, and he would have two long months in which to make an additional fight. He was not down yet. He would win his liberty. This jury was all wrong. A higher court would say so. It would reverse their verdict, and he knew it. He turned to Steger, where the latter was having the clerk poll the jury, in the hope that some one juror had been over-persuaded, made to vote against his will.

"Is that your verdict?" he heard the clerk ask of Philip Moultrie, juror No. 1.

"It is," replied that worthy, solemnly.

"Is that your verdict?" The clerk was pointing to Simon Glassberg.

"Yes, sir."

"Is that your verdict?" He pointed to Fletcher Norton.

"Yes."

So it went through the whole jury. All the men answered firmly and clearly, though Steger thought it might barely be possible that one would have changed his mind. The judge thanked them and told them that in view of their long services this night, they were dismissed for the term. The only thing remaining to be done now was for Steger to persuade Judge Payderson to grant a stay of sentence pending the hearing of a motion by the State Supreme Court for a new trial.

The Judge looked at Cowperwood very curiously as Steger made this request in proper form, and owing to the importance of the case and the feeling he had that the Supreme Court might very readily grant a certificate of reasonable doubt in this case, he agreed. There was nothing left, therefore, but for Cowperwood to return at this late hour with the deputy sheriff to the county jail, where he must now remain for five days at least–possibly longer.

The jail in question, which was known locally as Moyamensing Prison, was located at Tenth and Reed Streets, and from an architectural and artistic point of view was not actually displeasing to the eye. It consisted of a central portion–prison, residence for the sheriff or what you will–three stories high, with a battlemented cornice and a round battlemented tower about one-third as high as the central portion itself, and two wings, each two stories high, with battlemented turrets at either end, giving it a highly castellated and consequently, from the American point of view, a very prison-like appearance. The facade of the prison, which was not more than thirty-five feet high for the central portion, nor more than twenty-five feet for the wings, was set back at least a hundred feet from the street, and was continued at either end, from the wings to the end of the street block, by a stone wall all of twenty feet high. The structure was not severely prison-like, for the central portion was pierced by rather large, unbarred apertures hung on the two upper stories with curtains, and giving the whole front a rather pleasant and residential air. The wing to the right, as one stood looking in from the street, was the section known as the county jail proper, and was devoted to the care of prisoners serving short-term sentences on some judicial order. The wing to the left was devoted exclusively to the care and control of untried prisoners. The whole building was built of a smooth, light-colored stone, which on a snowy night like this, with the few lamps that were used in it glowing feebly in the dark, presented an eery, fantastic, almost supernatural appearance.

It was a rough and blowy night when Cowperwood started for this institution under duress. The wind was driving the snow before it in curious, interesting whirls. Eddie Zanders, the sheriff's deputy on guard at the court of Quarter Sessions, accompanied him and his father and Steger. Zanders was a little man, dark, with a short, stubby mustache, and a shrewd though not highly intelligent eye. He was anxious first to uphold his dignity as a deputy sheriff, which was a very important position in his estimation, and next to turn an honest penny if he could. He knew little save the details of his small world, which consisted of accompanying prisoners to and from the courts and the jails, and seeing that they did not get away. He was not unfriendly to a particular type of prisoner–the well-to-do or moderately prosperous–for he had long since learned that it paid to be so. To-night he offered a few sociable suggestions–viz., that it was rather rough, that the jail was not so far but that they could walk, and that Sheriff Jaspers would, in all likelihood, be around or could be aroused. Cowperwood scarcely heard. He was thinking of his mother and his wife and of Aileen.

When the jail was reached he was led to the central portion, as it was here that the sheriff, Adlai Jaspers, had his private office. Jaspers had recently been elected to office, and was inclined to conform to all outward appearances, in so far as the proper conduct of his office was concerned, without in reality inwardly conforming. Thus it was generally known among the politicians that one way he had of fattening his rather lean salary was to rent private rooms and grant special privileges to prisoners who had the money to pay for the same. Other sheriffs had done it before him. In fact, when Jaspers was inducted into office, several prisoners were already enjoying these privileges, and it was not a part of his scheme of things to disturb them. The rooms that he let to the "right parties," as he invariably put it, were in the central portion of the jail, where were his own private living quarters. They were unbarred, and not at all cell-like. There was no particular danger of escape, for a guard stood always at his private door instructed "to keep an eye" on the general movements of all the inmates. A prisoner so accommodated was in many respects quite a free person. His meals were served to him in his room, if he wished. He could read or play cards, or receive guests; and if he had any favorite musical instrument, that was not denied him. There was just one rule that had to be complied with. If he were a public character, and any newspaper men called, he had to be brought down-stairs into the private interviewing room in order that they might not know that he was not confined in a cell like any other prisoner.

Nearly all of these facts had been brought to Cowperwood's attention beforehand by Steger; but for all that, when he crossed the threshold of the jail a peculiar sensation of strangeness and defeat came over him. He and his party were conducted to a little office to the left of the entrance, where were only a desk and a chair, dimly lighted by a low-burning gas-jet. Sheriff Jaspers, rotund and ruddy, met them, greeting them in quite a friendly way. Zanders was dismissed, and went briskly about his affairs.

"A bad night, isn't it?" observed Jaspers, turning up the gas and preparing to go through the routine of registering his prisoner. Steger came over and held a short, private conversation with him in his corner, over his desk which resulted presently in the sheriff's face lighting up.

"Oh, certainly, certainly! That's all right, Mr. Steger, to be sure! Why, certainly!"

Cowperwood, eyeing the fat sheriff from his position, understood what it was all about. He had regained completely his critical attitude, his cool, intellectual poise. So this was the jail, and this was the fat mediocrity of a sheriff who was to take care of him. Very good. He would make the best of it. He wondered whether he was to be searched–prisoners usually were–but he soon discovered that he was not to be.

"That's all right, Mr. Cowperwood," said Jaspers, getting up. "I guess I can make you comfortable, after a fashion. We're not running a hotel here, as you know"–he chuckled to himself–"but I guess I can make you comfortable. John," he called to a sleepy factotum, who appeared from another room, rubbing his eyes, "is the key to Number Six down here?"

"Yes, sir."

"Let me have it."

John disappeared and returned, while Steger explained to Cowperwood that anything he wanted in the way of clothing, etc., could be brought in. Steger himself would stop round next morning and confer with him, as would any of the members of Cowperwood's family whom he wished to see. Cowperwood immediately explained to his father his desire for as little of this as possible. Joseph or Edward might come in the morning and bring a grip full of underwear, etc.; but as for the others, let them wait until he got out or had to remain permanently. He did think of writing Aileen, cautioning her to do nothing; but the sheriff now beckoned, and he quietly followed. Accompanied by his father and Steger, he ascended to his new room.

It was a simple, white-walled chamber fifteen by twenty feet in size, rather high-ceiled, supplied with a high-backed, yellow wooden bed, a yellow bureau, a small imitation-cherry table, three very ordinary cane-seated chairs with carved hickory-rod backs, cherry-stained also, and a wash-stand of yellow-stained wood to match the bed, containing a washbasin, a pitcher, a soap-dish, uncovered, and a small, cheap, pink-flowered tooth and shaving brush mug, which did not match the other ware and which probably cost ten cents. The value of this room to Sheriff Jaspers was what he could get for it in cases like this–twenty-five to thirty-five dollars a week. Cowperwood would pay thirty-five.

Cowperwood walked briskly to the window, which gave out on the lawn in front, now embedded in snow, and said he thought this was all right. Both his father and Steger were willing and anxious to confer with him for hours, if he wished; but there was nothing to say. He did not wish to talk.

"Let Ed bring in some fresh linen in the morning and a couple of suits of clothes, and I will be all right. George can get my things together." He was referring to a family servant who acted as valet and in other capacities. "Tell Lillian not to worry. I'm all right. I'd rather she would not come here so long as I'm going to be out in five days. If I'm not, it will be time enough then. Kiss the kids for me." And he smiled good-naturedly.

After his unfulfilled predictions in regard to the result of this preliminary trial Steger was almost afraid to suggest confidently what the State Supreme Court would or would not do; but he had to say something.

"I don't think you need worry about what the outcome of my appeal will be, Frank. I'll get a certificate of reasonable doubt, and that's as good as a stay of two months, perhaps longer. I don't suppose the bail will be more than thirty thousand dollars at the outside. You'll be out again in five or six days, whatever happens."

Cowperwood said that he hoped so, and suggested that they drop matters for the night. After a few fruitless parleys his father and Steger finally said good night, leaving him to his own private reflections. He was tired, however, and throwing off his clothes, tucked himself in his mediocre bed, and was soon fast asleep.

Chapter XLV

Say what one will about prison life in general, modify it ever so much by special chambers, obsequious turnkeys, a general tendency to make one as comfortable as possible, a jail is a jail, and there is no getting away from that. Cowperwood, in a room which was not in any way inferior to that of the ordinary boarding-house, was nevertheless conscious of the character of that section of this real prison which was not yet his portion. He knew that there were cells there, probably greasy and smelly and vermin-infested, and that they were enclosed by heavy iron bars, which would have as readily clanked on him as on those who were now therein incarcerated if he had not had the price to pay for something better. So much for the alleged equality of man, he thought, which gave to one man, even within the grim confines of the machinery of justice, such personal liberty as he himself was now enjoying, and to another, because he chanced to lack wit or presence or friends or wealth, denied the more comfortable things which money would buy.

The morning after the trial, on waking, he stirred curiously, and then it suddenly came to him that he was no longer in the free and comfortable atmosphere of his own bedroom, but in a jail-cell, or rather its very comfortable substitute, a sheriff's rented bedroom. He got up and looked out the window. The ground outside and Passayunk Avenue were white with snow. Some wagons were silently lumbering by. A few Philadelphians were visible here and there, going to and fro on morning errands. He began to think at once what he must do, how he must act to carry on his business, to rehabilitate himself; and as he did so he dressed and pulled the bell-cord, which had been indicated to him, and which would bring him an attendant who would build him a fire and later bring him something to eat. A shabby prison attendant in a blue uniform, conscious of Cowperwood's superiority because of the room he occupied, laid wood and coal in the grate and started a fire, and later brought him his breakfast, which was anything but prison fare, though poor enough at that.

After that he was compelled to wait in patience several hours, in spite of the sheriff's assumption of solicitous interest, before his brother Edward was admitted with his clothes. An attendant, for a consideration, brought him the morning papers, and these, except for the financial news, he read indifferently. Late in the afternoon Steger arrived, saying he had been busy having certain proceedings postponed, but that he had arranged with the sheriff for Cowperwood to be permitted to see such of those as had important business with him.

By this time, Cowperwood had written Aileen under no circumstances to try to see him, as he would be out by the tenth, and that either that day, or shortly after, they would meet. As he knew, she wanted greatly to see him, but he had reason to believe she was under surveillance by detectives employed by her father. This was not true, but it was preying on her fancy, and combined with some derogatory remarks dropped by Owen and Callum at the dinner table recently, had proved almost too much for her fiery disposition. But, because of Cowperwood's letter reaching her at the Calligans', she made no move until she read on the morning of the tenth that Cowperwood's plea for a certificate of reasonable doubt had been granted, and that he would once more, for the time being at least, be a free man. This gave her courage to do what she had long wanted to do, and that was to teach her father that she could get along without him and that he could not make her do anything she did not want to do. She still had the two hundred dollars Cowperwood had given her and some additional cash of her own—perhaps three hundred and fifty dollars in all. This she thought would be sufficient to see her to the end of her adventure, or at least until she could make some other arrangement for her personal well-being. From what she knew of the feeling of her family for her, she felt that the agony would all be on their side, not hers. Perhaps when her father saw how determined she was he would decide to let her alone and make peace with her. She was determined to try it, anyhow, and immediately sent word to Cowperwood that she was going to the Calligans and would welcome him to freedom.

In a way, Cowperwood was rather gratified by Aileen's message, for he felt that his present plight, bitter as it was, was largely due to Butler's opposition and he felt no compunction in striking him through his daughter. His former feeling as to the wisdom of not enraging Butler had proved rather futile, he thought, and since the old man could not be placated it might be just as well to have Aileen demonstrate to him that she was not without resources of her own and could live without him. She might force him to change his attitude toward her and possibly even to modify some of his political machinations against him, Cowperwood. Any port in a storm–and besides, he had now really nothing to lose, and instinct told him that her move was likely to prove more favorable than otherwise–so he did nothing to prevent it.

She took her jewels, some underwear, a couple of dresses which she thought would be serviceable, and a few other things, and packed them in the most capacious portmanteau she had. Shoes and stockings came into consideration, and, despite her efforts, she found that she could not get in all that she wished. Her nicest hat, which she was determined to take, had to be carried outside. She made a separate bundle of it, which was not pleasant to contemplate. Still she decided to take it. She rummaged in a little drawer where she kept her money and jewels, and found the three hundred and fifty dollars and put it in her purse. It wasn't much, as Aileen could herself see, but Cowperwood would help her. If he did not arrange to take care of her, and her father would not relent, she would have to get something to do. Little she knew of the steely face the world presents to those who have not been practically trained and are not economically efficient. She did not understand the bitter reaches of life at all. She waited, humming for effect, until she heard her father go downstairs to dinner on this tenth day of December, then leaned over the upper balustrade to make sure that Owen, Callum, Norah, and her mother were at the table, and that Katy, the housemaid, was not anywhere in sight. Then she slipped into her father's den, and, taking a note from inside her dress, laid it on his desk, and went out. It was addressed to "Father," and read:

Dear Father,–I just cannot do what you want me to. I have
made up my mind that I love Mr. Cowperwood too much, so I am
going away. Don't look for me with him. You won't find me
where you think. I am not going to him; I will not be
there. I am going to try to get along by myself for a
while, until he wants me and can marry me. I'm terribly
sorry; but I just can't do what you want. I can't ever
forgive you for the way you acted to me. Tell mama and Norah
and the boys good-by for me.
Aileen

To insure its discovery, she picked up Butler's heavy-rimmed spectacles which he employed always when reading, and laid them on it. For a moment she felt very strange, somewhat like a thief–a new sensation for her. She even felt a momentary sense of ingratitude coupled with pain. Perhaps she was doing wrong. Her father had been very good to her. Her mother would feel so very bad. Norah would be sorry, and Callum and Owen. Still, they did not understand her any more. She was resentful of her father's attitude. He might have seen what the point was; but no, he was too old, too hidebound in religion and conventional ideas–he never would. He might never let her come back. Very well, she would get along somehow. She would show him. She might get a place as a school-teacher, and live with the Calligans a long while, if necessary, or teach music.

She stole downstairs and out into the vestibule, opening the outer door and looking out into the street. The lamps were already flaring in the dark, and a cool wind was blowing. Her portmanteau was heavy, but she was quite strong. She walked briskly to the corner, which was some fifty feet away, and turned south, walking rather nervously and irritably, for this was a new experience for her, and it all seemed so undignified, so unlike anything she was accustomed to doing. She put her bag down on a street corner, finally, to rest. A boy whistling in the distance attracted her attention, and as he drew near she called to him: "Boy! Oh, boy!"

He came over, looking at her curiously.

"Do you want to earn some money?"

"Yes, ma'am," he replied politely, adjusting a frowsy cap over one ear.

"Carry this bag for me," said Aileen, and he picked it up and marched off.

In due time she arrived at the Calligans', and amid much excitement was installed in the bosom of her new home. She took her situation with much nonchalance, once she was properly placed, distributing her toilet articles and those of personal wear with quiet care. The fact that she was no longer to have the services of Kathleen, the maid who had served her and her mother and Norah jointly, was odd, though not trying. She scarcely felt that she had parted from these luxuries permanently, and so made herself comfortable.

Mamie Calligan and her mother were adoring slaveys, so she was not entirely out of the atmosphere which she craved and to which she was accustomed.

Chapter XLVI

Meanwhile, in the Butler home the family was assembling for dinner. Mrs. Butler was sitting in rotund complacency at the foot of the table, her gray hair combed straight back from her round, shiny forehead. She had on a dark-gray silk dress, trimmed with gray-and-white striped ribbon. It suited her florid temperament admirably. Aileen had dictated her mother's choice, and had seen that it had been properly made. Norah was refreshingly youthful in a pale-green dress, with red-velvet cuffs and collar. She looked young, slender, gay. Her eyes, complexion and hair were fresh and healthy. She was trifling with a string of coral beads which her mother had just given her.

"Oh, look, Callum," she said to her brother opposite her, who was drumming idly on the table with his knife and fork. "Aren't they lovely? Mama gave them to me."

"Mama does more for you than I would. You know what you'd get from me, don't you?"

"What?"

He looked at her teasingly. For answer Norah made a face at him. Just then Owen came in and took his place at the table. Mrs. Butler saw Norah's grimace.

"Well, that'll win no love from your brother, ye can depend on that," she commented.

"Lord, what a day!" observed Owen, wearily, unfolding his napkin. "I've had my fill of work for once."

"What's the trouble?" queried his mother, feelingly.

"No real trouble, mother," he replied. "Just everything–ducks and drakes, that's all."

"Well, ye must ate a good, hearty meal now, and that'll refresh ye," observed his mother, genially and feelingly. "Thompson"–she was referring to the family grocer– "brought us the last of his beans. You must have some of those."

"Sure, beans'll fix it, whatever it is, Owen," joked Callum. "Mother's got the answer."

"They're fine, I'd have ye know," replied Mrs. Butler, quite unconscious of the joke.

"No doubt of it, mother," replied Callum. "Real brain-food. Let's feed some to Norah."

"You'd better eat some yourself, smarty. My, but you're gay! I suppose you're going out to see somebody. That's why."

"Right you are, Norah. Smart girl, you. Five or six. Ten to fifteen minutes each. I'd call on you if you were nicer."

"You would if you got the chance," mocked Norah. "I'd have you know I wouldn't let you. I'd feel very bad if I couldn't get somebody better than you."

"As good as, you mean," corrected Callum.

"Children, children!" interpolated Mrs. Butler, calmly, looking about for old John, the servant. "You'll be losin' your tempers in a minute. Hush now. Here comes your father. Where's Aileen?"

Butler walked heavily in and took his seat.

John, the servant, appeared bearing a platter of beans among other things, and Mrs. Butler asked him to send some one to call Aileen.

"It's gettin' colder, I'm thinkin'," said Butler, by way of conversation, and eyeing Aileen's empty chair. She would come soon now–his heavy problem. He had been very tactful these last two months–avoiding any reference to Cowperwood in so far as he could help in her presence.

"It's colder," remarked Owen, "much colder. We'll soon see real winter now."

Old John began to offer the various dishes in order; but when all had been served Aileen had not yet come.

"See where Aileen is, John," observed Mrs. Butler, interestedly. "The meal will be gettin' cold."

Old John returned with the news that Aileen was not in her room.

"Sure she must be somewhere," commented Mrs. Butler, only slightly perplexed. "She'll be comin', though, never mind, if she wants to. She knows it's meal-time."

The conversation drifted from a new water-works that was being planned to the new city hall, then nearing completion; Cowperwood's financial and social troubles, and the state of the stock market generally; a new gold-mine in Arizona; the departure of Mrs. Mollenhauer the following Tuesday for Europe, with appropriate comments by Norah and Callum; and a Christmas ball that was going to be given for charity.

"Aileen'll be wantin' to go to that," commented Mrs. Butler.

"I'm going, you bet," put in Norah.

"Who's going to take you?" asked Callum.

"That's my affair, mister," she replied, smartly.

The meal was over, and Mrs. Butler strolled up to Aileen's room to see why she had not come down to dinner. Butler entered his den, wishing so much that he could take his wife into his confidence concerning all that was worrying him. On his desk, as he sat down and turned up the light, he saw the note. He recognized Aileen's handwriting at once. What could she mean by writing him? A sense of the untoward came to him, and he tore it open slowly, and, putting on his glasses, contemplated it solemnly.

So Aileen was gone. The old man stared at each word as if it had been written in fire. She said she had not gone with Cowperwood. It was possible, just the same, that he had run away from Philadelphia and taken her with him. This was the last straw. This ended it. Aileen lured away from home–to where–to what? Butler could scarcely believe, though, that Cowperwood had tempted her to do this. He had too much at stake; it would involve his own and Butler's families. The papers would be certain to get it quickly. He got up, crumpling the paper in his hand, and turned about at a noise. His wife was coming in. He pulled himself together and shoved the letter in his pocket.

"Aileen's not in her room," she said, curiously. "She didn't say anything to you about going out, did she?"

"No," he replied, truthfully, wondering how soon he should have to tell his wife.

"That's odd," observed Mrs. Butler, doubtfully. "She must have gone out after somethin'. It's a wonder she wouldn't tell somebody."

Butler gave no sign. He dared not. "She'll be back," he said, more in order to gain time than anything else. He was sorry to have to pretend. Mrs. Butler went out, and he closed the door. Then he took out the letter and read it again. The girl was crazy. She was doing an absolutely wild, inhuman, senseless thing. Where could she go, except to Cowperwood? She was on the verge of a public scandal, and this would produce it. There was just one thing to do as far as he could see. Cowperwood, if he were still in Philadelphia, would know. He would go to him–threaten, cajole, actually destroy him, if necessary. Aileen must come back. She need not go to Europe, perhaps, but she must come back and behave herself at least until Cowperwood could legitimately marry her. That was all he could expect now. She would have to wait, and some day perhaps he could bring himself to accept her wretched proposition. Horrible thought! It would kill her mother, disgrace her sister. He got up, took down his hat, put on his overcoat, and started out.

Arriving at the Cowperwood home he was shown into the reception-room. Cowperwood at the time was in his den looking over some private papers. When the name of Butler was announced he immediately went down-stairs. It was characteristic of the man that the announcement of Butler's presence created no stir in him whatsoever. So Butler had come. That meant, of course, that Aileen had gone. Now for a battle, not of words, but of weights of personalities. He felt himself to be intellectually, socially, and in every other way the more powerful man of the two. That spiritual content of him which we call life hardened to the texture of steel. He recalled that although he had told his wife and his father that the politicians, of whom Butler was one, were trying to make a scapegoat of him, Butler, nevertheless, was not considered to be wholly alienated as a friend, and civility must prevail. He would like very much to placate him if he could, to talk out the hard facts of life in a quiet and friendly way. But this matter of Aileen had to be adjusted now once and for all. And with that thought in his mind he walked quickly into Butler's presence.

The old man, when he learned that Cowperwood was in and would see him, determined to make his contact with the financier as short and effective as possible. He moved the least bit when he heard Cowperwood's step, as light and springy as ever.

"Good evening, Mr. Butler," said Cowperwood, cheerfully, when he saw him, extending his hand. "What can I do for you?"

"Ye can take that away from in front of me, for one thing," said Butler, grimly referring to his hand. "I have no need of it. It's my daughter I've come to talk to ye about, and I want plain answers. Where is she?"

"You mean Aileen?" said Cowperwood, looking at him with steady, curious, unrevealing eyes, and merely interpolating this to obtain a moment for reflection. "What can I tell you about her?"

"Ye can tell me where she is, that I know. And ye can make her come back to her home, where she belongs. It was bad fortune that ever brought ye across my doorstep; but I'll not bandy words with ye here. Ye'll tell me where my daughter is, and ye'll leave her alone from now, or I'll–" The old man's fists closed like a vise, and his chest heaved with suppressed rage. "Ye'll not be drivin' me too far, man, if ye're wise," he added, after a time, recovering his equanimity in part. "I want no truck with ye. I want my daughter."

"Listen, Mr. Butler," said Cowperwood, quite calmly, relishing the situation for the sheer sense of superiority it gave him. "I want to be perfectly frank with you, if you will let me. I may know where your daughter is, and I may not. I may wish to tell you, and I may not. She may not wish me to. But unless you wish to talk with me in a civil way there is no need of our going on any further. You are privileged to do what you like. Won't you come up-stairs to my room? We can talk more comfortably there."

Butler looked at his former protege in utter astonishment. He had never before in all his experience come up against a more ruthless type–suave, bland, forceful, unterrified. This man had certainly come to him as a sheep, and had turned out to be a ravening wolf. His incarceration had not put him in the least awe.

"I'll not come up to your room," Butler said, "and ye'll not get out of Philadelphy with her if that's what ye're plannin'. I can see to that. Ye think ye have the upper hand of me, I see, and ye're anxious to make something of it. Well, ye're not. It wasn't enough that ye come to me as a beggar, cravin' the help of me, and that I took ye in and helped ye all I could–ye had to steal my daughter from me in the bargain. If it wasn't for the girl's mother and her sister and her brothers–dacenter men than ever ye'll know how to be–I'd brain ye where ye stand. Takin' a young, innocent girl and makin' an evil woman out of her, and ye a married man! It's a God's blessin' for ye that it's me, and not one of me sons, that's here talkin' to ye, or ye wouldn't be alive to say what ye'd do."

The old man was grim but impotent in his rage.

"I'm sorry, Mr. Butler," replied Cowperwood, quietly. "I'm willing to explain, but you won't let me. I'm not planning to run away with your daughter, nor to leave Philadelphia. You ought to know me well enough to know that I'm not contemplating anything of that kind; my interests are too large. You and I are practical men. We ought to be able to talk this matter over together and reach an understanding. I thought once of coming to you and explaining this; but I was quite sure you wouldn't listen to me. Now that you are here I would like to talk to you. If you will come up to my room I will be glad to–otherwise not. Won't you come up?"

Butler saw that Cowperwood had the advantage. He might as well go up. Otherwise it was plain he would get no information.

"Very well," he said.

Cowperwood led the way quite amicably, and, having entered his private office, closed the door behind him.

"We ought to be able to talk this matter over and reach an understanding," he said again, when they were in the room and he had closed the door. "I am not as bad as you think, though I know I appear very bad." Butler stared at him in contempt. "I love your daughter, and she loves me. I know you are asking yourself how I can do this while I am still married; but I assure you I can, and that I do. I am not happily married. I had expected, if this panic hadn't come along, to arrange with my wife for a divorce and marry Aileen. My intentions are perfectly good. The situation which you can complain of, of course, is the one you encountered a few weeks ago. It was indiscreet, but it was entirely human. Your daughter does not complain–she understands." At the mention of his daughter in this connection Butler flushed with rage and shame, but he controlled himself.

"And ye think because she doesn't complain that it's all right, do ye?" he asked, sarcastically.

"From my point of view, yes; from yours no. You have one view of life, Mr. Butler, and I have another."

"Ye're right there," put in Butler, "for once, anyhow."

"That doesn't prove that either of us is right or wrong. In my judgment the present end justifies the means. The end I have in view is to marry Aileen. If I can possibly pull myself out of this financial scrape that I am in I will do so. Of course, I would like to have your consent for that–so would Aileen; but if we can't, we can't." (Cowperwood was thinking that while this might not have a very soothing effect on the old contractor's point of view, nevertheless it must make some appeal to his sense of the possible or necessary. Aileen's present situation was quite unsatisfactory without marriage in view. And even if he, Cowperwood, was a convicted embezzler in the eyes of the public, that did not make him so. He might get free and restore himself–would certainly–and Aileen ought to be glad to marry him if she could under the circumstances. He did not quite grasp the depth of Butler's religious and moral prejudices.) "Lately," he went on, "you have been doing all you can, as I understand it, to pull me down, on account of Aileen, I suppose; but that is simply delaying what I want to do."

"Ye'd like me to help ye do that, I suppose?" suggested Butler, with infinite disgust and patience.

"I want to marry Aileen," Cowperwood repeated, for emphasis' sake. "She wants to marry me. Under the circumstances, however you may feel, you can have no real objection to my doing that, I am sure; yet you go on fighting me–making it hard for me to do what you really know ought to be done."

"Ye're a scoundrel," said Butler, seeing through his motives quite clearly. "Ye're a sharper, to my way of thinkin', and it's no child of mine I want connected with ye. I'm not sayin', seein' that things are as they are, that if ye were a free man it wouldn't be better that she should marry ye. It's the one dacent thing ye could do–if ye would, which I doubt. But that's nayther here nor there now. What can ye want with her hid away somewhere? Ye can't marry her. Ye can't get a divorce. Ye've got your hands full fightin' your lawsuits and kapin' yourself out of jail. She'll only be an added expense to ye, and ye'll be wantin' all the money ye have for other things, I'm thinkin'. Why should ye want to be takin' her away from a dacent home and makin' something out of her that ye'd be ashamed to marry if you could? The laist ye could do, if ye were any kind of a man at all, and had any of that thing that ye're plased to call love, would be to lave her at home and keep her as respectable as possible. Mind ye, I'm not thinkin' she isn't ten thousand times too good for ye, whatever ye've made of her. But if ye had any sinse of dacency left, ye wouldn't let her shame her family and break her old mother's heart, and that for no purpose except to make her worse than she is already. What good can ye get out of it, now? What good can ye expect to come of it? Be hivins, if ye had any sinse at all I should think ye could see that for yerself. Ye're only addin' to your troubles, not takin' away from them–and she'll not thank ye for that later on."

He stopped, rather astonished that he should have been drawn into an argument. His contempt for this man was so great that he could scarcely look at him, but his duty and his need was to get Aileen back. Cowperwood looked at him as one who gives serious attention to another. He seemed to be thinking deeply over what Butler had said.

"To tell you the truth, Mr. Butler," he said, "I did not want Aileen to leave your home at all; and she will tell you so, if you ever talk to her about it. I did my best to persuade her not to, and when she insisted on going the only thing I could do was to be sure she would be comfortable wherever she went. She was greatly outraged to think you should have put detectives on her trail. That, and the fact that you wanted to send her away somewhere against her will, was the principal reasons for her leaving. I assure you I did not want her to go. I think you forget sometimes, Mr. Butler, that Aileen is a grown woman, and that she has a will of her own. You think I control her to her great disadvantage. As a matter of fact, I am very much in love with her, and have been for three or four years; and if you know anything about love you know that it doesn't always mean control. I'm not doing Aileen any injustice when I say that she has had as much influence on me as I have had on her. I love her, and that's the cause of all the trouble. You come and insist that I shall return your daughter to you. As a matter of fact, I don't know whether I can or not. I don't know that she would go if I wanted her to. She might turn on me and say that I didn't care for her any more. That is not true, and I would not want her to feel that way. She is greatly hurt, as I told you, by what you did to her, and the fact that you want her to leave Philadelphia. You can do as much to remedy that as I can. I could tell you where she is, but I do not know that I want to. Certainly not until I know what your attitude toward her and this whole proposition is to be."

He paused and looked calmly at the old contractor, who eyed him grimly in return.

"What proposition are ye talkin' about?" asked Butler, interested by the peculiar developments of this argument. In spite of himself he was getting a slightly different angle on the whole situation. The scene was shifting to a certain extent. Cowperwood appeared to be reasonably sincere in the matter. His promises might all be wrong, but perhaps he did love Aileen; and it was possible that he did intend to get a divorce from his wife some time and marry her. Divorce, as Butler knew, was against the rules of the Catholic Church, which he so much revered. The laws of God and any sense of decency commanded that Cowperwood should not desert his wife and children and take up with another woman–not even Aileen, in order to save her. It was a criminal thing to plan, sociologically speaking, and showed what a villain Cowperwood inherently was; but, nevertheless, Cowperwood was not a Catholic, his views of life were not the same as his own, Butler's, and besides and worst of all (no doubt due in part to Aileen's own temperament), he had compromised her situation very materially. She might not easily be restored to a sense of of the normal and decent, and so the matter was worth taking into thought. Butler knew that ultimately he could not countenance any such thing–certainly not, and keep his faith with the Church–but he was human enough none the less to consider it. Besides, he wanted Aileen to come back; and Aileen from now on, he knew, would have some say as to what her future should be.

"Well, it's simple enough," replied Cowperwood. "I should like to have you withdraw your opposition to Aileen's remaining in Philadelphia, for one thing; and for another, I should like you to stop your attacks on me." Cowperwood smiled in an ingratiating way. He hoped really to placate Butler in part by his generous attitude throughout this procedure. "I can't make you do that, of course, unless you want to. I merely bring it up, Mr. Butler, because I am sure that if it hadn't been for Aileen you would not have taken the course you have taken toward me. I understood you received an anonymous letter, and that afternoon you called your loan with me. Since then I have heard from one source and another that you were strongly against me, and I merely wish to say that I wish you wouldn't be. I am not guilty of embezzling any sixty thousand dollars, and you know it. My intentions were of the best. I did not think I was going to fail at the time I used those certificates, and if it hadn't been for several other loans that were called I would have gone on to the end of the month and put them back in time, as I always had. I have always valued your friendship very highly, and I am very sorry to lose it. Now I have said all I am going to say."

Butler looked at Cowperwood with shrewd, calculating eyes. The man had some merit, but much unconscionable evil in him. Butler knew very well how he had taken the check, and a good many other things in connection with it. The manner in which he had played his cards to-night was on a par with the way he had run to him on the night of the fire. He was just shrewd and calculating and heartless.

"I'll make ye no promise," he said. "Tell me where my daughter is, and I'll think the matter over. Ye have no claim on me now, and I owe ye no good turn. But I'll think it over, anyhow."

"That's quite all right," replied Cowperwood. "That's all I can expect. But what about Aileen? Do you expect her to leave Philadelphia?"

"Not if she settles down and behaves herself: but there must be an end of this between you and her. She's disgracin' her family and ruinin' her soul in the bargain. And that's what you are doin' with yours. It'll be time enough to talk about anything else when you're a free man. More than that I'll not promise."

Cowperwood, satisfied that this move on Aileen's part had done her a real service if it had not aided him especially, was convinced that it would be a good move for her to return to her home at once. He could not tell how his appeal to the State Supreme Court would eventuate. His motion for a new trial which was now to be made under the privilege of the certificate of reasonable doubt might not be granted, in which case he would have to serve a term in the penitentiary. If he were compelled to go to the penitentiary she would be safer–better off in the bosom of her family. His own hands were going to be exceedingly full for the next two months until he knew how his appeal was coming out. And after that–well, after that he would fight on, whatever happened.

During all the time that Cowperwood had been arguing his case in this fashion he had been thinking how he could adjust this compromise so as to retain the affection of Aileen and not offend her sensibilities by urging her to return. He knew that she would not agree to give up seeing him, and he was not willing that she should. Unless he had a good and sufficient reason, he would be playing a wretched part by telling Butler where she was. He did not intend to do so until he saw exactly how to do it–the way that would make it most acceptable to Aileen. He knew that she would not long be happy where she was. Her flight was due in part to Butler's intense opposition to himself and in part to his determination to make her leave Philadelphia and behave; but this last was now in part obviated. Butler, in spite of his words, was no longer a stern Nemesis. He was a melting man–very anxious to find his daughter, very willing to forgive her. He was whipped, literally beaten, at his own game, and Cowperwood could see it in the old man's eyes. If he himself could talk to Aileen personally and explain just how things were, he felt sure he could make her see that it would be to their mutual advantage, for the present at least, to have the matter amicably settled. The thing to do was to make Butler wait somewhere–here, possibly–while he went and talked to her. When she learned how things were she would probably acquiesce.

"The best thing that I can do under the circumstances," he said, after a time, "would be to see Aileen in two or three days, and ask her what she wishes to do. I can explain the matter to her, and if she wants to go back, she can. I will promise to tell her anything that you say."

"Two or three days!" exclaimed Butler, irritably. "Two or three fiddlesticks! She must come home to-night. Her mother doesn't know she's left the place yet. To-night is the time! I'll go and fetch her meself to-night."

"No, that won't do," said Cowperwood. "I shall have to go myself. If you wish to wait here I will see what can be done, and let you know."

"Very well," grunted Butler, who was now walking up and down with his hands behind his back. "But for Heaven's sake be quick about it. There's no time to lose." He was thinking of Mrs. Butler. Cowperwood called the servant, ordered his runabout, and told George to see that his private office was not disturbed. Then, as Butler strolled to and fro in this, to him, objectionable room, Cowperwood drove rapidly away.

Chapter XLVII

Although it was nearly eleven o'clock when he arrived at the Calligans', Aileen was not yet in bed. In her bedroom upstairs she was confiding to Mamie and Mrs. Calligan some of her social experiences when the bell rang, and Mrs. Calligan went down and opened the door to Cowperwood.

"Miss Butler is here, I believe," he said. "Will you tell her that there is some one here from her father?" Although Aileen had instructed that her presence here was not to be divulged even to the members of her family the force of Cowperwood's presence and the mention of Butler's name cost Mrs. Calligan her presence of mind. "Wait a moment," she said; "I'll see."

She stepped back, and Cowperwood promptly stepped in, taking off his hat with the air of one who was satisfied that Aileen was there. "Say to her that I only want to speak to her for a few moments," he called, as Mrs. Calligan went up-stairs, raising his voice in the hope that Aileen might hear. She did, and came down promptly. She was very much astonished to think that he should come so soon, and fancied, in her vanity, that there must be great excitement in her home. She would have greatly grieved if there had not been.

The Calligans would have been pleased to hear, but Cowperwood was cautious. As she came down the stairs he put his finger to his lips in sign for silence, and said, "This is Miss Butler, I believe."

"Yes," replied Aileen, with a secret smile. Her one desire was to kiss him. "What's the trouble darling?" she asked, softly.

"You'll have to go back, dear, I'm afraid," whispered Cowperwood. "You'll have everything in a turmoil if you don't. Your mother doesn't know yet, it seems, and your father is over at my place now, waiting for you. It may be a good deal of help to me if you do. Let me tell you–" He went off into a complete description of his conversation with Butler and his own views in the matter. Aileen's expression changed from time to time as the various phases of the matter were put before her; but, persuaded by the clearness with which he put the matter, and by his assurance that they could continue their relations as before uninterrupted, once this was settled, she decided to return. In a way, her father's surrender was a great triumph. She made her farewells to the Calligans, saying, with a smile, that they could not do without her at home, and that she would send for her belongings later, and returned with Cowperwood to his own door. There he asked her to wait in the runabout while he sent her father down.

"Well?" said Butler, turning on him when he opened the door, and not seeing Aileen.

"You'll find her outside in my runabout," observed Cowperwood. "You may use that if you choose. I will send my man for it."

"No, thank you; we'll walk," said Butler.

Cowperwood called his servant to take charge of the vehicle, and Butler stalked solemnly out.

He had to admit to himself that the influence of Cowperwood over his daughter was deadly, and probably permanent. The best he could do would be to keep her within the precincts of the home, where she might still, possibly, be brought to her senses. He held a very guarded conversation with her on his way home, for fear that she would take additional offense. Argument was out of the question.

"Ye might have talked with me once more, Aileen," he said, "before ye left. Yer mother would be in a terrible state if she knew ye were gone. She doesn't know yet. Ye'll have to say ye stayed somewhere to dinner."

"I was at the Calligans," replied Aileen. "That's easy enough. Mama won't think anything about it."

"It's a sore heart I have, Aileen. I hope ye'll think over your ways and do better. I'll not say anythin' more now."

Aileen returned to her room, decidedly triumphant in her mood for the moment, and things went on apparently in the Butler household as before. But those who imagine that this defeat permanently altered the attitude of Butler toward Cowperwood are mistaken.

In the meanwhile between the day of his temporary release and the hearing of his appeal which was two months off, Cowperwood was going on doing his best to repair his shattered forces. He took up his work where he left off; but the possibility of reorganizing his business was distinctly modified since his conviction. Because of his action in trying to protect his largest creditors at the time of his failure, he fancied that once he was free again, if ever he got free, his credit, other things being equal, would be good with those who could help him most–say, Cooke Co., Clark Co., Drexel Co., and the Girard National Bank–providing his personal reputation had not been too badly injured by his sentence. Fortunately for his own hopefulness of mind, he failed fully to realize what a depressing effect a legal decision of this character, sound or otherwise, had on the minds of even his most enthusiastic supporters.

His best friends in the financial world were by now convinced that his was a sinking ship. A student of finance once observed that nothing is so sensitive as money, and the financial mind partakes largely of the quality of the thing in which it deals. There was no use trying to do much for a man who might be going to prison for a term of years. Something might be done for him possibly in connection with the governor, providing he lost his case before the Supreme Court and was actually sentenced to prison; but that was two months off, or more, and they could not tell what the outcome of that would be. So Cowperwood's repeated appeals for assistance, extension of credit, or the acceptance of some plan he had for his general rehabilitation, were met with the kindly evasions of those who were doubtful. They would think it over. They would see about it. Certain things were standing in the way. And so on, and so forth, through all the endless excuses of those who do not care to act. In these days he went about the money world in his customary jaunty way, greeting all those whom he had known there many years and pretending, when asked, to be very hopeful, to be doing very well; but they did not believe him, and he really did not care whether they did or not. His business was to persuade or over-persuade any one who could really be of assistance to him, and at this task he worked untiringly, ignoring all others.

"Why, hello, Frank," his friends would call, on seeing him. "How are you getting on?"

"Fine! Fine!" he would reply, cheerfully. "Never better," and he would explain in a general way how his affairs were being handled. He conveyed much of his own optimism to all those who knew him and were interested in his welfare, but of course there were many who were not.

In these days also, he and Steger were constantly to be met with in courts of law, for he was constantly being reexamined in some petition in bankruptcy. They were heartbreaking days, but he did not flinch. He wanted to stay in Philadelphia and fight the thing to a finish–putting himself where he had been before the fire; rehabilitating himself in the eyes of the public. He felt that he could do it, too, if he were not actually sent to prison for a long term; and even then, so naturally optimistic was his mood, when he got out again. But, in so far as Philadelphia was concerned, distinctly he was dreaming vain dreams.

One of the things militating against him was the continued opposition of Butler and the politicians. Somehow–no one could have said exactly why–the general political feeling was that the financier and the former city treasurer would lose their appeals and eventually be sentenced together. Stener, in spite of his original intention to plead guilty and take his punishment without comment, had been persuaded by some of his political friends that it would be better for his future's sake to plead not guilty and claim that his offense had been due to custom, rather than to admit his guilt outright and so seem not to have had any justification whatsoever. This he did, but he was convicted nevertheless. For the sake of appearances, a trumped-up appeal was made which was now before the State Supreme Court.

Then, too, due to one whisper and another, and these originating with the girl who had written Butler and Cowperwood's wife, there was at this time a growing volume of gossip relating to the alleged relations of Cowperwood with Butler's daughter, Aileen. There had been a house in Tenth Street. It had been maintained by Cowperwood for her. No wonder Butler was so vindictive. This, indeed, explained much. And even in the practical, financial world, criticism was now rather against Cowperwood than his enemies. For, was it not a fact, that at the inception of his career, he had been befriended by Butler? And what a way to reward that friendship! His oldest and firmest admirers wagged their heads. For they sensed clearly that this was another illustration of that innate "I satisfy myself" attitude which so regulated Cowperwood's conduct. He was a strong man, surely–and a brilliant one. Never had Third Street seen a more pyrotechnic, and yet fascinating and financially aggressive, and at the same time, conservative person. Yet might one not fairly tempt Nemesis by a too great daring and egotism? Like Death, it loves a shining mark. He should not, perhaps, have seduced Butler's daughter; unquestionably he should not have so boldly taken that check, especially after his quarrel and break with Stener. He was a little too aggressive. Was it not questionable whether–with such a record–he could be restored to his former place here? The bankers and business men who were closest to him were decidedly dubious.

But in so far as Cowperwood and his own attitude toward life was concerned, at this time–the feeling he had–"to satisfy myself"–when combined with his love of beauty and love and women, still made him ruthless and thoughtless. Even now, the beauty and delight of a girl like Aileen Butler were far more important to him than the good-will of fifty million people, if he could evade the necessity of having their good-will. Previous to the Chicago fire and the panic, his star had been so rapidly ascending that in the helter-skelter of great and favorable events he had scarcely taken thought of the social significance of the thing he was doing. Youth and the joy of life were in his blood. He felt so young, so vigorous, so like new grass looks and feels. The freshness of spring evenings was in him, and he did not care. After the crash, when one might have imagined he would have seen the wisdom of relinquishing Aileen for the time being, anyhow, he did not care to. She represented the best of the wonderful days that had gone before. She was a link between him and the past and a still-to-be triumphant future.

His worst anxiety was that if he were sent to the penitentiary, or adjudged a bankrupt, or both, he would probably lose the privilege of a seat on 'change, and that would close to him the most distinguished avenue of his prosperity here in Philadelphia for some time, if not forever. At present, because of his complications, his seat had been attached as an asset, and he could not act. Edward and Joseph, almost the only employees he could afford, were still acting for him in a small way; but the other members on 'change naturally suspected his brothers as his agents, and any talk that they might raise of going into business for themselves merely indicated to other brokers and bankers that Cowperwood was contemplating some concealed move which would not necessarily be advantageous to his creditors, and against the law anyhow. Yet he must remain on 'change, whatever happened, potentially if not actively; and so in his quick mental searchings he hit upon the idea that in order to forfend against the event of his being put into prison or thrown into bankruptcy, or both, he ought to form a subsidiary silent partnership with some man who was or would be well liked on 'change, and whom he could use as a cat's-paw and a dummy.

Finally he hit upon a man who he thought would do. He did not amount to much– had a small business; but he was honest, and he liked Cowperwood. His name was Wingate–Stephen Wingate–and he was eking out a not too robust existence in South Third Street as a broker. He was forty-five years of age, of medium height, fairly thick-set, not at all unprepossessing, and rather intelligent and active, but not too forceful and pushing in spirit. He really needed a man like Cowperwood to make him into something, if ever he was to be made. He had a seat on 'change, and was well thought of; respected, but not so very prosperous. In times past he had asked small favors of Cowperwood–the use of small loans at a moderate rate of interest, tips, and so forth; and Cowperwood, because he liked him and felt a little sorry for him, had granted them. Now Wingate was slowly drifting down toward a none too successful old age, and was as tractable as such a man would naturally be. No one for the time being would suspect him of being a hireling of Cowperwood's, and the latter could depend on him to execute his orders to the letter. He sent for him and had a long conversation with him. He told him just what the situation was, what he thought he could do for him as a partner, how much of his business he would want for himself, and so on, and found him agreeable.

"I'll be glad to do anything you say, Mr. Cowperwood," he assured the latter. "I know whatever happens that you'll protect me, and there's nobody in the world I would rather work with or have greater respect for. This storm will all blow over, and you'll be all right. We can try it, anyhow. If it don't work out you can see what you want to do about it later."

And so this relationship was tentatively entered into and Cowperwood began to act in a small way through Wingate.

Chapter XLVIII

By the time the State Supreme Court came to pass upon Cowperwood's plea for a reversal of the lower court and the granting of a new trial, the rumor of his connection with Aileen had spread far and wide. As has been seen, it had done and was still doing him much damage. It confirmed the impression, which the politicians had originally tried to create, that Cowperwood was the true criminal and Stener the victim. His semi-legitimate financial subtlety, backed indeed by his financial genius, but certainly on this account not worse than that being practiced in peace and quiet and with much applause in many other quarters—was now seen to be Machiavellian trickery of the most dangerous type. He had a wife and two children; and without knowing what his real thoughts had been the fruitfully imaginative public jumped to the conclusion that he had been on the verge of deserting them, divorcing Lillian, and marrying Aileen. This was criminal enough in itself, from the conservative point of view; but when taken in connection with his financial record, his trial, conviction, and general bankruptcy situation, the public was inclined to believe that he was all the politicians said he was. He ought to be convicted. The Supreme Court ought not to grant his prayer for a new trial. It is thus that our inmost thoughts and intentions burst at times via no known material agency into public thoughts. People know, when they cannot apparently possibly know why they know. There is such a thing as thought-transference and transcendentalism of ideas.

It reached, for one thing, the ears of the five judges of the State Supreme Court and of the Governor of the State.

During the four weeks Cowperwood had been free on a certificate of reasonable doubt both Harper Steger and Dennis Shannon appeared before the judges of the State Supreme Court, and argued pro and con as to the reasonableness of granting a new trial. Through his lawyer, Cowperwood made a learned appeal to the Supreme Court judges, showing how he had been unfairly indicted in the first place, how there was no real substantial evidence on which to base a charge of larceny or anything else. It took Steger two hours and ten minutes to make his argument, and District-Attorney Shannon longer to make his reply, during which the five judges on the bench, men of considerable legal experience but no great financial understanding, listened with rapt attention. Three of them, Judges Smithson, Rainey, and Beckwith, men most amenable to the political feeling of the time and the wishes of the bosses, were little interested in this story of Cowperwood's transaction, particularly since his relations with Butler's daughter and Butler's consequent opposition to him had come to them. They fancied that in a way they were considering the whole matter fairly and impartially; but the manner in which Cowperwood had treated Butler was never out of their minds. Two of them, Judges Marvin and Rafalsky, who were men of larger sympathies and understanding, but of no greater political freedom, did feel that Cowperwood had been badly used thus far, but they did not see what they could do about it. He had put himself in a most unsatisfactory position, politically and socially. They understood and took into consideration his great financial and social losses which Steger described accurately; and one of them, Judge Rafalsky, because of a similar event in his own life in so far as a girl was concerned, was inclined to argue strongly against the conviction of Cowperwood; but, owing to his political connections and obligations, he realized that it would not be wise politically to stand out against what was wanted. Still, when he and Marvin learned that Judges Smithson, Rainey, and Beckwith were inclined to convict Cowperwood without much argument, they decided to hand down a dissenting opinion. The point involved was a very knotty one. Cowperwood might carry it to the Supreme Court of the United States on some fundamental principle of liberty of action. Anyhow, other judges in other courts in Pennsylvania and elsewhere would be inclined to examine the decision in this case, it was so important. The minority decided that it would not do them any harm to hand down a dissenting opinion. The politicians would not mind as long as Cowperwood was convicted–would like it better, in fact. It looked fairer. Besides, Marvin and Rafalsky did not care to be included, if they could help it, with Smithson, Rainey, and Beckwith in a sweeping condemnation of Cowperwood. So all five judges fancied they were considering the whole matter rather fairly and impartially, as men will under such circumstances. Smithson, speaking for himself and Judges Rainey and Beckwith on the eleventh of February, 1872, said:

"The defendant, Frank A. Cowperwood, asks that the finding of the jury in the lower court (the State of Pennsylvania vs. Frank A. Cowperwood) be reversed and a new trial granted. This court cannot see that any substantial injustice has been done the defendant. [Here followed a rather lengthy resume of the history of the case, in which it was pointed out that the custom and precedent of the treasurer's office, to say nothing of Cowperwood's easy method of doing business with the city treasury, could have nothing to do with his responsibility for failure to observe both the spirit and the letter of the law.] The obtaining of goods under color of legal process [went on Judge Smithson, speaking for the majority] may amount to larceny. In the present case it was the province of the jury to ascertain the felonious intent. They have settled that against the defendant as a question of fact, and the court cannot say that there was not sufficient evidence to sustain the verdict. For what purpose did the defendant get the check? He was upon the eve of failure. He had already hypothecated for his own debts the loan of the city placed in his hands for sale–he had unlawfully obtained five hundred thousand dollars in cash as loans; and it is reasonable to suppose that he could obtain nothing more from the city treasury by any ordinary means. Then it is that he goes there, and, by means of a falsehood implied if not actual, obtains sixty thousand dollars more. The jury has found the intent with which this was done."

It was in these words that Cowperwood's appeal for a new trial was denied by the majority.

For himself and Judge Rafalsky, Judge Marvin, dissenting, wrote:

"It is plain from the evidence in the case that Mr. Cowperwood did not receive the check without authority as agent to do so, and it has not been clearly demonstrated that within his capacity as agent he did not perform or intend to perform the full measure of the obligation which the receipt of this check implied. It was shown in the trial that as a matter of policy it was understood that purchases for the sinking-fund should not be known or understood in the market or by the public in that light, and that Mr. Cowperwood as agent was to have an absolutely free hand in the disposal of his assets and liabilities so long as the ultimate result was satisfactory. There was no particular time when the loan was to be bought, nor was there any particular amount mentioned at any time to be purchased. Unless the defendant intended at the time he received the check fraudulently to appropriate it he could not be convicted even on the first count. The verdict of the jury does not establish this fact; the evidence does not show conclusively that it could be established; and the same jury, upon three other counts, found the defendant guilty without the semblance of shadow of evidence. How can we say that their conclusions upon the first count are unerring when they so palpably erred on the other counts? It is the opinion of the minority that the verdict of the jury in charging larceny on the first count is not valid, and that that verdict should be set aside and a new trial granted."

Judge Rafalsky, a meditative and yet practical man of Jewish extraction but peculiarly American appearance, felt called upon to write a third opinion which should especially reflect his own cogitation and be a criticism on the majority as well as a slight variation from and addition to the points on which he agreed with Judge Marvin. It was a knotty question, this, of Cowperwood's guilt, and, aside from the political necessity of convicting him, nowhere was it more clearly shown than in these varying opinions of the superior court. Judge Rafalsky held, for instance, that if a crime had been committed at all, it was not that known as larceny, and he went on to add:

"It is impossible, from the evidence, to come to the conclusion either that Cowperwood did not intend shortly to deliver the loan or that Albert Stires, the chief clerk, or the city treasurer did not intend to part not only with the possession, but also and absolutely with the property in the check and the money represented by it. It was testified by Mr. Stires that Mr. Cowperwood said he had bought certificates of city loan to this amount, and it has not been clearly demonstrated that he had not. His non-placement of the same in the sinking-fund must in all fairness, the letter of the law to the contrary notwithstanding, be looked upon and judged in the light of custom. Was it his custom so to do? In my judgment the doctrine now announced by the majority of the court extends the crime of constructive larceny to such limits that any business man who engages in extensive and perfectly legitimate stock transactions may, before he knows it, by a sudden panic in the market or a fire, as in this instance, become a felon. When a principle is asserted which establishes such a precedent, and may lead to such results, it is, to say the least, startling."

While he was notably comforted by the dissenting opinions of the judges in minority, and while he had been schooling himself to expect the worst in this connection and had been arranging his affairs as well as he could in anticipation of it, Cowperwood was still bitterly disappointed. It would be untrue to say that, strong and self-reliant as he normally was, he did not suffer. He was not without sensibilities of the highest order, only they were governed and controlled in him by that cold iron thing, his reason, which never forsook him. There was no further appeal possible save to the United States Supreme Court, as Steger pointed out, and there only on the constitutionality of some phase of the decision and his rights as a citizen, of which the Supreme Court of the United States must take cognizance. This was a tedious and expensive thing to do. It was not exactly obvious at the moment on what point he could make an appeal. It would involve a long delay–perhaps a year and a half, perhaps longer, at the end of which period he might have to serve his prison term anyhow, and pending which he would certainly have to undergo incarceration for a time.

Cowperwood mused speculatively for a few moments after hearing Steger's presentation of the case. Then he said: "Well, it looks as if I have to go to jail or leave the country, and I've decided on jail. I can fight this out right here in Philadelphia in the long run and win. I can get that decision reversed in the Supreme Court, or I can get the Governor to pardon me after a time, I think. I'm not going to run away, and everybody knows I'm not. These people who think they have me down haven't got one corner of me whipped. I'll get out of this thing after a while, and when I do I'll show some of these petty little politicians what it means to put up a real fight. They'll never get a damned dollar out of me now–not a dollar! I did intend to pay that five hundred thousand dollars some time if they had let me go. Now they can whistle!"

He set his teeth and his gray eyes fairly snapped their determination.

"Well, I've done all I can, Frank," pleaded Steger, sympathetically. "You'll do me the justice to say that I put up the best fight I knew how. I may not know how–you'll have to answer for that–but within my limits I've done the best I can. I can do a few things more to carry this thing on, if you want me to, but I'm going to leave it to you now. Whatever you say goes."

"Don't talk nonsense at this stage, Harper," replied Cowperwood almost testily. "I know whether I'm satisfied or not, and I'd soon tell you if I wasn't. I think you might as well go on and see if you can find some definite grounds for carrying it to the Supreme Court, but meanwhile I'll begin my sentence. I suppose Payderson will be naming a day to have me brought before him now shortly."

"It depends on how you'd like to have it, Frank. I could get a stay of sentence for a week maybe, or ten days, if it will do you any good. Shannon won't make any objection to that, I'm sure. There's only one hitch. Jaspers will be around here tomorrow looking for you. It's his duty to take you into custody again, once he's notified that your appeal has been denied. He'll be wanting to lock you up unless you pay him, but we can fix that. If you do want to wait, and want any time off, I suppose he'll arrange to let you out with a deputy; but I'm afraid you'll have to stay there nights. They're pretty strict about that since that Albertson case of a few years ago."

Steger referred to the case of a noted bank cashier who, being let out of the county jail at night in the alleged custody of a deputy, was permitted to escape. There had been emphatic and severe condemnation of the sheriff's office at the time, and since then, repute or no repute, money or no money, convicted criminals were supposed to stay in the county jail at night at least.

Cowperwood meditated this calmly, looking out of the lawyer's window into Second Street. He did not much fear anything that might happen to him in Jaspers's charge since his first taste of that gentleman's hospitality, although he did object to spending nights in the county jail when his general term of imprisonment was being reduced no whit thereby. All that he could do now in connection with his affairs, unless he could have months of freedom, could be as well adjusted from a prison cell as from his Third Street office–not quite, but nearly so. Anyhow, why parley? He was facing a prison term, and he might as well accept it without further ado. He might take a day or two finally to look after his affairs; but beyond that, why bother?

"When, in the ordinary course of events, if you did nothing at all, would I come up for sentence?"

"Oh, Friday or Monday, I fancy," replied Steger. "I don't know what move Shannon is planning to make in this matter. I thought I'd walk around and see him in a little while."

"I think you'd better do that," replied Cowperwood. "Friday or Monday will suit me, either way. I'm really not particular. Better make it Monday if you can. You don't suppose there is any way you can induce Jaspers to keep his hands off until then? He knows I'm perfectly responsible."

"I don't know, Frank, I'm sure; I'll see. I'll go around and talk to him to-night. Perhaps a hundred dollars will make him relax the rigor of his rules that much."

Cowperwood smiled grimly.

"I fancy a hundred dollars would make Jaspers relax a whole lot of rules," he replied, and he got up to go.

Steger arose also. "I'll see both these people, and then I'll call around at your house. You'll be in, will you, after dinner?"

"Yes."

They slipped on their overcoats and went out into the cold February day, Cowperwood back to his Third Street office, Steger to see Shannon and Jaspers.

Chapter XLIX

The business of arranging Cowperwood's sentence for Monday was soon disposed of through Shannon, who had no personal objection to any reasonable delay.

Steger next visited the county jail, close on to five o'clock, when it was already dark. Sheriff Jaspers came lolling out from his private library, where he had been engaged upon the work of cleaning his pipe.

"How are you, Mr. Steger?" he observed, smiling blandly. "How are you? Glad to see you. Won't you sit down? I suppose you're round here again on that Cowperwood matter. I just received word from the district attorney that he had lost his case."

"That's it, Sheriff," replied Steger, ingratiatingly. "He asked me to step around and see what you wanted him to do in the matter. Judge Payderson has just fixed the sentence time for Monday morning at ten o'clock. I don't suppose you'll be much put out if he doesn't show up here before Monday at eight o'clock, will you, or Sunday night, anyhow? He's perfectly reliable, as you know." Steger was sounding Jaspers out, politely trying to make the time of Cowperwood's arrival a trivial matter in order to avoid paying the hundred dollars, if possible. But Jaspers was not to be so easily disposed of. His fat face lengthened considerably. How could Steger ask him such a favor and not even suggest the slightest form of remuneration?

"It's ag'in' the law, Mr. Steger, as you know," he began, cautiously and complainingly. "I'd like to accommodate him, everything else being equal, but since that Albertson case three years ago we've had to run this office much more careful, and—"

"Oh, I know, Sheriff," interrupted Steger, blandly, "but this isn't an ordinary case in any way, as you can see for yourself. Mr. Cowperwood is a very important man, and he has a great many things to attend to. Now if it were only a mere matter of seventy-five or a hundred dollars to satisfy some court clerk with, or to pay a fine, it would be easy enough, but—" He paused and looked wisely away, and Mr. Jaspers's face began to relax at once. The law against which it was ordinarily so hard to offend was not now so important. Steger saw that it was needless to introduce any additional arguments.

"It's a very ticklish business, this, Mr. Steger," put in the sheriff, yieldingly, and yet with a slight whimper in his voice. "If anything were to happen, it would cost me my place all right. I don't like to do it under any circumstances, and I wouldn't, only I happen to know both Mr. Cowperwood and Mr. Stener, and I like 'em both. I don' think they got their rights in this matter, either. I don't mind making an exception in this case if Mr. Cowperwood don't go about too publicly. I wouldn't want any of the men in the district attorney's office to know this. I don't suppose he'll mind if I keep a deputy somewhere near all the time for looks' sake. I have to, you know, really, under the law. He won't bother him any. Just keep on guard like." Jaspers looked at Mr. Steger very flatly and wisely–almost placatingly under the circumstances–and Steger nodded.

"Quite right, Sheriff, quite right. You're quite right," and he drew out his purse while the sheriff led the way very cautiously back into his library.

"I'd like to show you the line of law-books I'm fixing up for myself in here, Mr. Steger," he observed, genially, but meanwhile closing his fingers gently on the small roll of ten-dollar bills Steger was handing him. "We have occasional use for books of that kind here, as you see. I thought it a good sort of thing to have them around." He waved one arm comprehensively at the line of State reports, revised statutes, prison regulations, etc., the while he put the money in his pocket and Steger pretended to look.

"A good idea, I think, Sheriff. Very good, indeed. So you think if Mr. Cowperwood gets around here very early Monday morning, say eight or eight-thirty, that it will be all right?"

"I think so," replied the sheriff, curiously nervous, but agreeable, anxious to please. "I don't think that anything will come up that will make me want him earlier. If it does I'll let you know, and you can produce him. I don't think so, though, Mr. Steger; I think everything will be all right." They were once more in the main hall now. "Glad to have seen you again, Mr. Steger–very glad," he added. "Call again some day."

Waving the sheriff a pleasant farewell, he hurried on his way to Cowperwood's house.

You would not have thought, seeing Cowperwood mount the front steps of his handsome residence in his neat gray suit and well-cut overcoat on his return from his office that evening, that he was thinking that this might be his last night here. His air and walk indicated no weakening of spirit. He entered the hall, where an early lamp was aglow, and encountered "Wash" Sims, an old negro factotum, who was just coming up from the basement, carrying a bucket of coal for one of the fireplaces.

"Mahty cold out, dis evenin', Mistah Coppahwood," said Wash, to whom anything less than sixty degrees was very cold. His one regret was that Philadelphia was not located in North Carolina, from whence he came.

"'Tis sharp, Wash," replied Cowperwood, absentmindedly. He was thinking for the moment of the house and how it had looked, as he came toward it west along Girard Avenue–what the neighbors were thinking of him, too, observing him from time to time out of their windows. It was clear and cold. The lamps in the reception-hall and sitting-room had been lit, for he had permitted no air of funereal gloom to settle down over this place since his troubles had begun. In the far west of the street a last tingling gleam of lavender and violet was showing over the cold white snow of the roadway. The house of gray-green stone, with its lighted windows, and cream-colored lace curtains, had looked especially attractive. He had thought for the moment of the pride he had taken in putting all this here, decorating and ornamenting it, and whether, ever, he could secure it for himself again. "Where is your mistress?" he added to Wash, when he bethought himself.

"In the sitting-room, Mr. Coppahwood, ah think."

Cowperwood ascended the stairs, thinking curiously that Wash would soon be out of a job now, unless Mrs. Cowperwood, out of all the wreck of other things, chose to retain him, which was not likely. He entered the sitting-room, and there sat his wife by the oblong center-table, sewing a hook and eye on one of Lillian, second's, petticoats. She looked up, at his step, with the peculiarly uncertain smile she used these days–indication of her pain, fear, suspicion–and inquired, "Well, what is new with you, Frank?" Her smile was something like a hat or belt or ornament which one puts on or off at will.

"Nothing in particular," he replied, in his offhand way, "except that I understand I have lost that appeal of mine. Steger is coming here in a little while to let me know. I had a note from him, and I fancy it's about that."

He did not care to say squarely that he had lost. He knew that she was sufficiently distressed as it was, and he did not care to be too abrupt just now.

"You don't say!" replied Lillian, with surprise and fright in her voice, and getting up.

She had been so used to a world where prisons were scarcely thought of, where things went on smoothly from day to day without any noticeable intrusion of such distressing things as courts, jails, and the like, that these last few months had driven her nearly mad. Cowperwood had so definitely insisted on her keeping in the background– he had told her so very little that she was all at sea anyhow in regard to the whole procedure. Nearly all that she had had in the way of intelligence had been from his father and mother and Anna, and from a close and almost secret scrutiny of the newspapers.

At the time he had gone to the county jail she did not even know anything about it until his father had come back from the court-room and the jail and had broken the news to her. It had been a terrific blow to her. Now to have this thing suddenly broken to her in this offhand way, even though she had been expecting and dreading it hourly, was too much.

She was still a decidedly charming-looking woman as she stood holding her daughter's garment in her hand, even if she was forty years old to Cowperwood's thirty-five. She was robed in one of the creations of their late prosperity, a cream-colored gown of rich silk, with dark brown trimmings–a fetching combination for her. Her eyes were a little hollow, and reddish about the rims, but otherwise she showed no sign of her keen mental distress. There was considerable evidence of the former tranquil sweetness that had so fascinated him ten years before.

"Isn't that terrible?" she said, weakly, her hands trembling in a nervous way. "Isn't it dreadful? Isn't there anything more you can do, truly? You won't really have to go to prison, will you?" He objected to her distress and her nervous fears. He preferred a stronger, more self-reliant type of woman, but still she was his wife, and in his day he had loved her much.

"It looks that way, Lillian," he said, with the first note of real sympathy he had used in a long while, for he felt sorry for her now. At the same time he was afraid to go any further along that line, for fear it might give her a false sense as to his present attitude toward her which was one essentially of indifference. But she was not so dull but what she could see that the consideration in his voice had been brought about by his defeat, which meant hers also. She choked a little–and even so was touched. The bare suggestion of sympathy brought back the old days so definitely gone forever. If only they could be brought back!

"I don't want you to feel distressed about me, though," he went on, before she could say anything to him. "I'm not through with my fighting. I'll get out of this. I have to go to prison, it seems, in order to get things straightened out properly. What I would like you to do is to keep up a cheerful appearance in front of the rest of the family–father and mother particularly. They need to be cheered up." He thought once of taking her hand, then decided not. She noted mentally his hesitation, the great difference between his attitude now and that of ten or twelve years before. It did not hurt her now as much as she once would have thought. She looked at him, scarcely knowing what to say. There was really not so much to say.

"Will you have to go soon, if you do have to go?" she ventured, wearily.

"I can't tell yet. Possibly to-night. Possibly Friday. Possibly not until Monday. I'm waiting to hear from Steger. I expect him here any minute."

To prison! To prison! Her Frank Cowperwood, her husband–the substance of their home here–and all their soul destruction going to prison. And even now she scarcely grasped why! She stood there wondering what she could do.

"Is there anything I can get for you?" she asked, starting forward as if out of a dream. "Do you want me to do anything? Don't you think perhaps you had better leave Philadelphia, Frank? You needn't go to prison unless you want to."

She was a little beside herself, for the first time in her life shocked out of a deadly calm.

He paused and looked at her for a moment in his direct, examining way, his hard commercial business judgment restored on the instant.

"That would be a confession of guilt, Lillian, and I'm not guilty," he replied, almost coldly. "I haven't done anything that warrants my running away or going to prison, either. I'm merely going there to save time at present. I can't be litigating this thing forever. I'll get out–be pardoned out or sued out in a reasonable length of time. Just now it's better to go, I think. I wouldn't think of running away from Philadelphia. Two of five judges found for me in the decision. That's pretty fair evidence that the State has no case against me."

His wife saw she had made a mistake. It clarified her judgment on the instant. "I didn't mean in that way, Frank," she replied, apologetically. "You know I didn't. Of course I know you're not guilty. Why should I think you were, of all people?"

She paused, expecting some retort, some further argument–a kind word maybe. A trace of the older, baffling love, but he had quietly turned to his desk and was thinking of other things.

At this point the anomaly of her own state came over her again. It was all so sad and so hopeless. And what was she to do in the future? And what was he likely to do? She paused half trembling and yet decided, because of her peculiarly nonresisting nature–why trespass on his time? Why bother? No good would really come of it. He really did not care for her any more–that was it. Nothing could make him, nothing could bring them together again, not even this tragedy. He was interested in another woman–Aileen–and so her foolish thoughts and explanations, her fear, sorrow, distress, were not important to him. He could take her agonized wish for his freedom as a comment on his probable guilt, a doubt of his innocence, a criticism of him! She turned away for a minute, and he started to leave the room.

"I'll be back again in a few moments," he volunteered. "Are the children here?"

"Yes, they're up in the play-room," she answered, sadly, utterly nonplussed and distraught.

"Oh, Frank!" she had it on her lips to cry, but before she could utter it he had bustled down the steps and was gone. She turned back to the table, her left hand to her mouth, her eyes in a queer, hazy, melancholy mist. Could it be, she thought, that life could really come to this–that love could so utterly, so thoroughly die? Ten years before–but, oh, why go back to that? Obviously it could, and thoughts concerning that would not help now. Twice now in her life her affairs had seemed to go to pieces–once when her first husband had died, and now when her second had failed her, had fallen in love with another and was going to be sent off to prison. What was it about her that caused such things? Was there anything wrong with her? What was she going to do? Where go? She had no idea, of course, for how long a term of years he would be sent away. It might be one year or it might be five years, as the papers had said. Good heavens! The children could almost come to forget him in five years. She put her other hand to her mouth, also, and then to her forehead, where there was a dull ache. She tried to think further than this, but somehow, just now, there was no further thought. Suddenly quite outside of her own volition, with no thought that she was going to do such a thing, her bosom began to heave, her throat contracted in four or five short, sharp, aching spasms, her eyes burned, and she shook in a vigorous, anguished, desperate, almost one might have said dry-eyed, cry, so hot and few were the tears. She could not stop for the moment, just stood there and shook, and then after a while a dull ache succeeded, and she was quite as she had been before.

"Why cry?" she suddenly asked herself, fiercely–for her. "Why break down in this stormy, useless way? Would it help?"

But, in spite of her speculative, philosophic observations to herself, she still felt the echo, the distant rumble, as it were, of the storm in her own soul. "Why cry? Why not cry?" She might have said–but wouldn't, and in spite of herself and all her logic, she knew that this tempest which had so recently raged over her was now merely circling around her soul's horizon and would return to break again.

Chapter L

The arrival of Steger with the information that no move of any kind would be made by the sheriff until Monday morning, when Cowperwood could present himself, eased matters. This gave him time to think–to adjust home details at his leisure. He broke the news to his father and mother in a consoling way and talked with his brothers and father about getting matters immediately adjusted in connection with the smaller houses to which they were now shortly to be compelled to move. There was much conferring among the different members of this collapsing organization in regard to the minor details; and what with his conferences with Steger, his seeing personally Davison, Leigh, Avery Stone, of Jay Cooke Co., George Waterman (his old-time employer Henry was dead), ex-State Treasurer Van Nostrand, who had gone out with the last State administration, and others, he was very busy. Now that he was really going into prison, he wanted his financial friends to get together and see if they could get him out by appealing to the Governor. The division of opinion among the judges of the State Supreme Court was his excuse and strong point. He wanted Steger to follow this up, and he spared no pains in trying to see all and sundry who might be of use to him–Edward Tighe, of Tighe Co., who was still in business in Third Street; Newton Targool; Arthur Rivers; Joseph Zimmerman, the dry-goods prince, now a millionaire; Judge Kitchen; Terrence Relihan, the former representative of the money element at Harrisburg; and many others.

Cowperwood wanted Relihan to approach the newspapers and see if he could not readjust their attitude so as to work to get him out, and he wanted Walter Leigh to head the movement of getting up a signed petition which should contain all the important names of moneyed people and others, asking the Governor to release him. Leigh agreed to this heartily, as did Relihan, and many others.

And, afterwards there was really nothing else to do, unless it was to see Aileen once more, and this, in the midst of his other complications and obligations, seemed all but impossible at times–and yet he did achieve that, too–so eager was he to be soothed and comforted by the ignorant and yet all embracing volume of her love. Her eyes these days! The eager, burning quest of him and his happiness that blazed in them. To think that he should be tortured so–her Frank! Oh, she knew–whatever he said, and however bravely and jauntily he talked. To think that her love for him should have been the principal cause of his being sent to jail, as she now believed. And the cruelty of her father! And the smallness of his enemies–that fool Stener, for instance, whose pictures she had seen in the papers. Actually, whenever in the presence of her Frank, she fairly seethed in a chemic agony for him–her strong, handsome lover–the strongest, bravest, wisest, kindest, handsomest man in the world. Oh, didn't she know! And Cowperwood, looking in her eyes and realizing this reasonless, if so comforting fever for him, smiled and was touched. Such love! That of a dog for a master; that of a mother for a child. And how had he come to evoke it? He could not say, but it was beautiful.

And so, now, in these last trying hours, he wished to see her much–and did–meeting her at least four times in the month in which he had been free, between his conviction and the final dismissal of his appeal. He had one last opportunity of seeing her–and she him–just before his entrance into prison this last time–on the Saturday before the Monday of his sentence. He had not come in contact with her since the decision of the Supreme Court had been rendered, but he had had a letter from her sent to a private mail-box, and had made an appointment for Saturday at a small hotel in Camden, which, being across the river, was safer, in his judgment, than anything in Philadelphia. He was a little uncertain as to how she would take the possibility of not seeing him soon again after Monday, and how she would act generally once he was where she could not confer with him as often as she chose. And in consequence, he was anxious to talk to her. But on this occasion, as he anticipated, and even feared, so sorry for her was he, she was not less emphatic in her protestations than she had ever been; in fact, much more so. When she saw him approaching in the distance, she went forward to meet him in that direct, forceful way which only she could attempt with him, a sort of mannish impetuosity which he both enjoyed and admired, and slipping her arms around his neck, said: "Honey, you needn't tell me. I saw it in the papers the other morning. Don't you mind, honey. I love you. I'll wait for you. I'll be with you yet, if it takes a dozen years of waiting. It doesn't make any difference to me if it takes a hundred, only I'm so sorry for you, sweetheart. I'll be with you every day through this, darling, loving you with all my might."

She caressed him while he looked at her in that quiet way which betokened at once his self-poise and yet his interest and satisfaction in her. He couldn't help loving Aileen, he thought who could? She was so passionate, vibrant, desireful. He couldn't help admiring her tremendously, now more than ever, because literally, in spite of all his intellectual strength, he really could not rule her. She went at him, even when he stood off in a calm, critical way, as if he were her special property, her toy. She would talk to him always, and particularly when she was excited, as if he were just a baby, her pet; and sometimes he felt as though she would really overcome him mentally, make him subservient to her, she was so individual, so sure of her importance as a woman.

Now on this occasion she went babbling on as if he were broken-hearted, in need of her greatest care and tenderness, although he really wasn't at all; and for the moment she actually made him feel as though he was.

"It isn't as bad as that, Aileen," he ventured to say, eventually; and with a softness and tenderness almost unusual for him, even where she was concerned, but she went on forcefully, paying no heed to him.

"Oh, yes, it is, too, honey. I know. Oh, my poor Frank! But I'll see you. I know how to manage, whatever happens. How often do they let visitors come out to see the prisoners there?"

"Only once in three months, pet, so they say, but I think we can fix that after I get there; only do you think you had better try to come right away, Aileen? You know what the feeling now is. Hadn't you better wait a while? Aren't you in danger of stirring up your father? He might cause a lot of trouble out there if he were so minded."

"Only once in three months!" she exclaimed, with rising emphasis, as he began this explanation. "Oh, Frank, no! Surely not! Once in three months! Oh, I can't stand that! I won't! I'll go and see the warden myself. He'll let me see you. I'm sure he will, if I talk to him."

She fairly gasped in her excitement, not willing to pause in her tirade, but Cowperwood interposed with her, "You're not thinking what you're saying, Aileen. You're not thinking. Remember your father! Remember your family! Your father may know the warden out there. You don't want it to get all over town that you're running out there to see me, do you? Your father might cause you trouble. Besides you don't know the small party politicians as I do. They gossip like a lot of old women. You'll have to be very careful what you do and how you do it. I don't want to lose you. I want to see you. But you'll have to mind what you're doing. Don't try to see me at once. I want you to, but I want to find out how the land lies, and I want you to find out too. You won't lose me. I'll be there, well enough."

He paused as he thought of the long tier of iron cells which must be there, one of which would be his–for how long?–and of Aileen seeing him through the door of it or in it. At the same time he was thinking, in spite of all his other calculations, how charming she was looking to-day. How young she kept, and how forceful! While he was nearing his full maturity she was a comparatively young girl, and as beautiful as ever. She was wearing a black-and-white-striped silk in the curious bustle style of the times, and a set of sealskin furs, including a little sealskin cap set jauntily on top her red-gold hair.

"I know, I know," replied Aileen, firmly. "But think of three months! Honey, I can't! I won't! It's nonsense. Three months! I know that my father wouldn't have to wait any three months if he wanted to see anybody out there, nor anybody else that he wanted to ask favors for. And I won't, either. I'll find some way."

Cowperwood had to smile. You could not defeat Aileen so easily.

"But you're not your father, honey; and you don't want him to know."

"I know I don't, but they don't need to know who I am. I can go heavily veiled. I don't think that the warden knows my father. He may. Anyhow, he doesn't know me; and he wouldn't tell on me if he did if I talked to him."

Her confidence in her charms, her personality, her earthly privileges was quite anarchistic. Cowperwood shook his head.

"Honey, you're about the best and the worst there is when it comes to a woman," he observed, affectionately, pulling her head down to kiss her, "but you'll have to listen to me just the same. I have a lawyer, Steger–you know him. He's going to take up this matter with the warden out there–is doing it today. He may be able to fix things, and he may not. I'll know to-morrow or Sunday, and I'll write you. But don't go and do anything rash until you hear. I'm sure I can cut that visiting limit in half, and perhaps down to once a month or once in two weeks even. They only allow me to write one letter in three months"–Aileen exploded again–"and I'm sure I can have that made different–some; but don't write me until you hear, or at least don't sign any name or put any address in. They open all mail and read it. If you see me or write me you'll have to be cautious, and you're not the most cautious person in the world. Now be good, will you?"

They talked much more–of his family, his court appearance Monday, whether he would get out soon to attend any of the suits still pending, or be pardoned. Aileen still believed in his future. She had read the opinions of the dissenting judges in his favor, and that of the three agreed judges against him. She was sure his day was not over in Philadelphia, and that he would some time reestablish himself and then take her with him somewhere else. She was sorry for Mrs. Cowperwood, but she was convinced that she was not suited to him–that Frank needed some one more like herself, some one with youth and beauty and force–her, no less. She clung to him now in ecstatic embraces until it was time to go. So far as a plan of procedure could have been adjusted in a situation so incapable of accurate adjustment, it had been done. She was desperately downcast at the last moment, as was he, over their parting; but she pulled herself together with her usual force and faced the dark future with a steady eye.

Chapter LI

Monday came and with it his final departure. All that could be done had been done. Cowperwood said his farewells to his mother and father, his brothers and sister. He had a rather distant but sensible and matter-of-fact talk with his wife. He made no special point of saying good-by to his son or his daughter; when he came in on Thursday, Friday, Saturday, and Sunday evenings, after he had learned that he was to depart Monday, it was with the thought of talking to them a little in an especially affectionate way. He realized that his general moral or unmoral attitude was perhaps working them a temporary injustice. Still he was not sure. Most people did fairly well with their lives, whether coddled or deprived of opportunity. These children would probably do as well as most children, whatever happened—and then, anyhow, he had no intention of forsaking them financially, if he could help it. He did not want to separate his wife from her children, nor them from her. She should keep them. He wanted them to be comfortable with her. He would like to see them, wherever they were with her, occasionally. Only he wanted his own personal freedom, in so far as she and they were concerned, to go off and set up a new world and a new home with Aileen. So now on these last days, and particularly this last Sunday night, he was rather noticeably considerate of his boy and girl, without being too openly indicative of his approaching separation from them.

"Frank," he said to his notably lackadaisical son on this occasion, "aren't you going to straighten up and be a big, strong, healthy fellow? You don't play enough. You ought to get in with a gang of boys and be a leader. Why don't you fit yourself up a gymnasium somewhere and see how strong you can get?"

They were in the senior Cowperwood's sitting-room, where they had all rather consciously gathered on this occasion.

Lillian, second, who was on the other side of the big library table from her father, paused to survey him and her brother with interest. Both had been carefully guarded against any real knowledge of their father's affairs or his present predicament. He was going away on a journey for about a month or so they understood. Lillian was reading in a Chatterbox book which had been given her the previous Christmas.

"He won't do anything," she volunteered, looking up from her reading in a peculiarly critical way for her. "Why, he won't ever run races with me when I want him to."

"Aw, who wants to run races with you, anyhow?" returned Frank, junior, sourly. "You couldn't run if I did want to run with you."

"Couldn't I?" she replied. "I could beat you, all right."

"Lillian!" pleaded her mother, with a warning sound in her voice.

Cowperwood smiled, and laid his hand affectionately on his son's head. "You'll be all right, Frank," he volunteered, pinching his ear lightly. "Don't worry—just make an effort."

The boy did not respond as warmly as he hoped. Later in the evening Mrs. Cowperwood noticed that her husband squeezed his daughter's slim little waist and pulled her curly hair gently. For the moment she was jealous of her daughter.

"Going to be the best kind of a girl while I'm away?" he said to her, privately.

"Yes, papa," she replied, brightly.

"That's right," he returned, and leaned over and kissed her mouth tenderly. "Button Eyes," he said.

Mrs. Cowperwood sighed after he had gone. "Everything for the children, nothing for me," she thought, though the children had not got so vastly much either in the past.

Cowperwood's attitude toward his mother in this final hour was about as tender and sympathetic as any he could maintain in this world. He understood quite clearly the ramifications of her interests, and how she was suffering for him and all the others concerned. He had not forgotten her sympathetic care of him in his youth; and if he could have done anything to have spared her this unhappy breakdown of her fortunes in her old age, he would have done so. There was no use crying over spilled milk. It was impossible at times for him not to feel intensely in moments of success or failure; but the proper thing to do was to bear up, not to show it, to talk little and go your way with an air not so much of resignation as of self-sufficiency, to whatever was awaiting you. That was his attitude on this morning, and that was what he expected from those around him–almost compelled, in fact, by his own attitude.

"Well, mother," he said, genially, at the last moment–he would not let her nor his wife nor his sister come to court, maintaining that it would make not the least difference to him and would only harrow their own feelings uselessly–"I'm going now. Don't worry. Keep up your spirits."

He slipped his arm around his mother's waist, and she gave him a long, unrestrained, despairing embrace and kiss.

"Go on, Frank," she said, choking, when she let him go. "God bless you. I'll pray for you." He paid no further attention to her. He didn't dare.

"Good-by, Lillian," he said to his wife, pleasantly, kindly. "I'll be back in a few days, I think. I'll be coming out to attend some of these court proceedings."

To his sister he said: "Good-by, Anna. Don't let the others get too down-hearted."

"I'll see you three afterward," he said to his father and brothers; and so, dressed in the very best fashion of the time, he hurried down into the reception-hall, where Steger was waiting, and was off. His family, hearing the door close on him, suffered a poignant sense of desolation. They stood there for a moment, his mother crying, his father looking as though he had lost his last friend but making a great effort to seem self-contained and equal to his troubles, Anna telling Lillian not to mind, and the latter staring dumbly into the future, not knowing what to think. Surely a brilliant sun had set on their local scene, and in a very pathetic way.

Chapter LII

When Cowperwood reached the jail, Jaspers was there, glad to see him but principally relieved to feel that nothing had happened to mar his own reputation as a sheriff. Because of the urgency of court matters generally, it was decided to depart for the courtroom at nine o'clock. Eddie Zanders was once more delegated to see that Cowperwood was brought safely before Judge Payderson and afterward taken to the penitentiary. All of the papers in the case were put in his care to be delivered to the warden.

"I suppose you know," confided Sheriff Jaspers to Steger, "that Stener is here. He ain't got no money now, but I gave him a private room just the same. I didn't want to put a man like him in no cell." Sheriff Jaspers sympathized with Stener.

"That's right. I'm glad to hear that," replied Steger, smiling to himself.

"I didn't suppose from what I've heard that Mr. Cowperwood would want to meet Stener here, so I've kept 'em apart. George just left a minute ago with another deputy."

"That's good. That's the way it ought to be," replied Steger. He was glad for Cowperwood's sake that the sheriff had so much tact. Evidently George and the sheriff were getting along in a very friendly way, for all the former's bitter troubles and lack of means.

The Cowperwood party walked, the distance not being great, and as they did so they talked of rather simple things to avoid the more serious.

"Things aren't going to be so bad," Edward said to his father. "Steger says the Governor is sure to pardon Stener in a year or less, and if he does he's bound to let Frank out too."

Cowperwood, the elder, had heard this over and over, but he was never tired of hearing it. It was like some simple croon with which babies are hushed to sleep. The snow on the ground, which was enduring remarkably well for this time of year, the fineness of the day, which had started out to be clear and bright, the hope that the courtroom might not be full, all held the attention of the father and his two sons. Cowperwood, senior, even commented on some sparrows fighting over a piece of bread, marveling how well they did in winter, solely to ease his mind. Cowperwood, walking on ahead with Steger and Zanders, talked of approaching court proceedings in connection with his business and what ought to be done.

When they reached the court the same little pen in which Cowperwood had awaited the verdict of his jury several months before was waiting to receive him.

Cowperwood, senior, and his other sons sought places in the courtroom proper. Eddie Zanders remained with his charge. Stener and a deputy by the name of Wilkerson were in the room; but he and Cowperwood pretended now not to see each other. Frank had no objection to talking to his former associate, but he could see that Stener was diffident and ashamed. So he let the situation pass without look or word of any kind. After some three-quarters of an hour of dreary waiting the door leading into the courtroom proper opened and a bailiff stepped in.

"All prisoners up for sentence," he called.

There were six, all told, including Cowperwood and Stener. Two of them were confederate housebreakers who had been caught red-handed at their midnight task.

Another prisoner was no more and no less than a plain horse-thief, a young man of twenty-six, who had been convicted by a jury of stealing a grocer's horse and selling it. The last man was a negro, a tall, shambling, illiterate, nebulous-minded black, who had walked off with an apparently discarded section of lead pipe which he had found in a lumber-yard. His idea was to sell or trade it for a drink. He really did not belong in this court at all; but, having been caught by an undersized American watchman charged with the care of the property, and having at first refused to plead guilty, not quite understanding what was to be done with him, he had been perforce bound over to this court for trial. Afterward he had changed his mind and admitted his guilt, so he now had to come before Judge Payderson for sentence or dismissal. The lower court before which he had originally been brought had lost jurisdiction by binding him over to to higher court for trial. Eddie Zanders, in his self-appointed position as guide and mentor to Cowperwood, had confided nearly all of this data to him as he stood waiting.

The courtroom was crowded. It was very humiliating to Cowperwood to have to file in this way along the side aisle with these others, followed by Stener, well dressed but sickly looking and disconsolate.

The negro, Charles Ackerman, was the first on the list.

"How is it this man comes before me?" asked Payderson, peevishly, when he noted the value of the property Ackerman was supposed to have stolen.

"Your honor," the assistant district attorney explained, promptly, "this man was before a lower court and refused, because he was drunk, or something, to plead guilty. The lower court, because the complainant would not forego the charge, was compelled to bind him over to this court for trial. Since then he has changed his mind and has admitted his guilt to the district attorney. He would not be brought before you except we have no alternative. He has to be brought here now in order to clear the calendar."

Judge Payderson stared quizzically at the negro, who, obviously not very much disturbed by this examination, was leaning comfortably on the gate or bar before which the average criminal stood erect and terrified. He had been before police-court magistrates before on one charge and another–drunkenness, disorderly conduct, and the like–but his whole attitude was one of shambling, lackadaisical, amusing innocence.

"Well, Ackerman," inquired his honor, severely, "did you or did you not steal this piece of lead pipe as charged here–four dollars and eighty cents' worth?"

"Yassah, I did," he began. "I tell you how it was, jedge. I was a-comin' along past dat lumber-yard one Saturday afternoon, and I hadn't been wuckin', an' I saw dat piece o' pipe thoo de fence, lyin' inside, and I jes' reached thoo with a piece o' boad I found dey and pulled it over to me an' tuck it. An' aftahwahd dis Mistah Watchman man"–he waved his hand oratorically toward the witness-chair, where, in case the judge might wish to ask him some questions, the complainant had taken his stand–"come around tuh where I live an' accused me of done takin' it."

"But you did take it, didn't you?"

"Yassah, I done tuck it."

"What did you do with it?"

"I traded it foh twenty-five cents."

"You mean you sold it," corrected his honor.

"Yassah, I done sold it."

"Well, don't you know it's wrong to do anything like that? Didn't you know when you reached through that fence and pulled that pipe over to you that you were stealing? Didn't you?"

"Yassah, I knowed it was wrong," replied Ackerman, sheepishly. "I didn' think 'twuz stealin' like zackly, but I done knowed it was wrong. I done knowed I oughtn' take it, I guess."

"Of course you did. Of course you did. That's just it. You knew you were stealing, and still you took it. Has the man to whom this negro sold the lead pipe been apprehended yet?" the judge inquired sharply of the district attorney. "He should be, for he's more guilty than this negro, a receiver of stolen goods."

"Yes, sir," replied the assistant. "His case is before Judge Yawger."

"Quite right. It should be," replied Payderson, severely. "This matter of receiving stolen property is one of the worst offenses, in my judgment."

He then turned his attention to Ackerman again. "Now, look here, Ackerman," he exclaimed, irritated at having to bother with such a pretty case, "I want to say something to you, and I want you to pay strict attention to me. Straighten up, there! Don't lean on that gate! You are in the presence of the law now." Ackerman had sprawled himself comfortably down on his elbows as he would have if he had been leaning over a back-fence gate talking to some one, but he immediately drew himself straight, still grinning foolishly and apologetically, when he heard this. "You are not so dull but that you can understand what I am going to say to you. The offense you have committed–stealing a piece of lead pipe–is a crime. Do you hear me? A criminal offense–one that I could punish you very severely for. I could send you to the penitentiary for one year if I chose–the law says I may–one year at hard labor for stealing a piece of lead pipe. Now, if you have any sense you will pay strict attention to what I am going to tell you. I am not going to send you to the penitentiary right now. I'm going to wait a little while. I am going to sentence you to one year in the penitentiary–one year. Do you understand?" Ackerman blanched a little and licked his lips nervously. "And then I am going to suspend that sentence–hold it over your head, so that if you are ever caught taking anything else you will be punished for this offense and the next one also at one and the same time. Do you understand that? Do you know what I mean? Tell me. Do you?"

"Yessah! I does, sir," replied the negro. "You'se gwine to let me go now–tha's it."

The audience grinned, and his honor made a wry face to prevent his own grim grin.

"I'm going to let you go only so long as you don't steal anything else," he thundered. "The moment you steal anything else, back you come to this court, and then you go to the penitentiary for a year and whatever more time you deserve. Do you understand that? Now, I want you to walk straight out of this court and behave yourself. Don't ever steal anything. Get something to do! Don't steal, do you hear? Don't touch anything that doesn't belong to you! Don't come back here! If you do, I'll send you to the penitentiary, sure."

"Yassah! No, sah, I won't," replied Ackerman, nervously. "I won't take nothin' more that don't belong tuh me."

He shuffled away, after a moment, urged along by the guiding hand of a bailiff, and was put safely outside the court, amid a mixture of smiles and laughter over his simplicity and Payderson's undue severity of manner. But the next case was called and soon engrossed the interest of the audience.

It was that of the two housebreakers whom Cowperwood had been and was still studying with much curiosity. In all his life before he had never witnessed a sentencing scene of any kind. He had never been in police or criminal courts of any kind–rarely in any of the civil ones. He was glad to see the negro go, and gave Payderson credit for having some sense and sympathy–more than he had expected.

He wondered now whether by any chance Aileen was here. He had objected to her coming, but she might have done so. She was, as a matter of fact, in the extreme rear, pocketed in a crowd near the door, heavily veiled, but present. She had not been able to resist the desire to know quickly and surely her beloved's fate–to be near him in his hour of real suffering, as she thought. She was greatly angered at seeing him brought in with a line of ordinary criminals and made to wait in this, to her, shameful public manner, but she could not help admiring all the more the dignity and superiority of his presence even here. He was not even pale, as she saw, just the same firm, calm soul she had always known him to be. If he could only see her now; if he would only look so she could lift her veil and smile! He didn't, though; he wouldn't. He didn't want to see her here. But she would tell him all about it when she saw him again just the same.

The two burglars were quickly disposed of by the judge, with a sentence of one year each, and they were led away, uncertain, and apparently not knowing what to think of their crime or their future.

When it came to Cowperwood's turn to be called, his honor himself stiffened and straightened up, for this was a different type of man and could not be handled in the usual manner. He knew exactly what he was going to say. When one of Mollenhauer's agents, a close friend of Butler's, had suggested that five years for both Cowperwood and Stener would be about right, he knew exactly what to do. "Frank Algernon Cowperwood," called the clerk.

Cowperwood stepped briskly forward, sorry for himself, ashamed of his position in a way, but showing it neither in look nor manner. Payderson eyed him as he had the others.

"Name?" asked the bailiff, for the benefit of the court stenographer.

"Frank Algernon Cowperwood."

"Residence?"

"1937 Girard Avenue."

"Occupation?"

"Banker and broker."

Steger stood close beside him, very dignified, very forceful, ready to make a final statement for the benefit of the court and the public when the time should come. Aileen, from her position in the crowd near the door, was for the first time in her life biting her fingers nervously and there were great beads of perspiration on her brow. Cowperwood's father was tense with excitement and his two brothers looked quickly away, doing their best to hide their fear and sorrow.

"Ever convicted before?"

"Never," replied Steger for Cowperwood, quietly.

"Frank Algernon Cowperwood," called the clerk, in his nasal, singsong way, coming forward, "have you anything to say why judgment should not now be pronounced upon you? If so, speak."

Cowperwood started to say no, but Steger put up his hand.

"If the court pleases, my client, Mr. Cowperwood, the prisoner at the bar, is neither guilty in his own estimation, nor in that of two-fifths of the Pennsylvania State Supreme Court–the court of last resort in this State," he exclaimed, loudly and clearly, so that all might hear.

One of the interested listeners and spectators at this point was Edward Malia Butler, who had just stepped in from another courtroom where he had been talking to a judge. An obsequious court attendant had warned him that Cowperwood was about to be sentenced. He had really come here this morning in order not to miss this sentence, but he cloaked his motive under the guise of another errand. He did not know that Aileen was there, nor did he see her.

"As he himself testified at the time of his trial," went on Steger, "and as the evidence clearly showed, he was never more than an agent for the gentleman whose offense was subsequently adjudicated by this court; and as an agent he still maintains, and two-fifths of the State Supreme Court agree with him, that he was strictly within his rights and privileges in not having deposited the sixty thousand dollars' worth of city loan certificates at the time, and in the manner which the people, acting through the district attorney, complained that he should have. My client is a man of rare financial ability. By the various letters which have been submitted to your honor in his behalf, you will see that he commands the respect and the sympathy of a large majority of the most forceful and eminent men in his particular world. He is a man of distinguished social standing and of notable achievements. Only the most unheralded and the unkindest thrust of fortune has brought him here before you today–a fire and its consequent panic which involved a financial property of the most thorough and stable character. In spite of the verdict of the jury and the decision of three-fifths of the State Supreme Court, I maintain that my client is not an embezzler, that he has not committed larceny, that he should never have been convicted, and that he should not now be punished for something of which he is not guilty.

"I trust that your honor will not misunderstand me or my motives when I point out in this situation that what I have said is true. I do not wish to cast any reflection on the integrity of the court, nor of any court, nor of any of the processes of law. But I do condemn and deplore the untoward chain of events which has built up a seeming situation, not easily understood by the lay mind, and which has brought my distinguished client within the purview of the law. I think it is but fair that this should be finally and publicly stated here and now. I ask that your honor be lenient, and that if you cannot conscientiously dismiss this charge you will at least see that the facts, as I have indicated them, are given due weight in the measure of the punishment inflicted."

Steger stepped back and Judge Payderson nodded, as much as to say he had heard all the distinguished lawyer had to say, and would give it such consideration as it deserved–no more. Then he turned to Cowperwood, and, summoning all his judicial dignity to his aid, he began:

"Frank Algernon Cowperwood, you have been convicted by a jury of your own selection of the offense of larceny. The motion for a new trial, made in your behalf by your learned counsel, has been carefully considered and overruled, the majority of the court being entirely satisfied with the propriety of the conviction, both upon the law and the evidence. Your offense was one of more than usual gravity, the more so that the large amount of money which you obtained belonged to the city. And it was aggravated by the fact that you had in addition thereto unlawfully used and converted to your own use several hundred thousand dollars of the loan and money of the city. For such an offense the maximum punishment affixed by the law is singularly merciful. Nevertheless, the facts in connection with your hitherto distinguished position, the circumstances under which your failure was brought about, and the appeals of your numerous friends and financial associates, will be given due consideration by this court. It is not unmindful of any important fact in your career." Payderson paused as if in doubt, though he knew very well how he was about to proceed. He knew what his superiors expected of him.

"If your case points no other moral," he went on, after a moment, toying with the briefs, "it will at least teach the lesson much needed at the present time, that the treasury of the city is not to be invaded and plundered with impunity under the thin disguise of a business transaction, and that there is still a power in the law to vindicate itself and to protect the public.

"The sentence of the court," he added, solemnly, the while Cowperwood gazed unmoved, "is, therefore, that you pay a fine of five thousand dollars to the common-wealth for the use of the county, that you pay the costs of prosecution, and that you undergo imprisonment in the State Penitentiary for the Eastern District by separate or solitary confinement at labor for a period of four years and three months, and that you stand committed until this sentence is complied with."

Cowperwood's father, on hearing this, bowed his head to hide his tears. Aileen bit her lower lip and clenched her hands to keep down her rage and disappointment and tears. Four years and three months! That would make a terrible gap in his life and hers. Still, she could wait. It was better than eight or ten years, as she had feared it might be. Perhaps now, once this was really over and he was in prison, the Governor would pardon him.

The judge now moved to pick up the papers in connection with Stener's case, satisfied that he had given the financiers no chance to say he had not given due heed to their plea in Cowperwood's behalf and yet certain that the politicians would be pleased that he had so nearly given Cowperwood the maximum while appearing to have heeded the pleas for mercy. Cowperwood saw through the trick at once, but it did not disturb him. It struck him as rather weak and contemptible. A bailiff came forward and started to hurry him away.

"Allow the prisoner to remain for a moment," called the judge.

The name, of George W. Stener had been called by the clerk and Cowperwood did not quite understand why he was being detained, but he soon learned. It was that he might hear the opinion of the court in connection with his copartner in crime. The latter's record was taken. Roger O'Mara, the Irish political lawyer who had been his counsel all through his troubles, stood near him, but had nothing to say beyond asking the judge to consider Stener's previously honorable career.

"George W. Stener," said his honor, while the audience, including Cowperwood, listened attentively. "The motion for a new trial as well as an arrest of judgment in your case having been overruled, it remains for the court to impose such sentence as the nature of your offense requires. I do not desire to add to the pain of your position by any extended remarks of my own; but I cannot let the occasion pass without expressing my emphatic condemnation of your offense. The misapplication of public money has become the great crime of the age. If not promptly and firmly checked, it will ultimately destroy our institutions. When a republic becomes honeycombed with corruption its vitality is gone. It must crumble upon the first pressure.

"In my opinion, the public is much to blame for your offense and others of a similar character. Heretofore, official fraud has been regarded with too much indifference. What we need is a higher and purer political morality–a state of public opinion which would make the improper use of public money a thing to be execrated. It was the lack of this which made your offense possible. Beyond that I see nothing of extenuation in your case." Judge Payderson paused for emphasis. He was coming to his finest flight, and he wanted it to sink in.

"The people had confided to you the care of their money," he went on, solemnly. "It was a high, a sacred trust. You should have guarded the door of the treasury even as the cherubim protected the Garden of Eden, and should have turned the flaming sword of impeccable honesty against every one who approached it improperly. Your position as the representative of a great community warranted that.

"In view of all the facts in your case the court can do no less than impose a major penalty. The seventy-fourth section of the Criminal Procedure Act provides that no convict shall be sentenced by the court of this commonwealth to either of the penitentiaries thereof, for any term which shall expire between the fifteenth of November and the fifteenth day of February of any year, and this provision requires me to abate three months from the maximum of time which I would affix in your case–namely, five years. The sentence of the court is, therefore, that you pay a fine of five thousand dollars to the commonwealth for the use of the county"–Payderson knew well enough that Stener could never pay that sum–"and that you undergo imprisonment in the State Penitentiary for the Eastern District, by separate and solitary confinement at labor, for the period of four years and nine months, and that you stand committed until this sentence is complied with." He laid down the briefs and rubbed his chin reflectively while both Cowperwood and Stener were hurried out. Butler was the first to leave after the sentence–quite satisfied. Seeing that all was over so far as she was concerned, Aileen stole quickly out; and after her, in a few moments, Cowperwood's father and brothers. They were to await him outside and go with him to the penitentiary. The remaining members of the family were at home eagerly awaiting intelligence of the morning's work, and Joseph Cowperwood was at once despatched to tell them.

The day had now become cloudy, lowery, and it looked as if there might be snow. Eddie Zanders, who had been given all the papers in the case, announced that there was no need to return to the county jail. In consequence the five of them–Zanders, Steger, Cowperwood, his father, and Edward–got into a street-car which ran to within a few blocks of the prison. Within half an hour they were at the gates of the Eastern Penitentiary.

Chapter LIII

The Eastern District Penitentiary of Pennsylvania, standing at Fairmount Avenue and Twenty-first Street in Philadelphia, where Cowperwood was now to serve his sentence of four years and three months, was a large, gray-stone structure, solemn and momentous in its mien, not at all unlike the palace of Sforzas at Milan, although not so distinguished. It stretched its gray length for several blocks along four different streets, and looked as lonely and forbidding as a prison should. The wall which inclosed its great area extending over ten acres and gave it so much of its solemn dignity was thirty-five feet high and some seven feet thick. The prison proper, which was not visible from the outside, consisted of seven arms or corridors, ranged octopus-like around a central room or court, and occupying in their sprawling length about two-thirds of the yard inclosed within the walls, so that there was but little space for the charm of lawn or sward. The corridors, forty-two feet wide from outer wall to outer wall, were one hundred and eighty feet in length, and in four instances two stories high, and extended in their long reach in every direction. There were no windows in the corridors, only narrow slits of skylights, three and one-half feet long by perhaps eight inches wide, let in the roof; and the ground-floor cells were accompanied in some instances by a small yard ten by sixteen–the same size as the cells proper–which was surrounded by a high brick wall in every instance. The cells and floors and roofs were made of stone, and the corridors, which were only ten feet wide between the cells, and in the case of the single-story portion only fifteen feet high, were paved with stone. If you stood in the central room, or rotunda, and looked down the long stretches which departed from you in every direction, you had a sense of narrowness and confinement not compatible with their length. The iron doors, with their outer accompaniment of solid wooden ones, the latter used at times to shut the prisoner from all sight and sound, were grim and unpleasing to behold. The halls were light enough, being whitewashed frequently and set with the narrow skylights, which were closed with frosted glass in winter; but they were, as are all such matter-of-fact arrangements for incarceration, bare–wearisome to look upon. Life enough there was in all conscience, seeing that there were four hundred prisoners here at that time, and that nearly every cell was occupied; but it was a life of which no one individual was essentially aware as a spectacle. He was of it; but he was not. Some of the prisoners, after long service, were used as "trusties" or "runners," as they were locally called; but not many. There was a bakery, a machine-shop, a carpenter-shop, a store-room, a flour-mill, and a series of gardens, or truck patches; but the manipulation of these did not require the services of a large number.

The prison proper dated from 1822, and it had grown, wing by wing, until its present considerable size had been reached. Its population consisted of individuals of all degrees of intelligence and crime, from murderers to minor practitioners of larceny. It had what was known as the "Pennsylvania System" of regulation for its inmates, which was nothing more nor less than solitary confinement for all concerned–a life of absolute silence and separate labor in separate cells.

Barring his comparatively recent experience in the county jail, which after all was far from typical, Cowperwood had never been in a prison in his life. Once, when a boy, in one of his perambulations through several of the surrounding towns, he had passed a village "lock-up," as the town prisons were then called–a small, square, gray building with long iron-barred windows, and he had seen, at one of these rather depressing apertures on the second floor, a none too prepossessing drunkard or town ne'er-do-well who looked down on him with bleary eyes, unkempt hair, and a sodden, waxy, pallid face, and called—for it was summer and the jail window was open:

"Hey, sonny, get me a plug of tobacco, will you?"

Cowperwood, who had looked up, shocked and disturbed by the man's disheveled appearance, had called back, quite without stopping to think:

"Naw, I can't."

"Look out you don't get locked up yourself sometime, you little runt," the man had replied, savagely, only half recovered from his debauch of the day before.

He had not thought of this particular scene in years, but now suddenly it came back to him. Here he was on his way to be locked up in this dull, somber prison, and it was snowing, and he was being cut out of human affairs as much as it was possible for him to be cut out.

No friends were permitted to accompany him beyond the outer gate—not even Steger for the time being, though he might visit him later in the day. This was an inviolable rule. Zanders being known to the gate-keeper, and bearing his commitment paper, was admitted at once. The others turned solemnly away. They bade a gloomy if affectionate farewell to Cowperwood, who, on his part, attempted to give it all an air of inconsequence—as, in part and even here, it had for him.

"Well, good-by for the present," he said, shaking hands. "I'll be all right and I'll get out soon. Wait and see. Tell Lillian not to worry."

He stepped inside, and the gate clanked solemnly behind him. Zanders led the way through a dark, somber hall, wide and high-ceiled, to a farther gate, where a second gateman, trifling with a large key, unlocked a barred door at his bidding. Once inside the prison yard, Zanders turned to the left into a small office, presenting his prisoner before a small, chest-high desk, where stood a prison officer in uniform of blue. The latter, the receiving overseer of the prison—a thin, practical, executive-looking person with narrow gray eyes and light hair, took the paper which the sheriff's deputy handed him and read it. This was his authority for receiving Cowperwood. In his turn he handed Zanders a slip, showing that he had so received the prisoner; and then Zanders left, receiving gratefully the tip which Cowperwood pressed in his hand.

"Well, good-by, Mr. Cowperwood," he said, with a peculiar twist of his detective-like head. "I'm sorry. I hope you won't find it so bad here."

He wanted to impress the receiving overseer with his familiarity with this distinguished prisoner, and Cowperwood, true to his policy of make-believe, shook hands with him cordially.

"I'm much obliged to you for your courtesy, Mr. Zanders," he said, then turned to his new master with the air of a man who is determined to make a good impression. He was now in the hands of petty officials, he knew, who could modify or increase his comfort at will. He wanted to impress this man with his utter willingness to comply and obey—his sense of respect for his authority—without in any way demeaning himself. He was depressed but efficient, even here in the clutch of that eventual machine of the law, the State penitentiary, which he had been struggling so hard to evade.

The receiving overseer, Roger Kendall, though thin and clerical, was a rather capable man, as prison officials go—shrewd, not particularly well educated, not over-intelligent naturally, not over-industrious, but sufficiently energetic to hold his position.

He knew something about convicts–considerable–for he had been dealing with them for nearly twenty-six years. His attitude toward them was cold, cynical, critical.

He did not permit any of them to come into personal contact with him, but he saw to it that underlings in his presence carried out the requirements of the law.

When Cowperwood entered, dressed in his very good clothing–a dark gray-blue twill suit of pure wool, a light, well-made gray overcoat, a black derby hat of the latest shape, his shoes new and of good leather, his tie of the best silk, heavy and conservatively colored, his hair and mustache showing the attention of an intelligent barber, and his hands well manicured–the receiving overseer saw at once that he was in the presence of some one of superior intelligence and force, such a man as the fortune of his trade rarely brought into his net.

Cowperwood stood in the middle of the room without apparently looking at any one or anything, though he saw all. "Convict number 3633," Kendall called to a clerk, handing him at the same time a yellow slip of paper on which was written Cowperwood's full name and his record number, counting from the beginning of the penitentiary itself.

The underling, a convict, took it and entered it in a book, reserving the slip at the same time for the penitentiary "runner" or "trusty," who would eventually take Cowperwood to the "manners" gallery.

"You will have to take off your clothes and take a bath," said Kendall to Cowperwood, eyeing him curiously. "I don't suppose you need one, but it's the rule."

"Thank you," replied Cowperwood, pleased that his personality was counting for something even here. "Whatever the rules are, I want to obey."

When he started to take off his coat, however, Kendall put up his hand delayingly and tapped a bell. There now issued from an adjoining room an assistant, a prison servitor, a weird-looking specimen of the genus "trusty." He was a small, dark, lopsided individual, one leg being slightly shorter, and therefore one shoulder lower, than the other. He was hollow-chested, squint-eyed, and rather shambling, but spry enough withal. He was dressed in a thin, poorly made, baggy suit of striped jeans, the prison stripes of the place, showing a soft roll-collar shirt underneath, and wearing a large, wide-striped cap, peculiarly offensive in its size and shape to Cowperwood. He could not help thinking how uncanny the man's squint eyes looked under its straight outstanding visor. The trusty had a silly, sycophantic manner of raising one hand in salute. He was a professional "second-story man," "up" for ten years, but by dint of good behavior he had attained to the honor of working about this office without the degrading hood customary for prisoners to wear over the cap. For this he was properly grateful. He now considered his superior with nervous dog-like eyes, and looked at Cowperwood with a certain cunning appreciation of his lot and a show of initial mistrust.

One prisoner is as good as another to the average convict; as a matter of fact, it is their only consolation in their degradation that all who come here are no better than they. The world may have misused them; but they misuse their confreres in their thoughts. The "holier than thou" attitude, intentional or otherwise, is quite the last and most deadly offense within prison walls. This particular "trusty" could no more understand Cowperwood than could a fly the motions of a fly-wheel; but with the cocky superiority of the underling of the world he did not hesitate to think that he could. A crook was a crook to him–Cowperwood no less than the shabbiest pickpocket. His one feeling was that he would like to demean him, to pull him down to his own level.

"You will have to take everything you have out of your pockets," Kendall now informed Cowperwood. Ordinarily he would have said, "Search the prisoner."

Cowperwood stepped forward and laid out a purse with twenty-five dollars in it, a pen-knife, a lead-pencil, a small note-book, and a little ivory elephant which Aileen had given him once, "for luck," and which he treasured solely because she gave it to him. Kendall looked at the latter curiously. "Now you can go on," he said to 'the "trusty," referring to the undressing and bathing process which was to follow.

"This way," said the latter, addressing Cowperwood, and preceding him into an adjoining room, where three closets held three old-fashioned, iron-bodied, wooden-top bath-tubs, with their attendant shelves for rough crash towels, yellow soap, and the like, and hooks for clothes.

"Get in there," said the trusty, whose name was Thomas Kuby, pointing to one of the tubs.

Cowperwood realized that this was the beginning of petty official supervision; but he deemed it wise to appear friendly even here.

"I see," he said. "I will."

"That's right," replied the attendant, somewhat placated. "What did you bring?"

Cowperwood looked at him quizzically. He did not understand. The prison attendant realized that this man did not know the lingo of the place. "What did you bring?" he repeated. "How many years did you get?"

"Oh!" exclaimed Cowperwood, comprehendingly. "I understand. Four and three months."

He decided to humor the man. It would probably be better so.

"What for?" inquired Kuby, familiarly.

Cowperwood's blood chilled slightly. "Larceny," he said.

"Yuh got off easy," commented Kuby. "I'm up for ten. A rube judge did that to me."

Kuby had never heard of Cowperwood's crime. He would not have understood its subtleties if he had. Cowperwood did not want to talk to this man; he did not know how. He wished he would go away; but that was not likely. He wanted to be put in his cell and let alone.

"That's too bad," he answered; and the convict realized clearly that this man was really not one of them, or he would not have said anything like that. Kuby went to the two hydrants opening into the bath-tub and turned them on. Cowperwood had been undressing the while, and now stood naked, but not ashamed, in front of this eighth-rate intelligence.

"Don't forget to wash your head, too," said Kuby, and went away.

Cowperwood stood there while the water ran, meditating on his fate. It was strange how life had dealt with him of late–so severely. Unlike most men in his position, he was not suffering from a consciousness of evil. He did not think he was evil. As he saw it, he was merely unfortunate. To think that he should be actually in this great, silent penitentiary, a convict, waiting here beside this cheap iron bathtub, not very sweet or hygienic to contemplate, with this crackbrained criminal to watch over him!

He stepped into the tub and washed himself briskly with the biting yellow soap, drying himself on one of the rough, only partially bleached towels. He looked for his underwear, but there was none. At this point the attendant looked in again. "Out here," he said, inconsiderately.

Cowperwood followed, naked. He was led through the receiving overseer's office into a room, where were scales, implements of measurement, a record-book, etc. The attendant who stood guard at the door now came over, and the clerk who sat in a corner automatically took down a record-blank. Kendall surveyed Cowperwood's decidedly graceful figure, already inclining to a slight thickening around the waist, and approved of it as superior to that of most who came here. His skin, as he particularly noted, was especially white.

"Step on the scale," said the attendant, brusquely.

Cowperwood did so, The former adjusted the weights and scanned the record carefully.

"Weight, one hundred and seventy-five," he called. "Now step over here."

He indicated a spot in the side wall where was fastened in a thin slat–which ran from the floor to about seven and one half feet above, perpendicularly–a small movable wooden indicator, which, when a man was standing under it, could be pressed down on his head. At the side of the slat were the total inches of height, laid off in halves, quarters, eighths, and so on, and to the right a length measurement for the arm. Cowperwood understood what was wanted and stepped under the indicator, standing quite straight.

"Feet level, back to the wall," urged the attendant. "So. Height, five feet nine and ten-sixteenths," he called. The clerk in the corner noted it. He now produced a tape-measure and began measuring Cowperwood's arms, legs, chest, waist, hips, etc. He called out the color of his eyes, his hair, his mustache, and, looking into his mouth, exclaimed, "Teeth, all sound."

After Cowperwood had once more given his address, age, profession, whether he knew any trade, etc.–which he did not–he was allowed to return to the bathroom, and put on the clothing which the prison provided for him–first the rough, prickly underwear, then the cheap soft roll-collar, white-cotton shirt, then the thick bluish-gray cotton socks of a quality such as he had never worn in his life, and over these a pair of indescribable rough-leather clogs, which felt to his feet as though they were made of wood or iron–oily and heavy. He then drew on the shapeless, baggy trousers with their telltale stripes, and over his arms and chest the loose-cut shapeless coat and waistcoat. He felt and knew of course that he looked very strange, wretched. And as he stepped out into the overseer's room again he experienced a peculiar sense of depression, a gone feeling which before this had not assailed him and which now he did his best to conceal. This, then, was what society did to the criminal, he thought to himself. It took him and tore away from his body and his life the habiliments of his proper state and left him these. He felt sad and grim, and, try as he would–he could not help showing it for a moment. It was always his business and his intention to conceal his real feelings, but now it was not quite possible. He felt degraded, impossible, in these clothes, and he knew that he looked it. Nevertheless, he did his best to pull himself together and look unconcerned, willing, obedient, considerate of those above him. After all, he said to himself, it was all a play of sorts, a dream even, if one chose to view it so, a miasma even, from which, in the course of time and with a little luck one might emerge safely enough. He hoped so. It could not last. He was only acting a strange, unfamiliar part on the stage, this stage of life that he knew so well.

Kendall did not waste any time looking at him, however. He merely said to his assistant, "See if you can find a cap for him," and the latter, going to a closet containing numbered shelves, took down a cap–a high-crowned, straight-visored, shabby, striped affair which Cowperwood was asked to try on. It fitted well enough, slipping down close over his ears, and he thought that now his indignities must be about complete. What could be added? There could be no more of these disconcerting accoutrements. But he was mistaken. "Now, Kuby, you take him to Mr. Chapin," said Kendall.

Kuby understood. He went back into the wash-room and produced what Cowperwood had heard of but never before seen–a blue-and-white-striped cotton bag about half the length of an ordinary pillow-case and half again as wide, which Kuby now unfolded and shook out as he came toward him. It was a custom. The use of this hood, dating from the earliest days of the prison, was intended to prevent a sense of location and direction and thereby obviate any attempt to escape. Thereafter during all his stay he was not supposed to walk with or talk to or see another prisoner–not even to converse with his superiors, unless addressed. It was a grim theory, and yet one definitely enforced here, although as he was to learn later even this could be modified here.

"You'll have to put this on," Kuby said, and opened it in such a way that it could be put over Cowperwood's head.

Cowperwood understood. He had heard of it in some way, in times past. He was a little shocked–looked at it first with a touch of real surprise, but a moment after lifted his hands and helped pull it down.

"Never mind," cautioned the guard, "put your hands down. I'll get it over."

Cowperwood dropped his arms. When it was fully on, it came to about his chest, giving him little means of seeing anything. He felt very strange, very humiliated, very downcast. This simple thing of a blue-and-white striped bag over his head almost cost him his sense of self-possession. Why could not they have spared him this last indignity, he thought?

"This way," said his attendant, and he was led out to where he could not say.

"If you hold it out in front you can see to walk," said his guide; and Cowperwood pulled it out, thus being able to discern his feet and a portion of the floor below. He was thus conducted–seeing nothing in his transit–down a short walk, then through a long corridor, then through a room of uniformed guards, and finally up a narrow flight of iron steps, leading to the overseer's office on the second floor of one of the two-tier blocks. There, he heard the voice of Kuby saying: "Mr. Chapin, here's another prisoner for you from Mr. Kendall."

"I'll be there in a minute," came a peculiarly pleasant voice from the distance. Presently a big, heavy hand closed about his arm, and he was conducted still further.

"You hain't got far to go now," the voice said, "and then I'll take that bag off," and Cowperwood felt for some reason a sense of sympathy, perhaps–as though he would choke. The further steps were not many.

A cell door was reached and unlocked by the inserting of a great iron key. It was swung open, and the same big hand guided him through. A moment later the bag was pulled easily from his head, and he saw that he was in a narrow, whitewashed cell, rather dim, windowless, but lighted from the top by a small skylight of frosted glass three and one half feet long by four inches wide. For a night light there was a tin-bodied lamp swinging from a hook near the middle of one of the side walls. A rough iron cot, furnished with a straw mattress and two pairs of dark blue, probably unwashed blankets, stood in one corner. There was a hydrant and small sink in another. A small shelf occupied the wall opposite the bed. A plain wooden chair with a homely round back stood at the foot of the bed, and a fairly serviceable broom was standing in one corner. There was an iron stool or pot for excreta, giving, as he could see, into a large drain-pipe which ran along the inside wall, and which was obviously flushed by buckets of water being poured into it. Rats and other vermin infested this, and it gave off an unpleasant odor which filled the cell. The floor was of stone. Cowperwood's clear-seeing eyes took it all in at a glance. He noted the hard cell door, which was barred and cross-barred with great round rods of steel, and fastened with a thick, highly polished lock. He saw also that beyond this was a heavy wooden door, which could shut him in even more completely than the iron one. There was no chance for any clear, purifying sunlight here. Cleanliness depended entirely on whitewash, soap and water and sweeping, which in turn depended on the prisoners themselves.

He also took in Chapin, the homely, good-natured, cell overseer whom he now saw for the first time–a large, heavy, lumbering man, rather dusty and misshapen-looking, whose uniform did not fit him well, and whose manner of standing made him look as though he would much prefer to sit down. He was obviously bulky, but not strong, and his kindly face was covered with a short growth of grayish-brown whiskers. His hair was cut badly and stuck out in odd strings or wisps from underneath his big cap. Nevertheless, Cowperwood was not at all unfavorably impressed–quite the contrary– and he felt at once that this man might be more considerate of him than the others had been. He hoped so, anyhow. He did not know that he was in the presence of the overseer of the "manners squad," who would have him in charge for two weeks only, instructing him in the rules of the prison, and that he was only one of twenty-six, all told, who were in Chapin's care.

That worthy, by way of easy introduction, now went over to the bed and seated himself on it. He pointed to the hard wooden chair, which Cowperwood drew out and sat on.

"Well, now you're here, hain't yuh?" he asked, and answered himself quite genially, for he was an unlettered man, generously disposed, of long experience with criminals, and inclined to deal kindly with kindly temperament and a form of religious belief– Quakerism–had inclined him to be merciful, and yet his official duties, as Cowperwood later found out, seemed to have led him to the conclusion that most criminals were innately bad. Like Kendall, he regarded them as weaklings and ne'er-do-wells with evil streaks in them, and in the main he was not mistaken. Yet he could not help being what he was, a fatherly, kindly old man, having faith in those shibboleths of the weak and inexperienced mentally–human justice and human decency.

"Yes, I'm here, Mr. Chapin," Cowperwood replied, simply, remembering his name from the attendant, and flattering the keeper by the use of it.

To old Chapin the situation was more or less puzzling. This was the famous Frank A. Cowperwood whom he had read about, the noted banker and treasury-looter. He and his co-partner in crime, Stener, were destined to serve, as he had read, comparatively long terms here. Five hundred thousand dollars was a large sum of money in those days, much more than five million would have been forty years later. He was awed by the thought of what had become of it–how Cowperwood managed to do all the things the papers had said he had done. He had a little formula of questions which he usually went through with each new prisoner–asking him if he was sorry now for the crime he had committed, if he meant to do better with a new chance, if his father and mother were alive, etc.; and by the manner in which they answered these questions–simply, regretfully, defiantly, or otherwise–he judged whether they were being adequately punished or not. Yet he could not talk to Cowperwood as he now saw or as he would to the average second-story burglar, store-looter, pickpocket, and plain cheap thief and swindler. And yet he scarcely knew how else to talk.

"Well, now," he went on, "I don't suppose you ever thought you'd get to a place like this, did you, Mr. Cowperwood?"

"I never did," replied Frank, simply. "I wouldn't have believed it a few months ago, Mr. Chapin. I don't think I deserve to be here now, though of course there is no use of my telling you that."

He saw that old Chapin wanted to moralize a little, and he was only too glad to fall in with his mood. He would soon be alone with no one to talk to perhaps, and if a sympathetic understanding could be reached with this man now, so much the better. Any port in a storm; any straw to a drowning man.

"Well, no doubt all of us makes mistakes," continued Mr. Chapin, superiorly, with an amusing faith in his own value as a moral guide and reformer. "We can't just always tell how the plans we think so fine are coming out, can we? You're here now, an' I suppose you're sorry certain things didn't come out just as you thought; but if you had a chance I don't suppose you'd try to do just as you did before, now would yuh?"

"No, Mr. Chapin, I wouldn't, exactly," said Cowperwood, truly enough, "though I believed I was right in everything I did. I don't think legal justice has really been done me."

"Well, that's the way," continued Chapin, meditatively, scratching his grizzled head and looking genially about. "Sometimes, as I allers says to some of these here young fellers that comes in here, we don't know as much as we thinks we does. We forget that others are just as smart as we are, and that there are allers people that are watchin' us all the time. These here courts and jails and detectives–they're here all the time, and they get us. I gad"–Chapin's moral version of "by God"–"they do, if we don't behave."

"Yes," Cowperwood replied, "that's true enough, Mr. Chapin."

"Well," continued the old man after a time, after he had made a few more solemn, owl-like, and yet well-intentioned remarks, "now here's your bed, and there's your chair, and there's your wash-stand, and there's your water-closet. Now keep 'em all clean and use 'em right." (You would have thought he was making Cowperwood a present of a fortune.) "You're the one's got to make up your bed every mornin' and keep your floor swept and your toilet flushed and your cell clean. There hain't anybody here'll do that for yuh. You want to do all them things the first thing in the mornin' when you get up, and afterward you'll get sumpin' to eat, about six-thirty. You're supposed to get up at five-thirty."

"Yes, Mr. Chapin," Cowperwood said, politely. "You can depend on me to do all those things promptly."

"There hain't so much more," added Chapin. "You're supposed to wash yourself all over once a week an' I'll give you a clean towel for that. Next you gotta wash this floor up every Friday mornin'." Cowperwood winced at that. "You kin have hot water for that if you want it. I'll have one of the runners bring it to you. An' as for your friends and relations"—he got up and shook himself like a big Newfoundland dog. "You gotta wife, hain't you?"

"Yes," replied Cowperwood.

"Well, the rules here are that your wife or your friends kin come to see you once in three months, and your lawyer—you gotta lawyer hain't yuh?"

"Yes, sir," replied Cowperwood, amused.

"Well, he kin come every week or so if he likes—every day, I guess—there hain't no rules about lawyers. But you kin only write one letter once in three months yourself, an' if you want anything like tobaccer or the like o' that, from the store-room, you gotta sign an order for it, if you got any money with the warden, an' then I can git it for you."

The old man was really above taking small tips in the shape of money. He was a hold-over from a much more severe and honest regime, but subsequent presents or constant flattery were not amiss in making him kindly and generous. Cowperwood read him accurately.

"Very well, Mr. Chapin; I understand," he said, getting up as the old man did.

"Then when you have been here two weeks," added Chapin, rather ruminatively (he had forgot to state this to Cowperwood before), "the warden 'll come and git yuh and give yuh yer regular cell summers down-stairs. Yuh kin make up yer mind by that time what y'u'd like tuh do, what y'u'd like to work at. If you behave yourself proper, more'n like they'll give yuh a cell with a yard. Yuh never can tell."

He went out, locking the door with a solemn click; and Cowperwood stood there, a little more depressed than he had been, because of this latest intelligence. Only two weeks, and then he would be transferred from this kindly old man's care to another's, whom he did not know and with whom he might not fare so well.

"If ever you want me for anything—if ye're sick or sumpin' like that," Chapin now returned to say, after he had walked a few paces away, "we have a signal here of our own. Just hang your towel out through these here bars. I'll see it, and I'll stop and find out what yuh want, when I'm passin'."

Cowperwood, whose spirits had sunk, revived for the moment.

"Yes, sir," he replied; "thank you, Mr. Chapin."

The old man walked away, and Cowperwood heard his steps dying down the cement-paved hall. He stood and listened, his ears being greeted occasionally by a distant cough, a faint scraping of some one's feet, the hum or whir of a machine, or the iron scratch of a key in a lock. None of the noises was loud. Rather they were all faint and far away. He went over and looked at the bed, which was not very clean and without linen, and anything but wide or soft, and felt it curiously. So here was where he was to sleep from now on–he who so craved and appreciated luxury and refinement. If Aileen or some of his rich friends should see him here. Worse, he was sickened by the thought of possible vermin. How could he tell? How would he do? The one chair was abominable. The skylight was weak. He tried to think of himself as becoming accustomed to the situation, but he re-discovered the offal pot in one corner, and that discouraged him. It was possible that rats might come up here–it looked that way. No pictures, no books, no scene, no person, no space to walk–just the four bare walls and silence, which he would be shut into at night by the thick door. What a horrible fate!

He sat down and contemplated his situation. So here he was at last in the Eastern Penitentiary, and doomed, according to the judgment of the politicians (Butler among others), to remain here four long years and longer. Stener, it suddenly occurred to him, was probably being put through the same process he had just gone through. Poor old Stener! What a fool he had made of himself. But because of his foolishness he deserved all he was now getting. But the difference between himself and Stener was that they would let Stener out. It was possible that already they were easing his punishment in some way that he, Cowperwood, did not know. He put his hand to his chin, thinking–his business, his house, his friends, his family, Aileen. He felt for his watch, but remembered that they had taken that. There was no way of telling the time. Neither had he any not, pen, or pencil with which to amuse or interest himself. Besides he had had nothing to eat since morning. Still, that mattered little. What did matter was that he was shut up here away from the world, quite alone, quite lonely, without knowing what time it was, and that he could not attend to any of the things he ought to be attending to–his business affairs, his future. True, Steger would probably come to see him after a while. That would help a little. But even so–think of his position, his prospects up to the day of the fire and his state now. He sat looking at his shoes; his suit. God! He got up and walked to and fro, to and fro, but his own steps and movements sounded so loud. He walked to the cell door and looked out through the thick bars, but there was nothing to see–nothing save a portion of two cell doors opposite, something like his own. He came back and sat in his single chair, meditating, but, getting weary of that finally, stretched himself on the dirty prison bed to try it. It was not uncomfortable entirely. He got up after a while, however, and sat, then walked, then sat. What a narrow place to walk, he thought. This was horrible–something like a living tomb. And to think he should be here now, day after day and day after day, until–until what? Until the Governor pardoned him or his time was up, or his fortune eaten away–or–

So he cogitated while the hours slipped by. It was nearly five o'clock before Steger was able to return, and then only for a little while. He had been arranging for Cowperwood's appearance on the following Thursday, Friday, and Monday in his several court proceedings. When he was gone, however, and the night fell and Cowperwood had to trim his little, shabby oil-lamp and to drink the strong tea and eat the rough, poor bread made of bran and white flour, which was shoved to him through the small aperture in the door by the trencher trusty, who was accompanied by the overseer to see that it was done properly, he really felt very badly. And after that the center wooden door of his cell was presently closed and locked by a trusty who slammed it rudely and said no word. Nine o'clock would be sounded somewhere by a great bell, he understood, when his smoky oil-lamp would have to be put out promptly and he would have to undress and go to bed. There were punishments, no doubt, for infractions of these rules–reduced rations, the strait-jacket, perhaps stripes– he scarcely knew what. He felt disconsolate, grim, weary. He had put up such a long, unsatisfactory fight. After washing his heavy stone cup and tin plate at the hydrant, he took off the sickening uniform and shoes and even the drawers of the scratching underwear, and stretched himself wearily on the bed. The place was not any too warm, and he tried to make himself comfortable between the blankets–but it was of little use. His soul was cold.

"This will never do," he said to himself. "This will never do. I'm not sure whether I can stand much of this or not." Still he turned his face to the wall, and after several hours sleep eventually came.

Chapter LIV

Those who by any pleasing courtesy of fortune, accident of birth, inheritance, or the wisdom of parents or friends, have succeeded in avoiding making that anathema of the prosperous and comfortable, "a mess of their lives," will scarcely understand the mood of Cowperwood, sitting rather gloomily in his cell these first days, wondering what, in spite of his great ingenuity, was to become of him. The strongest have their hours of depression. There are times when life to those endowed with the greatest intelligence–perhaps mostly to those–takes on a somber hue. They see so many phases of its dreary subtleties. It is only when the soul of man has been built up into some strange self-confidence, some curious faith in its own powers, based, no doubt, on the actual presence of these same powers subtly involved in the body, that it fronts life unflinchingly. It would be too much to say that Cowperwood's mind was of the first order. It was subtle enough in all conscience–and involved, as is common with the executively great, with a strong sense of personal advancement. It was a powerful mind, turning, like a vast searchlight, a glittering ray into many a dark corner; but it was not sufficiently disinterested to search the ultimate dark. He realized, in a way, what the great astronomers, sociologists, philosophers, chemists, physicists, and physiologists were meditating; but he could not be sure in his own mind that, whatever it was, it was important for him. No doubt life held many strange secrets. Perhaps it was essential that somebody should investigate them. However that might be, the call of his own soul was in another direction. His business was to make money–to organize something which would make him much money, or, better yet, save the organization he had begun.

But this, as he now looked upon it, was almost impossible. It had been too disarranged and complicated by unfortunate circumstances. He might, as Steger pointed out to him, string out these bankruptcy proceedings for years, tiring out one creditor and another, but in the meantime the properties involved were being seriously damaged. Interest charges on his unsatisfied loans were making heavy inroads; court costs were mounting up; and, to cap it all, he had discovered with Steger that there were a number of creditors–those who had sold out to Butler, and incidentally to Mollenhauer–who would never accept anything except the full value of their claims. His one hope now was to save what he could by compromise a little later, and to build up some sort of profitable business through Stephen Wingate. The latter was coming in a day or two, as soon as Steger had made some working arrangement for him with Warden Michael Desmas who came the second day to have a look at the new prisoner.

Desmas was a large man physically–Irish by birth, a politician by training–who had been one thing and another in Philadelphia from a policeman in his early days and a corporal in the Civil War to a ward captain under Mollenhauer. He was a canny man, tall, raw-boned, singularly muscular-looking, who for all his fifty-seven years looked as though he could give a splendid account of himself in a physical contest. His hands were large and bony, his face more square than either round or long, and his forehead high. He had a vigorous growth of short-clipped, iron-gray hair, and a bristly iron-gray mustache, very short, keen, intelligent blue-gray eyes; a florid complexion; and even-edged, savage-looking teeth, which showed the least bit in a slightly wolfish way when he smiled. However, he was not as cruel a person as he looked to be; temperamental, to a certain extent hard, and on occasions savage, but with kindly hours also. His greatest weakness was that he was not quite mentally able to recognize that there were mental and social differences between prisoners, and that now and then one was apt to appear here who, with or without political influences, was eminently worthy of special consideration. What he could recognize was the differences pointed out to him by the politicians in special cases, such as that of Stener–not Cowperwood. However, seeing that the prison was a public institution apt to be visited at any time by lawyers, detectives, doctors, preachers, propagandists, and the public generally, and that certain rules and regulations had to be enforced (if for no other reason than to keep a moral and administrative control over his own help), it was necessary to maintain–and that even in the face of the politician–a certain amount of discipline, system, and order, and it was not possible to be too liberal with any one. There were, however, exceptional cases–men of wealth and refinement, victims of those occasional uprisings which so shocked the political leaders generally–who had to be looked after in a friendly way.

Desmas was quite aware, of course, of the history of Cowperwood and Stener. The politicians had already given him warning that Stener, because of his past services to the community, was to be treated with special consideration. Not so much was said about Cowperwood, although they did admit that his lot was rather hard. Perhaps he might do a little something for him but at his own risk.

"Butler is down on him," Strobik said to Desmas, on one occasion. "It's that girl of his that's at the bottom of it all. If you listened to Butler you'd feed him on bread and water, but he isn't a bad fellow. As a matter of fact, if George had had any sense Cowperwood wouldn't be where he is to-day. But the big fellows wouldn't let Stener alone. They wouldn't let him give Cowperwood any money."

Although Strobik had been one of those who, under pressure from Mollenhauer, had advised Stener not to let Cowperwood have any more money, yet here he was pointing out the folly of the victim's course. The thought of the inconsistency involved did not trouble him in the least.

Desmas decided, therefore, that if Cowperwood were persona non grata to the "Big Three," it might be necessary to be indifferent to him, or at least slow in extending him any special favors. For Stener a good chair, clean linen, special cutlery and dishes, the daily papers, privileges in the matter of mail, the visits of friends, and the like. For Cowperwood—well, he would have to look at Cowperwood and see what he thought. At the same time, Steger's intercessions were not without their effect on Desmas. So the morning after Cowperwood's entrance the warden received a letter from Terrence Relihan, the Harrisburg potentate, indicating that any kindness shown to Mr. Cowperwood would be duly appreciated by him. Upon the receipt of this letter Desmas went up and looked through Cowperwood's iron door. On the way he had a brief talk with Chapin, who told him what a nice man he thought Cowperwood was.

Desmas had never seen Cowperwood before, but in spite of the shabby uniform, the clog shoes, the cheap shirt, and the wretched cell, he was impressed. Instead of the weak, anaemic body and the shifty eyes of the average prisoner, he saw a man whose face and form blazed energy and power, and whose vigorous erectness no wretched clothes or conditions could demean. He lifted his head when Desmas appeared, glad that any form should have appeared at his door, and looked at him with large, clear, examining eyes—those eyes that in the past had inspired so much confidence and surety in all those who had known him. Desmas was stirred. Compared with Stener, whom he knew in the past and whom he had met on his entry, this man was a force. Say what you will, one vigorous man inherently respects another. And Desmas was vigorous physically. He eyed Cowperwood and Cowperwood eyed him. Instinctively Desmas liked him. He was like one tiger looking at another.

Instinctively Cowperwood knew that he was the warden. "This is Mr. Desmas, isn't it?" he asked, courteously and pleasantly.

"Yes, sir, I'm the man," replied Desmas interestedly. "These rooms are not as comfortable as they might be, are they?" The warden's even teeth showed in a friendly, yet wolfish, way.

"They certainly are not, Mr. Desmas," replied Cowperwood, standing very erect and soldier-like. "I didn't imagine I was coming to a hotel, however." He smiled.

"There isn't anything special I can do for you, is there, Mr. Cowperwood?" began Desmas curiously, for he was moved by a thought that at some time or other a man such as this might be of service to him. "I've been talking to your lawyer." Cowperwood was intensely gratified by the Mr. So that was the way the wind was blowing. Well, then, within reason, things might not prove so bad here. He would see. He would sound this man out.

"I don't want to be asking anything, Warden, which you cannot reasonably give," he now returned politely. "But there are a few things, of course, that I would change if I could. I wish I might have sheets for my bed, and I could afford better underwear if you would let me wear it. This that I have on annoys me a great deal."

"They're not the best wool, that's true enough," replied Desmas, solemnly. "They're made for the State out here in Pennsylvania somewhere. I suppose there's no objection to your wearing your own underwear if you want to. I'll see about that. And the sheets, too. We might let you use them if you have them. We'll have to go a little slow about this. There are a lot of people that take a special interest in showing the warden how to tend to his business."

"I can readily understand that, Warden," went on Cowperwood briskly, "and I'm certainly very much obliged to you. You may be sure that anything you do for me here will be appreciated, and not misused, and that I have friends on the outside who can reciprocate for me in the course of time." He talked slowly and emphatically, looking Desmas directly in the eye all of the time. Desmas was very much impressed.

"That's all right," he said, now that he had gone so far as to be friendly. "I can't promise much. Prison rules are prison rules. But there are some things that can be done, because it's the rule to do them for other men when they behave themselves. You can have a better chair than that, if you want it, and something to read too. If you're in business yet, I wouldn't want to do anything to stop that. We can't have people running in and out of here every fifteen minutes, and you can't turn a cell into a business office–that's not possible. It would break up the order of the place. Still, there's no reason why you shouldn't see some of your friends now and then. As for your mail–well, that will have to be opened in the ordinary way for the time being, anyhow. I'll have to see about that. I can't promise too much. You'll have to wait until you come out of this block and down-stairs. Some of the cells have a yard there; if there are any empty–" The warden cocked his eye wisely, and Cowperwood saw that his tot was not to be as bad as he had anticipated–though bad enough. The warden spoke to him about the different trades he might follow, and asked him to think about the one he would prefer. "You want to have something to keep your hands busy, whatever else you want. You'll find you'll need that. Everybody here wants to work after a time. I notice that."

Cowperwood understood and thanked Desmas profusely. The horror of idleness in silence and in a cell scarcely large enough to turn around in comfortably had already begun to creep over him, and the thought of being able to see Wingate and Steger frequently, and to have his mail reach him, after a time, untampered with, was a great relief. He was to have his own underwear, silk and wool–thank God!–and perhaps they would let him take off these shoes after a while. With these modifications and a trade, and perhaps the little yard which Desmas had referred to, his life would be, if not ideal, at least tolerable. The prison was still a prison, but it looked as though it might not be so much of a terror to him as obviously it must be to many.

During the two weeks in which Cowperwood was in the "manners squad," in care of Chapin, he learned nearly as much as he ever learned of the general nature of prison life; for this was not an ordinary penitentiary in the sense that the prison yard, the prison squad, the prison lock-step, the prison dining-room, and prison associated labor make the ordinary penitentiary. There was, for him and for most of those confined there, no general prison life whatsoever. The large majority were supposed to work silently in their cells at the particular tasks assigned them, and not to know anything of the remainder of the life which went on around them, the rule of this prison being solitary confinement, and few being permitted to work at the limited number of outside menial tasks provided. Indeed, as he sensed and as old Chapin soon informed him, not more than seventy-five of the four hundred prisoners confined here were so employed, and not all of these regularly–cooking, gardening in season, milling, and general cleaning being the only avenues of escape from solitude. Even those who so worked were strictly forbidden to talk, and although they did not have to wear the objectionable hood when actually employed, they were supposed to wear it in going to and from their work. Cowperwood saw them occasionally tramping by his cell door, and it struck him as strange, uncanny, grim. He wished sincerely at times since old Chapin was so genial and talkative that he were to be under him permanently; but it was not to be.

His two weeks soon passed–drearily enough in all conscience but they passed, interlaced with his few commonplace tasks of bed-making, floor-sweeping, dressing, eating, undressing, rising at five-thirty, and retiring at nine, washing his several dishes after each meal, etc. He thought he would never get used to the food. Breakfast, as has been said, was at six-thirty, and consisted of coarse black bread made of bran and some white flour, and served with black coffee. Dinner was at eleven-thirty, and consisted of bean or vegetable soup, with some coarse meat in it, and the same bread. Supper was at six, of tea and bread, very strong tea and the same bread–no butter, no milk, no sugar. Cowperwood did not smoke, so the small allowance of tobacco which was permitted was without value to him. Steger called in every day for two or three weeks, and after the second day, Stephen Wingate, as his new business associate, was permitted to see him also–once every day, if he wished, Desmas stated, though the latter felt he was stretching a point in permitting this so soon. Both of these visits rarely occupied more than an hour, or an hour and a half, and after that the day was long. He was taken out on several days on a court order, between nine and five, to testify in the bankruptcy proceedings against him, which caused the time in the beginning to pass quickly.

It was curious, once he was in prison, safely shut from the world for a period of years apparently, how quickly all thought of assisting him departed from the minds of those who had been most friendly. He was done, so most of them thought. The only thing they could do now would be to use their influence to get him out some time; how soon, they could not guess. Beyond that there was nothing. He would really never be of any great importance to any one any more, or so they thought. It was very sad, very tragic, but he was gone–his place knew him not.

"A bright young man, that," observed President Davison of the Girard National, on reading of Cowperwood's sentence and incarceration. "Too bad! Too bad! He made a great mistake."

Only his parents, Aileen, and his wife–the latter with mingled feelings of resentment and sorrow–really missed him. Aileen, because of her great passion for him, was suffering most of all. Four years and three months; she thought. If he did not get out before then she would be nearing twenty-nine and he would be nearing forty. Would he want her then? Would she be so attractive? And would nearly five years change his point of view? He would have to wear a convict suit all that time, and be known as a convict forever after. It was hard to think about, but only made her more than ever determined to cling to him, whatever happened, and to help him all she could.

Indeed the day after his incarceration she drove out and looked at the grim, gray walls of the penitentiary. Knowing nothing absolutely of the vast and complicated processes of law and penal servitude, it seemed especially terrible to her. What might not they be doing to her Frank? Was he suffering much? Was he thinking of her as she was of him? Oh, the pity of it all! The pity! The pity of herself–her great love for him! She drove home, determined to see him; but as he had originally told her that visiting days were only once in three months, and that he would have to write her when the next one was, or when she could come, or when he could see her on the outside, she scarcely knew what to do. Secrecy was the thing.

The next day, however, she wrote him just the same, describing the drive she had taken on the stormy afternoon before–the terror of the thought that he was behind those grim gray walls–and declaring her determination to see him soon. And this letter, under the new arrangement, he received at once. He wrote her in reply, giving the letter to Wingate to mail. It ran:

My sweet girl:–I fancy you are a little downhearted to think I cannot be with you any more soon, but you mustn't be. I suppose you read all about the sentence in the paper. I came out here the same morning–nearly noon. If I had time, dearest, I'd write you a long letter describing the situation so as to ease your mind; but I haven't. It's against the rules, and I am really doing this secretly. I'm here, though, safe enough, and wish I were out, of course. Sweetest, you must be careful how you try to see me at first. You can't do me much service outside of cheering me up, and you may do yourself great harm. Besides, I think I have done you far more harm than I can ever make up to you and that you had best give me up, although I know you do not think so, and I would be sad, if you did. I am to be in the Court of Special Pleas, Sixth and Chestnut, on Friday at two o'clock; but you cannot see me there. I'll be out in charge of my counsel. You must be careful. Perhaps you'll think better, and not come here.

This last touch was one of pure gloom, the first Cowperwood had ever introduced into their relationship but conditions had changed him. Hitherto he had been in the position of the superior being, the one who was being sought–although Aileen was and had been well worth seeking–and he had thought that he might escape unscathed, and so grow in dignity and power until she might not possibly be worthy of him any longer. He had had that thought. But here, in stripes, it was a different matter. Aileen's position, reduced in value as it was by her long, ardent relationship with him, was now, nevertheless, superior to his–apparently so. For after all, was she not Edward Butler's daughter, and might she, after she had been away from him a while, wish to become a convict's bride. She ought not to want to, and she might not want to, for all he knew; she might change her mind. She ought not to wait for him. Her life was not yet ruined. The public did not know, so he thought–not generally anyhow–that she had been his mistress. She might marry. Why not, and so pass out of his life forever. And would not that be sad for him? And yet did he not owe it to her, to a sense of fair play in himself to ask her to give him up, or at least think over the wisdom of doing so?

He did her the justice to believe that she would not want to give him up; and in his position, however harmful it might be to her, it was an advantage, a connecting link with the finest period of his past life, to have her continue to love him. He could not, however, scribbling this note in his cell in Wingate's presence, and giving it to him to mail (Overseer Chapin was kindly keeping a respectful distance, though he was supposed to be present), refrain from adding, at the last moment, this little touch of doubt which, when she read it, struck Aileen to the heart. She read it as gloom on his part–as great depression. Perhaps, after all, the penitentiary and so soon, was really breaking his spirit, and he had held up so courageously so long. Because of this, now she was madly eager to get to him, to console him, even though it was difficult, perilous. She must, she said.

In regard to visits from the various members of his family–his mother and father, his brother, his wife, and his sister–Cowperwood made it plain to them on one of the days on which he was out attending a bankruptcy hearing, that even providing it could be arranged he did not think they should come oftener than once in three months, unless he wrote them or sent word by Steger. The truth was that he really did not care to see much of any of them at present. He was sick of the whole social scheme of things. In fact he wanted to be rid of the turmoil he had been in, seeing it had proved so useless. He had used nearly fifteen thousand dollars thus far in defending himself–court costs, family maintenance, Steger, etc.; but he did not mind that. He expected to make some little money working through Wingate. His family were not utterly without funds, sufficient to live on in a small way. He had advised them to remove into houses more in keeping with their reduced circumstances, which they had done–his mother and father and brothers and sister to a three-story brick house of about the caliber of the old Buttonwood Street house, and his wife to a smaller, less expensive two-story one on North Twenty-first Street, near the penitentiary, a portion of the money saved out of the thirty-five thousand dollars extracted from Stener under false pretenses aiding to sustain it. Of course all this was a terrible descent from the Girard Avenue mansion for the elder Cowperwood; for here was none of the furniture which characterized the other somewhat gorgeous domicile–merely store-bought, ready-made furniture, and neat but cheap hangings and fixtures generally. The assignees, to whom all Cowperwood's personal property belonged, and to whom Cowperwood, the elder, had surrendered all his holdings, would not permit anything of importance to be removed. It had all to be sold for the benefit of creditors. A few very small things, but only a few, had been kept, as everything had been inventoried some time before. One of the things which old Cowperwood wanted was his own desk which Frank had had designed for him; but as it was valued at five hundred dollars and could not be relinquished by the sheriff except on payment of that sum, or by auction, and as Henry Cowperwood had no such sum to spare, he had to let the desk go. There were many things they all wanted, and Anna Adelaide had literally purloined a few though she did not admit the fact to her parents until long afterward.

There came a day when the two houses in Girard Avenue were the scene of a sheriffs sale, during which the general public, without let or hindrance, was permitted to tramp through the rooms and examine the pictures, statuary, and objects of art generally, which were auctioned off to the highest bidder. Considerable fame had attached to Cowperwood's activities in this field, owing in the first place to the real merit of what he had brought together, and in the next place to the enthusiastic comment of such men as Wilton Ellsworth, Fletcher Norton, Gordon Strake–architects and art dealers whose judgment and taste were considered important in Philadelphia. All of the lovely things by which he had set great store–small bronzes, representative of the best period of the Italian Renaissance; bits of Venetian glass which he had collected with great care–a full curio case; statues by Powers, Hosmer, and Thorwaldsen–things which would be smiled at thirty years later, but which were of high value then; all of his pictures by representative American painters from Gilbert to Eastman Johnson, together with a few specimens of the current French and English schools, went for a song. Art judgment in Philadelphia at this time was not exceedingly high; and some of the pictures, for lack of appreciative understanding, were disposed of at much too low a figure. Strake, Norton, and Ellsworth were all present and bought liberally. Senator Simpson, Mollenhauer, and Strobik came to see what they could see. The small-fry politicians were there, en masse. But Simpson, calm judge of good art, secured practically the best of all that was offered. To him went the curio case of Venetian glass; one pair of tall blue-and-white Mohammedan cylindrical vases; fourteen examples of Chinese jade, including several artists' water-dishes and a pierced window-screen of the faintest tinge of green. To Mollenhauer went the furniture and decorations of the entry-hall and reception-room of Henry Cowperwood's house, and to Edward Strobik two of Cowperwood's bird's-eye maple bedroom suites for the most modest of prices. Adam Davis was present and secured the secretaire of buhl which the elder Cowperwood prized so highly. To Fletcher Norton went the four Greek vases–a kylix, a water-jar, and two amphorae–which he had sold to Cowperwood and which he valued highly. Various objects of art, including a Sevres dinner set, a Gobelin tapestry, Barye bronzes and pictures by Detaille, Fortuny, and George Inness, went to Walter Leigh, Arthur Rivers, Joseph Zimmerman, Judge Kitchen, Harper Steger, Terrence Relihan, Trenor Drake, Mr. and Mrs. Simeon Jones, W. C. Davison, Frewen Kasson, Fletcher Norton, and Judge Rafalsky.

Within four days after the sale began the two houses were bare of their contents. Even the objects in the house at 931 North Tenth Street had been withdrawn from storage where they had been placed at the time it was deemed advisable to close this institution, and placed on sale with the other objects in the two homes. It was at this time that the senior Cowperwoods first learned of something which seemed to indicate a mystery which had existed in connection with their son and his wife. No one of all the Cowperwoods was present during all this gloomy distribution; and Aileen, reading of the disposition of all the wares, and knowing their value to Cowperwood, to say nothing of their charm for her, was greatly depressed; yet she was not long despondent, for she was convinced that Cowperwood would some day regain his liberty and attain a position of even greater significance in the financial world. She could not have said why but she was sure of it.

Chapter LV

In the meanwhile Cowperwood had been transferred to a new overseer and a new cell in Block 3 on the ground door, which was like all the others in size, ten by sixteen, but to which was attached the small yard previously mentioned. Warden Desmas came up two days before he was transferred, and had another short conversation with him through his cell door.

"You'll be transferred on Monday," he said, in his reserved, slow way. "They'll give you a yard, though it won't be much good to you–we only allow a half-hour a day in it. I've told the overseer about your business arrangements. He'll treat you right in that matter. Just be careful not to take up too much time that way, and things will work out. I've decided to let you learn caning chairs. That'll be the best for you. It's easy, and it'll occupy your mind."

The warden and some allied politicians made a good thing out of this prison industry. It was really not hard labor–the tasks set were simple and not oppressive, but all of the products were promptly sold, and the profits pocketed. It was good, therefore, to see all the prisoners working, and it did them good. Cowperwood was glad of the chance to do something, for he really did not care so much for books, and his connection with Wingate and his old affairs were not sufficient to employ his mind in a satisfactory way. At the same time, he could not help thinking, if he seemed strange to himself, now, how much stranger he would seem then, behind these narrow bars working at so commonplace a task as caning chairs. Nevertheless, he now thanked Desmas for this, as well as for the sheets and the toilet articles which had just been brought in.

"That's all right," replied the latter, pleasantly and softly, by now much intrigued by Cowperwood. "I know that there are men and men here, the same as anywhere. If a man knows how to use these things and wants to be clean, I wouldn't be one to put anything in his way."

The new overseer with whom Cowperwood had to deal was a very different person from Elias Chapin. His name was Walter Bonhag, and he was not more than thirty-seven years of age–a big, flabby sort of person with a crafty mind, whose principal object in life was to see that this prison situation as he found it should furnish him a better income than his normal salary provided. A close study of Bonhag would have seemed to indicate that he was a stool-pigeon of Desmas, but this was really not true except in a limited way. Because Bonhag was shrewd and sycophantic, quick to see a point in his or anybody else's favor, Desmas instinctively realized that he was the kind of man who could be trusted to be lenient on order or suggestion. That is, if Desmas had the least interest in a prisoner he need scarcely say so much to Bonhag; he might merely suggest that this man was used to a different kind of life, or that, because of some past experience, it might go hard with him if he were handled roughly; and Bonhag would strain himself to be pleasant. The trouble was that to a shrewd man of any refinement his attentions were objectionable, being obviously offered for a purpose, and to a poor or ignorant man they were brutal and contemptuous. He had built up an extra income for himself inside the prison by selling the prisoners extra allowances of things which he secretly brought into the prison. It was strictly against the rules, in theory at least, to bring in anything which was not sold in the store-room–tobacco, writing paper, pens, ink, whisky, cigars, or delicacies of any kind. On the other hand, and excellently well for him, it was true that tobacco of an inferior grade was provided, as well as wretched pens, ink and paper, so that no self-respecting man, if he could help it, would endure them. Whisky was not allowed at all, and delicacies were abhorred as indicating rank favoritism; nevertheless, they were brought in. If a prisoner had the money and was willing to see that Bonhag secured something for his trouble, almost anything would be forthcoming. Also the privilege of being sent into the general yard as a "trusty," or being allowed to stay in the little private yard which some cells possessed, longer than the half-hour ordinarily permitted, was sold.

One of the things curiously enough at this time, which worked in Cowperwood's favor, was the fact that Bonhag was friendly with the overseer who had Stener in charge, and Stener, because of his political friends, was being liberally treated, and Bonhag knew of this. He was not a careful reader of newspapers, nor had he any intellectual grasp of important events; but he knew by now that both Stener and Cowperwood were, or had been, individuals of great importance in the community; also that Cowperwood had been the more important of the two. Better yet, as Bonhag now heard, Cowperwood still had money. Some prisoner, who was permitted to read the paper, told him so. And so, entirely aside from Warden Desmas's recommendation, which was given in a very quiet, noncommittal way, Bonhag was interested to see what he could do for Cowperwood for a price.

The day Cowperwood was installed in his new cell, Bonhag lolled up to the door, which was open, and said, in a semi-patronizing way, "Got all your things over yet?" It was his business to lock the door once Cowperwood was inside it.

"Yes, sir," replied Cowperwood, who had been shrewd enough to get the new overseer's name from Chapin; "this is Mr. Bonhag, I presume?"

"That's me," replied Bonhag, not a little flattered by the recognition, but still purely interested by the practical side of this encounter. He was anxious to study Cowperwood, to see what type of man he was.

"You'll find it a little different down here from up there," observed Bonhag. "It ain't so stuffy. These doors out in the yards make a difference."

"Oh, yes," said Cowperwood, observantly and shrewdly, "that is the yard Mr. Desmas spoke of."

At the mention of the magic name, if Bonhag had been a horse, his ears would have been seen to lift. For, of course, if Cowperwood was so friendly with Desmas that the latter had described to him the type of cell he was to have beforehand, it behooved Bonhag to be especially careful.

"Yes, that's it, but it ain't much," he observed. "They only allow a half-hour a day in it. Still it would be all right if a person could stay out there longer."

This was his first hint at graft, favoritism; and Cowperwood distinctly caught the sound of it in his voice.

"That's too bad," he said. "I don't suppose good conduct helps a person to get more." He waited to hear a reply, but instead Bonhag continued with: "I'd better teach you your new trade now. You've got to learn to cane chairs, so the warden says. If you want, we can begin right away." But without waiting for Cowperwood to acquiesce, he went off, returning after a time with three unvarnished frames of chairs and a bundle of cane strips or withes, which he deposited on the floor. Having so done–and with a flourish–he now continued: "Now I'll show you if you'll watch me," and he began showing Cowperwood how the strips were to be laced through the apertures on either side, cut, and fastened with little hickory pegs. This done, he brought a forcing awl, a small hammer, a box of pegs, and a pair of clippers. After several brief demonstrations with different strips, as to how the geometric forms were designed, he allowed Cowperwood to take the matter in hand, watching over his shoulder. The financier, quick at anything, manual or mental, went at it in his customary energetic fashion, and in five minutes demonstrated to Bonhag that, barring skill and speed, which could only come with practice, he could do it as well as another. "You'll make out all right," said Bonhag. "You're supposed to do ten of those a day. We won't count the next few days, though, until you get your hand in. After that I'll come around and see how you're getting along. You understand about the towel on the door, don't you?" he inquired.

"Yes, Mr. Chapin explained that to me," replied Cowperwood. "I think I know what most of the rules are now. I'll try not to break any of them."

The days which followed brought a number of modifications of his prison lot, but not sufficient by any means to make it acceptable to him. Bonhag, during the first few days in which he trained Cowperwood in the art of caning chairs, managed to make it perfectly clear that there were a number of things he would be willing to do for him. One of the things that moved him to this, was that already he had been impressed by the fact that Stener's friends were coming to see him in larger numbers than Cowperwood's, sending him an occasional basket of fruit, which he gave to the overseers, and that his wife and children had been already permitted to visit him outside the regular visiting-day. This was a cause for jealousy on Bonhag's part. His fellow-overseer was lording it over him–telling him, as it were, of the high jinks in Block 4. Bonhag really wanted Cowperwood to spruce up and show what he could do, socially or otherwise.

And so now he began with: "I see you have your lawyer and your partner here every day. There ain't anybody else you'd like to have visit you, is there? Of course, it's against the rules to have your wife or sister or anybody like that, except on visiting days–" And here he paused and rolled a large and informing eye on Cowperwood–such an eye as was supposed to convey dark and mysterious things. "But all the rules ain't kept around here by a long shot."

Cowperwood was not the man to lose a chance of this kind. He smiled a little– enough to relieve himself, and to convey to Bonhag that he was gratified by the information, but vocally he observed: "I'll tell you how it is, Mr. Bonhag. I believe you understand my position better than most men would, and that I can talk to you. There are people who would like to come here, but I have been afraid to let them come. I did not know that it could be arranged. If it could be, I would be very grateful. You and I are practical men–I know that if any favors are extended some of those who help to bring them about must be looked after. If you can do anything to make it a little more comfortable for me here I will show you that I appreciate it. I haven't any money on my person, but I can always get it, and I will see that you are properly looked after."

Bonhag's short, thick ears tingled. This was the kind of talk he liked to hear. "I can fix anything like that, Mr. Cowperwood," he replied, servilely. "You leave it to me. If there's any one you want to see at any time, just let me know. Of course I have to be very careful, and so do you, but that's all right, too. If you want to stay out in that yard a little longer in the mornings or get out there afternoons or evenings, from now on, why, go ahead. It's all right. I'll just leave the door open. If the warden or anybody else should be around, I'll just scratch on your door with my key, and you come in and shut it. If there's anything you want from the outside I can get it for you–jelly or eggs or butter or any little thing like that. You might like to fix up your meals a little that way."

"I'm certainly most grateful, Mr. Bonhag," returned Cowperwood in his grandest manner, and with a desire to smile, but he kept a straight face.

"In regard to that other matter," went on Bonhag, referring to the matter of extra visitors, "I can fix that any time you want to. I know the men out at the gate. If you want anybody to come here, just write 'em a note and give it to me, and tell 'em to ask for me when they come. That'll get 'em in all right. When they get here you can talk to 'em in your cell. See! Only when I tap they have to come out. You want to remember that. So just you let me know."

Cowperwood was exceedingly grateful. He said so in direct, choice language. It occurred to him at once that this was Aileen's opportunity, and that he could now notify her to come. If she veiled herself sufficiently she would probably be safe enough. He decided to write her, and when Wingate came he gave him a letter to mail.

Two days later, at three o'clock in the afternoon–the time appointed by him–Aileen came to see him. She was dressed in gray broadcloth with white-velvet trimmings and cut-steel buttons which glistened like silver, and wore, as additional ornaments, as well as a protection against the cold, a cap, stole, and muff of snow-white ermine. Over this rather striking costume she had slipped a long dark circular cloak, which she meant to lay off immediately upon her arrival. She had made a very careful toilet as to her shoes, gloves, hair, and the gold ornaments which she wore. Her face was concealed by a thick green veil, as Cowperwood had suggested; and she arrived at an hour when, as near as he had been able to prearrange, he would be alone. Wingate usually came at four, after business, and Steger in the morning, when he came at all. She was very nervous over this strange adventure, leaving the street-car in which she had chosen to travel some distance away and walking up a side street. The cold weather and the gray walls under a gray sky gave her a sense of defeat, but she had worked very hard to look nice in order to cheer her lover up. She knew how readily he responded to the influence of her beauty when properly displayed.

Cowperwood, in view of her coming, had made his cell as acceptable as possible. It was clean, because he had swept it himself and made his own bed; and besides he had shaved and combed his hair, and otherwise put himself to rights. The caned chairs on which he was working had been put in the corner at the end of the bed. His few dishes were washed and hung up, and his clogs brushed with a brush which he now kept for the purpose. Never before, he thought to himself, with a peculiar feeling of artistic degradation, had Aileen seen him like this. She had always admired his good taste in clothes, and the way he carried himself in them; and now she was to see him in garments which no dignity of body could make presentable. Only a stoic sense of his own soul-dignity aided him here. After all, as he now thought, he was Frank A. Cowperwood, and that was something, whatever he wore. And Aileen knew it. Again, he might be free and rich some day, and he knew that she believed that. Best of all, his looks under these or any other circumstances, as he knew, would make no difference to Aileen. She would only love him the more. It was her ardent sympathy that he was afraid of. He was so glad that Bonhag had suggested that she might enter the cell, for it would be a grim procedure talking to her through a barred door.

When Aileen arrived she asked for Mr. Bonhag, and was permitted to go to the central rotunda, where he was sent for. When he came she murmured: "I wish to see Mr. Cowperwood, if you please"; and he exclaimed, "Oh, yes, just come with me." As he came across the rotunda floor from his corridor he was struck by the evident youth of Aileen, even though he could not see her face. This now was something in accordance with what he had expected of Cowperwood. A man who could steal five hundred thousand dollars and set a whole city by the ears must have wonderful adventures of all kinds, and Aileen looked like a true adventure. He led her to the little room where he kept his desk and detained visitors, and then bustled down to Cowperwood's cell, where the financier was working on one of his chairs and scratching on the door with his key, called: "There's a young lady here to see you. Do you want to let her come inside?"

"Thank you, yes," replied Cowperwood; and Bonhag hurried away, unintentionally forgetting, in his boorish incivility, to unlock the cell door, so that he had to open it in Aileen's presence. The long corridor, with its thick doors, mathematically spaced gratings and gray-stone pavement, caused Aileen to feel faint at heart. A prison, iron cells! And he was in one of them. It chilled her usually courageous spirit. What a terrible place for her Frank to be! What a horrible thing to have put him here! Judges, juries, courts, laws, jails seemed like so many foaming ogres ranged about the world, glaring down upon her and her love-affair. The clank of the key in the lock, and the heavy outward swinging of the door, completed her sense of the untoward. And then she saw Cowperwood.

Because of the price he was to receive, Bonhag, after admitting her, strolled discreetly away. Aileen looked at Cowperwood from behind her veil, afraid to speak until she was sure Bonhag had gone. And Cowperwood, who was retaining his self-possession by an effort, signaled her but with difficulty after a moment or two. "It's all right," he said. "He's gone away." She lifted her veil, removed her cloak, and took in, without seeming to, the stuffy, narrow thickness of the room, his wretched shoes, the cheap, misshapen suit, the iron door behind him leading out into the little yard attached to his cell. Against such a background, with his partially caned chairs visible at the end of the bed, he seemed unnatural, weird even. Her Frank! And in this condition. She trembled and it was useless for her to try to speak. She could only put her arms around him and stroke his head, murmuring: "My poor boy—my darling. Is this what they have done to you? Oh, my poor darling." She held his head while Cowperwood, anxious to retain his composure, winced and trembled, too. Her love was so full—so genuine. It was so soothing at the same time that it was unmanning, as now he could see, making of him a child again. And for the first time in his life, some inexplicable trick of chemistry—that chemistry of the body, of blind forces which so readily supersedes reason at times—he lost his self-control. The depth of Aileen's feelings, the cooing sound of her voice, the velvety tenderness of her hands, that beauty that had drawn him all the time—more radiant here perhaps within these hard walls, and in the face of his physical misery, than it had ever been before–completely unmanned him. He did not understand how it could; he tried to defy the moods, but he could not. When she held his head close and caressed it, of a sudden, in spite of himself, his breast felt thick and stuffy, and his throat hurt him. He felt, for him, an astonishingly strange feeling, a desire to cry, which he did his best to overcome; it shocked him so. There then combined and conspired to defeat him a strange, rich picture of the great world he had so recently lost, of the lovely, magnificent world which he hoped some day to regain. He felt more poignantly at this moment than ever he had before the degradation of the clog shoes, the cotton shirt, the striped suit, the reputation of a convict, permanent and not to be laid aside. He drew himself quickly away from her, turned his back, clinched his hands, drew his muscles taut; but it was too late. He was crying, and he could not stop.

"Oh, damn it!" he exclaimed, half angrily, half self-commiseratingly, in combined rage and shame. "Why should I cry? What the devil's the matter with me, anyhow?"

Aileen saw it. She fairly flung herself in front of him, seized his head with one hand, his shabby waist with the other, and held him tight in a grip that he could not have readily released.

"Oh, honey, honey, honey!" she exclaimed, pityingly feverishly. "I love you, I adore you. They could cut my body into bits if it would do you any good. To think that they should make you cry! Oh, my sweet, my sweet, my darling boy!"

She pulled his still shaking body tighter, and with her free hand caressed his head. She kissed his eyes, his hair, his cheeks. He pulled himself loose again after a moment, exclaiming, "What the devil's got into me?" but she drew him back.

"Never mind, honey darling, don't you be ashamed to cry. Cry here on my shoulder. Cry here with me. My baby–my honey pet!"

He quieted down after a few moments, cautioning her against Bonhag, and regaining his former composure, which he was so ashamed to have lost.

"You're a great girl, pet," he said, with a tender and yet apologetic smile. "You're all right–all that I need–a great help to me; but don't worry any longer about me, dear. I'm all right. It isn't as bad as you think. How are you?"

Aileen on her part was not to be soothed so easily. His many woes, including his wretched position here, outraged her sense of justice and decency. To think her fine, wonderful Frank should be compelled to come to this–to cry. She stroked his head, tenderly, while wild, deadly, unreasoning opposition to life and chance and untoward opposition surged in her brain. Her father–damn him! Her family–pooh! What did she care? Her Frank–her Frank. How little all else mattered where he was concerned. Never, never, never would she desert him–never–come what might. And now she clung to him in silence while she fought in her brain an awful battle with life and law and fate and circumstance. Law–nonsense! People–they were brutes, devils, enemies, hounds! She was delighted, eager, crazy to make a sacrifice of herself. She would go anywhere for or with her Frank now. She would do anything for him. Her family was nothing–life nothing, nothing, nothing. She would do anything he wished, nothing more, nothing less; anything she could do to save him, to make his life happier, but nothing for any one else.

Chapter LVI

The days passed. Once the understanding with Bonhag was reached, Cowperwood's wife, mother and sister were allowed to appear on occasions. His wife and the children were now settled in the little home for which he was paying, and his financial obligations to her were satisfied by Wingate, who paid her one hundred and twenty five dollars a month for him. He realized that he owed her more, but he was sailing rather close to the wind financially, these days. The final collapse of his old interests had come in March, when he had been legally declared a bankrupt, and all his properties forfeited to satisfy the claims against him. The city's claim of five hundred thousand dollars would have eaten up more than could have been realized at the time, had not a pro rata payment of thirty cents on the dollar been declared. Even then the city never received its due, for by some hocus-pocus it was declared to have forfeited its rights. Its claims had not been made at the proper time in the proper way. This left larger portions of real money for the others.

Fortunately by now Cowperwood had begun to see that by a little experimenting his business relations with Wingate were likely to prove profitable. The broker had made it clear that he intended to be perfectly straight with him. He had employed Cowperwood's two brothers, at very moderate salaries–one to take care of the books and look after the office, and the other to act on 'change with him, for their seats in that organization had never been sold. And also, by considerable effort, he had succeeded in securing Cowperwood, Sr., a place as a clerk in a bank. For the latter, since the day of his resignation from the Third National had been in a deep, sad quandary as to what further to do with his life. His son's disgrace! The horror of his trial and incarceration. Since the day of Frank's indictment and more so, since his sentence and commitment to the Eastern Penitentiary, he was as one who walked in a dream. That trial! That charge against Frank! His own son, a convict in stripes–and after he and Frank had walked so proudly in the front rank of the successful and respected here. Like so many others in his hour of distress, he had taken to reading the Bible, looking into its pages for something of that mind consolation that always, from youth up, although rather casually in these latter years, he had imagined was to be found there. The Psalms, Isaiah, the Book of Job, Ecclesiastes. And for the most part, because of the fraying nature of his present ills, not finding it.

But day after day secreting himself in his room–a little hall-bedroom office in his newest home, where to his wife, he pretended that he had some commercial matters wherewith he was still concerned–and once inside, the door locked, sitting and brooding on all that had befallen him–his losses; his good name. Or, after months of this, and because of the new position secured for him by Wingate–a bookkeeping job in one of the outlying banks–slipping away early in the morning, and returning late at night, his mind a gloomy epitome of all that had been or yet might be.

To see him bustling off from his new but very much reduced home at half after seven in the morning in order to reach the small bank, which was some distance away and not accessible by street-car line, was one of those pathetic sights which the fortunes of trade so frequently offer. He carried his lunch in a small box because it was inconvenient to return home in the time allotted for this purpose, and because his new salary did not permit the extravagance of a purchased one. It was his one ambition now to eke out a respectable but unseen existence until he should die, which he hoped would not be long. He was a pathetic figure with his thin legs and body, his gray hair, and his snow-white side-whiskers. He was very lean and angular, and, when confronted by a difficult problem, a little uncertain or vague in his mind. An old habit which had grown on him in the years of his prosperity of putting his hand to his mouth and of opening his eyes in an assumption of surprise, which had no basis in fact, now grew upon him. He really degenerated, although he did not know it, into a mere automaton. Life strews its shores with such interesting and pathetic wrecks.

One of the things that caused Cowperwood no little thought at this time, and especially in view of his present extreme indifference to her, was how he would bring up this matter of his indifference to his wife and his desire to end their relationship. Yet apart from the brutality of the plain truth, he saw no way. As he could plainly see, she was now persisting in her pretense of devotion, uncolored, apparently, by any suspicion of what had happened. Yet since his trial and conviction, she had been hearing from one source and another that he was still intimate with Aileen, and it was only her thought of his concurrent woes, and the fact that he might possibly be spared to a successful financial life, that now deterred her from speaking. He was shut up in a cell, she said to herself, and she was really very sorry for him, but she did not love him as she once had. He was really too deserving of reproach for his general unseemly conduct, and no doubt this was what was intended, as well as being enforced, by the Governing Power of the world.

One can imagine how much such an attitude as this would appeal to Cowperwood, once he had detected it. By a dozen little signs, in spite of the fact that she brought him delicacies, and commiserated on his fate, he could see that she felt not only sad, but reproachful, and if there was one thing that Cowperwood objected to at all times it was the moral as well as the funereal air. Contrasted with the cheerful combative hopefulness and enthusiasm of Aileen, the wearied uncertainty of Mrs. Cowperwood was, to say the least, a little tame. Aileen, after her first burst of rage over his fate, which really did not develop any tears on her part, was apparently convinced that he would get out and be very successful again. She talked success and his future all the time because she believed in it. Instinctively she seemed to realize that prison walls could not make a prison for him. Indeed, on the first day she left she handed Bonhag ten dollars, and after thanking him in her attractive voice–without showing her face, however–for his obvious kindness to her, bespoke his further favor for Cowperwood– "a very great man," as she described him, which sealed that ambitious materialist's fate completely. There was nothing the overseer would not do for the young lady in the dark cloak. She might have stayed in Cowperwood's cell for a week if the visiting-hours of the penitentiary had not made it impossible.

The day that Cowperwood decided to discuss with his wife the weariness of his present married state and his desire to be free of it was some four months after he had entered the prison. By that time he had become inured to his convict life. The silence of his cell and the menial tasks he was compelled to perform, which had at first been so distressing, banal, maddening, in their pointless iteration, had now become merely commonplace–dull, but not painful. Furthermore he had learned many of the little resources of the solitary convict, such as that of using his lamp to warm up some delicacy which he had saved from a previous meal or from some basket which had been sent him by his wife or Aileen. He had partially gotten rid of the sickening odor of his cell by persuading Bonhag to bring him small packages of lime; which he used with great freedom. Also he succeeded in defeating some of the more venturesome rats with traps; and with Bonhag's permission, after his cell door had been properly locked at night, and sealed with the outer wooden door, he would take his chair, if it were not too cold, out into the little back yard of his cell and look at the sky, where, when the nights were clear, the stars were to be seen. He had never taken any interest in astronomy as a scientific study, but now the Pleiades, the belt of Orion, the Big Dipper and the North Star, to which one of its lines pointed, caught his attention, almost his fancy. He wondered why the stars of the belt of Orion came to assume the peculiar mathematical relation to each other which they held, as far as distance and arrangement were concerned, and whether that could possibly have any intellectual significance. The nebulous conglomeration of the suns in Pleiades suggested a soundless depth of space, and he thought of the earth floating like a little ball in immeasurable reaches of ether. His own life appeared very trivial in view of these things, and he found himself asking whether it was all really of any significance or importance. He shook these moods off with ease, however, for the man was possessed of a sense of grandeur, largely in relation to himself and his affairs; and his temperament was essentially material and vital. Something kept telling him that whatever his present state he must yet grow to be a significant personage, one whose fame would be heralded the world over–who must try, try, try. It was not given all men to see far or to do brilliantly; but to him it was given, and he must be what he was cut out to be. There was no more escaping the greatness that was inherent in him than there was for so many others the littleness that was in them.

Mrs. Cowperwood came in that afternoon quite solemnly, bearing several changes of linen, a pair of sheets, some potted meat and a pie. She was not exactly doleful, but Cowperwood thought that she was tending toward it, largely because of her brooding over his relationship to Aileen, which he knew that she knew. Something in her manner decided him to speak before she left; and after asking her how the children were, and listening to her inquiries in regard to the things that he needed, he said to her, sitting on his single chair while she sat on his bed:

"Lillian, there's something I've been wanting to talk with you about for some time. I should have done it before, but it's better late than never. I know that you know that there is something between Aileen Butler and me, and we might as well have it open and aboveboard. It's true I am very fond of her and she is very devoted to me, and if ever I get out of here I want to arrange it so that I can marry her. That means that you will have to give me a divorce, if you will; and I want to talk to you about that now. This can't be so very much of a surprise to you, because you must have seen this long while that our relationship hasn't been all that it might have been, and under the circumstances this can't prove such a very great hardship to you–I am sure." He paused, waiting, for Mrs. Cowperwood at first said nothing.

Her thought, when he first broached this, was that she ought to make some demonstration of astonishment or wrath: but when she looked into his steady, examining eyes, so free from the illusion of or interest in demonstrations of any kind, she realized how useless it would be. He was so utterly matter-of-fact in what seemed to her quite private and secret affairs–very shameless. She had never been able to understand quite how he could take the subtleties of life as he did, anyhow. Certain things which she always fancied should be hushed up he spoke of with the greatest nonchalance. Her ears tingled sometimes at his frankness in disposing of a social situation; but she thought this must be characteristic of notable men, and so there was nothing to be said about it. Certain men did as they pleased; society did not seem to be able to deal with them in any way. Perhaps God would, later–she was not sure. Anyhow, bad as he was, direct as he was, forceful as he was, he was far more interesting than most of the more conservative types in whom the social virtues of polite speech and modest thoughts were seemingly predominate.

"I know," she said, rather peacefully, although with a touch of anger and resentment in her voice. "I've known all about it all this time. I expected you would say something like this to me some day. It's a nice reward for all my devotion to you; but it's just like you, Frank. When you are set on something, nothing can stop you. It wasn't enough that you were getting along so nicely and had two children whom you ought to love, but you had to take up with this Butler creature until her name and yours are a by-word throughout the city. I know that she comes to this prison. I saw her out here one day as I was coming in, and I suppose every one else knows it by now. She has no sense of decency and she does not care–the wretched, vain thing–but I would have thought that you would be ashamed, Frank, to go on the way that you have, when you still have me and the children and your father and mother and when you are certain to have such a hard fight to get yourself on your feet, as it is. If she had any sense of decency she would not have anything to do with you–the shameless thing."

Cowperwood looked at his wife with unflinching eyes. He read in her remarks just what his observation had long since confirmed–that she was sympathetically out of touch with him. She was no longer so attractive physically, and intellectually she was not Aileen's equal. Also that contact with those women who had deigned to grace his home in his greatest hour of prosperity had proved to him conclusively she was lacking in certain social graces. Aileen was by no means so vastly better, still she was young and amenable and adaptable, and could still be improved. Opportunity as he now chose to think, might make Aileen, whereas for Lillian–or at least, as he now saw it–it could do nothing.

"I'll tell you how it is, Lillian," he said; "I'm not sure that you are going to get what I mean exactly, but you and I are not at all well suited to each other any more."

"You didn't seem to think that three or four years ago," interrupted his wife, bitterly.

"I married you when I was twenty-one," went on Cowperwood, quite brutally, not paying any attention to her interruption, "and I was really too young to know what I was doing. I was a mere boy. It doesn't make so much difference about that. I am not using that as an excuse. The point that I am trying to make is this–that right or wrong, important or not important, I have changed my mind since. I don't love you any more, and I don't feel that I want to keep up a relationship, however it may look to the public, that is not satisfactory to me. You have one point of view about life, and I have another. You think your point of view is the right one, and there are thousands of people who will agree with you; but I don't think so. We have never quarreled about these things, because I didn't think it was important to quarrel about them. I don't see under the circumstances that I am doing you any great injustice when I ask you to let me go. I don't intend to desert you or the children–you will get a good living-income from me as long as I have the money to give it to you–but I want my personal freedom when I come out of here, if ever I do, and I want you to let me have it. The money that you had and a great deal more, once I am out of here, you will get back when I am on my feet again. But not if you oppose me–only if you help me. I want, and intend to help you always–but in my way."

He smoothed the leg of his prison trousers in a thoughtful way, and plucked at the sleeve of his coat. Just now he looked very much like a highly intelligent workman as he sat here, rather than like the important personage that he was. Mrs. Cowperwood was very resentful.

"That's a nice way to talk to me, and a nice way to treat me!" she exclaimed dramatically, rising and walking the short space–some two steps–that lay between the wall and the bed. "I might have known that you were too young to know your own mind when you married me. Money, of course, that's all you think of and your own gratification. I don't believe you have any sense of justice in you. I don't believe you ever had. You only think of yourself, Frank. I never saw such a man as you. You have treated me like a dog all through this affair; and all the while you have been running with that little snip of an Irish thing, and telling her all about your affairs, I suppose. You let me go on believing that you cared for me up to the last moment, and then you suddenly step up and tell me that you want a divorce. I'll not do it. I'll not give you a divorce, and you needn't think it."

Cowperwood listened in silence. His position, in so far as this marital tangle was concerned, as he saw, was very advantageous. He was a convict, constrained by the exigencies of his position to be out of personal contact with his wife for a long period of time to come, which should naturally tend to school her to do without him. When he came out, it would be very easy for her to get a divorce from a convict, particularly if she could allege misconduct with another woman, which he would not deny. At the same time, he hoped to keep Aileen's name out of it. Mrs. Cowperwood, if she would, could give any false name if he made no contest. Besides, she was not a very strong person, intellectually speaking. He could bend her to his will. There was no need of saying much more now; the ice had been broken, the situation had been put before her, and time should do the rest.

"Don't be dramatic, Lillian," he commented, indifferently. "I'm not such a loss to you if you have enough to live on. I don't think I want to live in Philadelphia if ever I come out of here. My idea now is to go west, and I think I want to go alone. I sha'n't get married right away again even if you do give me a divorce. I don't care to take anybody along. It would be better for the children if you would stay here and divorce me. The public would think better of them and you."

"I'll not do it," declared Mrs. Cowperwood, emphatically. "I'll never do it, never; so there! You can say what you choose. You owe it to me to stick by me and the children after all I've done for you, and I'll not do it. You needn't ask me any more; I'll not do it."

"Very well," replied Cowperwood, quietly, getting up. "We needn't talk about it any more now. Your time is nearly up, anyhow." (Twenty minutes was supposed to be the regular allotment for visitors.) "Perhaps you'll change your mind sometime."

She gathered up her muff and the shawl-strap in which she had carried her gifts, and turned to go. It had been her custom to kiss Cowperwood in a make-believe way up to this time, but now she was too angry to make this pretense. And yet she was sorry, too–sorry for herself and, she thought, for him.

"Frank," she declared, dramatically, at the last moment, "I never saw such a man as you. I don't believe you have any heart. You're not worthy of a good wife. You're worthy of just such a woman as you're getting. The idea!" Suddenly tears came to her eyes, and she flounced scornfully and yet sorrowfully out.

Cowperwood stood there. At least there would be no more useless kissing between them, he congratulated himself. It was hard in a way, but purely from an emotional point of view. He was not doing her any essential injustice, he reasoned–not an economic one–which was the important thing. She was angry to-day, but she would get over it, and in time might come to see his point of view. Who could tell? At any rate he had made it plain to her what he intended to do and that was something as he saw it. He reminded one of nothing so much, as he stood there, as of a young chicken picking its way out of the shell of an old estate. Although he was in a cell of a penitentiary, with nearly four years more to serve, yet obviously he felt, within himself, that the whole world was still before him. He could go west if he could not reestablish himself in Philadelphia; but he must stay here long enough to win the approval of those who had known him formerly–to obtain, as it were, a letter of credit which he could carry to other parts.

"Hard words break no bones," he said to himself, as his wife went out. "A man's never done till he's done. I'll show some of these people yet." Of Bonhag, who came to close the cell door, he asked whether it was going to rain, it looked so dark in the hall.

"It's sure to before night," replied Bonhag, who was always wondering over Cowperwood's tangled affairs as he heard them retailed here and there.

Chapter LVII

The time that Cowperwood spent in the Eastern Penitentiary of Pennsylvania was exactly thirteen months from the day of his entry to his discharge. The influences which brought about this result were partly of his willing, and partly not. For one thing, some six months after his incarceration, Edward Malia Butler died, expired sitting in his chair in his private office at his home. The conduct of Aileen had been a great strain on him. From the time Cowperwood had been sentenced, and more particularly after the time he had cried on Aileen's shoulder in prison, she had turned on her father in an almost brutal way. Her attitude, unnatural for a child, was quite explicable as that of a tortured sweetheart. Cowperwood had told her that he thought Butler was using his influence to withhold a pardon for him, even though one were granted to Stener, whose life in prison he had been following with considerable interest; and this had enraged her beyond measure. She lost no chance of being practically insulting to her father, ignoring him on every occasion, refusing as often as possible to eat at the same table, and when she did, sitting next her mother in the place of Norah, with whom she managed to exchange. She refused to sing or play any more when he was present, and persistently ignored the large number of young political aspirants who came to the house, and whose presence in a way had been encouraged for her benefit. Old Butler realized, of course, what it was all about. He said nothing. He could not placate her.

Her mother and brothers did not understand it at all at first. (Mrs. Butler never understood.) But not long after Cowperwood's incarceration Callum and Owen became aware of what the trouble was. Once, when Owen was coming away from a reception at one of the houses where his growing financial importance made him welcome, he heard one of two men whom he knew casually, say to the other, as they stood at the door adjusting their coats, "You saw where this fellow Cowperwood got four years, didn't you?"

"Yes," replied the other. "A clever devil that–wasn't he? I knew that girl he was in with, too–you know who I mean. Miss Butler–wasn't that her name?"

Owen was not sure that he had heard right. He did not get the connection until the other guest, opening the door and stepping out, remarked: "Well, old Butler got even, apparently. They say he sent him up."

Owen's brow clouded. A hard, contentious look came into his eyes. He had much of his father's force. What in the devil were they talking about? What Miss Butler did they have in mind? Could this be Aileen or Norah, and how could Cowperwood come to be in with either of them? It could not possibly be Norah, he reflected; she was very much infatuated with a young man whom he knew, and was going to marry him. Aileen had been most friendly with the Cowperwoods, and had often spoken well of the financier. Could it be she? He could not believe it. He thought once of overtaking the two acquaintances and demanding to know what they meant, but when he came out on the step they were already some distance down the street and in the opposite direction from that in which he wished to go. He decided to ask his father about this.

On demand, old Butler confessed at once, but insisted that his son keep silent about it.

"I wish I'd have known," said Owen, grimly. "I'd have shot the dirty dog."

"Aisy, aisy," said Butler. "Yer own life's worth more than his, and ye'd only be draggin' the rest of yer family in the dirt with him. He's had somethin' to pay him for his dirty trick, and he'll have more. Just ye say nothin' to no one. Wait. He'll be wantin' to get out in a year or two. Say nothin' to her aither. Talkin' won't help there. She'll come to her sinses when he's been away long enough, I'm thinkin'."

Owen had tried to be civil to his sister after that, but since he was a stickler for social perfection and advancement, and so eager to get up in the world himself, he could not understand how she could possibly have done any such thing. He resented bitterly the stumbling-block she had put in his path. Now, among other things, his enemies would have this to throw in his face if they wanted to–and they would want to, trust life for that.

Callum reached his knowledge of the matter in quite another manner, but at about the same time. He was a member of an athletic club which had an attractive building in the city, and a fine country club, where he went occasionally to enjoy the swimming-pool and the Turkish bath connected with it. One of his friends approached him there in the billiard-room one evening and said, "Say, Butler, you know I'm a good friend of yours, don't you?"

"Why, certainly, I know it," replied Callum. "What's the matter?"

"Well, you know," said the young individual, whose name was Richard Pethick, looking at Callum with a look of almost strained affection, "I wouldn't come to you with any story that I thought would hurt your feelings or that you oughtn't to know about, but I do think you ought to know about this." He pulled at a high white collar which was choking his neck.

"I know you wouldn't, Pethick," replied Callum; very much interested. "What is it? What's the point?"

"Well, I don't like to say anything," replied Pethick, "but that fellow Hibbs is saying things around here about your sister."

"What's that?" exclaimed Callum, straightening up in the most dynamic way and bethinking him of the approved social procedure in all such cases. He should be very angry. He should demand and exact proper satisfaction in some form or other–by blows very likely if his honor had been in any way impugned. "What is it he says about my sister? What right has he to mention her name here, anyhow? He doesn't know her."

Pethick affected to be greatly concerned lest he cause trouble between Callum and Hibbs. He protested that he did not want to, when, in reality, he was dying to tell. At last he came out with, "Why, he's circulated the yarn that your sister had something to do with this man Cowperwood, who was tried here recently, and that that's why he's just gone to prison."

"What's that?" exclaimed Callum, losing the make-believe of the unimportant, and taking on the serious mien of some one who feels desperately. "He says that, does he? Where is he? I want to see if he'll say that to me."

Some of the stern fighting ability of his father showed in his slender, rather refined young face.

"Now, Callum," insisted Pethick, realizing the genuine storm he had raised, and being a little fearful of the result, "do be careful what you say. You mustn't have a row in here. You know it's against the rules. Besides he may be drunk. It's just some foolish talk he's heard, I'm sure. Now, for goodness' sake, don't get so excited." Pethick, having evoked the storm, was not a little nervous as to its results in his own case. He, too, as well as Callum, himself as the tale-bearer, might now be involved.

But Callum by now was not so easily restrained. His face was quite pale, and he was moving toward the old English grill-room, where Hibbs happened to be, consuming a brandy-and-soda with a friend of about his own age. Callum entered and called him.

"Oh, Hibbs!" he said.

Hibbs, hearing his voice and seeing him in the door, arose and came over. He was an interesting youth of the collegiate type, educated at Princeton. He had heard the rumor concerning Aileen from various sources–other members of the club, for one–and had ventured to repeat it in Pethick's presence.

"What's that you were just saying about my sister?" asked Callum, grimly, looking Hibbs in the eye.

"Why–I–" hesitated Hibbs, who sensed trouble and was eager to avoid it. He was not exceptionally brave and looked it. His hair was straw-colored, his eyes blue, and his cheeks pink. "Why–nothing in particular. Who said I was talking about her?" He looked at Pethick, whom he knew to be the tale-bearer, and the latter exclaimed, excitedly:

"Now don't you try to deny it, Hibbs. You know I heard you?"

"Well, what did I say?" asked Hibbs, defiantly.

"Well, what did you say?" interrupted Callum, grimly, transferring the conversation to himself. "That's just what I want to know."

"Why," stammered Hibbs, nervously, "I don't think I've said anything that anybody else hasn't said. I just repeated that some one said that your sister had been very friendly with Mr. Cowperwood. I didn't say any more than I have heard other people say around here."

"Oh, you didn't, did you?" exclaimed Callum, withdrawing his hand from his pocket and slapping Hibbs in the face. He repeated the blow with his left hand, fiercely. "Perhaps that'll teach you to keep my sister's name out of your mouth, you pup!"

Hibbs's arms flew up. He was not without pugilistic training, and he struck back vigorously, striking Callum once in the chest and once in the neck. In an instant the two rooms of this suite were in an uproar. Tables and chairs were overturned by the energy of men attempting to get to the scene of action. The two combatants were quickly separated; sides were taken by the friends of each, excited explanations attempted and defied. Callum was examining the knuckles of his left hand, which were cut from the blow he had delivered. He maintained a gentlemanly calm. Hibbs, very much flustered and excited, insisted that he had been most unreasonably used. The idea of attacking him here. And, anyhow, as he maintained now, Pethick had been both eavesdropping and lying about him. Incidentally, the latter was protesting to others that he had done the only thing which an honorable friend could do. It was a nine days' wonder in the club, and was only kept out of the newspapers by the most strenuous efforts on the part of the friends of both parties. Callum was so outraged on discovering that there was some foundation for the rumor at the club in a general rumor which prevailed that he tendered his resignation, and never went there again.

"I wish to heaven you hadn't struck that fellow," counseled Owen, when the incident was related to him. "It will only make more talk. She ought to leave this place; but she won't. She's struck on that fellow yet, and we can't tell Norah and mother. We will never hear the last of this, you and I–believe me."

"Damn it, she ought to be made to go," exclaimed Callum.

"Well, she won't," replied Owen. "Father has tried making her, and she won't go. Just let things stand. He's in the penitentiary now, and that's probably the end of him. The public seem to think that father put him there, and that's something. Maybe we can persuade her to go after a while. I wish to God we had never had sight of that fellow. If ever he comes out, I've a good notion to kill him."

"Oh, I wouldn't do anything like that," replied Callum. "It's useless. It would only stir things up afresh. He's done for, anyhow."

They planned to urge Norah to marry as soon as possible. And as for their feelings toward Aileen, it was a very chilly atmosphere which Mrs. Butler contemplated from now on, much to her confusion, grief, and astonishment.

In this divided world it was that Butler eventually found himself, all at sea as to what to think or what to do. He had brooded so long now, for months, and as yet had found no solution. And finally, in a form of religious despair, sitting at his desk, in his business chair, he had collapsed–a weary and disconsolate man of seventy. A lesion of the left ventricle was the immediate physical cause, although brooding over Aileen was in part the mental one. His death could not have been laid to his grief over Aileen exactly, for he was a very large man–apoplectic and with sclerotic veins and arteries. For a great many years now he had taken very little exercise, and his digestion had been considerably impaired thereby. He was past seventy, and his time had been reached. They found him there the next morning, his hands folded in his lap, his head on his bosom, quite cold.

He was buried with honors out of St. Timothy's Church, the funeral attended by a large body of politicians and city officials, who discussed secretly among themselves whether his grief over his daughter had anything to do with his end. All his good deeds were remembered, of course, and Mollenhauer and Simpson sent great floral emblems in remembrance. They were very sorry that he was gone, for they had been a cordial three. But gone he was, and that ended their interest in the matter. He left all of his property to his wife in one of the shortest wills ever recorded locally.

"I give and bequeath to my beloved wife, Norah, all my property of whatsoever kind to be disposed of as she may see fit."

There was no misconstruing this. A private paper drawn secretly for her sometime before by Butler, explained how the property should be disposed of by her at her death. It was Butler's real will masquerading as hers, and she would not have changed it for worlds; but he wanted her left in undisturbed possession of everything until she should die. Aileen's originally assigned portion had never been changed. According to her father's will, which no power under the sun could have made Mrs. Butler alter, she was left $250,000 to be paid at Mrs. Butler's death. Neither this fact nor any of the others contained in the paper were communicated by Mrs. Butler, who retained it to be left as her will. Aileen often wondered, but never sought to know, what had been left her. Nothing she fancied–but felt that she could not help this.

Butler's death led at once to a great change in the temper of the home. After the funeral the family settled down to a seemingly peaceful continuance of the old life; but it was a matter of seeming merely. The situation stood with Callum and Owen manifesting a certain degree of contempt for Aileen, which she, understanding, reciprocated. She was very haughty. Owen had plans of forcing her to leave after Butler's death, but he finally asked himself what was the use. Mrs. Butler, who did not want to leave the old home, was very fond of Aileen, so therein lay a reason for letting her remain. Besides, any move to force her out would have entailed an explanation to her mother, which was not deemed advisable. Owen himself was interested in Caroline Mollenhauer, whom he hoped some day to marry–as much for her prospective wealth as for any other reason, though he was quite fond of her. In the

January following Butler's death, which occurred in August, Norah was married very quietly, and the following spring Callum embarked on a similar venture.

In the meanwhile, with Butler's death, the control of the political situation had shifted considerably. A certain Tom Collins, formerly one of Butler's henchmen, but latterly a power in the First, Second, Third, and Fourth Wards, where he had numerous saloons and control of other forms of vice, appeared as a claimant for political recognition. Mollenhauer and Simpson had to consult him, as he could make very uncertain the disposition of some hundred and fifteen thousand votes, a large number of which were fraudulent, but which fact did not modify their deadly character on occasion. Butler's sons disappeared as possible political factors, and were compelled to confine themselves to the street-railway and contracting business. The pardon of Cowperwood and Stener, which Butler would have opposed, because by keeping Stener in he kept Cowperwood in, became a much easier matter. The scandal of the treasury defalcation was gradually dying down; the newspapers had ceased to refer to it in any way. Through Steger and Wingate, a large petition signed by all important financiers and brokers had been sent to the Governor pointing out that Cowperwood's trial and conviction had been most unfair, and asking that he be pardoned. There was no need of any such effort, so far as Stener was concerned; whenever the time seemed ripe the politicians were quite ready to say to the Governor that he ought to let him go. It was only because Butler had opposed Cowperwood's release that they had hesitated. It was really not possible to let out the one and ignore the other; and this petition, coupled with Butler's death, cleared the way very nicely.

Nevertheless, nothing was done until the March following Butler's death, when both Stener and Cowperwood had been incarcerated thirteen months—a length of time which seemed quite sufficient to appease the anger of the public at large. In this period Stener had undergone a considerable change physically and mentally. In spite of the fact that a number of the minor aldermen, who had profited in various ways by his largess, called to see him occasionally, and that he had been given, as it were, almost the liberty of the place, and that his family had not been allowed to suffer, nevertheless he realized that his political and social days were over. Somebody might now occasionally send him a basket of fruit and assure him that he would not be compelled to suffer much longer; but when he did get out, he knew that he had nothing to depend on save his experience as an insurance agent and real-estate dealer. That had been precarious enough in the days when he was trying to get some small political foothold. How would it be when he was known only as the man who had looted the treasury of five hundred thousand dollars and been sent to the penitentiary for five years? Who would lend him the money wherewith to get a little start, even so much as four or five thousand dollars? The people who were calling to pay their respects now and then, and to assure him that he had been badly treated? Never. All of them could honestly claim that they had not so much to spare. If he had good security to offer—yes; but if he had good security he would not need to go to them at all. The man who would have actually helped him if he had only known was Frank A. Cowperwood. Stener could have confessed his mistake, as Cowperwood saw it, and Cowperwood would have given him the money gladly, without any thought of return. But by his poor understanding of human nature, Stener considered that Cowperwood must be an enemy of his, and he would not have had either the courage or the business judgment to approach him.

During his incarceration Cowperwood had been slowly accumulating a little money through Wingate. He had paid Steger considerable sums from time to time, until that worthy finally decided that it would not be fair to take any more.

"If ever you get on your feet, Frank," he said, "you can remember me if you want to, but I don't think you'll want to. It's been nothing but lose, lose, lose for you through me. I'll undertake this matter of getting that appeal to the Governor without any charge on my part. Anything I can do for you from now on is free gratis for nothing."

"Oh, don't talk nonsense, Harper," replied Cowperwood. "I don't know of anybody that could have done better with my case. Certainly there isn't anybody that I would have trusted as much. I don't like lawyers you know."

"Yes–well," said Steger, "they've got nothing on financiers, so we'll call it even." And they shook hands.

So when it was finally decided to pardon Stener, which was in the early part of March, 1873–Cowperwood's pardon was necessarily but gingerly included. A delegation, consisting of Strobik, Harmon, and Winpenny, representing, as it was intended to appear, the unanimous wishes of the council and the city administration, and speaking for Mollenhauer and Simpson, who had given their consent, visited the Governor at Harrisburg and made the necessary formal representations which were intended to impress the public. At the same time, through the agency of Steger, Davison, and Walter Leigh, the appeal in behalf of Cowperwood was made. The Governor, who had had instructions beforehand from sources quite superior to this committee, was very solemn about the whole procedure. He would take the matter under advisement. He would look into the history of the crimes and the records of the two men. He could make no promises–he would see. But in ten days, after allowing the petitions to gather considerable dust in one of his pigeonholes and doing absolutely nothing toward investigating anything, he issued two separate pardons in writing. One, as a matter of courtesy, he gave into the hands of Messrs. Strobik, Harmon, and Winpenny, to bear personally to Mr. Stener, as they desired that he should. The other, on Steger's request, he gave to him. The two committees which had called to receive them then departed; and the afternoon of that same day saw Strobik, Harmon, and Winpenny arrive in one group, and Steger, Wingate, and Walter Leigh in another, at the prison gate, but at different hours.

Chapter LVIII

This matter of the pardon of Cowperwood, the exact time of it, was kept a secret from him, though the fact that he was to be pardoned soon, or that he had a very excellent chance of being, had not been denied–rather had been made much of from time to time. Wingate had kept him accurately informed as to the progress being made, as had Steger; but when it was actually ascertained, from the Governor's private secretary, that a certain day would see the pardon handed over to them, Steger, Wingate, and Walter Leigh had agreed between themselves that they would say nothing, taking Cowperwood by surprise. They even went so far–that is, Steger and Wingate did–as to indicate to Cowperwood that there was some hitch to the proceedings and that he might not now get out so soon. Cowperwood was somewhat depressed, but properly stoical; he assured himself that he could wait, and that he would be all right sometime. He was rather surprised therefore, one Friday afternoon, to see Wingate, Steger, and Leigh appear at his cell door, accompanied by Warden Desmas.

The warden was quite pleased to think that Cowperwood should finally be going out–he admired him so much–and decided to come along to the cell, to see how he would take his liberation. On the way Desmas commented on the fact that he had always been a model prisoner. "He kept a little garden out there in that yard of his," he confided to Walter Leigh. "He had violets and pansies and geraniums out there, and they did very well, too."

Leigh smiled. It was like Cowperwood to be industrious and tasteful, even in prison. Such a man could not be conquered. "A very remarkable man, that," he remarked to Desmas.

"Very," replied the warden. "You can tell that by looking at him."

The four looked in through the barred door where he was working, without being observed, having come up quite silently.

"Hard at it, Frank?" asked Steger.

Cowperwood glanced over his shoulder and got up. He had been thinking, as always these days, of what he would do when he did get out.

"What is this," he asked–"a political delegation?" He suspected something on the instant. All four smiled cheeringly, and Bonhag unlocked the door for the warden.

"Nothing very much, Frank," replied Stager, gleefully, "only you're a free man. You can gather up your traps and come right along, if you wish."

Cowperwood surveyed his friends with a level gaze. He had not expected this so soon after what had been told him. He was not one to be very much interested in the practical joke or the surprise, but this pleased him–the sudden realization that he was free. Still, he had anticipated it so long that the charm of it had been discounted to a certain extent. He had been unhappy here, and he had not. The shame and humiliation of it, to begin with, had been much. Lattery, as he had become inured to it all, the sense of narrowness and humiliation had worn off. Only the consciousness of incarceration and delay irked him. Barring his intense desire for certain things– success and vindication, principally–he found that he could live in his narrow cell and be fairly comfortable. He had long since become used to the limy smell (used to defeat a more sickening one), and to the numerous rats which he quite regularly trapped. He had learned to take an interest in chair-caning, having become so proficient that he could seat twenty in a day if he chose, and in working in the little garden in spring, summer, and fall. Every evening he had studied the sky from his narrow yard, which resulted curiously in the gift in later years of a great reflecting telescope to a famous university. He had not looked upon himself as an ordinary prisoner, by any means– had not felt himself to be sufficiently punished if a real crime had been involved. From Bonhag he had learned the history of many criminals here incarcerated, from murderers up and down, and many had been pointed out to him from time to time. He had been escorted into the general yard by Bonhag, had seen the general food of the place being prepared, had heard of Stener's modified life here, and so forth. It had finally struck him that it was not so bad, only that the delay to an individual like himself was wasteful. He could do so much now if he were out and did not have to fight court proceedings. Courts and jails! He shook his head when he thought of the waste involved in them.

"That's all right," he said, looking around him in an uncertain way. "I'm ready."

He stepped out into the hall, with scarcely a farewell glance, and to Bonhag, who was grieving greatly over the loss of so profitable a customer, he said: "I wish you would see that some of these things are sent over to my house, Walter. You're welcome to the chair, that clock, this mirror, those pictures–all of these things in fact, except my linen, razors, and so forth."

The last little act of beneficence soothed Bonhag's lacerated soul a little. They went out into the receiving overseer's office, where Cowperwood laid aside his prison suit and the soft shirt with a considerable sense of relief. The clog shoes had long since been replaced by a better pair of his own. He put on the derby hat and gray overcoat he had worn the year before, on entering, and expressed himself as ready. At the entrance of the prison he turned and looked back–one last glance–at the iron door leading into the garden.

"You don't regret leaving that, do you, Frank?" asked Steger, curiously.

"I do not," replied Cowperwood. "It wasn't that I was thinking of. It was just the appearance of it, that's all."

In another minute they were at the outer gate, where Cowperwood shook the warden finally by the hand. Then entering a carriage outside the large, impressive, Gothic entrance, the gates were locked behind them and they were driven away.

"Well, there's an end of that, Frank," observed Steger, gayly; "that will never bother you any more."

"Yes," replied Cowperwood. "It's worse to see it coming than going."

"It seems to me we ought to celebrate this occasion in some way," observed Walter Leigh. "It won't do just to take Frank home. Why don't we all go down to Green's? That's a good idea."

"I'd rather not, if you don't mind," replied Cowperwood, feelingly. "I'll get together with you all, later. Just now I'd like to go home and change these clothes."

He was thinking of Aileen and his children and his mother and father and of his whole future. Life was going to broaden out for him considerably from now on, he was sure of it. He had learned so much about taking care of himself in those thirteen months. He was going to see Aileen, and find how she felt about things in general, and then he was going to resume some such duties as he had had in his own concern, with Wingate Co. He was going to secure a seat on 'change again, through his friends; and, to escape the effect of the prejudice of those who might not care to do business with an ex-convict, he was going to act as general outside man, and floor man on 'charge, for Wingate Co. His practical control of that could not be publicly proved. Now for some important development in the market–some slump or something. He would show the world whether he was a failure or not.

They let him down in front of his wife's little cottage, and he entered briskly in the gathering gloom.

On September 18, 1873, at twelve-fifteen of a brilliant autumn day, in the city of Philadelphia, one of the most startling financial tragedies that the world has ever seen had its commencement. The banking house of Jay Cooke Co., the foremost financial organization of America, doing business at Number 114 South Third Street in Philadelphia, and with branches in New York, Washington, and London, closed its doors. Those who know anything about the financial crises of the United States know well the significance of the panic which followed. It is spoken of in all histories as the panic of 1873, and the widespread ruin and disaster which followed was practically unprecedented in American history.

At this time Cowperwood, once more a broker–ostensibly a broker's agent–was doing business in South Third Street, and representing Wingate Co. on 'change. During the six months which had elapsed since he had emerged from the Eastern Penitentiary he had been quietly resuming financial, if not social, relations with those who had known him before.

Furthermore, Wingate Co. were prospering, and had been for some time, a fact which redounded to his credit with those who knew. Ostensibly he lived with his wife in a small house on North Twenty-first Street. In reality he occupied a bachelor apartment on North Fifteenth Street, to which Aileen occasionally repaired. The difference between himself and his wife had now become a matter of common knowledge in the family, and, although there were some faint efforts made to smooth the matter over, no good resulted. The difficulties of the past two years had so inured his parents to expect the untoward and exceptional that, astonishing as this was, it did not shock them so much as it would have years before. They were too much frightened by life to quarrel with its weird developments. They could only hope and pray for the best.

The Butler family, on the other hand, what there was of it, had become indifferent to Aileen's conduct. She was ignored by her brothers and Norah, who now knew all; and her mother was so taken up with religious devotions and brooding contemplation of her loss that she was not as active in her observation of Aileen's life as she might have been. Besides, Cowperwood and his mistress were more circumspect in their conduct than they had ever been before. Their movements were more carefully guarded, though the result was the same. Cowperwood was thinking of the West–of reaching some slight local standing here in Philadelphia, and then, with perhaps one hundred thousand dollars in capital, removing to the boundless prairies of which he had heard so much–Chicago, Fargo, Duluth, Sioux City, places then heralded in Philadelphia and the East as coming centers of great life–and taking Aileen with him. Although the problem of marriage with her was insoluble unless Mrs. Cowperwood should formally agree to give him up–a possibility which was not manifest at this time, neither he nor Aileen were deterred by that thought. They were going to build a future together–or so they thought, marriage or no marriage. The only thing which Cowperwood could see to do was to take Aileen away with him, and to trust to time and absence to modify his wife's point of view.

This particular panic, which was destined to mark a notable change in Cowperwood's career, was one of those peculiar things which spring naturally out of the optimism of the American people and the irrepressible progress of the country. It was the result, to be accurate, of the prestige and ambition of Jay Cooke, whose early training and subsequent success had all been acquired in Philadelphia, and who had since become the foremost financial figure of his day. It would be useless to attempt to trace here the rise of this man to distinction; it need only be said that by suggestions which he made and methods which he devised the Union government, in its darkest hours, was able to raise the money wherewith to continue the struggle against the South. After the Civil War this man, who had built up a tremendous banking business in Philadelphia, with great branches in New York and Washington, was at a loss for some time for some significant thing to do, some constructive work which would be worthy of his genius. The war was over; the only thing which remained was the finances of peace, and the greatest things in American financial enterprise were those related to the construction of transcontinental railway lines. The Union Pacific, authorized in 1860, was already building; the Northern Pacific and the Southern Pacific were already dreams in various pioneer minds. The great thing was to connect the Atlantic and the Pacific by steel, to bind up the territorially perfected and newly solidified Union, or to enter upon some vast project of mining, of which gold and silver were the most important. Actually railway-building was the most significant of all, and railroad stocks were far and away the most valuable and important on every exchange in America. Here in Philadelphia, New York Central, Rock Island, Wabash, Central Pacific, St. Paul, Hannibal St. Joseph, Union Pacific, and Ohio Mississippi were freely traded in. There were men who were getting rich and famous out of handling these things; and such towering figures as Cornelius Vanderbilt, Jay Gould, Daniel Drew, James Fish, and others in the East, and Fair, Crocker, W. R. Hearst, and Collis P. Huntington, in the West, were already raising their heads like vast mountains in connection with these enterprises. Among those who dreamed most ardently on this score was Jay Cooke, who without the wolfish cunning of a Gould or the practical knowledge of a Vanderbilt, was ambitious to thread the northern reaches of America with a band of steel which should be a permanent memorial to his name.

The project which fascinated him most was one that related to the development of the territory then lying almost unexplored between the extreme western shore of Lake Superior, where Duluth now stands, and that portion of the Pacific Ocean into which the Columbia River empties—the extreme northern one-third of the United States. Here, if a railroad were built, would spring up great cities and prosperous towns. There were, it was suspected, mines of various metals in the region of the Rockies which this railroad would traverse, and untold wealth to be reaped from the fertile corn and wheat lands. Products brought only so far east as Duluth could then be shipped to the Atlantic, via the Great Lakes and the Erie Canal, at a greatly reduced cost. It was a vision of empire, not unlike the Panama Canal project of the same period, and one that bade fair apparently to be as useful to humanity. It had aroused the interest and enthusiasm of Cooke. Because of the fact that the government had made a grant of vast areas of land on either side of the proposed track to the corporation that should seriously undertake it and complete it within a reasonable number of years, and because of the opportunity it gave him of remaining a distinguished public figure, he had eventually shouldered the project. It was open to many objections and criticisms; but the genius which had been sufficient to finance the Civil War was considered sufficient to finance the Northern Pacific Railroad. Cooke undertook it with the idea of being able to put the merits of the proposition before the people direct—not through the agency of any great financial corporation–and of selling to the butcher, the baker, and the candlestick-maker the stock or shares that he wished to dispose of.

It was a brilliant chance. His genius had worked out the sale of great government loans during the Civil War to the people direct in this fashion. Why not Northern Pacific certificates? For several years he conducted a pyrotechnic campaign, surveying the territory in question, organizing great railway-construction corps, building hundreds of miles of track under most trying conditions, and selling great blocks of his stock, on which interest of a certain percentage was guaranteed. If it had not been that he knew little of railroad-building, personally, and that the project was so vast that it could not well be encompassed by one man, even so great a man it might have proved successful, as under subsequent management it did. However, hard times, the war between France and Germany, which tied up European capital for the time being and made it indifferent to American projects, envy, calumny, a certain percentage of mismanagement, all conspired to wreck it. On September 18, 1873, at twelve-fifteen noon, Jay Cooke Co. failed for approximately eight million dollars and the Northern Pacific for all that had been invested in it–some fifty million dollars more.

One can imagine what the result was–the most important financier and the most distinguished railway enterprise collapsing at one and the same time. "A financial thunderclap in a clear sky," said the Philadelphia Press. "No one could have been more surprised," said the Philadelphia Inquirer, "if snow had fallen amid the sunshine of a summer noon." The public, which by Cooke's previous tremendous success had been lulled into believing him invincible, could not understand it. It was beyond belief. Jay Cooke fail? Impossible, or anything connected with him. Nevertheless, he had failed; and the New York Stock Exchange, after witnessing a number of crashes immediately afterward, closed for eight days. The Lake Shore Railroad failed to pay a call-loan of one million seven hundred and fifty thousand dollars; and the Union Trust Company, allied to the Vanderbilt interests, closed its doors after withstanding a prolonged run. The National Trust Company of New York had eight hundred thousand dollars of government securities in its vaults, but not a dollar could be borrowed upon them; and it suspended. Suspicion was universal, rumor affected every one.

In Philadelphia, when the news reached the stock exchange, it came first in the form of a brief despatch addressed to the stock board from the New York Stock Exchange– "Rumor on street of failure of Jay Cooke Co. Answer." It was not believed, and so not replied to. Nothing was thought of it. The world of brokers paid scarcely any attention to it. Cowperwood, who had followed the fortunes of Jay Cooke Co. with considerable suspicion of its president's brilliant theory of vending his wares direct to the people–was perhaps the only one who had suspicions. He had once written a brilliant criticism to some inquirer, in which he had said that no enterprise of such magnitude as the Northern Pacific had ever before been entirely dependent upon one house, or rather upon one man, and that he did not like it. "I am not sure that the lands through which the road runs are so unparalleled in climate, soil, timber, minerals, etc., as Mr. Cooke and his friends would have us believe. Neither do I think that the road can at present, or for many years to come, earn the interest which its great issues of stock call for. There is great danger and risk there." So when the notice was posted, he looked at it, wondering what the effect would be if by any chance Jay Cooke Co. should fail.

He was not long in wonder. A second despatch posted on 'change read: "New York, September 18th. Jay Cooke Co. have suspended."

Cowperwood could not believe it. He was beside himself with the thought of a great opportunity. In company with every other broker, he hurried into Third Street and up to Number 114, where the famous old banking house was located, in order to be sure. Despite his natural dignity and reserve, he did not hesitate to run. If this were true, a great hour had struck. There would be wide-spread panic and disaster. There would be a terrific slump in prices of all stocks. He must be in the thick of it. Wingate must be on hand, and his two brothers. He must tell them how to sell and when and what to buy. His great hour had come!

Chapter LIX

The banking house of Jay Cooke Co., in spite of its tremendous significance as a banking and promoting concern, was a most unpretentious affair, four stories and a half in height of gray stone and red brick. It had never been deemed a handsome or comfortable banking house. Cowperwood had been there often. Wharf-rats as long as the forearm of a man crept up the culverted channels of Dock Street to run through the apartments at will. Scores of clerks worked under gas-jets, where light and air were not any too abundant, keeping track of the firm's vast accounts. It was next door to the Girard National Bank, where Cowperwood's friend Davison still flourished, and where the principal financial business of the street converged. As Cowperwood ran he met his brother Edward, who was coming to the stock exchange with some word for him from Wingate.

"Run and get Wingate and Joe," he said. "There's something big on this afternoon. Jay Cooke has failed."

Edward waited for no other word, but hurried off as directed.

Cowperwood reached Cooke Co. among the earliest. To his utter astonishment, the solid brown-oak doors, with which he was familiar, were shut, and a notice posted on them, which he quickly read, ran:

September 18, 1873.

To the Public–

We regret to be obliged to announce that, owing to
unexpected demands on us, our firm has been obliged to
suspend payment. In a few days we will be able to present a
statement to our creditors. Until which time we must ask
their patient consideration. We believe our assets to be
largely in excess of our liabilities.

Jay Cooke Co.

A magnificent gleam of triumph sprang into Cowperwood's eye. In company with many others he turned and ran back toward the exchange, while a reporter, who had come for information knocked at the massive doors of the banking house, and was told by a porter, who peered out of a diamond-shaped aperture, that Jay Cooke had gone home for the day and was not to be seen.

"Now," thought Cowperwood, to whom this panic spelled opportunity, not ruin, "I'll get my innings. I'll go short of this–of everything."

Before, when the panic following the Chicago fire had occurred, he had been long– had been compelled to stay long of many things in order to protect himself. To-day he had nothing to speak of–perhaps a paltry seventy-five thousand dollars which he had managed to scrape together. Thank God! he had only the reputation of Wingate's old house to lose, if he lost, which was nothing. With it as a trading agency behind him–with it as an excuse for his presence, his right to buy and sell–he had everything to gain. Where many men were thinking of ruin, he was thinking of success. He would have Wingate and his two brothers under him to execute his orders exactly. He could pick up a fourth and a fifth man if necessary. He would give them orders to sell–everything–ten, fifteen, twenty, thirty points off, if necessary, in order to trap the unwary, depress the market, frighten the fearsome who would think he was too daring; and then he would buy, buy, buy, below these figures as much as possible, in order to cover his sales and reap a profit.

His instinct told him how widespread and enduring this panic would be. The North- ern Pacific was a hundred-million-dollar venture. It involved the savings of hundreds of thousands of people–small bankers, tradesmen, preachers, lawyers, doctors, wid- ows, institutions all over the land, and all resting on the faith and security of Jay Cooke. Once, not unlike the Chicago fire map, Cowperwood had seen a grand prospectus and map of the location of the Northern Pacific land-grant which Cooke had controlled, showing a vast stretch or belt of territory extending from Duluth–"The Zenith City of the Unsalted Seas," as Proctor Knott, speaking in the House of Representatives, had sarcastically called it–through the Rockies and the headwaters of the Missouri to the Pacific Ocean. He had seen how Cooke had ostensibly managed to get control of this government grant, containing millions upon millions of acres and extending fourteen hundred miles in length; but it was only a vision of empire. There might be silver and gold and copper mines there. The land was usable–would some day be usable. But what of it now? It would do to fire the imaginations of fools with–nothing more. It was inaccessible, and would remain so for years to come. No doubt thousands had subscribed to build this road; but, too, thousands would now fail if it had failed. Now the crash had come. The grief and the rage of the public would be intense. For days and days and weeks and months, normal confidence and courage would be gone. This was his hour. This was his great moment. Like a wolf prowling under glittering, bitter stars in the night, he was looking down into the humble folds of simple men and seeing what their ignorance and their unsophistication would cost them.

He hurried back to the exchange, the very same room in which only two years before he had fought his losing fight, and, finding that his partner and his brother had not yet come, began to sell everything in sight. Pandemonium had broken loose. Boys and men were fairly tearing in from all sections with orders from panic-struck brokers to sell, sell, sell, and later with orders to buy; the various trading-posts were reeling, swirling masses of brokers and their agents. Outside in the street in front of Jay Cooke Co., Clark Co., the Girard National Bank, and other institutions, immense crowds were beginning to form. They were hurrying here to learn the trouble, to withdraw their deposits, to protect their interests generally. A policeman arrested a boy for calling out the failure of Jay Cooke Co., but nevertheless the news of the great disaster was spreading like wild-fire.

Among these panic-struck men Cowperwood was perfectly calm, deadly cold, the same Cowperwood who had pegged solemnly at his ten chairs each day in prison, who had baited his traps for rats, and worked in the little garden allotted him in utter silence and loneliness. Now he was vigorous and energetic. He had been just sufficiently about this exchange floor once more to have made his personality impressive and distinguished. He forced his way into the center of swirling crowds of men already shouting themselves hoarse, offering whatever was being offered in quantities which were astonishing, and at prices which allured the few who were anxious to make money out of the tumbling prices to buy. New York Central had been standing at 104 78 when the failure was announced; Rhode Island at 108 78; Western Union at 92 12; Wabash at 70 14; Panama at 117 38; Central Pacific at 99 58; St. Paul at 51; Hannibal St. Joseph at 48; Northwestern at 63; Union Pacific at 26 34; Ohio and Mississippi at 38 34. Cowperwood's house had scarcely any of the stocks on hand. They were not carrying them for any customers, and yet he sold, sold, sold, to whoever would take, at prices which he felt sure would inspire them.

"Five thousand of New York Central at ninety-nine, ninety-eight, ninety-seven, ninety-six, ninety-five, ninety-four, ninety-three, ninety-two, ninety-one, ninety, eighty-nine," you might have heard him call; and when his sales were not sufficiently brisk he would turn to something else–Rock Island, Panama, Central Pacific, Western Union, Northwestern, Union Pacific. He saw his brother and Wingate hurrying in, and stopped in his work long enough to instruct them. "Sell everything you can," he cautioned them quietly, "at fifteen points off if you have to–no lower than that now–and buy all you can below it. Ed, you see if you cannot buy up some local street-railways at fifteen off. Joe, you stay near me and buy when I tell you."

The secretary of the board appeared on his little platform.

"E. W. Clark Company," he announced, at one-thirty, "have just closed their doors."

"Tighe Company," he called at one-forty-five, "announce that they are compelled to suspend."

"The First National Bank of Philadelphia," he called, at two o'clock, "begs to state that it cannot at present meet its obligations."

After each announcement, always, as in the past, when the gong had compelled silence, the crowd broke into an ominous "Aw, aw, aw."

"Tighe Company," thought Cowperwood, for a single second, when he heard it. "There's an end of him." And then he returned to his task.

When the time for closing came, his coat torn, his collar twisted loose, his necktie ripped, his hat lost, he emerged sane, quiet, steady-mannered.

"Well, Ed," he inquired, meeting his brother, "how'd you make out?" The latter was equally torn, scratched, exhausted.

"Christ," he replied, tugging at his sleeves, "I never saw such a place as this. They almost tore my clothes off."

"Buy any local street-railways?"

"About five thousand shares."

"We'd better go down to Green's," Frank observed, referring to the lobby of the principal hotel. "We're not through yet. There'll be more trading there."

He led the way to find Wingate and his brother Joe, and together they were off, figuring up some of the larger phases of their purchases and sales as they went.

And, as he predicted, the excitement did not end with the coming of the night. The crowd lingered in front of Jay Cooke Co.'s on Third Street and in front of other institutions, waiting apparently for some development which would be favorable to them. For the initiated the center of debate and agitation was Green's Hotel, where on the evening of the eighteenth the lobby and corridors were crowded with bankers, brokers, and speculators. The stock exchange had practically adjourned to that hotel en masse. What of the morrow? Who would be the next to fail? From whence would money be forthcoming? These were the topics from each mind and upon each tongue. From New York was coming momentarily more news of disaster. Over there banks and trust companies were falling like trees in a hurricane. Cowperwood in his perambulations, seeing what he could see and hearing what he could hear, reaching understandings which were against the rules of the exchange, but which were nevertheless in accord with what every other person was doing, saw about him men known to him as agents of Mollenhauer and Simpson, and congratulated himself that he would have something to collect from them before the week was over. He might not own a street-railway, but he would have the means to. He learned from hearsay, and information which had been received from New York and elsewhere, that things were as bad as they could be, and that there was no hope for those who expected a speedy return of normal conditions. No thought of retiring for the night entered until the last man was gone. It was then practically morning.

The next day was Friday, and suggested many ominous things. Would it be another Black Friday? Cowperwood was at his office before the street was fairly awake. He figured out his program for the day to a nicety, feeling strangely different from the way he had felt two years before when the conditions were not dissimilar. Yesterday, in spite of the sudden onslaught, he had made one hundred and fifty thousand dollars, and he expected to make as much, if not more, to-day. There was no telling what he could make, he thought, if he could only keep his small organization in perfect trim and get his assistants to follow his orders exactly. Ruin for others began early with the suspension of Fisk Hatch, Jay Cooke's faithful lieutenants during the Civil War. They had calls upon them for one million five hundred thousand dollars in the first fifteen minutes after opening the doors, and at once closed them again, the failure being ascribed to Collis P. Huntington's Central Pacific Railroad and the Chesapeake Ohio. There was a long-continued run on the Fidelity Trust Company. News of these facts, and of failures in New York posted on 'change, strengthened the cause Cowperwood was so much interested in; for he was selling as high as he could and buying as low as he could on a constantly sinking scale. By twelve o'clock he figured with his assistants that he had cleared one hundred thousand dollars; and by three o'clock he had two hundred thousand dollars more. That afternoon between three and seven he spent adjusting his trades, and between seven and one in the morning, without anything to eat, in gathering as much additional information as he could and laying his plans for the future. Saturday morning came, and he repeated his performance of the day before, following it up with adjustments on Sunday and heavy trading on Monday. By Monday afternoon at three o'clock he figured that, all losses and uncertainties to one side, he was once more a millionaire, and that now his future lay clear and straight before him.

As he sat at his desk late that afternoon in his office looking out into Third Street, where a hurrying of brokers, messengers, and anxious depositors still maintained, he had the feeling that so far as Philadelphia and the life here was concerned, his day and its day with him was over. He did not care anything about the brokerage business here any more or anywhere. Failures such as this, and disasters such as the Chicago fire, that had overtaken him two years before, had cured him of all love of the stock exchange and all feeling for Philadelphia. He had been very unhappy here in spite of all his previous happiness; and his experience as a convict had made, him, he could see quite plainly, unacceptable to the element with whom he had once hoped to associate. There was nothing else to do, now that he had reestablished himself as a Philadelphia business man and been pardoned for an offense which he hoped to make people believe he had never committed, but to leave Philadelphia to seek a new world.

"If I get out of this safely," he said to himself, "this is the end. I am going West, and going into some other line of business." He thought of street-railways, land speculation, some great manufacturing project of some kind, even mining, on a legitimate basis.

"I have had my lesson," he said to himself, finally getting up and preparing to leave. "I am as rich as I was, and only a little older. They caught me once, but they will not catch me again." He talked to Wingate about following up the campaign on the lines in which he had started, and he himself intended to follow it up with great energy; but all the while his mind was running with this one rich thought: "I am a millionaire. I am a free man. I am only thirty-six, and my future is all before me."

It was with this thought that he went to visit Aileen, and to plan for the future.

It was only three months later that a train, speeding through the mountains of Pennsylvania and over the plains of Ohio and Indiana, bore to Chicago and the West the young financial aspirant who, in spite of youth and wealth and a notable vigor of body, was a solemn, conservative speculator as to what his future might be. The West, as he had carefully calculated before leaving, held much. He had studied the receipts of the New York Clearing House recently and the disposition of bank-balances and the shipment of gold, and had seen that vast quantities of the latter metal were going to Chicago. He understood finance accurately. The meaning of gold shipments was clear. Where money was going trade was–a thriving, developing life. He wished to see clearly for himself what this world had to offer.

Two years later, following the meteoric appearance of a young speculator in Duluth, and after Chicago had seen the tentative opening of a grain and commission company labeled Frank A. Cowperwood Co., which ostensibly dealt in the great wheat crops of the West, a quiet divorce was granted Mrs. Frank A. Cowperwood in Philadelphia, because apparently she wished it. Time had not seemingly dealt badly with her. Her financial affairs, once so bad, were now apparently all straightened out, and she occupied in West Philadelphia, near one of her sisters, a new and interesting home which was fitted with all the comforts of an excellent middle-class residence. She was now quite religious once more. The two children, Frank and Lillian, were in private schools, returning evenings to their mother. "Wash" Sims was once more the negro general factotum. Frequent visitors on Sundays were Mr. and Mrs. Henry Worthington Cowperwood, no longer distressed financially, but subdued and wearied, the wind completely gone from their once much-favored sails. Cowperwood, senior, had sufficient money wherewith to sustain himself, and that without slaving as a petty clerk, but his social joy in life was gone. He was old, disappointed, sad. He could feel that with his quondam honor and financial glory, he was the same–and he was not. His courage and his dreams were gone, and he awaited death.

Here, too, came Anna Adelaide Cowperwood on occasion, a clerk in the city water office, who speculated much as to the strange vicissitudes of life. She had great interest in her brother, who seemed destined by fate to play a conspicuous part in the world; but she could not understand him. Seeing that all those who were near to him in any way seemed to rise or fall with his prosperity, she did not understand how justice and morals were arranged in this world. There seemed to be certain general principles– or people assumed there were–but apparently there were exceptions. Assuredly her brother abided by no known rule, and yet he seemed to be doing fairly well once more. What did this mean? Mrs. Cowperwood, his former wife, condemned his actions, and yet accepted of his prosperity as her due. What were the ethics of that?

Cowperwood's every action was known to Aileen Butler, his present whereabouts and prospects. Not long after his wife's divorce, and after many trips to and from this new world in which he was now living, these two left Philadelphia together one afternoon in the winter. Aileen explained to her mother, who was willing to go and live with Norah, that she had fallen in love with the former banker and wished to marry him. The old lady, gathering only a garbled version of it at first, consented.

Thus ended forever for Aileen this long-continued relationship with this older world. Chicago was before her–a much more distinguished career, Frank told her, than ever they could have had in Philadelphia.

"Isn't it nice to be finally going?" she commented.

"It is advantageous, anyhow," he said.

Concerning Mycteroperca Bonaci

There is a certain fish, the scientific name of which is Mycteroperca Bonaci, its common name Black Grouper, which is of considerable value as an afterthought in this connection, and which deserves to be better known. It is a healthy creature, growing quite regularly to a weight of two hundred and fifty pounds, and lives a comfortable, lengthy existence because of its very remarkable ability to adapt itself to conditions. That very subtle thing which we call the creative power, and which we endow with the spirit of the beatitudes, is supposed to build this mortal life in such fashion that only honesty and virtue shall prevail. Witness, then, the significant manner in which it has fashioned the black grouper. One might go far afield and gather less forceful indictments–the horrific spider spinning his trap for the unthinking fly; the lovely Drosera (Sundew) using its crimson calyx for a smothering-pit in which to seal and devour the victim of its beauty; the rainbow-colored jellyfish that spreads its prismed tentacles like streamers of great beauty, only to sting and torture all that falls within their radiant folds. Man himself is busy digging the pit and fashioning the snare, but he will not believe it. His feet are in the trap of circumstance; his eyes are on an illusion.

Mycteroperca moving in its dark world of green waters is as fine an illustration of the constructive genius of nature, which is not beatific, as any which the mind of man may discover. Its great superiority lies in an almost unbelievable power of simulation, which relates solely to the pigmentation of its skin. In electrical mechanics we pride ourselves on our ability to make over one brilliant scene into another in the twinkling of an eye, and flash before the gaze of an onlooker picture after picture, which appear and disappear as we look. The directive control of Mycteroperca over its appearance is much more significant. You cannot look at it long without feeling that you are witnessing something spectral and unnatural, so brilliant is its power to deceive. From being black it can become instantly white; from being an earth-colored brown it can fade into a delightful water-colored green. Its markings change as the clouds of the sky. One marvels at the variety and subtlety of its power.

Lying at the bottom of a bay, it can simulate the mud by which it is surrounded. Hidden in the folds of glorious leaves, it is of the same markings. Lurking in a flaw of light, it is like the light itself shining dimly in water. Its power to elude or strike unseen is of the greatest.

What would you say was the intention of the overruling, intelligent, constructive force which gives to Mycteroperca this ability? To fit it to be truthful? To permit it to present an unvarying appearance which all honest life-seeking fish may know? Or would you say that subtlety, chicanery, trickery, were here at work? An implement of illusion one might readily suspect it to be, a living lie, a creature whose business it is to appear what it is not, to simulate that with which it has nothing in common, to get its living by great subtlety, the power of its enemies to forefend against which is little. The indictment is fair.

Would you say, in the face of this, that a beatific, beneficent creative, overruling power never wills that which is either tricky or deceptive? Or would you say that this material seeming in which we dwell is itself an illusion? If not, whence then the Ten Commandments and the illusion of justice? Why were the Beatitudes dreamed of and how do they avail?

The Magic Crystal

If you had been a mystic or a soothsayer or a member of that mysterious world which divines by incantations, dreams, the mystic bowl, or the crystal sphere, you might have looked into their mysterious depths at this time and foreseen a world of happenings which concerned these two, who were now apparently so fortunately placed. In the fumes of the witches' pot, or the depths of the radiant crystal, might have been revealed cities, cities, cities; a world of mansions, carriages, jewels, beauty; a vast metropolis outraged by the power of one man; a great state seething with indignation over a force it could not control; vast halls of priceless pictures; a palace unrivaled for its magnificence; a whole world reading with wonder, at times, of a given name. And sorrow, sorrow, sorrow.

The three witches that hailed Macbeth upon the blasted heath might in turn have called to Cowperwood, "Hail to you, Frank Cowperwood, master of a great railway system! Hail to you, Frank Cowperwood, builder of a priceless mansion! Hail to you,

Frank Cowperwood, patron of arts and possessor of endless riches! You shall be famed hereafter." But like the Weird Sisters, they would have lied, for in the glory was also the ashes of Dead Sea fruit–an understanding that could neither be inflamed by desire nor satisfied by luxury; a heart that was long since wearied by experience; a soul that was as bereft of illusion as a windless moon. And to Aileen, as to Macduff, they might have spoken a more pathetic promise, one that concerned hope and failure. To have and not to have! All the seeming, and yet the sorrow of not having! Brilliant society that shone in a mirage, yet locked its doors; love that eluded as a will-o'-the-wisp and died in the dark. "Hail to you, Frank Cowperwood, master and no master, prince of a world of dreams whose reality was disillusion!" So might the witches have called, the bowl have danced with figures, the fumes with vision, and it would have been true. What wise man might not read from such a beginning, such an end?

Manufactured By: RR Donnelley
                     Momence, IL USA
                     July, 2010